RANI

Jaishree Misra is the best-selling author of *Ancient Promises*, *Accidents Like Love and Marriage* and *Afterwards*. She lives in London and works at the British Board of Film Classification.

Rani

JAISHREE MISRA

PENGUIN BOOKS

PENGUIN BOOKS
Published by the Penguin Group
Penguin Books India Pvt. Ltd, 11 Community Centre, Panchsheel Park,
New Delhi 110 017, India
Penguin Group (USA) Inc., 375 Hudson Street, New York, New York 10014, USA
Penguin Group (Canada), 90 Eglinton Avenue East, Suite 700, Toronto,
Ontario, M4P 2Y3, Canada (a division of Pearson Penguin Canada Inc.)
Penguin Books Ltd, 80 Strand, London WC2R 0RL, England
Penguin Ireland, 25 St Stephen's Green, Dublin 2, Ireland
(a division of Penguin Books Ltd)
Penguin Group (Australia), 250 Camberwell Road, Camberwell,
Victoria 3124, Australia (a division of Pearson Australia Group Pty Ltd)
Penguin Group (NZ), 67 Apollo Drive, Rosedale, North Shore 0632,
New Zealand (a division of Pearson New Zealand Ltd)
Penguin Group (South Africa) (Pty) Ltd, 24 Sturdee Avenue, Rosebank,
Johannesburg 2196, South Africa

Penguin Books Ltd, Registered Offices: 80 Strand, London WC2R 0RL, England

First published by Penguin Books India 2007

Copyright © Jaishree Misra 2007

10 9 8 7 6 5 4 3 2 1

ISBN-13: 978-0-14310-210-6   ISBN-10: 0-14310-210-9

This is a work of fiction. All situations, incidents, dialogue and characters, with the
exception of some well-known historical and public figures mentioned in this novel, are
products of the author's imagination and are not to be construed as real. They are not
intended to depict actual events or people or to change the entirely fictional nature of
the work. In all other respects, any resemblance to persons living or dead is entirely
coincidental.

Typeset in PalmSprings by SÜRYA, New Delhi
Printed at Pauls Press, New Delhi

Author's Note

There cannot be many people put through the Indian educational system who will fail to recall mindlessly chanting lines from a Subhadra Kumari Chauhan poem: *'Bundele harbolon ke mukh humne suni kahani thi, Khoob ladi mardani woh toh Jhansi wali rani thi'* ('I have heard from the mouths of the Bundelas her story, the brave queen of Jhansi who fought so hard she bravely sacrificed her life'). I was among those schoolchildren, a bored seven-year-old who was, sadly, neither interested in Hindi poetry nor in Indian history. But, many years later, while searching for an inspiring female character to explore a new genre, the old verse was inexplicably dredged up from a barely revisited corner of my mind. Rani Lakshmibai seemed a promising candidate for a big historical novel.

After early trawls through some excellent internet sites and tentative forays into the India section of the British Library, I found myself swept into the morass of shifting perspectives that is colonial history. Here, up against all that I had been taught as an Indian schoolgirl of the brave queen who had taken on early British imperialists, were reports of a massacre of innocent British women and children at Jhansi Fort that I had either slept through or that my history teachers had failed to mention. Quite suddenly the grainy sketch of a sword-wielding female warrior rearing up on her horse, even today a favourite of primary school textbooks in India, sat uneasily against words like 'mutineer' and 'murderer', so recurrent in older British sources. Statues like those of General Hugh Rose in Kensington and Henry Havelock at Trafalgar Square, passed every day on my way to work, took on a new meaning and led to renewed puzzlement at why hardly anyone outside India today knew the name of Rani Lakshmibai, India's Boudica, whom even her British victors would come to grudgingly describe as an 'Indian Joan of Arc'.

I felt caught between British chroniclers of the time, who loathed and scapegoated Lakshmibai for the part she played in the 1857 massacres and uprising—a nasty blot on Victorian imperialist ideals— and Indian nationalist writers who, emerging a few years later, eulogized her, almost as undeservingly, in order to use her as an energizing and necessary inspiration to the freedom movement that would follow. It was with more than a little trepidation that I took my own steps into Lakshmibai's world. To my astonishment, what I found was a fascinatingly modern woman, with passions and relationships that were completely recognizable and a story with enormous appeal for our own times. Suddenly the idea that a young, capable woman like her had dared to take on the might of an invading army, laying down her life for a cause that was already lost, was no longer so inexplicable.

Even the most exacting historians will find it hard to assess how closely my Lakshmibai resembles the real woman who lived and died 150 years ago, there being no authentic photographs and little personal detail available in primary sources and also because time and perspective would have done much in a century and a half to freely colour fact. But readers of this book—like all fans of historical fiction— will nevertheless want to know *exactly* how much of the story is true. I can assure them that the dates and important historical events within which the story takes shape are based on recorded details and that all the main characters existed in real life. To breathe life into those characters and offer explanations for how they might have come to make their decisions was, I believe, my main task as a novelist and, in order to achieve this, I have had to create imaginary conversations and scenarios. Certain events and timeframes—such as the move of Peshwa-sahib's court from Bithur to Varanasi and Moropant's move to Jhansi—have been either collapsed or extended for the sake of narrative neatness and pace. Similarly, creative licence has been taken with the ages of Tantia and Nana, there being too many discrepancies in available records anyway. Some characters have also been elided from the story; Moropant's second wife, for instance, and visitors to Lakshmibai's court, such as Robert Hamilton and John Lang, the latter, in fact, an invaluable chronicler used by many who have written of her. Readers who are keen on knowing more about such deliberately omitted facts and figures would be well-advised to read some of the books listed in the bibliography and make their own way through that complex and contentious part of history for themselves, rather than rely on a work of historical fiction as this is.

Fiction was the form I consciously chose, not just because it is my natural literary home, but also because of the entry it offers into characters' deepest thoughts and most private conversations, those realms always denied to even the finest non-fiction writers. Primary sources on Rani Lakshmibai are not plentiful; her personal letters were never found after the battle at Kotah-ki-Sarai and many relevant papers would no doubt have been destroyed during the assault on Jhansi. It would also, understandably, not have been in her supporters' interests to preserve anything that would have aligned them to rebel activity in newly colonized India, post-1858. Love for Lakshmibai lived on mostly in the safety of folk songs and ballads, some going as far as suggesting that she never died in battle at all. But, in terms of actual research material, all that remains now are pages of official correspondence between Jhansi and Government House in the run-up to Jhansi's annexation and the most fascinating of these relate to the support that Lakshmibai received from her British political agent in her darkest days.

It was on my first research trip to the National Archives in New Delhi that I read a letter written by an irate Lord Dalhousie to Major Ellis, curtly informing him that news of his conduct had been received by Calcutta 'with much dissatisfaction'. There may have been many noble reasons for which Jhansi's political agent made the decisions he did and what I write is merely interpretation as, in the end, all historical writing is. I have taken further liberties with Ellis's story. The last recorded fact I could find on him was his punishment posting to Panna soon after Jhansi's annexation but, after that, and rather frustratingly, the trail went cold. The rest of his story in this book springs entirely from my imagination and from various writings by a handful of British men and women of the time, brave enough and clear-sighted enough to see the cruelties perpetrated by their government in this terrible conflict.

Of course, in placing a love story—albeit unspoken and unfulfilled—at the core of this book, I was concerned that I would be upsetting those Indian sentiments that have been carefully schooled into seeing Rani Lakshmibai as virtuous and valiant and no more. But I was in no doubt that I had to find the woman behind the warrior and, as various serendipitous events unfolded during the creative process, I convinced myself that the spirit of Rani Lakshmibai was hovering benevolently around me somewhere. She could surely only have been pleased to see how utterly inspired I was by her lonely courage, and how moved by the idea that she was, strangely, a little bit like every woman I know.

London 2007

JAISHREE MISRA

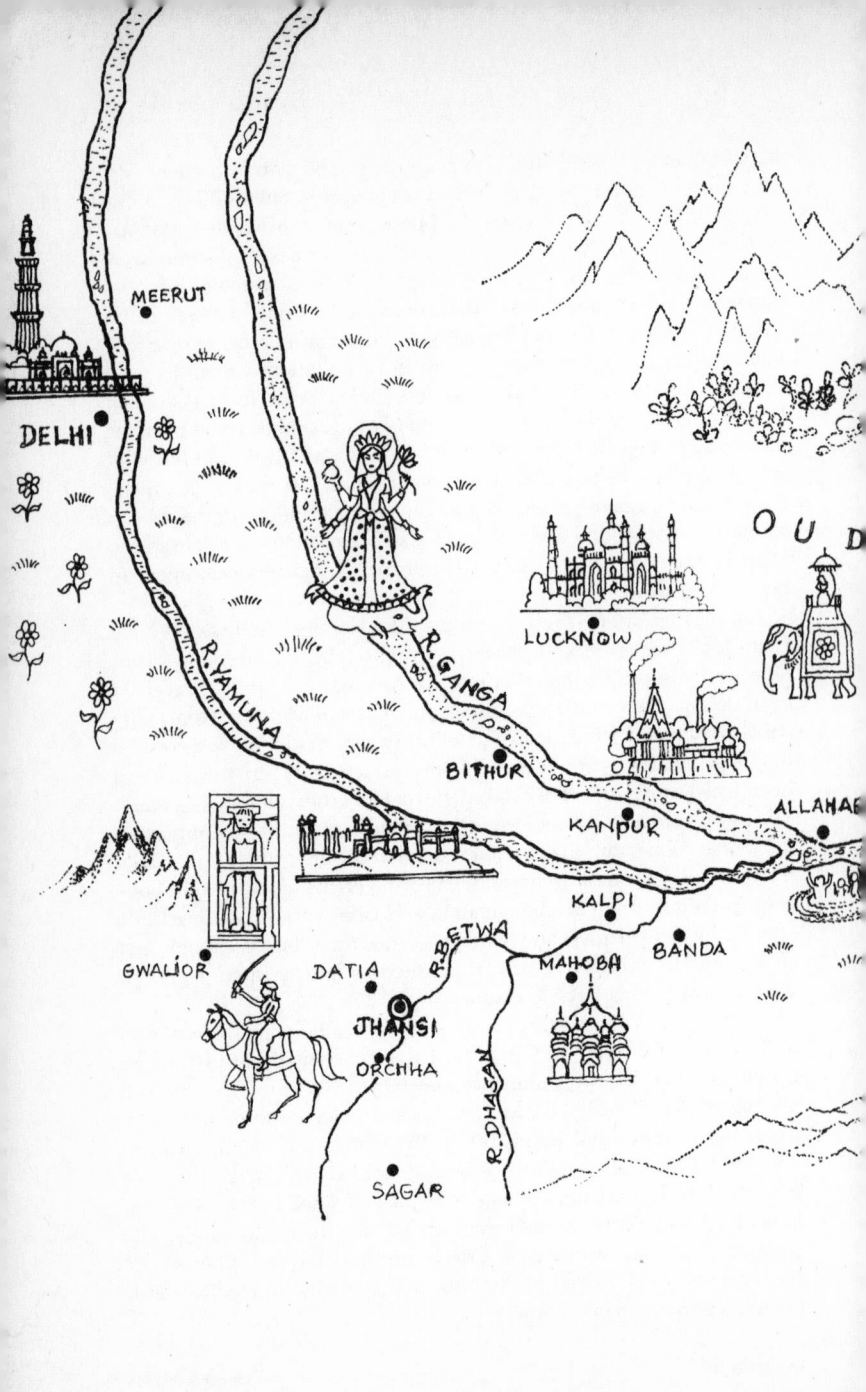

DELHI

MEERUT

R. YAMUNA

GWALIOR

DATIA

JHANSI

ORCHHA

SAGAR

R. BETWA

R. DHASAN

R. GANGA

LUCKNOW

O U D

BITHUR

KANPUR

ALLAHA

KALPI

MAHOBA

BANDA

CALCUTTA

When the nightingale sings with the crow
Light of my eyes, to our garden I will go
Where lilies and roses once more blossom and grow
There, as streams in silent forests, so too love will flow.

Jalaluddin Rumi

Prologue

A woman steps out of her carriage, brass bells on its hood chinking like a dancer's anklets. She surveys the crowded bazaar through her veil, seeing the festival crowds, the scrubbed smiling faces, and feels her heart lift. A cloud of cardamom wafts across from a nearby halwai preparing delicacies that will be consumed at sundown, when the Eid fast breaks. She inhales in pleasure but knows she must not linger. First she must make for Bara Bazaar to buy a length of muslin and then take it to the embroiderers who sit gossiping under the silk-cotton tree. Her request will be simple—perhaps a tiny edging of flowers or a paisley shape to decorate a corner. After buying a few glass bangles from a hawker, she starts to walk up a narrow street, smiling at the thought that what she really wants is to peek at the newest designs the weavers will have conjured up for wives of the town's wealthy merchants: gold zardozi roses on Kashmiri silk, gossamer silver threads entwined with rice pearls.

On her way she passes the jeweller's store but his wares she can only admire from afar. She has never stepped through his door, but today, in the glass display case, there is a beautiful necklace that momentarily halts her steps. Breath catches in her throat as she sees a length of rubies, fit for a queen, each bead like a drop of blood glinting in the evening light. Who will buy it, she wonders. Perhaps an English memsahib who will have it fastened around her long white neck by an adoring husband. She imagines the memsahib dropping a kiss on her husband's hand as it brushes past her face...

She sighs briefly, lifting the folds of her burkha to walk on. Then she spots him. On the far side of the street, his tall figure obscured off and on by the milling crowds. Her heart starts to race, blood pounds in her ears. She last saw him in a distant time, in another world. He has changed little; eyes the colour of monsoon clouds, his hair crisp and golden like Bundelkhand's summer sands. But it is like seeing a ghost, a visitation from another time, long gone. It was nearly ten years ago that he had returned to his country, sailing the black waters to reclaim his place and his people. What could have brought him back now? When the wounds of their land had subsided and all was finally peace. Why in heaven's name had he returned?

She stands, poised uncertainly between past and future, and sees him take a step towards her. Yes, he has seen her too.

✌ 1 ✎

Robert Ellis stood at the prow of his steamer, watching Brunswick dock appear over oily black waters. All he could feel at this moment was disbelief at having completed the journey from India without turning back. As warehouses and cranes materialized out of the murk, his entire being filled with a churning rage, now more anger than sorrow. It was constricting his stomach, making his mouth turn bitter and his head throb so hard he had to tighten his grip on the metal rail of the deck.

Where would he even begin to count his losses? Everything was gone, everything he had known since boyhood: love, honour, career, identity, even the claim he should have had to both the lands he loved.

Evening was falling as a hired hansom drove him down crowded London streets to the Northumberland Hotel. The view offered by his carriage window could not have seemed more removed from the small sunlit town he had left behind. A freezing fog was beginning to settle over the taller buildings and spires, men wrapped in greatcoats were emerging from offices, clinging to their hats as they hurried to their homes or clubs. Some were boarding elegant phaetons that gleamed with ornate brass trimmings. He ought to feel proud of this great metropolis, grown even greater by its trade with India. He ought to take heart in the thought that he too had contributed to that endeavour. The city had certainly grown handsomer but, like him, it was somehow more knowing and less forgiving. It wore the air of the wealthy, fat and sleek and comfortable but strangely listless, and was shrouded this winter evening in a cloak of gloom.

After paying off the cab driver, he followed a porter up the carpeted steps to his room, knowing already that the hotel was too plush, too grand—not just for what he was accustomed to but also for what he was minded to enjoy any more. Someone was playing a faintly recognizable piece on a piano but it was a tune that no longer had the power to soothe as it may have done once in childhood. He would have to get out before the comforts made him grow soft again. A boarding house in the vicinity of East India House should not be hard to find, a set of rooms austere and functional. That would give him something to do first thing in the morning.

He slipped a coin into the palm of the porter before pulling shut the door to his room, kicking off his boots and throwing himself on the bed. Wretched, that was how he felt. Wretched and wasted. He put his forearm over his eyes, trying to shut out the glow from the gas lamp on the street outside, and pressed it down as he felt, mortifyingly, the grief held so carefully at bay through the long journey now well up uncontrollably in his chest. Not once so far had he allowed himself the luxury of sorrow but tonight there may be no escape. Tonight there was no longer the slap of waves against the hull of a boat, reminding him that he could always disembark at the next port and turn back. No longer the serene warmth of a Jhansi night, the crickets in the long grass and the night call of the chakwa bird. Tonight his lullabies were to be the unfamiliar tooting of an omnibus and the endless drone of a mighty city trying to forget itself in slumber.

Hours later, and still wide awake, he rose. Perhaps it was hunger that prevented sleep. He had not even divested himself of the clothes worn on his voyage when he had fallen onto his bed and so he merely pulled on his boots and hat before abruptly leaving the room. He made his way through the hotel's now hushed lobby and emerged onto the cold street again. The wind whipped upwards, its icy fingers stabbing at his face, causing his eyes to smart and water. The clock on the spire of St. Martin-in-the-Fields showed ten minutes to the midnight hour as he walked under its looming shadow, negotiating a path through narrow roads to Covent Garden market. How strange that he should remember the way after all these years.

The market was all life and bright lights, despite the lateness of the hour. A costermonger was loading his barrow with boiled prunes and nearby a group of boys huddled around a smoking fire, thumbing a set of torn and dirty cards. One of them shouted an unintelligible word of abuse at a ragpicker for disturbing their game of cribbage. From the next street there were cries of children still at work, 'Ni-ew mackerel, six-a-shilling! All large and alive-o!' The shrill music of their calls did not seem that different from the cries of hawkers in Jhansi's bazaar. There it was sour black chana in leaf plates or pretty glass bangles sold by the dozen...

He walked on, finding a small tavern serving pie and mash. Only the dregs were left but the serving girl, seeing the look on his face, silently scraped as much as she could get out of the bowl before clattering a plate down before him. He fished a few extra coins out of his pocket and was rewarded with a wedge of bread and two pickled eggs. The meal was satisfying enough and, after he had finished, he looked around, absently crumbling the unfinished crust onto his plate. He drained his pint of stout, noticing that a woman was watching him. Crimson lips parted in a wide smile as she took in his silk cravat, his skin browned by the eastern sun. He got up abruptly to leave but she was quicker than him, pressing him against the door, whispering something about a few shillings and a room upstairs. Her hand was swift on his trouser front and, despite his numbness, he felt himself go hard under her searching fingers. But, much to the woman's annoyance, he pulled himself away and ducked out of the warm tavern, almost stumbling on its wet stone steps in his haste to leave.

A snow flurry had engulfed the street and the gas lamps were now smudged blurs of light. He pulled his collar up and wrapped his cape around his cold aching body. Should he walk on, seek out the river and hope that its black snaking length did not remind him of the silver one he had left behind? Or should he return to the hotel and try, once again, to get some sleep? How long, he wondered, how long before he would escape the torment of her memory?

A snowflake prickled on his face before melting near his ear. He had tried to describe snow to her once, recounting stray stories about his Shropshire boyhood that he had told no one else, desperate to cheer her in those dark days following the annexation. She had listened attentively, her eyes softening as her own memories began seeping out of her in a sad, low voice. They were sitting under the harsinghaar tree in the walled garden at Motibagh and she had told him of her riverside childhood, of the two boys she had grown up with and the father she had adored. Little Mani, with a destiny looming over her that no one knew about. What strange fates had conspired to bring them together; a girl who was to become queen and a young British officer destined to wrest her land from her. A land they had both grown to love and would both come to lose.

He remembered their sudden burst of laughter, echoing eerily in the walled garden, when they realized that their joys as children had been identical—riding horses and climbing trees. But he had heard the wistfulness in her laughter, seen the depths of unhappiness she could no longer hide. Though filled with his own regrets, he had felt a sudden surge of hope that perhaps they were not really completely divided. He wanted to take her hands and tell her that it was possible for worlds riven apart by everything else to be coupled, however tenuously, by shared memories of childhood. By trust and love. But she was by then lost in her memories and it was as if he had already lost her to them.

❧ 2 ❧

India, 1835

'Mani! Mani!' Angry voices rang through the dense silence of the mango orchard making the little girl curl her body tightly, cradling it in a gnarled arm of her tree. She would have to stay very still for any sharp movement would set the parrots flying out of the treetop in a sudden clapping explosion of green.

Through the lattice of branches, the summer sky looked like butter melting onto the parched earth below. Mani could not feel the heat, crouched as she was in the cool dark heart of her giant tree. She was safe nestled in these branches because nobody else was nimble enough to climb as high as she could. Her father was too old, Nana too fat and Tantia...well, Tantia would never go where Nana could not. From the day Mani's mother had suddenly gone, transformed from a warm smiling presence to a waxen-faced doll stretched out on a funeral bier, it was the womb of this tree, fragrant with ripening fruit, that had become her sanctuary.

She peered again through the darkness, adjusting her eyes to the brass-yellow heat haze beyond and this time saw two pairs of legs walking towards the tree. Both were clad in shorts and slippers, one set of knees scuffed and skinny like knobbly tamarind twigs and the other chubby with dimpled fat. The boys' heads were obscured by dusty leaves but Mani hastily pulled herself back when she heard Tantia's high voice, closer than she had thought.

'Nana, maybe she's gone back into Saturday House.'

Tantia's whining tone told her that he would not last long in this search. He hated these games when people hid from sight, their disappearance being filled with terrors that Mani could not completely understand.

Poor Tantia. So overawed by Nana who saw him merely as a shadow with no feelings of its own. Nana would never go indoors until the afternoon heat finally penetrated his bristly coconut head, reminding him of icy khus sherbets or the great chunks of watermelon being kept cool for them under wet gauze. Mani hoped it would not be a very long wait. Much as she loved her leaf-haven, there were only so many green mangoes she could nibble on to stave off her hunger and, with the sun so high in the sky, her meal was now surely congealing in the dining hall. How had Nana not succumbed yet to the call of hunger? It was almost always Nana's appetite that brought their games to a halt, Mani and Tantia clicking their tongues in shared frustration while Nana's plump frame disappeared into the kitchens in search of spicy namkeen.

Mani froze as Nana's voice emerged from right under the tree in an angry growl, 'She's here, I know she's here. I saw her running this way…badmash girl, so infuriating!'

They had been speaking in Marathi but Nana now broke into English, as he always did when he wished to sound really outraged. 'She had no cause to steal my diary,' he said stridently, obviously hoping he was striking dread in her heart if she was up in the tree, 'she knows it is my personal and private property.'

So fond of pompous English words. Always trying to show how much cleverer than both her and Tantia he was, especially in front of Mr Todd, their English tutor. Although Tantia was easily impressed, Mani had no qualms in reminding Nana that he knew more than them only because he was ten while they were six and seven. She knew she would soon catch up—already she was better at some things, especially horse riding. But Tantia always seemed a little unsure when she tartly threw that in Nana's face, never taking her side against Nana either out of loyalty or fear, Mani never knew which.

It was Tantia's querulous voice that rose up through the branches this time. 'Maybe she has only *borrowed* your diary, Nana,' he pleaded.

Though briefly touched by this unlikely defence, Mani knew that it had been offered only because Tantia was desperate to end their search for her so he could return indoors. Once in the kitchens he would stick very close to one of the maids until Mani showed up again. And, on finally seeing her, he would hide his relief under a huge sulking face.

'*Borrowed it*?' Nana screeched before repeating the offending word sarcastically, 'Borrowed? I think both of you should remember that everything you have and eat and wear is borrowed from my father and me anyway. It is only because we have given you permission to live in our palace that you are here at all. Understand that, Tantia?'

Through the leaf screen, she saw Tantia nod his bullet head glumly before he set off after Nana again, dragging his feet noisily through the dry undergrowth. They were going in the direction of the water wells but Mani knew they would retrace their steps to the orchard if they did not find her there. It was safest to stay hidden a while longer.

Settling into the familiar crevices of the branch, Mani sighed deeply, wondering why Nana was such a bully and why Tantia was always so eager to win his approval. She had even tried asking Tantia that once, after a particularly unpleasant altercation with Nana, sitting close by him and stretching her arm up to put it around his shoulders. But he had mutely shaken his head and pushed her hand away to wipe snot and tears on his sleeve.

Tossing a cluster of tiny new mangoes between her hands, she repeated the unfamiliar English word Nana had used, feeling the soft puff of it against her lips. English was such a funny language—words that were almost exactly the same sometimes had nothing to do with each other at all. Such as 'purse' and 'person'. Now here was 'personal'. She would have to ask her father what it meant or perhaps Mr Todd when he came on Wednesday for the English lesson. Already, she was Mr Todd's favourite in the schoolroom. Unlike the other tutors, he was less inclined to be lenient with Nana just because Nana was the Peshwa's son. Most people in the court relegated her and Tantia to lowly second-class citizens but Mr Todd was different. At first Mani had found the English tutor's careful neutrality most charming but, lately, she had worked out that he was dismissive of Nana because it was the British who had taken away Peshwa-sahib's powers after he had been defeated by them in battle.

Mani slid up the branch on which she had been reclining to smack her forehead angrily. She was constantly forgetting the awful possibility that Nana may well become the next Peshwa soon. Even though there was all that talk about the British never allowing anyone to hold the title of Peshwa ever again, Peshwa-sahib was doing everything in his power for Nana to inherit. And, after all, Peshwa-sahib would not be around forever. These days he too was always falling ill as Mani's own mother had done before she died and, if he did die, and if Nana did indeed become Peshwa someday, then Mani would most likely be the first person to be banished from *his* kingdom.

She felt a sudden rush of remorse at having stolen Nana's diary and read all those scribblings about how he would become a powerful ruler and train an army that would take on the British. And take on the Maharaja of Gwalior who, Nana had written, was just a 'buddhoo chamcha' of his British Resident. He had even paraphrased the English translation of that ('idiot lackey') and signed off using the official title he would inherit—'Peshwa Nanasahib Dhondu Pant', rather than just Nana. He behaved sometimes as though he were already the Peshwa, parroting his adoptive father's views: complaining yesterday of how unfair it was that the British could rob the Maratha clans of their land and birthright merely by having bigger armies. Even though Nana had not been born when the war and the eviction took place, he talked as though he remembered every detail, declaring sombrely that their life could never compare to what they once had in Pune.

Whatever the truth, however, Mani often felt something inside her chest grow tight and cold whenever she heard people in the court talk about the British in whispered and sometimes urgent voices. Worrying that those red-uniformed giants may order them to move out of Saturday House too, if anyone did anything to upset them. She could not even imagine living anywhere else but in this house that sprawled so lazily by the river, and hoped her father was right when he said that the British were generally even-handed and fair. He had told her that the whispering in court was only because it was always wise to control one's tongue—especially when one lived in 'an uncertain world'.

Feeling a renewed clutch of fear, Mani briefly contemplated shinning down the tree trunk to return Nana's diary so that she could reclaim her two friends again. But her better instincts were instructing her to take a less honourable path. She cocked her head to one side, hearing nothing but the parrots scraping their beaks on the branches above and the squirrels rustling frantically amidst the dried leaves below. Quite sure that the boys would by now have wandered down to the river from the old well, she nimbly dropped down onto the soft earth under the tree. Tucking Nana's diary into the waistband of her skirt and smoothing her small silk blouse over it, she carefully picked her way over the leaves underfoot, stopping each time her feet snapped a twig. Great-aunt Asharfi-bua too would no doubt be cross with her for having left the house without wearing her slippers.

Once at the edge of the orchard, Mani stopped to examine the soles of her feet, her heart sinking at the sight of the black mud caking them. That would take at least twenty minutes to scrub clean, by which time Nana and Tantia would have arrived in the schoolroom for their tuitions. It was not easy to decide whose wrath she wished to avoid more, Nana's over the diary or her great-aunt's over the state of her feet. Finally resolving that Asharfi-bua could be more easily won over with a profusion of smiles and promises, Mani ran into the back door of Saturday House, making her way through the warren of corridors around the kitchens and servants quarters before scuttling across the shadowed quadrangle to get to the part of the palace that was occupied by Nana and his family. Having arrived unseen at her destination, she peered around the door of the schoolroom. It was empty. She made her way hastily to Nana's pile of books and slipped his diary amongst them before wiping her sticky palms on the back of her skirt. Careless as Nana was with his belongings, he would be easily fooled into believing that it was he who had brought it out of his room by mistake. Heart thumping now with the knowledge of how narrowly her crime had escaped detection, Mani scurried swiftly out of the room.

A clock chimed six times somewhere in the bowels of the palace. Mani made a quick mental calculation, deciding that she still had a few minutes to wash her feet before joining Asharfi-bua for her prayers. Luckily it was Tuesday and not Wednesday, which meant it was Karim-teacher's history class and not Mr Todd's weekly English lesson. Karim-teacher, not as much of a stickler for punctuality as the Englishman, would hopefully not scowl at her and make disapproving English throat-clearing noises if she turned up for tuition just a few minutes late. Pleased with herself at escaping just about everybody's anger, Mani hurried back down the corridor in the direction of her father's quarters, silk skirt billowing behind her like a pink sail. She knew she ought to slow down, her father having asked her wearily just this morning why she could not simply *walk* like everyone else. She had been tumbling pell-mell down the stairs and he had looked up from his papers to ask why she always behaved as though wild animals were chasing her. Baba's occasional rebukes, so mildly delivered, could never really worry her though.

Mani called her father Baba, although the rest of the court knew him as Moropant. As political advisor to the deposed Peshwa, he was one of the most trusted courtiers but, according to his small daughter, much too occupied with his work. It was an unfair accusation as, whatever the events of the day, Moropant always found the time to take Mani down to the river for their evening walk. Once within sight of the rolling river Ganga, they would settle on a bench under the amaltash tree, Mani sometimes perching on her Baba's lap to be able to grab his face between her hands and ensure he could not escape her more urgent questions.

On one of those evenings, with one hand on her shoulder, he had captured an amaltash flower as it spun down from the tree. They both looked at the small yellow bloom lying on his palm but Mani knew he was speaking to himself as he said softly, 'The heat has come early again and, see, it is these poor flowers that must pay the price. Drifting helplessly towards uncertain fates, just like us.' He looked up at Mani before adding, 'How like the flowers we are, beti, knowing nothing of the fate we simply inherit from others.'

He had lifted her off his lap at this point to walk on but Mani, trotting along beside him, wondered whether by 'others' he meant the British or people in Peshwa-sahib's court. She did not like to quiz her father too much on days like this when he seemed to be talking more to himself than to her but this seemed important.

She tugged at his hand, 'Is that why Peshwa-sahib gazes so sadly out of the windows sometimes, Baba? Is it his fate he is thinking of?'

Moropant smiled down at her, 'Yes, I suppose it is, beti. It is his Pune homeland he remembers as he looks out at our Varanasi countryside. And the many Maratha clans he had been leader of not so long ago.'

Those were things her father had already told her about—of the war with the East India Company's army and Peshwa-sahib's subsequent exile to Varanasi.

'But Saturday House is the best place on earth to be, Baba,' she protested. 'And you said once that the British are good jailers, did you not? I like this jail and so do Nana and Tantia.'

Moropant laughed. 'Oh the British are charitable jailers alright. Better than the Mughals would have been. And they pay Peshwa-sahib a pension generous enough for his entire retinue to live comfortably here at Saturday House.'

'Perhaps they give us money because they like us,' Mani said confidently.

'I think it would be fair to say that they do not *dislike* us, beti. All they want is that we promise them compliance and stay out of their way.'

'Then that must be why they live far away from us too.'

'The Europeans like to have their own little enclaves of Christian life and some of them distance themselves from local traditions. But there's nothing wrong with that, is there, Mani? We all feel safer gathering amongst our own. No, the British respect us much more than those Muslim invaders of yore. We have much to be grateful for.'

Mani nodded. Apart from Mr Todd and the occasional visitor to the court, the only time she saw Europeans was on her occasional jaunts into town. She could not help staring at them from her carriage windows; tall men in buttoned uniforms hung with gold braid and women who looked like overblown roses in their huge silk gowns. They looked fabulous to her wondering gaze but it was clear that great gulfs separated her world from theirs. Her first knowledge that there may be things to fear from these strange, other-worldly beings was to come only two years later.

Eight-year-old Mani was settled on the floor at the back of the hall, stringing a heap of jasmines on a silk thread she had pulled off the edge of her skirt. Once the garland was ready, Asharfi-bua would help to wind it into her braid. It would perfume her hair for at least two days if she fooled Asharfi-bua into believing she had washed it by patting a little water on the top of her head. Busy with her task, she barely noticed Moropant walking in. He too had not seen her small figure curled amongst the damask curtains as he strolled to the bay windows, his back turned to the hall. The Ganga was visible from all the windows in this wing and Mani knew that the sight of the great river never failed to delight her father. 'The timelessness of our Ganga-ma confers peace and calm on the troubled soul,' he would say, his eyes sometimes clouding with sudden pensiveness.

Mani returned to her flowers when she saw that her father was today only observing some fishermen struggling to control their bamboo boats. A large Company steam sloop was blowing a loud horn to clear them from its path and the small fishing vessels rocked dangerously in the choppy brown waves left in its wake.

The guards at the entrance of the hall opened the big brass doors again, this time letting Peshwa-sahib and his younger brother through. Their day's business in the court must have concluded early, Mani thought, as she watched the servants setting up the hookah pipes and spittoons. After a flurry of activity, the servants retired from the room, walking backwards, leaving only the three men behind.

From the sight of the sun being slowly swallowed up by the glittering river, Mani knew that the men lingered in the hall only to await their summons for the dusk prayers and meal. They settled themselves on capacious gaddas, tucking their silk dhotis under them while wall hangings swayed gracefully in the evening breeze. A whiff of incense drifted in from somewhere. Peshwa-sahib pulled a hookah towards himself and filled its bowl with a pinch of cinnamon from a silver box. He fixed his favourite jade mouthpiece onto the pipe before taking a long pull and, as he leaned back on his bolster, Mani saw that the expression on his face was troubled. She wondered why, as her Baba so often said exasperatedly, people just *forgot* to notice their blessings. As Peshwa-sahib opened the conversation, his despondent voice reverberated hollowly across the empty hall.

'Like riverside melon vines, they are,' Mani heard him say, 'at first sending soft and sweet tendrils out so tentatively. Then, finding the richness of our soil, they grow and spread before our very eyes and, before we know it, those very tentacles are winding around our throats.'

His brother responded soothingly, 'We have no choice but to accept that the Company is invincible, Bhai-sahib. The power of its army protects its trade and that trade pays for the army.'

Peshwa-sahib emitted a humourless laugh. 'So beautifully simple. And now new territories come under their control without anyone putting up even the semblance of a fight.'

'What is the point of a fight?' Moropant offered. 'We have tried that and failed. Even though my own Maratha pride rebels against this state of affairs, it seems we now have no choice but to remain on the Company's right side. We must avail of the opportunities that lie in friendship with them, even if others accuse us of being false and self-seeking.'

'Granted, Moropant, but should that cause us to turn on our fellow Maratha clans?'

'Of course, it is in the Company's interests to cause infighting amongst us Marathas. We can only hope that they will not be able to fragment such an ancient clan as ours so easily.'

'Hope? Even as we play further and further into British hands?' Peshwa-sahib snorted scornfully. 'Can you not see how easily they divide us—a whisper here, a treaty there. Before you know it, brother will be pitted against brother. And the Honourable East India Company is the great puppeteer, pulling all our strings.'

'What can one do, Bhai-sahib? Things have come to such a pass that it is now the British we must turn to, even to parley with our own Maratha brothers.'

Peshwa-sahib turned on his brother sharply, 'Just because we cannot keep our own houses in order, why should we put our faith in firangis who neither like us nor understand us? Isn't it naïve to hope they will help? Haven't we already tried that and found our negotiator becoming the bigger enemy instead?'

Mani sank behind the curtains, trying to stay hidden from view. She hated it when either Peshwa-sahib or Baba got angry. Luckily, however, Peshwa-sahib's younger brother was putting aside his hookah to mollify them. 'We must admit that there are good men among the British, Bhai-sahib, men of honour willing to fight their own government's injustices. And not all British reforms have worked against us. The practices of sati and child sacrifice followed by the Rajputs…age-old…only the British can curb them.'

Moropant voiced his support, 'Quite. Bentinck was an able man who had a genuine interest in bettering things. Did it matter that he was British when there were benefits to be had for all of us from his administration?'

Peshwa-sahib remained silent as his brother replied, 'If you ask me, these white firangis are much better than the dissolute Mughals and those Afghan devils who plagued us in the past. Those Mussalmans loathed us Marathas and made no effort to hide the fact. At least the British are, by and large, civil and respect our good traditions while advocating change where necessary. If they want to control the trade, let them, I say.'

But Peshwa-sahib's mouth remained downcast as he vehemently spewed a jet of betel juice into a spittoon. 'How can you be so blind, my brothers?' he asked bitterly, irritatedly dismissing the servant who had been sent to summon them for the evening meal. The annoyed flick of Peshwa-sahib's hand made the jewels in his rings flash angry red across the room. Mani watched the servant hastily back away.

'Can you not see that when the British proscribe practices like sati, it is merely part of a concerted Christian attack on Hindu values?' Peshwa-sahib continued. 'You think William Bentinck really cared about some grieving widow throwing herself on her husband's funeral pyre? After all how many such cases happen in reality? Tell me. Maybe just one or two a year? And only among the Rajput landowners. And are not our people already trying to bring about the same social reforms?'

Moropant nodded. 'It is true there are Hindus in Bengal also fighting the practice of sati, but Peshwa-sahib—'

Peshwa-sahib cut him short. 'There is no "but", Moropant. Nobody—least of all the British administration—wants to acknowledge the good that our own people are doing. The point is that the East India Company must show everybody what a degenerate people we are, establish in the eyes of the world—their Board of Directors, their Parliament, their people, even themselves—how desperately we need *them* to come and enlighten *us*. To prove that Christianity is the only way to create a good and decent society.'

'Are you saying that all their social reforms are just an elaborate screen for conversions to Christianity?'

'Yes!' Peshwa-sahib cried, 'presented to us as gifts we must be grovellingly grateful for. Why, have they not got brigands and highwaymen in their own countries just like the Thugs here? But they make our thuggee out to be somehow connected with evil Kali worship—because it suits their purposes to have *our* religion seem cruel and insane. So that they can come and civilize us and, yes, *convert* us, Moropant. Do we not know that they use children to work in inhuman conditions in their own factories and workhouses? But do you ever hear them talk about their social evils over here?'

Moropant shook his head as Peshwa-sahib continued speaking, leaning forward and using his hookah pipe to jab agitatedly into the smoky air, 'How can you even for one moment believe that it is the betterment of our people that they desire? When we have had flourishing civilizations in our lands for over four thousand years. Four thousand years, Moropant! No, what they covet are our land and our possessions and they will take those from under our noses even while we stand and admire the good we think *they* are doing *us*!'

Mani, frightened by the flashing anger in her beloved Peshwa-sahib's eyes, heard his brother gently chide him. 'Forgive me, Bhai-sahib, but how can one not believe that at least their desire to respect our ways is genuine. I was shown a Company handbook that has recently been produced for their officers serving in India that instructs them to accept Hindu and Muslim practices, even if they find them offensive.'

At this Peshwa-sahib thumped his fist on his arm bolster, his voice growing even shriller with frustration. 'See, that is exactly what I mean! *Even if they find it offensive*! Is it not arrogance to be in someone else's land and decide what is offensive and what is not? While we are expected to blindly accept their practices as being good and civilized? Did we not hear that their latest method of punishing insubordination within their ranks is to tie the offender onto the mouth of a cannon before blowing him to bits? Did they not do exactly that to four of their sipahis in Madras just last month? *That* is civilized behaviour but their outlawing of sati and thuggee is to be lauded!'

As Peshwa-sahib sat back, visibly exhausted by his rage, Mani clutched her flower chain to her thumping chest. Peshwa-sahib's face was ashen and she knew how much the doctors worried about his health. He would *die*, just like her mother, if he flew into such rages. To her relief, her father spoke up, his voice calm and measured as always.

'Forgive me, Peshwa-sahib. But we have already lost the battle and cannot turn the clock back. Now, for our children's sake, it is peace we must strive for. I know I would be willing to sacrifice a little of my pride and a few of our customs if only for our children to enjoy a better world than ours.'

There was silence for a few minutes and Mani was sure that they could hear the drumbeats of her heart echo across the room. But Moropant sat up to rearrange the folds of his shawl, changing his tone to a more light-hearted one as he added, 'In fact, I think it is the children I now hear, no doubt coming to fetch us for the meal.'

Mani knew this was a lie, as Nana and Tantia had gone to

Sarnath for the day and she was crouched right here in this corner, but the cue was taken by Peshwa-sahib's brother. 'And, if we do not depart for the dining hall after this second summons, I fear we will be in very grave trouble with the ladies.'

At this Peshwa-sahib raised himself reluctantly from his bolsters, saying wryly, 'And that, we all know, is just not worth the trouble, is it? Worse even than annoying the British.'

There was general laughter as the men got up but Mani could not still the beating of her heart as she followed them out of the hall at a safe distance. They were strolling down the darkening veranda and she saw to her relief that Peshwa-sahib had slung an arm around the shoulders of the two men accompanying him. She caught up as they entered the dining chamber and heard Peshwa-sahib now speak quietly, his voice filled more with sadness than anger, 'What makes me fearful, my brothers, is that there is no limit to human greed. And that is just a universal truth that applies to all of us, not merely the British. At first they only wanted to trade and keep other Europeans away from their trading posts; then they turned their attentions to us indigenous rulers, enticing our soldiers away by offering better pay and pensions. After that it became too tempting to keep the lands that were bringing them such untold wealth and, along with that, they took our self-respect. Can you not see how much they need India ever since they lost America? You mark my words, Moropant, in the end they will get not just India's territory and treasures but much, much more. Things that we cannot even dream of at present. And when they take what they want, it will be with great stealth, like a breeze that will blow into our houses, seeming to offer succour even while it poisons us in our sleep.'

Through the meal, Mani could barely swallow the food placed before her as dread continued to knock at the walls of her stomach. She pushed the bowl of shrikhand away and tried to shake off Asharfi-bua who was holding a damp palm against her forehead to ensure she was not ill. Peshwa-sahib's anger with the British was so confusing. After all, one could not ask for more from this peaceful happy life they all enjoyed at Saturday House. Her father had always said that anyone who brought and kept peace in the land was welcome and that the British deserved praise for bringing order as the Mughal line waned and everyone started fighting for control. After all, they were all fortunate to live in lands so blessed with riches. Enough for them all, if it was distributed fairly.

After the meal, her father took her down to the western garden as usual. Still disturbed by the argument she had overheard earlier,

Mani noticed that her Baba too was unusually quiet, his eyes focussing somewhere in the far distance. The park all around them was covered in long gentle shadows and Saturday House, lying at the edge of it, was basking silently in the warm moonlight. But Moropant suddenly looked down at her with a strange expression on his face, shadows plunging his eyes into holes.

'I know you and Nana and Tantia fight and make up all the time, beti,' he said abruptly, his voice unusually thick, 'but you must always remember that they are your friends, your brothers, Mani.'

Mani nodded obediently. She had heard this lecture many times before and knew exactly at which points to nod. But today her father would not be easily appeased, continuing to speak in a tone of frightening urgency, as though the whole world were just about to collapse around them. 'You three children will always have to look after each other, even after you grow up, Mani. There must be no more of this childish quarrelling.' He put his arm around her shoulder and sighed deeply. When he spoke again, his grip on her shoulder had relaxed and his voice was gentler, 'Think about it, Mani. If you fight, then how will you protect each other when faced with a real enemy? You will not think it possible now but it is to each other you will turn when a bigger adversary comes along.'

Mani thought about who a *real* enemy to her might be, bigger than even Nana and Tantia put together, and could think of none. She knew she ought not to argue with her Baba when he was upset but she had to set him right on one matter. 'Baba, even if *I* agreed not to fight with Nana and Tantia, you would never be able to get them to agree,' she protested. '*Even* if I remained as calm and peaceful as I possibly could, they would just end up fighting with each other. Especially Nana with Tantia.'

Moropant shook his head ruefully and sighed again, 'Poor Tantia. What would have happened to him, had Peshwa-sahib not taken him in to be Nana's companion? I have never told you this, beti, but when Tantia's parents died in the cholera epidemic, none of his relatives could be persuaded to take care of him. The poor fellow was sent from house to house, no one being willing to take responsibility for an orphan child left without any means. I sometimes worry what that sense of abandonment may have done to him...the wounds of childhood sometimes lie seared across the mind like great raw welts that refuse to heal.'

'Maybe that is why Tantia is always so scared, Baba. And always so...so greedy for kind words.'

'You are absolutely correct, my clever little one. Greedy for kind words.' Moropant looked down at Mani who could not resist puffing up slightly at her father's approval. He was smiling at her now but his face faded again as he continued, 'I'm glad you can see what makes little Tantia the way he is, Mani. And have sympathy for him. Nana too would do well not to worsen Tantia's wounds with his teasing. The pain felt in childhood never fails to reach out through the years. It will take its revenge when it can.'

✿ 3 ✿

Far away from Varanasi, that same summer, young Robert Ellis stood looking up at the East Indiaman that was docked at Portsmouth harbour. The clamour and excitement before him seemed to reflect all his own inner feelings. He had just this month turned eighteen, received his rank of lieutenant and, now, before him was the vessel that was getting ready to carry him to his new life overseas. He would not deny his feelings were mixed but mostly they were buoyant, recent knowledge that the Company had agreed to pay for his passage to India quite setting the seal on his happiness.

He carried only a small case but watched with awe as some of the passengers—older officers, some travelling with their families and retinues—appeared to be loading the ship with enough worldly possessions to fill an entire house: boxes of clothes, hampers of food, beer and soda water, crates of china and glass, furniture, even a pet Highland terrier! It seemed a good thing to Ellis that the four-masted *Maidstone* was so huge—nine hundred tonnes, he had been told. But, as he watched crate after crate being stashed into the hold, he thought of the hapless East Indiaman *Kent* that, carrying HM's 31st foot regiment, had sunk in the Bay of Biscay only some years before.

Following a gentleman with the most impressive mutton-chop whiskers he had ever seen, Ellis stepped onto the gangplank. He would be one of the few officers on board not travelling with their regiments and his instructions were to sail the *Maidstone* up to Alexandria from where he was to take a Nile canal boat to Cairo and then a paddle-steamer belonging to the Peninsular and Oriental Steam Navigation Companyship to travel via Madras up the coast to Calcutta.

Ellis had exultantly gathered all those names these past weeks as though they were like the wildflowers he had sometimes collected as a child for his mother. There was still a dreamlike quality to the whole endeavour, even though it would soon be three years since his mother's death. Then, in that devastating winter of 1834, it was as though life had simply come to an end. There was no direction to be had from his grieving father and no prospects for the son of an impoverished curate with an unremarkable education in a small Welsh border town. Into that bleak world—miraculously it now seemed—had stepped an unlikely benefactor; his maternal uncle Herbert Peele, suddenly racked with guilt for having summarily cut off his only sister when she had made a hasty and unpromising marriage many years before. To a fifteen-year-old boy, it had seemed an awful pity that it had taken the horrible and painful death of his beloved mother to bring about such a wonderful prospect. But Ellis had not been able to resist leaping at the offer made by his Uncle Herbert at the funeral to nominate him for a commission at the East India Company's military seminary at Addiscombe.

That was how he had come to be here on this gentle August day, boarding a vessel due to take him to his new life in India. He had been informed back at the barracks that the *Maidstone* was one of the older Company ships and was also told to consider himself fortunate to be leaving it at Alexandria for a steamer. These East Indiamen offered, according to those better travelled than he, a notoriously poor service with crusty old officers who were 'dead against the passengers and dead against the India run'. But Ellis was too overjoyed to feel cowed by such cynicism and, on reaching the top of the gangplank, his optimism felt vindicated when the ship's captain, greeting his passengers, grabbed him by the hand and thumped him hard on the shoulder.

'Ah capital, *another* young officer,' the luxuriantly bearded commander roared genially, showing a set of huge tobacco-stained teeth. 'The more young guns on board, the better. Much more entertaining, I always say to the ladies. I'm in charge of this little dinghy here, in case you're wondering. Peter Roe's the name.'

Ellis moved on as Captain Roe turned to greet his next passenger, still booming with laughter. It was the boatswain who finally escorted him to his cabin amidst the confusion of boarding. This man was less rambunctious than his captain and Ellis guessed from his accent that he was either Danish or Swedish. Either way, like Captain Roe, he too seemed a first-rate man all round, cheerily answering all of Ellis's enquiries and even helping to stow his suitcase under the bunk. Ellis took only a quick look around his cabin; it was minuscule but he did not mind, given that he intended his time spent in it to be kept to a minimum. Eager to return to the deck so as not to miss even the smallest adventure, he made his way back through the melee.

An energetic sea breeze had picked up, mussing up his thatch of blonde hair, as he gazed around him, his heart surging with exhilaration and pride. A regiment was boarding the lower deck. Some of these young rankers looked even younger than him, no more than boys. Ellis heard Irish accents as they animatedly joshed with each other, everyone seeming gripped by the same infectious exultant spirit. He recalled what one of the directors at India House had said to him on the day he had received his commission, in a tone so nasal and snivelling Ellis had scarcely been able to understand him. 'Young man,' the old don had said, peering at him through a foggy monocle, 'India is a fine country for a young gentleman to raise a small fortune in, a very fine country indeed.' Having delivered this all-important piece of advice, the old man had merely harrumphed a few times before dismissing a befuddled Ellis from his room.

Stragglers were still boarding the top deck of the ship, bidding farewell to the people who had come to see them off. But, in less than an hour, and at the assigned time, the band was playing 'God Save the Queen', calls were being given to weigh anchor and the great bulk of the Maidstone was slowly pulling away from land.

Ellis found space at the railings amongst the hundreds of other passengers who were all waving and calling to the shrinking figures on the promenade as the busy docks of Portsmouth started to recede. There had been no one to come and see him off but Ellis too raised his arm and waved at a gaggle of children on a jetty who were whooping uproariously and waving their hats and scarves. They seemed happy enough to be seeing off a father or perhaps some other relative but Ellis could see the woman accompanying them wiping her eyes repeatedly on a handkerchief. Shortly, they were no more than tiny figures, the dockside buildings and warehouses like little doll-houses. Only a few seagulls stayed stubbornly with the Maidstone as it cut its slow wake across a pale green sea but, before long, they too had given up their pursuit, wheeling away and returning to shore.

In the distance, the green hump of the Isle of Wight stayed faintly visible for a while longer but soon even that gradually melted into the sea mist. Ellis considered marking his departure from homeland with momentous thought or word but he had given up praying a long time ago, much to his father's despair. And such a noisy and boisterous departure had not been conducive to grave contemplation of any sort. Though briefly tempted to lapse into some well-practiced prayer, Ellis finally looked at his last glimpse of land to say simply, 'Goodbye, England,' whispering the words rather self-consciously under his breath. He muttered again, more firmly, 'Goodbye England, thou shalt not miss me, nor me you.'

On that first day, Ellis was to discover that his fellow passengers offered mixed company; some, like him, on their maiden voyage, others old India hands, able to fluently speak up to two or three native languages, much to his envy. 'Sling the bat' someone termed it as they slipped in and out of English while conversing easily with each other in this exotic tongue. Ellis had managed to learn some Hindustani at Addiscombe, but this was different, fast-moving and thrilling, every unfamiliar word offering another tantalizing glimpse into the world that awaited him. He grabbed at the words swirling around him, *pawnee* and *doolie*, *churrie* and *nimmuck*, storing each one away carefully for future use.

Major Bundy was one of this breed, returning to rejoin his regiment at Lucknow, although his views on India shocked Ellis terribly. Already on the first night, the Major seemed to have taken it on himself to educate the others at their dinner table on the onerous task that lay before them, reserving his strongest views for the mild-mannered Reverend Waters. 'The Mahommedan can be made something of if a career is opened up to him,' Bundy offered, 'but those slimy treacherous Hindoos, with their castes and superstitions and horrid customs, constitute the real difficulty of our government and, indeed, our Church, Reverend.'

Ellis kept his eyes on his plate, startled by the discourtesy and wondering if anyone would counter it. The others around the table seemed unfazed, however, loudly complaining about the food and wine, both of which Ellis found perfectly passable. A joint and a steaming meat pie were followed by cheroots and brandy and what Major Bundy referred to as 'a fusillade of soda water' that was promptly mixed with sherbet and served up as Bombay Fizzer. After dinner, there were billiards in a large room kept wonderfully cool by a row of overhead cloth and bamboo fans. The fans, called 'punkahs', were kept moving by an elaborate system of pulleys that, Ellis discovered, ended in a small airless anteroom where the native punkah-wallahs were kept hidden away, tugging continually at their ropes.

Picking his way across to the prow that first night, Ellis could hear the cacophony of voices and singing emanating from the troop decks below. He knew that the soldiers would not have half the comforts of the officer class, probably crowded together and made to sleep in filthy hammocks, but they certainly appeared to be enjoying themselves, perhaps enlivened by tales of rich pickings the land of their destination was said to offer.

In just a few days, Ellis had exhausted the light literature available on board but there was still plenty to feast the senses on. It was getting warmer as they sailed east and the sea was turning strange shades of blue. Unfamiliar sea birds appeared whenever land was near and some of the officers had taken to shooting them for sport. One afternoon, there were loud cries of 'Look, look, just like a pack of hounds in full cry!' that made everyone rush to the decks. Looking down, Ellis saw a shoal of skipjacks, leaping out of the water and following each other with great rapidity across the head of the ship. A couple of the creatures flew right onto the deck, causing much screaming and skittering by the ladies, until, flapping piteously, the fish were swept back into the sea by the stewards.

The entertainments on board were varied and endless—games like pitch-and-toss, chess and backgammon and, on calm evenings, even quadrilles on the top deck. The two lieutenants Ellis had befriended, Cummings and Mansell, had both determinedly set their caps at the only single lady on board who seemed worthy of attention although Ellis had found her pallid beauty too fragile to be attractive. However, even she, it turned out, was sailing to join her fiancé in HM's 31st Light Infantry at Dinapur and so Mansell and Cummings, romantic hopes dashed, had joined Ellis to indulge each other with jolly japes to while away their time on board.

As young men who laughed easily and with tomfoolery their main preoccupation, the passage of the weeks was not cumbersome. One interlude that particularly amused Ellis was when Neptune and his wife came on board to make acquaintance with the ship's captain. The sea-god's chariot, fashioned out of a gun-carriage, was drawn by six half-naked seamen, Mansell amongst them, all painted to represent tritons. Ellis recognized the boatswain's mate under Neptune's long beard and cheered loudly with Cummings, as god presented captain with his offering of two tropical birds in a cage and a salted fish piercing the point of his trident.

A month later, the three young lieutenants, who were all due to board the *Oriental*, disembarked at Alexandria to catch a Nile boat bound for Cairo. Ellis observed how flat and featureless the land on either side of the river looked as they reached the teeming city. He hoped India's landscape would be more interesting and thought it fortunate that they had just one evening before meeting the *Oriental*. All he really wanted was to keep moving until they got to India. That was where all his dreams lay.

Nevertheless, in the lobby of the Shepherd Hotel that afternoon, he flopped down next to his friends, both of whom seemed to be suffering the gruelling effect of Cairo's heat.

'Does anyone fancy a trip out to see the Pyramids?' he asked half-heartedly.

'I hear they are ten miles from here,' Mansell responded doubtfully, peering out from under the soaked handkerchief he had spread on his forehead.

'Too much of an undertaking, old boy,' Cummings moaned, fanning himself with a newspaper, 'certainly with the roads in such a state of disrepair.'

'And they say old Sphinxy now wears a most sour aspect too,' Mansell laughed.

'Oh how age and neglect combine to impart unsightliness to the most lovely of countenances,' Cummings lamented in mock mournfulness.

'Better by far, I take it, to spend an evening with a gill full of stout than in the wasted pursuit of a once comely belle,' Ellis responded, taking up the joke. The Pyramids could wait for another day, after all the world was now his oyster. And there was India to look forward to.

They journeyed on, another seventy-two days of carefree pastimes and indulgences, occasionally passing Dutchmen and other vessels, until finally sailing within sight of the Car Nicobar isles and into the Bay of Bengal. It was Mansell who spotted the mainland of India first. Ellis had heard him yelling from the top deck one hot morning where people had gathered to avail of the sea spray, temperature gauges in some of the cabins showing 90 degrees before even midday. Looking across to where Mansell was pointing, Ellis saw India, at first a mere speck of green. He kept his eyes fixed on her, feeling a strange tingling on the back of his neck as he heard cries of pleasure from those gathering behind him. Despite Mansell's continuing noisy merriment, Ellis was suddenly silenced by awe as the speck spread and rose before them, growing slowly into a sun-washed stretch of land.

At first, it was India's multi-hued earth that Ellis noticed. Reds and yellows giving way to browns and even black as they sailed up the coast, every so often losing sight of land completely. As they approached Calcutta a few hours later, he saw a group of native children running and fluttering along an escarpment like thin colourful kites. Soon the vessel was approaching the mouth of a river Ellis knew to be the Hooghly and, instantly, a flotilla of smaller boats converged upon them—hawkers and vendors raucously selling all manner of goods and services. Some were the tiniest of rafts, consisting of no more than two palm trunks lashed precariously together by a length of rope. Some of the men occupying them were clad in the barest minimum, loin cloths only just covering their groins but the ladies on board the ship who had been to India before did not seem to mind, excitedly gathering on deck to make their purchases: coconuts and other exotic fruit and female accoutrements such as cowrie-bead necklaces and hair combs made of shell. The hawkers seemed happy to take anything that was offered in exchange—Indian or English coins, bottles of spirits, even old clothes and petticoat laces.

As the river narrowed, navigation became difficult, slowing the *Oriental* down to a crawl. From the deck, Ellis could now see mud huts, outside which peasants squatted. And, as they inched along, these gave way gradually to larger villages, better cultivated fields and two-storeyed brick houses with deep porticoes and verandas in which European women sat watching, waving their handkerchiefs in welcome. Finally the port of Calcutta came into view but the sandbanks seemed to be causing serious trouble by now. Amidst much shouting and confusion, it was decided that smaller vessels would be used to transport passengers to the ghats, native porters and coolies swarming on board to carry goods—and even people—ashore.

After bidding farewell to his companions who were both on their way to Berhampore, Ellis turned his attention to Calcutta. A day at the Auckland Hotel showed him, partly from the number and splendour of the equipages on view, how exceedingly wealthy the European community in Calcutta was. He saw traders, dealers, bankers and government officials, all of whom travelled in horse-drawn carriages that resembled colourful biscuit-tins on wheels. The hotel was commodious and luxurious, Ellis's room overlooking a busy street that resounded with the noise of commerce that went on into the wee hours of the morning. He could not have asked for a more comfortable bed after the bunk in the ship's cabin. It was an enormous four-poster shrouded with mosquito curtains and, though he could hear the wretched creatures whining all through the night, he was pleased to wake up in the morning and find that not one had been allowed even a little nibble.

By the end of the week he had stopped noticing the howling of jackals on the esplanade that had at first made the hair on his nape prickle and rise. The nightly calls of the watchmen guarding the European quarter had also gradually become a sound to soothe rather than disturb. Ellis could not have been more pleased to see how all of India's sights and smells and sounds were slowly becoming a part of his consciousness.

A servant had been assigned to him, a scrawny man called Lal whose skin hung from his frame as though about to fall right away. Ellis was astounded to discover that the man considered it his job to dress him as though he were a child—not a custom either familiar or desirable to one of his humble background. At first he thought he ought to permit Lal to do his job, allowing him even to massage the muscles on his arms and shoulders with bony fingers, but Ellis felt finally forced to order him to desist when a rough cloth was produced to rub his feet after he had been carefully divested of boots and socks. The poor man seemed not to understand at all, looking up at Ellis with a pained expression on his face, as though he might have made some terrible blunder. Frustrated, Ellis wished that he had the words to explain himself.

Dinner at the hotel was very well served with a variety of meats and roast game. There was also liver and bacon, served with Mosel, sherry and port and, to round everything off, Dodonean nuts and desserts. It was all so plentiful, Ellis could not resist smuggling a small parcel of food back for Lal, hoping to fatten him up slightly in the few weeks they would have together, but it was refused without explanation and this time it was Ellis's turn to feel a little hurt. There was still much to learn and understand.

Despite Calcutta's numerous charms, Ellis had no wish to tarry beyond the customary training period. He had enjoyed a most instructive and agreeable few months at Fort William, where he was taught rudimentary Urdu and Hindustani, but now he had grown impatient to take up his first posting. A place called Jhansi awaited him. A small state that, looking at a map of India, seemed to occupy its very heart.

The first part of Ellis's journey was by river, on board a large flat vessel called a budgerow that had a room built on it, complete with furniture and cooking facilities and servants. Disembarking at Allahabad, he was assigned a buggy to complete the last part of the journey overland, a horse-carriage, no bigger than a gig, with a syce running alongside in the dust. At Banda, he bided his time at a post bungalow to catch the weekly dak-gadi to Jhansi. This last was a covered wooden crate on wheels, rather resembling a baker's cart, with the primary function of delivering parcels and letters arriving by ship to remote addresses deep in the country. It was, Ellis was told, often pressed into use to ferry missionaries and other travellers like him who needed to get to these distant places.

Ellis's long journey to Jhansi had made it seem like an unreachable mirage at times and he knew not what to think when he finally saw it rise before him in the shimmering heat. It was the Fort he saw first, suspended hazily against a gleaming yellow sky. And, as he neared it, he saw too the city sprawled at its feet, a sprawling conurbation of houses and temples and lakes. This was Jhansi, and it was to become his home, the repository of all his hopes and ambitions. A sunlit city that would offer refuge from the cold grieving home in England that he had escaped. He looked at the Fort again, knowing already that he would grow to love Jhansi so much, it would not be long before he would make it his own.

✥ 4 ✥

On a hot Varanasi evening four summers later, Mani was asked to attend the grand durbar hall of Saturday House to greet a party just arrived from Jhansi. The maid sent to fetch her had surprised her by insisting she wear the green silk long-skirt and bodice that had been bought for her birthday. The brocade border sewn onto the sleeves of the bodice had cut into her arms even when she had been thinner last year and the idea of wearing it on such a humid day made Mani feel instantly grumpy. As she reluctantly pulled it on, she saw to her horror that the maid was reaching onto the top shelf of her almirah to pull out the heavily embroidered chunari in Tanchoi silk. The one reserved for the most special occasions.

'That one pricks my skin, I don't wish to wear it,' Mani objected, trying to be firm without sounding imperious. Her father disapproved terribly if she was ever high-handed with any of Peshwa-sahib's servants, constantly reminding her that they were not in their own employ. But this obstreperous maid was taking no notice at all of her request, insisting on winding the chunari around her shoulder, pinning it in place with a small pearl brooch. Now, as she hovered around waving the black kohl stick used to line the eyes, she was starting to annoy Mani greatly.

'Did I not say to you, I am busy reading my books and do not wish to be disturbed?'

The girl merely smiled mysteriously and replied softly, 'Peshwa-sahib has asked you to be dressed in your best for the Jhansi visitors.'

'Who are these Jhansi visitors anyway?' Mani asked, flouncing down onto a stool and succumbing to the maid's fussing fingers. Sitting back and blinking from the chilly sharpness of the kohl in her eyes, she considered how, increasingly, she was being presented, alongside Nana and Tantia, to visitors in the court. What made this summons unusual, though, was the uncompromising instruction to get so dressed up. Mani already had a pretty good suspicion what this was all about but the maid only smiled again as she attempted to glower at her through her stinging kohl-darkened eyes. After a sparkling jewelled bindi had been carefully stuck in the middle of Mani's forehead with a dab of rice-glue, she was ready and the two girls made their way down the stairs and across the quadrangle to the big hall.

Gaiety that Mani had not seen at Saturday House for many months now pervaded the large chamber. Every single crystal cup inside the grand chandelier contained a lit candle, even though it was still broad daylight, and, in a corner of the crowded hall, a musician was playing a sitar. Standing at the door, feeling unsure of herself in her unexpected finery, Mani managed to catch her father's eye. He smiled broadly as he spotted her and got up to escort her in, walking behind her as he held her by the shoulders. Peshwa-sahib, also looking absurdly happy, beckoned for them to walk across to where he sat before introducing her to one of the guests as 'his favourite girl, Manikarnika'.

That was her real name but she was always taken aback when someone addressed her by it. Mani tried not to scowl at the guest, an old man wearing a regal purple turban and a piercing gaze. Although nobody had told her yet exactly who he was, he enquired dourly what she had been doing to amuse herself. She was tempted to ask why that should be of such interest to him but a squeeze on her shoulder from Moropant warned her to be polite.

'I was reading. A book,' she said shortly.

Sharp eyes bored into her from beneath luxuriant white eyebrows. She had never seen eyebrows spring like that out of a face. They resembled two squashed birds and, as the man continued to stare, Mani imagined him choosing his eyebrows from a box full of cheeping creatures before carefully pasting on a pair every morning. He had obviously not been too impressed by her reply. Or perhaps he had thought her brevity rude, in which case her father would later look at her most reproachfully and not speak much over dinner. She hated silent meals like that and generally did her best to never earn them.

One small foot of hers crept unbidden over the other and she rubbed the ball of her foot over the toes of the other as though a sudden itch had developed there. As her anklets tinkled, a couple of the men in the room smiled reassuringly at her. But she felt embarrassed, violated even, by the way in which she was being examined by these strangers who were all looking her up and down in such an openly curious manner.

Of course she knew what all this was about, she was no fool. No wonder great-aunt Asharfi-bua had been in the kitchen all morning, wearing an anxious expression and barking orders at the cooks. Mani cursed herself for not enquiring earlier what the fuss was all about so that she could have hidden herself away in advance in her tree haven. Now it was too late to escape or even spare herself the disgusting sight of these men falling upon the succession of sweetmeats that was being dispatched from the kitchens. From the trouble that was being taken over them, it was clear that they had come with a marriage proposal although there was the faintest hope that they were people of political importance to Peshwa-sahib. The celebratory air of this gathering was not one befitting a serious political meeting, though. Those had become urgent and cheerless affairs, particularly in recent years, and people neither got dressed up nor ate so much at those gatherings anyway. And, if indeed this was a marriage proposal, then it had to be for her as there was no one else of marriageable age in Saturday House. Mani was furious that Asharfi-bua had not warned her of it, merely dismissing her cantankerously from the kitchen early this morning for being in the way. She vowed to lodge a complaint with her father as soon as possible but, for the moment, he too seemed completely preoccupied with the guests, laughing and jabbering with them as though they were the only people in the world who mattered. It peeved her enormously that, having planted her in front of the man with the bushy eyebrows, he was now not bothering to look in her direction at all.

Who were these people who spoke Marathi differently from the way in which it was spoken at Saturday House, mixed in with a lot more Hindustani. Such an odd assortment…old and young, tall and small, skinny and rotund, but mostly old and rotund, Mani thought ungraciously. They looked prosperous too and all of them, without exception, were overdressed in huge silk turbans and gaudy embroidered brocade kurtas.

She felt a poke in her shoulder and stepped aside for one of Peshwa-sahib's maids to hand around a silver thali full of hot crunchy jalebis, their sweetness oozing to form sticky pools on the bottom of the plate as they cooled. The central rosewood table was laden already with a stack of griddle-fried puranpoli and its accompanying pot of creamy shrikhand. Next to them was a platter holding an assortment of chewy halwas. These were the translucent green and red ones, square-cut and bright as jewels and covered today with sheets of the thinnest silver varkh that was only brought out of Asharfi-bua's cupboard for the most special occasions.

Finally, as though all that wasn't enough, Mani could see another maid enter with a tray full of her favourite sohan halwa. Everyone knew she loved these whirls of nut-flecked hard toffee for which the strong back teeth were needed and where bits would remain stuck till long afterwards, melting only after relentless probing by her tongue. Mani thought it unforgivable on Asharfi-bua's part to have not even told her that the sweets had been bought from the bazaar earlier today. The secrecy was quite probably for some silly reason such as worrying that she would eat too many and cause pimples to appear on her chin just before she was to be 'viewed'. They lay before her now, a whole plateful, gleaming golden and arranged in a spiral on a paraath, but if she helped herself to one now she would probably seem gluttonous before these guests and earn glares from both Baba and Peshwa-sahib.

Asharfi-bua was making her own entrance, waddling in with a platter of freshly fried daal-stuffed samosas, announcing ingratiatingly that they were for those without a sweet tooth. Mani noticed with satisfaction that her great-aunt was avoiding meeting her in the eye, even though she was openly scowling at her ample back. But there was no point in looking so intently at either Asharfi-bua or anyone else as, glancing around, Mani glumly observed the guests reach out greedily for everything, sweet or savoury, as though they had not seen such delicacies before. It was obvious that these affluent people were not unaccustomed to feasts and Mani wryly recognized the voracious behaviour typical of baraatis who liked nothing better than being indulged by prospective brides' families. She had even heard that the families of some extremely eligible bachelors actually toured the countryside, going from one bride-viewing to another for the sheer pleasure of being coddled and cosseted and fussed over in this horribly fawning way.

But which one of them was the prospective groom? Mani cast her eyes quickly around, not wishing to be seen staring, and picked out the youngest of them as the most likely candidate. He was muscular—which probably meant he rode well—but his head bore a ridiculously colourful three-cornered turban and he sported the biggest moustache Mani had ever seen at Saturday House. That was an impressive claim as some of Peshwa-sahib's courtiers had moustaches that, carefully waxed and shaped, resembled the curving grey horns on ancient bullocks' heads. This particular specimen was gleaming black and trembled magnificently as the man chomped on a hot jalebi. Mani felt a shudder of revulsion pass through her body. She did not want to get married and certainly not to a moustachioed jester like this one.

Looking around, she suddenly realized that Nana and Tantia had been left out of this gathering—quite possibly because Peshwa-sahib did not trust them to behave like proper young men at such an important event. Although feeling vaguely honoured to be considered more 'grown-up' and trustworthy than her two friends, she quickly quelled her pleasure, reminding herself sternly that it still did not mean she wanted to get *married*.

Later that night she overheard the argument between Asharfi-bua and her father that confirmed her suspicions. Disagreements between them were rare as Moropant usually allowed his formidable aunt to rule his household with no questions asked and Asharfi-bua's voice sounded frustrated rather than angry.

'Moropant Tambe, you are a fool, when will you accept that she is not a boy but a girl and one who has come of age too?'

'I know she must get married someday, Asharfi-bua, but why must she be expected to leave our house now? She is not even of fourteen years yet. Let her grow just a little bit more...maybe they can be persuaded to wait just a year or two...' Mani could hear the gentle pleading in her father's voice.

'Arrey, we are talking about a girl who has attained maturity two years ago and you want her to grow a little more! Girls who are allowed to grow too much before marriage only grow into trouble, Moropant. Especially when they are brought up not knowing if they are girl or boy, with all this horse riding and nonsense. You think Raja Gangadhar Rao will wait until *you* think she is old enough? Remember that he will have to get married soon because his first wife could not give him an heir and things like that cannot be made to wait. There will be hundreds of families more than willing to give their daughters away to him.'

Moropant was silent as Asharfi-bua stopped ranting to catch her breath. To Mani it seemed that she was not even giving her poor father time to think before setting off again. 'Listen, Moropant, you are only a courtier, and not even a courtier to proper royalty any more. Peshwa-sahib's powers are all gone, just like that, it is nothing but faded glory over here. We should be so honoured that a proposal like this has come for our Mani. All along we have known from her horoscope that a great marriage alliance was waiting for her. A *raja* for your daughter, and you will have the temerity to turn him down!'

At this, Moropant finally made an irritated sound in his throat. 'Asharfi-bua, even if the emperor in Delhi asked for Mani's hand, I would be saying the same thing,' he snapped. 'It is not status I am concerned with. I cannot help worrying that Raja Gangadhar is a widower and forty years old or more, almost my age...and anyway, I still feel Mani is too young...'

'Too young, too old, pah! The important thing is that the raja is a man with a reputation for being kind. Just consider, Moropant—even though his first rani could not bear him children, he did not take up with someone else when she was still alive. He could have had two or three wives using his wife's barrenness as an excuse? Why our own Peshwa-sahib has...' Asharfi-bua dropped her voice to a sibilant whisper at this point before deciding to return to her original point. 'Our Mani will not just be a queen, Moropant, she will be Raja Gangadhar's *first* queen and, from what we know of him, his only queen.'

Moropant made no comment and Mani confusedly wondered if she would be expected to join an array of barren wives. How many wives were rajas allowed to have? She had never given such matters any thought before! But Asharfi-bua had taken up her harangue again, now adopting a more placatory tone of voice.

'Moropant, we must remember too that we are not getting any younger. Both of us. I shudder to think of what will happen to our Mani once you and I are gone. I don't know about you but I certainly cannot bear to think of her treated like that Tantia is sometimes around here...'

Moropant seemed slumped in complete despair now, making no response at all as Asharfi-bua continued speaking quietly, 'Now that poor Rani Ramabai of Jhansi is dead, God rest her soul, the raja, understandably, wants another chance at marriage, my child. And who better than our Mani to be his wife and to be—think of it, Moropant—Rani of Jhansi!'

Mani could hear the awe and wonder in her great-aunt's voice as she pronounced those words, *Rani of Jhansi*, and felt a prickle run down her spine.

'Rani of Jhansi,' Mani whispered to herself, leaning her hot forehead on the cool marble trellis of the window after her father and great-aunt had retired to their separate rooms, their dispute unresolved. Where was this Jhansi anyway? And how could she become a rani of anywhere with no warning or training? She would never know what to do or even where to start. Feeling unbearably confused, Mani looked down at the gently flowing river and, seeing the fallen stars struggling in the dark waters of the Ganga, felt there was a certain justice in that. How could the world that was such a happy place so suddenly turn upside down? She did not want to get married, she certainly did not want to be queen of Jhansi or anywhere else for that matter. Even as a little girl she had never particularly enjoyed dressing up, preferring to join Nana and Tantia in their boyish pursuits of gilli-danda and pitthoo. She was happy here in Saturday House. It was the only home she had ever known and she belonged *here*, not in some unknown place called Jhansi. But Mani knew no one more determined than Asharfi-bua and feared that her gentle father would weaken before the sheer force of the tearful desperation she had heard in her great-aunt's voice. Mani's only other girlfriend, a cousin of Nana's, was married two years ago, at exactly the same age that Mani was now. She should have known that it was only a matter of time before which her family would start looking for a match for her too. But she had never seriously thought about leaving Varanasi and, worse, Saturday House. The shock of hearing that conversation between her father and Asharfi-bua was making her stomach churn terribly, although that could also be the three chunks of sohan halwa she had consumed earlier, after the guests had gone.

A horrifying thought occurred to Mani when she had crawled into bed, and she was still struggling to sleep two hours later: that moustachioed man could not have been the groom, for Jhansi's raja would surely have been seated at the very centre of the room. Which one was the raja then? Not that wrinkled old man with the purple turban and chicken feathers for eyebrows? Forty was so *old*, it was positively ancient. Mani felt frantic fingers clutching at her belly, making her want to vomit.

She was still feeling ill in the morning, an uneasy pain lurking in the pit of her stomach, reminding her of the previous day's events the moment she awoke. As her eyes unglued, Tantia's figure materialized in the window seat.

'I have been waiting hours for you to wake up, Mani,' he complained nasally. These days his voice moved scales most alarmingly, squeaky one moment and guttural the next.

'What are you doing here?' Mani demanded, rubbing her eyes and stretching her arms before propping herself up on one elbow. She had only recently started agreeing with Asharfi-bua that it was really quite inappropriate for Nana and Tantia to come unbidden into her room, prodding and poking her things with their dirty fingers and with sticks as they had done since they were children.

'Nana is having his bath and I was bored,' Tantia said, getting up to wander across the room and examine the contents of Mani's writing bureau.

'Stop prying among my things,' she said indignantly, before switching over to what she thought may be a supercilious English accent, 'Have you not got any shame to be looking at the things belonging to a girl?'

'Girl, hanh?' Tantia chuckled. 'Old woman would be more like it. Nearly about to be married...'

'If you're not careful, I'll have you blown from a cannon when I'm Rani of Jhansi,' Mani retorted archly.

'Ha, so it's true then?'

Mani looked away, refusing to be drawn as Tantia waggled his eyebrows at her, a silly smile splitting his face in half. 'So, is it true, my dear Mani, that the raja of Jhansi sent his ministers to get a good look at you yesterday, so that they could confirm that you had the longest nose and biggest head this side of the Ganga?'

Tantia ducked, adroitly avoiding the cushion that hurtled his way. But Mani did not want to chase him away, for it was possible he would be carrying vital information. 'Were those Jhansi's *ministers* then?' she asked, pulling another cushion onto her lap and leaning forward on it.

'Of course, pagli, what did you think, that they would let you become a rani without having Jhansi's entire council of ministers assess your weight and height and measure the width of your nose and the length of your every hair? And rajas are hardly likely to go wandering around the countryside in search of brides, are they, buddhoo?'

Mani beamed at Tantia, sitting back in relief, 'So that old crumbly with the waggling eyebrows was not the raja after all!'

Tantia fell onto the cushioned window seat, chortling loudly, 'You thought Baba Dixit was your bridegroom? He's the prime minister of Jhansi, buddhoo, and he must be at least one hundred years old!' Tantia screeched with renewed merriment as he realized the advantage he could take of this. 'Wait till I tell Nana! You thought Baba Dixit...'

He got up and was still laughing as he ran down the corridor, almost crashing into Asharfi-bua who was heaving her bulk up the stairs.

'Curses to that child,' Asharfi-bua puffed as she came into Mani's room, trying to catch her breath, 'nearly knocking me down the stairs, just like that. Shooting past as though he has important state business waiting for him. But at least he's woken you up. Come on get up now and clean your teeth, Mani-beti. I've had some fresh new neem sticks and sandalwood paste placed along with your bathwater downstairs. Remember to keep the sandalwood paste on your face for at least fifteen minutes before washing it off. You must start looking after that pretty face of yours now...no more of this tomboy tomfoolery of yours.'

'Why, Bua?' Mani asked. Perhaps wide-eyed innocence would get her the information she wanted.

'Why? Because you are now no longer a child and because big-big proposals of marriage have started coming from near and far.'

'Was that a proposal that came yesterday then? From those men in turbans who could not stop eating.' Mani hoped that Asharfi-bua would not miss the sarcasm in her voice. She really ought not to forget her annoyance towards her great-aunt for having failed to tell her what was going on yesterday.

Asharfi-bua sat down on the edge of Mani's bed and took her chin between fingers smelling of ghee. She looked into her niece's eyes and Mani felt suddenly uncomfortable to see tears in her old aunt's rheumy gaze. Even Asharfi-bua's normally strident voice seemed to have taken on a suddenly uncharacteristic wobbliness as she said, 'Yes, jaan, that was a proposal for you. And an exceedingly honourable one too. From the raja of Jhansi, no less. He had heard about your beauty from Peshwa-sahib and wanted to find out for himself if you were as lovely as he had been told.'

'My beauty *and* my brains, please Bua,' Mani reminded her.

'Yes-yes, jaan, your beauty and your brains. The ministers have gone away from here very happy, Mani. Now we have to wait to see what the raja says. He may want to see you for himself, imagine that!'

'What about me, when will I get to see him?' Mani asked.

'Chee, chee, what sort of forward talk is this? You see *him*, just like that? You will see him when the time is right, that is how it is done.' Asharfi-bua got up and started to wheeze agitatedly again, making a hash of trying to fold Mani's discarded quilt before stuffing it into the almirah.

'Is he very...tall, Bua?' Mani had meant to say 'old' rather than 'tall' and felt gripped by a sudden unfamiliar shyness.

Luckily Asharfi-bua did not seem to have noticed Mani's blushes as she carried on waddling about the room, straightening and clearing things, grumbling under her breath. 'He will be as all men are, Mani, two legs, two hands, eyes in his head and that is all you need to know. What is important is that I have heard that he is kind and wise and devotedly tended his poor wife till her dying day. Men like that are rare, child. Or would you rather we found some strapping young fellow who cannot keep his hands off the palace maids and courtesans, as happened to our poor Mangaladevi, hanh? They thought they were marrying her off to some high-ranking nobleman but what a rogue he turned out to be and the poor girl's life was finished after her marriage, just like that.'

Having delivered that ominous line, Asharfi-bua shuffled away to terrorize another part of the household, her bottom wobbling like giant watermelons inside her sari. Mani stayed in bed, even more confused than before. On the one hand, the very sound of words like 'marriage' and 'husband' made her want to retch but, on the other hand, she rather liked the idea of a raja coming from a faraway land to seek her hand in marriage. If truth were to be told, she had already attributed the raja of Jhansi with a face—oldish, but in a nice benign way and with soft, kind eyes that were devoted, already, to her. She imagined keeping him waiting a few weeks before giving him her answer that would finally be a 'yes' because…well, because she couldn't think of a good enough reason to say 'no' right away. Except—and this she was quite sure about—she would ask that he wait until she had grown up a bit more and learnt everything there was to know about horsemanship. She was only just getting to master the art of riding with the reins between her teeth and not using her hands at all, a skill that both Nana and Tantia were extremely envious of, even though they could scarcely bring themselves to admit it.

Mani was still contemplating the possibility of being a queen as she had her bath a little later, rubbing the neem stick vigorously against her teeth and gums while the sandalwood paste dried and tightened on her face. Unhooking her blouse before taking off her clothes, she felt the temperature of the water before adding some more hot water from the copper cauldron in the corner under which coals were still glowing. With a small brass lota she splashed warm water to soften the dried mask on her face before rubbing it off, fragrant drops running down her neck and dripping off the tips of her small erect nipples. Using her loofah, she started to scrub some gram flour onto her arms and back, wondering whether, as Rani of Jhansi, she would be able to get someone else to do all these boring tasks for her such as rubbing her back and scrubbing her feet clean of the dirt they gathered when she went out to play in the mango orchard with Nana and Tantia.

Mani was sure her father would shortly wish to discuss the matter directly with her and was not surprised when he offered to conduct her riding lesson the following day, dismissing the old Pathan who normally supervised the session. Moropant waited patiently for Mani to complete all her usual exercises, nodding approvingly as she flew effortlessly over the highest bar and laughing at her efforts to control the horse without using her hands. But it was only when they were trotting at a gentle pace back to the stables at the end of the lesson that he finally touched on the topic that had lain unspoken between them so far.

He cleared his throat before speaking slowly and carefully, as though about to discuss the most politically sensitive matter in the world. 'Mani-beti, your Asharfi-bua tells me that you know about the wedding proposal from Jhansi and have not indicated any major objection to it. Is that correct?'

Like Moropant, Mani kept her eyes fixed firmly on the horizon, wondering at how embarrassed she suddenly felt before her beloved Baba. But she knew he was waiting anxiously to hear her response and so she replied, equally carefully, 'Yes, Baba, I know of it and cannot think of any major objection but...'

As she trailed off, Moropant responded nervously, 'But? But what, beti?'

'You see, Baba, I am a little concerned that I have not learnt all the things I need to finish learning first.'

'And what might that be?' Moropant asked, now sounding a little more amused than worried.

'Well, for one I'm not as expert a horse rider as I would like to be yet and Pathan-ji says that, with a few more months of practice, I will be able to leap over hedges with the reins held in my mouth...'

Moropant laughed out loud. 'If it's horsemanship you're worried about, Mani, it may interest you to know that the Jhansi stables are supposed to be amongst the finest in Bundelkhand.'

Mani turned to look at him open-mouthed. This was starting to be a lot less bad than she had anticipated.

'Stables full of horses, and they would all belong to *me*?' she asked disbelievingly.

Moropant nodded sagely. 'Well, to whoever marries the raja of Jhansi, beti. It would be nice not to have to beg Nana for your turn on his horses, wouldn't it? I have even heard it said that Jhansi has a small stable of elephants...'

Mani knew that Moropant was reminding her of the time Nana had been so unkind, refusing to let her go up in the Peshwa's elephant howdah with him just to look at the view.

As Mani lapsed into confused silence, Moropant felt faintly ashamed of his machinations, although this was diluted considerably by the knowledge that his daughter would indeed acquire numerous luxuries that he, a mere courtier, would never be able to afford. His voice dropped a note as he continued speaking, 'Peshwa-sahib has always been generous to a fault with you, Mani, but we both know that you will never really be Nana's equal here at Saturday House. And now before this poor father lies the chance to elevate his daughter's position to one of royalty. How can I spurn such a remarkable offer, I ask you, beti? How?'

Guilt washed briefly over Moropant as he deftly shifted the burden of his decision onto Mani but, shooting a swift look in her direction, saw that the troubled lines on her brow had cleared away. Perhaps it was the thought of a stable full of horses, which would be the most dreadfully frivolous reason to accept a marriage proposal. He wished he had not dangled that possibility before her so thoughtlessly. After all, she was still in many ways just a child.

After returning their horses, they walked down the path that would take them to the main entrance of Saturday House, Mani remaining silent on the subject of the marriage proposal. Despite her uncustomary silence, Moropant could sense her growing acquiescence to it. He knew he ought to be feeling relieved at how easily it had been brought about but, irrationally, found himself wishing too that Mani would rail just a little bit against getting married and leaving her old father behind. Instead, as they walked up the main stairs, she blurted, 'Baba, I will be married to whomever you choose. To the raja of Jhansi, if you so wish.'

She had not looked at him as she said this but he saw a smile on her face as she lifted the hem of her skirt and raced up the last few stairs at her usual speed. Moropant, watching his daughter's fleeing figure melt into the dark shadows of the house, scolded himself for feeling suddenly inexplicably robbed.

Later in the evening, Moropant heard Mani stoutly defending the man she was due to marry. Nana had been teasing her mercilessly all through the meal, finally declaring that all kings of Jhansi, past and present, were British 'chamchas' and lackeys.

Mani's voice rose in passionate anger in protest, 'They are not with the British. They are an independent state!' Turning to her father, she had pleaded, 'It is not true what Nana says, is it, Baba?'

'Well, Nana is partially right, beti,' Moropant replied. 'Raja Gangadhar is indeed friendly with the British but only because one of his ancestors helped to bring some anti-British rebels under control.'

'See, I told you, buddhoo. He *is* a British lackey,' Nana crowed triumphantly.

Mani, red in the face, retorted hotly, 'You are only sore because the British are not welcome in this court, Nana. If the British allow the raja of Jhansi to rule his state and even remain friendly with him, then there must be good reason to do. Maybe he is just a very good ruler.'

Moropant, both touched and worried at his daughter's spirited defence of her future husband, wondered when she would start asking him awkward questions about Jhansi's political status, a matter he too felt quite unsure of at the moment.

A fortnight after his party had visited Saturday House, the raja of Jhansi sent his final approval of the match. His letter was delivered to Saturday House on a close, pre-monsoonal evening. Mani, watching the unfamiliar man arrive on horseback at the gates, had known instantly that he was the personal messenger whose arrival from Jhansi was being eagerly anticipated. Following him at a safe distance, Mani watched the visitor hand over a khureeta in court. She could not hear his words but knew that he would be making poetic and elaborate addresses to Peshwa-sahib's court. Peering through a pair of tasselled brocade curtains at the back of the big hall, she saw Peshwa-sahib open an embroidered mauve silk purse containing the inscribed piece of parchment that would seal her fate. He was nodding and smiling broadly, handing the messenger a few silver mohurs to indicate his pleasure. Mani felt a quiver run through her body, a mix of exhilaration and nervousness that made her go hot and cold all at once.

It was best to flee back to her room before she was spotted. Running up the backstairs, she threw open her door before flinging herself onto the window seat, hardly able to breathe for the gnawing at her stomach. Outside, Ganga-ma was rolling brown and turbulent in anticipation of the monsoons and Mani, hanging her head out of the window, marvelled at the way in which her river always managed to reflect her moods. She took a deep breath, trying to calm herself. It was odd that the raja had not asked to see her first, merely accepting his ministers' view of her. Perhaps that was because the Jhansi contingent had delivered the most glowing report of both her beauty and her brains, as Asharfi-bua had indicated. She pulled her head back in and cast a glance at herself in the mirror above the cabinet— at the moment she looked far from beautiful, her face all hot and flushed, tangled hair hanging over her cheeks. She had to put on a calm visage before someone came in search of her to break the news. Picking up the embroidery hoop that Asharfi-bua had started for her earlier, she soon threw it down in disgust as she pricked her fingers twice before managing even one stitch. There was no telling if her apprehension was one of fear or joy for she had never known such a strange mix of emotions before. By the time a maid came in to tell her that she was summoned to the courtroom by Peshwa-sahib, she thought she was ready to collapse from exhaustion.

Feigning nonchalance, she wandered into the hall with what she imagined was an expression of neutral curiosity on her face. But when she saw her father holding the khureeta, she could bear it no longer. She snatched it out of his hands, her ears burning from the shouts of laughter that she could hear from both Peshwa-sahib and Baba as she fled their presence.

Mani tucked the silk purse into her blouse as she hurried back to her room, hoping desperately that Nana and Tantia were busy elsewhere in the palace. Reoccupying her window seat again, she struggled with the gold strings wrapped around the pouch with trembling fingers. Even her breath felt short in her chest and she knew that it was nothing to do with having run up the winding backstairs as she never went at a sedate pace either up or down them, much to Asharfi-bua's chagrin. But now she could hear someone coming down the corridor to her room. Clicking her tongue in frustration, Mani hastily pushed the purse back into her blouse before leaping up. This was like being a hunted deer in a forest with no trees. Shoving past a baffled Asharfi-bua, she picked up her skirts and ran down the corridor to leave the house by the main stairway this time. Even in such a large house, it was impossible sometimes to find a quiet corner. She knew, however, exactly where to go, and slowed down only once she reached the gates leading to the mango orchard.

Once at the foot of her beloved old tree, she expertly looped her long skirt between her legs before tucking the end into her waistband. Effortlessly finding all her familiar footholds, she was up in her private sanctum within a matter of minutes and, when finally completely hidden from view by branches and leaves, she delved into her blouse to pull out the khureeta, now damp and warm from her exertions. Leaning on the great central trunk, she fumbled with the knots, shaking her head to rid it of its thumping drumbeats.

The letter was addressed to Peshwa-sahib and said, in a most elegant script, that Gangadhar Rao, raja of Jhansi, was pleased to renew his alliance with the Peshwa's court by marrying Manikarnika Tambe, daughter of his senior political advisor, Moropant Tambe. Mani's eyes scanned rapidly over the next bit that went on at length about how the rajas of Jhansi had been entrusted long ago by Peshwa-sahib's ancestors to be the state's subedars, expressing in different flowery ways how pleased the raja was to be presented with the opportunity to be allowed to return that ancient favour. None of that interested Mani much and she skipped through the remainder of the letter, looking for more mention of her name. When she found none, she sat back, scolding herself for having such unbecomingly eager thoughts about this stranger whom she had not even seen. Just because he wanted her to be his wife and queen. Running her finger over the brown ink letters and the seal at the bottom, she wondered if Raja Gangadhar had sat down to write it personally or given it to one of his court writers to compose. She imagined that he would have formed a picture in his mind of what she looked like from the descriptions given to him by his ministers. At least he had that. Perhaps a portrait of hers would be sent as well. She, on the other hand, had no idea at all what sort of a face she was to give him in her thoughts.

Marriage was not something Mani had given much thought to before and it was so very odd that, since hearing of the marriage proposal, she had been able to think of little else. Lying back in the comforting hollow carved by her growing body over the years, she placed the letter over her face, screening away the sun-drenched leaves and branches now shorn of their burden of summer fruit. She inhaled the smell of the paper and ink, willing the letter to give up the secrets it contained of the man who had sent it, imagining how his hands would have put pen to paper and carefully folded it before sending it on its way to her, his bride.

❧ 5 ❧

Observing his daughter in the weeks that followed, Moropant could see, to his growing relief, that Mani had come not just to accept the idea of marriage but seemed even to be relishing it. How inexplicable young girls' minds sometimes were, he thought, knowing that it was best not to probe and reminding himself to be pleased that Mani was not as traumatized by the idea of leaving Saturday House as he had at first feared. Asharfi-bua had been right when she described Mani as having a wise soul, quite unlike other children her age. Why, even her horoscope destined greatness. Perhaps he should have bowed earlier to his old aunt's superior knowledge of the child she had brought up so carefully and wished, not for the first time in the past few days, that his poor wife had still been alive to share their joy.

He had today requested Peshwa-sahib to talk Mani through the wedding plans. Not merely because it was Peshwa-sahib's old connection with the Maratha subedars of Jhansi that had brought about this proposal, but also because Moropant knew how much Mani adored Peshwa-sahib, endowing him with a sort of grandfatherly status.

Moropant now watched them from the window of his quarter in Saturday House as the pair walked around the gardens awash with evening light. Mani was holding Peshwa-sahib's hand around her shoulder, partially to give him support, looking up at him and laughing as he made some observation and Moropant could imagine the wry humour with which Peshwa-sahib would explain to her the importance of this alliance. He had always been better with these young people than Moropant, despite having no children of his own. After adopting Nana, he had seemed to enjoy surrounding himself more and more with young people, not just for Nana's sake but his own, Moropant suspected. Perhaps in their carefree joys, he had been able to forget some of his own tribulations. Moropant's heart warmed as he heard the distant tinkle of Mani's laughter, her figure now obscured from view behind the rows of chameli bushes in the western garden.

Mani, for her part, did not notice the heavy perfume of the chameli flowers as she listened carefully to Peshwa-sahib. He was talking of his hopes that her presence at Jhansi would lead to a renewal of old and valued ties between the two royal houses. Looking up at his dear old face and seeing his eyes glaze over with sudden tears, she found herself wishing desperately that she would indeed be able to do something to revive Peshwa-sahib's diminished fortunes once she became rani of Jhansi. Perhaps she could help to improve his abysmal relationship with the British, seeing that her future husband was close to them. Future husband—no matter how many times she said it, the words still remained strange and daunting.

As they reached the gates at the end of the garden, Mani cast a look out at the rice fields lying beyond them—they had been a silver sheet of water just a few months ago. Now they were knee-high and jade green, readying themselves for harvest. How quickly the seasons changed and moved on, taking her life with it. She had not even noticed the years pass and had only just learnt that, being a girl, she ought to have watched over and treasured the few years she would have in her childhood home. How would she be able to bear exchanging this house, its quiet mango orchards and her beloved river, for some distant land? What if her new family did not like her? What if she could never find herself able to belong to that new home and all those people she was meant to rule over?

There was something in her that still quaked at the thought of becoming a queen and, even worse, wife to someone she had never seen. But, as she tightened her hold around Peshwa-sahib's waist, Mani told herself fiercely that getting married to achieve the happiness of this dear old man and her father was as honourable a reason as any. How could she ever doubt that they, who loved her so much, would ever put her in a situation that could cause her harm?

'So you are happy, little Mani?' Peshwa-sahib asked, feeling her sudden hug.

Mani nodded demurely in response, although it would probably have been more accurate to say that she was not *unhappy*. With Peshwa-sahib, she felt she could be honest. 'I am not against the idea of marriage, Badey Baba. Asharfi-bua would never let me escape it anyway.'

Peshwa-sahib laughed in agreement but persisted, 'I fear I hear a "but" in there...'

Mani looked up at him beseechingly. 'Oh Badey Baba, I just wish I did not have to go quite so far away from Saturday House and all of you.'

'I understand that, beti. That is the burden of being born a girl. Our daughters are flower buds given so briefly to us, their perfume reserved for their husband's homes where they blossom. Jhansi no doubt eagerly awaits its queen. Moropant will tell you about the history of the state before your journey there. And, once you are in Jhansi, you will learn all that you need to know from your future husband; I know him to be a kind and tolerant man.'

Mani, suddenly shy, said softly, 'But I will not be able to bear being far away from all of you...'

Peshwa-sahib laughed. 'All girls say that before they leave their homes. And then, once they are in paradise with their husbands, they suffer from sudden loss of memory about their parental homes. I can wager you anything, beti, that we will be thinking and talking of you much more often than you will ever remember us. As queen, you will have so much to see and learn, I fear that you will soon forget all about Saturday House and those you have left behind.'

'That will never happen, Badey Baba! You will all be in my thoughts every day. I promise you that.'

'Well, I certainly want you to remember us. But maybe not every day, Mani,' the old man said, eyes twinkling, before he added more seriously, 'You will have far more important things to consider. Marriages are unions between not just two people but entire families and communities. In your case, it also includes the union of states and royal lines, which puts a heavy burden on your young shoulders. But we would never have expected you to take on all that if we had not thought you capable of it. I have every confidence in you. Now, if it had been either Nana or Tantia...'

They laughed together at the thought of Nana and Tantia being cast into positions of responsibility. Ever since her marriage had been fixed, the pair had become suddenly almost deferential to Mani—no longer ordering her about and even seeking her opinion on important matters. That, she decided, had been the most agreeable part of it all so far.

Raja Gangadhar had decreed that it was fitting for the nuptials to take place at Jhansi and so Saturday House was soon filled with the excitement of, not just the wedding, but also the long journey that awaited the bridal party across the vast stretch of Bundelkhand. But, before that, there were clothes to be stitched and jewellery to be made. Mani was amazed at just how many dressmakers and embroiderers existed in Varanasi as endless battalions of them trooped in and out of the house in the weeks leading up to the wedding. There were trips into the nearby town too: exciting visits to shops bursting with silks and precious stones and filigreed silver. As she was taken by Asharfi-bua to Varanasi's finest tailoring establishments for her clothes to be fitted and every inch of her was carefully scrutinized and measured to get her new trousseau made to perfection, Mani swung from feeling excited to being unbearably exhausted. On one such trip into Varanasi, thrilled by the cacophony of conch-shells and temple bells amidst the energetic bustle on the ghats and the myriad smells of unfamiliar foodstuffs wafting in from crowded bazaars, Mani thought suddenly of how empty the drowsy routine of life at Saturday House really was. She could not wait to escape it, especially as she could see how much Nana and Tantia envied her all the adventures her new life would bring.

Asharfi-bua had told her that Raja Gangadhar Rao wanted this second marriage of his be kept simple, his first wife having not been long dead, but that did not seem to dampen anyone's enthusiasm at Saturday House. The household seemed to talk of nothing but *the wedding* and *the journey* these days. Raja Gangadhar had undertaken to send enough horse-carriages and palanquins for the bridal party to make the journey from Varanasi to Jhansi in comfort. The expedition would take some ten days and, as they would be travelling west, occasionally through forests and ravines notorious for Thugs and dacoits, a small party of armed guards was being sent as well.

On the day the party from Jhansi were due to arrive, Nana and Tantia, watching eagerly from the upper windows of Saturday House, announced their arrival with loud whoops and yells. Mani joined them at their lookout post to see a small caravan winding its way down the road leading to the Peshwa's palace, two shehnai players leading the way as they played their reedy music. An elephant, painted with elaborate designs followed them, grandly pulling a large enclosed wooden carriage that looked like a small room on wheels, arched windows at the front and back covered with silk curtains. Following its slow, stately progress were half a dozen horse-drawn carriages and covered bullock carts, male servants carrying palanquins across their shoulders and an army of matchlock-men and guards bearing spears, jezails and muskets gleaming shiny in the sun. As they inched their way slowly down the road that cut its way through the neat rustling squares of rice fields, Mani felt her first frisson of genuine fear at the impending nuptials. She looked at the distant horizon, where the road vanished as green fields melded into blue skies, and wondered what lay beyond.

Just yesterday, she had looked at Jhansi on the survey map in their schoolroom, making sure no one was around to see her slowly trace the roads leading to it with her fingertip. Like Varanasi, it seemed to sit near a river, the Betwa, and Mani wondered if she would derive comfort from that fact once she was far from her own riverside home and everyone she knew and loved. How she wished that the map would talk and tell her about the town and its people, the palace she would live in and, most of all, about the man she was to marry. She felt suddenly anxious again and annoyed with herself for the confusion of her feelings that seemed to change from one moment to the next with no warning at all.

Three days after the raja's party had arrived at Saturday House, they declared themselves ready for the return journey. Mani had not been given the opportunity to make any friendly overtures to the people who had come from Jhansi, Asharfi-bua keeping her on a tight rein with stern reminders not to attempt befriending those who were soon to become her retainers. She had, however, enviously heard Nana's and Tantia's reports of how Siddhabaksh the elephant was being strengthened for the return journey, being fed enormous salted wheat-cakes, his ears and feet being carefully oiled to prevent them from cracking in the heat of the sun.

No one could predict exactly how long the journey back to Jhansi would take, and so it was agreed that the departure should take place sooner rather than later. The idea was to travel as quickly as possible to Orchha where they would then bide their time until the most auspicious day for the wedding.

Mani awoke early on the morning of her departure from Saturday House and watched the sunlight creep over the wall next to her bed.

Every little crack and pit on that stretch of wall was so well known, it was impossible to believe that she would not be waking up to its familiarity any more. Turning over, she looked at her small writing desk in the corner, covered with the schoolbooks that she had not had the time for these past few weeks, having been kept busy with new clothes to be stitched, jewellery to be ordered and hundreds of visitors to Saturday House, all bearing gifts and blessings for the new young queen of Jhansi. The weeks leading up to this day had passed in a whirl of unfamiliar experiences, leaving no time for fears or doubts. Suddenly now they were crowding in on Mani as she lay on her bed, making her feel weak and physically unable to get up. She could hear footsteps outside and saw Asharfi-bua come in to wake her up as she always did.

Mani watched her great-aunt from her bed, as she fussed and fretted in her usual style, although today it seemed like a huge effort for her to say all the usual things—get up, get up…brush your teeth with a fresh neem twig…don't forget the sandalwood on your face— as though it was just another day and not the last time she would be saying all those things she had chanted like a morning mantra ever since she had taken over Mani's care, ten years ago.

Mani dragged herself up in bed and reached out her arms to her elderly great-aunt, not trusting herself to speak without descending into sobs. But, as Asharfi-bua sat next to her and gathered her into her large soft bosom, both of them dissolved into helpless tears.

'Who will wake me up in my new home, Asharfi-bua? What will I do without you?' Mani inhaled tearfully from the smell of ghee and gram flour that always enveloped Asharfi-bua, an aroma that she would forevermore associate with motherly love. 'Please change your mind and come with me to Jhansi, Bua,' she pleaded.

'I am too old to make the long journey, jaan,' Asharfi-bua said, her voice wobbling as she tried to hold back her tears. 'I would have done anything to see my darling Mani-beti become a beautiful bride but a journey of so many days would finish me off just like that, I fear, beti.'

'We should have asked for the wedding to take place here at Saturday House, then you could have attended it too. Surely the raja would have understood…I should have written him a personal letter…'

Asharfi-bua pulled herself away and Mani saw a familiar look overcome her great-aunt's face, a look that told her that Asharfi-bua would never stop worrying about her, even when she had become queen of Jhansi.

'Write suggestions to the raja indeed! You will just have to learn to do the raja's bidding, Mani-beti!' she scolded. 'He is not like your father or Peshwa-sahib is to you, child, indulging your every whim. *Even* if silly ideas like that occur to you, you will just have to learn to tuck them away somewhere deep in your mind, promise me that!'

The urgency in her voice made Mani laugh through her tears but she could see how earnestly Asharfi-bua meant what she said. Her aunt was clutching her by the shoulders now and looking searchingly into her face. 'Promise me you will not say or do anything to upset Raja Gangadhar, Mani-beti. *Especially* in the first few months. Until you know him well and he has learnt to love you. He is a *raja*, don't forget that. And your husband, *not* a loving father or uncle.'

Poor dear anxious Asharfi-bua, Mani thought, wiping her own tears away as she smiled wanly. 'Bua, I promise you I will do everything the raja says,' she said solemnly before flashing a mischievous look at Asharfi-bua, unable to resist adding cheekily, 'and read his mind and do all those things also that he does not say...'

Asharfi-bua flapped her sari pallav at Mani's face in mock anger. 'Departing home to become a rani and still being impudent to your poor old aunt,' she said, blowing her nose fiercely on her pallav and laughing as she got up to help Mani out of bed.

But, after Mani had joined the rest of the wedding party assembling under the front porch of Saturday House, the two of them clung to each other one last time, now with real sorrow, as the time came for everyone to board their waiting carriages. Moropant, having just dealt with Nana and Tantia's latest altercation over which of them would travel in Mani's wooden chariot, felt his knees grow weak as he watched the farewell between his daughter and his aunt. How selflessly Asharfi-bua had cared for Mani ever since the child had lost her mother, making her welfare the very mission of her own widowed life. He did not have the heart to separate them now but, after a few minutes, Nana's mother gently disengaged the two, reminding everyone of the long journey that lay ahead.

Mani embraced Peshwa-sahib, who was also not attending the wedding because of his own poor health, and bent to touch his feet for a final blessing. Putting both his hands on her head, he whispered a Vishnu mantra for good luck before helping her into the waiting carriage. Mani, gripping the open window frame, looked out with a tear-stained face at Peshwa-sahib and Asharfi-bua and all the guards and courtiers who had congregated under the main portico of Saturday House to see the bridal party off for Jhansi. But it was her great-aunt's hands that she could not release as the mahout clicked his tongue in his throat to alert the elephant to their departure. Hands, now so gnarled, that had for years braided her hair and had even, on occasion, sharply tapped a copper lota on her head to quieten her during childhood baths.

'Bua!' Mani wailed as the carriage lurched forward and those beloved old fingers slipped out of her grip. Poor Asharfi-bua would never be able to keep up with the others who were running alongside the slowly plodding elephant. Mani craned her neck out of the window, trying to see over the heads of the guards and the servants. Through streaming eyes, she could barely see Asharfi-bua standing just behind Peshwa-sahib, both of them looking unbearably old in their white garments. As the gates were opened, her last glimpse of her great-aunt was blocked by the waving crowd before her carriage turned out of the gates and Saturday House and all its occupants vanished abruptly from view. Now all Mani could see were rippling stretches of rice plants and a murky pond in which the village buffalo was already wallowing in lazy anticipation of the day's heat.

Mani's tears had dried by the time the carriages trundled slowly past the stone ghats and she saw the sacred spot on the Ganga after which she had been named. A bereaved family was preparing to float the ashes of a loved one into the river but today Ganga-ma seemed oblivious to Mani's mood, flowing serenely on as though she did not really care who came and who went. Boatmen, repairing their barges in the cool half-light of the morning, looked up only briefly, accustomed to the sight of wealthy parties travelling in their caravans of elephants and horses through this prosperous town. Pilgrims to Varanasi's many temples were amassing on the steps leading down to the water and Mani wondered what had brought all these people to Varanasi even as she left it, their heads bobbing at the water's edge as they awaited the first rays of dawn to make their morning ablutions.

Willing herself to cry as all departing brides must, she recalled the trips she had made in her childhood to the Vishveshwar temple, balanced on the edge of the ghats, her father carrying a tray of flowers and coconuts as offerings for the gods. A stray memory drifted into her mind of helping to immerse her own mother's ashes in the river one uncomprehending summer evening. As she was overcome in a renewed bout of tears and hiccoughs, Nana, sitting next to her, patted Mani's arm. But she barely noticed his attempt at comfort, swinging around to look again through the tiny window on the back wall of the wooden carriage. She saw the spires of myriad temples and the dome of Aurangzeb's vaulting mosque turn to sudden gold as they caught the first glimmerings of dawn. Unable to tear her gaze away, she watched the sun inch slowly over golden Varanasi. Her vision, already blurred by tears, was blinded by its brilliance and she wept even harder at the thought that she had been deprived thus of even her very last glimpse of her birthplace.

Soon, she slept, exhausted from her uncustomary tears. Nana slept too, his head lolling comically, which brought the smile back to Mani's lips when she awoke some hours later. Even though Nana was nearly seventeen, and exceedingly proud of the spreading stain under his nose, he still looked like a boy to Mani, short and plump as he would always be. Tantia had outshot him in height last year, but had not outgrown his awe of the older boy, gloomily accepting Nana's orders this morning to find room in one of the lesser carriages as Nana had wanted to sit in this elephant-drawn one along with Mani. Realizing with sudden and rather agreeable surprise that these carriages were technically more hers than Nana's, Mani decided she would search for Tantia as soon as they came to their first halt and revoke Nana's attempts to ban him from sitting in the best carriage. She felt guilty at having been so overcome with sorrow to be leaving Asharfi-bua and Peshwa-sahib that she had quite forgotten to consider poor Tantia's feelings and could not wait to compensate for her omission as soon as possible. How strange but how very delightful to be able to legitimately supersede Nana's haughty orders to her and Tantia!

She knew it was around midday as the sun was now high in the sky and the air had grown hot and still, except for the whine of a fly trapped inside the carriage somewhere. The caravan seemed to be slowing down amongst a lot of shouting from the grooms and mahouts and, looking out of the small window, Mani guessed that they were stopping for lunch to be served. As the carriages came to a grinding halt beside a small rapidly flowing river, Nana was made to get up by one of his retainers and stumbled sulkily to where the stream had broken up into a series of waterfalls. Mani followed him to the water's edge, looking for Tantia downriver where the horses were already being refreshed and people were wading with relief into the cool, bubbling brook, splashing fresh water on their face and arms with cries of delight. She waved as she spotted his bullet head but he was already walking hurriedly to join Nana and the other menfolk in their manly preoccupations. Perhaps he had not seen her.

She stood alone at the edge of the river, watching it flow over a quartz bed, looking for her reflection. Only the flaming orange of her silk achkan, painstakingly stitched for her in Jhansi style, was discernible in the rushing waters, her face a mere blur. Mani, completely forgetting Asharfi-bua's advice on looking after her new clothes, sat down on the riverbank to plunge her legs into the water and felt the mossy granite bed of the stream soft and cool against her feet. Throwing a few stray pebbles into the bubbling waters, she decided that she would someday (but only *after* she had got to know the raja of Jhansi better) ask him if she could have Asharfi-bua over to stay with them. For now, though, mindful of her many promises, Mani knew she had no choice but to hold firm in her decision to be neither disrespectful nor forward with her new husband. She looked into the water again and, seeing glimpses of a young worried face, hoped desperately that it would not turn out to be too difficult, this whole business of being married to a raja. She wished she knew more about him. Not just what he looked like but what he would *be* like as well...

She saw Nana and Tantia on the other side of the camp, hanging around the syces, admiring their horses, and felt a twinge of envy at their freedom. They wouldn't have to worry about marriages for a long time yet and would probably never have to leave their childhood home. It felt most unjust to Mani to be burdened thus for being born a girl. Peshwa-sahib's exhortations about daughters being like flower buds really brought no comfort at all.

Voices were calling her name and Mani got up to return to where everyone was settling down for lunch. This first meal had been prepared and packed by the cooks back at Saturday House and would be eaten cold, although Mani had heard her father making elaborate arrangements for advance parties of servants and cooks to be ready with tents and food before the wedding party arrived at each night stop. As the food was laid out, Mani's heart melted as she saw that Asharfi-bua had remembered to include the black lime pickle she knew she enjoyed with her parathas. Seating herself cross-legged on a duree that had been spread under a tree and spreading her banana leaf out in front of her, she sipped at the glass of buttermilk that had been poured for her before tearing off a piece of paratha to wrap around the pickles. Servants waved flies away with their yak-tail fans, stirring the still air. Mani felt her spirits rise when Nana and Tantia flopped down on the bolsters next to her, full of eager excitement.

'Have you heard, Mani, the next part of the trip is going to be through dense woodland and forests?'

'The syces were telling us that these forests teem with nilgai and wild boar.'

'And one of them even said that it would not be uncommon for a tiger to be spotted if we were lucky.'

Mani smiled at them both. Even though their excitement was infectious, she could not help thinking that in some odd way, the things that thrilled them now seemed strangely remote to her. Was it possible for friends to grow apart so suddenly and in a matter of just a few days, she pondered, watching Nana poke Tantia hard in the ribs with a long stick he had found under a tree. While Tantia started to holler and Nana disclaimed all knowledge of his bruise, receiving a tetchy rebuke from his mother nonetheless, Mani knew she had already left her childhood playfellows far behind.

Nevertheless she was pleased when the pair piled into her carriage as the journey recommenced, the caravan soon entering the first of the forested areas that would be covered on the journey. Mani shivered and pulled a woollen shawl around her as the trees closed over their heads and the air grew dark and cold. Here and there, she could hear the sound of rushing water before seeing, as the carriages wound along the twists of the muddy track, tiny silver cascades of water just visible through the trees. The heavy silence of the forest was broken only by the creaking of their carriages and the occasional screeching of parrots. The carriage rocked from side to side as she peered out of the windows, scouring the passing forest for the promised wildlife. But, apart from a few swinging monkeys and the occasional deer that scuttled away through the vines and shrubs at the sound of the carriage wheels, there was no sight of either boars or tigers and Mani laughed at the collective sigh of disappointment emitted by Nana and Tantia as the procession emerged unscathed into the sunlight a few hours later.

She stretched herself in exhaustion as the evening drew in and the caravan started to slow down again. She hoped they were about to stop as her arms and legs ached from being cooped up in such a confined space. What a weary thought that they had covered only one tenth of their journey so far. How very far Jhansi was from home! Mani wondered how different it would be in terms of customs and practices. She knew that her bridegroom's people, being Maratha, would speak more or less the same languages as her own family, although she expected there would be differences in the dialect. The foods and the traditions also did not generally differ greatly from one Hindu royal family to another so she hoped she would not have to struggle with anything too unusual. Asharfi-bua had told her that Gangadhar's immediate family, like hers, was very small. His parents had died many years before and he had just one older brother who had been overlooked by the British when Gangadhar had been offered the throne on their uncle's death. There had apparently been some squabbling over the succession, but Asharfi-bua had been unclear on the details and it was one of the things that Mani had resolved to ask her father during this long journey to Jhansi. He had seemed so preoccupied with the wedding arrangements in the past few weeks but had no excuse now. Without Peshwa-sahib being around to occupy his attentions, Mani knew this was her best opportunity for all her questions about Jhansi and its raja.

They were drawing in now to the outskirts of a town to make their first night stop. The advance party of tent-pitchers and cooks sent on ahead had taken longer than expected to get the fires going and buy local ingredients for the meal and Mani was told to wait in the carriage when they came to a halt at the site marked out for their night-camp. She watched from the window as servants bustled about an escarpment overlooking the Ganga. Piqued that Nana and Tantia had been given permission to help feed Siddhabaksh the elephant, she cheered up as her father climbed into her carriage to keep her company instead. He carefully drew the tissue-silk curtains on the windows and Mani guessed it was to keep the local townspeople, who may have heard that this was the wedding party en route to Jhansi, from peeping in on her. On the other hand, perhaps he too, like her, was unsure of whether she would henceforth have to spend her life in purdah, the fate and choice of so many royal women.

'Look Mani,' Moropant said, pointing out the large wharf area visible below, 'that is Mirzapur, the highest point on the river that can be reached by the new Company steamers.'

Mani looked down at a huge moored boat and the endless stream of men disembarking from it with loads on their heads. She had so many important questions to ask her Baba but, for the time being, it was simpler to stick to the safety of impersonal concerns.

'Do you suppose those bales are indigo, Baba?' she asked.

'I'm not sure, beti, but I think them more likely to be cotton, gathered from the surrounding districts. The steamer will carry it to England or perhaps China.'

The sun was sinking beyond the river, sending flaming orange ripples across the water surface. Mani watched the buildings on its banks slowly grow dark, their edges fading and gradually becoming invisible against the night as windows started to glow with the blurred light of candles and lanterns within. Some of the houses looked as though they belonged to affluent merchants, especially the brick structures surrounded by deep, pillared verandas and crowned with pyramid-shaped maize thatches.

'Who do you think the dwellers of such elegant houses are, Baba?'

'Those big mansions? Almost certainly European indigo merchants, beti, or perhaps opium traders. The boatmen and dockhands will be the occupants of the smaller huts you see there, on the opposite bank of the river.'

Mani looked at the pinpricks of light, feeling faintly ashamed that she almost never stopped to think much about anonymous people and lives outside her tiny circle of acquaintances at Varanasi. Some of her lessons in the schoolroom at Saturday House had been interesting enough and she had always concentrated better than either Nana or Tantia but actually seeing those places unfold before her eyes now made the world seem far bigger than she had ever considered before. At the end of that horizon, lay Jhansi. She still did not know exactly how to broach the really important subjects with her father.

Outside, the servants continued going about the arduous business of setting up camp, assisted by a few local people who had turned up to help. Amidst loudly shouted instructions, tent-pegs were being hammered, ropes firmly tied, carpets rolled out and laid, while bhistis went around, refreshing the workers from goat-skin water bags. On the other side of the camp, large fires were being lit so that the cooking of the evening meal could begin. Mani could hear the chop-chop-chop of the khansamas preparing the vegetables that had been bought from nearby villages. As the smell of frying onions rose into the air, Mani guessed that the meal would take at least another hour to prepare. She took a deep breath. There was no putting off any more the questions she really wanted to ask, not just about Jhansi but also the man she was due to marry in less than ten days' time.

She had already gathered all the boring details, mostly by reading the books that Karim-teacher had recommended. She knew that Jhansi state was once part of the neighbouring kingdom of Orchha and that it was an erstwhile raja of Orchha who had built the grand fort at Jhansi in the seventeenth century. Karim-teacher had also told her that the Peshwas' land had once included Jhansi but they had given it over to Raja Gangadhar's subedar ancestors as their own kingdom grew. Of course, Karim-teacher, being such a sycophant of Nana's, had waxed eloquent about the generosity of the Peshwas but Mani had read that those early subedars of Jhansi had been such able administrators that they had eventually become the rulers of Jhansi. The most popular of these was Raja Gangadhar's uncle, Ramachandra Rao, who had earned British support by helping to control a Maratha rebellion against them. She had laughed as she saw the ridiculous title that a grateful Lord Bentinck had bestowed on him: 'Devoted Servant of the Glorious King of England'. Perhaps *that* was the information to use in order to open up the subject with Baba.

Despite the growing darkness, Mani kept her gaze out of the

window as she blurted abruptly, 'Did I tell you, Baba, what a pompous title the raja of Jhansi was given once? *Devoted Servant of the Glorious King of England*, imagine! I hope I don't get a name like that.'

Moropant smiled. 'I don't think they give titles like that any more. And England has a Queen now—Queen Victoria. She too is young and newly married even though she must be at least ten years older than you.'

Baba was refusing to be pinned down. He was now helping himself to a drink of cool water from the earthen surahi that had been placed in their carriage and Mani found herself chafing at his stubbornness. She worried that Nana or Tantia would barge into their carriage with some inane interruption, completely preventing her from being able to ask the really vital questions that still lay unanswered.

As Moropant sipped at his water, she made another attempt. 'Karim-teacher told me that Jhansi has suffered some really hard times, Baba. Is that true?'

'He's absolutely correct, beti. There was a famine in Jhansi and Jalaun many moons ago. And, partly due to it, you see, the cotton trade to China just died away. Many of Jhansi's poor starved to death at the time.'

Mani wondered at how saddened she suddenly felt. Almost as though someone close to her had suffered a terrible loss. 'But, why did Jhansi suffer so, Baba, when it had been so prosperous before? It doesn't make sense.'

'You're right, it doesn't make any sense. There is no need for anyone to starve to death in such plentiful lands as ours, beti. It all comes down to how the grain trade is managed and distributed and sometimes even kings have no control over that.'

'Surely that trade must have picked up again,' Mani said, brow still furrowed. She gestured to the steamer that was still being loaded on the jetty below, illuminated now by large lanterns.

'I'm sure it has, Mani. But, more recently, Jhansi suffered an uprising over land rights that had been manipulated by the neighbouring Rajput kings of Orchha and Datia.'

'Why would they do that, Baba? After all Jhansi was part of Orchha once.'

'Well, friendships between neighbouring states wax and wane like the moon, beti. It does not help that Jhansi is a Maratha kingdom with Rajput neighbours. There has recently been a little jealousy over Jhansi's good relations with the British too.'

'So what happened to that uprising then?'

'Raja Gangadhar's uncle, who was Jhansi's king then, had to call upon the British to help him subdue the landlords and ended up mortgaging a part of his kingdom to pay for the support received from them.'

Mani sighed deeply. She suddenly felt queasy at the thought that being a queen would mean worrying endlessly about things that would be completely out of her control much of the time. And there was still so much to learn, with not that many days to learn them in.

Moropant, looking at the lengthening shape of his daughter's normally cheerful face, felt something squeeze at his heart. He ought to spare her the worries but he also knew this was his best chance to teach her some invaluable lessons. He had never wanted her to be one of those zenana women who knew and cared little about matters of state, even if there were certain blessings in that kind of ignorance.

'Not everything is out of a ruler's control, though, beti,' he continued gently. 'The ways of individual kings and queens count for a lot too. You see, the previous raja of Jhansi, Raghunath Rao, unleashed a sadly inefficient administration on the state, bringing it to the verge of bankruptcy. He had also been an immoral man, openly flaunting his concubines and illegitimate children before his unfortunate wife. Which was why...' Moropant paused, now choosing his words carefully, '... on the death of Raghunath Rao four years ago, the British chose his nephew, Raja Gangadhar, from the two or three other contenders for the throne, believing that he was best suited to lead the state back to prosperity.'

Mani wanted to ask her father about concubines and wives but, gripped by sudden shyness, asked instead, 'Has he succeeded, Baba?'

Moropant looked at the worried expression on Mani's face and smiled reassuringly at her. He was glad he had never allowed Mani's natural intelligence to wither and die, just for having had the misfortune of being born a girl. Both he and Peshwa-sahib, in deciding that Mani would be educated alongside Nana and Tantia, had never for a moment regretted that she had turned out to be brighter and more perceptive than both of them put together. At least, as Peshwa-sahib had said on the day Mani's wedding had been fixed, they had done the people of Jhansi a great service by giving them a queen who came with the blessings of education.

'Prosperity is such a relative thing, beti,' Moropant said, as Mani still awaited a reply to her question. 'Jhansi, if you compare it with the Mughal court in Delhi or that of the Nawabs of Awadh, or even what our Peshwa-sahib once had in Pune, is not very wealthy. What Gangadhar Rao should be most commended for is that he has brought peace and stability, not just to Jhansi but to the entire region. Only after peace is established, can one hope for prosperity.'

'And how does he keep peace, Baba? Does he ride before a large army?' Mani queried.

'Oh no,' Moropant laughed. 'Fortunately he has followed a much more sensible path than that! Raja Gangadhar, on taking the throne, very sensibly accepted the condition laid by the British that he would accept their doctrine of power without responsibility...'

'What sort of power is that?' Mani cried. 'I hope it's not like our Peshwa-sahib's so-called "arrangement" with the British where everyone knows he really has no powers! Is it Baba?'

Moropant searched for the right words. 'Peshwa-sahib's present burdens come from some unfortunate old decisions he made, it has to be said, Mani-beti. No, from all accounts, Raja Gangadhar is a sagacious man. Rulers like him, who have accepted the British doctrine, are allowed to keep their wealth and their privileges and even have the freedom to run their states and rule their people, provided they do nothing to upset the British in any way and are quite willing to let the local British agents make all critical decisions.'

'Agents?'

'Political agents of the Governor-General in Calcutta, beti. They are called that in smaller principalities, although they are no different from the Residents in more important places, like Delhi or Kanpur.'

Moropant felt immensely relieved as a maid thrust her head through the door of the carriage to inform them that their tents were now ready to be occupied. Even though it was important for Mani to know the history of the state whose queen she was so shortly due to become, Moropant preferred his daughter's opinions to come from the man who was to become her husband. The last thing he wanted was to blight the good relationship that existed between Jhansi and the British with any careless comments, especially having struggled all these years to control the abysmal relationship between Peshwa-sahib and his own agents. In truth, though, he feared deeply for his daughter, about to walk straight into the seething cauldron of uncertainties and mistrust that royal life invariably was. Despite Peshwa-sahib's encouragement and Asharfi-bua's coercions, it had not been an easy decision for him to send his daughter into a life whose pressures were likely to outweigh its comforts and he felt his heart wring itself in sudden and silent foreboding. Did one rejoice or lament when a loved one, dearer than life itself, was to become part of a land's future history.

He emerged from the carriage into the cool grey evening, his limbs feeling suddenly weary from the long day's travel they had endured. Looking up and stretching himself, he saw that Mani's descent behind him was causing a small commotion among the crowd of locals that had been waiting at the fringes of the camp, hoping to catch a glimpse of the royal bride. Observing her suddenly frightened expression, he pulled Mani's silk chunari over her head and hustled her out of sight into her tent. As he closed the canvas flap behind them, Moropant felt a clutch of fear at how much his daughter's life had already changed. He could not bear the thought of her being consigned to purdah, her lively spirit and shining acumen locked away behind ivory screens forever. Nor could he contemplate a royal life outside the zenana where Mani's every move would be noticed and watched, not always sympathetically.

Feeling sick at heart, he bent over a hurricane lamp to adjust its wick, reflecting on how, despite Asharfi-bua's assurances and Mani's own apparent confidence, he had not been able to overcome his earlier fears that the man chosen to wed his daughter was so much older than her. How many times he had wished for the chance to meet Raja Gangadhar before the betrothal but Peshwa-sahib's growing conviction in the suitability of the match had prevented him from requesting it. He had prayed endlessly since then that the difference in their ages would not cause an unbridgeable chasm between them, both as man and woman as well as king and queen. Mani, he knew, was self-assured and intelligent and interested enough to cope with new experiences. But so much of her future happiness now depended on Gangadhar. On his willingness to guide a new, young wife gently into her new role. Allowing her, with the patience and fortitude that only a parent would normally impart willingly, to shed her childish preoccupations and teach her to spread her wings. It terrified Moropant to think that Gangadhar may be impatient with his precious daughter, dismissing her nascent interest in history and politics as folly, keeping her shut away in the zenana—those cloistered quarters filled with the kind of cruelties that only women would perpetrate on other women.

Lighting the lamp with a taper, Moropant scolded himself for being overjoyed one moment at Mani's good fortune in marrying a king and fearful the very next at that very same thought. So far he had managed to use the preparations for this wedding journey as a distraction from hundreds of different worrisome possibilities, but the effort had worn him out more than he had imagined possible.

As the lamp's wick flared, the interior of Mani's tent sprang to life. The servants had already laid the carpet and placed enough furniture to make it more of a room than a tent. As a procession of scurrying maids moved Mani's personal belongings out of the carriage, Moropant turned to look at his daughter, now sitting on the edge of a khaat, swinging her legs and eagerly awaiting more meaningful conversations with him. Despite his fatigue, he knew he owed it to his daughter to allay whatever fears she too may brook about her new life to come but now he was just too tired. As he stroked the top of her head, about to tell her to get some rest before dinner, she shaped her mouth into a small, disappointed moue, guessing what he was about to say.

'Do you not think, Mani-beti, that after this long journey, you and I both deserve some rest,' he asked pleadingly. 'Where is that daughterly concern that should be instructing this poor old father to go instantly to his own tent and stretch himself out on a comfortable bed?'

'Oh Baba, please, just one more question and then I promise I will let you go to your tent,' she said instead.

'Well, fair enough, one question only—what is it?' he asked uneasily, half-expecting her to ask him some personal question about Gangadhar that he would not have the answer to. He wanted of course to be able to tell her everything that she wanted to know, as he had always striven to do, erasing every last doubt from her mind. But now here he was, confused unbearably by his own cursed vacuity where it came to knowledge of his daughter's future life. Luckily for him, though, she seemed still too overcome by her own shyness to open up any awkward lines of enquiry, sticking to the safety of innocuous questions instead.

'Just tell me this, Baba,' she now queried, her smooth young brow breaking into an exaggeratedly vexed frown again, 'why is it that our Maratha nobles *allowed* the British to become so powerful in the first place? *Especially* seeing that the Mughals lost the power they once had…'

'That's not one question!' Moropant laughed loudly. 'That's one hundred questions lumped into one!'

'No, it is just a very clever question, Baba,' Mani retorted. 'You promised! Oh Baba please!'

'Well, you tell me, you're the one who has been attending all this tuition along with Nana and Tantia that our Peshwa-sahib pays good money for. You should know all this already. Let me ask you a question instead—which was the first place, tell me, to be taken over by the British?'

'I know, that's easy, Bengal!' Mani cried as though back in competition with Nana and Tantia at Karim-teacher's class. 'The

British defeated the Nawab there who had killed many of their people at Calcutta when they had a disagreement. I remember Mr Todd called it the Black Hole of Calcutta but Karim-teacher said that was just English exaggeration.'

Moropant chuckled. 'Yes he would, wouldn't he! Well Bengal was the first and the British became what is called "de jure" masters of Bengal in 1765. And—what can one say—from then on the East India Company has been rather like a river in spate that swallows up everything in its path almost as though it cannot help it.'

Moropant seemed to have forgotten his earlier one-question rule and now hitched up his dhoti to settle himself on a soft goat-skin gadda, much to Mani's delight. She quickly moved up to make room for him as he continued. 'I suppose it goes all the way back to the time the traders of the East India Company first arrived in India on their ships, Mani. The British king at the time granted the Company virtually sovereign rights—to raise an army, mint coinage, exercise civil and criminal jurisdiction and, yes, to wage wars too. He must have had little choice because India is so far from England and it would have been impossible for their government over there to control things here. It's easier now, of course, with new kinds of ships that have cut down the journey time for people and goods to be sent. But also too late to change established patterns.'

'So does that mean the East India Company will just grow and grow and take over even more states as they have been doing, Baba? Like our Ganga River swallowing fields and trees when she floods!'

Moropant laughed. 'Well, the British don't really want the states that will bring them little benefit, beti. The ones they want are those that share borders with feared enemies, like Afghanistan and Russia. And, of course, they would like control of those states that enjoy great riches, like Awadh.'

'And how is it that they just get what they want, Baba? That's what I have never understood.'

'Well, treaties are drawn up that allow for "annexation" of places like Mirzapur here and even our own Varanasi.'

Mani looked puzzled. 'But how is it, Baba, that some of these rajas just give up so easily. At least our Peshwa-sahib fought a war to try save his crown.'

'Well, sometimes royal families don't have much of a choice, beti. Take Nawab Wazir Ali, for instance—he was told to choose between his kingdom and his life. Now what sort of choice is that?' Moropant smiled gently at the look of astonishment on his daughter's face.

'Well, I know what I'd have chosen,' she replied tartly, tossing her braid over one shoulder, eyes flashing indignantly alongside dancing gold eardrops.

'Ah, Mani-beti, what moves your heart are the ideals of youth. Don't forget that, by the time it happened, Wazir Ali was not a young man any more. He agreed quietly to go and died without ever seeing his beloved kingdom again.'

Moropant looked at his daughter's face, lit by the soft ochre of glowing lanterns. Her dark eyes were still crowded with doubt, despite now being shaded with sleep. He knew that anything he said to her would only generate many more questions. Questions that he wanted Mani to put to her new husband and not to him, a tired old courtier full of cynical views. Moropant had never felt more aware that he was not just a mere courtier but courtier to a powerless Peshwa stripped of all past glories. All his knowledge in the end came to nothing. Perhaps his little Mani, marrying a raja, would have more control over her own fate...

For the time being, however, she was not a queen but still his obstinate little daughter. He slapped his knees and, getting up, said very firmly, 'Well, I think that's more than enough for one night.' He stretched himself with a loud groan. 'I must say your Karim-teacher would have been most astounded at this sudden interest of yours in his subject, Mani.'

He smiled as Mani grimaced in memory of some of the soporific history lessons she had endured back in the schoolroom at Saturday House. Turning the wick of the brass hurricane lamp down, Moropant allowed the glow in the tent to dim to near darkness before lifting the canvas flap and feeling the cool night air brush his face.

Looking back at Mani who had already flopped down on the pile of silk coverlets on her nivaar cot, he added, 'I will have food sent to you here. Don't forget, we have to have an early start tomorrow too, so that we can try to make the distance up to Allahabad. It would be auspicious to offer worship at Prayag before we proceed on our way to Jhansi—and that will give you a chance for you to bathe in your favourite Ganga again. Now I have to go and find out what those two scoundrels Nana and Tantia are up to. Put on a fresh set of clothes, beti, and have something to eat before you fall asleep. I'll send one of the maids in to help you.'

After Moropant had departed, Mani continued to lie on her bed, a hundred thoughts swimming confusingly around her. She wondered why she had felt so uncommonly bashful to ask her father the many questions she had about Gangadhar himself, his appearance and character and family background. It was possible the journey would present further opportunities but, for the time being, general questions were all she felt able to ask Moropant and even his replies to those had left her feeling muddled and confused.

She turned to face the candle whose flame resembled a dancer on tiptoe. Suddenly some of Karim-teacher's lessons were starting to make sense too—particularly the ones in which he made fervent declarations about his Awadh homeland that would invariably be mimicked later by Nana. Nana, with a carefully inked upper lip and chin, and Tantia, wearing tufts of glued-on cotton for whiskers and affecting the mincing manners of Mr Todd, would occasionally have mock arguments once the lessons were over, sending Mani into hysterical giggles. They had all grown up accepting that, sometimes in the course of just one morning, they would have to listen to two completely polarized views of not just the current situation but historical events as well. Oh it was all so confusing it was giving her a headache!

A young woman slipped through the tent flap and smiled shyly at the sight of Mani with her head hanging upside down over the wooden edge of the cot. Mani recognized one of two girls who had been sent by the raja of Jhansi to be her chief handmaidens. The girl was fair skinned and pretty: possibly belonging to a high-caste family that may have fallen on hard times. Mani sat up on her khaat, pleased to welcome the girl into her tent, hoping to put the remainder of her questions about life in Jhansi to her. Possibly *she* would be able to tell her something more about the man she was due to marry in a fortnight, Mani thought, quite forgetting Asharfi-bua's careful instructions on not being overly friendly with the retainers.

She had not, however, bargained for how the journey so far would have fatigued her. As the maid carefully unbraided and brushed out the tangles in Mani's mass of curly hair, gently rubbing coconut oil into her scalp, Mani could feel the tent around her start to rock with sleep. She tried to focus on the sweet-faced maid she could see in her mirror but her head was already spinning with all the things she had learnt and all the things she was suddenly painfully conscious of still having to learn. History, politics, the psychology of men's minds...none of these were things that had ever entered Mani's head with any seriousness of purpose before. Additionally, as queen of Jhansi, she would have no choice but to heed the advice that Asharfi-bua had tried to instil in her from babyhood, which was to *think* before opening her mouth to speak, and to consider *all* options before taking *any* decisions—habits that had never come easily to Mani. She was glad that this long journey would provide her with the time to find out more about Jhansi. There was still so much she wanted to know, but now she just wanted to lay her head down on her pillow and sleep. She mumbled in gratitude to the maid as she felt her gentle hands lower her onto the bed. Even as the softness of a silk razai covered her, Mani had already floated into the deepest slumber.

As she woke in the morning, feeling the warmth of the sun's rays creep over the colourful canvas of the tent, it was as though a new Mani had grown overnight in her head. She lay on her back for a few moments, seeing not the embroidered appliquéd flowers on the roof of the tent but all the responsibilities that lay ahead of her. Although she knew she ought to be feeling frightened by them, she was strangely unruffled. Having grown up with Peshwa-sahib's regrets about his poor relationship with the British, Mani felt grateful for the knowledge garnered last night that Raja Gangadhar enjoyed a much happier relationship with them. It was just sensible not to antagonize those who were so powerful. She hoped he would help her become a wise ruler too. That was what she wanted more than anything else at the moment; to be a devoted and efficient queen to the people of Jhansi.

It was no wonder then to find, as they continued on their journey that day, that Tantia's and Nana's company felt suddenly both puerile and irritating. The pair just could not seem to stop their constant bickering as they alternated between excitement and boredom, tired already with the rigours of travel.

When the caravan of carriages drew in at Allahabad at dusk on the second day, Mani decided to use the planned holy dip at Prayag to cleanse herself, not of her sins—for she was sure she had collected only very few of those—but of all childish preoccupations instead. Moropant had returned from paying the necessary tax to the local British authority for the wedding party to enjoy the privilege of bathing in this holy confluence of rivers and everyone was disembarking from their carriages. As Mani descended from hers, she turned to face the river, enjoying the feel of its breeze on her face. While the tents were being pitched and the large retinue busied itself again, Mani picked her way across the white riverbed, followed closely by the two new maids who had been assigned to her. They looked out to where the two streams of the Ganga and the Yamuna joined each other. The distinction between the two rivers was clear to see, almost as though an invisible line had been drawn to separate gentle serene Yamuna from her spirited sister Ganga, bubbling and frothing as though in a very great hurry to get somewhere. Mani knew that the third mythical river, Saraswati, joined their union from below.

Mani smiled as she thought suddenly of how like the rivers before them her two new companions were. She had already worked out that Sundar was the soft-spoken and dreamy one while Kashi was much more ebullient. Already it felt delightful to be in the company of two pleasant and clever girls after years of competing with Nana and Tantia only to be left out of their games the minute she got better than them.

'Come, hold my hands, Sundar and Kashi,' she said, 'and we shall go look for Saraswati-ma too. Maybe she is the most beautiful of these three river-sisters which is why she hides her face away!'

Linking hands, the three girls walked in, feeling the water's playful tugs on their feet and anklets as it rushed between the folds of their silk skirts.

'How do the waters of these rivers not rush and merge into one, I wonder?' Mani cried happily, lifting her soaking skirt.

'Oh Rani-sahiba, this is what marriages must be like,' Sundar replied. 'See how the two rivers lie side by side with each remaining so different from the other. One the colour of polished silver and the other like old unvarnished gold. But each the more beautiful for being next to its companion.'

'Sundar, you should be writing poetry!' exclaimed Kashi. She too turned towards Mani, her eyes shining. 'But is she not right, Rani-sahiba, look at how the two rivers are coming together and conjoining without letting go of each other. Even the gods could not separate them if they tried!'

৵ 6 ৽

As Mani's bridal procession travelled westwards across the north Indian plains, she saw the fabric of the countryside change and grow more rocky and parched. The slowly plodding hooves of their horses and bullocks were churning up a great cloud of sand that now followed their caravan like a gloomy brown shadow. They passed places with strange names—Chitrakoot and Banda and Mahoba—and here, looking out of the carriage windows, were things Mani had never seen before; ravines and rocky outcrops and tall date palms, silent sentinels eerily guarding a barren land.

She gazed in awe at the dun-coloured expanse of earth, its vastness broken by the contrasting wonders of flimsy anthills and giant boulders. Apart from occasional brown veils of dust that rose lazily from the earth only to fall and cover another part of it further away, there was hardly any movement in the landscape. Mani wondered if it was the stillness of the land surrounding them that was responsible for the strange ennui that seemed to have settled over the wedding party these past two days. Certainly, the excitement with which they had set off from Saturday House twelve days ago had long evaporated.

'Just look at that rock, Nana,' Mani whispered, 'nearly as big as a house.'

'And those massive fissures in the earth there. Siddhabaksh's mahout was telling me that some of the larger chasms actually hold small hidden villages.'

A few hours later, as the landscape changed character again, they passed a small walled village nestled in the shadow of an imposing mud fort.

This time it was Moropant's voice that broke the silence. 'Forts like that belong to small chieftains and landowners who rule not just the villages at their feet but entire swathes of land stretching beyond. And you see those ravines in the distance? Canyons like that have become notorious in recent times, providing handy hiding places for dacoits and thugs who stay easily concealed while observing unsuspecting travellers.' He laughed at the expression on Mani's and Nana's faces, adding with mock seriousness, 'If you sit very still, you will feel them—a hundred eyes watching us pass, all saluting the future rani of Jhansi.'

A ripple of excitement finally passed through the procession as it drew into Jhansi district. Mani tried to calm a sudden attack of nerves by gazing up at the sky. It looked almost white with heat, but they were drawing under mercifully thick leaf cover again. At least the Jhansi kings of yore had been wise enough to bestow their travellers with shade, Mani thought.

'Sal trees,' Moropant observed, looking at the knotted trunks and soft green-blue leaves. Pointing to the great bunches of flowers hanging downwards and close enough to touch, he added, 'Red dyes are extracted from these and used for the cotton threads by Jhansi's weavers.'

As they emerged from the sal forests, the landscape gave way once more to thorny keekar and khakhrak trees and great tussocks of kans grass. Siddhabaksh's mahout, now back on his own familiar territory, shouted excitedly down to them, 'Jhansi city! See, the cenotaphs of the old rajas of Jhansi if you look over there—in the far distance to the east!'

Mani craned her neck but could only see the taller spires of a distant row of temples and mausoleums from her low-slung carriage. She would have to bide her time before seeing Jhansi as the caravan was now turning off the main road, as had been planned, heading towards the city of Orchha. Tonight they were to be the guests of its raja as Peshwa-sahib had sought his permission for the wedding party to make their final preparations in the comfort of one of Orchha's many palaces.

Mani hoped that Jhansi would be at least half as beautiful as Orchha, a city that seemed to be rising out of the waters of the Betwa as they approached it. It was built on an island separated from the mainland by an arm of the river but, as they drew closer, Mani could see that an air of passed splendour covered the profusion of moss-covered citadels and palaces beyond the city walls. Even the great main archway had been walled up and the carriages had to enter carefully through a narrow postern gate. Mani supposed that the glory of the old Rajput kingdom had faded as Mughal power had been on the ascendant in past centuries.

The raja of Orchha had arranged for the bridal retinue to stay in a wing of Jehangir Mahal, a huge sandstone palace that had been built by one of his ancestors in honour of an old Mughal benefactor. Mani had never seen a palace so big: it spread over four floors, each with its own warren of rooms, courtyards and balconies, surmounted by arching cupolas that seemed to have no purpose other than look beautiful. While the menfolk departed to pay their respects to Raja Sujan Singh, Mani and the other women were led to an enchanting little palace, once home to a famed Orchha dancer, that lay in the shadow of Jehangir Mahal.

Mani walked into Phool Bagh, a garden of flowers in the midst of which the dancer's palace nestled. She looked around her, sighing in pleasure, 'It is clear to see from where the garden has taken its name, Sundar,' she said, 'just bursting with flowers, is it not?'

'Oh how beautiful those pomegranate trees look, laden with fruit, Rani-sahiba.'

'Like hundreds of little hanging jewels!'

Mani stopped short, clutching Sundar's arm in delight as she spotted a peacock preening amidst the foliage. For one startled moment they stared at each other, before the bird stood tall and unfanned a jewelled train of sapphire and turquoise over its head.

'A fitting obeisance to a future queen,' Sundar whispered, smiling.

But, as the two girls continued wandering through the overgrown gardens, Mani saw that the trees and flowers were being choked gradually by entwining, looping vines. The fountains were empty of water, their hydraulic system of pipes crumbling with disuse. Suddenly she felt saddened by the idea that even the greatest of glories were transient things that would eventually pass away.

As night fell over Orchha, Mani sat with Sundar on a balcony of the dancing girl's palace, watching a silver moon rise over the darkened silhouettes of Chatrabhuj Temple's chattris and spires. She felt silenced by the story Sundar had just finished telling her, of the Mughal emperor, Jehangir, who had fallen so deeply in love with the beautiful dancer, Rai Parveen, that he had built this lovely palace for her even though she would not go to stay with him in his capital city.

'People knew so much more about love and sacrifice in those days, Sundar,' Mani said, sighing deeply.

'Love has always been the same, Rani-sahiba. The same today as at the start of time.'

'Imagine how beautiful Rai Parveen must have been, Sundar, to have earned such adoration from the great Mughal emperor. He could have had anyone he desired.'

'Maybe it was not just Rai Parveen's beauty that attracted the emperor, Rani-sahiba, but her gift for music and poetry. And her purity too. All of that put together must have seemed irresistible to him.'

'But why do you think Rai Parveen rejected the emperor's advances, when he declared his love so generously? She could have had a life of limitless luxury in Delhi.'

'I am sure it was because she preferred to remain in her home town, Rani-sahiba, where she was respected for her accomplishments. In the eyes of the Delhi court, she would have forever been seen as just another of the emperor's concubines, even if his own love had been true.'

Mani breathed a satisfied sigh. 'How brave and how principled Rai Parveen must have been, Sundar, to have chosen her own destiny so bravely.'

Sundar pulled her shawl over her shoulders with a delighted shiver. 'Do you not agree, my Rani-sahiba, that stories of *unrequited* passion are much, much better than straightforward love stories?'

'Yes, I do like sad stories! Unspoken passions, doomed love, those make the best stories. Although I suppose we should be thankful we are not characters who have to live in them!'

They laughed at that, throwing their heads back and causing the cloud of fireflies hovering over their heads to dart away into the night. Despite calls from indoors, the two girls lingered on Rai Parveen's balcony, continuing to muse over whether the great emperor was more likely to have been insulted by the dancing girl's courage of conviction or impressed by her lack of avarice. A satisfying conclusion had not been reached before they were finally ordered to bed.

The following morning, Mani was woken before daybreak. It was so early, the sky had not lost its pearly mist yet. Even the birds were still asleep. She tried to rouse herself as Nana's mother clucked around her bed in the half-darkness, issuing directions to the maids: there were so many things to be done, it sounded as though the bridal preparations would take hours. But Mani, longing for another few minutes' solitude, snuggled back under her silk razai in an effort to recapture the dream she had been enjoying of the talented and brave Rai Parveen. It was perhaps not the most fitting image in which to take refuge on an occasion as auspicious as this, but Mani liked the thought that the spirit of a long-gone emperor's lover was watching over her today.

She ought to get up to tell Sundar that she had finally deduced that clever beautiful Rai Parveen had, in fact, immortalized Emperor Jehangir's love by refusing him. Only half-listening to Nana-ma's irritating stream of instructions, Mani reasoned, with eyes still squeezed tightly shut, that, had the dancer accepted Jehangir's offer, the very thing that had made her so attractive to him would have been lost: her purity, her unattainability. She snuggled her face further into her feather pillow, wanting to muse over these romantic notions some more but Nana's mother was not to be dissuaded from her mission and finally Mani reluctantly unglued her eyes at the playful threat that she would miss her own wedding if she languished in her bed a moment longer.

Sundar and Kashi came in and set about their preparations. After helping Mani out of bed, they proceeded to disrobe her, gently buffing and massaging her skin with a paste of turmeric and sandalwood until it took on the lustre of gold. After the fragrant ochre paste had been sponged away, she was led to the adjoining bath chamber. Here a huge copper cauldron had been filled with warm water and, from small vials, the attar of rose and jasmine were added before Mani stepped gingerly in. As she submerged herself, handfuls of rose petals that had been scattered across the surface of the water gathered around her body. Their fragrance, caught in the rising steam, was intoxicating. Mani was permitted to linger now, her thoughts suspended with the rising steam, the sweet perfume of the oils calming her nerves. When Sundar and Kashi returned, they massaged Mani's limbs once more, before lifting her out of the warmth of the bath to gently dry her. Mani felt strangely shy now in the company of these girls—she had not been prepared for the intimacy and care they showed her, less still for the rush of anxiety she was now experiencing as her body was prepared for the gaze of another.

Yet still they were not finished, for now they turned their attention to her hair, washing it with soap-nut and shikakai, vigorously rubbing and squeezing each tendril before finally winding it up in a soft white Persian towel. Mani returned to the bedchamber, her legs feeling heavy and her heart beating so quickly, she thought she might faint.

Once Mani's hair had been dried over the smoke from an incense-filled brazier, the business of her make-up began: touches of vermilion and cinnabar on her cheeks and lips, kohl in her eyes and hundreds of tiny red and white dots to frame her face in the Maratha bridal style. She then stepped into the embroidered lehnga that was being held up by both the maids because it was so heavy, its skirt of gold tissue weighed down with hundreds of tiny pearls that had been painstakingly embroidered onto the fabric at a tiny shop in one of Varanasi's backstreets.

Through all this, Nana's mother was busy with the large wooden jewellery boxes that she had guarded with her life throughout the journey. Amongst the elaborate meena-worked bangles being slipped on to Mani's wrists were green glass ones that signified matrimony, covering Mani's arms all the way from her delicate wrist to the point of her elbow. Each of her fingers would carry a ring, while two—the shape of curved fishes—were for her toes. A pair of gold anklets with minuscule hanging bells was wound around her feet.

Once Mani's hair had been combed back, peacock-shaped earrings were screwed into her earlobes and then hooked into her hair to spare her ears for these were weighty pieces. Even as Mani thought she might collapse under the weight of this jewellery, another piece, a gift from Peshwa-sahib, was brought out and carefully placed on her head—a sarpech that swept up her hairline from behind her ears, rising into a small, paisley-shaped peak at the top of her forehead and framing her face with a profusion of tiny spinel beads. A teeka rested in the middle of her forehead, the delicate gold filigree catching the light of the first cool rays of dawn, just visible now through the narrow windows.

Then, when Mani could not believe that there was an inch of her body left to adorn, a nose-pin encrusted with diamonds was clipped to the side of her nose while Nana's mother bent over the last box to draw out the final piece. It was a pearl tanmani that had once belonged to Mani's mother. As it was fastened around her neck, Mani

caught her first glimpse in the bevelled looking-glass and felt her
courage rise: perhaps the spirits of both Rai Parveen and her mother
were watching over her today—one providing her with gentle courage,
the other with protection.

As she turned from the mirror, the others stepped back to take it
all in.

Nana's mother nodded her head with satisfaction. 'You look just
beautiful, Mani-beti, every inch a queen.'

'Our Rani-sahiba glows like a gilded flower,' Kashi said as
Sundar lifted her young queen's hand to kiss it gently, too overcome
with emotion to speak.

'Sundar, Kashi, quickly fetch a smoking lamp and ask one of the
maids for a handful of dry chillies,' Nana's mother said, 'the evil eye
of all that behold their new queen's beauty today must be warded off.'

'Don't worry, Nana-ma, this veil will cover our Rani-sahiba's face
from all prying eyes, evil or not-so-evil,' Kashi laughed as the final
accoutrement was carefully draped over Mani's head.

Mani took a last look at herself, her face now barely visible
beyond her chin, her mother's pearl necklace framing it below.
Childhood was over but, as she stepped out of the dressing chambers,
the certainty of youth told her that the onward journey could not
possibly fail to be as joyous.

Mani pressed her face against the half-shuttered window of the bridal
chariot carrying her into Jhansi. Before her rose the citadel in which
Orchha's and then Jhansi's kings had lived for centuries. From a
distance, the fort looked as though it had been carved out of the crest
of the large rock on which it stood but, as they neared it, battlements
and turrets and grey-ramparted walls slowly took shape. Washed by
the rains that had fallen during the night, the granite now glowed
silver in the sun. It took another few minutes for Mani to realize, as
an invisible hand clutched at her heart, that this was her final
destination. Jhansi Fort—inside which waited her husband and her
new home.

The carriage wheels were churning sun-filled puddles on the
road leading up to the town into soft tea-brown sludge. Mani looked
up again at the forbidding stone structure as they drew closer and
took some comfort from the welcoming sight of hundreds of tiny red
and green flags cheerfully fluttering themselves dry on the ramparts.
There were people standing under a big tasselled pennant in crimson
silk; she could see their colourful robes and even a British uniform but
could not discern any faces. She wondered who they were and if the

king was amongst them. Jhansi Fort was neither as large nor as beautiful as the one at Orchha but, as Mani gazed up at the approaching structure, she was awed nonetheless at the thought that all the secrets of her future life were held inside it.

The town walls too were made of grey granite, at least twenty-five feet high and, as the carriages swept under a pair of huge brass-studded wooden gates, they were jostled by curious and happy crowds filling the streets. On the far side of the road leading to the fort were gardens and a lake but the procession turned down a road flanked by large mansions and houses, the windows and gateways of which were all filled with people waving and cheering the visitors from Varanasi. Nana's mother was quick to draw the silken curtains before anyone could see the bride and Mani sat back on her seat, feeling suddenly nervous.

The bridal party had been asked to make its way to Khanderao Darwaza, the fort's main gate where the raja's reception party was waiting to welcome them. As the elephant pulling Mani's carriage plodded its way majestically up the sweeping road, shehnai players, drummers and buglers, massed on the ramparts above, trumpeted a thunderous welcome to the bridal party. Another pair of massive gates was thrown wide open and the procession came to an abrupt stop.

The first of the ceremonies was due to take place in the gardens just outside the Ganesh temple where a colourful shamiana protected the welcoming party from the rapidly climbing sun. As the men in the bride's party disembarked, Mani and the other women watched the proceedings from behind the safety of their curtained carriages. Men from both sides hugged and draped each other with marigold garlands and Mani saw the old prime minister, who had led the party that visited Saturday House, embrace her father.

'Is the raja among those men, Nana-ma?' Mani whispered. She was clutching Nana-ma's plump arm so hard, she was leaving reddened imprints of her fingers on flesh.

'Don't be silly, pagli,' Nana-ma laughed, patting her arm, 'he won't be here.' She then added mischievously, 'In a hurry to see your bridegroom, are you?'

Mani pinched her, this time deliberately, making Nana's pretty mother smack her wrist smartly. 'You may soon be a very grand rani but for the time being you're still our little Mani, so behave, my child.'

The two of them peered out at the ceremonies again. Now the men from the bride's side were taking off their embroidered jootis so that one of the raja's men could pour water from a brass jug onto their feet, while another followed him, wiping the water using a soft muslin cloth. Even Nana and Tantia were having their feet washed alongside the men and looked as though they were greatly enjoying the fuss. Once this was done, the women were invited to enter the Ganesh temple.

Mani felt sudden terror at the prospect of leaving the safe womb of Siddhabaksh's carriage and clung to Nana-ma's arm, worried that the people of Jhansi would compare her unfavourably with their previous queen for whom they might still be grieving. Although she knew it was not important, she could not help wondering if that queen too had been beautiful. She watched Moropant make his way through the crowd towards her.

'Come, beti, it is the auspicious time for the ceremony,' he said, his eyes softening at the sight of his tomboyish daughter transformed into a queen. Taking his hand, Mani rose, tottering a little at first from the unaccustomed weight of her clothes and jewels. But, as she stepped out of the carriage, she heard the sharp intake of breath from the crowd milling around the temple and standing on the ramparts of the fort above, all of them straining for a first glimpse of their new young queen. The sun, shining brightly on the gilt howdahs atop a row of caparisoned elephants, dazzled and blinded Mani but, as the elephants knelt in homage, she saw gold bands wrapped around their tusks and howdahs swaying precariously, their occupants all bowing their heads in her direction. The shrill blowing and beating of the shehnai and dholak players filled the air.

With Moropant leading her by the hand and Nana's mother holding her from behind by her shoulders, Mani walked slowly up to the temple, hearing the ululations and the exultant cheers of the people of Jhansi ringing in her ears. All doubts were laid to rest— these people already loved her, merely for being their raja's wife. She could see their faces shining with happiness, the tinsel they were throwing up in the air falling around her like silver rain.

The cheering receded as she stepped through the arched door of the temple and was replaced by chanting of priests. The inner courtyard of the temple was so smoky with camphor and incense fumes, Mani thought for a minute that she may choke. She could barely see the people who were crowding the canopied archways and cloisters but it did not look as though the raja had restricted the invitees to just his closest relations and ministers, as Asharfi-bua had thought likely. Mani had to keep her feet from slipping on the oil-glazed stone floor as, head veiled and bowed, she followed the row of earthen jars, filled alternately with silver coins, turmeric and vermilion, which would lead her to the wedding mandap. As they arrived at a curtain of flower garlands, she knew that before her was the pavilion inside which her bridegroom waited.

Fat pillars of jasmines and marigolds, held together by fine silver threads and emanating heady cloying scents, had to be pushed aside for her to enter the mandap and, lifting the heavy silk skirts of her lehnga, she stepped in with her right foot. Hands helped to lower her onto white cushions laid in readiness before the holy fire. Once she was seated, she became aware that the raja was sitting right next to her on the cushion, although he and the people standing beyond him were not visible to her through the red silken antarpaat, the dividing cloth that would be kept between them until the main incantations were over. She could only glimpse the glitter of his jewellery and, occasionally, his right forearm as he reached out for libations being dispensed by the chief priest. Those first signs were not propitious— his arm was thin, heavily veined and with a sparse covering of hair at its wrist. He was wearing a few gem-studded bangles around his hand that clunked with each move.

The interminable ceremonies wound on, with the priests invoking the forces of nature, the strength of the planets and the blessings of God to bless the raja's union. Every so often, the chanting would be interrupted for the head priest to use his silver ladle to spoon some more ghee or throw a handful of perfumed salts into the fire. Mani's eyes smarted from the smoke and her head throbbed from the weight of the sarpech. It was with immense relief that she realized that the libations were over when Nana's mother helped her up again. It was time now for the varmala ceremony when the dividing silk cloth would be taken down and she and the bridegroom would behold each other for the first time. Not daring to look up, Mani bowed her head as she felt a heavy flower garland positioned gently on her neck. The priest was putting a similar garland in her own hands with instructions to raise it over her husband's head. She did this, still not looking up at his face, overcome with shyness as the people surrounding them smiled and cheered, sprinkling rice grains and throwing cloudy red kumkum powder into the air. Given further instructions by the priest, she extended her right hand that was covered in the elaborate henna designs painted on by the maids at Orchha. A large ring was pushed onto one finger and, as Mani felt her husband's hands on hers, she wondered whether she would faint from the heat and the clamour and the various thoughts rushing through her head. She blamed Asharfi-bua who had valiantly attempted telling her before she had left Varanasi about wedding nights and what men and women did when they got married. Hastily trying to clear her head of impure thoughts, Mani furiously concentrated on the mangal ashtaka that was being recited by the priest, the eight wedding verses full of good advice for couples embarking on matrimony as the black-beaded mangalsutra was placed around her neck.

It was nearly time for the saptapadi, the ritual seven steps taken together that would complete the wedding ceremony. Now more able to dart a few curious glances in the groom's direction through the embroidered tissue of her veil, Mani saw that he was bare-chested, except for a huge gold necklace that virtually spanned his upper body. Despite the jewellery, he did not look kingly or warrior-like at all but small and puny. Mani's first observation of the raja was of how narrow-framed he was which, though making him seem boyish for his age, had the effect of turning him into a wizened, sickly little boy. She felt a deep pang of disappointment. Even though she had pictured her new husband in many different sizes and shapes in her daydreams back at Saturday House, trying him out with different faces and figures, she had never thought he would be so small. Now, standing next to him, she was acutely aware that she may even be taller than him. She hunched her own body in an effort to shrink inside her bridal robes and felt a sudden shameful pricking of tears behind her eyelids. Trying to squeeze them back with a few large blinks and swallows, she desperately hoped that no one had noticed her sudden unhappiness.

The chanting from the priests sitting across the quadrangle rose a notch in volume, echoing eerily through the cloisters, as the saptapadi commenced. The raja was instructed to take his bride's hand while the ends of their respective garments were knotted together as a symbol of two people being united in matrimony. Mani felt his hand tighten over her own. She turned towards her new husband and met his gaze through her veil for the first time. His face was thin and sallow and his hair wispy grey. But, perhaps sensing her discomfiture, his eyes twinkled as he grinned in a conspiratorial smile that turned the corners of his mouth upwards in a comical way.

She felt her spirits rise slightly with this unexpected sign of friendship and thought she ought to say something pleasant in return. 'Tie that knot firmly,' she said to the junior priest, trying to sound affable, although she noticed Nana-ma's eyes widen in horror at the impertinence so unbecoming of a bride. Mani felt her face flush hot and bit her lip at her unintended indiscretion, imagining Asharfi-bua's wrath had she been present. But, luckily for her, the raja seemed amused by her unexpected audacity and Mani was sure she heard him emit a high-pitched chuckle as they took their first step together.

Once the ceremonies at the temple were over, Mani, still seated in one of the cloisters, saw that her new husband had now donned a brilliant brocade angarkha over his white silk dhoti. On his head he wore the three-cornered Maratha turban that made him appear a few inches taller and, although he still seemed painfully thin, Mani was relieved to see that he carried himself with dignity. He appeared to be popular with his people too who, waiting patiently outside the temple, broke into exultant cries and cheers as the royal couple emerged into the sunshine, Mani walking two steps behind. Conch-shells were being blown furiously and the two cannons above the main gates of the fort were firing celebratory shots to announce the conclusion of the nuptials. Women in colourful skirts stood on the ramparts, holding trays from which they were throwing huge handfuls of dried scented petals and unhusked rice onto the bridal pair and the crowd below.

The noise receded slightly as Mani was taken through the main doorway of the fort. Once out of sight of the townspeople, the red cloth that had bound Gangadhar and her garments together was untied by the priest and Mani was led away by a group of women. Though relieved that she did not have to sit with her new husband and make small-talk, Mani wondered anxiously where she was being taken next as she was told to step into a waiting palanquin. Carried up a sloping road, she saw gardens laden with flowers and fruit on either side and, a few minutes later, she was before Panch Mahal, the palace within the fort that was the royal residence. The ceremony to welcome her to her new home was to take place with just the women present, according to local custom, and Mani was relieved to see that Nana's mother was still accompanying her. The bridegroom, thankfully, appeared to have vanished for the time being.

Panch Mahal was five storeys high with curlicued windows overlooking a small rectangular artificial lake filled with red lotus flowers. As the noisy, colourful contingent walked into the palace, giggling and cracking lewd jokes about marriage, Mani was tempted to join in their laughter but remained mindful of Asharfi-bua's numerous and increasingly frantic bits of advice in the past few weeks. Instead, she kept a straight face while an older woman performed an aarti by circling her face and figure with a silver platter that held a brass oil lamp, silver and gold coins and pots of antimony and turmeric. She did all that she was told to do, including having her feet immersed in vermilion and knocking over, with her right foot, a rice measure filled with grain before stepping over the main doorway into the palace. After her mouth had been sweetened with jaggery, she was led through a courtyard into an airy carpeted hall.

Here were walls painted over in vegetable dyes with pictures of mythological characters and stories. Friezes over the doors had pictures of paired swans, tigers and elephants and the figures of gods and goddesses entwined with each other in passionate embraces, some with thrusting bare breasts boldly on display. Mani wondered nervously if the paintings had been done at her husband's request but decided that they were far more likely to be the product of the fevered imagination of the dissolute ancestor Moropant had told her about who had enjoyed keeping concubines.

After Mani had been seated on a large silver and velvet swing, her bridal kankans and bracelets were taken off her hands to the accompaniment of gentle songs. The morning wore on with the womenfolk of the two families acquainting themselves with each other, their chatter interspersed with singing and dancing. A couple of female entertainers had been called in as a part of the day's amusements and Mani watched her relatives fall about with laughter as the comediennes lampooned the manners of Varanasi folk with good-humoured and occasionally lewd jokes. Mani wondered where the men were. She hoped her father was not worrying about her unnecessarily as she was having a much more enjoyable time than she had expected, even though she was now quite tired. She thought too of the glimpse she had got of her new husband, frightened suddenly at the thought of being left alone with him when this crowd dispersed. He had looked so old in that one glimpse she had got of him, older even than her father. But Mani pushed the thought out of her head, straining to concentrate instead on the entertainers' jests through suddenly pounding ears. It was no use, though, and, when one of her maids asked if she wished to be taken to a resting chamber, she nodded her grateful assent.

While the remaining women continued to enjoy their entertainments, Mani was led away to a large room whose walls, decorated with a profusion of tiny mirrors and crystal pieces, sent a thousand little images of herself ricocheting about the room the moment she stepped in. Mani guessed from the clothes and jewels of the women accompanying her that they were either wives of local nobles or perhaps Gangadhar's relations and she hoped desperately that Sundar and Kashi were bringing up the rear of this unfamiliar group. She did not know what to make of these women who, away from the crowd, were now giggling at quips she could barely understand, their bangles clinking noisily as they nudged each other with their elbows and shoulders. When one of them remarked that it was advisable for the rani-sahiba to take as much rest as possible lest the raja should want to summon her this very night, they roared with raucous laughter as though that had been a fine joke indeed. Mani could only summon up a weak smile, knowing that they referred to the same things Asharfi-bua had warned her about. It was safest to pretend a sudden interest in the murals of birds and trees decorating the far side of the room.

This large chamber was very unlike the spartan comforts of her father's quarters back at Saturday House, every wall and corner softened by brocaded cushions and long damask drapes. It was— Mani searched for the unfamiliar word in her head—it was how she had imagined women with loose morals might live, a sort of boudoir, a kotha. There was something faintly immodest about the opulence of her surroundings although, having looked around some more in amazement, Mani decided that there was something about its effrontery that she liked.

She wasn't sure she liked the noblewomen very much, though— uncomfortably imagining they were laughing at her—and was relieved when they departed the chamber as abruptly as they had come, in a flurry of tinkling anklets and laughter. Only Kashi and Sundar were left and Mani was thankful for their sympathetic silence as they started to divest her of her bridal trappings. The jewels and the lehnga had started to itch and to feel as though they weighed twice as much as they had in the morning. Mani allowed her body to sag against Sundar's as the young maid rubbed perfumed oil onto her neck and ears to remove sight of the bruises left by the heavy jewellery. She was then helped into a thin cotton chemise, by now barely able to stand, before being led to the large four-poster bed that was set in the middle of the room. Kashi covered her with a soft sheet, whispering as she did that her rani-sahiba was to sleep for the remainder of the afternoon as she would not be required to be seen until the evening prayers at sundown.

After the two girls had withdrawn with a soft swishing of skirts, Mani lay on her bed, suddenly wide awake. A moment ago, she had been fighting to keep her eyes from closing, the womb-like rocking of the carriage, still trapped within her body, making her sway with sleep. But, left on her own for the first time in the day, she told herself in sudden panic to stay alert. There could be all sorts of unforeseen events. Perhaps the raja would choose this moment to walk in. Perhaps this was when he would demand his conjugal rights. She was not entirely sure what those were but did not even have the energy to get up and pay obeisance to the raja, leave alone think about conjugal rights.

Uneasily, she eyed the mirrored wall. Her own many reflections seemed to be watching her lying on this strange bed. It was as though she had suddenly split into a hundred different selves, each of which knew nothing of the other. If the rani of Jhansi came across little Mani of Saturday House now, would they even know what to say to each other? The two could not be further apart.

In order to calm herself, she started to chant the names of all the places she had passed on her long journey to Jhansi...Karchana, Kaushambi, Karwi...Chitrakoot, Mahoba, Kulpahar...Oran, Charkhari, Orchha...all those places that lay between Jhansi and home. Like lines from a poem, the music of their names lulled Mani until the mirrors started to fade slowly and she fell into an exhausted sleep.

✌ 7 ✊

In the Army cantonment that lay six miles east of the fort, Captain Ellis was mulling over the wedding ceremony he had attended in the morning. As Jhansi's political agent, he had been invited by the king to watch the arrival of the bridal procession along with the rest of the court and had stood with the ministers on the fort's ramparts, watching the caravan appear over the dusty horizon. The chariot bearing the new young queen was welcomed in a blaze of firecrackers and trumpets as it passed under the town gates but the bride, of course, had been carefully masked from view.

For days the city had worn a celebratory air, trees on either side of the rutted road leading to it festooned with flags and flower chains. Raja Gangadhar had ordered festivities to be laid out for his people for a whole week leading up to the wedding and every day the town had been entertained by cockfights and elephant races, traders flocking in from miles around to set up stalls selling sweetmeats and firecrackers.

Much of the expenditure involved had contravened Captain Ellis's early advice to the king. Jhansi's treasury had not yet recovered from Raghunath Rao's dissolute reign and was still teetering on the verge of bankruptcy. Although a royal wedding was a welcome distraction for Jhansi's people, orders received from Calcutta had been unambiguous: Ellis was, like many other officers in his position, expected to curb the excesses of native royals, their eccentricities and extravagances sometimes the sole reason for some states being so sapped of progress. It was not always easy and, seeing how delighted old Raja Gangadhar was to be getting married again, Ellis had on this occasion not had the heart to press the issue. He had gone as far as lending the cantonment's brass bands for the morning's festivities but had been less pleased to hear about the huge wedding banquet that was being laid on in the evening.

He had never enjoyed being contrary with Raja Gangadhar. They were essentially friends and had developed a respect and a liking for each other that did not always exist between native royalty and the Company officials attached to their court. Ellis had been genuinely pleased when the widowed king, who always cut a rather lonely figure, had voiced his desire to marry again. He had sat in on some of the discussions Raja Gangadhar had had with his prime minister on the matter of his second marriage and had agreed with them that a royal liaison was not of primary importance as territorial expansion was not imperative for Jhansi. He had seen a portrait of the most suitable bride that Prime Minister Baba Dixit had brought back from Varanasi, painted on a miniature sliver of ivory. The picture showed a face that was both pretty and intelligent, endowed with a pair of luminous dark eyes. Ellis had only looked briefly at it, awkwardly recognizing that he would never be allowed to lay eyes on the rani of Jhansi who would always remain in purdah in the presence of Englishmen. He certainly had no reason not to wish the king much luck with this new marriage of his.

The sound of the screen doors slamming at the back of the bungalow indicated that Karamchand had returned from the ice-house. Ellis got up to mix his drink as his orderly came in bearing his basket of precious cargo—a block of ice carefully wrapped in gunny sacking.

'Sahib, the abdaar in charge of the ice-pits is saying that this year's ice might not last through the summer. The nights have not been cold enough to freeze the pans,' Karamchand said as he placed his basket down on the bar.

Ellis, lifting the edge of the gunny, chipped a piece off the block straight into his glass with a small ice-pick. 'Ah, what a tragedy it would be, Karamchand, to be unable to comfort a parched palate with a tall glass of iced soda water.' He swilled a peg of whisky over the ice and grinned. 'Or, better still, an iced whisky-pawney, eh?'

Karamchand smiled toothlessly. He was lucky to have a sahib like Captain Ellis who, unlike some of the other sahibs, was easygoing, rarely had an angry word for him and, best of all, secretly slipped him the occasional whisky drink when they sat outside on the veranda together, but only after the lanterns had been dimmed.

'Sahib you will go for the raja's wedding feast soon? I shall run your bath?' Karamchand enquired.

'Yes, no rush,' Ellis replied, flopping down on his wicker chair. He felt a bit cheerless tonight, having been assigned the duty of accompanying Major Malcolm to the wedding banquet at the fort. Word had reached Ellis that the major had already arrived from Gwalior in the afternoon but so far Ellis had lain low, managing to avoid him. Major Malcolm's company was never one Ellis actively sought but he could not put it off any more. Already he was late.

He threw a resentful look at the clock above the mantelpiece, trying to rouse himself. 'I think I'll have another glass of that, Karamchand,' he said instead, adding, 'And fetch your glass too from the kitchen, old boy. You may as well have a peg while I'm at it.'

As Karamchand busied himself at the bar, Ellis leaned his head back and eyed the swaying punkah above his head, suddenly feeling rather gloomy about his own single status. It was a thought that had been recurring with alarming frequency in recent months. Twenty-four in the autumn and life's joys seemed to be passing him by, especially since he had been seconded to the civil service. Recently he seemed to have been spending inordinate amounts of time touring the areas surrounding Jhansi to assess the Company's system of revenue collection. It had already proven a mind-numbing task, providing little interaction with anyone of a like disposition and Ellis hoped he would not have to continue it for long.

'So Karamchand, your raja is a married man again,' he said, lifting his glass off the proffered tray. 'You've got to give it to the old codger. Never say die and all that. Second time round. Beating both you and me to the matrimonial stakes *again*.' He looked at the chunk of ice glinting in the golden liquor, unable to contain his smile as he asked, 'And tell me once more, Karamchand, why is it that *you* will not marry?'

He had asked his faithful orderly that question a few times these past few days and had never failed to be amused by Karamchand's stock reply: 'I will marry when you marry, sahib. This house needs a nice memsahib for putting flowers and teaching me how to bake the cakes.'

Tonight, however, Karamchand too seemed in a somewhat maudlin mood and sighed loudly before replying. 'Sahib, to tell the truth, I don't get married because for me marriage will be like that chakwa bird you can hear,' he said mournfully.

Ellis was puzzled. 'Chakwa bird?'

'You don't know chakwa bird, sahib? That is the one going "aw, aw" under the shehthooth tree. That is the male bird and the female will say "n'aich" when she returns to him by the riverside in the morning...' Karamchand trailed off but Ellis was still looking at him, baffled by his explanation. He knew the birds Karamchand referred to—there were a few curious red–brown wild ducks on the banks of the Betwa—the biological name being *Anus Caesarca*, if he was not mistaken. A pair was occasionally to be seen grubbing around at the bottom of his own garden.

'Sahib,' Karamchand said patiently, 'you are not understanding? The chakwa birds are always together in the daytime but, at night, they are doomed to be apart. The female flies across the river and that is why the male cries all through the night, "aw, aw" until she comes back to him.'

'Jolly silly thing to do, if you ask me, especially seeing what models of constancy they are in the daytime,' Ellis exclaimed.

But Karamchand refused to be cheered. 'It is the curse of Lord Ram on the chakwa birds, sahib. When Lord Ram was wandering the earth, looking for his Sita, he had asked the forests for her whereabouts and they had sighed, sharing his bereavement. Then he asked the stars who dimmed their beams. But, when he asked the chakwa birds, they showed no sorrow, happy as they were in their own love, saying that they knew of no Sita. So the grieving Lord Ram cursed them to be divided by the waters every night. Since then, there is no sleep for the poor chakwa bird who must bemoan his lost love all night, hoping she will find him again in the morning.'

Ellis shook his head. 'That's a terrible story, Karamchand. Imagine burdening me with that before I go off to attend a wedding banquet! The only thing that can possibly comfort me now is a bath.'

Karamchand shuffled out of the room while Ellis took a final resigned swig of his drink. He put his glass down on the walnut table and got up from his chair. Padding across the cool floor of his cavernous bedroom in bare feet, he peeled off his damp clothes. Old Karamchand certainly hadn't helped to lighten his own mood. Chakwa birds crying through the night, indeed. He certainly didn't need his mood worsened tonight. Major Malcolm's presence in Jhansi and the state of his job and life were bad enough, really.

It was hard to recall exactly when he had grown out of his early enthusiasm for the position he had felt so lucky to be offered not that long ago. At first it had all been so exciting; especially the gradual and painstaking process of winning the confidence of Jhansi district's corrupt zamindars, men who controlled vast swathes of the region's land. It had, at the time, been a source of immense pride to carry on the traditions and high standards of public duty set by other British administrators before him. But, this past year, he had grown unsure of which was worse: the constant touring and living out of tents with a retinue of servants and soldier–sepoys as they went from village to village, meeting headmen and farmers, or the days spent back here at Jhansi when the hours would stretch interminably ahead, filled with nothing other than the most enervating boredom.

There were occasional good days, of course. Today had not been too bad. After the king's wedding ceremony, Ellis had taken up Captain Martin's offer of riding down to the riverside and had felt an immense sense of pleasure when they returned, sweating and tired at sundown, with a brace of black partridge that had been eagerly received by the khansama in the mess kitchens. But the delights of hunting, the lifeblood of most officers in India, had never quite revealed themselves to Ellis for reasons he had never been able to fathom. Perhaps his inability to properly enjoy that life stemmed from his quiet upbringing in Shropshire, even though he had not for one moment regretted his escape from it after Mama's death. Indeed, he ought not to forget that, on first arriving in Calcutta and being taught to speak Hindustani at Fort William, he had considered himself the luckiest lad alive.

Karamchand had finished running the bath and Ellis stepped into it, balancing himself with a hand on the wall. 'Perhaps you're right about those bloody chakwa birds, Karamchand,' he said, sliding into the cool water with a groan, 'I certainly empathize with that poor sod going "aw, aw" outside. Not that I have a female chakwa awaiting me but who'd have thought it was possible to get so bloody lonely in the midst of such a beautiful land, eh?'

'But it is a good world for English sahibs,' Karamchand said firmly. 'You have your clubs and your bungalows and your shikaar and fishing...'

The man sounded almost terse, Ellis thought, feeling both peeved and amused by the lack of sympathy. But it was daft to expect poor Karamchand to understand. India offered innumerable pleasures, but—even though Ellis sometimes enjoyed going out hunting and hawking—he found himself increasingly spending his evenings either working or reading at home, unable to shake off those old habits instilled in him as a child. He leaned back in the cool water, acknowledging to himself that the regulated, rather humdrum life led by his parents, once so suffocating, had obviously permeated him far more than he had ever thought likely.

'I blame my parents, Karamchand,' he grinned, 'for making me such a prisoner of habit and allegiance. And perhaps you're right after all. A memsahib's presence would be nice. Not for the flowers and cake, of course.'

Ellis rubbed soap vigorously over his chest and thighs, feeling the ache from the hard ride he had undertaken with Martin slowly leave his body as his muscles relaxed. However lonely it got, the idea of making surreptitious trips to the brothels in town frequented by the rankers had never attracted him. Only once had he allowed Major Malcolm to drag him along to one of the better class kothas that specialized in nautch performances. Tawny-skinned women, reeking of musk oil and attar, had sung and danced into the night and Malcolm had eagerly told him of how easily these women could be 'persuaded' into regular sexual liaisons, with just a few favours bestowed in the form of alcohol or, oddly enough, cigars. That sort of diversion repulsed him, the fear of contracting syphilis that the barracks were rife with being just one of the deterrents.

Putting down the block of Windsor soap, he signalled to Karamchand that he was ready to have his back scrubbed. As he leaned forward to allow his orderly to tend to his neck and shoulders, he was relieved to hear him speak up again. The old man had hopefully regained his equanimity after those earlier mournful ramblings about the chakwa birds.

'Will the new rani-sahiba be at the wedding feast, sahib?' he asked.

Ellis peered into the tepid grey water, thinking of the bridal figure clad in cerise that he had briefly seen disembarking her chariot at the temple. She had been completely veiled but he recalled the whisperings in the cantonment of Raja Gangadhar's new bride being very young, barely a child. He knew, though, that the most important priority faced by the king at the moment was to provide an heir for his line to continue and the younger the bride, the better he probably thought his chances would be.

'I think not, Karamchand. I have heard the king say that she will be in purdah, at least for the first few months.'

'Let us hope she bears him the heir Jhansi needs, sahib,' Karamchand said, lathering his horsehair brush from a small pot of shaving powder. Ellis leaned back in the bath, angling his face towards the lantern, and closed his eyes.

Yes, heirs and children, that was the other thing to consider. Ellis had once seriously contemplated a dalliance with an Indian beauty, when Malcolm had pointed out the careful attention being paid to them by the daughter of a high-ranking nobleman at the Gwalior king's court. She had certainly seemed willing, almost embarrassingly so, flashing knowing glances in his direction from the women's section of the court. But relationships between British officers and native bibis were being increasingly frowned upon by the Company's Board of Directors and Ellis had considered it wise not to scupper his career prospects. Nor, for that matter, did he want to father a brood of half-caste children. He had often wondered what it was like for the half-caste Eurasians who found it so difficult to fit in anywhere. Everyone knew that the poor Eurasian bastards who had enlisted with the 77th Royal Field Artillery were treated like dirt, even by the native irregulars, excluded from the most prestigious battalions, despite being fine soldiers, some of them. Many had been reduced to becoming fifers, drummers and farriers. And yet the most pitiable part to Ellis was that they still considered themselves to be socially above the natives, ending up as a laughing stock in both British and Hindustani societies. The only ones who did survive the mixing of blood were usually from the British upper classes, where powerful families and established orders served to erase all signs of Hindu or Muslim blood, the children being given proper English names before being sent to receive the right sort of education back home, sometimes with a complete severance of ties with the Indian half of their families.

Karamchand had finished the shave and Ellis sunk his face into the steaming hot flannel. He waited while the orderly ended his toilette with the customary head massage and pomade before heaving himself out of the bath. Stepping onto the wooden floor and tying a bath sheet around his waist, he concluded that his only chance of finding love was to either try for a term back home or perhaps seek a posting to one of the bigger cantonments. Everyone was talking about how more and more young English ladies were daring to make the voyage these days, some plainly in search of husbands, now that the newer steamers had cut the journey time down so considerably. 'Fishing fleets' Malcolm had called them, no doubt smugly imagining himself a rather fine catch for some young hopeful travelling out from England. They were all gathering in the presidencies, though, and Ellis couldn't see any of them braving the journey to somewhere as remote as Jhansi.

He emerged from the bathroom to find that the dependable Karamchand had already laid out his ceremonial red and gold tunic on the bed. His heart sank as he remembered how constricted his shoulders had felt the last time he'd worn the accursed thing. It was obvious that the Company needed its officers to be elaborately braided and befrogged to leave no doubt about their superior status to the native princes but someone could surely have come up with a more sensible design for their uniforms, he had often thought. Given half a chance, Ellis knew he would slip into a loose-fitting muslin kurta on a night as sultry as this.

He struggled into his plus-fours, feeling its fabric straining against his already perspiring legs despite the punkah's best efforts overhead. As he held out his arms, Karamchand pulled the cross-belt around his chest before buckling the webbed sword belt in place. Today he would have to be fitted with the ceremonial sword in recognition of the importance of the event he was to attend. His boots, blacked and shined, their leather gleaming in the light from the lanterns, were ready and waiting in a corner of the room and he sat on his bed, bracing himself with a hand on Karamchand's shoulder, as he helped to pull them on. Ellis worried sometimes at how dependent he had become on his quiet and devoted orderly but knew he was not as bad as officers like Malcolm, who needed their entire retinue of servants dancing attendance on them during their baths and toilette. Patting Karamchand's arm in appreciation, Ellis got up and stamped on the wooden floorboards a couple of times to adjust his feet inside the stiff leather of the boots. Karamchand sat back on his haunches and looked up at him, circling his thumb and forefinger in a spontaneous gesture of appreciation. Ellis responded with a smiling grimace and a rueful shake of his head. They both knew this was a pantomime that had to be endured every so often.

Ellis fastened his new watch and chain to his uniform and caught a glimpse of himself in the mirror above the dresser. He'd nearly forgotten the last item that Karamchand was now holding out—his white pith helmet with its gleaming gold spike.

Pulling it on and linking the metal strap just above the chin rather than under it, as regulation demanded, Ellis grinned at his reflection, wondering if the Company would know how futile it was to even attempt competing sartorially with Raja Gangadhar. With an incurable penchant for the brightest of silks even on ordinary days, tonight he would no doubt be resembling a prize cockatoo. They would all be there—the Rajput kings of nearby Orchcha and Datia and Malcolm's exceedingly wealthy friend, Maharaja Scindia of Gwalior—preening in their best finery and covered from head to toe in jewels and silks. Raja Gangadhar would want to spare no expense on such an occasion, despite the privations of the Jhansi household and Ellis's constant warnings not to overstretch the treasury. But it had been hard to grudge him his desire to celebrate his wedding and, already Ellis could feel his spirits rising slightly. Perhaps it would be an idea to ride to the fort rather than use the small hansom carriage available at the mess that only served to make him feel claustrophobic.

The Officers' Mess was not far from Ellis's bungalow and, after handing his horse over to one of Major Malcolm's vast retinue, Ellis ran up the stairs of the building, startled to see Malcolm already standing on its veranda. He was struggling with his cravat, his eyes glittering in the moonlight, having clearly imbibed far too much whisky for his own good.

He spoke as soon as he saw Ellis, without any of the usual preliminary banter, 'Have you heard the news, Ellis? The North West frontier?'

Ellis noticed instantly that his voice lacked its normal self-assured tone.

'No, sir, been down at the riverside all afternoon. I haven't seen anyone but young Martin today,' Ellis replied. 'What is it, sir?'

Ellis was startled to hear a tremble in Malcolm's voice as he lowered it to a whisper, 'Elphinstone, Burnes, the lot of them, they're all dead. Dead, Ellis, would you believe it? Wiped out by the Afghans. Tricked into it apparently by the son of Dost Mohammed...and Burnes had considered the man his friend, ha!'

Malcolm swivelled around to return indoors, throwing over his shoulder in his more typical drawl, 'Never trust a man in a turban I always say.'

Following him in consternation, Ellis felt the floor of the room rock slightly and regretted for a moment the third glass of whisky downed just before leaving his bungalow. This was horrible news, even though all the rumours that had trickled down from the North West Frontier had been grim for a while now.

'What the devil could have gone wrong, sir, you said there'd never been a greater force...'

It was less than three years ago that Malcolm had boasted of the fanfare with which General Elphinstone's Army of the Indus had set out from Peshawar—'an entire bridge of boats built to cross the mighty Indus,' he had said and, later, 'Kandahar captured'...'the Bolan and Khyber passes crossed without any trouble at all'—it had never been bad news.

'For God's sake, sir,' Ellis continued, 'they'd taken Kabul without as much as a murmur...'

Malcolm was unusually silent and Ellis suddenly realized that it was a subject he did not want discussed in front of the orderly summoned to help him with his necktie. He turned and pushed open a window shutter to get some fresh air and the room filled instantly with the raucous chirping of night crickets. Their cheerful sound made him feel sick at heart as he gazed sightlessly into the darkness. That silent, almost timorous, fall of Kabul had sent ripples of excitement across British cantonments all over India. To get there before the slippery Russians entrenched themselves, that had been the main concern. Certainly Lord Auckland had made it his top priority in recent years, even going personally to Lahore to negotiate with Maharaja Ranjit Singh of the Punjab and flag off their combined forces.

Ellis turned to see the orderly standing on tiptoe, carefully brushing Malcolm's moustache and side-whiskers into luxuriant fullness. Malcolm was right, it was best to be prudent before the Indian servants as it was impossible to know how much they understood or cared. But Ellis could not contain his incredulity and he sought Malcolm's bloodshot gaze again, dropping his voice to a whisper. '*Burnes*?' he asked, hoping somehow that he may have misheard.

As Malcolm nodded, Ellis felt his stomach constrict. He had met an exceedingly likable young Captain Burnes at a merchant's house at Calcutta no more than a year ago. Nephew of Alexander Burnes. And, talking to him, had been filled with admiration for how their entire clan had grown devoted to the upliftment of these lands. Apparently suffering from none of the superciliousness of newer Company men who had little desire to understand the places they came out to govern but filled with a genuine desire to do good. For one of such a family to die in the course of selfless service?

Ellis took a deep breath. 'Perhaps we just overreached ourselves on that border, sir,' he said finally, hearing his own voice emerge hoarse and almost inaudible.

The orderly had finished brushing the jacket and withdrawn silently from the room. Wincing as he tried to loosen his collar, Malcolm came up to Ellis, keeping his voice low. 'Dash it Ellis,' he said, 'you remember the size of the force that had set out, don't you?'

Ellis nodded silently. There had been nothing like it before— thirty thousand men and twenty thousand camels, elephants, horsemen, artillery, engineers, military bands. In addition there had been the servants—water bearers, brass polishers, cooks, coolies, dhobis—those apocryphal tales had even reached Jhansi of every regiment having six hundred native stretcher bearers of its own and every platoon its own troop of men and women to polish their brasses and wash their clothes. Some of them had even taken their families along and there had been rumours of prostitutes being part of the entourage too.

'And how many would you wager made it back to Jalalabad?' Malcolm demanded.

Ellis shook his head, he could not even venture a guess. It was odd though how Malcolm seemed to be almost relishing recounting the ghastly news.

'One!' Malcolm said with a flourish, holding up his forefinger and repeating dramatically, 'One poor sod. A doctor...Brydon, Bryson, or some such. Escaped the murderers by the skin of his teeth apparently before riding hell for leather across the pass and reaching Jalalabad only barely alive.'

Ellis shook his head in disbelief. All those lives, all that time and effort and expense...what had been the point of it?

He dragged his attention back to Malcolm who was still prattling agitatedly as he threw a last look at the mirror, smoothing his hair down with some spittle. 'They kept bonfires burning outside Jalalabad Fort for days, sounding the bugle, hoping some poor bugger still struggling his way across the mountains would hear them. But not another soul was to return. It's confirmed now, wiped out, the whole bleeding lot of them. The Army of the Indus defeated by a bunch of scimitar-wielding, bearded, bloodthirsty savages.'

He picked up his keys and Ellis stepped out onto the veranda. Malcolm's orderly was awaiting further orders outside but melted away into the night as Malcolm dismissed him with a wave of his hand and bolted shut the door to his room, tugging at the lock a couple of times. The front yard was quiet, the crickets in the long grass at the back of the building inaudible from here. All that could be heard now was the distant yapping of jackals and the gentle snuffling of their tethered horses.

The two men mounted their horses, Malcolm still fulminating under his breath, his earlier shock seeming to have turned now to anger. 'Bunch of yahoos, the Afghans, with all their humbug beliefs,' he muttered. 'I'll never understand what possessed Burnes to have faith in them. Wouldn't trust them within an inch of my own life, personally. Hot-tempered tribesmen who spend their lives lurching from blood-feud to blood-feud. And now trying to play a double game between Russia and us. But, you take this from me, Ellis, we're sure to be able to win this game, given time. Subdue the worst of them. Show them what's good for them.'

'It's the Pashtun tribal code of honour that we haven't managed to get our heads around yet, I imagine, sir. But I suppose we have to be grateful that the people in these central states are, by and large, a docile bunch, willing to work with us,' Ellis said, suddenly keen to calm Malcolm, anxious that, in such a mood, he was likely to say something unfortunate at the king's wedding banquet. 'It's only rational to expect that the men will be harder and more ruthless the further north one travels, sir. Something to do with the terrain—the protection their mountains have always given them from outsiders perhaps.'

'If you ask me though, Ellis, there's nothing to praise in the local natives either. Servile and conniving, a worse blend cannot be found.' Malcolm's manner sometimes grated terribly with Ellis but he was on a roll now and nothing would stop him. 'Can't say which I mind more,' he continued, 'these grinning Bundeli niggers or the Pathans and the Afghans who are, well, ruffians and hooligans, but at least make no pretence to being anything else. But you mark my words, old chap, we'll get them all in the end, yes we will. Round them up every last one, teach them a thing or two and blow to smithereens all those that don't do their salaam sahibs properly.'

Ellis felt cold fingers run down his spine even though he was well accustomed to Malcolm's malevolence. He knew better, however, than to get into an argument before reaching the palace as that would only worsen the major's ill-temper. It would certainly not help to have him say something unfortunate to any of the maharajas tonight as who could tell how they would receive news of an English defeat in Afghanistan. There might even be some among them who would rejoice to see British noses rubbed in it for once.

They rode on in the direction of the fort, the only sound breaking the stillness of the night being the laboured breathing of Malcolm's syce running alongside and the rhythmic thudding of his bare heels on the road. Ellis was always loath to have syces trotting along beside him and tonight it bothered him even more than usual. He thought again of those poor souls in Afghanistan, killed or mutilated or worse, their bodies turning the snows of those inhospitable wastes beyond the mountain passes red with English blood. They would have set out on their journey, as all travellers do, with hope and anticipation, never imagining there would be no coming back. And what of loved ones who awaited them at home? Ellis had a sudden flash of the lovelorn chakwa bird cries in his head. There seemed suddenly something very dark and gloomy about the night as the two horses clip-clopped their way through the opaque heat, the syce panting behind them as they covered the six-mile distance to the fort.

Ellis thought he knew every tree and stone on this road but, tonight, he found himself noticing things he had never seen before—that clump of thorny shrubs behind the mess, the ghostly shapes of the water tanks, dark undulations of the land behind which people could so easily hide in wait. Jhansi had so far been a haven of peace— almost too quiet for its own good—but, for the first time, it suddenly felt...he searched for the words...foreign, full of menace.

It was with more than relief that Ellis finally greeted the sight of Raja Gangadhar's fort atop its hillock as the horses ambled around a corner and the lights from enormous celebratory bronze lanterns adorning Khanderao Darwaza blazed into view.

Talk of the English defeat on the Afghan front floated through the men's section of the banquet that night, weaving through the king's grand durbar hall. Occasional bursts of high-pitched laughter from the women who were seated in the neighbouring room punctured the low hum of conversation. There was no sign of the young queen who was no doubt being carefully kept in purdah, as befitted a new bride. Among the menfolk, it was as though a distant massacre had not taken place at all as the festivities took over. Everyone seemed to know of the English defeat and it was spoken of and passed on and repeated as heads nodded and eyes widened and decanters were passed around, but in a casual, careless, callous way, as one might comment unthinkingly on a passing event of no consequence at all to the living and the present. It was all too faraway and too remote and too unlikely to happen anywhere as peaceful as this small, sleepy town. But Ellis could not seem to forget his earlier misgivings as the last toasts were drunk and royalty and army, Indian and European, sat down to dine in the dripping radiance of the dozens of chandeliers hanging above their heads.

As the raja's liveried servants brought out the dishes one by one, in a sudden fanciful moment, Ellis felt he could actually see the news rise up like an invisible evil thought, to dance around the resplendent chandeliers, before being carried like sly little whispers into the kitchens and outside the palace and over the very walls of the city. Already the news would be trickling through to the barracks and the villages in and around Jhansi as in other parts of the country. People never seemed to need newspapers for news to spread in India. Perhaps only a few local people, like the raja's old Afghani retainer, Khuda Baksh, would have actual connections with those faraway names—Jalalabad...Kandahar...Kabul. Ellis had so often talked to the old man about his homeland, watching his rheumy old eyes moisten with memories.

But there would always be someone who knew someone who had accompanied the British on their mission to Afghanistan. A son, a father, brother, husband. And Ellis knew that it was only a matter of time before those people asked why their men had been sent to fight in a battle that was not theirs? Our enemy is not their enemy, he thought, trying to suppress his illogically rising gall, our fight is not their fight and our victory will certainly not be their gain. For how long would they continue to send their children to fight in others' wars? For how long would they stand by the British so unthinkingly, forgiving all that was asked of them?

❧ 8 ❧

Mani winced as Sundar tried to extricate the kaanphool that was snagged in her hair. As the maid painstakingly unhooked strands of hair that were wound around the fine gold chains, she looked apologetically at the young queen who was sitting patiently waiting for her to finish, biting her lip but making no other expression of pain.

'Please forgive me, Rani-sahiba, I will try not to hurt you,' Sundar said, bending double to see better in the candlelight.

'Don't worry, Sundar,' Mani replied with eyes closed, 'it's not your fault.' She took another sharp intake of breath as she felt the skin on her hairline being pulled again. Mani opened her eyes to gaze blearily at her reflection. Far away, she could hear the clock in the hallway chime…was it eleven or midnight…Mani could not remember a single night that she had been able to go to bed before eleven o'clock in the fortnight she had already been at Jhansi. Every evening had brought either a banquet or some other ceremony in honour of various visiting dignitaries eager to meet the new rani. She had taken her position at all of them next to her new husband who, though pleased to have her beauty praised, had otherwise paid her scant attention.

Today's functions had revolved around her renaming ceremony. She was now no longer Mani but Lakshmibai, Rani of Jhansi. Mani knew that all Maratha brides took on new names when they got married. She had a vague memory of having been admonished once for neglecting to address Nana's cousin Hema as 'Mangaladevi' after she had got married. 'I now belong to my husband's house,' Hema had protested, 'and I am no more the Hema who used to play with you.' It had puzzled Mani at the time but now, of course, she understood it all.

Poor Sundar had managed to extricate the earring but was now trying to unclasp the kundan-work choker around her neck. Mani looked at her crumpled nine-yard paithani sari and the antimony smudged around her tired eyes, wondering at how unfamiliar she still looked to herself. She closed her eyes and heaved a sigh of relief as she felt Sundar finally remove the necklace that had been pricking at her throat all evening, allowing her to lift it carefully over her head.

The mound of jewellery on the marble top of the dressing table was growing before her eyes. Picking up the choker, she examined the simple elegance of the piece. The maid had told her that it had once belonged to the raja's mother. In the glass teardrops of the old necklace were more tiny reflections of her figure. All of them, little Lakshmibais.

She said her new name under her breath, trying to make it stick, stretching out the soft sound of the 'ksh' before the second syllable. The maid smiled at her in the mirror.

'Raja Gangadhar has personally chosen the name, Rani-sahiba, as he has no parents to act on his behalf. How happy they would have been today, had they lived to see these happy times...'

'Had you ever seen them, Sundar? The raja's parents?'

'No, Rani-sahiba, for they both died in our poor raja-sahib's infancy.'

Mani stopped to reflect how heart-breaking it must have been for her husband to have lost both parents when he was a child. She, at least, had a beloved father who had never once allowed her to mourn the loss of her mother. But perhaps she was not to ask the maid too many more questions about the king.

'Do you suppose my name comes from the goddess Mahalakshmi, Sundar?'

'Yes, Rani-sahiba, our town's goddess; for it is she who protects our Jhansi.'

This maid, sweet as she was, was not given to garrulous chatter unlike the other one. Though frustrated by it, Mani was determined to strike up a warm conversation. 'Did you know, Sundar, the custom of new names comes from girls having to subsume their personalities and pasts along with their childhood names...my Asharfi-bua told me that.'

She closed her eyes as Sundar started to rub the bruises on her neck with gentle hands. Although she could have sat there forever, she soon raised her hand to signal that it was enough. The poor maid had been awake and tending to her since early in the morning and needed to sleep too.

As she got up to allow Sundar to unwind her sari, she addressed the solemn young maid again, 'Your hands are always so careful, Sundar, as though I were a china doll and not a real person at all.'

Sundar smiled in reply, keeping her eyes on the folds and pins of the sari. 'Rani-sahiba is always praising me. I am sure the maids in Varanasi must have been at least as gentle as I am.'

'I did not use the maids in Peshwa-sahib's palace so much,

Sundar, but turned to my Asharfi-bua for everything. She brought me up as my own mother, although it was always with a kind of serious purpose rather than tenderness!'

The maid laughed and Mani, wishing not to seem ungrateful for her poor great-aunt's care, added quickly, 'But I know now that my bua's scolding and advising was merely another form of love. She must have worried that too much love would soften me and make me unable to leave my father's home.'

'My rani-sahiba, it is my greatest pleasure to tend to your needs. I hope there will be no reason for you to ever miss your Asharfi-bua's love.'

Stepping into the cotton chemise Sundar was holding up, the newly named Lakshmibai allowed the maid to tie her hair back in a loose braid before she was helped into her bed. She was now so tired, she felt a sudden surge of tears rise within her chest as she was gently covered with her pashmina quilt. Pulling the coverlet over her mouth and nose, she watched Sundar walk around the chambers, snuffing out all the candles and lowering the lanterns, until the room was nearly dark.

'Goodnight, my rani-sahiba, sleep well and please call me if you need anything, I am not far,' she heard the maid say.

'You sleep well too, Sundar, you work so hard...' she replied, imagining the pretty girl smiling as she shut the door behind her.

Mani stared into the darkness, unable to quell her tears any more. Using the edge of the quilt to wipe her suddenly streaming eyes and nose, she scolded herself for being ungrateful for her many new blessings. She was becoming just like Peshwa-sahib, unhappy even when surrounded by comforts most people could only dream of.

'Lakshmibai,' she whispered softly. Her voice sounded like the pathetic quaver of a reed pipe. She raised it and said more firmly, 'Lakshmibai, Rani of Jhansi.' That was better. 'Queen Lakshmibai of Jhansi...Rani-sahiba Lakshmibai.'

Her father had already taken to calling her Rani Lakshmibai. She had looked for the twinkle in his eye when he had first said it, but had seen only seriousness. Perhaps he too thought the title would make her feel important, in control. Mani was only a silly little pet-name anyway and her new husband had quite rightly declared it ill-fitting for a queen of her stature. Even Manikarnika had not been good enough for him.

She had last seen her husband at the ceremony that had been conducted this morning at Jhansi's main temple. The raja's special *suvarna mena* had been summoned to take her there, a golden palanquin carried today by four female bearers. They bore her weight lightly, using only an arm each, twirling silver-handled ostrich-feather fans as they carried her through the cobbled streets of the town. Through the gauze of the curtains, Lakshmibai could see that they were all young and pretty in tight bodices and colourful skirts, embroidered nagra slippers on their feet. They chatted with each other like old friends and occasionally responded to a hailed greeting from the crowd. A band of drummers and shehnai players preceded them and those musicians seemed to be enjoying themselves too, nodding their heads in appreciation of each other's skills. The people of Jhansi seemed similarly full of good cheer, summoned by the celebratory trumpeting and crowding onto windows and balconies from where they awaited another glimpse of their new queen.

Arriving at the grand old temple, Lakshmibai saw that it was built on the banks of a vast peaceful lake that was full of darting silver fish. Although she longed to run up to its edge and feed them with the puffed rice being carried as offerings for the temple, she disembarked and waited demurely by her palanquin while the raja emerged from his own carriage. He gave her only a brief smile before walking slowly up the column of stairs and she followed, careful to keep a few feet behind him as instructed by Asharfi-bua.

The darkened sanctum sanctorum resounded with the soft chanting of priests as they walked in. The stone idol of the goddess was dressed in a new silk skirt, her face covered with a silver mask. Lakshmibai, taking her cue again from the raja, paid obeisance and watched while he stepped forward to drape the idol with a necklace, his thanksgiving for the nuptials. Milk, offered to the goddess during the morning prayers, was then sprinkled on Lakshmibai's head and a pinch of sindoor smeared in the central parting of her hair. She was seated and a platter of rice placed on her lap with instructions for her new name to be written on it. Raja Gangadhar, who seemed to know the routine, sat next to her and took her hand in order to guide her finger through the rice. Lakshmibai, who had not been touched yet by her husband since the wedding ceremonies, felt her face burn. He had quite probably been through this routine with his previous wife before and seemed to know exactly what to do. Finally, the crown worn by generations of queens before her was placed on her head while prayers were chanted to bless the auspicious occasion.

When she finally emerged, blinking, from the darkened hall, she heard the temple bells pealing deafeningly to proclaim to all that Maharani Lakshmibai had been crowned before the eyes of the goddess. A prickle of fear and excitement ran down her back at the thought.

Perhaps this was what the raja was waiting for before fully considering her his wife.

Still following the raja, she was given coins in small silk pouches to hand over to the temple priests for their efforts, before descending the steps of the temple to give alms to the beggars, the poor and the sick, who were sitting in long patient rows along the road leading to the temple. Later, she walked around amongst the crowd that had gathered, allowing the women to touch her arm or the edge of her sari. Some of them seemed overawed by her jewellery and her clothes and she had wanted to reassure them that she was really no different from them. Only the children seemed oblivious to her status as she handed out laddoos to them. Enjoying herself, she had held the children's outstretched hands for as long as she could before they were pulled away to stuff the confections into their mouths. She had also enjoyed distributing new clothes to the elderly, some of whom had even reached out to hug her. In one shy glimpse, she had seen her husband smile at her and had felt pleased at his obvious pride. He could, after all, have been envious of all the attention that was now focussed on her. Instead, he asked Lakshmibai to hand the clothes and blankets out, seeming not to mind at all that she was suddenly at the receiving end of everyone's gratitude. She felt touched by this and, even though her husband had barely spoken more than a few words to her, she knew she really had no cause for complaint.

Within her first few days in the court, Lakshmibai discovered to her relief that Gangadhar was not insistent that she remain behind purdah. Although she had not seen much of him yet, regular instructions were being sent through her handmaidens and it was Sundar who had told her that the raja only expected his queen to be in purdah when European men were present in court. Even on those occasions, it was to be no more than a symbolic gesture, consisting of either a carved ivory screen or the presence of two guards who would stand in between her and the male guests, holding up an embroidered silk sheet.

Lakshmibai had already met, in this manner, some of the city's European merchants, the British army officers of the Jhansi regiment and also the political agents of Jhansi and other nearby districts. She had not found much to say to them so early on but her father, who had agreed to stay in Jhansi until she was settled, assured her that conversation was not expected of new brides and so presumably nobody had found her silence insulting.

If anyone had asked, however, she would have declared quite openly that the best day in Jhansi so far had been when she was taken to visit the Army regiments at Sagar. She had been required to attend the function in purdah, following a small tunnel of silk cloth to get from her carriage to an enclosure that had been partitioned off for women of the royal household. But, even from behind the screens, she had been able to see sleekly groomed horses marching in perfectly arrayed ranks. Their riders too were wearing fabulous uniforms— short red tunics with gold trimmings, worn over black leggings and boots, ceremonial swords hanging by their sides, while on their heads were turbans of intertwining red, black and gold silk. The man leading them, a British officer, wore a white helmet with a magnificent plume that emerged from its crest like a cloud.

The Englishwomen too had been so charming, their pretty pink faces smiling shyly at her from behind parasols and bonnet brims. No one approached to speak to her but Lakshmibai thought it was probably due to uncertainties over her own rules of purdah. In a corner of a large parade ground, a brass band was playing jaunty tunes and beyond them she could see a yellow church with a spire and a row of houses with tiled gables and deep verandas, their gardens bursting with flowers. Under a cloudless sky, with the sun shining down on brass instruments and colourful uniforms and frocks, Lakshmibai felt as though she had travelled entire worlds away from sleepy old Saturday House to reach some wonderful place resembling paradise.

She stole a look at Gangadhar who was seated on a sofa at the head of the crowd, smiling and talking animatedly with a couple of British officers. They looked tall and handsome in their bright red uniforms next to the frail figure of her husband but it was for him that she felt a sudden wave of affection and pride. She had married a man who clearly maintained an excellent relationship with the British, seeing how cordial their welcome to her had been so far. How unlike poor dear Peshwa-sahib back at Varanasi, too full of honour and vanity to have known better.

The following morning, a group of Christian missionaries from Jhansi's new Church of St Jude's assembled to pay their respects. Lakshmibai had received them too from behind purdah but when one of the nuns asked to stay back and have a private conference with the new queen, Gangadhar consented, smiling and nodding encouragingly at Lakshmibai which, for some inexplicable reason, made her feel suddenly cross with him.

Trying to quell the panic she felt at her first solo official meeting, she led the nun into one of the ladies' chambers where they could be seated comfortably. Even though Lakshmibai had met Europeans like her tutor Mr Todd at Varanasi, none had been women and she felt herself relax slightly as she beheld a tiny, pointed grey-eyed face shining earnestly from under a white wimple. The nun was only a young woman herself, her thin figure free of all female appurtenances. Lakshmibai felt very overdressed, clad as she was in a silk angarkha with a shimmering blue georgette dupatta draped over her head, pieces of jewellery attached to all the visible parts of her body.

'I should be delighted if you called me Sister Agnes, Rani-sahiba,' the diminutive nun opened up in accented but otherwise near-perfect Hindustani that both startled and pleased Lakshmibai.

She recalled being told by her father that new Company laws now allowed unrestricted access to missionaries arriving in India and clearly her husband wished to be friendly to them too. Determined not to let either her father or her husband down, she thought she ought to offer hospitality in her own best English, a combination of Mr Todd's and Asharfi-bua's careful tutelage coming to the fore.

'Sister Agnes, please can I serve you something to drink on such a hot day, so that you can tell me about your work once you are refreshed?' Lakshmibai said, scrunching her toes in embarrassment at how she had stumbled through that sentence. She knew she had sounded gauche, her hospitality clumsy and rehearsed, but Sister Agnes seemed charmed and smiled broadly at her, nodding eager assent. And so, while the maids served them tall silver glassfuls of frothing pink watermelon sherbet, the two women settled back on the bolsters of a velvet sofa to strike up a tentative conversation.

Lakshmibai, unable to resist her curiosity, opened up with a directness she was not sure she would have mustered in open court or in her husband's presence, 'Tell me please, Sister Agnes, how long have you been in Jhansi and how did it come to be that you travelled to a country so faraway from your own? You must have had such a long journey to make.'

'Ah, Rani-sahiba, I know you too have made a long overland journey from your own home town,' the Englishwoman replied warmly. 'Perhaps, though, you are lucky to have not had any seas to cross. My voyage on the steamer—oh so many moons ago—did not suit my constitution all and has since provided me with very good reason to never return to England!' She laughed and then, seeing that an answer was still awaited, continued more shyly, 'I do not have a very exciting story to tell, Rani-sahiba, nothing like yours, I am sure. I was born Amy Johnson to a poor family in the East End of London and was sent to join the Church as a sixteen-year-old. Within just a year I was chosen to come here, to India, to propagate the message of Christ. And that is the sum total of it, I fear.'

'And how did you come to be in Jhansi?' Lakshmibai persisted.

'Ah, that was more a matter of good fortune than good planning. Just two days after arriving in Calcutta, I joined a group of missionaries who were setting out to build churches in the more remote areas of central India. I had not planned to be in Jhansi but this is where we ended up and the truth is that I have never for one moment regretted it, Rani-sahiba.'

'How odd that you too, like me, had to change your name to start your new life. From Amy Johnson, you became Sister Agnes. And Manikarnika has had to become Rani Lakshmibai!'

'Indeed, Rani-sahiba, ours is church practice. A worthy custom that enables one to remember that the old self has been shed and that an entirely new life awaits.'

'I think I understand, Sister Agnes,' Lakshmibai said solemnly, ringed fingers folded neatly in her lap. Little Mani certainly belonged to another age and would never have sat here so obediently and gracefully and so very beautifully dressed.

The nun added reassuringly, 'It is a transition easily made once one has accepted one's calling in life, Rani-sahiba. My life as Amy Johnson in a crowded London workhouse ended so suddenly. I too was young and had never spent a night away from my mother. And, on those terrible nights on the high seas when the ship would roll so far that I was sure my end had come, oh how I longed for just one glimpse of my mother's gentle face again. I could never have dreamt then that here, in Jhansi, a whole new family would be awaiting me— whose love would so enrich me so fully that the old life would simply fade away. I can barely remember my mother's face now but I'm sure the Lord loves me more for it.'

'Oh but how brave you are, not just to leave your blood-family but also to make such a long voyage by sea, Sister Agnes!' Lakshmibai said, conscious that her own recent journey across dusty Bundelkhand held no comparison. 'I have learnt that all rivers, including the beloved Ganga I grew up with, flow into the sea, but I have never even laid eyes on the "black water" that our people so fear to cross.'

'Forgive me, Rani-sahiba, but I think of *you* as being brave to have set out on such an important task—marriage and queenship—at your tender age!' the nun replied solemnly.

'Ah, but that is my duty, Sister Agnes, as a daughter and, now, a wife.'

'Isn't it curious that I saw myself as having a duty to perform too, Rani-sahiba. A duty to my God and to my Church.'

'Yes, that is true,' Lakshmibai said, after a pause, 'we are each following our own destinies it seems to me. But tell me, Sister Agnes, was the church at Jhansi built after you came here?'

'Oh no, Rani-sahiba, the church building that you saw in the cantonment took us more than five years to build. We worked out of a tin shed for many years, but the East India Company has in recent years grown helpful, having overcome their earlier fears that their trade could be adversely affected if local people objected to us.'

'Has the palace too given you assistance in your work?'

'Raja Gangadhar has been kindness itself, ever since he became king, Rani-sahiba,' the nun replied, 'but I'm afraid we haven't always had such cooperation. Some kings have felt rather threatened by us. Such as Raja Raghunath Rao, who hated us to such an extent that he actually gave refuge to some wicked Thugs here in this very fort.' Sister Agnes waved her hand at the sunlit quadrangle in which they sat.

'Perhaps Raja Raghunath felt he ought to protect their beliefs. Not all were as evil as people say...' Lakshmibai offered hesitantly. This was unfamiliar ground and the dead raja whom she had never known was, after all, a relative of her husband's.

'I think it was more out of pique against Christians than anything else, my dear Rani-sahiba. Raja Raghunath Rao simply did not like the missionaries whose work to save fallen souls he always resented.'

Taken aback by Sister Agnes's candour, Lakshmibai was not sure at all what to say in reply. She had not heard Gangadhar criticize his uncle, the old raja, nor mention the Thugs. But she thought she was beginning to see the reasons for which Gangadhar followed the policies he did. The British had placed him on the throne of Jhansi specifically because they knew he would be different from his uncle and supportive of their work. And, as long as their work did not interfere directly with his court, he had probably thought it sensible to allow them to carry on their reforms and businesses and trade, even their missionary work.

Lakshmibai guessed that she too was being assessed by the nun who was no doubt wondering what sort of influence she would bring to bear on the king. She would never know, of course, that he had barely spoken to her so far.

Lakshmibai sat up in her chair, trying to look queenly. 'I think you can be sure, Sister Agnes, that my presence in this court will be one that will only help and assist my husband, the king. The church· and the palace must work together to create a better life for the citizens of Jhansi. If that is a shared mission, then we have no reason to disagree on anything at all.'

She could feel her heart pound with the sweeping boldness of her statement, wondering if Raja Gangadhar would think it forward of her. But surely a sincere avowal to support him in every way could not be taken amiss. Well, Sister Agnes certainly looked very happy. She saw the nun thump her hands on her knees with a satisfied air indicating that her business was done and she was about to leave. But it appeared she had not finished yet. With a big smile on her face, she picked up a valise and placed it on the marble table before pulling out a bundle wrapped in paper. Eagerly tearing it open, she revealed two copies of the Bible, one translated into Persian and the other into Sanskrit. 'For you, Rani-sahiba,' Sister Agnes declared proudly, getting to her feet and handing them over carefully as though they were made of glass.

Lakshmibai took the proffered books, not at all sure if it was correct and proper to be accepting them. But she ran her fingers over the leather covers saying politely, 'They are so beautiful. I thank you, Sister Agnes.'

'Please read them when you can, Rani-sahiba, there is much comfort to be had in their pages.'

Lakshmibai nodded. Perhaps the clever little nun had sensed that she was a little bit in need of comfort but surely Jhansi's court would not be pleased at all if their new queen was to receive it from the Bible! She put the books back carefully on the table, watching the nun hurry out of the courtyard, accompanied by a maid.

Before leaving the court, Sister Agnes paid tribute to Raja Gangadhar's choice of bride and Moropant's heart swelled with joy as he heard her shower praises on his daughter's education and upbringing in open court. He shot a look at the king who too looked pleased, inclining his head at the nun's generous words.

In the month since the wedding ceremony, Moropant had been alternately admiring and astonished at the manner in which his daughter had risen to the challenges placed before her so unexpectedly. He had seen her observing all the proceedings in the court quietly and astutely, without the slightest sign of boredom and straining to hear every word when seated behind the purdah. If she was so determined to be a good queen, then he was sure she was going to make a resounding success of it. How foolish and unnecessary all his fears before the wedding had been!

Looking at her now as she reoccupied her place by her husband's side, he thought proudly of how she now even looked every inch a queen, her blue silk dupatta framing her solemn face. He could not wait to tell Asharfi-bua how right she had been about their Mani's capacity to be a competent wife and queen.

Despite his sense of satisfaction, however, Moropant felt himself grow anxious again as the day approached for his return to Varanasi. On the morning of his departure, he made a small formal speech to all the courtiers, pledging the assistance of the Peshwa-sahib and his retinue to the royal house of Jhansi. Raising his head, he dared not look up at his daughter who was seated on her throne next to Gangadhar's, fearful that she would be in tears. He was deeply touched when Raja Gangadhar, noticing how overcome he was, tactfully suggested that father and daughter be given a little time alone together before it was time for him to leave.

Moropant and Lakshmibai were escorted into one of the antechambers and he saw to his distress that, for the second time since coming to Jhansi, his daughter was overwhelmed by sorrow. Although she had cried grievously on the day that Nana and Tantia and the rest of the bridal party had returned to Varanasi, she had soon composed herself, taking comfort from her father's presence. Raja Gangadhar had invited Moropant to stay in Jhansi as long as he liked but Moropant knew that it would not be fitting to remain any longer. Already it had been four weeks since the wedding and he worried that, apart from the impropriety, Lakshmibai would become too accustomed to having him near her. He was also anxious about Peshwa-sahib and Asharfi-bua, both of whom he had left in such poor health. Even though Lakshmibai had accepted all those reasons for him to return to Varanasi days ago, she was now crying in earnest, slumped in his arms and clutching him as though terrified to let go.

'Raja Gangadhar is a fine, kind man, beti,' he said, patting her back feebly, trying to keep his voice cheerful, 'and that is the only reason that I feel I can leave you in his care.'

Lakshmibai would not be consoled and continued to weep, leaning her forehead on her father's chest and wiping her dripping nose with the back of her hand. As one of her new rings snagged at her nose, she cried afresh and Moropant wondered at his continuing inability to bear seeing her in pain, even though she was not really his to worry about any more. He held his daughter by the shoulders and raised her chin, dabbing at her nose with a silk handkerchief and trying to get her to focus her brimming eyes on his.

'You are destined for greater things than any of the rest of us, beti,' he said, composing his voice before adding carefully, 'and it is those of us destined for greatness that must leave life's smaller joys behind. You are to be not just a good wife to Raja Gangadhar but also a great queen to Jhansi. I know you will do both to the best of your abilities...already I feel so proud of you...'

There was no other way to do this but to leave her very quickly; words would only make it worse. He dropped his hands and turned away from his daughter, feeling as though his anchor had been ripped away, cutting him adrift of the only thing that had ever been of any importance at all.

Moropant boarded his waiting carriage. When it started to move, he dared not look over his shoulder at the receding palace lest Mani be standing at a window. Instead, he remained unbending and dry-eyed as they passed under the great gates of the fort. But, as the horses picked up speed, he sank his head between his hands, reflecting that the rolling sound of the wheels carrying him away from his daughter must surely be the saddest sound in the world.

Jhansi was slowly left behind. How, he wondered, could he possibly return to a Saturday House that would be robbed of the sound of his daughter's laughter and play. Was it selfish that it was for himself rather than his daughter that he grieved?

His conviction that Mani would be well cared for by her new husband was a conclusion on which his own survival depended. Raja Gangadhar had certainly revealed himself to be a wise and tolerant man and Moropant had observed his daughter being treated with respect in the Jhansi court, thankfully not one in which women were all but invisible. The concern he had initially felt at Raja Gangadhar being nearly his own age had been forced into relief that his daughter's husband was not a callow and unthinking youth that a younger man would almost certainly have been. Yes, Asharfi-bua was almost certainly right—a handsome young bridegroom might well have brought Mani unhappiness. Moropant had also forced himself to mind less that Gangadhar was not, by the looks of things, in the best of health. Life never offered any guarantees; he, widowed at a young age, ought to know that.

Uncharacteristically, however, Moropant had not thought to ask his daughter what she felt about the new life thrust on her so abruptly. Perhaps that had been deliberate too for he could never have exposed himself to the possible knowledge of her unhappiness. That would have been just too unbearable for a loving father to abide.

৵ 9 ৵

In the days following Moropant's departure from Jhansi, Lakshmibai learnt her lessons fast, allowing loneliness to creep around her only in the darkness of the night. On such nights, she would lie awake, listening to the haunted cries of jackals from the forests beyond the city walls as the palace around her seemed to fall into restless slumber. Two full months after her wedding, she continued to lie on her bed after the maids had left, wondering whether this would be the night her husband would come. Sometimes, even after she had drifted into sleep, she would come awake with a start, imagining sounds of approaching footsteps. But so far Gangadhar had not made an appearance in her chambers and she was still not very sure whether to be upset by his absence or not.

At least a pattern had emerged to her days. The mornings were spent with the maids who helped her with her bath and toilette. After visiting the temple, she would join the court where either her husband or one of his ministers would patiently explain the proceedings. Efforts were being made to include her in meetings with ministers and councillors and she guessed that this was on the order of her husband. He had so far seemed kind and respectful, even turning to her at a recent meeting to ask her opinion about a petitioner seeking a loan.

They were not left in private very much but, on one of those occasions, her husband had teased her gently at her eastern use of Hindustani, the expression on his face indicating affection rather than cruelty. Lakshmibai had not known how to reciprocate, confused by the memories of Asharfi-bua's frantic pieces of advice. But, despite her great-aunt's fears, Gangadhar had so far been nothing but kindness and courtesy and, if anyone had asked, Lakshmibai would have found it genuinely hard to point to a single flaw in his manner towards her.

She could see that he was serious when it came to state business but also fond of the arts. Almost every evening, there was some form of entertainment lined up for the courtiers; outdoor music mehfils by the steps of the lotus tank or travelling jesters, even, on some occasions, plays in the palace's baradari, the pillared stone canopy surrounded by an amphitheatre on the eastern edge of the fort.

Theatre appeared to be Gangadhar's great passion and Lakshmibai had watched, amused, as one evening, seeming utterly inspired by the actors, he had sprung up from the cushions on which they had been reclining, and insisted on playing a part himself. A few seconds later, he had emerged from the wings, dressed in the garb of a woman, much to the hilarity and appreciation of the actor's troupe and the audience. Lakshmibai thought he played his role surprisingly well, as he preened and strutted through the pillars of the baradari, every inch a petulant Radha, annoyed with Krishna, her lover, for flirting with the gopikas.

Later, face flushed from his artistic efforts and still dressed in his costume, Gangadhar had collapsed on the cushions next to her, eager for her praise. When she had told him how well he had acted, he wanted to know how he had looked and when she had, observed jokingly at how fine a figure he cut as a woman, he had seemed elated, playfully pinching her cheek and being more demonstrative to her than he had ever been before.

Lakshmibai tossed on her bed again, unable to sleep. Her cotton chemise clung to her damp body and the velvet drapes around her silver bedstead felt claustrophobic on such a warm night. Reluctant to get up and walk around a palace that she was still not entirely familiar with and anxious to not rouse the entire household of maids and guards if she made a noise, she decided, once again, that she certainly could never attempt leaving the women's quarters in search of her absent husband. Asharfi-bua would disapprove terribly of such brazenness.

It was puzzling that her husband had so far not shown any desire to exert his conjugal rights. Perhaps, she mulled, he was waiting for her to grow up a bit more before attempting to share her bed. Asharfi-bua had told her all about a man sharing a woman's bed, telling her that although it would hurt at first, she would soon learn to enjoy it— 'it' being a circumstance Lakshmibai could only vaguely imagine at this point. The possibility also existed that Gangadhar, being such a considerate man, simply did not like the idea of hurting her since she was still so young. Well, that was certainly a more palatable thought than the idea that he might not find her attractive!

Staring into the murky darkness, Lakshmibai was bemused by the thought that she should suddenly think it so important for her husband to find her beautiful. Especially as it would have been quite untruthful for her to say she felt attracted by poor Gangadhar's appearance! But maybe that was what love was, she pondered, that wondrous thing whose virtues she had heard extolled in so many poems and lyrics in her schoolroom. Why, she had once glimpsed a glint of tears even in doughty old Mr Todd's eyes when he had recited a love poem to them. Nana and Tantia had not noticed, merely snorting hysterically when she later told them.

But how was she supposed to tell if it was indeed love that now assailed her so confusingly? She had no other explanation for how had it come to be that she—who had never before been concerned with dressing up—now found herself choosing her clothes so carefully, even wondering whether Gangadhar would prefer her hair braided in the Ambarha style or with beads and flowers entwined into a chignon. Luckily, Sundar and Kashi knew exactly what to do, choosing what she wore to her various functions, carefully matching the right necklaces, earrings, pendants and even little embroidered silken slippers to go with them. They knew what sort of clothes Gangadhar would like to see her in.

Lakshmibai, her small figure dwarfed atop the huge bed, wished she could pull a curtain over these annoying thoughts so that sleep would come. Angry with herself for suddenly missing her childhood friends and old life at Saturday House, she flung her face away from the windows. Those empty squares of darkness were too often a reminder that they were all still there, just beyond the moonlit horizon; all together in Varanasi, while she was here by herself.

She tossed her body around on the bed with a thump again. No, she was quite certain she liked Jhansi, and liked being its queen. Sundar and Kashi were *much* better company than Nana and Tantia had ever been. Everyone she had met so far had been gentle and chivalrous and respectful, even the British who had so kindly arranged that parade for her. Gangadhar had been more than generous, giving her all the jewellery that had once belonged to his deceased mother and wife, even mentioning plans to refurbish the Newalkar palace in the city that she could design and that would henceforth be called Ranimahal in her honour.

It was ungenerous of her, in spite of all that, to still wish she did not have these lonely nights to face. Back at Saturday House, Asharfi-bua had slept in the chamber adjoining her room and, whenever sleep evaded, she had known she could always crawl into her bed. Even though it was something she rarely did, at least she knew she *could*. Unlike here at Jhansi, where, if her husband decided he did not want to come to her at night, she merely had to accept it without question. How strange it was. On the one hand, sharing her bed was an eventuality she felt apprehensive and quite terrified of but, on the other hand (and really very perplexingly), she knew that it was an important part of being someone's wife and could find no pleasure in escaping it more than absolutely necessary.

Yesterday she had caught herself looking at the frescoes in the eastern hallways of Panch Mahal, feeling a curious anticipation, excitement even, in the pit of her stomach knowing that she too would soon learn to use her body in that way. Curving and thrusting to accommodate her husband's body, feeling his passion unravel her own. Oh, hurry up and grow, she chided herself, flopping over and burying her face in a pillow, maybe then Gangadhar would be more able to think of her as a proper wife.

In his rooms on the upper storey of Panch Mahal, Gangadhar sat before a gilded dressing table hung with a large oval mirror, candlelight flickering on his face. He took a pinch of surmai from a tiny silver box and smeared it first into one eye and then the other. Blinking slightly from the sudden cooling sharpness, he sat back a minute before leaning forward again. Opening another miniature silver box carefully, so as not to spill its contents, he dipped his forefinger into it and smeared a little pink powder over his left cheekbone. Rubbing it into the flesh, he angled his face slightly to see if it was visible. Satisfied with the subtle tone it cast over his cheek, he repeated the procedure on the other side of his face and then on his lips, first the top, then the bottom, spreading a little extra rouge beyond the lipline to make the mouth seem fuller, more feminine. Gangadhar sat back and gazed at his reflection. He knew his subjects expected members of the royal family, even the men, to look fairer and more beautiful than their people—which provided him with ample reason to take care of his appearance when going out in public. But it had soon become a nightly ritual he had come to enjoy too. Once the day's work was done and the palace slumbered peacefully, he could finally be himself, relaxed and shielded from public gaze in the soothing solitude of his chambers and take on whichever guise suited his fancy for the night.

Getting up and walking across to his costume chambers, he divested himself of his dressing gown before pulling out a beautiful silk robe embroidered with blue and gold paisleys. Pulling it around him, and revelling in the feel of the soft Benarsi silk on his skin, he glanced over his shoulder at the three full-length angled mirrors he had had imported specially from Belgium two years ago. He was pleased with what he beheld. If he narrowed his eyes to blur his reflection, the amber light of the candles made him appear lovelier than ever before. He thought he looked wraith-like, fragile, womanly. Leaning over to the racks behind those on which his royal robes hung, glinting and shimmering in the half-light, he pulled out the heavy silk skirt of a lehnga. His dead wife had been as slender as himself and he had helped her choose the fabric and the silk threads, brought to their court by a renowned Chinese merchant. It was a richly embroidered ensemble and Gangadhar had, much to his wife's delight, painstakingly explained to the court tailor exactly how the fabric must fall when the skirt was worn, clinging to the waist but swirling out into deep, generous folds that would open up like a peacock-feather fan as the body turned.

He was content in a way that he had not felt all day. In fact, if it were not for the fact that he knew he could escape into his nightly reveries, he sometimes wondered if he could have coped with the pressures of his life at all.

As Gangadhar pirouetted before his mirror, a bright sparkling figure in the gloom of his chambers, it was clear that he had all but forgotten about his new young bride awaiting him in the women's wing only a short walk away.

Lakshmibai was not unhappy in those early months at Jhansi, soon forming a little routine and amusing herself in ways she had grown used to, even as a child. Her maids had orders to rouse her before daybreak but she would lie in bed for a while, using the slant of the sun's rays to indicate the time of morning and watching the bright bars of light creep slowly over the Persian rug on the floor, unhurriedly bringing deer and trees and flowers to life out of its velvet weave. After either Sundar or Kashi had brought her tray of tea, she would sip on the strong brew, inhaling its aromas of cardamom and wood-smoke while looking out across the battlements to the amethyst hills that blanketed the countryside north of Jhansi, remembering sometimes the long journey through Bundelkhand that had brought her here. Sometimes Raja Gangadhar would join her on the balcony and they would talk like old friends, stories of her rough and tumble childhood with Nana and Tantia always bringing a smile to his lips. Often the day's business awaiting them would be discussed, matters about irrigation, crop rotation, sanitation and, of course, British policies for Jhansi.

Then the raja would return to his chambers, leaving her to attend to the rituals of her bath. Accompanied by her maids, she would descend to the newly constructed bathing pool in the private walled Amod Garden that was reserved entirely for the female members of the household. After her hair and body had been oiled, Lakshmibai insisted that she and her handmaidens bathe together, preferring the laughing companionship of the women as they splashed and swam in the cool water to the solitary bath she was entitled to as queen. They dried themselves on the steps leading down to the pool only when sunshine started trickling through the flower trees, Lakshmibai submitting to the careful ministrations of her maids as they ran fingers through her mass of curls, gently untangling knots and rubbing her scalp with jasmine tincture. While Kashi plucked starry white mogra flowers off the nearby shrubs and wove them into a garland for her hair, Sundar would sit on a footstool and decorate her fingers and toes with henna patterns and dye the soles of her feet in a platter of deep red vermilion.

Bathed and dressed, she would then accompany Gangadhar and his retinue on a visit to one of Jhansi's many temples for the morning prayers before which the matters of state administration could not commence. Most mornings were spent in meetings of state that took place, along with the ministers, in the pillared hall of the Diwan-i-Khas. She tried to attend as many of these as possible, eager to learn about administrative matters, although Raja Gangadhar also insisted that his young wife be given plenty of opportunities away from court, to ride her horses and develop the equestrian skills he knew she loved. After her daily rides, she enjoyed nothing more than discussing the horses' well-being with the head-groom and indulging in friendly banter with the syces. She had picked a young doe-eyed mare called Sarangi to be her own, riding her further and further away from the fort as she gained confidence. But, in those early days she did not go far and, after returning Sarangi to the grooms, she made it a point to slip into the elephant stables next door, in order to personally feed Siddhabaksh a large clutch of sugar cane sticks. Sometimes she patted his trunk and looked into his small shy eyes, wondering whether he remembered the long journey that had brought her to Jhansi. At first it was not without sorrow, as she still missed her family and especially her father. But, as the months passed, she felt her mourning lift and clear as naturally as the day's mists respond to the warmth of the sun. Soon she could scarcely remember a time when Jhansi had not been her home.

In those days of discovery, Lakshmibai saw how her husband came into his own in the evenings, laughing and joking as the revelries would begin in the baradari or on the banks of the lotus tank, its dark water glowing with the reflections of brass kerosene lanterns that lined the carved perimeter. Even the preparations excited Gangadhar and he sometimes came out to personally supervise everything, making sure that the ground was sprinkled with fragrant water before carpets were laid and scattered with cushions and flower petals, insisting that only the best wine and sherbet be served. It was as though no expense was too much for these soirées. It amused Lakshmibai to see her husband unable to contain himself as the performances would commence, restlessly clapping his hand on his thigh as the singers and musicians settled themselves on colourful rugs and durees, tuning their sitars and hammering lightly on the strings of their tablas before beginning to play. On other nights, when dancers wearing shimmering costumes and bells on their feet would perform, Gangadhar was almost delirious with joy. It was an infectious passion and, one moonless night, when torches were lit and the whirling dancers looked like small glittering insects about to perish on those flickering flames, even Lakshmibai felt completely bewitched by the beauty of it all.

Sometimes a visiting group of qawwals from Lahore or Peshawar would be invited to declare praises to Allah in rich abundant voices. As their voices rang out in unison over the ramparts of the fort, Lakshmibai wondered if they filtered through to the people of Jhansi living in their huts and houses beyond the fort. Finally, of course, there were the plays and the skits, comedies and tragedies unfolding with the darkened Panch Mahal as their backdrop. Lakshmibai knew these were Gangadhar's favourite events as he sat, evening after evening, rapt with attention, seeming almost to become one with the emotions playing out before them. Occasionally he would join in, although Lakshmibai could never be persuaded to do so, content to watch this strange side to her husband, boyish in his enthusiasm, exultant in some inexplicable joy. She was not sure she entirely accepted his obsession, being far too pragmatic to give herself over to similar flights of imagination. But she envied Gangadhar his enthusiasm, wishing she could understand his passions better.

Her own preferred evenings were the anonymous excursions into town, she and Gangadhar undertaking a secret monthly ritual of donning old clothes and covering their heads with veils so as not to be recognized. Gangadhar had learnt from his own father that there was no better way to gain insight into their people's lives than by actually mingling with them anonymously in the streets and bazaars and now passed on to Lakshmibai too the perspective that public assemblies alone could never bring. Lakshmibai adored her husband and the father-in-law she had never known for having considered it so important to assess the true welfare of their people. And, as she walked veiled by her husband's side, revelling in her anonymity for those few hours, she observed the people of Jhansi, developing an unspoken affection for them as they went about their businesses— grocers selling grain and spices, halwais expertly puffing up poories in smoking hot oil and serving them to excited children, women buying bangles, haggling over prices, getting household utensils mended. It was in this world of everyday joys and sorrows, the commonplace and the mundane, that Lakshmibai knew that her own calling lay. Being queen would forever preclude her from the pleasures of ordinariness but, on such delightful days, she did not miss them at all.

She had it in her heart, however, to feel compassion for Gangadhar whose joys came from things even further removed from reality. She knew already, from having seen the unhappiness creep over Peshwa-sahib's face during her childhood, that it was truly tragic to be trapped in a life that failed to fit. It was ironic too that a ruler like Peshwa-sahib, deprived of his realm, never ceased to mourn it while Gangadhar was so burdened by the one that had been thrust on him. Without being told, Lakshmibai could see her husband labouring under the weight of his role and the slyness he employed to escape its responsibilities whenever he could. Already there were moments when she both pitied him and wanted to help him but she had found her own calling, taking Jhansi to her bosom as a mother would a motherless child.

~ 10 ~

It was three months after the wedding that Captain Ellis first had occasion to speak directly to the new queen. Riding towards the fort from the cantonment one blazing morning, he surveyed the stark countryside, considering how very burnt it looked. Jhansi's black soil, called 'mar' by the locals, was suited to nothing better than pulses and gram in these hot months, although Ellis had done his best to revive the once thriving cotton cultivation in those areas that lay closer to the Betwa and Pahuj rivers. He mulled over the possibility of trying oilseeds too at some point. Something about the challenge presented by these rolling dark wastes appealed enormously to him—not just the satisfaction of seeing black soil turn lush green when given the right kind of irrigation and care, but also the progress he had seen being made by the people of this land, some of whom had previously scratched a pitifully meagre living from keeping chickens and reaping just a few sacks of millet every year.

As his roan picked its way across the rutted mud tracks, he felt the sun beat down on the back of his neck, the old sola topee as usual providing woefully inadequate protection on such a hot day. Though tempted to postpone this visit to King Gangadhar by another week, by which time some much-hoped for rain may have fallen, it had seemed to Ellis prudent not to put it off any more than absolutely necessary. He had still not given the king any information about the man appointed as Governor-General after Lord Auckland's departure, a post of enormous significance to Indian royals who remained in a state of permanent nervousness about likely changes to their positions when new officials descended from England, each with exciting new ideas for this country and often armed with a raft of new laws. Not that Gangadhar had too much to worry about, shared power with the British working as well as it ever could, thankfully. From what Ellis could see, there were no immediate changes on Jhansi's horizon.

As he was escorted into the grand pillared hall, the king rose, as was his wont whenever he saw Captain Ellis, extending his hand in the European manner. It had not escaped Ellis's notice that this was a courtesy the king almost never extended to Major Malcolm whom he had quite obviously disliked from the moment he had laid eyes on him. It was a mutual abhorrence and Ellis had always been grateful for enjoying the goodwill of Raja Gangadhar who clearly welcomed his visits.

'Good morning, my dear man,' he called cheerfully as Ellis strode up to the throne to take his proffered hand.

'Raja-sahib, you look very well,' Ellis replied, a little unsure if the ruddy colour on the raja's cheeks was make-up or good health before deciding it must be the former. He knew that Indian royalty had an odd fondness for powders and rouges and remembered that Gangadhar was a man not normally known to be in the pink of health.

'So kind of you, so kind,' the king murmured, waving Ellis to his customary chair carved in French style and rather gaudily upholstered in gold tapestry. He seated himself, faintly surprised to hear the king turn to one of his courtiers and instruct him to summon the queen. As always, Raja Gangadhar was courteous to a fault, 'Please request Rani Lakshmibai to grace us with her presence in the Diwan-i-Khas. Remind her to be in purdah as Captain Ellis is in court.' So it looked like the new queen attended court regularly, quite unlike the previous queen whom Ellis had never once set eyes on in the court. It was interesting that she was being trained in administrative affairs.

As the guard departed, a silver platter bearing the customary paan-supari and a glass of sherbet materialized as usual at Ellis's elbow without anyone's bidding. He politely turned down the chewing tobacco and betel nut, as he always did when anticipating a political discourse or discussion, but picked up the glass of sherbet and took a long swallow of its contents, feeling instantly revived. The paan leaves were especially brought in from nearby Mahoba but Ellis decided that, one of these days, he would find out from that excellent Afghani retainer of the raja's what it was that went into these summertime drinks served at the palace. Always redolent with peppermint and lime, they seemed able to wash away the dust and the heat of the day with just one sip. The reprieve from the fearsome sun outside was a welcome one as a huge embroidered punkah swayed sleepily above their heads. The palace and this assembly hall next door to it were always filled with fresh cool air, their archways and windows carefully covered with vetiver tatties that were soaked in perfumed water during the summer months. He stretched his legs and sat back in his seat, surprised that the raja appeared to be awaiting the arrival of the queen before beginning his business.

The people assembled in the court rose again as there was a small flurry of movement at one of the doors. The queen was being escorted in, accompanied by a couple of her handmaidens and the purdah bearers. Ellis quickly put his glass down to stand up as well and waited respectfully until he heard the tinkling of anklets and bangles behind the intricately carved ivory screen subside. He bowed in the direction of the screen before saying politely, 'Good morning, Rani-sahiba.' He had spoken in English as was his custom whenever in Raja Gangadhar's company but wished instantly that he had remembered to make his initial address in Hindi for the benefit of the young queen.

His surprise must have shown when a soft voice responded from behind the screen, wishing him good morning in English too. She had not spoken at all the last time she had attended court in his presence. Her voice was low-pitched and she did not sound as young as he had expected. He felt gratified to hear her speak in English, remembering that the prime minister had talked of the private education received by the prospective bride in the Peshwa's household at Varanasi. Although his own Hindi and Urdu were passable, Ellis preferred to conduct his work in English, particularly when tact was called for and suddenly he was confused about which language to use. But Raja Gangadhar opened up again in English as a maid cleared Ellis's empty glass away.

'So, to what do we owe the pleasure of your visit, Captain Ellis?' he queried.

'Ah yes,' Ellis replied, gathering his thoughts, 'I need to tell you, Raja-sahib, about developments at Calcutta.'

'Let me guess, Captain Ellis. Lord Auckland was recalled, wasn't he?'

Ellis nodded. 'You're quite right, Raja-sahib. I suppose we were all expecting it, although it was a little abrupt when it came.'

'It was because of the English defeat at Afghanistan?' Gangadhar asked.

Before he could reply, Ellis heard the queen add in slightly hesitant English, 'We heard that the British Army suffered many losses in the mountain passes...'

He was startled to hear Rani Lakshmibai speak up. Perhaps it had been hasty of him to assume that, like the previous queen, Gangadhar's second wife would also stay away from the business of the court and Ellis felt suddenly unnerved at the prospect of having her engage him in conversation. Not that it was necessarily a bad thing to have the new queen involved in Jhansi's administration but he needed to be sure that she was not going to interfere with the excellent camaraderie that had been carefully built up with the king. Unsure if it was to him or to her husband that the remark had been addressed, he hesitated and cleared his throat before replying.

'You are quite right, Rani-sahiba, it is the dreadful business of the reverses we suffered on that front. Which are, I daresay, being viewed in London as a personal misjudgement on the part of Lord Auckland and General Elphinstone.'

'Many lives were lost, we heard,' the Rani said again softly, 'many soldiers, both Hindustani and European.'

'Yes, Rani-sahiba, losses to the Bengal Army have been grave indeed. And, I agree, there is no sadder business than war and its attendant loss of life,' Ellis replied gravely.

'Do we know much about the new Governor-General, Captain Ellis?' Raja Gangadhar asked, looking anxious.

'Ah yes, Raja-sahib. The new Governor-General is Lord Ellenborough. Edward Law, Baron of Ellenborough.'

Gangadhar looked enquiringly at the political agent and Ellis nodded reassuringly, aware of how worried the king would rightly be about the repercussions any changes in Calcutta could have on his own fortunes. 'I'm afraid I do not know very much personally about Lord Ellenborough yet, Raja-sahib, except that he has had a stint on the Company's Board of Control in London.' Ellis smiled apologetically, adding what he hoped would sound encouraging to the raja, 'I think, Raja-sahib, we can all be quite sure that Lord Ellenborough's efforts will lie in consolidating progress within India rather than in expansionism.'

'How can it be that nothing at all is known of him, my dear Captain Ellis, you conceal something from me,' the raja protested. 'Come now, you must know something about the man that you can tell us. I see that you are smiling!'

Ellis took quick stock of the situation. He knew of the raja's fondness for the occasional bit of gossip and often indulged it where it could do no harm. Quite often, it provided useful distraction, although he was always scrupulously careful not to say anything that would show the British officer class in poor light. There was also an unspoken understanding between Raja Gangadhar and him that absolutely nothing of a personal nature would ever be discussed in Major Malcolm's presence. But now, recalling the tabloid publicity that had surrounded the Ellenboroughs' divorce back in England, there seemed no reason to be overly reticent in this matter. Some light conversation may even serve to ward off Raja Gangadhar's understandable apprehension.

'Oh I do not seek to conceal anything from you, Raja-sahib! It is the truth when I say that little is known of Lord Ellenborough here in India and the only reason I smile is that it would have been worthy to say the same of Lady Ellenborough. Perhaps I ought to say, the erstwhile Lady Ellenborough, for they are now divorced, I hear, and the new Governor-General has arrived in India on his own.'

Gangadhar emitted his high-pitched laugh that, no matter how many times Ellis heard it, always served to make him cringe a little.

'Aha, I knew there was something more you could tell me. I do hope you are going to tell us too, my friend, why the erstwhile Lady Ellenborough is so well known in society circles!'

Ellis felt his colour rise. Idle chatter with the raja was one thing, but the presence of the new queen just behind the ivory screen was another matter altogether. Principally as he had heard that one of the reasons for which the Ellenboroughs' marriage had floundered so spectacularly was because of the considerable age difference between Lord Ellenborough and his young wife. Not unlike that between the couple seated before him now.

Raja Gangadhar, seeing the hesitation on his face, smiled encouragingly. 'Do not worry, Captain Ellis, Rani-sahiba will be as discreet as I am and whatever you say will remain safe with us.'

Ellis did not like to point out to the raja that his courtroom was heaving with courtiers and servants. However, as their dialogue was taking place in English, the assembled company had already drawn away from the main area to retire into small hookah-smoking huddles in the archways and bay windows. Hardly anyone seemed interested in their conversation, getting on with their own businesses in disparate groups, some taking seat on the mattresses and bolsters scattered around the court.

Raja Gangadhar could usually be trusted to remain discreet and so Ellis continued but not without dropping his voice and shifting slightly self-consciously on his chair. 'Well, Raja-sahib, Lord Ellenborough was a widower when he married the young Jane Digby, daughter of a wealthy Norfolk businessman...' He could sense the attentiveness of the rani behind her purdah as he continued hesitantly,

'Who can ever tell what goes on inside a marriage, but some say that it was Lord Ellenborough's own philanderings that led Lady Ellenborough to strike up a raging and extremely public love affair with the prince of Austria. Rumour has it that she followed him all the way across Europe although it was also said that by then the prince of Austria did not reciprocate her feelings and tried very hard to get rid of her, a matter he finally succeeded in, much to his relief and her chagrin of course...'

Ellis was startled to hear the rani emit a small spontaneous burst of laughter as her husband sat back and shrieked shrilly. Although he was pleased to see that the queen shared Gangadhar's sense of humour, he felt a sudden and curious sense of panic. It was the most peculiar thing to be sitting on this garish brocade seat, sharing gossip about a distant Englishwoman's peccadilloes with the newly crowned rani of Jhansi whom he could not even see. Even though his tenure in India had resulted in some eccentric moments, surely this was a prize one. Luckily for Ellis, however, Gangadhar seemed bored already with the subject and was leaning forward on his throne as though eager now to put an end to flippant talk and get on with more important things.

'My dear Captain Ellis,' he said, his voice dropping to a near whisper, 'I am pleased that you graced us with a visit today because there is something I have been wanting to ask you.'

'Please do and I shall try to be of assistance, Raja-sahib,' Ellis replied, hoping it was not going to be an awkward request. The whole business of maintaining cordial relations with the raja while not letting Major Malcolm suspect he might be going all soft and 'native' was never an easy one.

'My dear fellow, just this week I heard some bad news about my friend and compatriot in Nagpur, Maharaja Raghu-ji. There has again been talk of Nagpur being annexed by the British. I remember the Resident...Cavendish?...his name was Cavendish, wasn't it? Do you remember when he came up with this notion first?' Ellis nodded but Gangadhar had turned to where the rani was seated and was now talking to her, his manner suddenly agitated, 'Despite a treaty being signed, very similar to our own, that the Bhonsles would rule in perpetuity, this Cavendish had the temerity to suggest, about five years ago, that Nagpur be taken over by the British. Luckily, the maharaja managed to fight off the claim then but now I hear that it could be resurfacing, despite the departure of Cavendish. Is that true, Captain Ellis?'

Captain Ellis was relieved. This he did know the answer to,

having only recently heard about the case from Malcolm and he was pleased that it was not bad news he had to relay. 'I can tell you on authority, Raja-sahib, that the new Resident has taken a decidedly sympathetic stance to the royal family of Nagpur. This man, Wilkinson, has vowed to help the Bhonsle family retain their claim to the throne. So far, and as far as I am aware, Government House does not have any trouble with his recommendation.'

Gangadhar sat back on his throne, his thin face seeming only partially reassured, two rouge spots highlighted in his pale sallow skin. 'I have it on good authority that, after Nagpur, it will be Jhansi's turn next. We are all very worried, you know, Nagpur, Satara, Jhansi...we are small states, with nothing like the might of Awadh and Gwalior. But we try to help the Company as much as we can so that we can all survive and jointly carry out the administration of this land. Rumours like this are most unhelpful and make me lose sleep at night, Captain Ellis. My health suffers as a consequence.'

'I wonder where they come from, Raja-sahib, certainly not from the British camp because they are quite untrue,' Ellis replied soothingly.

'Are we sure that we do not have enemies within our own court?'

Once again, the voice emerging from behind the purdah was the rani's. Ellis had to strain to hear her softly spoken words as she continued.

'Enemies within the court had always been one of Peshwa-sahib's biggest concerns, which is why he trusted men like my father whom he had known since his own childhood.'

Ellis wondered if she was blessed with genuine perspicacity or had just happened to make an extremely accurate guess and looked around quickly to see who may have overheard her. He noted with relief that the raja's brother, Krishna Rao, was fortuitously absent from court. It was no surprise that Krishna Rao continued to simmer with hatred for the British since their decision on the succession and it was certainly possible that he was behind these new rumours of Nagpur's annexation.

Raja Gangadhar was deep in discussion now with his new queen and Ellis watched them for a few minutes, intrigued by the idea of such a young woman already involved in state matters. Although he thought it most commendable of the king to be making an effort to include his new bride in court affairs, Ellis hoped again that it was not going to affect his own relationship with the Jhansi throne. Certainly it was reassuring to know that the new queen was educated and able to converse intelligently and he knew he ought to feel pleased on behalf of Raja Gangadhar that she seemed willing too to help her husband in matters of state governance. Perhaps his fears were irrational.

As Ellis got up to leave a few minutes later, he heard the rani's voice bid him goodbye. He bowed deeply, averting his eyes from the ivory screen that masked her from view. Suddenly, absurdly, he felt overwhelmed by curiosity about the queen's appearance. He wondered whether she would have been able to observe him from where she sat. He had the strangest notion that she was watching him depart the assembly hall as he strode down the central passage before running briskly down its old stone steps.

Krishna Rao, riding in from the Gwalior Road with his guards, saw Captain Ellis leave the walled city on horseback. The two men nodded tersely at each other and Krishna Rao tried to suppress his customary quiver of irritation at the sight of Jhansi's political agent. He had never seen any reason to mask either his hatred for the British or his contempt for his younger brother's obsequiousness towards them. When would Gangadhar realize that all his bowing and scraping was never going to prevent the eventual annexation of Jhansi.

Watching Ellis cantering towards the cantonment, Krishna Rao remembered the words he had used to Gangadhar after the British Commission had despatched its decision about Jhansi's throne. 'They would rather have you whom they scorn than the rightful heir whom they fear and respect,' he had said, pleased to see Gangadhar hang his head in shamed acknowledgement of the truth.

Even though it was clear to see why the British had favoured Gangadhar over him, Krishna Rao had failed to understand why his younger brother had so willingly accepted the crown. Even as a child, Gangadhar had shown scant interest in affairs of the state, a nervous little boy always preferring to escape into strange unnamed reveries and artistic pleasures that Krishna himself had little time for. There were times when Krishna wondered if Gangadhar had taken the unforeseen offer only to prevent his brother's accession, fearful of the direction in which he would certainly have taken Jhansi. Most definitely, not one single Englishman would ever have been allowed to set foot beyond these gates.

Krishna Rao turned to ride on towards the palace only when Captain Ellis had passed through the main gate. Not for the first time, he wished he could have spurned Gangadhar's conciliatory attempt to make him a minister. It was a job that brought little comfort and offered too many glimpses into the treacherous cordiality his foolish brother insisted on extending to the British. 'You will come to regret your "friendship",' he had snarled at Gangadhar just yesterday. 'That

Ellis whom you call friend is nothing better than a snake in the grass.'
It always gave immense pleasure to see Gangadhar turn so easily back
into the pale sickly child he had been since their parents had died, his
continuing anxieties obvious in those fluttering hands and bulging
coward's eyes.

But now there was this Lakshmibai girl. Krishna Rao threw his
new sister-in-law a contemptuous look as he strode into the court
room. She was always sitting there these days, surrounded by a bunch
of tittering women. The courtroom was no place for fashion and
fripperies, he had always held, but now he felt forced to hold his
tongue. Despite her youth, he had to admit that—unlike Gangadhar's
dead wife—this one was not politically uncomprehending. Her quick
grasp of complex matters was apparent already and it was clear that
most of Gangadhar's court had already found the interest she was
displaying in state matters affecting and almost touching. Stupidly,
the courtiers all liked her and it was going to be harder to garner
support for a rebellion against Gangadhar with this new queen being
so unfailingly pleasant and respectful to them all. He had to grudgingly
admit that even he could find little fault with the young rani at the
moment. But he was willing to bide his time.

Although Lakshmibai had already been warned of the often
public quarrels between Gangadhar and Krishna Rao, frustratingly
she could press nothing more out of the discreet Sundar who so
determinedly avoided tittle-tattle. But, that morning, she was to witness
one of those notorious rows herself. Seated a few feet away from the
area in court where the main business was being conducted, she had
seen Krishna Rao striding into the hall to take his place among the
ministers gathered around Gangadhar. She had been only half-listening
when his voice had lashed like a whip across the room.

'What do you mean, I cannot send the letter?' Krishna Rao's
already ruddy face had turned an angry shade of purple.

'We don't want to annoy them, Krishna-bhai, this sort of letter
will do no good,' Gangadhar said pacifyingly. 'Months of careful
bridge-building could be lost in one moment if a letter like this,
written with such careless anger, is sent to Calcutta. What do we hope
to achieve from it?'

'So you are willing to let this resumption of rent-free lands just
continue, are you?'

'It was set in place by Sir William Bentinck many years ago. And
he was not a bad man, he did plenty of good for us too. Sometimes,
Krishna-bhai, we must simply learn to take the good with the bad.'

'But even if every other policy is a good one, should we not at least attempt to do something about the bad ones? Or do we say, "Ah, such good men," and take everything that the British choose to put our way?'

'No, Krishna-bhai, all I am saying is that we have to wait and see; that is all.'

Lakshmibai was proud to see how calm and dignified her poor husband looked, though she could see, even from where she sat, that his hand was shaking, the paper he held trembling like a leaf.

It was clear that Krishna Rao was only more enraged to see his younger brother stand his ground. He rose from his chair, his body swelling with rage, 'So...so we will wait until every one of our peasants is reduced to complete poverty...until our own treasury is emptied and even then we will be saying, "Oh, but they are my friends oh but they helped to eradicate sati." Will we? *Will we*?!'

One of the older ministers, attempting to pacify him, was rudely shaken off.

'Our peasants are not beggars yet and our treasury has not looked so healthy in years.' Gangadhar spat the words out before clamping his jaw, as though fearful of saying too much. Lakshmibai could see a vein throbbing in his temple and she clenched her fists, feeling his tension flood her own body.

The court fell silent. Except for the punkah-wallahs slowly moving their large feather fans, no one moved. From some of Kashi's prattlings, Lakshmibai had gathered that this was not an unusual spectacle in the court. Arguments between the two brothers were, she had been told, fairly commonplace, with Krishna Rao shouting and fulminating and Gangadhar usually adopting a conciliatory tone. But she wondered if it was unusual for her husband to be as quietly livid as this.

After a minute's silence, during which Gangadhar remained outwardly implacable, Krishna Rao managed to collect himself, but it was clear he was not ready to give up just yet.

'And what about this latest gem from Captain Ellis?' Krishna Rao had picked up a letter from the central table and was waving in the air.

'Unless you tell me what it is, how do you expect me to inform you?' Gangadhar replied calmly.

'Oh you know what I'm talking about. English being made compulsory in all our schools. Bringing up our children to be little brown Englishmen—just so that they can be used by the Company to do the work their own officers will not deign to do. Making our children fit into their mould. Eventually they will even *think* like them—is that what you want? Do you know how upset both the

Sanskrit pandits and the Muslim maulvis already are with your friend
Ellis's efforts to bring this about? As if the missionaries' meddling
alone was not enough. But, of course we will merely ignore the
anxieties of our own people in our haste to obey British commands.
Why is this court in such a hurry to fall in with their invidious
designs? We made no pledge. They just come up with new ways to
enslave us and we accept whatever is put our way without question.'

'Well, we have not yet made English compulsory in the schools,
have we?'

'That is exactly what Ellis wants us to remedy with immediate
effect!'

'Krishna-bhai, I have already spoken to Captain Ellis about this
matter and he has said he only wrote the letter to satisfy Calcutta.
What we do in actual practice, he will be willing to overlook. Do not
forget he is our friend. And we have much more to gain by maintaining
that friendship rather than losing it by putting him in an awkward
position with his superiors. Leave it to me and I will get Rao Bande
to draft a careful letter addressing the matter today. After all, he is in
charge of our educational policies. And then I will have a quiet word
with Captain Ellis too, I do not foresee any problems there.'

Krishna Rao was temporarily silenced, probably reminded that
Captain Ellis had often conceded to discreet requests put to him
before. But Lakshmibai looked anxiously at her husband's face,
rendered pallid and clammy from his dispute. In the midst of her own
feelings of panic at having witnessed such a shameful public argument
between the brothers, she made a mental note to have Gangadhar see
the doctor. Perhaps a skilled vaid would be able to prescribe some
herbal medicines to bring him strength. He was so painfully thin
compared to his strapping brother, it did not seem fair at all. She had
also recently noticed that Gangadhar's left leg had developed a tremor
whenever he sat in the court, although the spasms seemed considerably
reduced when he was relaxing at one of the evening soirées. Whatever
his ailment, Lakshmibai was determined to help shield her husband
from the stresses that his brother so nastily exposed him to. Perhaps
it was deliberate, carefully crafted to slowly destroy Gangadhar's
spirit so that Krishna Rao could one day claim the crown for himself.
She felt a fierce and uncharacteristic rage suddenly for her brother-in-
law, claiming to speak up for Jhansi but caring only about himself.

Lakshmibai barely noticed as these busy months passed and
Jhansi slipped silently into her first winter. The last of her homesickness
melted into the crisp clear air as she delighted in Panch Mahal's
winter rituals. The evenings were the best when fallen eucalyptus and

neem leaves in the compound of the fort were swept up and burnt in spicy smelling bonfires and all the womenfolk gathered around to warm their fingers and chatter about the day's events.

As the nights drew in and grew chilly, the outdoor mehfils and theatrical performances were moved from the starlit outdoor baradari to the great hall next door to Panch Mahal that was easier to keep warm with charcoal braziers and woollen durees laid on the floor. Conversely, the daytime public assemblies now took place outdoors, in the town's central square, Gangadhar's guards setting up chairs and tables under the giant neem tree so that petitioners could warm themselves in the weak winter sunshine as they awaited audience with their raja-sahib and rani-sahiba. Increasingly, Gangadhar was making his young wife sit beside him during these meetings, so that she would learn the business of state administration. Her presence seemed to thrill the townsfolk and Lakshmibai hoped that it had not escaped Gangadhar's notice that more and more female petitioners were coming to the assemblies, choosing to bring their problems to their rani-sahiba, confident that she, as a woman, would understand them better. To Lakshmibai this was all immensely thrilling and she treasured the thought that her husband, by tutoring her so carefully in the arts of administration, was convinced by her talent for it. He was, in fact, so good at explaining things to her in simple and understandable terms, that of late she hardly ever stopped to miss her dearest father and Peshwa-sahib any more. How lucky she was to have gained from her husband the kind of protection and love that she had been so anxious about losing when she had left her father's home. Already she had learnt that there was so much to love in her husband—his kindness and his courtesy, his obviously growing confidence in her. Why should it matter if, given all that, he had still not spent a night of love with her?

∾ 11 ∾

Even though Raja Gangadhar had given instructions during Lakshmibai's first year in Jhansi for the palace in the city to be refurbished, it took another whole year for the project to begin. Lakshmibai, still unaccustomed to her exalted position after the passage of two years, had not liked to ask the reason for the delay but conjectured that her husband was waiting for revenues to be raised.

She was by now, however, quite convinced that it would be

beneficial to move out of Panch Mahal as soon as possible. It was surely something to do with the way in which Panch Mahal had been constructed that made it difficult for her to break existing patterns of life in that palace. Gangadhar still occupied the men's wing on a different floor, which meant that she was always left in the position of awaiting a visit from her husband, never able to freely go into his chambers. Even though Gangadhar often came into her room to share breakfast or tea with her, she had grown to recognize that she ought to do something that would encourage him to visit her at night too. She had not worked out yet exactly what ploy to use, distracted by the plans for the new palace which, she sometimes hoped, would provide the solution to her dilemma.

On a bright April morning, Lakshmibai accompanied Gangadhar on the short walk from Panch Mahal to the construction site in the town. As she maintained the protocol of keeping a few paces behind the raja, she observed how well her husband looked today. Sundar walked next to Lakshmibai, holding a large silk parasol to protect her from the sun, and together they slowly traversed their way down the sloping road that led out of the fort. As they emerged from the great gates into the crowded city streets, criers parted the bazaar crowds for the royal party while horses and carriages waited, their wealthy occupants bowing their greetings. They made slow progress, stopping to talk to all who approached them but, even as the raja conducted a seemingly interminable conversation with an elderly merchant, Lakshmibai and Sundar exchanged a glance that was full of exhilaration caused by this new spring day.

A few minutes later, they walked into the old Newalkar palace that had been built by an ancestor of Gangadhar's over fifty years before. Lakshmibai looked up at its ceiling. Now that it had been cleaned of its cobwebs, its state of disrepair was clearer. Paint had peeled over the years, forming bulges and rolls that looked as though someone had painstakingly stuck old parchment paper onto all the ceilings and walls. Underfoot, the old marble floor lay cracked and uneven, with weeds springing out of gaping fissures.

While the priests conducted purification ceremonies in the main hall to rid the building of all its old ghosts, Lakshmibai looked around the derelict haveli, already seeing indented arches where there were now broken-down doorways and carved inlaid marble columns where there were dusty pillars. She would have the entire front courtyard tessellated in the style of Peshwa-sahib's private garden back at Saturday House, except that hers would have fountains playing in them all through the day to keep Jhansi's summer heat at bay. The inner walls would be decorated with floral creepers made of onyx and rose quartz and jade from Jaipur. Each room would be illuminated by scores of mirror-backed brass sconces and the main hallways would have the most magnificent crystal chandeliers that would have to be specially ordered from Lucknow. Every one of the many annexes that were being planned by the architects would have their own gardens and arbours with mosaic floors. One annexe would be used as a public assembly hall, another as a house for guests who visited. As soon as the guest annexe was ready, she would have her father and Asharfi-bua and even Peshwa-sahib come over to stay so that she could lavish on them the love and care she was now in a position to give. She would make sure it had the most charming walled courtyard, filled with songbirds and white flowering shrubs and trees—harsinghaar and jasmine and queen of the night—it would be named Motibagh, garden of pearls...

Lakshmibai saw her husband smile at her and realized that he had spotted the delirious expression on her face as all these thoughts flashed through her head. Dear Gangadhar—she knew he was embarking on all this at least partially to gladden her heart and she could not wait to express her gratitude as she watched him stroll across the room to speak to her.

'You look as happy as a humming bird, my little rani,' he said softly so that no one but Sundar could hear.

'I *am* very happy, my lord, and so eager to start overseeing this project. How can I thank you for allowing me to be in charge of it,' Lakshmibai said, eyes shining.

'Well, it may keep you busy for more time to come than you imagine,' Gangadhar laughed, tapping her gently on her cheek. He then addressed Lakshmibai's companion, 'Which consequently means you will be kept very busy too, Sundarbai.'

Lakshmibai turned to Sundar and saw that she was smiling shyly as she said proudly, 'We will make this a palace of such beauty, people will come from near and far to study its architecture and exclaim over its artistry, Raja-sahib.'

'Yes, we must all strive to leave behind something that will outlive us,' Gangadhar said thoughtfully, already thinking of something else as he moved on.

Lakshmibai, who was feeling too overjoyed to be drawn into his sudden pensiveness, clutched Sundar's arm as she suddenly remembered the lovely palace of Rai Parveen that they had stayed at on their way to Jhansi. 'We'll make this palace better than the grand old edifices of Orchha, Sundar! It may not be as big as their Jehangir

Mahal, but it will be exquisite and, unlike poor Rai Parveen's palace, this one will not be allowed to slowly fade into obscurity but will be loved forever. It is in your hands and mine, Sundar, and we will make it a palace that travellers will cross the rivers and mountains of Bundelkhand to see.'

Lakshmibai did not know it but it was Ellis, recently promoted to the rank of major, who was in control of the money to be spent on the project. He, for his part, had no knowledge of the queen's impatience, never once guessing how frustratingly slow the progress on the new palace would seem to her. On one of his occasional visits to the town, a whole year after construction had started, he saw that, although some of the walls had already grown to head-height, foundations were still being laid to the annexes and the planned gardens still lay fallow. Raja Gangadhar had the previous week indicated his requirement of extra funds and Major Ellis had had to tell him that he was fairly certain Government House would not sanction a loan. As such, he was perturbed to see one June morning that the construction site was a hive of activity, masons and artisans toiling under the midday sun. Sitting atop his horse, he listened to the echoing tap-tap-tap of chisels and hammers, wondering who had given orders for the construction to resume. Considering the gravity with which he still took his role, he could not see reason enough to lobby Government House with what may appear to be a flippant request, especially at a time when the extravagances of native royals were being seriously curtailed. King Gangadhar would have to be informed that Panch Mahal inside the fort was for the time being large enough to accommodate his retinue. There was no immediate urgency for a new palace.

Lakshmibai returned to the fort feeling dejected. Every day for the past year she had religiously made an evening visit to the construction site but saw less and less progress each time she went. Today the number of artisans at the site also seemed depleted to half, although nobody could tell her why. She drew her silk chunari around her as she felt the cold air of Panch Mahal's darkened interior envelop her as soon as she walked in. She had often scolded herself for her eagerness to flee this palace, embarrassed at the haste with which she had forgotten how sumptuous its chambers had seemed when she had first seen them and compared their lavishness to her father's spartan quarters at Saturday House. She was not ungrateful for the many blessings she enjoyed in her married life but could not find the words to explain why she felt so choked by Panch Mahal's dark corridors and echoing lonely silences.

Escaping onto a balcony, she stood holding a low balustrade and gazed down at the gardens below through unseeing eyes. Despite urging herself to enjoy their lush beauty, she could feel a rush of familiar sadness wash over her again. It was the kind of sadness that could not even induce tears, robbing her completely of energy. On some days, she even felt too fatigued to rouse herself from her bed, which was most unlike her. The poor head gardener had asked her days ago to tell him how best to improve the view she had of the western garden from her private balcony and she felt suddenly ashamed that she still had not found the time to do so.

Her mornings were invariably occupied by the public meetings that Gangadhar had insisted took place every day and that she was now almost entirely in charge of. In addition, Gangadhar had also suggested that she take charge of reorganizing Jhansi's state library that had been founded by another of his philanthropic relatives and most of her afternoons these past few months had been spent examining and sorting the treasure of silk-bound manuscripts, books and maps from the ancient University of Nalanda that had recently been bought at auction. She had sent for art restorers to embark upon the delicate task of repairing the library's series of paintings from southern Tanjore and employed local bookbinders to cover with silk and brocade the exquisite old copies of the *Bhagwad Gita* she had also found in the library. But, busy as she was, a hollow was growing inside her somewhere that ached as though desperate to be filled with something she could not name.

More than anything else, it concerned Lakshmibai that, even after nearly two years of personally overseeing Gangadhar's medications, her husband's health did not seem to be improving. She had made enquiries and summoned the most renowned vaid available in the area, even sending one of the royal carriages to fetch the man every week from his vaidyasala in Gwalior. But the tremors had spread to Gangadhar's hands and even the muscles in his face contorted into strange spasms whenever he was under stress. Lakshmibai was sure it was the strain of court life and particularly Krishna Rao's obstreperousness that rendered Gangadhar so unwell and, unless the causes for his illness were removed, how could he possibly get better?

Hardly noticing the fragrance of mogra wafting on the evening breeze, she bounced tight fists against the balustrade, vowing to discuss with her husband the possibility of having Krishna Rao moved out of Jhansi to some other place. Parola perhaps. It would not be easy. Krishna Rao was not without his share of supporters, invariably using new British policies to help spread disaffection. But perhaps Gangadhar would be able to create a role for him somewhere outside of the court. She would have to consider all the options carefully before presenting the idea to her husband though. It was quite possible that, despite feeling so oppressed by his brother's presence, Gangadhar himself would resist her plans. It would be typical of his sentimental nature to place family loyalties above political decisions.

Lakshmibai turned away from the balcony to return to her room. Someone had lighted all the oil lamps and the sconces were causing long shadows to dance up and down the painted walls. Easing her feet out of her embroidered slippers, she walked barefoot across the cool floor. How like her beloved old Peshwa-sahib Gangadhar sometimes was, she reflected, equally prone to responding emotionally rather than pragmatically to the welfare of his huge retinue. She had so often heard her father despair over some sentimental and expensive decision made by Peshwa-sahib and found it ironic that now she was cast in a similar role with Gangadhar. Picking up a miniature portrait of her husband from her bureau, she gazed at his benign countenance, feeling her annoyance soften. How could she help loving her husband, especially since he was unfailingly kind and sweet-tempered with her...but, by the end of next spring, she would have been in Jhansi for three full years and still she lay alone in her bedchamber at night.

Replacing the picture on its ivory stand, she walked to a tall mirror, unwinding her sari and observing her figure materialize from amidst its folds. How odd it was that all the influence she exerted over her husband in the daytime came to naught once the evening revelries were over and he repaired to his own chambers while she was escorted to hers. She was not sure if she had imagined it, but even her maids seemed to be dropping hints that it was a matter she ought to resolve, as they giggled and laughed during their morning baths down at the Amod Garden water tanks. Just yesterday, the old masseuse had commented on how beautifully the queen's breasts were developing as she oiled her body, laughing good-naturedly at the raja's enjoyment of them. The old woman had stopped short in some confusion only when Sundar glared at her but Lakshmibai had not failed to see the exchange of looks all around.

Bewildering and vexing as it was, Lakshmibai felt quite certain that it was not a concubine whose company Gangadhar preferred to hers. For one, she was sure that Sundar, though the soul of discretion, was too fond of her queen to let the presence of a concubine in the king's life remain unmentioned. The more forthcoming Kashi too would surely have said something. There was little that escaped palace maids of the goings-on, both inside the zenana and outside it. And Lakshmibai was as confident as it was possible to be that her husband was not likely to take up with a concubine when she, Lakshmibai, had never done anything to discourage him to come to her. Why, he was such a good man that he was considerate about the welfare of even those whom he knew conspired against him!

Undoing the pleats at her waistband, she smiled ruefully at her reflection in the half-murk. Was she not pretty enough...or enticing enough...had she not been chosen for this marriage because she was beautiful? In the candlelight, what she saw was a face grown prettier since her girlhood; cheekbones had emerged where once was baby fat, her hair was longer and smoother, her gait grown languid and graceful. Surely Gangadhar could not fail to notice all this. Or was it best to remain grateful for her husband's quiet friendship, tutoring herself not to expect anything more? What too of the increasingly compelling fact that she needed to produce the child that his first wife had been unable to give him? Had not Asharfi-bua made it plain to her all that time ago that one of her most important duties would be to provide Jhansi with an heir to its throne? Poor Asharfi-bua had even wept as she had instructed her little Mani to allow Raja Gangadhar to do whatever he had to do to her, even if it hurt, as it was so imperative for a queen to produce a healthy heir quickly.

Lakshmibai turned away from her reflection with an annoyed click of her tongue. She did not need to be told how complicated the issue of succession could become where there was no direct heir. Why, even Krishna Rao's hostility towards Gangadhar was because there had been no clarity of succession after Jhansi's previous king had died.

She had gradually pieced together the story from the things that various people had mentioned. The previous king, Gangadhar's uncle Raghunath Rao, had never had children with his own wife although his mistress, the ex-dancing girl Roshan, had managed to produce a son. Lakshmibai had seen that 'son'—Ali Bahadur—once and had remembered instantly the whisperings she had heard of the dead king's impotence. It was a credible story as Ali Bahadur, with his pale grey eyes and burly physique, bore no resemblance whatsoever to the paintings that hung in the palace of the old king.

When she had overheard two of the older maids whisper about

the various licentious activities that still took place at the palatial house built by the old king for his mistress, she had been unable to mask her curiosity. Demanding to be taken past Roshan's residence on her way back from the Mahalakshmi temple, she had been driven through Bara Bazaar and had peered out of her carriage windows to see paan-chewing eunuchs guarding the gates of a grand old haveli. Their tall flat figures were bedecked in glittering clothes as they lounged haughtily against the gateposts and it occurred to Lakshmibai that the old king had obviously left his mistress enough money to continue living in extravagance. The ex-concubine they guarded was now quite probably an absurd figure, her powers enfeebled by the death of her royal benefactor, but still those faithful eunuchs continued to protect those gates as though a precious jewel lived within it. How powerful a beautiful woman's authority could be, Lakshmibai thought, feeling a twinge of envy. The mansion that Kashi scornfully described as 'a house of ill-repute', where the old king had been so regular a visitor, was not visible behind its gates but Lakshmibai imagined the decrepit old man, whose picture still hung in the main hallway at Panch Mahal, visiting it. Willing to risk losing everything for the sexual pleasures he could not find with his wife.

Lakshmibai seated herself on the edge of her bed, recalling how she had wormed out of Kashi stories of the intrigue and the plotting that had overwhelmed the court after Raghunath Rao's death. Kashi had even told her of how Roshan had arrogantly appeared at the palace soon after the old king's funeral, accompanied by two of her eunuch friends, raucously demanding Ali Bahadur's share of the royal jewellery. Lakshmibai wondered what it might have been like for the childless widow of the old king to see the younger woman flaunting in her face the ripe crass beauty that had so captivated her husband and, worse, parading in front of everyone the strapping son that earthy allure had earned her. Although she had once tried asking Gangadhar about those incidents, he had merely looked embarrassed and shrugged off her enquiries and she guessed that it was because he always found it difficult to say anything demeaning about anybody. She had not pressed him, still mindful of her promise to Asharfi-bua that she would not behave in a forward manner with her husband.

Although it was well past the time for her evening prayers, Lakshmibai lay back on her pillows. Asharfi-bua had been right about many things; Gangadhar was a man too gracious and far too mannerly to even think of making his wife suffer in such a degrading manner as his thoughtless uncle had done. Lakshmibai was certain that she would never have to worry about concubines ensnaring her husband

and putting her to the kind of shame that the old king's widow had endured. But, despite that knowledge, Lakshmibai felt a familiar sense of exasperation at Gangadhar's lack of interest in consummating their relationship. Surely he could see that she was not a child any more, especially as neither he nor anyone else at Jhansi treated her as one in any other matter?

She sprang out of bed to place a candelabra on the shelf. Slipping off her robes, she examined her body closely in the full-length three-way mirror. What she could see were well-rounded breasts and hips that had filled out, making her waist look even slimmer than before. She had, over recent months, seen the areolae of her nipples grow and darken, becoming soft discs of dark gold against the wheaten sheen of her skin; the triangle at the base of her stomach turn to secretive black velvet. She angled her face against the light from the candles to confirm that her face had long lost its youthful chubbiness, taking on lines that made her eyes look ever more limpid than before. Surely, her husband would find her beautiful if he would only care to look! And did he not want her to bear his child: was that not why he had married her? There were no more excuses she could make on his behalf. If he was still waiting for her to grow up, then maybe it fell upon her to show him how mature she now was. It was time to share a full conjugal life with her husband and, for the first time ever, Lakshmibai was going to make that decision for both of them.

Gangadhar sat up in surprise on the bolsters of his bed as he heard voices in the outer chambers followed by the unfamiliar sound of anklets. Putting down the papers he had been leafing through, he called out for his guards. But it was Lakshmibai who appeared through the door.

'What is it, my dearest wife? You here? Why didn't you call me to your chambers if you wanted to speak to me?'

'Because I wanted to see you here, in your own bedchambers, where you sleep every night,' Lakshmibai replied softly, sliding a flirtatious sidelong look at him before adding with a laugh, 'Faiz Ali nearly would not let me in, until I reminded him who was queen!'

'Those are my orders to him, my rani, for no other reason than that, when I am resting after the day's work, I do not like being disturbed.'

Gangadhar said this with a smile so that there was no edge to his words but, even if there had been, Lakshmibai was feeling bold enough to have ignored it. She now kicked off her silk slippers and climbed onto Gangadhar's high silver four-poster, causing him to have to make room for her. She ran her hand in admiration over the beautiful amber-coloured headrest made of stretched rhinoceros skin before making herself comfortable, rearranging the cushions to lean on them. Looking at her husband, she smiled at his confused expression.

'Oh don't look so bewildered,' she laughed, 'it is only a wife trying to sleep next to her husband, that's all, nothing out of the ordinary!'

'But why, Lakshmibai? Are you not comfortable there? Do you need new chambers? Or a better bed? Don't forget that, with the palace being refurbished in the city, you will be able to plan your new chambers in exactly the way you want them to be.'

'It is none of those things, my husband, please don't fret. I just wanted to spend some time alone with you and find out how you were…is that so unusual from a wife?'

Gangadhar smiled, looking more relaxed. He leaned over to cup his hand gently on the side of Lakshmibai's face, 'I am just fine, and much better now. It's possible the vaid's medicines are working. See, you can hardly see the tremors now.' He held up his hand and it pained Lakshmibai to see that, even as he did so, his hand was visibly shaking in the candlelight.

But this was not the time to think of all that. Already so much time had been lost in worrying about her husband's health. Lakshmibai raised her arm to slip her own hand into Gangadhar's and pulled it gently down to rest on the curve of her left breast. She felt his arm become rigid momentarily before he closed his eyes, as though in pain. He had gone very still. She then reached out for his left hand that was even now holding onto a few sheets of paper. Extricating them slowly from between his fingers and making him drop them onto the floor, she pulled his hand over her other breast, effectively trapping both his hands with her own. For a few seconds, they lay next to each other, face-to-face, Gangadhar's palms frozen over Lakshmibai's breasts. It was so quiet, the sound of their combined breathing filled the room. The cloth punkah above their heads moved with metronomic regularity, the punkah-wallah in the next room unaware of such unusual events taking place in the raja's bedchamber.

Using her hands, Lakshmibai made Gangadhar's cupped palms move in a circular motion and, as she felt her nipples respond to being rubbed, she closed her own eyes for a few moments, feeling an unfamiliar sensation low down in the pit of her stomach. Opening her eyes again, she realized that Gangadhar had his own eyes tightly squeezed. But it was as though something was hurting him. She could see no pleasure on his face. The corners of his mouth had turned white, his lips were pale and clenched. Stopping the movement of their hands abruptly, Lakshmibai asked anxiously, 'What is it, Gangadhar-ji, are you all right, are you in pain?'

Gangadhar's eyes flew open and Lakshmibai could see, alarmingly, that tears had welled up in them.

'What is it? What is it, you are in pain, aren't you?' she asked, concern written all over her face.

Gangadhar nodded, as though words were too much effort for him. Lakshmibai touched his forehead with her fingers. 'You are running a high fever, you are not well at all! Why didn't you tell me?'

She got up, adjusting her blouse and rearranging her dupatta around her shoulder, blaming herself in a frantic voice, 'You should have told me, Gangadhar-ji, rather than letting me disturb your rest. And, without knowing, I have now made you worse. Let me go and fetch a doctor for you.'

Getting up from the bed, she pulled on her slippers quickly before opening the door to the outer chamber, 'Faiz Ali,' she said urgently, 'come in here and stay with the raja, he has been taken unwell, I am going to get help.'

She did not see the expression of utter desolation come across her husband's face as he watched her run out of the room in search of help.

☙ 12 ❧

Ellis reread the new directive with incredulity. The contents of the mailbag that had just been delivered by the dak-gadi were strewn across his desk but everything else would have to wait.

'The brutes, the wretched brutes, what do they think this is going to achieve?' he muttered to himself, throwing the letter down onto the clutter before him. Taking a few breaths to calm himself, he reached out for the peon's bell on his desk and rang for Panna Ram. When the man came in, bowing and scraping in a manner he had been given numerous instructions not to, Ellis snapped, 'Are the officers back from the parade ground yet?'

'I don't know sir, I will find out, give me please just one minute, sir,' Panna Ram replied, bowing his way out backwards and nearly tripping over the doormat.

'Bloody fool,' Ellis muttered, pulling a letter pad across the desk before scribbling a note: *Bentinck's 1835 order to ban corporal punishment of sepoys rescinded by Lord Hardinge. I think we need to meet to discuss implications for both 12th Bengal and 13th Irregular.*

He signed his name at the bottom and rolled the blotter over the note before folding it up and pushing it into an envelope. On hearing Panna Ram's footsteps outside, Ellis swiftly changed his mind. Taking the note out of the envelope again, he proceeded to quickly tear it into little shreds, suddenly unsure of whether to trust the oily little peon not to steam open the envelope to have a look inside. This was a sensitive matter and he certainly did not want the sepoys getting wind of this before their officers were informed.

'Yes sir, they are all back, sir, shall I call them here, sir?' Panna Ram asked.

'Well, tell Captain Martin I'd like to see him soon. In the billiards room. Five o'clock.'

After methodically perusing the last of his documents, Ellis gathered his papers together and tied them up with a piece of twine. Getting up from his chair, he knocked on the thin partition wall as a signal to the punkah-wallah to cease his fanning. He shut the door behind him and stepped out into the oppressive evening air. The monsoons were expected any time now, a time of year when the evenings were always airless and heavy with expectation. He yanked on his collar to loosen it, already feeling his shirt grow clammy and stick to his perspiring back and chest. With as much briskness as he could muster, he walked down a path that had been created a few years ago, on his instructions, with orange earth flanked on either side by Jhansi's naturally dark mud. It had been a source of fascination for Ellis once that soil came in so many different colours in India, but it was now one of those little things that he had stopped noticing and taking delight in.

The billiards room was empty, the balls gleaming and shiny on their green felt bed. Ellis tried to remember when he had last picked up a cue, straightening as he heard footsteps coming down the corridor.

'Ah Martin,' Ellis addressed the smart young captain entering the room, 'apologies for such short summons, but I had something important to show you. I thought it best not to wait for Major Royle's return from the hills.' He took the letter from Calcutta out of the sheaf in his hands and handed it to Martin. He watched the younger man's face as he read it but its expression was impenetrable.

'What do you think?' Ellis asked as it was handed back to him.

Martin cocked his eyebrows and seemed to consider his words for a moment, before saying, 'Well, it finally gives us something to use against obstreperous sepoys, sir. Lord Bentinck's attempt to cast them in a class apart from our own rankers had never seemed too fair to me.'

Ellis tried not to let his surprise show. He liked Martin well enough and had always thought he was made of better stuff than the newer breed of griffin coming these days to India—men of a different class, plainly attracted to service in India only because of the tales of rich pickings that were no doubt trickling back home. Not even taught Hindustani any more, officers arrived these days with barely any understanding of the men they were to command. Even worse was their astonishing lack of respect for native traditions.

'Come, Martin, you know as well as I do that Bentinck's apparent bias was only because the Bengal Army was made up of high-caste Hindu sepoys of many years' service. To subject them to the same treatment as young British and Irish rankers—butchers and cordwainers, men accustomed to a harder way of life—would have been ill-advised to say the least.'

Martin remained unmoved, saying flatly, 'It's a prejudice our men would only have taken up to a point, sir.'

'Yes, of course, we can't be seen to discriminate. But it isn't as if floggings take place regularly—I can't even remember when we last conducted one in these parts. What worries me, Martin, is the slippery slope. As it is, there have been complaints recently that some newer officers openly call the sepoys insulting names, even boxing their ears or conjuring up amusing punishments for not doing as they are told.'

'Only in extreme cases, sir, and only to maintain the discipline of the Army.'

'There hasn't been any recent trouble, surely?' Ellis asked.

'Well in the Punjab, sir, our problem with the Sikhs, sepoys organizing their own panchayats to demand new rights. Such insurrections must be dealt with firmly, sir. Before they get out of hand.'

'Yes, but what have the Sikh wars got to do with our men here, Martin?' Ellis responded wearily.

'Forgive me, sir, but our men here come to hear these things inevitably. And, perhaps because of it, there are reports that they have already stated their refusal to go to the Punjab to fight. Before even receiving orders, sir.'

'Why on earth not? I know they didn't like the idea of sailing to Burma...'

'It's the same business about losing one's caste if made to cross the sea. Now it's even the River Indus, apparently! The Bengal

Infantry sepoys have always been the worst offenders with this sort of poppycock, sir.'

Ellis recalled a time, not that long ago, when these deep-seated beliefs would have been respected. Now, of course, it was poppycock, superstitious mumbo-jumbo that had to be beaten out of errant sepoys. He could not for the life of him imagine when the shift had started taking place but worried that, rather like a disease, it would catch him too unawares one day. He had never had time for the evangelical zeal of some British officers who thought they could 'tame' their sepoys and instil proper Christian values in them but some of the recently emerged Utilitarian ideas had seemed to make some sense even to him.

Martin was droning on, 'The artillery fellows who went to Kabul have even tried telling us that they were forcibly converted to Islam but that's obviously nonsense, sir. Any yarn to gain sympathy, I suppose.'

'Yes of course, Martin, but caution may not be a bad idea. From what I gather, minor rebellions have already broken out in the Bengal Army. I hear that sepoys there were furious at their overseas allowances being stopped once Sind was taken because, technically, we don't describe the Sind as being overseas any more. That is a prickly issue, certainly, when you think it was at least partially their efforts that helped conquer Sind!'

'Yes, sir, but foremost must come their duty as soldiers. And if not, corporal punishment remains the sole guarantee for maintaining the discipline and regulation of the Army.'

The bloody man sounded like a walking directive, Ellis thought. Using corporal punishment as security against military distemper was as foolish as the worst native superstitions. What could have happened to change even a man like Martin? Sepoys were men of high birth, of yeoman stock. Already they had been expected to accept unquestioningly that a native subedar–major, equivalent in rank to a British captain, now earned half the salary and had none of the privileges accorded to a captain, merely because he was not white-skinned. Ellis had so often found himself mulling over how these people had allowed Englishmen like him, officers who sometimes used their power with cruelty and hauteur, to wield such control over their lives. It was possible, of course, that generations of Mughal rule had simply inured the native population to servitude. And he had concluded that perhaps the British had just got lucky to find themselves suddenly in charge of a people already schooled in humiliation. But there was no point discussing any of that with Martin. Already Ellis suspected that he was seen in some quarters as being far too permissive to the sepoys and their various complaints. It was best not to make his opinion too openly known.

'Well, Martin,' Ellis said, picking up his papers from the baize table, 'I'll leave it to you to break the news of this new directive to Major Royle and Major Mead when they return from Simla. It's safest to wait till they are back, and fully briefed, before the sepoys of both regiments are informed.' He waited till Martin had clicked his heels together and left the room before departing it himself, feeling even more downcast than before.

As Ellis stepped out onto the veranda of the officers' mess, he smelt it before he saw it. That unmistakable smell of wet earth, both heavy and refreshing, wafting through the air. A light westerly breeze had picked up and was making the leaves in the upper reaches of the giant peepul trees dance and flutter. He heard a distant low rumble and looked up over the western horizon. There would be no sunset tonight as the sky had already turned a dark churning black. The monsoons had arrived at last but Ellis felt none of his customary joy as the first few raindrops spattered, fat and warm, on the parched earth at his feet.

Lakshmibai thought she had never heard of anything so dreadful. 'They can't flog the sipahis at will!' she cried indignantly, making her husband look nervously over his shoulder to see who may have overheard. Luckily, the small group of Company soldiers that had presented the petition in the assembly hall had now left.

'My dear rani, they are the Company's soldiers, not ours,' Gangadhar reminded her gently.

'Can you imagine us even contemplating such a travesty to the soldiers in our army? Kshatriyas, men from the warrior caste?' Lakshmibai looked aghast at her husband who looked away, shifting slightly in his seat.

'I agree, rani. It does seem like such an unnecessary reversal on the good that has been achieved. I'm surprised Ellis never informed me about this. He is usually quite conscientious in letting me know before I hear from some other source.'

'It really does make me wonder. On the one hand, people like Sister Agnes tell us that our Hindu customs are brutal and, on the other hand, the Company is allowed to use their degrading punishments? What makes them believe sipahis will do their bidding only if they are whipped? They have had sipahis in the Company's Army for over one hundred years!'

'My dear Lakshmibai, I have immense sympathy for the sipahis too. But we can only hope that the old directive has been changed only in name and will never actually be put into practice. I do not see what we, sitting here, can do anyway.'

Lakshmibai felt a familiar twinge of irritation at her husband's attitude. She had, in recent times, found herself chafing more and more at Gangadhar's acquiescent attitude to Major Ellis. On the one hand, she had no time for Krishna Rao's acerbic non-compliance over anything that came from the British, knowing that his rebellion against their authority sprang less from a sense of righteousness than plain bitterness. The right path in dealing with the British lay somewhere halfway between the polarized attitudes of the two brothers and Lakshmibai felt annoyed at the restrictions she had so far placed on herself. She agreed with Gangadhar when he pointed out that British policies were not all bad but she could also see, unlike him, that the Company only really acted in their own commercial and military interests. She was tiring of the unthinking obedience her husband seemed willing to give the British, so unthinking indeed that she sometimes wondered if his belief in their goodness was genuine. Lakshmibai made up her mind to have a word with Ellis when he next visited the palace on this business of floggings. It did not matter what Gangadhar may think.

She cast a glance at her husband who had got up from his chair and was now making his way across the hall with help from Faiz Ali, thereby ending the conversation. She knew she ought to stem her rush of exasperation, knowing that she had probably annoyed him with her outspokenness. Perhaps his apparent lack of fervour was because of his ill-health. But then, how could she explain the disappearance of that apathy when it was time to attend the nightly theatricals on the steps of the baradari?

Lakshmibai took a deep breath before getting up and walking out of the assembly hall back to her chambers in Panch Mahal. If her husband was more interested in arts and theatre than in matters of state, it was even more incumbent on her to ensure that Jhansi did not suffer as a consequence of it.

The issue of the corporal punishment of sepoys was to remain unresolved for another two weeks as Major Ellis's next visit to the Fort, at the invitation of Raja Gangadhar, was to attend a nautch performance to celebrate the rani's seventeenth birthday. The only Englishman honoured with an invitation, Ellis took his place on the middle tier surrounding the baradari canopy with the familiar curious sensation of being watched.

Lakshmibai, seated behind the silken curtains along with the other women who were in purdah, observed the Englishman seat himself on the carved gilt chair reserved for foreign visitors. She had seen him many times over the years but the features she had glimpsed had always been fragmented by the tiny apertures of her ivory screen purdah. She knew that he had hair the colour of a young deer's pelt and eyes like grey rain-clouds. Suddenly she was curious to see his entire face and peered through the thin silk, leaning forward. Through the blue gauze of the purdah, his countenance seemed pleasant enough, if a little ghostly as one half of his face was illuminated by the light of a nearby hurricane lamp while the rest was plunged in shadows. His tall figure, wearing a black suit and red cummerbund, arranged itself awkwardly on the high-backed chair as he crossed and uncrossed one booted foot over the other and Lakshmibai wondered if he would have been more comfortable merely reclining on the cushions like Gangadhar and his ministers nearby.

She looked at Ellis's face again; despite the sharpness of his features, he had an air of gentleness about him. He did not have Gangadhar's fastidious air about him, wearing his suit as though it were an imposition to be so dressed up but his face had a rather melancholic, faraway expression. Even as the master of ceremonies entertained the gathering with a series of jokes, there was the barest flicker of a smile on Ellis's mouth. What sorrows were those that afflicted the Englishman, Lakshmibai wondered, recalling that he never sounded as though he were really enjoying himself, even when narrating tales for Gangadhar's amusement.

From their conversations in the court, she had gathered the impression of an honourable and well-intentioned man who was almost as fond of Jhansi as she herself was. His affection for Gangadhar seemed genuine and he never failed to respect Hindustani traditions and ways. She was less sure, though, of Major Ellis's ability to hold faith with his convictions and had sometimes wondered if he would possess the courage to stand up to his senior officers if that became necessary. Although he was probably powerless in the face of directives from Calcutta and London, she resolved to ask him for a reassurance that corporal punishment would not be used on sipahis in Jhansi. She would send a message to the cantonment first thing in the morning. Ellis was a good man and she felt suddenly confident of being able to appeal directly to his humanity, even if Gangadhar had so far shied away from the task. Perhaps she would not even inform Gangadhar of her intention to meet Ellis for all the interest he was showing in state matters these days.

The meeting between Lakshmibai and Ellis that followed three days later was a fraught one and Ellis returned from it feeling sick at heart. As he sat alone in the mess that night, Major Malcolm took the chair opposite his and Ellis tried to contain his dismay. He had been trying unsuccessfully to avoid the man all day but was well stuck with him now. Malcolm wore a crotchety air about him and was clearly keen to discuss their visit to the palace but Ellis sipped again on his tumbler of whisky, determined not to be the one to break the silence.

The warren of buildings that was the Officers' Mess was the only sanctuary on a night like this and Ellis could not realistically have hoped to get away from Malcolm as he had awaited his supper in the anteroom. He sat sunk low on the sofa, gazing into the empty grate, noticing that the faint smell of kedgeree served at breakfast still hung in the dank air. Ornately framed oil paintings of past Governors-General lined the walls of the cavernous room, self-assured expressions indicating their pleasure at having earned places within those gilt-edged frames. Five stuffed birds in a glass box joined them in staring sightlessly at no one in particular. Their expressions always seemed either angry or sulky to Ellis, loathing as he did this new fashion of stuffing dead birds and mounting them in cabinets.

Outside, in the darkness of the night, the pouring rain sounded as though a river were flowing off the roof and dropping like a small waterfall into the garden below. Despite the deep ledge constructed over the window, Ellis could feel a fine cool spray waft across his face and hands and looked down to see that his jacket had acquired the finest sheen of moisture. The monsoon was a favourite season, putting an end to the seemingly endless sight of parched earth and dust-laden trees. Normally, Ellis would have stood at the window to breathe in the welcome scent of wet earth but Malcolm's kill-joy presence was a real imposition tonight.

He had not wanted Malcolm to accompany him to the palace at all but the man had insisted on accompanying him, no doubt because the cantonment had emptied as it usually did in the summer months and there was absolutely no one around for Malcolm to call on or make merry with. Ellis was sure the visit would have gone off more amicably had he attended the court alone, Malcolm's abrasive manner never contributing positively to any discussions.

Malcolm's nasal twang rose above the sound of the rain. 'So Her Grand Highness is not to be trifled with, eh Ellis? That was no less than a ticking off, I daresay. Dashed impudence on her part, if you ask me, to imagine she can just summon us to give us a piece of her mind like that. Quite preposterous, didn't you think?'

Malcolm's tone was casual enough and Ellis guessed that all he wanted was to break the silence that had descended on them. His own thoughts were so dark that he considered staying silent long enough for Malcolm to imagine he had not heard him. Perhaps the man would even feel obliged to get up and wander away in search of better company, though the prospect was not good on a night as wet as this.

But Malcolm's beady eyes remained fixed on Ellis's face, leaving him with no choice but to pull himself up on the sofa before replying curtly, 'Well, she's less afraid of us than the king is, I suppose.'

Ellis was not sure why he had allowed his meeting with Rani Lakshmibai to make him feel so morose. She had at first, quite unsurprisingly, expressed her displeasure with the new directive regarding the floggings and, unlike her husband who always beat around the bush when he had a complaint about British policies, had not hesitated to speak her mind. To do her credit, she had made it clear that it was the government she was furious with rather than Ellis himself, only wanting her views to be passed on to his superiors in Calcutta. Left to himself, Ellis knew he could have expressed the sympathy he genuinely felt and offer to use the directive sparingly on a local level. But Malcolm had stepped in at that point, behaving like a belligerent terrier.

Even Ellis had been taken aback when the rani's response had reduced the redoubtable Malcolm to a glowering silence. Wasted, of course, seeing that she could not have seen his scowls through the purdah. It was not pleasant and Ellis wondered why Raja Gangadhar had chosen not to be present, even though he had heard that Rani Lakshmibai had started playing a more active role in the administration of Jhansi in recent days as the raja had been taken ill again.

Malcolm uncoiled his legs lazily. 'Don't know about you but I find her lack of fear a bit impertinent, old chap. Maybe we *ought* to make her a little afraid...should be easy enough.'

Ellis felt chilled suddenly at the nastiness in his voice. 'What do you mean?' he asked warily.

Malcolm was now sitting up in his chair, getting increasingly animated. 'Oh just throw something her way that'll rattle her. You know how fond our magistrate is of pettifogging little details—we could ask him to chuck some directive her way that'll make her crawl, show the brazen little termagant who's ruling whom around here. I'm certainly not standing for some jumped-up Jezebel telling us our business, the cheek of it! These native chiefs would do well to remember that it's their weakness for luxury and superstition and…and bloody *humbug* that has sapped this country of progress. A little reminder of the debt they owe us for bringing order and advancement to their provinces wouldn't be out of order, I believe.'

'Come, sir, I'm sure she wasn't trying to tell us our business, just voicing her own feelings on what is, after all, a rather iniquitous business. We're just not used to hearing their opinions especially as the king's usually so reticent.'

'Well, he's a prize chump, isn't he? I mean, you know the man better than I do, Ellis, but, for God's sake, it's ghastly seeing the poor creature tricked out in tinsel like that, all face paint and dripping jewellery—like a ruddy French whore.'

Ellis finally smiled wryly, recognizing the truth in Malcolm's description. 'He's certainly overdressed sometimes, old Gangadhar. Thoroughly decent chap, though. You have to grant him that. Genuinely anxious about the well-being of his people…and in that matter quite unlike some of the other native royals we know of. Also charmingly trusting of our intentions, don't you think?' After a short pause, suddenly feeling a desperate need to lighten the tone of the conversation, Ellis added, 'Besides, he's awfully generous with his collection of cigars.'

'Well, he's never offered me one, I'd have you know,' Malcolm snapped back. 'And as for her…Jezebel…unfailingly beastly and condescending. Seldom deigns to greet me properly, despite speaking the lingo perfectly well…' Malcolm trailed off, his whiskers bristling with imagined insults. He took another sip of his whisky, grinning suddenly, a gold incisor gleaming in the half-light. 'Wouldn't you want to know what she looked like behind that dashed screen? Tough as old boots, probably, although they tell me she isn't a day over eighteen. Seems hard to square up that brassy voice with such a young woman.'

'She's always seemed old for her years,' Ellis replied. 'Admirable political instinct too. I'd say she already rules the place with more vigour than her husband does.'

'Well, that wouldn't take much effort seeing what a feeble dolt he is,' Malcolm drawled before fixing his gaze again on Ellis. 'I say, Ellis, I wonder if it's true what they say about the king being…you know…a queer? Or a pederast, perhaps. As fishy as Dick's hatband, I'd be inclined to believe.' He squinted in the half-light over the rim of his glass, trying to read the expression on Ellis's face.

'Nothing in his demeanour has ever indicated any sexual perversions, I have to say,' Ellis replied after a moment, the starchiness of his voice audible even to his own ears.

'Well, there's no sign of children yet, is there? In both his marriages, come to think of it. I certainly think it's not beyond the bounds of...'

Their conversation was interrupted by the arrival of a party at the outer door. Cries of pleasure and triumph at having braved the rain floated into the anteroom as the doors swung open and a foursome came into view, surrounded by a retinue of fussing servants shaking out umbrellas and brushing raindrops off clothes and hats. A maid was kneeling before two ladies, helping to squeeze the rainwater from the edges of dresses and petticoats and wiping their shoes clean. Ellis's heart sank further as he recognized the Meads and the Royles.

'Why if it isn't Major Malcolm!' Harriet Mead trilled cheerily from the veranda as she spotted him, adding swiftly, 'Oh, and Major Ellis.'

The men put their glasses down and stood up, Malcolm beaming from ear to ear.

'Exactly the people who will fill us in on the gossip we might have missed in our weeks away from Jhansi, Belinda,' Harriet said to her companion before raising her voice again to call out, 'I shall be exceedingly cross if you say we've missed any intrigues while we were up in Simla, Major Malcolm!'

Harriet Mead, wife of the commanding officer of the Jhansi garrisons, allowed a turbaned bearer to take her bonnet away to be dried before she bustled into the room, trailing a cloud of damp verbena after her. The rather less effusive figures of her husband and Major and Belinda Royle followed her into the room a few moments later. Smiling brightly, Harriet offered a damp gloved hand to the men in turn as they moved around to accommodate her plump little figure. Seating herself on the edge of a leather armchair, she delicately peeled off her gloves and mopped a face gone pink from its recent exertions. The delicate handkerchief looked completely inadequate for its task and, had Harriet used it only to display her expensive Honiton lace, the ploy was completely lost on Ellis.

Belinda Royle looked distinctly less amused by her dousing. She rubbed pale hands vigorously together before trying to rearrange thin brown ringlets that were lying wet and stringy across the back of her neck. Briefly she bobbed at both men. 'Rotten luck to be caught in such a downpour,' she said in her customary brisk manner. 'Could we have a fire, do you think, Major Malcolm? It does get so awfully chilly when it rains.'

'Shall I get the punkah-wallah to stop his fanning?' Malcolm asked, instantly solicitous, clearly delighted at being presented so unexpectedly with female company.

'Oh no, my dear Belinda,' Harriet Mead protested cheerily as she plopped back onto her sofa, 'it may be cold tonight but at least the punkah keeps the infernal insects away.'

'Hard to think it's just September, isn't it?' Major Mead said, shaking hands as the club bearers fussed around with chairs and tables, trying to accommodate the group. Malcolm clicked his fingers and pointed at the empty grate. One of the bearers bowed obsequiously before scurrying off.

Malcolm turned back to the group, beaming so hard his whiskers were quivering. Recognizing what a dour mood he had been in all evening, Ellis thought he could hardly blame his companion for being so pleased at the unexpected company of this rather jolly foursome. Major Mead had always seemed a likable fellow, good for an evening's company. Although even he, loquacious and good-humoured as he had shown himself capable of being after a few stiff shots of brandy, was as content as most of the others in the cantonment to slide into indulgent nodding silence when in the presence of his ebullient wife.

Harriet Mead, arranging the damp folds of her frock, was eager to get the conversation swiftly moving on. 'Oh, do let's all settle down quickly so that Major Malcolm and Major Ellis can tell us about whom they were talking when we came in—we're here for an evening of scandal, rumour and tittle-tattle, aren't we Belinda?'

The bearer returned to the room, carrying a tray of coals and paper for the fire. Belinda Royle rolled her eyes in the man's direction and cleared her throat meaningfully. She dropped her voice to a whisper, 'Well...after whatsisname's gone, of course. I hear they all know English now, although they always pretend not to.'

'Now darling,' Major Royle remonstrated fondly.

'You know it's true,' Belinda replied sharply, causing her husband to lapse back into embarrassed silence.

Harriet, as was her wont, was quick to diffuse the tension. 'Oh but what would poor Major Royle know of our domestic concerns, Belinda,' she said in a tone of mock petulance. 'Gentlemen always assume rather erroneously that our domestic brigade operates like an obedient regiment of sepoys, even though we all know it's not the same at all.'

With the departure of the bearer, Belinda allowed her voice to ring freely around the room, 'More's the pity, Harriet. The sepoys know their place in the hierarchy and are grateful for it but the cooks and gardeners and dhobis *we* have to deal with sometimes behave as though it's such an awful imposition to be in our employ. And *so* unwilling to learn anything new, I find myself constantly astonished by their obstinacy.'

Harriet replied soothingly, 'Ah my dear Belinda, I know there are those beastly days when the servants seem to be conspiring to get everything wrong. But, it's not all bad, really...' She giggled before adding, 'You'll never believe how I spent my morning—teaching my khansama how to say, "Tea is served, memsahib", rather than bellow "Chotta haziri ready!" What a spot of fun that was.'

They fell silent again as the bearer returned to the room to blow into the smouldering coals through a metal pipe. A small fire leapt to life and the warmth from it licked comfortingly around the dampness of carpet and hems and collars. Harriet stretched her fingers out in pleasure and, glancing at the servant's retreating figure, laughed, 'Well, now that he's gone, it's perfectly safe to tell us about whom you were gossiping, Major Malcolm.'

Ellis was amused to see Malcolm turn a fine shade of plum under his ginger whiskers. He didn't think even Malcolm, always eager to partake of juicy scandal, would be inclined to discuss the king of Jhansi's sexual proclivity with their two lady companions. He watched wryly as his suave older colleague avoided the question completely by getting up and elaborately proffering his seat to Belinda Royle for its proximity to the fire.

'Oh you're just bashful about our enquiries, Major Malcolm,' Belinda Royle laughed sportingly as she exchanged places with Malcolm. 'You must forgive us but we've only this morning returned from the hills and have become rather accustomed to a good dose of gossip with our evening drink. It's quite dreadful really.' She sat back in her chair and brushed a few remaining raindrops off her crinoline lap and onto the carpet underfoot.

Harriet Mead turned to Ellis at this point, blue eyes shining gleefully. 'Oh I cannot begin to tell you all what an absolutely charming time we had in Simla, Major Ellis! It's just the place for a handsome young man like you. Have you ever been? It was such a riot when the officers and writers came up from Calcutta too. Weren't those evenings strolling on the Mall just perfectly enchanting, Belinda?'

Her friend, whose pinched features had relaxed considerably with the warmth of the fire, smiled. 'One may be forgiven for wishing to *never* come back. Oh how very dreadful the mofussil is during the rains.'

After everyone had ordered their drinks and the bearer had left the room, Ellis thought he should display some interest in the ladies' recent perambulations. 'Was the new Governor-General in residence too at Simla?' he enquired politely of Harriet.

'The Governor-General, his wife and two of her sisters too, in addition to their son who is, I believe, acting as private secretary to his father, Major Ellis. A most charming young man called Charles. And, of course, their whole coterie of staff and helpers. And this year, they threw a party to celebrate the birthday of one of Lady Hardinge's sisters to which we were all invited. My, what a spectacle it was, wouldn't you say, Belinda? The gowns and the jewels, sumptuous and glittering and, oh goodness, what an array of fine food and wine was on offer—I spotted enormous boxes with the Wilson's "Hall of all Nations" labels on them being unloaded…proper Yorkshire hams and pork pies, pheasant and grouse and game of all description…quite splendid indeed.' Harriet beamed happily at the memory.

'The fashions from Calcutta never fail to make me feel a frightful frump, though, I have to say,' Belinda said ruefully.

'Oh my dear,' Harriet replied, 'we couldn't *hope* to compete with the Presidency set when they descend on the hills like flocks of peacocks at the start of the season. Didn't they look just marvellous in their fabulous gowns? Swansdown trimmings seemed to be all the rage and, oh, did you see that adorable little bonnet trimmed with orange blossom that Lady Hardinge wore to church the day we left? I have it on good authority that her chiffons and taffetas are brought straight out from Paris to be tailored at Calcutta's finest establishments. We can barely keep up when all we have here is our little darjiwallah sitting on the veranda of the house with his tin-pot sewing machine. But that's just the way it's always been in the mofussil and there's no point complaining, I always say.'

Ellis's ears always started to ring a few minutes into conversation with Harriet Mead, but he found himself smiling with the rest. She was not a dislikeable lass—pretty, with large blue eyes and blessed with a disarming effervescence that was genuinely quite infectious. Ellis had heard it said before of girls like Harriet Mead that every dreary mofussil town needed one to keep everyone sane and in good spirits and tonight she certainly played her part with aplomb.

'Well, as long as they don't look down their noses at people like us from the mofussil, I don't really mind I suppose,' Belinda Royle responded mildly.

'I have to say it was most objectionable when the Fort William writers wouldn't as much as look at us once the Presidency girls had arrived! But, seeing what young devils some of them are, I don't suppose we should grumble. Darling James, you're quite safe on that score!'

Ellis saw Major Mead give his wife an indulgent look before he turned to him. 'It's easy to see why people have started going up to the Himalayan foothills despite Darjeeling's proximity to Calcutta, Ellis. It's all rather jolly there, certainly the best way to break the back of the summer.'

'I've unfortunately not yet had occasion to visit Simla,' Ellis replied.

Malcolm cut in. 'It's Tudor mixed in with Surrey if you can imagine that. Perfectly charming.'

'It's easy to imagine being back at home when the mists roll in over the mountains.'

'The cottage we stayed in even had a gabled roof covered in wisteria. And a quite delightful garden just bursting with hollyhocks and dahlias.'

'Sounds exactly like the home I grew up in,' Ellis smiled at Harriet before adding, 'But I must confess just a little concern over this conspiracy to turn Indian hill-towns into copies of the Lake District or Dovedale.'

Major Mead laughed at that but Ellis noticed no one else did. The two ladies fell silent as the men discussed a local matter regarding the sepoys and Ellis wondered if they were suddenly despondent at how fast their summer season in Simla had passed. They sat in silence for a few minutes, sipping on glasses of Mosel as the rain continued to pour outside, turning the flat landscape around Jhansi to a muddy bog.

'Sounds like it may never stop,' Belinda Royle remarked finally as they listened to the rat-a-tat gunfire of raindrops leaping off the tin roofs of the cookhouse and latrines that surrounded the club.

'Well it can never manage to drizzle on the plains, can it? Buckets of rain just come chucking down from the heavens,' Major Malcolm said.

'I once counted three whole days before one benighted downpour had decided to stop during the last monsoon,' Mead agreed, 'and, when it did stop, that had been abrupt too. Halting without tailing off into a drizzle and leaving behind a steaming hot earth that reeked with all manner of sodden smells.'

Belinda shuddered, clutching her arms around her thin person. 'If you ask me, it's these monsoon nights that are the most disagreeable and the host of new and unfamiliar insects they bring. I don't know whether it's worse hearing them whining all around in the darkness or having them fall everywhere with that horrid burnt waxy smell from flying too close to the candles.'

'It's the creepy-crawlies I loathe,' Harriet contributed, 'snakes and scorpions and—did I tell you about the bullfrog that I found in my veranda the other day...so large he seemed almost human as he looked me up and down as though wondering what I was doing there!'

'Oh yes, there's certainly something decidedly vicious about the rain in India, blessed with none of the gentleness with which it alights on English roofs and trees.'

'I do try for your sake, my dear James, but I must say there are days when I yearn for some of those things that you could never hope to see in this scrubby hard brown land where it's either bakingly hot or pouring madly with rain. It's so hard to imagine that it's been nearly three years since I left home.'

A flash of lightning lit the faces of the group huddled around the fire followed by a furious crack of thunder. Harriet jumped visibly and Ellis suddenly felt sorry for her. If he sometimes missed the sight of English mists hanging over soft wet gardens and other innumerable small things, such as the smell of freshly mown summer grass, he knew it was always much worse for the ladies.

However, the irrepressible Harriet had already pulled herself up in her armchair, her face brightening again. 'BUT,' she said loudly, 'like my darling papa who never fails to remind me in each of his letters, I say there's no point in moping, is there? Honestly, if you think about it, there's plenty to be quite grateful for.'

She was clearly determined to rouse the group out of all homesickness and Ellis braced himself for another of her cheery remarks. Fortunately, her husband beat her to it, changing the subject with a question directly addressed to him.

'By the way, I've been meaning to ask you, Ellis—it can't be true what they're saying about Kashmir, can it?'

'Kashmir?' Malcolm cut in, looking sharply at his companion. Ellis winced at his obvious displeasure in not being the first to hear the news but waited for the bearer to finish refilling the empty glasses before replying to Mead's question in a low voice. 'I think it may well be true, if you're referring to Gulab Singh,' he said. 'We're giving Kashmir away to him. For services rendered in the Sikh wars.'

Malcolm turned to the two women, returning swiftly to his former expansive self. 'Gulab Singh is the king of Jammu who assisted us rather ably in the Punjab,' he explained.

Mead and Royle still looked puzzled. 'Why on earth would Gulab Singh be given Kashmir? He's a Hindoo, isn't he?' Royle asked.

'Well, after Ranjit Singh's death, Gulab Singh's influence was apparently invaluable in negotiating between the Sikhs and us. So he's due his reward which I heard is going to be, yes, who'd have thought—Kashmir.'

'Surely he can't just be *given* it!' Belinda Royle exclaimed disbelievingly. 'I know the gifts given in this country can seem quite monstrous sometimes but, for heaven's sake, an entire province?'

'Well, it is meant to look like a sale,' Ellis laughed. 'No doubt money will change hands so that it doesn't look like an embarrassing endowment.'

'Wouldn't it also seem a bit anomalous to have a Hindoo king suddenly rule over Muslim subjects?' Major Mead asked, inadvertently echoing Ellis's thoughts on the subject.

'Only as peculiar I suppose as Muslim nawabs in Hyderabad and Awadh ruling over Hindoos,' Malcolm replied airily. 'These natives are used to their strange mishmash of cultures and religions. Can't see that being a problem.'

'How much do you suppose is the price they've placed on Kashmir? A token sum, I take it?' Major Royle enquired, putting his glass down.

'From what I heard, the price being asked from Gulab Singh is a paltry seventy lakh rupees. Oh, and, yes, a horse, six goats and a pair of cashmere shawls,' Ellis replied, unable to hide his amusement at the looks of incredulity covering the faces before him.

His inability to mask his feelings about the sheer unthinking stupidity of Calcutta's recent decision was perhaps unwise, for, out of the corner of his eye, he saw Belinda Royle nudge Harriet Mead with the tip of her shoe.

❧ 13 ❧

On Lakshmibai's eighteenth birthday Gangadhar imparted the best piece of news she had received in the four years she had been married to him. He was taking her to Varanasi so that she could see everybody at Saturday House again! She knew he had probably quietly planned for this auspicious day to come before making his announcement to her, waiting too for the temple pujas to be done with and all their well-wishers to have departed, leaving them in a rare moment alone together on her balcony.

He had said it casually, almost as though it were only a passing thought but smiled broadly as she sat up on the velvet seat of her silver swing, making the bells on its corners jingle loudly as though they too were as surprised and delighted as she.

'My lord, my sweetest husband, when did you plan this? A journey to my beautiful Varanasi!' she cried, quelling a sudden desire to cry.

'Well, my little rani, the truth is that people have for long tried to get me to go on pilgrimages to, not just Varanasi, but also Prayag and Puri. And I manage to make some excuse to escape them each time. My best excuse in recent years being that Varanasi is too full of my dear wife's relatives to be an attraction at all!' He laughed, his thin face covered in delight as Lakshmibai thumped a cushion gently on his back.

'You cannot fool me, Gangadhar-ji! You long to make pilgrimages to all these places, I know, and would be travelling to see beautiful goddesses all over the land if your health did not prevent you. But, Varanasi! And Saturday House!'

'It is most certainly true. Having married a daughter of Mother Ganga, it would appear that the goddess will spare me no longer. She came into my dreams last night, virtually commanding me to go. You will get your wish...I know how often you must have yearned to see your family and childhood friends again.'

A couple of cushions fell to the floor as Lakshmibai sprang to wrap her arms around Gangadhar's waist, squeezing him gently before resting her cheek lovingly on the silken back of his kurta. 'I cannot even imagine how wonderful it would be to see them all again. Baba and Peshwa-sahib and Nana–Tantia—they must be proper young men now...I wonder whether they now have great big coiled moustaches like all good Maratha men!'

Gangadhar smiled at her. 'You can bring your two brothers back here with you, if you like. I won't mind even if they have great big coiled moustaches, bigger than mine.'

Lakshmibai laughed delightedly. 'No thank you—they always drove me to distraction, those two, and will never let me get on with my various duties here. But, if Asharfi-bua is well enough to travel, perhaps we can bring her back. You'll adore her—especially as she makes the most delicious shrikhand in Varanasi.'

'Yes, the time is right to meet the bua you speak of so lovingly, my rani. We could send Khuda Baksh and some of the others up ahead to open up my house at Kashi. I last saw it as a child, imagine that! We would be quite comfortable there and you would not be too far from your beloved Saturday House.'

The sun and shade played with each other on the balcony, evening breezes carrying the scent of distant rain. Lakshmibai looked at the Jhansi plains stretching beyond the town walls, folding up into shallow brown hills to the east. Beyond them somewhere lay her homeland—the one she had wept to leave as a young bride and that, as Peshwa-sahib had predicted, she barely stopped to remember now. It was only at night, when the day's work was done and she lay alone on her bed, that thoughts of Saturday House would sometimes drift back to her. No longer with restless craving but with the same sort of unspoken and resigned acceptance she had brought to her mother's sudden absence when she had been a mere child.

Lakshmibai smiled gently at her husband. 'If we waited for the winter to set in, you would find it less fatiguing than travelling under the September sun. But I have to say, my dear husband, even though we may have a few months yet, I am going to write to my family and start preparations for our journey without delay. It's far too exciting to have to wait!'

'My sweetest rani,' Gangadhar said, turning to hold Lakshmibai's chin in his hand and tilting her face up to his, 'will you ever know how much joy it gives me to see you happy. How patient you have been with my ill-health, how brave and strong.' He laughed before releasing her face. 'But, before you start making arrangements for the trip, do not forget the preparations for the forthcoming Vijayadashami festival. I know it is one of your favourite celebrations. This year perhaps we will travel into Orchha district for it.'

'Do you know that the Jhansi style of celebrating it is unheard of in Varanasi? We will certainly observe Vijayadashami with special pomp this year. For me it will be a personal celebration too of the turn your health has taken for the better, my dear Gangadharji.'

But, a month later, Gangadhar was ill again. The Vijayadashami celebrations that involved the kings of Orchha, Datia and Jhansi riding across their respective borders in symbolic remembrance and forgiveness of past incursions, had proved too much for him. Sitting down with his guards and courtiers to a picnic banquet under the shade of Orchha trees, he had felt the cramps in his stomach grow and seize his body and soon he was convulsed in juddering pain. Lakshmibai called for the raja's carriage and cradled her husband's fevered head in her lap as they rushed back to the fort, sending one of the guards up ahead to fetch Dr Allen from the English camp. Whether Gangadhar liked it or not, she was going to have to administer English medicines. His illness, whatever it was, had raged too far ahead for the slow effects of his ayurvedic medications to suffice any more. As she wiped his brow with her sari, she could see that the spasm had returned to his face, freezing the left side of it into a distressed grimace. Bending down to put her mouth close to his ear, she muttered his favourite mantras, not knowing what else to say.

Even though she knew it was wrong and selfish of her to think of her own needs in the midst of her husband's anguish, some of the tears escaping her eyes as she bent over her husband were for her own loss. How she had been looking forward to the planned pilgrimage for Varanasi. It would not happen now, not if Gangadhar was going to suffer a relapse just as the winter months approached. It would also not be correct for her to go on her own, leaving a sick husband behind—her own father and Peshwa-sahib, and not to mention Asharfi-bua, would never forgive her such a misdemeanour. She would have no choice but to swallow her disappointment once more. As she looked out at the rocky landscape of Jhansi passing the window of the carriage, she wondered sadly if she would ever see her childhood home in this life again.

It was Lakshmibai's day to receive petitioners in the public durbar in the city palace, set up by Gangadhar, and increasingly popular ever since she had taken over five years ago. Although a light breeze blew occasionally through the open pillared hall, the summer heat was intense and Lakshmibai felt for those people who had been standing and waiting to speak to her all morning. Giving an order for the remaining people to sit down and for water to be distributed, she turned her attentions back to the farmer whose turn it was next.

Even as he approached her, his eyes started to brim over. Accustomed to having people approach her in various states of distress, Lakshmibai nodded kindly at the old man, waiting for him to speak. Trying to compose himself, he launched into a tearful diatribe, 'Rani-sahiba, my ancestors have tilled our few bighas of soil for as far back as anyone can remember. That land has been in our family for generations. What gives the British the right to take it away just like that?'

The old farmer was almost wailing as tears rolled down his fissured face, his hands folded in a gesture of supplication. Lakshmibai waited for his heaving sobs to subside before saying gently, 'The British sahibs have always had difficulty understanding our practices of ownership by farming and tenancy, accustomed as they are to having papers and deeds for everything. You do not have to worry about that as our local tax officials respect the recommendations made by this court. But that does not explain why you did not cultivate your land last year? The threat of confiscation is because you have not paid the taxes, is that not so?'

'Rani-sahiba, my wife had been ill, her treatment took up all my time and all my money. I did not think they would insist on the tax when I have not even been able to cultivate anything this season. I have had to sell my bullock, all my seed-corn and utensils just to survive. Where will the money for the tax come from? And I never thought they could take away my land like that.'

'How can you not know that!' Lakshmibai tried to control the impatience in her voice. How carefully she and Dewan Rao Bande had negotiated to remove the zamindari system in Jhansi, knowing that feudal landlords merely kept all the profits from farming for themselves. 'The system of ryotwari was brought in for farmers like you to be able to own their lands. All you had to do was grow your crops and pay taxes directly to the British collector, without the fear that some middleman maybe siphoning away the fruits of your labour. But how can I protect you if you have failed to do that?'

'Forgive me, but the taxes the angrez have set are so high, Rani-sahiba. Despite all my efforts, sometimes I grow enough to only be able to pay the taxes, with nothing left for myself and my family. And, failure to pay tax, even for just one year, can lead to arrest and their taking away my lands?'

The farmer was growing distraught again and Lakshmibai stayed silent. She had genuinely believed that the system put in place by Major Ellis had been a better one for her people, far better than leaving them at the mercy of the zamindars. And had agreed then that there ought to be some sanction against non-payment of taxes. Confiscation and arrest was punitive but the British needed their taxes, to recoup the cost of administration and, of course, to cover the cost of their growing army, even though Ellis never stated that openly.

'What use is my land to them anyway, Rani-sahiba? Will they come and cultivate it themselves?'

This time it was the prime minister, Dewan Rao Bande, who replied, 'They rent such tracts of land to tenant farmers from whom they get even better revenue than by the normal system of taxation. It is, in the end, no different to zamindari...'

The man started to weep helplessly, his shoulders shaking in his thin muslin shirt. Lakshmibai, knowing she would later have cause to regret it, gestured to her prime minister that he was to give the farmer the amount he needed out of her own personal funds. Charity was not beneficial in the long run but, sometimes, there was no other recourse.

By the time the small crowd of supplicants had left the rani's durbar, it was well past midday but the farmer was still on Lakshmibai's mind when she turned to the grey-haired Dewan Rao Bande. He had proven his worth as a trusted minister for many years but, as Jhansi's newly appointed prime minister, the queen had come to rely increasingly on his quiet wisdom.

'Dewan-ji, have we done wrong with this revenue system? We try to bend policy and luckily we have a sympathetic ear in Major Ellis, although I suspect that his powers are quite limited too when he is up against some distant British official sitting in the government offices at Calcutta. Those are the people making all these decisions, not the officers here, like Major Ellis, who are themselves helpless in the face of their superiors.'

'Rani-sahiba, we know that this Company's main source of wealth has now become Hindustan. Ever since their wretched India Act imposed free-trade doctrines on the East India Company, it has had to relinquish its commercial monopolies. So how else can they raise money but through taxation of our peasants?'

'The system itself is not a bad one but what does make it seem heartless is that some people sitting in a distant Parliament make those decisions. What can they know of our tribulations here? In such cases, expediency will always overrule compassion, do you not think?'

'I agree, Rani-sahiba. How the British imagine it possible to make decisions on behalf of a people without once even looking into their faces is beyond me.'

Lakshmibai got up from her throne. 'Well, that poor farmer's face will certainly not leave my mind for the rest of the day and that is the curse of the ruler who knows her subjects as people. But,' she added, turning to face dewan-ji, 'at least I have the consolation that I can try to help those who remain in need of special assistance, weighing up individual circumstances where necessary.'

Dewan Rao Bande followed Lakshmibai to the door. 'And that, Rani-sahiba, is *exactly* where British policy fails our people. They may well be successful at maintaining order but when they look at India, all they see are their own opportunities that lie within it. Where is the room then for individual circumstances? The rani is right to consider charity to that old farmer. A law can never be all-encompassing and, where it fails, to continue to seek answers in that body of law is both foolish and cruel. That is when the monarch is called upon to act with grace and compassion. It was a British poet who once said that a monarch's acts of mercy become him better than his crown.'

The guards stepped aside as they started to walk out of the pillared hall together and Lakshmibai nodded at them before speaking again. 'Dewan-ji, I hear that in Awadh there is a radical reformation of the revenue collection system going on. Is it something we can adopt for our Jhansi?'

Waiting until they had walked down a few steps, dewan-ji replied thoughtfully, 'This is a method that the British appear to have picked up from their experiences in the provinces of the north-west frontier, Rani-sahiba, whereby their officers deal directly with the cultivators, not so unlike our own ryotwari system. The difference is that in Awadh, the system of zamindari and taluqdari has been far more established than ours and goes back many generations. This new system is, in fact, turning all the erstwhile taluqdars against the British whom they see as bullies, meddling in a system that had worked well for them for as far back as anyone can remember. The taluqdars are powerful people with tentacles spreading deep into the land. If I were the British Collector in Awadh, I would be very fearful of what people are saying there.'

Lakshmibai emitted a short laugh as they reached the gates to her palace. 'Fearful? Do the British even know the meaning of the word, Dewan-ji? A people so confident of being born to rule, they cannot even comprehend that anyone might be unhappy to be ruled by them.'

'Oh I agree absolutely, Rani-sahiba. Why, even in their own country their aristocracy seem so sanguine about their place in society, not concerned at all by the revolutionary spirit sweeping across Europe. Does one call that confidence or self-assuredness or just arrogance?' The old prime minister shook his grey head ruefully. 'Some of their own poor are trying to gain more rights; we read about the Chartist movement in the *Times* newspaper, if you remember, Rani-sahiba. But, how cleverly those nobles keep their population subdued, so contented with age-old imbalances. I cannot say I understand at all how the English people remain so accepting, so magnanimous in the face of such iniquities.'

Lakshmibai nodded and sighed. 'How can we then wonder, Dewan-ji, that they come to our lands and, finding a people so compliant and so timid, seem not to know the word "fear" at all.'

But fear was exactly what Major Ellis felt when, in the unseasonably harsh winter of 1848, word arrived that Lord Dalhousie had landed in

Calcutta to become India's thirteenth Governor-General. At thirty-five, he was the youngest man appointed to the post and his mettle had already been proven as president of the Board of Trade in Sir Robert Peel's government. Ellis had no doubt that the man had been carefully picked for his staunch belief in the benefits of Utilitarianism. Certainly his reputation for being an imperious and impatient young workaholic had preceded his arrival at Government House. Even though Ellis knew that news from Calcutta reached Jhansi's court well before his own announcements, he rode out one chilly January morning to bear the news officially to the palace.

As the purdah bearers were summoned, Lakshmibai watched Ellis climb up the stairs to the durbar hall, knowing already from Dewan Rao Bande's source in Calcutta what he was here to say. Through the carved ivory purdah, she saw that his gait was measured and, as he neared, that the drowsy grey of his eyes seemed shaded with unhappiness. Gangadhar had roused himself for the political agent's visit although, increasingly, his appearances in the durbar were now restricted only to special occasions or for Ellis's rare visits.

It had not escaped Lakshmibai's notice too that Ellis had adopted a more guarded approach in recent months. His reserve today was in stark contrast to the cheery announcements he had made about Lord Ellenborough's and Hardinge's appointments a few years ago, and she could not help a sudden feeling of foreboding as he withdrew into a chilly silence while she persisted with questions about the new Governor-General. Lakshmibai could not tell if Ellis had merely grown more cautious with the passage of the years or whether he was on orders from his superiors in Calcutta to withdraw his friendship from Jhansi's court. But, apart from telling them that the new Governor-General was young, enthused by what he called 'Utilitarian principles' and fired with genuine conviction in the benefits that both India and Britain could have in his appointment, Ellis simply would not be pressed for a more personal opinion.

'I have never met Lord Dalhousie, Rani-sahiba,' he said finally, signalling politely that Lakshmibai's insistence would not force him to reveal more, adding politely a few seconds later, 'but I have absolutely no doubt in our new Governor-General's capabilities, Rani-sahiba. He will waste no time in coming to grips with the challenges of his new task here.'

Lakshmibai was frustrated by Ellis's reticence but resolved to find out more about Dalhousie by using Dewan Rao Bande's contacts with other princely states.

She did not have long to wait—a mere three months after

Dalhousie's arrival in India, there were rumblings of trouble again in the Punjab. The news had been brought to Jhansi by a travelling drama troupe that had been invited to stay in the artiste's quarters for a few days. Though the openly stated reason was that they were present for the entertainment of Jhansi's convalescing raja, Lakshmibai knew that travellers like them were an invaluable source of information on events taking place in distant parts of the country.

In the baradari that night, courtiers and merchants gathered for the performance as the Punjabi actors satirized the recent story of the Dewan Mulraj of Multan who, pressurized by the British at Lahore to pay one million pound sterling as a price for holding office, had resisted and been summarily dismissed from his post. As the jester playing the role of the British Resident, Frederick Currie, appeared onstage, his face covered in rice powder and his voice taking on a strange English accent, the entire court at Jhansi fell about in merriment. Delighted to hear Gangadhar laugh out loud next to her, Lakshmibai watched the actor ham up the role of a confused and terrified Englishman searching for a friendly native prince to replace the old dewan. There was another burst of hilarity as a jester suggested they travel as far as Jhansi where a certain Raja Gangadhar was sure to make a suitable candidate and Lakshmibai joined in the applause as Gangadhar raised himself on his cushions to make a gracious bow towards the stage.

The play proceeded with another prince found but, as the character was shown being escorted to Lahore by two young English officers, all three were set upon by Mulraj's irate men and killed. This too was represented in comic fashion, with enormous swords being wielded and loud exaggerated cries emanating from the assassinated Englishmen. Lakshmibai saw that the audience was still laughing, their faces shining happily in the light of the lanterns and felt a sudden chill envelop her. Was no one stopping to think that these events were not fictitious but actually taking place in another state? Suddenly the Punjab seemed very near. If such things could happen there, surely they were possible in Jhansi too?

Later, questioning the actors, Lakshmibai found them unclear on the details of what may have happened after the two English officers had been murdered since the troupe had left the Punjab soon after the event. But one of the actors thought that Lord Dalhousie was now seeking an alliance with the governor of Hazara instead of the dewan of Multan and Lakshmibai deduced that the British were determined to control Punjab, despite the setbacks suffered so far.

As more news trickled in over the following few weeks,

Lakshmibai heard that the governor of Hazara too had defected to Multan's side, having seen the depth of anti-British sentiment among both their peoples. She wondered whether the new Governor-General was surprised when the people of Multan finally rose in revolt against British rule, mere months within his arrival in India.

When word went around that Dalhousie was initially doing nothing to control the insurgency, Dewan Rao Bande's theory was that it was because of the fierceness of the summers in the north-west. 'The British are too canny to have their troops try to take on soldiers far hardier than theirs and more accustomed to the heat,' he said to Lakshmibai.

But she was doubtful. 'That does not fit in with everything else we hear about him, Dewan-ji,' she said. 'I think the delay in action is because Dalhousie may have a bigger prize in his sights. From all we hear, he is not just a careful man but also fiercely ambitious on behalf of British interests. He must think he can safely ignore these minor revolts and the animosity of unimportant, small-time nobles. Those are only small irritations to a man like him who will use them to lead to what he really wants. I think what he needs is for this to grow into a full-scale war. Only then will he be able to justify total and final control of all Punjab. Surely he cannot fail to desire the riches of that state?'

Lakshmibai's prime minister was astonished at the sagacity of his young queen when events over the next few weeks proved her hunch to be absolutely right. It was only when the Sikhs moved in on Peshawar and formed an alliance with the Afghans, still puffed up from their rout of the British in Kabul, that Dalhousie made it obvious that he would wait no more.

He made his announcement at a private ball for senior British officers holidaying in the rarefied cool climes of Simla and, by the time Dalhousie had descended from the hills, British troops were already lined up and waiting on the borders of the Punjab plains. The order to march was given and the Second Anglo-Sikh War was underway. It already looked set to be bigger both in scale and in outcome than the first war and everyone waited for events to unfold, some with excitement and a few others, like Major Ellis, with a terrible apprehension.

It was with immense regret that Ellis heard, weeks later, that more than three thousand Company soldiers, both European and Hindustani, had lost their lives fighting the Sikhs in Chillianwala on the banks of the Jhelum. He knew that casualties among the Sikhs would have been even higher and it was with trepidation that he made enquiries about the fortunes of the royal family of Punjab, knowing that the raja and rani of Jhansi would query him specifically on that. From reading between the lines of accounts in the papers, it was all too clear that the token ruler of the state, Maharaja Duleep Singh, only ten years old, and his mother, Rani Jindan, had not needed much persuasion after the war to sign the Treaty of Lahore. Ellis marvelled that it could not have been easier for Dalhousie than if he had carefully planned every inch of the campaign. The annexation order was drawn up at Government House even before war ended and, in the spring of 1849, Dalhousie rode triumphantly into Lahore to claim for himself the wealth and the prestige of the Punjab.

Soon afterwards, Ellis heard of the various 'prizes' that were being claimed by the British according to the Treaty of Lahore. Chief amongst these was the Koh-i-Noor diamond, large as a turtle's egg, that had been in the possession of Maharaja Ranjit Singh for years. No one knew for certain its origins, although those who had read the ancient *Baburnama*, swore that it was the gem described in that text as 'mountain of light', with a value equivalent to 'two and a half days' food for the entire world'. Ellis had read the *Baburnama* in his Fort William days and knew too of the legend of the Koh-i-Noor that stated that its owner would either face imminent extinction or rule over the world. He remembered this with a shiver, a year after Lahore had been taken, when word went around that Lord Dalhousie had derived great pleasure in delivering the great Koh-i-Noor personally to Queen Victoria at her palace in London.

14

Rani Lakshmibai paced around her chambers, feeling the knot in her stomach tighten further. The news about Punjab's hapless royal family had been bad enough and she could now feel her anger multiply with this letter just arrived from her old childhood friend, Nana. He had addressed it to Rani Lakshmibai of Jhansi, making her wonder for a moment if he too, like everyone else, had forgotten her old pet name of Mani. But, reading through to the end of the letter, she noticed that, despite the elaborate seal, he had signed the letter simply 'Nana'. As a boy, he had insisted on using the full title he had always assumed would be his and Lakshmibai found it rather sad that he had stopped doing so, now that it mattered more than ever before. His childish rounded handwriting had not changed much, however, and she felt herself suddenly melt with old affections.

The letter bore Peshwa-sahib's address of Bithur near Kanpur, the idyllic life they had all spent together at Saturday House having come to an abrupt end soon after her own departure from it. Poor frail Peshwa-sahib, never entirely giving up hope of regaining his Pune kingdom, had moved his court to Bithur further up the Ganga some years before and Moropant's letters had indicated that Peshwa-sahib believed his chances of rebuilding his damaged relationship with the British would be better there. It was certainly true that not much was ever likely to happen in the quiet, holy town of Varanasi, whereas the thrusting new commercial energies of Kanpur, with its big British garrison, busy factories and splendid mansions, held much better scope for developing the associations and connections needed to ensure Nana's future as the next Peshwa.

Now, from Nana's letter, Lakshmibai gathered that her beloved old Peshwa-sahib was ill and possibly even dying. Keen to get some kind of reassurance from the local British Resident regarding the future of his son before he died, Peshwa-sahib had, according to Nana, apparently been granted reluctant audience only to be peremptorily informed that automatic succession of his title could not be guaranteed. The main sticking point was that Nana was not Peshwa-sahib's real son but merely adopted. Her chest heaving from suppressed indignation, Lakshmibai read the paragraph again...

> *Rani Lakshmibai, you know how beloved my father is to me and I to him. Never once has the word 'adopted' ever escaped his lips and never once has he given me any less love and affection than I would have received had I been his natural son. That these people can now attempt to demean that bond is beyond belief. Do they not know of the sorrow of childlessness, do they not see the honour of an adopted son, have they no heart?*

Lakshmibai turned to Sundar who was busy refilling the oil lamps at one corner of the room. Her voice was bleak, 'My dear brother is in trouble, Sundar, and I must think of some help to offer.'

'Trouble, Rani-sahiba?' Sundar, wearing a worried expression, walked across the chamber as she wiped her hands on a rag.

'Trouble with their British Resident in Kanpur who is questioning Nanasahib's rights as an adopted son. My poor Peshwa-sahib has never been blessed with the kind of support from his Resident that we are lucky to receive from our Major Ellis.'

Lakshmibai looked out of the window, remembering not just the relationship she had personally witnessed between Peshwa-sahib and

Nana but also the love and generosity that had been showered on her in the years she had spent with them.

'I have told you haven't I, Sundar, of how Peshwa-sahib always treated me as though I were his daughter? Indulging my every wish alongside that of Nana's. Can these British really not understand that such affection does not necessarily spring from ties of blood?'

But, even as she asked the question, Lakshmibai knew that it was not really the state of Peshwa-sahib's relationship with his son, adopted or otherwise, that was at stake. She looked at Sundar, speaking more to herself than to her maid, 'What the British have to do is reduce Nana to a nobody. So that they can curtail the pension they have been giving Peshwa-sahib's family ever since they took over his kingdom.'

'Is it possible for someone to be refused a birthright merely because he is adopted? Adopted children are one's own, are they not, Rani-sahiba?'

'Oh it is only an excuse being employed by the British, Sundar. And happening everywhere. If not outright war, as in the Punjab, the Company is either questioning the adoptions of heirs by rulers or throwing paternity into doubt or sometimes even, most insultingly of all, just stating that certain rulers do not have the capacity to rule. Anything that will provide an excuse for them to take over lands and titles.'

Lakshmibai was sure that Nana knew of these ulterior motives but she understood that the slur on his filial ties with the Peshwa-sahib probably hurt just as much as the potential for losing his pension and the final hope, however remote, of regaining his father's title.

'That is what makes me so angry, Sundar,' Lakshmibai continued, 'not the Company's greed for expansion. That has always been there. But the unfeeling carelessness of the methods they employ sometimes. I do not know which it is: that the British imagine Hindustani nobles are too artless to recognize what is being done to them or that they are so indifferent they will not even pretend they cared.'

'Perhaps our Raja-sahib will be able to put in a word with Major Ellis? He is, as you say, a fair-minded man who respects our ways and he might be able to take up the case with his counterpart in Kanpur?'

Lakshmibai smiled gently at Sundar's optimism. She did not want to voice her feelings before her maid any more than necessary but she knew that there would be little point in asking Gangadhar whether he would help Nana. She could almost hear his plaintive voice, 'Lakshmibai, we should not burden Major Ellis with these things. It is the prerogative of those Company officers who administer

Kanpur to make such decisions. Why, even we merely depend on the goodwill of Major Ellis and the achievements of our ancestors. It is imperative that we stay on the right side of the British. What is the point of fighting other people's battles?'

'We will have to see what we can do, Sundar,' Lakshmibai said, sitting down at her desk to compose a reply to Nana. Choosing a sheet of paper, she turned away from her maid, 'There is no point agitating Raja Gangadhar with further bad news, Sundar. He needs his rest. By the way, has his new batch of medication arrived from Gwalior yet?'

After the serious attack of blood dysentery that Gangadhar had suffered a few months back, he had been falling ill with alarming frequency of late and news of British annexations invariably filled him with dread and anxiety. Lakshmibai, unable to sleep one night, had found Gangadhar wandering around the palace gardens, muttering and fretting, his eyes wide open but glazed with sleep. It was fortunate that she had been standing on the balcony of Panch Mahal, in an attempt to escape the heat of her cloistered chambers. Spotting a white-cloaked figure moving around in the gardens below and recognizing Gangadhar's frail form straightaway, she had rushed downstairs with Sundar and Kashi to return him to the safety of the palace. They had gently coaxed him back to his room, trying not to cause a commotion for fear that word would spread of all not being well with the raja. That sort of information would be far too opportune for the Krishna Rao faction in court.

Taking him back into his room and laying out his thin body on the vastness of the carved silver bed, Lakshmibai could not help wondering, as she only sometimes allowed herself to do, at the ironies of the state of her marriage. Despite her occasional exasperation with Gangadhar, she still grieved at the nameless torments suffered by her gentle husband, and yet it appeared that she was powerless to soothe him.

She determined to stay by his side. She did not need to seek anyone's permission—it was her duty as his wife to ensure he did not wander out again. Requesting Sundar and Kashi to sleep outside the bedchamber and to chastise Faiz Ali severely for having allowed his attention to lapse, she lay down next to her husband, keeping a basin of rosewater at hand to sprinkle periodically on his burning forehead.

That same night, while the rest of the palace slept, Lakshmibai finally consummated her marriage to Gangadhar. It was eight whole years after their wedding ceremony at the Ganesh temple. She had been just thirteen then and could barely remember the frightened ingénue she must have seemed in her heavy wedding lehnga and kilos of bridal jewellery. Now she was three weeks short of her twenty-first birthday, not a child any more in any aspect of her life. Old enough to know what made people behave the way they did, mature enough to understand the ways of the world. As she later disengaged herself from her husband's supine body, she turned her back on him, curling herself up tightly and wrapping her arms around her shoulders to keep away the sudden chill. She squeezed her eyes shut, trying to keep her despair at bay, but finally, witnessed only by the tranquil moonlight pouring ceaselessly through an open window, she wept for the very first time at the loneliness of her married life.

It was her husband's increasing frailty that finally gave Lakshmibai reason to move into his wing of the palace, as she had always wanted. Though she occasionally regretted that it had taken his growing illness and dependency to bring about the life she had craved, there was solace in the knowledge that she finally had the semblance of the marriage and the life she had always hoped to have. The public assemblies kept her busier than ever and, increasingly, it was incumbent on her to receive Major Ellis in the absence of her husband in order to discuss matters of state. During these meetings, she maintained the court etiquette of purdah, delivering her views in a soft but firm voice from behind the ivory screen, even though Major Ellis seldom gave her cause for complaint.

But, more than anything else, what brought her pleasure was the new togetherness she finally enjoyed with her husband. It became her wont in those days to make straight for Gangadhar's chambers every evening, to tell him of the day's events as she sat on his bed, folding up squares of fragrant paan or playing chess. She made her ailing husband laugh by narrating some of the lighter moments of the day, even though it later gave her a stab of pain to imagine that she had never been more contented than in those last months of Gangadhar's life.

Those months passed swiftly for Major Ellis too and his visits to the court were leaving him more and more impressed with Jhansi's young queen who, it was clear, was quite ably ruling the state in lieu of her husband. As another monsoon came to a close, healing previously parched fields and refilling dried riverbeds, there were two further reasons for celebrations in the city of Jhansi. It was Diwali, the night that commemorated the return of Lord Ram from exile and also signified the start of the cooler winter months. And the raja and rani of Jhansi had chosen that holy day to make an announcement by special decree and with much fanfare. Rani Lakshmibai was pregnant with child.

The people of Jhansi were in jubilant mood and sweets and clothes were being distributed all across the city from specially constructed stalls. Raja Gangadhar had even sent two separate cartloads of sweet laddoos and jalebis to the 12th Bengal Native Infantry and even the 13th Irregular Cavalry army garrisons six miles away, so great was his joy.

When Major Ellis visited the town that evening, he saw people thronging to the Mahalakshmi temple to thank their goddess for peace and prosperity and wondered if they heard any of the news of war and uprisings that trickled through to his office from distant states. It was clear that they did not wish to remember their rani's frequent warnings that the Jhansi treasury was in a sadly depleted state, nor that they had to pay their taxes whether the harvest had been good or not, nor even all that talk of their raja gradually losing his mind.

As evening fell, the fort and the city came to life as never before. Every available niche in the walls of houses held candles or oil lamps; parapets and balconies and window ledges lined with tiny flickering flames. Lake Lachhmitaal that stretched across the northern part of the city, looked like a sea of light, covered as it was with hundreds of floating diyas, each carrying somebody's wish for something. Men and women, clad in their new clothes, came out onto the streets to help their children light the firecrackers and sparklers bought from the bazaar. The palace had ordered a special fireworks display in the gardens outside the Ganesh temple and people had been gathering from early evening in anticipation of this special event. As night fell and enormous fountains of fire whooshed up in the air, a series of explosions in bright hot colours lit up the night sky, causing cries of delight and wonder to rise from the crowd.

Ellis would have been quite content to celebrate this wonderful festival with the people of Jhansi—some of whom he had come to know like personal friends over the years—but it would have been considered odd, both by them and by his own people in the cantonment, the times having created all these new barriers. And so, having paid his respects at the court, he called for his horse and rode slowly back to his house.

Lakshmibai insisted on coming out to watch the fireworks, despite protestations by Sundar and Kashi that she ought to be resting and staying away from the public gaze. As she stepped out onto the ramparts above the main entrance to the fort, people craned their necks to see if her pregnancy was visible and a sigh went up from the crowds amassed below as they saw their young queen resplendent in a gold-edged ochre sari, her swelling belly signifying a whole new era for Jhansi.

Raja Gangadhar too stepped out for a few minutes onto the ramparts and together the royal couple waved to their delighted people crowding the slopes of the hillocks, by now euphoric to see for themselves that rumours of the raja's illness were completely untrue.

To Lakshmibai, looking down at the city bathed in the light of sparklers and oil lamps, it felt like the happiest moment of her life. Even as a child, she had no memory of ever being so satisfied, so filled with a feeling of being blessed.

Most encouragingly of all, Gangadhar's condition seemed to have improved in the past few weeks. The last major breakdown had been over a year ago, when they had heard of Dalhousie's annexation of Satara, the old heartland of the great Maratha kingdom. Lakshmibai knew that Satara, ruled by Shivaji's successors since the seventeenth century, had always been beloved to Maratha kings as a symbol of their resistance to Mughal powers. But Governor-General Dalhousie had, in his very first year, decided to annexe it, using some pretext so thin that Lakshmibai could not even remember it now. That business had led to Gangadhar's tremors and the night sweats again but Lakshmibai had seen him through all that, spending sleepless nights tending him back to health.

Standing on the balcony, Gangadhar took Lakshmibai's arm and they both smiled at the roar of appreciation from the crowd below. 'It is for you they cheer, my rani,' he said softly, 'they know, like I do, that I hold so painfully onto my kingship only because I am able to unburden so many of my duties onto you.'

'Jhansi is my duty too, Raja-sahib,' she replied, 'and certainly not a burden.'

'And soon there will be a prince to help you share it, yes?' Gangadhar grinned his lopsided smile.

Lakshmibai's face was radiant in the glow from the bonfires and Gangadhar, moved by her beauty, added more sombrely, 'Never has an heir to our throne been more important, Lakshmibai. Never.'

She nodded, looking down at the people milling below the fort's ramparts. 'It is certainly wise to be circumspect about British intentions, Raja-sahib. And Krishna-bhai's machinations make me fearful too. I cannot honestly say which outweighs the other in my mind right now.'

'Ah yes, I saw the look that passed over Krishna-bhai's countenance when news of your pregnancy was announced to the court. Like a cloud passing over the winter sun, almost imperceptible at first. But I felt the sudden chill in the air, Rani-sahiba, there was no mistaking it. Even though poor Krishna-bhai gathered his composure soon enough to add his tributes to those of the other ministers.'

Lakshmibai shivered as she pulled her sari pallav around her shoulders. Perhaps she ought not to expose herself to the evening air any more. They bowed again to their people, folding their hands together in deep namastes, before Lakshmibai instructed Faiz Ali to assist the raja in leaving the balcony. Following him indoors, she waited while Faiz Ali settled her husband back into his chair, noticing how the small amount of exertion had caused Gangadhar's face to look drawn and ashen again. His eyes were closed as though in pain but he opened them to give her a look that made her stomach constrict in alarm. How quickly the celebratory air of the evening had turned into something full of unease.

'My dear Lakshmibai,' Gangadhar said, his voice almost a whisper, 'I give you my word that neither you nor our child will ever lose Jhansi if anything happens to me. My word.'

Three months later, news arrived to convince Lakshmibai that her foreboding on Diwali night had not been unfounded.

'Baji Peshwa Rao is dead, my beloved Peshwa-sahib is dead...' Lakshmibai cried, running into Gangadhar's rooms, tears streaming down her face. Normally, she saw it as her duty to shield him from all bad news but this sorrow was too much to bear and it was one of those rare occasions when she needed her husband's succour. Gangadhar knew that the Peshwa-sahib had been like a second father to Lakshmibai in her childhood and that she had loved him as dearly as Moropant, writing letters to both men with equal regularity every month. He reached out his arms and she clung to him, her body racked with sobs.

'My Rani...you must be careful, in your condition...these tears...'

But she was inconsolable and Gangadhar called out for Sundar and Kashi who took her back to her chambers where her face and body were massaged and wiped with towels soaked in aloe juice. The two women wound down the khus mats over the windows, urging the rani to sleep but, after a mere five minutes on her bed, she had sprung up again.

'Sundar, I cannot rest until I have written to Nana and to my baba, who must also be grieving the loss of his oldest friend.'

'Rani-sahiba, the rider from Bithur will wait until you are ready to send your reply. There is no rush.'

'Yes, but Nana's letter says that, once his father's last rites had been performed, there are matters of secrecy and urgency that he needs to discuss face to face. I cannot delay an invitation to Jhansi.'

'Oh my rani-sahiba, I will call the court writer now but you must promise that you will take some rest after that.'

'I do not need the writer, just bring me my portable bureau, Sundar,' Lakshmibai said, already composing in her mind the words with which she would express her condolences. 'I need to let Nanasahib know that, as my brother, he is welcome to not just visit but stay at Jhansi for as long as he needs.'

Despite the heat of the morning, Lakshmibai insisted on walking out to the gates of the fort in order to greet the old friend she had not seen for nearly nine years. As Nanasahib's carriage pulled up at Khanderao Darwaza, he could not contain his delight, tumbling out of its doors before it had come to a proper halt and throwing his guards into consternation. He hugged Lakshmibai as tears streamed down his plump face. Lakshmibai wept too, remembering how casually she had seen Nana off from Jhansi as a thirteen-year-old bride, not considering at all that so many years would pass before she saw him again. She recalled with sorrow her last glimpse of Peshwa-sahib, who had looked so anxiously at her through the carriage window as she had departed Saturday House for Jhansi. Never once imagining they would never see each other again.

Gangadhar was waiting inside Panch Mahal to extend his own welcome and, as the carriages rolled into the portico, he made a huge effort to walk down the few steps of the palace. Greeting the younger man with folded hands, he said, 'Jhansi welcomes its rani's brother, though with immense sorrow at the passing of our beloved Peshwa-sahib.' As Nanasahib acknowledged him with a deep bow, he added, 'Rani Lakshmibai's desire to see her family in all these years must never be in doubt. It is my ill health that is to blame. That and matters of state have consumed all her energies these many years. But now I am pleased, my brother, that you have so kindly given me the opportunity to apologize in person for such a grave omission in my duties.'

Nanasahib responded with his own request for forgiveness.

'Despite the presence of such a loving sister and brother here in Jhansi, it had sadly not been possible for me to visit this beautiful city and palace, mainly because of my own father's health and our preoccupations about the succession. But there is time for all that later and I feel we have put you to enough strain already, Raja Gangadhar-ji.'

Nana watched as Lakshmibai and a guard steered Gangadhar up the stairs and onto a chair in the hall, arranging his limbs into a seated position. Although he had heard of the raja of Jhansi's illness, it was still shocking to see for himself how like a ghoul the old man looked, particularly next to Lakshmibai who had blossomed into a glowing and serene beauty. He watched her minister to her husband, smiling at his decrepit figure without any trace of revulsion, before turning her attention back to him. How had it come to be that petulant, hot-headed little Mani had grown so gracious?

Lakshmibai seemed overcome with emotion at Nana's presence in Jhansi, trying to hold back her tears as she sat down before him. Finally gathering her emotions, she said, 'Imagine, Nana, apart from Baba's one visit many moons ago, this is the first time I have had a family member come to my home. But, before anything else, you must tell me about my beloved Peshwa-sahib. Please tell me he was at peace in his final days and suffered no pain.'

'Oh, I wish I could, Mani, but it would be false to claim that Baba died anything but a broken man. By taking over the case for my succession, I had hoped to relieve him of his never-ending struggle. Even our move to Bithur was calculated to achieve that. But every disappointment, every setback only seemed to worsen his burden. He knew, even as his soul departed us, that he was taking the title of Peshwa with him. Dalhousie was like a wall of stone on that matter.'

'We will talk of that later, Nana. You must now tell me what news you have of my father and my dearest Asharfi-bua in Varanasi.'

From the expression on Lakshmibai's face, Nana guessed that his disputed succession was a subject she did not wish to discuss in her husband's presence. Although he was not sure why, he dutifully answered her questions about Moropant and Asharfi-bua, adding, 'And that other brother of yours will arrive here tomorrow too.'

He saw Lakshmibai's eyes widen with renewed pleasure as she said, '*Tantia* is coming to Jhansi too?'

Nana nodded, pleased to behold her joy, but suddenly he felt conscious that their fervent conversation could be tiring Raja Gangadhar. He turned to Raja Gangadhar and said light-heartedly, 'Perhaps we should reserve all further conversation for when Tantia is here or we will end up having to repeat everything for his benefit, Raja-sahib. That means saying everything at least three times over for poor Tantia can only grasp matters when they have been repeated very slowly a few times.' As they all laughed, Nana said to Gangadhar, his eyes twinkling, 'Perhaps my sister has told you about Tantia's slightly limited intellectual abilities but you can assess them for yourself when he arrives tomorrow, Raja-sahib. It is always best to be forewarned to prevent the shock.'

Lakshmibai turned to Sundar. 'Have the quarters at Motibagh palace been made ready to receive our honoured guests, Sundar? Send Khuda Baksh with Nanasahib's retainers to show them where everything is.'

After Nana had begged leave to refresh himself after the long journey, Lakshmibai warned, 'I will come and visit you in Motibagh once you have settled in. Do you know it is newly constructed and that you are to be its first occupants? It could not give me more pleasure to think that the first people to occupy it are my own family members and I will have to come to personally supervise your comforts.'

Nana made his way from the palace to Motibagh in his carriage, followed by an entourage. He wondered, as they drove through Jhansi's crowded streets, if it had been inconsiderate of him to turn up with such high hopes that Lakshmibai would be able to help with his problems. She obviously had her hands full with a husband so sick. But Jhansi was still independent and, to Lakshmibai's credit, had remained on the right side of the British so far.

As his carriage pulled into the porch of an elegant new haveli, Nana could see construction in progress on its far side. Stepping out and surveying the sprawling new complex with one hand shielding his eyes from the sun, he nodded as the groom explained that it was the new palace being built by the rani so that she could move out of Panch Mahal inside the fort in order to be closer to the public assembly halls. It was gratifying to see Lakshmibai's efficacy as a ruler and Jhansi's ongoing prosperity for himself. Yes, his little sister Mani was exactly the kind of ally he needed at this time.

The following day, Nana watched Lakshmibai's unbounded joy as she threw herself into the newly arrived Tantia's arms. Being closer in age, she had always held a special fondness for the younger boy and Nana remembered with amusement the way in which the two of them had sometimes united against him during their childhood squabbles.

'Tantia, my little brother,' Lakshmibai said, finally pulling away from him and wiping away her tears of joy.

Tantia was indignant. 'Little?' he queried as they all laughed, looking up at his strapping frame. 'I am neither littler than you in size, nor in age, my dear Mani, in case you've forgotten!'

'Perhaps only in intellect, then,' Lakshmibai shot back, earning a loud laugh from Nana.

Observing the affectionate banter, Nana felt moved to see the ease with which they had all three slipped back into the camaraderie of their childhood days, memories of Saturday House and their schoolroom coming flooding back to his weary mind, like balm on a wound.

Lakshmibai's attentions were now turned to him. 'Please tell me, Nana, if my Motibagh met all your needs last night. As you know, it is brand new and its comforts have not been tested yet.'

Nana put his arm around her shoulder. 'There can only be one place more wonderful than this beautiful mansion and that, as you know Mani, is our Saturday House.'

Through his laughing tone, Lakshmibai discerned the sorrow in his voice at those words and her own face grew serious as she said, 'I have to leave you, my brothers, to attend to my duties for the day but we will talk of old times and shed a few tears for Saturday House and for my dear Peshwa-sahib when I return from my durbar in the evening.'

It was only later that evening, as the night deepened and the old friends' conversation grew solemn, that Nana was finally able to tell Lakshmibai about his recent troubles. Recalling the last painful days of his father's life, Nana described how Lord Dalhousie had promptly terminated the last of his inherited rights on the very day of the Peshwa's death.

'As an adopted son, I am only allowed to lay claim to some of my father's personal effects and property, Mani. The title of "Peshwa" and the pension that has accompanied it so far have already been withdrawn,' he said, his voice breaking as he spoke.

'Is there no recourse, Nana?' Lakshmibai asked. 'Is it not worth trying to lodge an appeal with Calcutta, or even London? Perhaps I can help you find someone who may make a good emissary.'

'I have the best emissary, Mani. A man called Azimullah who could not have better credentials to deal with the British. He is the cleverest man I know, speaks English better than an Englishman and—'

'And loathes Englishmen more than anyone else in the world!' Tantia laughed.

'What is the reason for such a loathing?' Lakshmibai asked.

'He does not talk of it very much,' Nana replied, 'only told me once that he was born to an impoverished Muslim family in Peshawar and had seen a beloved younger sister starve to death in the famine of 1837. That same year, unable to pay the punitive taxes being demanded by the local British collector, his father too killed himself and it had apparently fallen upon Azimullah, who was only a boy then, to untie his father's emaciated body that was found hanging from the branches of the shethooth tree just yards from their backdoor. I have never seen such bitterness on a man's face as when Azimullah recounted that incident to me. He said the collector had ridden up to see what the commotion was about but Azimullah, looking up from where he was squatting by his father's body, said he could only see the brightness with which the English official's brass buttons shone and the gleaming polish on his shoes and bridle. According to him, he had felt a yawning hole inside his stomach fill up with a churning, gushing rage. It would appear that he has carried that hatred within him ever since.'

'There's more to his story. I once got it out of him,' Tantia chipped in eagerly. 'Azimullah said that, to escape the famine, he and his mother and sister travelled many days on foot, eventually fetching up in Kanpur as starving refugees. They were taken in by a local Christian missionary and Azimullah helped in the kitchens of the orphanage to earn a place in the Free School. Seeing the boy's aptitude for learning, the Reverend had offered to help pay for further education but—yes, only if he converted to Christianity. Typical Christian kindness!'

'But that is the way it always is, Tantia. Even our missionary school here in Jhansi converts its children before taking them in. It is a small price to pay for being fed and educated, I always say,' Lakshmibai said.

But Nana shook his head. 'It's a price one does not recognize straightaway, Mani, but Azimullah was too clever, even as a boy, to be ignorant of it. He says that although he was tempted to further his own prospects, he refused the Reverend's offer only to see the good Christian transform instantly from a kindly benefactor into a cold and disinterested stranger.'

'Then how did he gain his education?'

'Ah, when ordered to leave the Reverend's employ, Azimullah managed to get a job as an accountant with Brigadier Ashburnham in the cantonment. But, all the while he was teaching himself both English and French, knowing he would need the language of his oppressors if he wished to fight them back someday.'

On seeing the fascinated expression on Lakshmibai's face, Tantia could not resist cutting in again, 'Do you know, when Azimullah resisted the advances of one of the brigadier's assistants, he was thrown out of that establishment as well—on this occasion charged with bribery and corruption!'

'And, as you can imagine, Mani, by this time, Azimullah's loathing for the British was not only genocidal, it was set in stone,' Nana said.

'When he heard of Peshwa-sahib's case against the British, he came to our court with an offer of assistance. It was I who first received him and brought him before Nana,' Tantia said proudly.

'And has he had any success with the appeal, Nana?' Lakshmibai asked.

'The hearing in Calcutta came to nothing, but I had held out more hope for London.'

'Azimullah went to London too?' Lakshmibai asked in surprise.

'Yes, to appeal to the Company's Board of Directors. But it was to no avail at all. After his final unsuccessful visit to the Company offices on Leadenhall Street, he asked to be taken to the British Parliament. He describes it as a huge beautiful building made of carved gold. And says he stood there for hours, silently gazing up at its magnificent walls and secretive narrow windows, filled with the same rage he had felt towards that English collector when he had been just a boy.'

Lakshmibai sighed. 'How indeed has it come to be that those men so faraway rule the fortunes of people like us, Nana?'

'Not just in India, Mani, but Azimullah tells me that far-flung places—Canada, Jamaica—also have their local economies being crushed by these new ideas of "Free Trade" that are in fact free for no one but the British.'

'Oh you should hear Azimullah's stories of London someday, Mani,' Tantia cut in, 'and the wealth that flows from our coffers to theirs. He described the iron-grey river they have there, with twice the traffic that you see on our Ganga; ships and barges and steam sloops, the naval might that has brought us all into the Englishman's grip.'

'Yes, poor Azimullah said that, out of sheer frustration, he had hired a hansom carriage and gone up and down the thronging roads of the city that day, unable to quell his multiplying anger. Everything he saw only served to make it worse; a gleaming steel and glass mountain rising out of a park—a Great Exhibition Hall apparently commissioned by Queen Victoria's husband to celebrate Britain's achievements abroad, just think of that.'

'Things we cannot even imagine, Mani,' Tantia continued, 'a locomotive, a huge steam engine pulling a row of carriages into a railway station; men in frock-coats travelling on omnibuses twice the height of our carriages; and ladies more beautiful than the ones they send here, all dripping pearls and wearing jewel-bright gowns...'

'Made, yes, of our silks,' Nana said dryly. 'Azimullah talked of London's nobles who do not even know that their fine clothes come from India. Why, he says they know nothing even of their own miserable brethren, toiling in workhouses far from the fashionable parts of the city. He said his stomach turned at the pictures he saw in the *Illustrated London News* of gaunt-faced starving Irish peasants, remembering the famine that had killed his own sister and father. Oh yes, he says that all the wealth and vigour and power of London could not make it seem any less vicious and uncaring a place than he already knew it to be.'

After a long pause, Lakshmibai said quietly, 'I can imagine the desperation he must have felt so far from home. And having to return with no good news for you, Nana.'

'None at all, Mani,' Nana replied sadly. 'Azimullah returned with empty hands and the next thing I knew was that I had been sent a curt letter from London, confirming Dalhousie's decision to stop my pension and remove my title.'

As silence enveloped the group again, Nanasahib recalled Azimullah's advice to him before he had left Bithur, 'The rani of Jhansi will not be ready to join us at the moment, regardless of her loyalty to you. She has too much to cope with right now, her husband's illness, her expected child...people join revolutions only when they have personal reason to and Rani Lakshmibai, for the time being, has no real grievances against the British.' Nanasahib could see how right he was. At the moment, Mani's friendship with her British agent would only confuse her, make her unwary and credulous. There was no doubt that Jhansi too would one day face its trials but, until then, he would have to bide his time.

'No, my dear, Mani,' Nana repeated sadly, 'even a man as clever as Azimullah has no solution for me at the moment.'

'How can British ministers possibly know, from so faraway, of what great rulers the Peshwas once were, Nana,' Lakshmibai said, taking Nana's hand in hers.

'From the time of Shivaji's death, Mani,' Nanasahib said, his eyes filling with tears again, 'my ancestors had toiled to keep our stronghold from falling into Mughal hands. It was we Peshwas who gave back the Marathas their power and that was how we came to rule and give direction to our people. But it seems that all that history and all our glorious past can just be taken away like that, plucked out of our grasp. Like children fighting over a plaything.'

As tears started rolling down his face in earnest, Lakshmibai put her arms around Nana. She placed her cheek against his shoulder, unable to find the necessary words of comfort, and feeling frightened to see such uncustomary tears from her old playmate.

Tantia leapt up from his seat and pulled out the stiletto knife that he had taken to carrying in a small sheath hanging from his belt. 'We will not let them!' he cried agitatedly, 'we will not let the foreigner walk on our lands in his filthy big boots, defiling and destroying everything he can lay his hands on!'

'Oh stop being so dramatic, Tantia,' Nana snapped irritatedly and Lakshmibai could see that their relationship had changed little in the intervening years—Tantia still as eager to please Nana and Nana as dismissive of that loyalty as ever.

'Be calm, Tantia, my brother,' Lakshmibai said more gently, pulling Tantia down to sit next to her again. 'Aggression will not achieve anything. The British are more powerful than perhaps our ancestors should ever have allowed them to become. The best thing is to play the game in the way they do. With calmness and determination and with the use of sweet temperate words that betray little emotion. That is their key to success and that is what we should aspire to.'

Nana looked at her hopefully. He trusted Mani's judgement—despite her husband's illness, she had taken such impressive charge over their kingdom. His own advisors, even Azimullah, had not been much help so far. Tantia, of course, was never of any use at all, always too eager to strike a belligerent attitude rather than consider a rational course of action. Yes, he felt grateful indeed to have a friend like Mani and wished, with half-amused regret, that he had been kinder to her when she was a little girl.

Two months after Nana and Tantia had departed Jhansi, and a month before her time, Lakshmibai recognized the first spasms of labour as she concluded the day's business at her durbar in the city palace. It was Sundar whom she called first and the maid, taking one look at her queen's face twisted with pain, needed no further explanation. Maids were summoned to lift the rani bodily and carefully place her in a palanquin before it was rushed through the city streets to Panch

Mahal. Sundar ran ahead to prepare the labour chamber and rouse the midwives.

After being placed on a wooden slatted bed, cleared of its bedding and mattresses, Lakshmibai watched the room around her become a hive of activity. In the room next door, the midwife was ordering a junior maid to boil cauldrons of water with pepper pods fresh from the tree. Through increasingly unbearable spasms in her back and legs, Lakshmibai heard Sundar ask for castor oil to be warmed and for fresh cotton clothes for both herself and the expected baby to be made ready. A spoonful of ghee mixed with honey was fed to her to ease labour but the bands of white-hot pain gripping her waist and back were only growing tighter and stronger. She wanted to vomit and even the gentle touch of Sundar's hand on her forehead seemed suddenly an insufferable interference.

Had there ever been an agony so terrible, Lakshmibai wondered as the throbbing, wrenching spasms gripped her entire body…it was as though she were being pushed to the very limit of her endurance but the new life at the end of it would be worth it, she reminded herself desperately, clutching Sundar's hands. Through her delirium of pain, her back, her legs, now her entire being on fire, she remembered the mother she herself had hardly known and some of her tears were for that poor soul who had been through all this for a mere four years of motherhood. Sundar's face was looming over hers, anxious, pleading but she could hardly hear the words she was uttering for the anguish.

Minutes stretched into hours as pain engulfed her…she had no idea how long she writhed on that bed before she felt that final tearing and pushing that even she could recognize as the final contractions of childbirth. And then from a far distance, she heard a thin cry followed by the laughter of the maids before she gave way to merciful darkness.

❧ 15 ❧

Major Ellis was amongst the first to receive notification of the prince's birth:

> *A Prince is born. Rani Lakshmibai of Jhansi is blessed with a male child, son of Gangadhar Rao, Raja of Jhansi. The Prince is named Rajkumar Damodar Vasudev Rao. All hail the new Prince, long live the King!*

As he rode to the palace to personally congratulate the king and queen, he could hear the town criers calling out at street corners and bazaars. The people of Jhansi were gathered in small huddles, chattering excitedly. Their joy was clear to see: it was a boy, the raja's line would be perpetuated. When the last queen had died childless, they had worried for their future. It was clear that it was not just the British who had no desire to see either Krishna Rao or Ali Bahadur succeed Gangadhar with their false claims to Jhansi's throne. When eight years had passed in the raja's marriage to Rani Lakshmibai, Ellis was sure that the whisperings and rumours would have started again. But now, the new hope that filled the city was palpable, swelling through the streets and bazaars. People were thronging to the temples to make their thanksgiving, bearing platters full of flowers and coconuts and jaggery. In that tiny new life that had just been awakened in the palace, lay the aspirations and dreams that the people of Jhansi had for their own children's lives. And, of course, it was Major Ellis's job to enquire of Government House what its intentions would be for the new prince.

Inside the palace, Lakshmibai lay in her chamber, looking in wonder at the life she had created. He was tiny but perfect. He had arrived too early and labour had seemed so long and frantic but, when he had finally come, it was as though he had shyly slipped out without wishing to be noticed at all. Lakshmibai knew she must have fainted in the final throes of labour as she had not known she had delivered a male child until Sundar had appeared at her side, wreathed in smiles and holding a bundle in her arms. The midwife had already cleaned him but there were still traces of blood...her blood, their blood...on the edges of his hairline and in the creases of his tiny feet and hands. Lakshmibai sat up to take him from Sundar. She gathered his tiny person to her, impatiently moving aside the fresh cotton cloth in which he was wrapped, wanting to feast her eyes on his every tiny limb and appendage. He was very still, with eyes tightly closed and she looked up at Sundar, every new mother's anxiety writ large all over her face.

'Rani-sahiba, don't fret,' the young woman said, 'the baby prince is tired too from all his efforts. Both he and you need to sleep.'

'I can't stop holding him, Sundar,' Lakshmibai whispered, 'I never want to let go.'

Kashi, returning to the room, smiled when she saw the queen with her baby. 'My dearest rani-sahiba, I was here too at the moment of our prince's birth, but I ran to tell raja-sahib. He will be coming soon. Are you tired, my rani?'

'Of course I am, pagli, wouldn't you be after so many hours of labour,' the queen mumbled affectionately, reaching out to squeeze the hands of her two maids. The poor girls had not slept all night. 'What would I do without the two of you,' she said softly before asking, 'Is raja-sahib well? Is he coming?'

'Soon, Rani-sahiba, and then you must take some rest,' Sundar said, stroking Lakshmibai's hair, still damp from the sweat of her labour. 'Kashi, bring a basin of warm water with those rose-coloured crystals dissolved in it, as Dr Allen had said. We need to sponge Rani-sahiba down before she sleeps.'

Through alternating waves of bliss and sleep and fatigue, Lakshmibai floated in an ethereal world, only barely aware of Gangadhar coming in and kissing her forehead. Through vision blurred by exhaustion, she saw her husband lift up his son and weep for joy, sinking his face into the baby's coddling clothes, before that perfect picture dissolved and she slept again. She could feel Sundar and Kashi gently sponge her and dry her and she wondered at the empty feeling inside her body so accustomed to carrying life within it—until she remembered that he was there, somewhere near her, alive—such wonder to imagine that she had actually spawned a whole new life. The prince, her son, who would one day be her support and Jhansi's future. Lakshmibai's last thoughts as she drifted off to sleep were for her baby son. Grow up soon, little one. I need you to stand by my side, and to be tall and strong for the people of Jhansi when your father and I are gone. That is the duty you are born with and that will have to be your life...

Lakshmibai smiled at Kashi and Sundar who were jostling each other as they bent over the baby in his crib. Sundar won this time, triumphantly raising herself with the tiny mewling prince in her arms, causing Kashi to go into a mock-sulk. Lifting a silver beaker with an elongated spout, that had been ordered last week from the royal jeweller, Sundar tried to pour a few drops of milk and honey into the baby's mouth. Kashi, unable to stay away too long, sprang to help, holding his head tenderly to one side so that Sundar could attempt to get the spout into the side of his tightly clamped mouth again. 'Oh sweet baby prince, pure gold had been ground into this to make you strong, please drink it,' she crooned liltingly but still little Damodar spluttered the mixture out, spraying Sundar's clothes with it, now crying in a high-pitched, weak wail.

How patient these girls are, Lakshmibai thought, feeling faintly guilty at her own lack of maternal instinct. Perhaps it's because I cannot remember my own mother, she thought. Perhaps it will grow on me, like all these other things have—being queen, being Gangadhar's wife. Who would have thought then that little Mani, only bothered about riding horses once, was capable of all these things. And now, motherhood too.

In the first few weeks of her baby's life, Lakshmibai found her maternal spirit surge unbidden, awed at the manner in which her breasts brimmed, growing heavy and wet whenever her baby cried. Holding him to her breast, she remembered half-forgotten songs to sing, unable to recall if she may have heard them from her own mother. Now the routines of the court and public assemblies that had so captivated her all these years paled into insignificance against the simple joy of walking up and down her chamber, holding the warm body of her baby against her own. Climbing one day to the highest balcony of Panch Mahal, she looked out at the brown hills and distant forests and imagined teaching her son how to ride through them, just as her father had taught her in the grounds of Saturday House. Once her son was as expert a rider as her, she would proudly traverse the countryside, the young prince by her side, showing him the land he would rule and, in turn, showing the land and its people the handsome young prince they, like her, were so fortunate to have.

It thrilled her too to see Gangadhar's contentment. Like all things hard-won, she had at first worried that it may only be ephemeral, another theatrical role that Gangadhar would enjoy playing only for a while. But, as the days passed, she could slowly feel the tightened coils inside her unwind as a new confidence in Gangadhar's love tentatively unfurled. Her husband's eagerness to spend all his time with her and their son was real and tangible, not something he could tire of or discard like a robe. It was almost as though he had surprised himself in his delight at discovering the pleasures that were available in being a husband and a father, each of those roles feeding blissfully off the other. And, even though it had come so late, Lakshmibai felt filled with gratitude to be finally blessed with the kind of family life that had eluded her, even when she had herself been a child.

She watched now, her face brimming with pleasure, as Gangadhar lay stretched out next to his baby infant, willing him to flop over onto his belly.

'You can do it, little one,' he was laughing, gently tugging at one tiny arm flailing up in the air. 'Look Lakshmibai, he has done it again!' They both laughed at the startled expression on Damodar's face as, having flipped over, he looked astonished to be bobbing above the silken quilt before sinking his face back into its soft folds, exhausted by his efforts.

Gangadhar tenderly picked up the tiny body and laid it on his own stomach as he too lay back on his cushions. Lakshmibai knew that his exertions were wearing him out too, but did not have the heart to tell him to leave the baby's nursery to get some rest. She had not seen such bliss on his face ever before but, as she watched him cup one hand gently over Damodar's small head, she suddenly felt that old tautness overcome her at the thought of such unaccustomed happiness. So unfamiliar and unforeseen that she could not help fearing it may be transient.

And so when, just four months after his birth, little Damodar fell ill, Lakshmibai wondered why she was not less shocked, less able to accept that her happiness had indeed been short-lived. A raging fever had overtaken her baby's frail body, making his eyes roll upwards, leaving empty white eyeballs like those of a child already dead. Nonetheless, his chest heaved with racking great breaths, as though a battle to stay alive were being waged inside that tiny frame.

It had appeared as though from nowhere, leaving no time for thought. A distraught Lakshmibai frantically sent men in every direction, with orders to fetch the best doctors who could come quickly. The English doctor who arrived first thought it was meningitis and the Indian doctor, a few hours later, said it was more likely to be a filarial fever. Before a third opinion could be sought, however, little Damodar, three days short of being four months old, was dead. His body taking one last heaving breath before going limp and silent, a rag doll in his mother's arms. Lakshmibai shook him gently a few times, before succumbing to harder, desperate shoves, knowing with each frantic thrust that failed to open his eyes that she could not hurt him. And yet a part of her was refusing to believe in the finality of his stillness, refusing to accept the horrible knowledge that he was gone.

'NO! *It can't be*! He is alive, he is my son. A mother knows. *He is alive*!' Lakshmibai screamed, now furiously shaking the lifeless body as though she could thereby will it to live, a weeping Sundar trying to restrain her from damaging the fragile frame of her dead child.

Gangadhar, summoned from his chambers, came stumbling into the room as soon as he heard the news. But, with one look at the tiny grey face of his son, he seemed to accept instantly what Lakshmibai could not and collapsed into Faiz Ali's arms. As his faithful bodyguard picked him up to carry him back to his room, cradling him tenderly as though he were himself a child, Sundar desperately wished for Rani Lakshmibai too to be given the luxury of unconsciousness. But Lakshmibai continued to scream over her child's body, as if by doing so her desperation would bring him back to life. Her pain seemed physical and Sundar could see that it would fall upon her again to do whatever she could for her queen. There would be no comfort to be had from Raja Gangadhar.

As Sundar had guessed, Gangadhar, accustomed to carrying his sorrows trapped within himself, did not emerge from his chambers for the rest of the day, while Sundar, tears running down her face, attempted again and again to take the baby away from the rani. But Lakshmibai continued to cling to her son's small corpse, putting it repeatedly to her face and to her chest, trying to breathe life into its deathly silence and rapidly stiffening limbs. Convinced that she had deprived Damodar of life for having lacked maternal spirit, she wailed on and on, asking to be pardoned, begging for forgiveness, in racking, heartrending sobs that Sundar was sure could be heard all over the town and even beyond the city walls.

But, by nightfall, it was as though an endless well of tears had abruptly dried up. For a while, Lakshmibai still moaned, dry tearless sounds emerging from her throat before she went slowly silent, her face against her pillow, her baby's body still clutched in the crook of her arm. She raised her head and looked around at Sundar, and the maid knew that it had finally dawned on her rani that, by indulging her own sorrow, she merely intensified the suffering of everyone around her. As Kashi approached timorously to pick the baby up from the bed, Sundar saw Lakshmibai take one last look at his face, now tinted blue with the cold hue of death, and bend over to place a final kiss on his forehead. Sundar felt her throat clog as she thought of how many such tender kisses the child would have received, growing up with the love of a mother like Lakshmibai. But Fate, capricious and unthinking, never seemed to know where to send its cruellest shafts and the women were silent as Kashi quietly took the tiny feather-light body away from his mother and out of the room.

Sundar remained with Lakshmibai, unsure of what to say, knowing there was no real comfort she could offer. She ran her fingers through Lakshmibai's long hair, gently untangling its knots. But Lakshmibai, who usually loved this routine, had not even noticed the ministering hands, getting up abruptly from her bed to leave the room. Following her, Sundar saw the rani walk into the courtyard that led to Amod Gardens, a lonely wraithlike figure among the trees bleached white by the faded light of the moon. Lakshmibai sat down on a marble bench, at first not noticing Sundar appear by her side. But an hour later, she lay down, her head silently seeking the comfort of Sundar's lap and that was where Kashi found them as dawn broke, the soothing night scents of the jasmines having failed to bring them both sleep.

Sundar and Kashi and the other maids in the palace broke down and wept only later that morning when the rani finally agreed to get some rest, for how could they show their grief when the queen herself had found the power to shut her love for her dead son away? But Sundar feared that what the rani had closed away would slowly consume her from within. Looking out from the upper windows of the palace, she observed that the queen's silent grief had made the whole countryside fall still. Suddenly there was no music, no temple bells, no sounds of children at play in the streets, not even the lowing of cows in the evening hour. Maybe, she said later to Kashi, all those things knew that the little prince would never grow up to enjoy them and had, in sorrow and deference, shut themselves away. The whole city was struck with something that was spreading like a slow poison from the palace into every home and to the dun countryside beyond. And it felt to Sundar as though that pall of despair would spread and beget more desolation and more pain with every day that passed.

The cremation took place the following day under a soft pink sky on the banks of Lake Lachhmitaal, where a small sandalwood pyre, drenched in ghee, had been made ready to receive the minuscule figure shrouded in white. Sundar and Kashi held onto Lakshmibai's quivering figure, but there were no more of the tearful screams of the previous day. The people of Jhansi were gathered in shocked and silent sympathy on nearby hillocks and temple steps and the maids knew Rani Lakshmibai was thinking of them as she stood with her back straight and stiff, her face a mask of sorrowing courage. When Raja Gangadhar was brought out of his carriage, Sundar saw that he was being lifted straight off the ground by Faiz and Mohammed Ali, each of whom had taken an arm to hoist him up. She had heard that the king's tremors had returned in the night, and so severely that he could barely walk. Sundar had silently wondered if, like so many men, the king had found himself unable to face his wife's anguish and merely taken refuge in his own afflictions instead. She watched him now as he took the wick that was being held out by the priest. His guards still holding him from both sides, he reached out with shaking hands and lit his baby son's pyre. As the fire took, a wail went up from the crowd. Still the rani was silent as she gazed in the direction of her husband lighting the flame that would soon consume her dead child.

Lakshmibai looked at Gangadhar as though he were a stranger, for a moment loathing him for not having thought of comforting her in the night. It was *his* child that had died, the loss was of the heir to *his* throne. Had that made him forget that she had lost her most precious gift too? Even as she tried to quell her raging blame, she felt a renewed abhorrence as she remembered how difficult it had been to conceive their baby in the first place. Her reproach of a husband whom she had always yearned to regard as blameless now pierced so hard within her, she wondered if he could feel its shafts from where he stood. She detested the thought that she had been so young and foolish that she had satisfied herself for years with receiving just his friendship and not a husband's love. She wondered too if there was some bleak symbolism in the fact that their baby's life, so difficult to create and holding so brief and tenuous a love together, had been so very easy to lose. Indeed, if by losing their baby their love had come to an end too, Lakshmibai felt she could not really care. There was simply no further unhappiness to expend.

Sundar, her tears now falling unchecked, felt angry quivers pass through the rani's erect body as she held her close and grieved at the tortured thoughts she knew must be passing through her queen's mind.

What Lakshmibai was thinking—how could she not—was that the death of her child was the death, not just of this child but of all others that may have come. It was the death of motherhood, the death of hope, of a future line of kings, of Jhansi's expectations, a death...yes, a death of life itself.

❧ 16 ❧

News of the death of his grandchild reached Moropant only days after the event and, that very night, he made his decision to return to Jhansi. Soon after Peshwa-sahib's passing, Lakshmibai had invited him to join her court but he had prevaricated at the time. Now, with this heartbreaking news, he could feel his daughter's need for support beckon across the miles. For months he had done nothing more useful than shuttle between Bithur and Varanasi anyway, trapped between Peshwa-sahib's and Asharfi-bua's fading lives. But poor Asharfi-bua—who could sense Moropant's growing despondence—now insisted that his daughter needed him more than she did and he had gratefully agreed.

Leaving his old aunt in the care of Peshwa-sahib's younger brother and his kindly wife, Moropant finally bade farewell to Varanasi. Peshwa-sahib had gone, his title was defunct, Nana had moved with his own younger set of courtiers to Bithur. There was nothing left for

Moropant in Varanasi except the care of his ailing aunt. Saturday House had long fallen into lassitude with the departure of all its children. Moropant couldn't help feeling that disappointment was stalking their lives in various guises like some evil beast.

Making almost the same journey from Varanasi to Jhansi that he had made with Mani's bridal procession, he wondered at how the countryside had changed in just ten years. It was not the trees or the hills or the rolling grace of the river Ganga, those had all stayed the same. It was everything else—the roads were smoother and more numerous, some were even macadamized. There were also a great many more horses and carriages about, travelling busily between towns. The cities themselves had become thriving, bustling places bright with men in colourful uniforms and English ladies travelling grandly in their landau carriages and sedan chairs.

As Moropant approached Jhansi, he saw that it too had grown. He noticed cotton fields stretching beyond the city's lake in all directions while newly planted barley and wheat formed quilted squares in different shades of brown and green closer to the town walls. There were more houses, the city spilling out from the confines of the fort and spreading into what had previously been just dry dusty land. Maybe it was true that his daughter had brought prosperity to Jhansi. But Moropant wished with the desperation of a father's heart that Jhansi would bring Lakshmibai the happiness she deserved too.

As his carriage neared the gates of the fort, he wondered what words he would find to comfort his bereaved daughter, his gut churning at the unjustness of dearly worshipped gods who did not know where it was merciful to take a life and where to grant it.

Lakshmibai was awaiting him, a small lonely figure dwarfed by the pillared hall of Panch Mahal. Moropant hurried up the stairs to take his daughter in his arms. Her strong young figure was still that of a woman in the prime of her life and her face, despite everything, still shone with the good health of youth, but Moropant could see depths in his daughter's eyes that had never existed before as they drew apart. Depths and shadows that told him she was now grown old in experience and grief if not in age. His heart was heavy as he realized that her losses had now outstripped his. He had heard too about Gangadhar's illness and wondered bleakly whether the death of their child would make their already incomplete union worse.

In Jhansi's court, it was clear to see that Rani Lakshmibai was now almost entirely in charge. Gangadhar had all but retired from active politics, only occasionally appearing to sign some papers or if his old friend Major Ellis was calling, visits that continued to confer a special lucidity on him. Moropant could tell that his daughter was liked and respected by all her ministers. Even the formidable Krishna Rao seemed to have become feeble, the fire in his belly grown cold.

Within a month of arriving in Jhansi, Moropant was put in charge of security and one of his main tasks was to reorganize the state's small army of guards.

'Times have changed, Baba,' Lakshmibai said. 'We need to be ready to defend ourselves if the tide turns against us. At the moment our fortunes are satisfactory, the British are content with our friendship and our Rajput neighbours are busy with their own concerns. But we must still be prepared.'

Moropant could not tell if this was common sense or whether a new pessimism had crept into Lakshmibai's mind, borne from her recent loss. But he set about developing the previously rag-tag palace army that had never had to face any real aggressions. It pleased him when Lakshmibai sometimes joined him in his training of the troops, observing that she had not forgotten her old horsemanship skills. Together they would ride out into the countryside and, as they raced through the nearby forests and glens, their horses panting in tandem, he once heard her laughter rise above the sound of their hooves and was thrilled at the thought that he had his rambunctious child back again instead of some distant and quietly grieving queen.

It was not just the loss of her baby and the illness of her husband; British policies and their effect on Jhansi gave her cause for worry too. Moropant remembered the foolishness with which he had dismissed the anxieties of his old friend Peshwa-sahib so many years ago. But he had been young then. Young and hasty and too unwise to imagine that the plant watered and tended in the backyard would not just grow but one day send its tentacles right through the windows of their house.

There were days when Moropant worried that his daughter would buckle under the strain, days when she looked tired and wan and would not speak to him about matters of state. At times like that, he tried not to mind if she rode out alone. If there were any comforts to help her overcome these difficult times, they were not his to give.

Major Ellis received news of Moropant's arrival in Jhansi with apprehension, aware that the rani's father had for many years been political advisor to the old deposed Peshwa. The British had never enjoyed a good relationship with the last Peshwa, a weak man who had proven his slipperiness more than once during the Anglo-Maratha wars. But Ellis comforted himself with a reminder that Rani Lakshmibai had never indicated an unwholesome attitude towards the British. His relationship with Jhansi remained one of trust and affection. Her father had quite obviously moved to Jhansi to help her in her times of sorrow. There was nothing to be fearful of.

But, in those months, Dalhousie's annexations continued apace. Satara had been followed by Sambalpur and Sambalpur by Baghat— each of those announcements causing Raja Gangadhar to retreat further and further into a state of almost childlike incomprehension.

European goods were flooding the markets. Ellis read in the papers that England had become the most industrialized country in the world. New machines that could do the work of ten handloom workers meant that cloth could be made even more cheaply in Lancashire mills and nobody was buying the once famed Chandela muslins made locally out of Nurma and Kharua cottons any more. Trade in blue Dessaun stuffings had trickled to virtually nothing too. Rani Lakshmibai had informed him that her public durbars were full of people clamouring for her to do something to protect their livelihoods but that was not something Ellis could help her with. Even the rupee coins that everyone carried and used in the bazaar were now the standardized ones created by the British, the old Jhansi rupee having become nearly defunct. A new bank had also been formed in Bombay to make trade easier between India and the Company but Calcutta's instructions were for the British to concern themselves only with their own profits, not with the tribulations of local weavers and handloom workers.

It pained Ellis deeply to relay such bad tidings to Jhansi's court and the effort to refrain from giving his own feelings away was becoming a terrible burden. The rani's manner had given him cause for concern on his last visit to the court too. Where she normally sounded brisk and businesslike, he now noted a new depth in her voice that indicated her own crowding sorrows. It was not hard to guess how heavily the loss of her child would lie on her heart and Ellis wished he could find some good tidings to alleviate her pain.

Usually, the annual visit to Sister Agnes's Mission School was one that Lakshmibai looked forward to but this year, mere months after the death of her baby, she watched the school building approach from her carriage window with an unfamiliar weight in the pit of her stomach. Through the sheer curtains, she saw that blue distempered walls had been decorated with ropes of marigold flowers and roses.

Strains of a hymn floated towards her as the carriage rolled into the neat, newly swept compound. The children were all gathered under the shade of a mulberry tree, the school's two Eurasian teachers waving thin white arms as they kept time. Small voices wavered with uncertainty as Rani Lakshmibai descended from the carriage but she smiled and made a gesture for them to carry on their singing. Their voices rose again, a few cracking on the higher notes as they gathered enthusiasm again.

Lakshmibai watched them intently, remembering her reaction on first hearing about the local church's practice of taking in Indian orphans, alongside European and Eurasian children, and converting them to Christianity before offering them an education. Although at first uncertain about the motives of the missionaries, she had soon found herself arguing with Krishna Rao over his desire to see her take issue with Sister Agnes over the matter. 'She thinks she can buy their faith by offering Christian food and Bible lessons,' Krishna Rao had expostulated angrily but Lakshmibai had retorted by pointing out that a far worse indignity than being Christian lay in the simple fact of being poor. From then on, stubbornly, she had insisted on assisting Sister Agnes and the Protestant Mission in whatever way she could.

After the hymn was concluded, Sister Agnes seemed not to be able to resist her natural urge to reach out to embrace Lakshmibai warmly as guards unloaded baskets of pomegranates, custard apples and oranges from the bullock carts that had accompanied the royal carriage to the school. New uniforms, stitched by the royal tailors, had already been despatched to the school in neatly ironed piles over two weeks ago and Lakshmibai looked at the children, observing how smart they looked in starched shorts and skirts. As they were herded back into the schoolroom for the rest of the day's lessons, Lakshmibai tried not to think of the childhood that her Damodar would never have. She followed Sister Agnes into her office to be shown the school's latest reports.

Sister Agnes waited until they were alone in her room before opening up with her customary directness, 'Rani-sahiba, I prayed so hard for you in your recent loss. Please assure me that you are as much at peace with your bereavement as you appear.'

Lakshmibai considered her reply, grateful for the nun's candour. 'Thankfully, I still have my work, Sister Agnes,' she replied finally.

'My duties keep me so busy I fall into my bed at night with no energy left to dwell on selfish sorrows.'

Sister Agnes nodded. 'There is no better cure than hard work, Rani-sahiba. Hard work and prayer. Those have always been my credo.'

Lakshmibai laughed. 'Prayer...I must admit I'm less good at that, Sister. Maybe that's a problem shared by all energetic people. It just makes me feel impatient if I have to sit and listen to prayers for too long.'

'I think I understand that, Rani-sahiba...' The nun's voice dropped to a whisper as she confided, 'I must admit I sometimes chafe if the Padre's Sunday sermon goes on for too long as I sit in church thinking about all the things I need to get on with.'

The two women laughed and Sister Agnes placed her hand on Lakshmibai's arm. 'I am truly filled with admiration for your courage, Rani-sahiba. Promise me you will tell me if there's ever anything I can do for you...'

Lakshmibai nodded, unable to speak for a sudden lump in her throat. Sister Agnes saw tears rise and tremble in the Rani's dark eyes and patted her arm, for once lost for words. She had liked Jhansi's young queen from the very moment she had set eyes on her small bejewelled figure all those years ago. She waited a few moments for the rani to compose herself.

Managing a weak smile, Lakshmibai finally replied, 'It feels so odd, Sister, and so sad that here, at the Mission, you have all these orphaned little ones while I sit alone in my palace, rocking Jhansi's empty cradle.'

'These children bring me unending comfort, Rani-sahiba, whenever I feel far from home. Or uncertain about my vocation. They are as much mine as they would have been borne from my own womb.'

Lakshmibai nodded but her voice was small as she replied, 'I too have tried reminding myself that my people are like my children, Sister. That I may have been deprived of my baby in order to learn to love them more. But that is small comfort, especially when faced with the question of the raja's title. The people of Jhansi need an heir to their throne, for the sake of their children's futures. My devotion to them cannot be enough.'

Sister Agnes hesitated before saying gently, 'Maybe it is too soon to talk of these things. But might you consider adopting a child, Rani-sahiba? Could that not be a solution to the issue of inheritance? I don't know, of course, what the restrictions in your religion are...'

'There are no restrictions at all on adoption among Hindus, Sister

Agnes. There is very old acceptance of that practice, mainly because a Hindu needs someone to perform his death rites without which there can be no eternal salvation. We have practised it quite respectably for centuries—I was even brought up in a house where adoption was considered a most honourable thing. Yes, I have thought about adoption many times these past few weeks, Sister. Of course, you realize that I could not come here to St. Jude's. I will have to find someone from within the raja's gotra, you know, his clan. It would have to be a child who was a blood relation so that the line can be perpetuated. As a royal family, we have to think about those things as well.'

Sister Agnes looked admiringly at Lakshmibai as she explained so stoically how she planned to deal with her loss. She had heard rumours that the king had been lapsing in and out of a state of mental breakdown these past few weeks. How fortunate Jhansi was to have a queen like Lakshmibai. It was less than a month ago that Agnes had visited the mission in Lucknow and been horrified to hear stories of the licentious behaviour of the nawab and his multiple begums and concubines there. The sisters there had said that there were rumours too of orgies involving young boys and prostitutes from the city—apparently a Sodom and Gomorrah in the heart of India. Agnes did not envy the task those poor Lucknow missionaries had cut out for them.

Once the school reports had been perused, Lakshmibai chose a small painted papier mâché parrot from the children's handiwork as a keepsake before leaving the building. Sister Agnes helped Lakshmibai up the steps of the royal carriage, insisting on arranging her jamawar shawl over her knees. Stepping back down into the school compound, the nun watched as the carriage bore the queen away, waving along with her children until it had vanished down the dusty road.

It was August by the time Major Ellis was finally sent a summons from the court and he knew its primary purpose was to ensure that the prince's death had not changed the government's policy towards Jhansi.

It pained him to see the parlous state Raja Gangadhar was in as he was bodily carried into the private anteroom and placed on his throne. He attempted a small smile but to Ellis the expression looked more like a grimace of pain.

'My dear Raja-sahib, I can always call at another time if you feel...'

Gangadhar waved away his concern with a thin hand. 'No, no my man,' he said haltingly and Ellis saw to his horror a sliver of saliva begin to drip out of the side of the raja's half frozen mouth before one of his guards hastily wiped it away. 'You know...how I depend on you to come and...tell me all that is going on in the state and...the country.'

There was a small flurry and as the guards bearing a silken purdah came through the doors, Ellis knew they were about to be joined by the rani. He stood up as the customary sound of tinkling anklets and bangles heralded her arrival.

'Good morning, Major Ellis,' he heard her say briskly. The tone of her voice made it sound as though she had overcome her recent anguish.

'Good morning and namaskar, Rani-sahiba. I was just telling his Highness that I can call at a more opportune moment if that is your preference.'

'Major Ellis, it is a pleasure to receive you here and you always bring us such important news. But first, please have your drink,' the rani said.

Ellis sipped at the glass of mint sherbet before placing the silver tumbler back on its tray. 'I hope you will find today's news of interest to you both,' he began. 'As usual I have a mix of the good and the not-so-good to offer, but I think it is mainly good news.'

'Oh we are so pleased to hear it, Major Ellis,' Rani Lakshmibai said. 'Sometimes it feels as though we only ever get to hear bad news sitting in this court. Please do tell us what good tidings you carry for us today.'

'First of all, Rani-sahiba, you will be pleased to know of our successes in Burma. Just today I have received the message that Rangoon and Page have been taken.'

'Oh that is glad news. I know many of our local sipahis had been fearing the call to serve on that front so far away.'

'That had been looking less likely after the annexation of Punjab anyway, Rani-sahiba. Lord Dalhousie's orders had been to recruit as many Sikh soldiers as possible into our army and the Sikhs—forgive me my bluntness—they are less burdened by superstitions, Rani-sahiba, than our Hindu Bengal Army soldiers who feel hampered to travel for religious reasons.'

'Do...do the...the Sikh recruits join the...Company's forces?' Gangadhar asked, his speech slurred and halting.

'As far as I am aware, Raja-sahib, they are forming what they are calling the Punjab Irregular Frontier Force,' Ellis replied. 'Lord

Dalhousie has got the Board of Administration to authorize the Lawrence brothers, now governing the Punjab, not just to take up this task but also to undertake all manner of administrative and social reforms in that state. Apparently, it is all going down rather well with the local people.'

'I would think the Muslims there would be eager to see their mosques and schools restored. You know, the Sikh rulers had not just persecuted them for years but had even taken to using their mosques as ammunition stores during the Sikh wars,' the rani said before adding, 'But don't let me interrupt your good news, Major Ellis, you did say you had more?'

'Ah yes, another order of Lord Dalhousie's. A truly exciting one. The rail locomotive is being brought to India. I hear the first line is to be from Bombay to Thana. Once a company is hired to lay the tracks, it will be a wonderful resource for India. I think it is going to change the face of this country, Rani-sahiba.'

'Oh that is certainly thrilling!' Lakshmibai said. 'Nanasahib had told me that his emissary had returned with fabulous stories of London—especially the new railway and a motorized carriage he called an omnibus. Although there are bound to be those who will remain determined to oppose change, I think I approve heartily of scientific progress coming to our land. This Lord Dalhousie of yours, he certainly sounds like a reformer and I would be pleased to see all these things brought to our Jhansi too.'

'He's young, Rani-sahiba, and full of ideas and plans for this country. I know he has pained your friend Nanasahib greatly but, all in all, his intentions are good. He is what I would call a "modernizer" in the best sense of that word. Railways, road improvements, posts and telegraphs, schools and hospitals—his plans are big and India can only benefit by them...' Ellis could hear the slightly forced exhilaration in his own voice and paused momentarily as he wondered if the rani may notice it. She made as if to speak again. Over the years, Ellis had heard her grow increasingly confident in expressing her views through her purdah but now she seemed to hesitate for a minute, as though uncertain of whether she trusted him enough to voice new doubts.

He heard her take a long breath, her voice turn suddenly pensive as she said, 'But tell me, Major Ellis, tell me in *truth* whether you think Lord Dalhousie is bringing the rail locomotive for our mutual benefit or for the Company to be able to trade more easily and thereby only for the Company's profits to improve?' Before Ellis could reply, she continued, speaking more swiftly as she gained confidence. 'Is it not true that industries in England have become dependent on this country to sell their goods? I have already told you of how, at my public assemblies, our weavers come and tell us that no one will buy their wares any more. Because cheaper cloth is being sent from mills in your country where you have machines to make them. Will these railways not simply make local workers' situations worse? If you were honest, I think you would admit that the railways are being brought so that your goods can be spread more easily around the country and so that your troops can be transported to take over more lands. How will *my* people profit from it?'

Ellis wondered whether to remind her that her people were his people too—that he too had worked untiringly all these years to help uplift Jhansi but Raja Gangadhar had already chipped in, smiling a little nervously at his wife's forthrightness. 'Now it is...your turn...to forgive the rani her candour, my friend!' he said pleadingly.

Ellis acknowledged the raja's apology with a nod. He felt faintly embarrassed, having heard it said that Dalhousie's intention was in fact to free India's poor from the yoke of their native royalty who, he believed implacably, had always ground their people down for their own selfish ends. There was certainly some truth in the rani's statement but he could not openly admit it and said only, 'Rani-sahiba makes a valid point. Yes, of course, that is how it will appear to people who trust our intentions with difficulty but please do believe me when I say that Lord Dalhousie's purpose is an honourable one. Sometimes he comes up against obstacles of his own, of course...but that was to be my final bit of news, unfortunately not very good.' He sensed the attention with which his words were being absorbed from behind the purdah and continued speaking carefully. 'Just a couple of months ago Lord Dalhousie had asked for Indian nobles to be included in the governance of this country. You may have heard of the India Act, although attempts were being made to keep it quiet until a decision had been made. Well, I have it on very good authority that he had put in the request for his legislative council to include Indian aristocracy and intelligentsia, a most excellent idea according to me, but sadly...very sadly...he has been overruled in London.'

There was a rustling sound from behind the purdah, as though Lakshmibai had suddenly sat up, in either anger or surprise, he could not tell which. Her voice was sharp. 'So Hindustan, or all the states over which the British now have authority, will be governed by a council that has no representation from its own people whatsoever?' Ellis was silent and she continued, more softly, 'That seems so unreasonable, so high-handed. Is there no room for negotiation on that?'

'I would think not, Rani-sahiba,' Ellis mumbled, glad that he did not have to meet the rani's eyes, imagining the reproach he would have seen in them.

'Do you know,' she asked, although Ellis knew it was merely a rhetorical question from the meditative tone of her voice, 'that many of the old Mughal emperors employed Hindus…at *all* levels of government. Some of the most senior officials in the court of enlightened rulers like Akbar were very deliberately chosen from among local Hindus. They even married Hindu princesses, like the present emperor in Delhi, not just to consolidate their empires but also to show their willingness to embrace differences. And, in return, we Hindu rulers too try to keep Muslims involved at the highest levels of our administrations so that our Muslim people do not feel dispossessed. One can hope to maintain peace and stability only if the different peoples within a state feel secure and represented…'

There was a firm clink of bracelets as though the rani may have made an irritated gesture, realizing suddenly how futile it was to express such sentiments to an Englishman.

Ellis felt a twist of queasy shame in his stomach, tempered only by mild relief that he had refrained from telling Rani Lakshmibai the Board's stated reason for not including Indians on the governing council. The words had leapt off the page and stayed with him ever since he had read the report and he recalled them now, even as the rani got up and left the room accompanied by her entourage in what he imagined was a fit of pique. 'No two Indians can ever be found to represent adequately the diversity of Hindu and Muslim society,' Sir Charles Wood of the Board of Control had written. 'Exclusion of natives is therefore advised from all higher legislative and political forums in India.'

In a far happier meeting a few days later, Lakshmibai knelt before a child in a small silk sherwani. She took his small chin between her fingers and looked into a pair of long-lashed brown eyes that gazed back into hers enquiringly.

'Anand Rao?' she asked in a soft voice.

Even though it sounded more like a statement than a question, the small head nodded obligingly. He knew she was the rani. He had seen her many times before, she always spoke sweetly to him and she always smelt of jasmine flowers and cardamoms when she kissed his cheek.

Lakshmibai looked up at his father and said gently, 'He is the most beautiful child and I should be honoured to call him my own.'

The boy heard his father say, 'Rani-sahiba, the honour is ours that you have chosen our son to be Raja Gangadhar's heir, long may the raja live.'

Anand could see his mother's eyes shining with tears but he knew that she sometimes cried when she was happy and today felt none of the fear in his heart when he sensed that she was sad. Something told him they were all happy today as he saw the rani embrace his mother and both of them wiped their eyes. Even the old raja, who when Anand last saw him, scared him terribly with his pale face and ghostly black-ringed eyes, was now smiling from his bed and reaching out a thin hand towards him. He shrunk back into the safety of his father's dhoti, pressing his back into his legs, not wanting to go near one so sick. But now he was being propelled towards the raja. Gingerly stretching out his hand, he allowed his fingers to be grasped. The raja's skin felt dry and hot and papery in his sticky fist but he could not hear what the raja was whispering through his crooked half-mouth. The smell of medicines made him want to wrinkle his nose but he knew he must not. His father was nudging him with his knees to reply but he did not know what to say for he had not heard the question. Now his father was kneeling next to him and urging him to speak. Once again he looked enquiringly at the raja who repeated himself. This time he heard his rasping voice that sounded like the wrappers in which sweets from the bazaar were brought. 'Will you...promise...to look after the...rani for me?' he was asking. Anand was puzzled. How could he be asked to look after the rani when she had so many maids to care for her and so many bodyguards who carried spears and guns in case anyone tried to hurt her? But he had heard too that the raja was mad. So maybe that was what made him ask such a silly question. He did not particularly want to speak to a madman but it felt as though all eyes in the room were looking at him and the waiting silence weighed heavily. It was also possible that the raja would have a mad fit if he refused his request. It was safest to quickly agree.

'I will look after the rani,' Anand Rao said firmly, and could tell straightaway that his reply had pleased everyone in the room. The ministers were all nodding, their shiny turbans and white beards glinting in the candlelight.

As he was lifted up in the air on his father's shoulder to be taken out of the raja's bedchamber, the rani announced, 'Tomorrow we will make the arrangements for the adoption ceremony. I will invite Major

Ellis and Captain Martin who is to be the new commanding officer of the barracks at Sagar to be our witnesses.'

The rani was smiling up at him now and he smiled back from his perch, feeling shy but eager to be friendly with her. Even though the raja was so scary and his room smelt so terrible, he did really like this rani. She wore a flowing red sari that had lots of gold flowers on it that shimmered and shone whenever she moved. As she walked up to him and stroked his dangling leg gently, he saw her dark eyes fill up with tears but she quickly blinked them back with a smile. Yes, he was glad he had promised to do whatever he possibly could to make the rani feel happy again.

✌ 17 ✍

The Meads had that summer received their transfer orders to Lucknow and, one evening shortly before their departure, Ellis was invited to tea. He felt weary as he rode the one-mile distance to their pretty bungalow adjoining the church and issued stern instruction to himself to be roused to at least a state of amicability by the time he got there. He had not been able to explain to himself reasons for which the joys and sorrows of his countrymen were beginning to seem more and more trifling by comparison with events elsewhere. Occasionally he chided himself for growing so detached but, as long as their annoyances were over causes no worse than errant servants who stole their victuals and the coming of the rains, it only wearied him and, indeed, disheartened him greatly to indulge them.

He was ushered into the Meads' commodious living room and saw instantly that even poor Harriet, usually so ebullient, was taking the strain of the move badly. She looked tired as she presided over her giant teapot, tendrils of blonde hair hanging limply across her brow, a few stray curls clinging to the back of her neck.

'Oh, this infernal climate,' her voice rose in an uncharacteristic whine, 'the damp air permeates every pore of my skin, reducing me by noon to exhaustion.'

Belinda Royle, as usual, had a better illustration of the humidity of this pre-monsoonal climate, 'My dear, you would never imagine it but just this morning I found my entire collection of shoes covered in mould. All of them; sitting there like little garden goblins, green and limp. No amount of brushing and polishing could revive them and I ended up giving away three perfectly decent pairs to the servants.

Three pairs. And perfectly decent ones, mind!' She broke off as she spotted Ellis, adding in a tone of some disapproval, 'Oh, here's Major Ellis.'

After the initial greetings had been exchanged, a crash in the adjoining dining room took Major Mead off in haste to investigate while Harriet continued with the tea, passing Ellis a generous slab of walnut cake. She smiled apologetically at him as another thud emerged from the dining room. 'I really should be supervising the packing myself; it's never wise to leave it to the servants, is it? But, having personally wrapped every single one of my china ornaments and daguerreotypes this morning, I seem to have used up the last ounce of my diminishing patience, I must say.'

'Oh it's enough to make one lose one's mind,' Major Royle cut in sympathetically, 'and your journey is sure to be quite abhorrent too. I'm afraid those doolies will provide precious little protection in the coming season of dust storms.'

'Oh never mind that,' Belinda cut in briskly, 'first things first, my dear Harriet. You make sure, dear girl, to instruct your orderly to wrap your dinner service in wads of newspaper and hay before they are put into the boxes and sent to Lucknow on those frightful bullock carts. Have I ever told you of how I lost my most treasured set of Waterford crystal?'

Ellis had heard the story before—as everyone else in the room probably had—but no one was impolite enough to say so and Belinda was already halfway through narrating it anyway.

'...turned to smithereens in a matter of moments—moments—as a clodpate coolie at the Calcutta docks swung the box off his head and onto the floor of the cart. On the very day we arrived in India, almost like a premonition. Oh I can still hear the heart-wrenching thump with which it landed ringing in my poor ears.'

Major Royle laughed. 'And I remember not just your tears but the wails of that coolie only too well. Had to save the poor bugger from getting the soundest kicking of his life from his overseer. Well, there'd have been no point in that, seeing it wasn't going to bring Belinda's crystal back.'

'But is that not the beautiful set I have seen at your table, Belinda?' Harriet queried politely, passing a cup of tea to her husband who had returned to the drawing room, flushed from his efforts at sorting out his servants' latest misdemeanour.

'Oh no, and it breaks my heart to think that I have never been able to find glasses as good,' Belinda replied, 'and that's not for want of trying, mind. The wine glasses you refer to my dear Harriet are horribly inferior replacements, bought at auction in Calcutta: our gain the loss of a recently bankrupted European merchant.'

'I think I'm going to have to do something about my dwindling collection of crockery too, so kindly bought for me from the most excellent Thomas Goode by my dear godmother. I seem to lose one every time we have company, thanks to the clumsiness of our khansama.'

'No doubt we will before long be resorting to the old camping style, instructing our dinner guests to bring their own plates!'

As everyone laughed and more cake was passed around, a card on the mantelpiece caught Belinda's eye. 'Goodness, you didn't tell me, Harriet!' she exclaimed as she got up to pluck it off the shelf before proceeding to read it, her face betraying excitement and more than a hint of envy.

Harriet blushed with pleasure and Ellis wondered if he was alone in receiving the impression that the card had been given such prominent place on the mantelpiece quite deliberately. It was obviously an invitation to some grand affair somewhere in Lucknow. Such was Ellis's weary cynicism in those days that he even thought it likely that Harriet's entire tea party had been set up purely for the purpose of having the card displayed to them all. It was now being passed around the company and, as it came to him, he too raised his brow in surprise to see the royal emblem of Awadh at the top. The name 'Harriet Mead' had been written with a thick calligraphy pen, the H and the M full of unfamiliar curls and whirls, making it look as though it might be some exotic Persian name and not English at all. He felt the paper between his fingers: thick creamy handmade paper, dusted with gold powder and scented with attar of roses. It was a perfume that he found altogether too cloying and even a little threatening. The whole room was now reeking of the powerful aroma as Harriet, now too thrilled to contain herself, brought out the envelope in which it had been delivered. Ellis saw a beautiful gold brocade khareeta and recognized, once again, the seal of Awadh.

'My goodness, what a beautiful purse—itself of some value, I should think. And, indeed, what a rare honour!' Major Royle exclaimed, reading the top line out loud, '"Begum Hazratmahal, chief wife of Nawab Wajid Ali Shah of Awadh, wishes to personally welcome Mrs Harriet Mead to the great city of Lucknow." I've never known anything like it!'

'My dear Harriet, the Oudh court is nothing like the dreary Jhansi one. Nothing,' Belinda Royle said knowledgeably. 'It's all awfully complicated there, with myriads of wives and concubines and eunuchs and not to mention having to watch for Moslem nawabi protocol too, jam-packed with do's and don'ts. But I have *every* confidence you'll manage it all *marvellously*.'

'Yes, it did seem to me that court life might be altogether rather more foreign in Lucknow than has been the case thus far in Jhansi,' a wide-eyed Harriet replied, putting her cup down nervously. 'Oh I do wish you could come with me, Belinda.'

'Oh stuff and nonsense, my dear. You'll manage perfectly well without me, I shouldn't doubt.'

Harriet cast her eye around the gathering. 'Of course, I shall miss you all terribly when we leave Jhansi. You have all been so kind and I'm sure we shan't ever make such good friends again.' As everyone demurred politely, she continued, her face brightening again, 'But I must say it will be such a relief to be leaving the tedium of the mofussil behind and I'm rather looking forward to a different kind of regimental life which sounds like so much fun with all the tales of parties and balls that James tells me of.'

'We hear of picnics and duck shoots and even paper chases, quite unlike *this* dreary cantonment,' Belinda added, unable to keep a note of envy out of her voice.

Harriet's response was swift, 'Oh but I must confess, Belinda, to being more than a little nervous about the begum's invitation, knowing so little about the peccadilloes of these native royals. They really are a rule unto themselves, aren't they? Despite the work of our Christian brothers and sisters. I'm not sure I want to be taken into the begum's zenana without either you or James to accompany me and tell me what to do.'

'Do not fret, my dear. We shall be trying to follow you to Lucknow as soon as possible. Although Kanpur also looks like a possibility for us. I hear it's a lot more exciting than even Lucknow. Have you had a special dress made for the begum?' Belinda asked, not waiting for a reply before continuing briskly, 'You'll need a new gown, of course. That old Satin de Mai frock of yours will most certainly not do for the begum of Oudh. You must be careful not to let the side down, my dear, when you're up against these native royals. I hear the begum's always festooned from head to toe with the most fabulous jewellery.'

Ellis felt sorry for Harriet whose face was now wearing a genuinely anxious expression. 'Well, I still have that copy of *Godey's Lady's Book* that you so kindly lent me last Christmas, Belinda. Perhaps I'll find something in there that the darji will be able to run up for me. I bought a bale of the most beautiful lilac grenadine from the cantonment store recently.'

'What a splendid idea. One of Godey's fashion plates has a frock with the dearest box-pleated flounces all along the waist. That would look fabulous on grenadine. You must let me instruct the darji before you let him loose on your new fabric, my dear.'

'Well, I've shown him how to use the Practical Dress Instructor already. He's such a clever, jolly little man, I'm sure we could persuade him to try his hand at box-pleats or even those marvellous little ruches sewed in points that you see these days.'

The conversation rose and fell around Ellis, rather like a well-practiced dance that always conspired to push him out to its fringes. Utterly bored, he looked around the room at the Meads' vast collection of oil paintings, all showing idyllic views of rural England—there were village ponds, wooden stiles, rosy-cheeked milkmaids attending the herd. Major Mead saw him gazing at them and smiled, trying to draw him into the gathering, 'All the things that remind people like us of home, eh? Harriet and I find them awfully comforting.' He nodded at the sturdy Friesians grazing stolidly in a Troyon painting, 'Rather different from the emaciated cattle that wander around the streets and bazaars here as though they have as much right to be there as people.'

'I daresay cattle have more rights than people in these Hindoo states,' Royle laughed.

'Aha, but one of the best things about moving from a Hindoo state to a Moslem one will be sinking my gnashers into a generous slab of beef steak, Royle,' Mead replied lightly.

Suddenly, despite the Meads' kindness at having attempted to include him in their tea party, Ellis felt unbearably suffocated both by the room and by their company. The khus tatties had been drawn tight and a servant was standing on the outside, keeping them drenched, but the scorching afternoon sun was still managing to make its presence felt in the stiflingly hot room. He put his cup down with a clatter and got up abruptly, feeling a complete cad at the look of consternation that came over Harriet Mead's pretty face.

'I'm ever so sorry, Mrs Mead, but I've just recalled an engagement elsewhere...' He felt terrible. It was not Harriet's fault, nor even that of people like the Royles, that made him so unable to fit in and Ellis hoped they would see that the blame lay entirely with him. Mumbling further excuses that he was sure no one believed, Ellis departed the Mead household. As he rode away, he knew that the party's attentions would turn to him in his absence, quite probably not sympathetically. It was hard to care much any more.

The following day, Major Ellis and Captain Martin took their places, on two high-backed chairs set to one side for them, alongside the ministers of the Jhansi court. The main durbar hall had been opened up for the adoption ceremony and the accompanying prayers had already commenced at one end. Smoky incense clouds rose towards the gilded ceiling of this vast pillared hall that echoed with the gentle chanting of bare-bodied priests grouped around a fire pit.

Looking around, Ellis spotted Krishna Rao amidst the crowd and they exchanged a curt nod. As soon as he looked away, Ellis leaned across to Martin who had noticed the exchange to mutter sotto-voce, 'Well, I must be doing something right to earn a nod rather than the customary glare, don't you think?'

'I'd have expected him to be in a foul temper over this adoption,' Martin replied, maintaining his impassive expression as carefully as Ellis. 'He surely can't be best pleased to be presented with yet another obstacle in his own thorny path to Jhansi's throne.'

'Quite. I reckon he'd have secretly opposed it but I'm not sure he would dare say anything to the queen, formidable that she herself is in many ways. Wise decision on her part, certainly, adopting a child and heir.'

'Yes sir, can't ever see Calcutta entertaining the idea of old Krishna Rao ascending the throne.'

Ellis shot a look around the room. They were too far from the ministers to be overheard, the prayer chanting masking all conversation. 'Well, they'd be a lot happier with the queen,' he replied, 'but she couldn't directly inherit the title, of course. Given the death of their baby, and in the light of the king's failing health, this adoption is a pragmatic step indeed.'

Ellis wondered if the queen had been behind the letter he had received from Raja Gangadhar just last week. He had recognized the king's faltering signature but the letter was in the elegant hand of an official court writer and was, essentially, a plea to present the king's adoption of his young relative to Calcutta as an entirely legal method for the royal lineage to continue.

'...God willing,' the letter had said, 'I hope to recover from my illness and regain my health. But if I fail to, I trust that you will take my loyalty to the British Government into account and show kindness to my son. Please acknowledge my widow as the mother of this boy during her lifetime. May the Government approve of her as Queen and ruler of Jhansi as long as this child is a minor. Please take care, my friend, to see that no injustice is done to them...'

Ellis's attention was drawn to the other end of the hall. A small boy, no more than four or five, was being led in by the hand. A tall man of serious appearance, who he guessed was the child's father, was helping to seat him on a snow-white mattress before the head-priest. As he drew away, the rani and her ladies-in-waiting assembled behind the purdah. Ellis could see the flashing and winking of their jewels through the thin silk of the curtains. Finally, the raja entered; carried in on a small silver bed, his feeble frame draped in an elaborately embroidered jamawar shawl. Even the pretence of hoisting him up and skimming his feet along the floor seemed to have been dispensed with as his illness had taken hold.

'Hadn't realized the old man was that far gone,' Captain Martin muttered under his breath, shifting uncomfortably.

Ellis nodded, not wishing to prolong the conversation for fear that people would guess they were commenting on the raja's piteous condition.

They lapsed back into silence, perched uncomfortably on their gilt chairs and looming above the other guests who sat cross-legged on carpets and durees on the floor. As the prayers progressed, Ellis marvelled at how obediently the child observed all the rituals, even chanting verses from a book of Vedas in a clear, high-pitched voice. He wished the child would fill the void that must surely exist in the rani's heart. From his calculations, he guessed that she could not be more than twenty-five now, but his estimate was based on all the conjecture he had heard about her when she had married the king.

An hour later the ceremony drew to a close with the priest sprinkling holy water on the boy's head and on Raja Gangadhar's. Both their hands were washed in the same silver bowl, after which the head-priest signalled to the crowd that they might now rise. Some people approached the raja and touched his feet. Ellis watched as some courtiers touched the feet of the newly adopted prince too. The expression on the child's face was one of bewildered acquiescence and Ellis felt sorry for him despite the sudden elevation in his stature. He had been advised that the boy was going to be renamed Damodar after the king's dead child. It was impossible to predict, in the current climate of busy expansionism, what might lie in store for this small principality and, consequently, for the fortunes of this prince. Jhansi had thus far not been important or wealthy enough to matter very much to the powers in Calcutta but its position, right in the middle of Bundelkhand, gave it a cachet it may one day wish it did not possess. Ellis took a deep breath before accompanying Martin across the hall, their tall figures shouldering their way through the crowd, to congratulate the raja and sign the requisite papers.

Raja Gangadhar was too weak to talk but he held onto Ellis's hand as he bent over him. He opened his mouth to speak but words would not come and Ellis squeezed his palm to indicate that he understood what he was trying to say. After what seemed like an age, he finally felt the raja relinquish his hand, allowing him to step away.

Moving away from the crowd, Ellis saw a small plump figure wend his way across the durbar hall, hailing him loudly, and recognized Nanasahib, the old Peshwa's son. He recalled having met the man once at the racecourse in Kanpur and knew that he had visited Jhansi recently. But he had not expected to see him at this ceremony and hoped he had managed to conceal his surprise by introducing him swiftly to Captain Martin. As the men shook hands, two other people in ceremonial dress stepped forward. They were presented as Nanasahib's friend, Tantia Tope, and their minister, Azimullah. Ellis wondered why Nanasahib, not even an ex-Peshwa, should be in need of a minister and resolved to ask Malcolm later, who was in Calcutta at the moment.

Both Nanasahib's companions greeted the Englishmen with unsmiling visages and Ellis suspected uneasily that they knew nothing of the warm relationship he shared with the royal family of Jhansi. Perhaps they assumed that he was here merely to snoop on behalf of the British. After a stiffly formal exchange of pleasantries, the party moved on, leaving Ellis disconcerted by the unfriendly demeanour of Nanasahib's aides, even though the man himself had seemed affable enough.

About to ask Captain Martin what he had thought of the odd little encounter, Ellis heard him slowly let out his breath and saw that Martin's eyes too were fixed on the departing backs of the three men. His voice was a hoarse whisper, 'I say, sir, was it just me or did you imagine that mullah chap would have been quite delighted to stick a small dagger in my stomach even as he shook my hand...'

Ellis did not reply but some instinct told him that this was not the last he would hear of Azimullah.

It was from Major Malcolm, who had in turn received his news from Belinda Royle, that Ellis heard the details of Harriet Mead's visit to Begum Hazratmahal a month after the Meads had reached Lucknow. Even Ellis, who normally shied away from the cantonment gossip, greeted the news with some curiosity, given the begum's notoriety. Starting off as one of the nawab of Awadh's hundred concubines, she had, having produced the son who would be heir, swiftly risen amongst the ranks of the wives to occupy a position of permanent and overweening power. She lived in the reputedly fabulous Qaiser Bagh Palace on the outskirts of Lucknow and it was to this palace that Harriet had been invited. According to Malcolm, the palace had turned out to be even more magnificent than Harriet had expected and, from the letter she had written Belinda, it appeared she had been utterly overwhelmed by it all.

Ellis could imagine poor Harriet disembarking from her carriage, resplendent in her new gown and dainty matching reticule, terrified at being greeted by one of the legions of African eunuchs purportedly employed by the nawab to mind his harem. According to Malcolm, Harriet had been whisked through fountained courtyards and walled gardens and room after room of the begum's Chaulakki Kothi, each carpeted and draped more opulently than the last. Finally deposited in an enormous curtained space, she had been asked to remove her shoes and her hat. Although entirely taken aback by this strange request and struggling somewhat to untie her laces, Harriet reported that she had not liked to question nawabi protocol, only wishing she had thought to bring one of her maids with her. Once her straw hat and shoes had been carefully carried away on a small bell-metal platter, she was taken in stockinged feet over yet more carpets and through further yards of silk curtains until she found herself facing a woman with pudding-soft flesh, 'as fair as any European's'.

The begum had apparently been all kindness and graciousness to Harriet and her letter had been full of this as well as elaborate descriptions of the harem. The commodious female quarter was, according to Harriet, filled with an air of great satiety and lassitude that seemed to be emanating from the begum herself. She had seen at least a score of women lounging around the zenana, playing card games and chess and carefully making up little green rectangles of paan that they chewed complacently on, resembling, as Harriet reported, a herd of colourfully arrayed cows.

Occasionally one of them shimmied to their side to enquire after the begum's comfort but Hazratmahal seemed happy to converse privately with Harriet, spending much of her time talking of a visit she had made to Queen Victoria, whom she referred to as 'your dear little Padishah', referring snidely to her appropriation of the Koh-i-Noor from the Punjab. Harriet thought it rather beastly of the begum to say such horrid things about her queen and had, consequently, been most relieved when the tea things were finally brought in by a succession of pretty young girls carrying platefuls of candied fruit and dainty little cakes. They were at this stage joined by the ladies of the harem who had finally roused themselves from their diwans and sofas to partake of the tea and, luckily for Harriet, the conversation changed course to much pleasanter matters.

The visit had ended, as visits to wealthy royal residences often did, with Begum Hazratmahal presenting Harriet with a small calf-skin leather box that Harriet swore she had tried her utmost to dissuade the begum from parting with. It was only later, as she opened the box in the privacy of her carriage, that she saw how expensive the gift was. Belinda had furnished Malcolm with the tiniest detail, almost as if she had been present too, and he later did a wonderful job of mimicking her nasal tone when repeating the story to Ellis: 'My dear, a thing of great beauty indeed. *Great* beauty. A bracelet of turquoise beads and opal drops like white pomegranate seeds, set alternately in delicate gold and silver pockets and strung together with the finest of chains. The turquoise exactly the colour of Harriet's eyes. *Exactly*. Imagine that!'

Ellis imagined Harriet lifting it out of the box and holding it against her wrist. Of course, she could not possibly have turned down such a gracious gift and risked offending the begum. Despite the rules, Ellis was certainly not going to enquire if Harriet had passed the bracelet onto the Toshakhana at Calcutta as protocol demanded. As far as he was concerned, Harriet had earned her bracelet by dint of all the effort she made to live in India, so very far from the comforts of England and home.

☙ 18 ❧

Seated at the writing desk in her room, Rani Lakshmibai looked up as Kashi entered the room followed by a smaller girl. This must be the playmate that Kashi had promised to recruit for Damodar, Lakshmibai thought, quickly putting her pen down and waiting for the two to be done with their namaskars. Lakshmibai smiled over the girl's head at Kashi, aware that the uncustomary depth of her obeisance today was for the benefit of the new maid as Lakshmibai had long before requested her retinue to dispense with the court formalities demanded of them by the previous queen.

'First things first, what is your name, my dear?' Lakshmibai asked the young girl standing before her, employing the local dialect and keeping her voice gentle for the child's terror was apparent.

'Kamlesh,' the girl mouthed so softly that Lakshmibai could barely hear her.

'What is that? Speak up, child. If you have no voice, how can I expect you to befriend my son, hmm?' she asked. The girl had a wide-eyed, honest look about her and Lakshmibai judged her to be the right age to act as both playmate and nursemaid for Damodar.

Kashi, standing behind the girl, gave her a poke in her back with her finger. 'She is Kamlesh and oh she has enough of a voice when you don't want to hear it, Rani-sahiba,' she laughed. 'I hear my aunt complain about it all the time!'

'Well, perhaps she will chatter to me too after she has found her voice again. Maybe it got lost on your way to the palace this morning. These things happen sometimes just to annoy us, yes?' The rani smiled at the girl and was pleased to see a shadow of a smile in response. She herself had not been much older than this chit of a girl when she had come to this house as Gangadhar's bride. How immature and fearful she too had been then, fretting constantly about how people perceived her rather than relying on her self-knowledge.

'She will lose her fear after just a few days, Kashi. Let her sleep in your room for the time being and make sure the other girls treat her well. Kamlesh, after a few days, you can come to me again and we can talk about how you can join in the prince's routine. He will be busy with his tuitions all morning but I think you might benefit by sitting with him at his lessons. It will be good for you to learn to read and write too. In the afternoon, he will rest with me for an hour before his play. Most evenings, you will have to take him to visit his parents who live across the city at Halwaipura.' The rani turned again to Kashi. 'I think that's enough instruction for now. For the next few days, either you or Sundar will continue taking Damodar to see his parents. Where is he now?'

'Sundar has gone to fetch him from his tuition, Rani-sahiba.'

'Well, after you have taken Kamlesh to show her the quarters, bring Damodar to me. We shall have lunch together and take some rest before I introduce him to his new companion. Child, you too will take some lunch and rest before the evening.'

Having signed the last of the papers brought to her by Dewan Rao Bande, Lakshmibai stood up, stiff from her day's work. Last night had been another restless one. Faiz Ali had woken her twice to say that Gangadhar had been asking to see her. For months now her husband barely left his chambers, leaving her responsible for Jhansi's affairs. But he so clearly looked forward to her visits, she knew she could not let him down and continued to give him nightly reports on all important events when the day's work was done. Sometimes she could not help feel annoyed at his abject dependency, especially when her own duties so consumed her energies. What exasperated most of all was that all the doctors agreed there was nothing physically wrong with Gangadhar. It was all in his mind, they said; a diagnosis Lakshmibai felt irked by, despite her best efforts to understand.

Her spirits rose as she heard Damodar's high-pitched voice echoing along the corridor. In a few moments her beautiful son would enter the room, looking unbearably smart in one of his princely achkans and, with a mere turn of his head, he would cause all her irritations to fall away. She smiled ruefully as she thought of motherhood's ability to make all else seem facile.

Damodar entered her chambers, holding Sundar's hand. His shy smile reminded her that he was still not entirely sure of her love even though she had so easily come to think of him as the baby she had lost not so long ago. He was only a few years older than her own Damodar would have been. That tiny ashen face of death would doubtless lie imprinted on her mind forevermore, but this smiling one before her now begged so sweetly to replace it; oh how could one fail to love again, she thought as Damodar ran into her outstretched arms.

'Here, my little raja,' she cried, 'up here on my lap so you can tell me about your lesson with the tutor.'

'Why do you always call me "raja", Ma? I am not the king,' Damodar asked, turning around to be pulled onto her lap.

'Because my darling, you are *my* little king and because, one day, every person in this land will have to call you Raja Damodar Rao, including me.'

'Really?'

'Really,' Lakshmibai promised firmly, enjoying the look of satisfaction she received for it.

'But when will I be king, Ma?'

'When Raja Gangadhar Rao steps down or passes away, that's when you become king, my darling.'

'I will be king and you will marry me and become my queen,' he said solemnly, making both Lakshmibai and Sundar peal with laughter.

'But...but only when the king passes away,' Damodar said hastily, confused by their mirth.

'Yes, jaan, when the king passes away,' Lakshmibai repeated more gravely, hoping that Damodar would not ask her when that would be. She turned to Sundar who was waiting to escort them to the dining room, 'Oh Sundar, couldn't lunch be brought in here for us? I really feel too tired to go to the dining hall.'

Damodar let out a cry of delight. 'I would like to eat in here. Can I sit with my feet up on the bed and be fed by Sundar?'

'No, you won't be eating on the bed, Chhotey Raja. You will sit at this little bureau here but we will pull it up to the bed and, yes, I think you can put your feet up.'

Damodar slid off her lap and kicked off his silk slippers before clambering onto the bed.

Lakshmibai turned to her maid. 'Sundar, please bring us only the simplest food. I will have just arahar ki daal with some rice and mango pickle. What would you like, Raja?'

'I will have potatoes,' Damodar said firmly.

Sundar watched in satisfaction as the rani sat next to Damodar on the bed, leaning against the soft cotton bolsters. The child wriggled himself next to her, tucking his head into the crook of her arm. Just a few months ago, Sundar had thought she would never again see that look of soft happiness on the rani's face but today it glowed like a flower that had bloomed overnight. Even Khuda Baksh's grey old head nodded in pleasure at the sight as he wheeled the lunch trolley into their chambers.

'I will serve rani-sahiba her food,' Sundar said to Khuda Baksh, 'you can return to your duties in the dining hall where the ministers await their lunch.'

After Sundar had carefully washed Damodar's hands in the silver bowls that had been placed in front of them, she patted them dry on a linen napkin. Then, picking up the rice platter, she scooped out a small measure for the rani's plate before attending to the prince.

'Bas, that's too much, Sundar,' the rani said, holding up her hand, 'you're always trying to secretly add more food to my plate.'

Sundar laughed as the prince too held up his hand in exactly the same manner, imitating too rani-sahiba's way of moving her rice to one side of the plate to place the small silver katori of daal next to it. However, as the rani accepted a small portion of roasted brinjal, the prince wrinkled his nose, pointing to the dish of potatoes instead. They had been fried to a crisp brown, in the way they all now knew Damodar liked them. Carefully lifting out a spoonful for Damodar's plate, Sundar stood watching while they ate, Damodar now prattling about the clever crow he had learnt about in his morning's lesson.

When they had finished eating, Sundar helped Damodar with the last fingerfuls of rice on his plate, scooping them into his mouth along with the last of the potatoes. Hands washed and plates cleared, Sundar attempted to wheedle the reluctant prince out of the rani's chamber, tempting him with the prospect of a new playmate called Kamlesh. But he had his arms firmly clasped around rani-sahiba's neck, extracting a promise of ten lovebirds that he could keep in the gardens adjoining his new room. The rani, for her part, seemed only too happy to submit to such a daring request and Sundar thought how delighted she would be to see the child's growing assurance in her love. But poor rani-sahiba looked fatigued today. Much as the child brought her pleasure, he needed to be extricated from the rani so that she could rest.

Lakshmibai lay back on her bed, tiredness flooding her as Sundar finally led Damodar away. She needed to catch some sleep before the evening public assembly and was grateful for Sundar's solicitousness. Their voices were still audible, floating down the corridor as they walked away from her chambers. First Sundar's musical tone: 'And then, with Kamlesh, we will go and visit your mother and father in their house, my little prince. You can show off your new friend to them too, and tell them about the lovebirds you are going to get.' And then little Damodar's high-pitched reply: 'Oh yes, Sundar, I want to go to my amma's house now, I really have missed my amma and my baba today...'

Lakshmibai turned her head away, trying not to let Damodar's words dim her contentment. Every so often she received a little reminder that Damodar was not really hers to call her own but maybe that would pass over the years. Closing her eyes, Lakshmibai placed her forearm over her face, hoping the cooing and warbling of the doves nesting in the alcoves outside would lull her to sleep. But an inexplicable restlessness was keeping her awake, her nerves tingling like pinpricks against her skin. She sighed and threw her arm over her head, looking at the coloured lozenges of light on the wall opposite the stained glass window. Filled with shimmering red and green sunlight, they looked like those oblong blocks of Karachi halwa she had loved looking at as a child. Although she had never liked eating them, preferring the burnt sugar flavour of sohan halwa instead, she remembered how she used to gaze into their translucence, always hoping to see something inside them that could not possibly exist. And, miraculously, grains of cardamom and slivers of nuts would transform into little people suspended forever in their sticky prisons. Once she had found them she would, of course, talk to them under her breath, offering them varied ideas to escape their imprisonment. When all resources were exhausted, she would finally bite carefully into the halwa and remove the nuts with her fingers to line them up on her plate, a messy teatime ritual that always annoyed Asharfi-bua for the sticky red fingerprints it left all over the table. What a silly child she had been, a little dreamer always looking for imaginary things to care for and worry about...so unlike practical sensible little

Damodar who just accepted whatever came his way with such unquestioning stoicism.

She closed her eyes again, willing herself to put aside these thoughts that were showing every sign of developing in an unwanted direction. Try to get some *rest* instead, she admonished herself, angry with such feeble wretchedness on her part. But why, she asked herself, had it always been so important to her to appear to be in charge of everything, trying to offer succour to other people, when the truth was there for all to see: that she was in fact one of the loneliest people she knew, someone who had none of the really important things in life—things that even the poorest of her subjects could have without asking—the love of a mother, the passion of a husband, a child to call one's own, not forgetting love and companionship and peace. All her wealth and her queenliness could not buy her those things and those...Lakshmibai could hardly bear to face the truth herself...those were the only things she wanted any more.

Infuriated with herself for having let her mind traverse all those thoughts she worked so hard to keep at bay, Lakshmibai jumped out of bed. She readjusted the folds of her sari in a fumbling rage before untying her braid and allowing her hair to tumble down to her waist. She did not need to call Sundar who was sometimes so slow and so gentle, she made Lakshmibai want to scream. Brushing her hair furiously, she could feel her scalp tingle as she dragged her hair back into a tight knot, jabbing a few jewelled pins to hold it in place. Without another glance at herself in the mirror, she left her chamber, letting the heavy wooden door close behind her with a satisfying crash.

But her thoughts would not turn themselves off even as she walked swiftly down the corridor. What was the point in being an admired and respected queen when she was not a proper wife to Gangadhar, but more like a sister or a friend? Nor really mother to Damodar, but a benevolent caretaker...why, she was not even a proper queen to Jhansi, just an obedient lackey to these British. If she thought about it, her marriage to Gangadhar was not too dissimilar to her relationship with Jhansi—empty, except for the outward trappings, futile in all but name.

❧ 19 ❧

Lakshmibai sat by Gangadhar's bedside, this time with the certain knowledge that she was losing him. Even the doctors had told her quite unequivocally to prepare for the end. Although the embroidered cloth punkah on the ceiling was creaking up and down interminably, she cooled Gangadhar's face with her own peacock feather fan. The November evenings were mercifully breezy but Lakshmibai had to do something with her restless hands. Every so often, her husband would rouse himself and open his eyes as though looking for her. Slowly focussing and seeing her still sitting there, he would let his lids drop again, satisfied. He was certainly dying. She recognized the heaving of his skeletal chest and the ashen grey pallor on his skin, so much like their own baby Damodar when he too had lain lifeless in her arms.

One by one the ministers came to pay their respects, including Krishna Rao and his young son, Sadashiv. Lakshmibai had expected Gangadhar's brother to cause her problems over Damodar's adoption but so far he had held his peace, surprisingly. She suspected, and her own father agreed, that the support she enjoyed from her ministers left little scope for fomenting a rebellion against her. Lakshmibai was pragmatic enough to know also that, with Dalhousie's policies wreaking such havoc, everything was in too much of a state of flux for any serious bids to be made for Jhansi's throne. If the British were to accept anyone's rule, it would be hers as regent until Damodar was old enough to rule. Krishna Rao had not even demurred as Gangadhar had signed the papers, with Major Ellis standing witness, declaring Damodar as his heir while all state administrative powers had been vested in her until Damodar gained his majority. Yet, whether it was hopelessness in the face of British hegemony or some bigger trick he had reserved for whenever Gangadhar died, Lakshmibai could not completely accept Krishna Rao's seeming placidity. For the time being, though, she was left with little choice but to wait and see whether that would turn after the raja's death.

The night deepened and Lakshmibai, seeking fresh air, stepped out onto the balcony that Gangadhar had not used for months. The winter sky was starless and clotted with dark scudding clouds. The trees around the palace, filled with night breezes, were whispering like gossipy old women, as though agitatedly trying to make up for her loneliness.

At least *they* recognized her loneliness, she thought, turning her face up towards them. Not everyone knew how Gangadhar had withdrawn into himself ever since their baby's death, his entire being collapsing into sorrow and illness. Those precious few months when they had enjoyed a full relationship had gone with the baby, their fragile and nascent passion dying with it. She had tried but not found herself able to keep from blaming her husband for his weakness. And mixed in with her grief was a frightening anger too—anger at how quickly he had taken the easier path of succumbing, never once thinking of her or of Jhansi. It was selfish, she thought, hating herself too for being so uncharitable to the husband who, she knew, had never intentionally hurt her and who now lay dying.

Yet, in spite of it all, she knew she would miss him too...his very presence in the palace had given her strength. How could she ever forget that she owed it entirely to him to have tutored her so generously and carefully in becoming a wise and good queen to Jhansi, more beloved of its people than he himself? Or had he handed over the reins of the state to her only because he had not been able to cope with the pressures of governance himself?

Wanting to stop the tortuous meanderings of her thoughts, she stepped back into the room, feeling revulsion at the overpowering smell of bromide and carbolic that, however potent, never seemed able to mask the sickly secretions of her husband's already decomposing body...

Twenty minutes after the clocks in the palace had chimed the midnight hour, Gangadhar finally died. Taking that same breath whose rattling, racking sound Lakshmibai thought she would never forget, having heard it so terrifyingly in the chest of her baby. As her husband's face went still, Lakshmibai looked on it vacantly, thinking how ugly a thing death was. She could never understand how people talked of peaceful repose in death. On both the occasions that she had seen it close at hand, it had seemed to have the power to make hideous even the memory of life.

Gangadhar's face now looked almost skull-like, his skin stretching waxy across his cheekbones, his jaw frozen into a permanent sideways grimace. Yes, he had gone. Lakshmibai got up from her bedside vigil and walked slowly down the long dark corridors back to her chamber. There was nothing more to do. Faiz Ali and Dewan Rao Bande would look after everything else, make all the arrangements for the public procession and cremation, they would inform Major Ellis too. She had done her duty as the raja's wife and would now be left alone to grieve.

As she opened her door, she felt almost surprised to see everything in her chamber exactly the same as before—the furniture, the drapes, the paintings, even her own lonely reflection in the mirrors on the far wall. She looked for a few minutes at her candlelit image and saw a woman still young, wearing the silks and jewels of a queen. Should there not be something to indicate that her life had changed indubitably and forever?

It would be foolish to cry, she thought as she lay down on her bed, feeling a dry painful heat behind her eyes. And what exactly would she be mourning? She turned and pressed her face into her pillow, reminding herself angrily that he had been kind, he had been gentle. How could she deny that he had, in his own way, loved her more than she could have ever hoped? Had it been wrong of her to have wanted more?

It was not the answer to that question but the fact that there was no one in the world she could have put that question to that finally made Lakshmibai draw in a huge sigh full of unshed tears before she wept as though she would never stop.

ॐ 20 ॐ

In attendance at Raja Gangadhar's funeral on the banks of the peaceful Lachhmitaal, Ellis was surprised at first to see that the rani was not in purdah any more. She had evidently chosen the misfortune of her widowhood on which to hang up that last ritual of submissive deference that had never seemed to suit her in the first place. Ellis had known Raja Gangadhar well enough to realize that purdah was not something he would have demanded of his wife and had also heard that the queen only observed it when in the company of the British. It had obviously been a duty the queen had imposed on herself for some reason. But now, on the death of her husband, she had found a moment most opportune to relinquish the custom. It occurred to Ellis that the act was a courageous gesture indicating that she was ready to deal with all the challenges that lay ahead of her. She was, however, in the white weeds of Indian widows, her bowed head covered by her sari.

Standing only a short distance away from the ceremonies taking place on the lakeside cremation ground, Ellis was able to observe Lakshmibai for the first time and was astonished to see how very young she was. Even though he had always known she was much younger than the king, he had, over the years, grown used to associating her voice from behind the purdah with the sallow and increasingly wrinkled face of Raja Gangadhar. But now, mere yards before him, was the firm curvaceous figure of a young woman, her skin glowing with good health. Her face was oval and wore a serious, unsmiling look that could not mask her beauty. At one point, when she looked up to murmur instructions to young Damodar who was bare-chested like the priest, Ellis saw dark luminous eyes and was startled as they flashed up at him across the marquee and over the heads of the other visiting dignitaries. He had not meant to be staring and, as their gaze briefly met, he hoped she would not misunderstand his intentions.

Lakshmibai could not fail to notice Major Ellis's look even from where he stood. Though distracted by having to instruct Damodar, she felt a flush of shame at how the frank appreciation in his gaze had made her pulse quicken instantly. Bending over to hold the burning torch for Damodar, she felt her breath grow shallow in her throat as though the fire had caused the air around it to grow thin. By the time she had straightened up and cast a quick glance over the crowd again, Ellis was looking, like everyone else, at the pyre of sandalwood now starting to spit and crackle angrily. The flames had taken hold and black clouds of smoke were billowing into the sky. Lakshmibai stared into the churning gold heart of the fire, trying desperately to remember Gangadhar's face when she had first looked upon it eleven years ago. Even as a young girl, she had been able to recognize the kindness in his eyes; his constant efforts to make her happy. That he had not always succeeded had been as much out of his control as hers and so how could one even begin to apportion blame, she thought, feeling that familiar wretchedness that gripped her every time she dwelt on the state of her marriage.

Following the journey being made by a plume of smoke floating up and dispersing into a benevolent blue sky, she tried to shake off her misery. It was impossible at this moment to tell if her aching grief was for the loss of her husband or the life she had never had with him. Deep down too was the realization that she only had herself to blame for putting her husband's needs before her own. She straightened her back, gripping the pallav of her sari against her shoulders as though its flimsy silk could somehow stave off the tumult of feelings inside her. Tempted terribly to seek out the warm approbation on Ellis's face again, she told herself bleakly that she had no reason at all to feel guilty in enjoying the pleasure of a man's admiring glance.

Later that morning, Major Ellis approached her, with Colonel Malcolm and Captain Martin following close behind. As he expressed their joint condolences, she looked into his blue-grey eyes. She listened carefully before briefly inclining her head and putting her palms together in a silent gesture of gratitude. Looking up again, she met his sympathetic look squarely with a grave expression in her own eyes. Then, for the first time she addressed him directly, saying softly, 'Thank you, Major Ellis. Your friendship was one my husband valued above all others and I am sure he would have been grateful for your presence here today.' She repeated her namaskar to the other two men without saying anything further and they bowed respectfully before moving on.

Three weeks were to pass before Ellis would encounter her again. He had packed his palette and paintbrushes early one morning and ridden the ten-mile distance to the abandoned castle that stood at the edge of Barhwa Sagar. It was Karamchand the orderly who, on one of their early exploratory rides, had shown him the crumbling castle that stood at the very edge of a vast sheet of water. And it had not been long before Ellis had taken to riding out to the lonely ruins whenever he tired of the cloistered life of the cantonment. No one had been able to tell him who had built this dwelling of such European appearance that it would not have looked out of place at all on the banks of the Rhine and he had not asked many questions for fear of losing the seclusion it offered him.

Although the stone construction was more or less intact, it looked as though the old castle was gradually being eaten away by dense forests on one side, while lapping silver waters of the lake washed against its eastern walls. Nearby were the ruins of an old Jain temple that was at least a thousand years old, going back to what Ellis guessed was probably the Gupta dynasty, judging by its undamaged stone friezes.

Despite Karamchand's protestations that the castle was likely to be the haunt of bandits and dakoos, Ellis had recently taken to escaping at least once a week to Barhwa Sagar. There was something about such stubborn remnants of long-forgotten glories that offered a permanence increasingly hard to find elsewhere. Sometimes, it was as if his only joy lay in these weekly escapes to the peaceful ruins, where the only sounds to disturb him were the geese and snipe at play in the water below. Occasionally, boys from the village beyond would bring their log canoes to the edge of the lake and their snatches of laughter would drift upwards as they raced each other, bringing a smile to his lips. It was on these heights, blissfully far from the cantonment, that he would set up his easel, safe in the knowledge that he would never be found even if the entire company were searching for him. It was true that his painting efforts were more fervent than accomplished but they provided him with an opportunity to make up for his peculiar disinheritance, these blank canvases allowing him the freedom to control things exactly as he wished; a power now virtually impossible in the real world.

That day, although the morning was still cold, Ellis set up his easel outdoors and took off his jacket, hanging it on a nearby tree. The best view of the Betwa flowing into the lake was from this crumbling eastern wing. He had heard that some poor soul had thrown himself into the river just last week, but one would never have guessed that tragedy could have any bearing on the silver ribbon lying sparkling across the horizon. His horse wandered untethered among the ruins, cropping at the grass that sprang between moss-covered stones. Morning breezes were making the surrounding forests rustle pleasantly.

It was when he was well into his stride, leaning over his canvas to carefully dot white flecks across the river's edge that he heard her voice. Even if he had not turned, he would have had little difficulty recognizing her by that soft and slightly musical intonation, as that was all he had known her by these many years. He swung around, experiencing the same disbelief he had felt at the raja's funeral on looking directly into her face. How strange and how pleasurable to see all of it, rather than merely catching tantalizing glimpses of eyes and mouth through the lacy ivory screens that had hidden her from view all these years.

She was sitting atop a chestnut mare, her face framed by a small red silk scarf. A few wisps of hair had managed to escape her scarf to play on her temples and neck. As she noticed his careful observations, Ellis saw her smile for the first time—a smile that he had 'heard' on many an occasion as he narrated small amusing stories to her and Raja Gangadhar, who enjoyed his occasional droll sense of humour. But seeing it now as it revealed a glimpse of teeth behind a shy smile, gave him the most curious sensation of warmth that he had not felt towards her before.

'I am sorry you did not hear us approach, Major Ellis,' she said apologetically, 'Sundar and I had no intention of startling you.'

Ellis, still holding his paintbrush, bowed to the queen and her companion. 'I need no particular concentration for such trifling recreation, Rani-sahiba,' he said, suddenly embarrassed at being caught with smudges of paint on his exposed forearms. He took a step to his left, attempting to block their view of his half-finished canvas.

'Your painting is quite beautiful, Major Ellis,' Lakshmibai said, smiling. 'I think you have captured the view of our river perfectly. Our Betwa never does travel anywhere in a hurry, does she?'

Ellis laughed, regaining his composure at the rani's friendly tone. 'Yes, I once tried painting the Betwa in the monsoon, but even then her mood seemed to remain unchanging and unhurried. Quite the sedate dowager lady, isn't she?' he said.

'If it is a restless river you are looking for, then it is our Ganga you want, Major Ellis. I was given one of her names, Manikarnika, born as I was at Varanasi. But later, when I was growing up, I used to wonder why they had named me after a goddess who had killed all her children.'

'I am not aware of that legend, Rani-sahiba. I have seen the Ganges at Kanpur but hadn't realized there was a story to explain her turbulence.'

'I don't tell stories very well, Major Ellis, but legend has it that Goddess Ganga agreed to marry King Shantanu on the condition that he would never question any of her decisions. But when she kept on drowning their children, he could finally bear it no more and begged her to stop.'

'How intriguing—and did she?'

'Shantanu saved the last child, a son who succeeded him as a mortal. All the others had been promised immortality through death, you see. But, as Ganga-devi's husband had broken his word to her, she vanished into the river to never return again.'

'That's a sad story indeed,' Ellis said, shaking his head ruefully. 'I have often wondered why this beautiful land produces such heartbreaking legends.'

'That's a very good question, Major Ellis, and certainly one for which I shall need time to think up an answer.' There was a small pause before Lakshmibai sat up in her saddle as though she had temporarily forgotten herself. 'But, Sundar and I will now ride on. We had not intended disturbing an artist at work.'

'Why, I wouldn't describe stirring stories as a disturbance at all. And I am truly touched by your kind compliments about my painting, Rani-sahiba. I'm normally much too diffident to show anyone my work.'

'Well, I would wish you to return to your painting, Major Ellis. We will now ride on.'

Ellis was in no hurry to terminate the conversation. 'I...I did not know that you rode, Rani-sahiba,' he said feebly.

'Oh, ever since I was a child. I love horses and try to ride every morning if I can manage the time.' There was another moment's hesitation before she added, 'And I did not know that you are a painter. It looks like there is a lot you and I do not know about each other, Major Ellis, despite your many visits to the palace over the years. I do not even seem to know your full name, having only ever seen your initials on government papers.'

'It is Robert, Rani-sahiba. Robert Walter Ellis.'

Lakshmibai smiled and said, 'So now I know both your name and your secret preoccupation, Major Ellis. Robert Walter Ellis, the painter.'

'I doubt I should ever describe myself as a painter, even though I do enjoy watercolours very much. There's something very comforting about the process of making the world seem a gentler place than it really is.'

'Perhaps then I should aspire to learning the skill from you someday,' she laughed.

'That would be my pleasure, Rani-sahiba, and perhaps, in return, you will allow me to come riding with you,' Ellis responded, wondering at his sudden boldness.

The rani looked down at him, her dark eyes suddenly inscrutable. 'That would be no trouble at all, Major Ellis,' she said evenly. She tugged on her horse's bridle before adding, 'I try to ride out every morning at around the same time and would be pleased to meet you here any morning that you are free to ride.'

Ellis bowed his head again as the two women turned their horses around. He watched them canter away feeling a strange thumping in his chest. He felt, for some odd reason, that he had just undertaken some huge risk, even though, going over the conversation in his mind, he knew it to be perfectly innocent. The queen and her companion were quite far along the escarpment now, going at a fair gallop, but still visible from where he stood. Both were wearing jodhpurs and silken tunics and, from this distance, could have been mistaken for men, sitting astride as they were, rather than side-saddle in the manner of English ladies.

The watery winter sun was gaining strength as Ellis returned to his painting. But the riverscape seemed quite the wrong thing to be painting now. The growing brilliance of the morning had taken the softness out of the scene. It had certainly been a distraction, meeting the rani unexpectedly like that. Ellis felt his mood had changed completely. He tore the paper from its easel and clipped on a fresh sheet. With just a few firm brushstrokes a face started to emerge, olive skinned, dark eyed and smiling. Her face had been against the sun and he was not sure if he ought to use black paint or brown to daub the eyes.

He half expected to never see her again on his rides but could not help a feeling of anticipation as he set out again the following morning for Barhwa Sagar. Much to his surprise and delight, however, she kept her word and, just as the sun had risen to tremble over the placid lake as though uncertain of which way to go next, he heard the crackling of leaves behind him. As he turned, he saw that her companion was with her again and, for a moment, he marvelled at how pretty a picture the two women made as their horses swayed gracefully in his direction, the dense green curtain of forest forming a barely moving backdrop.

'You do not paint today, Major Ellis?' Rani Lakshmibai called out by way of a laughing greeting.

He bowed courteously as they neared. 'I thought it far preferable to show you the environs of the lake if indeed you have not seen them before, Rani-sahiba,' he replied, unable to prevent displaying almost boyish pleasure at her having kept her promise to return.

Drawing in her reins, she said, 'You may be surprised, Major Ellis, to know how little of my land I have seen—although I do try to get around, sometimes without the knowledge of my subjects so that I acquire a sense of how things really are. I would be delighted now to have you show us this beautiful lake. Did you know it was man-made years ago in order to bring fertility to the surrounding areas?'

'Yes, by the eponymous Bir Singh Deo, I believe. The same king responsible for the citadel in which you live, if I am not mistaken.'

Ellis had merely presented received opinion and was taken aback as he was swiftly contradicted by Lakshmibai who said good-naturedly, 'Too much of the good done in Bundelkhand has been attributed to that no doubt great king, Major Ellis, but I do believe the idea for this jheel came from one of my husband's direct ancestors in an era anterior to Bir Singh Deo's. But, indeed, he built the fort in which I live.'

Even though her voice was firm, she smiled at him, signalling that she was not seriously upset with his error. Faintly discomfited, he mounted his roan briskly.

'Please lead the way down the embankment, Major Ellis,' Lakshmibai said as she and her maid drew their horses back to make way for him. He took the lead, carefully steering his horse down the slope, feeling granite scree and pebbles slip under its hooves, sending some rolling down the path ahead of them. He was going slowly enough for the two women to follow easily, even though it was clear that they were both expert horsewomen.

'They say there are crocodiles in the lake,' he called out over his shoulder, 'so I shall not be taking you too near if you do not mind, Rani-sahiba, but the jungles on the opposite shore that you can see from here are excellent hunting grounds for anyone who derives enjoyment from that occupation.'

They looked out over the expanse of water reflecting the thick forests at its far fringe as Ellis said, 'It always pleases me to see how well those trees guard the wealth of wildlife that live behind them.' The silence emanating from the forest was so deep, Ellis thought they might actually be able to hear it resounding but, below them, a flock of wild fowl shattered the peace quite suddenly as they broke into noisy play amidst the lotus leaves on the lake's surface.

'Have you no interest in the sport of the Englishmen, Major Ellis?' Rani Lakshmibai queried, drawing level with him as they reached flat ground. 'Your countrymen usually take great pleasure in hunting and fishing, which, for us Hindustanis, is more often conducted as a matter of need rather than entertainment.'

'I have been on many a hunt, Rani-sahiba. It is indeed, as you say, a social occasion in which one must sometimes take part, however unwillingly. It is not a favourite preoccupation of mine, I have to say, although one of my earliest hunting experiences in India took place on the opposite bank of this very lake.'

The bottom of the path had widened and they were now riding side by side. Lakshmibai had her head turned towards Ellis and he guessed she was waiting for him to elaborate. He cleared his throat self-consciously before starting his narration, aware that her eyes were fixed on his face.

'We had set out, a party of us from Sagar, to hunt some snipe, Rani-sahiba. But, overnight, one of our camels that had not been tied properly wandered down to the plain below and was found dead in the morning, killed by what was either a panther or a tiger, according to the local villagers. As you can imagine, there was great excitement and the poor camel's body was left as bait for the tiger the following night. The party was quite determined to avenge its death.'

'And did the tiger come back for it?' Lakshmibai asked. As Ellis turned to meet her gaze, he was close enough to see amber flecks dancing in soft dark eyes.

'Well, we took up our positions, with a couple of sowars carrying guns, in the branches of a tree just thirty yards from the camel but the only visitors we had in the night were jackals and hyenas. I still remember how deafening their howls and screams were as they set upon the carcass and I was sure that the caterwauling would keep the tiger away. But, at about one in the morning, it appeared at the edge of the clearing, eyes glittering and angry, as though loath to make an appearance until its passage was completely clear. What was quite amazing to behold was the manner in which the lesser animals gradually and reluctantly slunk away at the arrival of the master. His very presence at the edge of the clearing seemed enough warning to remove themselves. There is indeed an order laid down by Nature that is always respected, no matter how desirable the prize...'

'And did the bigger masters get their prize? I hope you are going to tell me that your party did not get the tiger?' Lakshmibai persisted.

'Well, if truth be told, I would have been truly content just to gaze on at the spectacle of that majestic creature transformed as it was to silver by the light of the moon. It was so near, I could actually hear its soft growling as it fell upon the camel to feast itself.'

'Oh how very sad—it must then have made such easy prey for its hunters.'

'On the contrary, Rani-sahiba. Some impatient fool started shooting wildly and it bounded away. We found traces of blood on the leaves near the clearing the next morning, which the men felt was likely to have been from a wound it had taken. But it escaped our guns, luckily, and probably still lives in the depths of the jungles on the other side.'

'Well, I certainly hope it does, Major Ellis. Somehow that is an inspiring thought, don't you think? An escaped tiger hiding forever from its would-be killers.'

'Perhaps even lying in wait for the day they return!' Ellis accepted laughingly.

He shot a look across at her smiling profile. Why had he never even imagined that this lovely, natural aspect to Rani Lakshmibai existed in the many years he had been visiting the palace? Even though he had often been impressed by her intellect and her grasp of politics, this warmth and charm had remained screened away behind her ivory purdah. She was looking away now, pointing in an easterly direction as she continued the conversation.

'There are beautiful forests on the way to Shivpuri too, Major Ellis,' she was saying, 'with only small wild animals, but filled with a wealth of birds of all descriptions, and the most magnificent old trees too. Seeing that, like me, you enjoy the pleasures of nature without harbouring the tiniest wish to destroy it, perhaps it will be my pleasure to show you around those forests tomorrow?'

Ellis bowed atop his horse, feeling incredibly flattered. 'I would be most honoured, Rani-sahiba,' he said, keeping his tone even.

As the sun disappeared behind a cloud, a rustling swept across the surrounding forest, lifting it like a soft green wave. Ellis looked up at the darkening sky.

'The wind seems to be picking up...it may rain,' he said, regretting almost immediately having so clumsily provided a reason for Rani Lakshmibai and her handmaiden to think of cutting short their ride.

He heard them commenting to each other in Marathi about the possible threat of rain and the distance that lay between them and Jhansi town and Lakshmibai seemed persuaded of the need to return to their palace. She smiled at him as she turned her horse around, her maid following her example.

'It is to be a hasty farewell today, Major Ellis,' she said apologetically.

'Of course. Goodbye, Rani-sahiba,' he said, bowing before watching them ride away as the wind rose some more, blowing hard through the leaves. He felt it lift his hair and run cool fingers down the skin on his neck and chest. The sound it made was one of angry rivers rushing over stone, as though suddenly impatient with the notion that anyone had ever considered this to be the most peaceful spot on earth.

Lakshmibai, galloping towards her fort with Sundar at her side, saw its granite mass rise gleaming on a shimmering horizon, untouched as yet by the approaching clouds. Gangadhar's royal standard was visible now, fluttering from its tall mast. As she rode on, she contemplated, as she had done all morning, her boldness in meeting Ellis outside the confines of her court and, more specifically, how uplifted the encounter had made her feel. She was determined not to feel guilty, having instructed herself many times since her husband's funeral to take the meagre delights that may now come to her, newly freed of the shackles that had been cast on her by matrimony and by Gangadhar's illness. Impetuosity had always been one of the flaws she most rued in herself, but, on this occasion, she was sure she had not made her decision lightly. Major Ellis was a faithful old friend of the Jhansi court. Gangadhar had trusted him even more implicitly than she herself had often been disposed to. Yes, she felt certain that her husband would only have derived satisfaction in this newfound ability to take control of her life and pleasures in a way that she had always allowed him to.

She raised her face to the sky as a few tentative streaks of rain fell and then wiped away a few small droplets that had fallen on Sarangi's golden mane. Now she could feel a couple of warm spatters on her bare forearms too. Pleased to believe they were numinous unspoken blessings from above, she spurred Sarangi to go faster, calling over her shoulder to Sundar who thrilled to hear the elated laughter of her queen float over the wind and the thudding of their horses' hooves.

A week after that encounter, Lakshmibai sat alone on her eastern balcony, watching the distant hills turn from purple to pale pink to a glorious rosy amber. She accepted the tumbler of cardamom tea brought by Sundar but, seeing that the rani's thoughts were faraway, the maid withdrew silently to her duties indoors. Lakshmibai's gaze rested on the sunrise unfurling before her but her thoughts were on the tall figure of Major Ellis who would, in an hour, be awaiting her at the lakeside. She blew on her tea, thinking of how sporting a figure he cut on horseback, even though his clothes always looked as though they had been thrown on in a hurry, his jodhpurs creased and shirtsleeves rolled carelessly to his elbow.

It had only been a few days since they had started taking their morning rides together but Lakshmibai could not help a small flutter of anxiety as she speculated on where they may lead. Surely it was improvident to expect that she, a newly widowed queen, could drift unthinkingly into a friendship with her British political agent in the way her husband had done. She ought not to forget that, as a woman and a widow, there would be mutterings about her conduct and the high opinion of her people mattered more to her than anything else. But, on the other hand, how could she deny that, although her official duties were keeping her busier than ever, and she had the companionship of both her son and her father, there was some unfathomable space within her that still waited to be filled.

She sipped her tea reflecting on how much she had started enjoying the Englishman's company, finding in his admiration of her a reminder that she too could have what other women enjoyed in such abundance. His candid appreciation made her feel alive, energized. How captivating it had been too to hear him talk about a distant world of which she had little acquaintance thus far. Yesterday, Ellis had told her of his upbringing in rural England and she had been spellbound by the picture he had drawn of snow on the field outside his home in wintertime. Closing her eyes, she had tried to imagine what it would be like to see soft frozen water drifting from the sky before shrouding the land in a white blanket—seeing a facet to, not just Ellis, but all English people that she had not given any thought to since first meeting Sister Agnes; of how far they were from their own land and all the things familiar to them. It was admirable indeed that people like Robert Ellis and Sister Agnes had left their homes in the pursuit of goals so big she almost could not understand them.

She twisted the silver tumbler around in her hands as her thoughts turned sombre. She had not been blind to the fact that, although Ellis had slowly grown comfortable telling her trivial things about himself, there was still an inner core within him that trapped his real thoughts and feelings. Gangadhar too had once made a rueful remark about Ellis's characteristic reserve but, unlike him, Lakshmibai found it a frustrating attribute. She wished she could ask Ellis about British plans for principalities like Jhansi, to explain better the British attitude to Indian nobilities and why things had come to such a pass that no one knew what the shape of the future would be. If only he would lose his innate pride for one moment and reveal perhaps his own disappointment with Calcutta's policies. Surely he must share some of her unease. But, on these subjects, Robert Ellis had so far remained reticent. She knew she ought not to feel hurt by it. Even after so many years of loyal friendship between Ellis and Gangadhar, there had always been a sense that they occupied essentially separate worlds. It was nothing personal, merely a reflection of the times in which they lived.

Lakshmibai put her tumbler down. The tea had grown cold and bitter while her thoughts had taken over. She wondered if, like everyone else, Ellis too saw her as wise and capable and not in need of his guidance at all. Even those who knew her best considered her strong and self-reliant. She smiled as she got up from her swing-seat, reflecting that perhaps she made it too easy for everyone to assume so blithely that she lacked the vulnerabilities of other women.

Standing before her mirror, she brushed out the night-time braids from her hair, imagining everyone's shock if she suddenly announced how much she too hungered sometimes for the small, mundane, everyday preoccupations that other women were so blessed with; the chance to choose pretty trinkets and bangles for herself from the bazaar stalls, buy favourite foods for her dear ones…even, indeed, beautify herself while awaiting a lover's footfall in the night.

Sundar had laid out her short green achkan jacket and cotton trousers and, as she pulled on her riding clothes, Lakshmibai thought again of the man she was preparing to meet so recklessly. How could she fail to notice his handsome bearing, his strong hands and shoulders? Even more than that, the boldness with which he sometimes took in her appearance, the way his drowsy gaze came to life as it alighted on her face. And how could she imagine that such an attraction would not lead them both someday to a place they may regret to find themselves in? She gave herself a long look in the mirror, seeing an unnatural glitter in her eyes, the stubborn set of her chin so rued once by poor Asharfi-bua. Then she wrapped her dupatta tightly over her head and turned to swiftly leave the room.

❧ 21 ❧

Ellis was aware, without even being told, of the unspoken understanding between Lakshmibai and him that they needed to be discreet about their morning rides together. The times they lived in were as tremulous and uncertain as the surface of the lake on whose banks they met and a friendship like theirs would only be misunderstood. There was nothing to be gained by allowing any speculation. Only Lakshmibai's companion, Sundar, knew of their encounters and Ellis was sure that she would not breathe a disloyal word to anyone, nor even suspect her rani's motives as being anything other than pure and principled.

It had been just over a fortnight that they had been meeting at the lakeside forests to ride together. Sometimes Lakshmibai was chaperoned by Sundar and sometimes she came alone. Ellis could not help wondering at her boldness but realized that her courtiers and people would probably forgive her anything, her popularity in Jhansi being what it was. It was he who would pay a high price if his superiors found out about these unofficial meetings with Rani Lakshmibai. Not that anything sensitive was ever discussed. Ellis was, by his very nature, too cautious to let any confidential information slip and Lakshmibai had seemed to respect that.

Instead, they talked of inconsequential things. As though, in a strange way, that was all one could depend on in times like this. Stray memories of childhood—Lakshmibai's of Varanasi and Ellis's of Shropshire. The passing of winter. Prince Damodar's academic progress. Each of their first impressions of Jhansi. They told each other the stories that had brought them both together; a young officer on board a ship for India and a girl travelling in a royal caravan to be crowned queen. Two journeys from different places that now linked them to the same piece of land and inextricably to each other.

He tried his utmost to keep from imagining a closer intimacy with her but, under the softly rustling canopies of trees, it was all too easy to picture their world transformed into one where hierarchies and barriers magically fell away. Ellis could not tell, however, what Lakshmibai was thinking. He knew she liked his company, but then she always had—taking on the trust and relative informality that her deceased husband had invested in him many years before. He could also tell that she enjoyed his admiration of her; that was obvious in the sudden downward curve of her lashes when he looked at her, that shy smile playing around the corners of her lips if he gazed a moment too long.

He now stood watching her gallop across the escarpment in his direction, her silk scarf fluttering in the wind behind her and entangling with a dark length of hair. How easy, how perilously easy to forget how separate their worlds were. She neared him, coming close enough for him to see her dark eyes shining exuberantly, the patina of perspiration on her skin. And then, in an unbidden flash of knowledge, he remembered the dangers; the knowledge of who they both were and what would be done to them. His gut twisted as she dismounted before him in one swift graceful movement. It took all he had, all his reserves of self-control and discipline, to keep from gathering her up in his arms to press kisses on her soft, smiling mouth. How horrible, how unjust to have to consider at a moment like this the great gulfs that would always separate them.

Having descended her horse, she was looking up at him, laughing. He wondered at her capacity to remain so casual and unperturbed for surely the expression on his face must give all his feelings away. But, just as suddenly, she had leapt onto her horse again, challenging him to race her across the plains. As he mounted his horse and galloped after her, unable to gain on her beautiful chestnut mare, he thought for one fleeting moment that the combined beating of their horses' hooves on the parched earth sounded like the warning drums of war. But the thought was quickly dispelled as they reached the edge of the forests and slowed to a canter.

After they had ducked into the forest and caught their breaths, Lakshmibai turned to Ellis, her eyes blazing from their exertions, to say with a sigh of pleasure, 'I could quite heedlessly ride my beautiful Sarangi all day, Major Ellis. Isn't that a terrible thing for the ruler of a state to say?'

He laughed and responded light-heartedly on the equal dastardliness of a Company official escaping his duties to produce second-rate watercolours at an abandoned castle.

She looked at him and he could hardly hear the question she asked next, distracted unbearably by the pretty picture she made sitting on her horse with golden motes of dust floating endlessly around her. Smiling, she repeated her enquiry about what else he enjoyed doing in his spare time.

Awkwardly he replied, 'Ah yes, inferior watercolours are not the only thing I preoccupy myself so vainly with, Rani-sahiba. I must admit a certain weakness for old Persian poetry too—when I can purchase texts from the auction houses in Meerut, that is.'

'Why, you should have told me, Major Ellis!' Lakshmibai cried, turning to him, her eyes shining. 'Our public library in Jhansi has a wonderful collection of Persian manuscripts gathered from all over Hindustan by one of my husband's ancestors. In fact, I spent many of my own early months in Jhansi helping to restore them. You would be very welcome to see them, if you wish.'

He was still distracted but summoned up some interest, 'Might there be Persian poetry books in your collection, Rani-sahiba?'

'What would any collection be worth without Persian poetry, Major Ellis,' Lakshmibai asked in mock reproof. 'I was captivated in those days by the verses of the great Persian poet Hafez and a Sufi mystic called Jalaluddin Rumi. You have heard of them? Of course, you have. Sadly, I get little time for such pleasures now. But you are, as I said, very welcome to borrow anything you like from my library.'

'I have always wanted to read more of Rumi and it is a most generous offer you make, Rani-sahiba.'

'Well then, I will give instructions for the library to be opened especially for you every Thursday afternoon, Major Ellis. It is usually kept shut at that time to encourage people to attend the assemblies instead. But I could certainly get someone to be present at the building for you. It would be no trouble.'

It was not merely the Persian texts that offered appeal. Ellis's secret hope was that working in the library would give him further opportunities for Lakshmibai's company too. Taking his chances, he asked swiftly, 'Would you allow me perhaps to help translate some of the older Persian poetry texts into English, Rani-sahiba? If you would agree to read them, I would be happy to get my humble efforts printed as well. That's if you find them any good!'

'We can agree it right now, if you will, Major Ellis,' Lakshmibai laughed. 'Every Thursday afternoon the library will be opened and made ready for your work. You have a queen's word.'

It was raining heavily on the afternoon of the first session but Ellis had ridden out nonetheless, delighted to find Lakshmibai awaiting him under the arches of the old building, accompanied by her archivist. She laughed when she saw the Englishman's dripping figure dismounting his horse and sent her guard in search of towels from the palace next door. But Ellis barely noticed the discomfort of his damp clothes as he ducked through the low door, elated to see that Lakshmibai intended to stay and help him with the translations.

As the rain persisted, pounding down on the tiled roof of the library, he riffled through the pile of manuscripts awaiting him,

choosing a book of Rumi's verses and reading the title out loud,
Kolliyaat-e-Shams-e-Tabrizi. He dared not attempt more than a single
couplet at first and cleared his throat before reading, stumbling once
on the throaty 'gh' sound but raising his voice as he regained
confidence:

> You are all held captive behind this veil, but if you escape
>   you will yet be Kings,
> The water of life speaks to all creatures, die for me, die on
>   the shores of my stream.

He could hear his own deep voice resound through the pillared
hall as he stopped and looked up to see Lakshmibai watching him
unfathomably from under shapely brows. As the last echoes were
absorbed into the book-lined walls, she lifted her head and he saw her
black eyes were sparkling. She clapped her hands before making a
graceful gesture of adaab in appreciation.

'Something tells me you would have heard Rumi far more
elegantly recited by your court poets, Rani-sahiba,' Ellis said
apologetically, closing the book to sit down next to her.

'Oh, court poets,' she said dismissively, 'too consumed by their
own vanity to be able to convey real feeling. Give me passion over
stylish correctness any day.'

'Have you always enjoyed Persian poetry, Rani-sahiba?'

'There was a time when I hated it,' she laughed. 'The tutor could
put me to sleep within minutes of starting his session in the schoolroom
back at Saturday House.'

'Saturday House? The Peshwa's residence, where you grew up,'
Ellis asked, even though he already knew the name from before her
arrival in Jhansi.

'Saturday House,' Lakshmibai nodded, smiling, her face softening
to an almost childlike expression suddenly as she added, 'the best
place in the world. Heaven, if there ever were a heaven on earth.'

'Do you still miss it?'

She threw him a momentarily surprised look but replied gently,
'I did, terribly, when I first came here. Such a beautiful house on the
riverside, deep verandas and endless corridors. An orchard full of
mango trees. Sometimes, even now, if I listen very carefully, I feel I
can hear the high-pitched sound of children's laughter echoing through
those memories.'

'A blissful childhood then, as one would imagine all childhoods
to be. Strange, when you consider how rare they really are.'

Lakshmibai turned to him as though eager to explain. 'It may sound peculiar for a girl who lost her mother at four to say she was happy, Major Ellis. But, believe me, I was not allowed to miss her at all. And, even though our court was imbued with the bitterness of spent power, I was given the best childhood possible, thanks to the combined attentions of my father and Peshwa-sahib.'

Ellis knew she referred to the last Peshwa, deposed after the third Anglo-Maratha war. Calcutta had distrusted him, his shilly-shallying and his shiftiness, but her tender recollection of the old man certainly offered a worthy lesson in the curious nature of perspective.

'I remember Raja Gangadhar saying that the Peshwa had afforded you the same education as his own adopted son,' he remarked.

'Same? Sometimes it felt like he gave me more love than he gave Nana, Peshwa-sahib's excuse being that daughters were passing treasures.' She stopped, seeming to recollect more memories before she continued, 'Of course, I remember that Peshwa-sahib's quarters were always grander than those I shared with my father and great-aunt—rooms full of colourful cushioned furniture and gilt-framed paintings and deep glass cabinets bursting with jewelled silver and copper artefacts. But Peshwa-sahib adored all three of us equally; Nana and Mani and even little Tantia—an orphan child, taken in to be Nana's companion. We all had the same tuition and the same riding lessons, and Peshwa-sahib's delight was genuine if either Tantia or I ever got better than Nana in any of our shared activities. Tantia always beat us both in archery and I was much better than both of them at equestrian sport.' She halted and smiled as a sudden thought occurred to her. 'Perhaps that was it—wise old Peshwa-sahib had used Tantia and me to ensure that Nana, adopted late in life, did not grow up with an exaggerated sense of his own importance. And, oh, how big *that* was!'

She paused, still smiling, but, seized by sudden shyness, said softly, 'Perhaps we should make a start on the poetry, Major Ellis. You don't really want me rambling on about my childhood. It is true what they say: the happiest childhoods are those where there's nothing of consequence to remember at all.'

Ellis would have wanted to ask her more about those memories that so animated her but obediently pulled his chair closer to the table to start the work. She was so close, he could smell the sandalwood and jasmine of her skin and hair as she leaned towards him. As she started to read, he summoned up all his powers of concentration to think of the words to write in his firm, spiky hand. The first line formed in brown ink, Persian words of passion and love, transformed into courtly English. She waited till he had finished before articulating the next line, her voice low and trembling slightly as though unused to hearing herself read. While she paused again for him to write, he heard her soft breathing, so near, and the gentle clink of the bangles on her wrists. He wished he could ask for such a moment to last forever but continued quietly with the work, forcing himself to concentrate on the task at hand. As they slowly worked their way through the first page, the rain outside gradually abated, softening to gentle taps and then eventual silence on the roof tiles above. For some reason that Ellis could not comprehend, the end of the shower seemed to alter the mood inside the library inexplicably too. He looked up at Lakshmibai, waiting for the next couplet, but she had put the book down to rise abruptly.

'The rain has stopped. I must beg your leave, Major Ellis,' she said, barely looking at him as she smoothed the folds of her sari. 'I nearly forgot. It is time for my public assembly.'

Ellis stood up, confused by Lakshmibai's sudden coldness. She turned away from him, walking swiftly through the musty gloom of the library before vanishing through a sunlit door, and he watched her, dismayed at how bereft he suddenly felt.

Lakshmibai stumbled out of the library, blinking in the sudden sharp sunlight. Giving her guards orders to wait, she ran into her adjoining palace. Of course she too had felt that arc of awareness pass between Robert Ellis and herself, a feeling so acute she knew she had to leave his presence before it weakened her. She trembled with fear as she thought of how closely she had watched his hands as he had rolled up his sleeves before starting to write, his fingers transforming to gentleness as he picked up the fragile paper. How nearly she had come to losing herself, she wondered aghast, with her guards standing just outside and the archivist of the library in the room next door. Why, at one point she had even squeezed her palms tightly in her lap to prevent them straying to the table where a muscle in his right arm tensed under the golden lamplight as he wrote.

The urgent chiming of the clock in the hallway reminded her that it was time for her assembly. But she ran towards her husband's portrait instead, standing before it for one appalled moment. She had always liked this portrait of Gangadhar's, the artist having subtly portrayed the wisdom and tolerance he had been so rich in. On occasion, she had used the sight of her husband's steady gaze in this picture to calm her restlessness. But today it was his forgiveness she sought. Forgiveness for disrespecting his memory, forgiveness for not having mourned him enough. Covering her eyes with her hands, she stood alone in the cavernous hallway, praying with all her heart to somehow find the strength she would need to turn all treacherous feelings away.

Throughout that evening's assembly, she heard her petitioners' voices as though through a tunnel, seeing their figures lapse in and out of a blurred dreamlike vision. It shamed her to feel so unable to focus on their concerns, all so much bigger and more urgent than hers. Here were people about to lose their homes and livelihoods, standing before her in expectation of help.

But later, after Damodar was turned in for the night and Sundar had snuffed out all the lights in her chamber, she felt its lonely spaces wind around her again, turning her body cold and suffocating her spirit. The night was still and the sky outside shorn of moon and stars. She could smell a storm brewing somewhere in the distance and waited, sleepless on her bed, for the rain that would soon fall.

Gangadhar was gone and custom demanded that her every last aspiration should have departed with him. All desires and longings seen off forever. But what did one do with expectations that refused so obstinately to die? Somehow it had been decreed that she should be denied the love of a man. Other people were deprived of other things; this was the gift she was simply not to have.

She woke early and found that rain had indeed fallen sometime in the night. Strangely, she had not heard it through what had felt like a fitful, fragmented sleep. Getting up from her bed, she walked to a near window and looked at the still slumbering countryside, now cleansed and shining green. A damp breeze drifted towards her through the trees and she wrapped the end of her sari against her cold and bare forearms. It was a perfect morning for a ride.

If she rode towards Barhwa Sagar, she may find all her resolutions melting as soon as she saw Robert Ellis again. She had known these past few days what her presence at the lakeside would indicate to him but had foolishly not stopped to consider the effect his expectancy would finally have on her.

There were other places she could ride to, forests and hillsides that would offer solitary peace, calm restorative reflection. Keep from throwing her back into the upheaval that had torn her apart yesterday.

She turned from the window, her mind made up. She had known the loss of happiness often enough to know it was never offered lightly. When it came, it was to be seized without guilt. She would find her own riding clothes, it was much too early to wake Sundar.

❧ 22 ❧

Their meetings became daily in those days. Every morning at dawn and sometimes in the dusty evening hours, when the cowherds and farmers were all returning home, they rode out to meet at the Barhwa Sagar forests. Ellis also continued making his weekly visits to the library and sometimes she joined him there. Nothing was voiced but Ellis took Lakshmibai's presence as a sign that she desired his company as much as he did hers. Like him, she too seemed content to let her feelings remain unspoken and the weeks passed thus, with neither of them willing to do anything that would disturb the surface of the unending depths that lay between them.

Then came the first day they failed to meet since their rendezvous had begun. It was a Thursday evening in early February and, for the first time ever, Ellis had failed to turn up for his appointment in her library. He had even forgotten that it was a Thursday as he sat alone in his darkening office with his head in his hands.

He picked up the paper and gazed sightlessly at the words before him, his eyes moving up and down the lines he had already read so often in the course of the afternoon, he knew them without even looking any more. The papers that lay spread out on the teak table before him had arrived by the dak-gadi from Calcutta that morning. And the document that he held in his hand was Dalhousie's announcement of the annexation of Jhansi.

Through the months of Raja Gangadhar's illness, it had not taken much to guess that it was coming and, even before the raja's death, Ellis had persuaded Rani Lakshmibai to send a letter to Government House informing them of Damodar's adoption and reminding Lord Dalhousie of Jhansi's steady loyalty to the British over the years. But, she had not received a reply—which he knew did not bode well. He could hardly deny, though, that in all the letters that had come to him on the subject, the hints and allusions had all pointed to the eventual annexation of Jhansi, trapped as it was in the midst of British-controlled territory. Malcolm had often talked about it as though it was fait accompli.

Ellis, on the other hand had thought or, more accurately, hoped that Lord Dalhousie, caught up with his own beloved wife's illness and death, would have had more sympathy for the plight of Raja Gangadhar's widow. But, in his saner moments he had known that Dalhousie was the sort of man who would never allow personal emotions to sway decisions made for the greater good. And so, here it finally was, the sorry piece of paper Ellis held in his hand. An order from the Governor-General's office in Calcutta that he, as political agent for Bundelkhand and Rewa district, be the first to inform Rani Lakshmibai that the Doctrine of Lapse was due to take effect in Jhansi now that the raja had died without leaving a proper heir. Prince Damodar's adoption was not to be recognized. Jhansi would pass into British hands.

Ellis got up abruptly, pacing around the small room a few times before settling heavily back on his chair, throwing his head back to utter a loud groan. How on earth was he supposed to break the news to her? he wondered agitatedly. He rubbed his fingers on that familiar pulsing pain that had taken hold again, deep beneath his left temple. Despite the air of inevitability about it, the news would crush her terribly, he was sure of that. She had been so optimistic, as though annexation was a distant travesty that could only happen in states that had annoyed the British in some way.

Mandavi, Kolaba, Jalaun, Surat, Satara...Ellis knew the list of annexed states so well, he could recite it backwards if necessary. Now the two principalities to be added to that list were Nagpur and Jhansi. Ellis had already studied the Nagpur case and Resident Wilkinson's bold support of Maharaja Raghu-ji in the forties that had eventually upheld his royal rights for perpetuity, hoping that he could do the same for Jhansi. But, according to this missive, Nagpur was due to be annexed on the thirteenth of March despite all past legal action. Government House lawyers had done it so easily—all previous treaties and agreements were merely to be summarily dismissed.

He read once again the copy of the letter that had been sent to him, ordering the current resident of Nagpur to take charge as its first commissioner with immediate effect, arranging too for the jewellery belonging to its royal family to be confiscated and auctioned in Calcutta. The fact that a copy had been made to him was like a warning that there would be absolutely no room for negotiation on Jhansi. If Nagpur's case had been so easily made, then Jhansi stood no chance at all. Not only was Lakshmibai about to lose her beloved land, it was to be Ellis's pitiless job to wrest it off her.

He got up again from his chair, scraping it over the wooden floor in sudden haste, suddenly feeling unbearably suffocated. He tried to quell the breathless and rather curious sense of urgency that was overwhelming him but did not want to stop to contemplate it as he knew he had to inform Lakshmibai of this before she heard about it from anyone else. Before the news trickled into Jhansi from Nagpur or Calcutta in that annoying manner in which bad news always seemed to get around in India. He banged on the partition wall for the punkah-wallah to stop his fanning and left the room, taking a few deep breaths and willing himself to calm down before going to meet her. As he made for his bungalow, taking the shorter route behind the cool shade of the water tank, he contemplated, with sudden shocking regret, how much easier it would have been to break this news to her had this foolish attraction not developed so carelessly in the interim.

A leaden weight took hold of his stomach as he walked up the steps of his veranda. Ducking under the profuse bunches of madhumalati blossoms hanging from its eaves, he entered his quiet bungalow and looked up at the clock on the mantelpiece. With sudden consternation, he realized he had missed his appointment to visit the library. It was nearly six o'clock now and much too late for that. Being a Thursday, Lakshmibai would by now be conducting her public durbar in the city palace. If he asked for a special audience with her, he had no doubt that she would make arrangements for him to be received in the assembly hall soon after her petitioners had left but he did not know whether it would be better to break the news of the annexation to her before all her ministers and courtiers or wait until he could see her in private.

Ellis paced around the living room, pulling off his jacket and loosening his collar. Karamchand had appeared at the door to ask when he wanted supper, saying something about needing to stock up on victuals. He could hardly hear him, both for the evening clamour of birds coming in to roost on the sheesham tree outside and for the throbbing headache that had been threatening all afternoon to descend and had now taken hold. He waved the orderly away and walked across to the cabinet to help himself to a shot of whisky from the decanter. Swilling the liquid around in his glass, he considered escaping Lakshmibai's grief by presenting the annexation papers to her in a public arena, knowing instantly that he simply could not bring himself to be so inconsiderate. It would be far kinder to tell her of it in private so that he could offer her words of comfort, for whatever they were worth.

The whisky wasn't going to help one jot, he thought irritably. Ringing his small brass bell, he asked Karamchand to bring him his tin of Holloway's balm. It would be better to try to sleep on the problem. He could hardly think straight for the bands of pain gripping his head. Perhaps after all it would be best to tell her when they went riding as usual the following morning.

He was early and, dismounting his horse, he found a broken piece of wall on which to sit while awaiting her. By the time she rode up, fifteen minutes later, Ellis had rehearsed many times over the words to use. Her handmaiden was not in attendance today, she was alone. She tied her horse to a tree and walked up to him, adjusting her head scarf. She looked so beautiful and so happy, he thought sadly. But her smile faded as she neared him and he stood up. She had been able to tell merely by the expression on his face that something was wrong.

'You have bad news for me, Major Ellis?' she asked in her customary direct fashion.

He nodded. 'I do, Rani-sahiba. It's very bad news.'

'Is it Jhansi? Not annexation? Please tell me quickly.'

'It is Jhansi. I am so sorry to be the person to tell you this, Rani-sahiba. Yes, Lord Dalhousie's order arrived in yesterday's dak.'

There was a short silence before she whispered, 'So they are to take my Jhansi.'

It was not a question being put to Ellis and he remained silently sympathetic.

'When is to take effect?' she asked, her voice shaking slightly.

'Next month. The twenty-first of March.'

'Barely a month. That's the reprieve they have given me?'

Again, she was making a statement rather than asking a question and so Ellis said nothing that would only demean her pain. He could, however, feel her anguish and wanted desperately to take her in his arms.

'All my years of rule and administration have come to nothing,' she said at last, quietly breaking the silence. Her voice was shaking as she seemed to speak to herself. 'I came as a child to live in Jhansi and made it my own. All that effort, everything can be taken away just like that, at the stroke of someone's pen? Without discussion, without consulting my people. Someone faraway in Calcutta or London. Someone who could not care less.' She looked directly at Ellis now as he heard the bitterness rise in her voice and catch at her throat, making her unable to say any more.

'I think the expectation is that you will continue to carry out the day-to-day administration of the state, Rani-sahiba...if that brings any comfort...' Ellis trailed off, knowing how hollow his words must sound.

'What exactly will I stand to lose?' she asked, a note of anger creeping into her voice.

'Mainly Prince Damodar's right to inherit. The right to raise taxes. Also...Rani-sahiba, control of the state's treasury will be handed over to us, to the British.'

'And how do you expect me to survive?' Now her eyes were

flashing like hard, bright jewels. Ellis could not discern if the glimmer was due to anger or unshed tears.

'There will be a pension. The figure of six thousand pounds per annum has been mentioned in this document. Perhaps that will be negotiable...' Ellis realized his voice sounded as though he were pleading, expecting her to actually understand and accept this travesty.

'That amount is expected to cover the running of my household and the court?' she snapped, and Ellis could hear both anger and hurt in her voice.

He nodded, biting his lip. 'I am so very sorry,' he said finally.

Ellis reached out an arm in her direction. He had never touched her before but this was not the time to think of protocol. She stepped back, as though his very touch would sting her and he dropped his arm down by his side again, feeling gauche and awkward. He saw that her chin and her mouth, always so ready to break into a smile, had crumpled and puckered. Her eyes, usually dancing with golden lights, were flooding over...but he dared not move towards her for fear of offending her again. It was as though even comfort from him would be too painful for her to bear.

She took the envelope Ellis was still holding in his hand, turned on her heel and returned to her horse without another word, tucking the letter into her belt. He watched as she struggled with the tether and guessed that she could not see what she was doing for her tears. But he knew he could neither help nor try to explain. Even if he had, he would not have known what to say. Silently and helplessly, Ellis watched her mount her horse in a swift movement before kicking its flanks and riding as hard as she could, back in the direction from which she had come.

Lakshmibai swung around from the window out of which she was gazing as her prime minister had been speaking. '*Main Jhansi nahin doongi*,' she declared slowly and defiantly, her diamond nose-pin gleaming angrily as it caught the sunlight from the windows.

She said it as though it was the easiest thing in the world. *I will not give up my Jhansi*. Dewan Rao Bande looked at her sadly. She had already been through so much, the death of her baby, the illness and the passing of her husband...she was just twenty-four and those were sorrows that did not belong to youth, he thought, feeling angry and helpless. He could sense her anguish emanate across the room. Sunlight was pouring in through the window behind her, making her look as though she were surrounded by an angry glow. Her figure was erect and her chin set, the silver threads in the white tissue-silk sari she wore ablaze with morning sunshine. The only overt sign of the stress she was suffering lay in fists clenched so tightly by her side, Dewan Rao Bande could see the bones of her knuckles through stretched translucent skin.

In his hands was the edict from Governor-General Dalhousie that she had handed over to him as soon as he had come into the courtroom this morning, declaring Damodar Rao an illegal heir and announcing that Jhansi was to be annexed by the Doctrine of Lapse.

Dewan Rao Bande's first thought was that this may be the final blow that would make the rani crumble. He was wise enough to know that, in many ways, it was her love of Jhansi that had helped her overcome all the other recent travails. But what resources could she call upon to help her surmount this loss? The child...even mothering the child was not as fulfilling a preoccupation as the dewan had hoped, the rani, typically, having insisted that Damodar not be torn completely away from the love of his natural parents.

But she looked composed now as she requested her prime minister to accompany her to the private chamber. Having sent for the court writer, they both waited in silence as she seated herself at her small rosewood writing bureau. Her fingers drummed distractedly on the delicate tracery of inlaid ivory, although she occasionally rubbed her temples, as though gathering her thoughts before the court writer arrived. Dewan Rao Bande had seen exactly the same expression of pertinacity on her face when she had written her first letter to Lord Dalhousie a few weeks ago, and knew he had to say something cautionary on this occasion.

He cleared his throat. 'Rani-sahiba, your previous letter may only have pre-empted the issue. I am not sure it will be of any use to write again.' His voice was gentle.

She raised her head and looked steadily at him. 'Dewan-ji, my previous letters to Calcutta were an attempt to thwart this annexation. Those may have had no effect but I am not ready to give up just yet. We still have work to do.'

The prime minister fell silent. There was no arguing with that determined look she wore. But he saw her face turn pensive and uncertain as she added slowly, 'Just think, Dewan-ji—I had imagined Lord Dalhousie to be a man with all the usual compassions of men. Having heard from Major Ellis that Dalhousie had been distraught when his wife died recently, I had hoped grief would have softened his heart. Hoped he would view my circumstances with kindness and consideration.'

She did not appear to be expecting a reply as she shook her head, unrolling a sheaf of paper before perusing it. It was a copy of the last letter she had written to Calcutta and her prime minister knew that she was searching desperately to find whatever it was whose inclusion or omission might have prompted the Governor-General to take his final decision. She started to carefully read its contents out loud:

To Marquess Dalhousie the Most Noble Governor-General of India

3rd December 1853

> *My most gracious compliments,*
> *Please allow me to begin by explaining the history between the state of Jhansi and the mighty British power we have grown to respect over three generations of rule. First, may I remind you of the services rendered by Shiv Rao Bhao, the father of my late husband, to the British government, even before its authority in this part of the country was established...*

Rani Lakshmibai read the rest of the letter under her breath before looking up at Dewan Rao Bande, uncertainty springing to her eyes again. 'Do you think, Dewan-ji, that I covered all the areas I should have done when I wrote it? I also feel that I should have been less emotional and avoided going over the history of our relationship with the British, concentrating more on the legality of their decision. I was in such a state when I dictated it, the raja's passing, the adoption, all that talk that was around at the time of the impending annexation...'

The dewan shook his head. 'I have tried everything and no approach seems to work with them, Rani-sahiba. Negotiation does not even come into it when they are intent on doing what is expedient to their own intentions. Not even attempts to negotiate by their own better men, such as Major Ellis. What is worse is that, while we have all seen their power and arrogance grow tenfold in the past ten years, some of us bear the guilt of having fed it on its way.'

Lakshmibai knew that her prime minister was alluding to Gangadhar's gentle acquiescence to British policies. She nodded but said firmly, 'I think even the raja would have accepted, Dewan-ji, that there was always the danger that the dog protecting our house may one day turn on us. But wasn't Raja Gangadhar helpless too? Even now, in some ways, we are merely seeking British protection. Now that both Krishna Rao and Sadashiv have made rival claims to Damodar's, who can tell what other plots may be brewing behind our backs? And, whether we like to admit it or not, the only people powerful enough to help us against our enemies are the British.'

'Rani-sahiba, you did well in asking both Krishna Rao and his son to leave the court after the raja's passing. There was nothing to be gained by entertaining their malign presence here. And, yes, as we predicted, see how they have now reared their heads, asking to be considered rightful heirs over Prince Damodar. But I do not think Government House will entertain the idea at all. In that matter at least, I think you will have their full support.'

'Well, they would not agree to my banishing the presence of father and son from Jhansi district altogether but that was not unreasonable, I suppose. Jhansi is Krishna Rao's home too and I, as a widow, cannot be seen to be so imperious to Gangadhar Rao's people. Oh yes, there are times when I have been grateful for British objectivity—and I would be the first to admit that. But, Dewan-ji, we must return to the matter of the letter to Lord Dalhousie. I feel we must give it one more chance. Let me rewrite this letter, explain our position better. There is still hope, I believe.'

The old dewan shook his head but said gently, 'Forgive an old man's pessimism, my rani. I will support you in your bid. We have nothing to lose.'

Rani Lakshmibai turned to her writer who was now ready with his paper and pens and writing stand. Waiting for him to sit down and announce his readiness by dipping his pen in the pot of ink, she began to slowly dictate, her hands twisting the embroidered silk purse in which the papers would later be conveyed to Calcutta:

Khureeta from Her Highness Lakshmibai, widow of Gangadhar Rao, late Raja of Jhansi

To Marquess Dalhousie the Most Honourable Governor General of India

Dated: Jhansi, 16th February 1854

My deepest compliments, sir

Distress at my recent bereavement when I last wrote to your Lordship on the 3rd December had prevented me from describing as fully as I ought to have done the circumstances of the adoption made by my late husband. I now beg leave to cover those few omissions...

Fifteen minutes later, as she continued to dictate, Dewan Bande Rao worried that Lord Dalhousie would not have the patience to peruse such lengthy letters. At the same time, he knew that it was important for the rani to pour all her feelings out onto paper. What was there to lose now that everything was already gone? And, if it gave the rani some comfort to imagine she had not given up without a fight, then he would not be the one to deny her such meagre comfort. Listening to her voice slowly dictate, he could hear her struggling to explain the legality of Prince Damodar's adoption...

...It cannot be denied that the terms Warisan [heirs] and Janishnian [successors], made use of in the second article of the treaty with Ramchandra Rao, refer to different parties; the term Warisan is confined in meaning to natural or collateral heirs, while Janishnian refers to the party adopted as heir and successor to the estate in the event of there being no natural or collateral heir entitled to the succession. Treaties are prepared with the utmost care before ratification; and it must be understood that both terms, Janishnian and Warisan, were deliberately introduced in this important document, for a specific reason. Fully believing that the concept of Janishnian had been well-established in the eyes of the British Government, my husband summoned Major Ellis and Captain Martin to Jhansi palace. In their presence, and in full Durbar, he proceeded to hand over Damodar Anand Rao, his lawfully adopted son, to the care and protection of the British Government, delivering at the same time a khureeta further declaring his wishes on this solemn occasion for communication to your Lordship.

I take the liberty of enclosing a list of some of the precedents that have occurred in Bundelkhand in which the right of a King or his widow to adopt a successor to the throne, in the absence of natural heirs, had been sanctioned.

It is with firm reliance on the integrity, fairness and justice of the British Government that I ask to be able to pass the days in peace and quietness, without any other care than to administer my state and prove my continuing loyalty, bringing up my son to take over the reins of the state when he has attained majority. Forgive me that I venture to express a hope that Jhansi, that has always supported you, will not now be considered undeserving of your favour and compassion.

It angered both Dewan Rao Bande and Moropant grievously that, when Rani Lakshmibai heard from Lord Dalhousie a month later, the Governor-General had not considered the kindness of a personal reply.

'This is only a copy of the report Dalhousie has received from his council, Dewan-ji, with not even a personal letter attached that might have explained things better!' Moropant cried, deeply injured on his daughter's behalf.

'I have no wish to defend him, Moropant-bhai, but perhaps all these annexations are keeping Government House too busy...' Dewan Rao Bande trailed off unconvincingly.

'It seems to me, Dewan-ji, that this is as a deliberate attempt to demean Jhansi further. A style this Governor-General seems remarkably adept at.'

Moropant read the report in his hand again, feeling the blood rush to his head. It galled him to think of the ungraciousness with which Dalhousie had completely overlooked all of Lakshmibai's achievements these many years. Recorded on this paper was no more than a litany of cold facts, strung together with the sole purpose of giving the British what they wanted.

February 1854

The adoption taken by Gangadhar Rao is absolutely without foundation.

The treaty of 1804 made with Gangadhar Rao's father, Shiv Rao Bhao, was a personal pact. In 1812, when Shiv Rao Bhao wanted to re-enact the same pact in the interests of his brother, Ramchandra Rao, the British government rejected it on the basis of an agreement that Peshwa Baji Rao II had made during the pact of 1804. The British were ruling Bundelkhand in place of the Peshwa at the time and Shiv Rao Bhao was in the Peshwa's service. The British did not want to renew in case it encroached on the Peshwa's rights.

Shiv Rao Bhao died in 1814. As by then the Peshwa had lost his possession of Bundelkand, a new treaty was established with Ramchandra Rao in 1817.

According to the second stipulation, Ramchandra Rao's claim as the descendent of Shiv Rao Bhao in Jhansi was accepted for future generations. Ramchandra Rao died in 1835, Raghunath Rao, the next ruler, died in 1838. There were then three new claimants—Krishna Rao (nephew of Raghunath Rao), Ali Bahadur (illegitimate son of Raghunath Rao) and Sankubai (the legally married wife of Raghunath Rao). To investigate these demands a commission was appointed with Lieutenant Colonel Speir (The Resident of Gwalior), Simon Frazer and Captain D. Ross, and Gangadhar Rao, younger nephew of Raghunath Rao, was selected by their verdict. This clearly proves the fact that Jhansi is one of those states that do lose autonomy in the absence of a male heir and hence are liable to be taken over by the government. (See the record of 28-10-1837 on adoption by the chieftains of Bundelkhand by Sir Charles Metcalfe.)

Rani Lakshmibai has cited the examples of Orchha, Datia and Jalaun where adoptions have been recognised. These bear no resemblance whatsoever to Jhansi. Orchha and Datia were always autonomous. The state of Jalaun was founded by a Maharashtrian chief from the Deccan. It was never under the Peshwa's rule despite its being a Maharashtrian kingdom. It is true that in 1832 a case of adoption was approved in Jalaun, but its terrible consequence prompted the British Government to take it over in 1840, and it has no wish to witness the autonomy of native rulers all over again.

๛ 23 ๛

Ellis rode into the city gates, considering that this was his second formal effort to meet Lakshmibai since telling her of the annexation order. He had made other attempts too, riding out every morning at dawn to Barhwa Sagar, but she had not shown up there either.

This was his first visit to the new palace and, as he approached it through the city gates, he looked up at the old fort, wondering if Lakshmibai had moved away from Panch Mahal after the raja's death in an endeavour to distance herself from her old life. Perhaps, on the other hand, it was merely to be nearer the public assembly halls so that she could be more accessible to her people. He supposed he would never be able to ask her such awkward questions, seeing how upset she already was. Besides, this morning Ellis was faced with the unenviable business of sealing the locks on Jhansi's treasury under a further set of instructions from Lord Dalhousie. A task he was not looking forward to at all.

Wrought iron gates led into the compound of the queen's new palace. They were unlocked, manned by a solitary guard, but Ellis knew that was the informal style Lakshmibai had always liked to adopt. After his horse was led away by one of the syces, he crossed into the main courtyard. There was still a smell of fresh plaster and lime-wash in the air, even though the palace had been completed over a year ago, lying unoccupied only because of the king's prolonged illness. He looked around at the creamy alabaster walls, inlaid with pale egg-shell blue lapis. This was all quite different from the deep vegetable dyes that most of Panch Mahal was decorated with, prettier and lighter, and Ellis remembered that Lakshmibai had been personally involved in the refurbishment project from the very start.

The main building he was approaching was not new, but the raja had once told him that a couple of annexes had been personally designed by Lakshmibai. It had taken many years to complete but Ellis could see that immense care had been taken to create a welcoming courtyard that led, through leaf-covered arches, to different wings. He thought it sad that his old friend Raja Gangadhar had not been able to move to this beautiful palace before his deepening illness. Who was to know—perhaps coming to these spacious, airy halls would have done him some good. Panch Mahal in the bowels of the fort had always had a dank and cheerless air about it.

Ellis paced around the pebbled courtyard, feeling restless at the indelicacy of the task that awaited him, even as the people of Jhansi went about their normal businesses just outside the gates. Even the gentle pitter-patter of the fountains could not serve to calm his nerves that felt as taut as the skin of a drum today. He looked up as footsteps approached but, much to his disappointment, saw that it was only Dewan Rao Bande. Rani Lakshmibai had, as before, sent her prime minister to receive him, pleading indisposition on her own part.

Frustrated at not being able to see her yet again and personally express his regret, Ellis left the city palace in the company of the dewan. Together, and in grim silence, they rode the one-mile distance to the gates of the fort and made their way up its steeply sloping road to the official vaults. Having examined the accounts for the two thousand rupees and fifteen annas of gold and silver coins that were left, Ellis gave the old keeper of the fort the signal to lock the treasury. Keys were turned in all the locks before they were tightly bound in pieces of muslin and sealed with a stick of red sealing wax.

Although Dewan Rao Bande stood by in decorous silence, Ellis knew how insulting this ritual would seem to the old man and wondered whether it had been on his advice that Rani Lakshmibai had declined to be present today. He wondered how much she revealed of her feelings to the dewan and whether he knew why she refused to see him. It was ridiculous to feel envious of the confidences she must share with her dignified old prime minister but Ellis did not possess the heart to look the old man in the face. Instead, he spoke a few words to the soldier from the 6th Scindia Contingent, who would henceforth guard the Jhansi treasury on behalf of the British, before calling for his horse and making his way back to the cantonment.

He rode slowly, accepting with a heavy heart that Lakshmibai was avoiding him. It could not be coincidence that she had been indisposed and unable to meet him on both the occasions that he had attempted meeting her since the annexation. There was no explanation either for her absences at Barhwa Sagar. Although he understood her anguish, it saddened him to think that she had not been able to separate him in her mind from those anonymous British powers at Government House who were responsible for Jhansi's annexation. Surely she would not blame him for their decisions?

It may have comforted Ellis to see Lakshmibai pacing around restlessly in her chambers after Dewan Rao Bande had left with him for the fort. Her pain was on many counts. She knew it was illogical to blame Robert Ellis for the annexation and was also aware of how powerless political agents were against the powers of Calcutta and London. But, in going over some of their conversations during their early morning rides at Barhwa Sagar, Lakshmibai had a growing realization of how loyal to his company and his country Ellis had always been. She could not remember even one stray remark he may have made, not a single careless moment that would have revealed his own unhappiness with the nefariousness of his government. All along, she and Gangadhar had assumed Ellis's sympathy, his good intentions towards them, the honour of his conscience. And now, wounded by these latest events, Lakshmibai wondered if they had been terribly wrong to do so.

She cursed her folly too in imagining that Ellis would be loyal to Jhansi merely because of his admiration for her. How could she have grown so close to an Englishman so unthinkingly when, in fact, they all so obviously held her in such low esteem? Every one of them. Even Ellis, who must have been assessing her all the time, encouraging her to tell him things she had never told anyone before. She wished she had never ridden out with him and spoken so much about herself and her childhood, seduced out of her more customary prudence by his concern and his seeming attraction towards her. Deeply ashamed now at having allowed her trust to grow in such unseemly directions, Lakshmibai was suddenly furious with herself for allowing the seductive peacefulness of the forests they had ridden in to cause her to forget where she came from and all that really mattered.

Stopping by her window and gazing out at Jhansi's busy, sun-filled streets, Lakshmibai felt strangely relieved at the thought that she would no longer be clandestinely meeting Robert Ellis. She could not deny how unhappy the surreptitiousness had made her feel, the need to keep secrets from people like her father who really had her welfare at heart. Only recently she had heard Moropant say that the world in which friendships with the British were possible had long gone. Wondering then if the words were aimed at her, she had felt unable to respond when he had next declared that those who still foolishly held fast onto such false relationships would soon find them turning rotten and treacherous in the poisoned air they all breathed.

She turned from her window as she heard Sundar coming in. Through a strangely ringing sound in her ears, she listened quietly as her faithful maid told her of how upset Major Ellis had looked at having had to leave the palace without seeing her again. She could hear the gentle unspoken rebuke in Sundar's tone but remained silent, her own face a mask. An inexplicable hollow of regret was forming somewhere deep inside her stomach but she turned away from Sundar's questioning eyes. She did not owe anyone any explanations and, keeping her eyes averted, she walked swiftly past Sundar and out of the room, telling herself firmly that her only regret should be for the fact that she had ever offered Robert Ellis her friendship at all.

❧ 24 ❧

Lakshmibai stood only a few yards further along the ramparts from Ellis as they watched her husband's ruby-red royal standard being brought down from the tallest turret of the fort. King Gangadhar's family insignia of the kettledrum and royal fan became visible one last time as the evening breeze picked up, unfurling the satin cloth for a moment before it was pulled down, folded and carried away. In its place, a large Union Jack was hoisted and Ellis, standing by the flagstaff, wondered if Lakshmibai had deliberately decided to stay in purdah today for fear of being seen with tears marring her face. She would surely not bear the idea of Colonel Malcolm seeing her in such a state.

The soldiers of the Jhansi army were assembled nearby, headed by Moropant Tambe. They had been summoned by Colonel Malcolm, who had been sent with special dispensation to hand out the soldiers' last salaries before their force was disbanded. As Malcolm supervised the payment, collecting signatures and receipts, some of the men showed their fury by throwing their firearms into the disused western well of the fort, making the rusted old well-wheel creak and rock angrily. Others merely wept, saluting the curtain behind which their rani stood.

Behind the silken screen, all was silent, although Ellis had been informed by Dewan Rao Bande that the rani had ordered another macabre ritual to take place on the far side of the fort, where all the king's theatre props, costumes and musical instruments had been removed from the underground storerooms of the palace to be made into a huge bonfire. According to the dewan, Rani Lakshmibai, who had never been as fond of the performing arts as her husband, now believed that the time for more serious pursuits was upon them. Ellis was not clear what exactly these pursuits may be, particularly as Lakshmibai would have even less responsibilities of governance after the annexation, and hoped desperately that Dewan-ji had not meant to sound as though he were issuing a threat.

Looking up, he felt the deepest of misgivings as he saw smoke from that ghastly fire rise over the eastern turrets of the fort. In that swirling black cloud were some of the gayest and happiest moments this fort had ever seen and Ellis wondered what Lakshmibai thought she gained by wilfully destroying their memory. It was imperative for him to try to talk to her in private; surely she would not refuse to see him ever again.

After Jhansi had officially passed into British hands, there followed, a few days later, yet another note from Calcutta, this time to clarify the inheritance rights of Damodar Rao:

25th March 1854

I apprehend that it is beyond the power of the Government to dispose of the property of the late Raja, which by law will belong to the son whom he adopted. The adoption, though good for the conveyance of private rights, does not affect the transfer of the Principality to the British government...

Moropant, reading under his breath, got to the end of the missive with a choking sound. He shook his head in disbelief before attempting to digest its contents again.

On the other side of the table, Dewan Rao Bande had been enumerating the slights already received from Government House: 'First they annex Jhansi and take away Prince Damodar's right to inherit the title, then they offer our rani a most paltry monthly stipend to live on and maintain her depleted court and army with. More recently, we get that insulting letter carrying Dalhousie's refusal to allow us to use money from Jhansi's treasury, even though it was for the specific purpose of conducting the prince's initiation ceremony. Calcutta, of course, never thinks it fit to provide any rationale, merely stating that the money in Jhansi's treasury has been frozen indefinitely for "undisclosed purposes"...what can these purposes be but to line their own coffers, I ask you, Moropant-bhai?'

His companion's concentration was on the directive before him and Dewan Rao Bande noticed that its contents had made Moropant's face turn an angry red. Smacking his hand on the paper, Moropant turned to him now to ask incredulously, 'Dewan-ji, just look at what is now being said about Prince Damodar's personal inheritance! Isn't this duality just typical of the British? On the one hand, Dalhousie had been so certain that Damodar could not succeed his father's throne because he was an adopted and not natural born child. But now here he is using the very *reverse* logic to have decided that the child *can* rightfully inherit Gangadhar's personal properties in Parola, Pune and Varanasi! You understand this sudden seeming generosity, don't you, Dewan-sahib? As Damodar is still a minor, this inheritance will take place only when he attains majority. And, until then, who holds these properties in custody—the *British*, of course.'

Dewan Rao Bande shook his head as though trying to clear it. 'Lord Dalhousie has always had this capacity for being both brilliant and cruel, Moropant-bhai. Yes, of course, I can see it—while seeming to make a magnanimous concession in recognizing at least some of Damodar's rights as an adopted son, he ensures that Rani Lakshmibai cannot touch these properties for more than ten years until the child gains majority...'

'If Dalhousie's intention has been to keep Jhansi's rani completely and humiliatingly under British control, then how easily he succeeds, Dewan-sahib!'

The prime minister clenched his shaking hands into a fist and held it to his forehead. He felt completely helpless in the face of this new injustice. And Moropant's ire did not help. On the one hand, he too, as Jhansi's prime minister, wanted to fight the British with every breath in his body but, on the other hand, he could see how powerless their position was. They had no army, no money and no legal standing, all of which the British were so rich in.

'Moropant-bhai, I fear that we have no recourse but to accept even this, however unjust it may be,' he said finally. Looking up, his heart quailed at the anger he could see on Moropant's face. Anger would only take them further away from the British, build even more barriers, transform an already perfidious adversary into a dangerous enemy. Even without earning their enmity, British treatment of them had been so harsh. What would happen if they were genuinely angered? He needed to go in search of Rani Lakshmibai and inform her of this new directive. It was his duty, as prime minister, to soothe her feelings, not inflame them as her father may do. Then he would need to address the delicate task of drawing up a decree to inform the people of Jhansi of these developments. It was possible that they would greet their fate with resignation as not much in their immediate lives was going to be altered by this. On the other hand, Dewan Rao Bande was sure that Jhansi would not take kindly to any behaviour on the part of the British that may seem like an affront to their rani. But how strong these emotions were likely to be, and what form it would take, was not within even the prime minister's ken to know.

Once appraised of the situation, Rani Lakshmibai wore a look of defeat. It was the first time that Dewan Rao Bande thought he saw the glint of tears in her eyes. Even when her husband had died, she had borne her grief stoically, too brave to feel bereft and too progressive in her outlook to contemplate retiring to a life of prayer behind purdah, normally expected of a widow. For some reason, no one had seemed to sit in judgement of the young queen when she continued to wear jewels and emerged from purdah even when communing with the British. Perhaps it was because the people of Jhansi so adored their brave rani that they were able to overlook her unusual behaviour, viewing it as a mark of her courage. Dewan Rao Bande himself had watched with respect as Jhansi's widowed queen had performed her duties with clarity and a confident sense of purpose. Like the people of Jhansi, he was immensely grateful for the fact that she was nothing like her peer who ruled not faraway, the wealthy and indulged Begum Hazratmahal of Awadh. Every time the dewan heard yet another story of excess emanating from the court of Awadh, he gave thanks for the discretion and dignity of his own young rani.

But today Lakshmibai sat very still as the dewan read Dalhousie's letter to her and, when he had finished and looked up at where she sat, he noticed that her normally erect carriage bore the look of something that had finally grown tired and wilted. She said nothing but her hands were twisting a corner of her sari pallav so hard, he could see the gold threads start to split and shred. 'I am sorry, my rani-sahiba, I am sorry we could not do more,' he said simply.

Her voice quivered slightly as she replied, 'I had so wanted to maintain the last shreds of my dignity by turning down their measly pension...but see how they have cornered me, Dewan-ji?' She took a deep breath before continuing, still speaking softly, with more sorrow than anger, making Dewan Bande Rao wonder if the flashes of anger and bursts of energy that had amounted to nothing in these past few days had finally worn her down.

'Please make an announcement to our people, we cannot keep them in the dark any more,' she said. 'I will write back to the Governor-General, accepting his proposals. I do not think we have a choice.'

Dewan Rao Bande nodded in relief. 'You are right, Rani-sahiba, we have little choice. It is best we play our cards with care rather than with anger when dealing with such powerful people.'

'Yes, we will continue the friendship that had been so hard-won by Raja Gangadhar and his ancestors, whatever my personal feelings maybe. That is in Jhansi's interests. And, who knows, perhaps one day the British will have to come to us for Jhansi's help. Certainly they will have few friends left when they treat people with such high-handed arrogance.'

Rani Lakshmibai spoke sadly but straightened herself, pulling her sari pallav around her shoulders as though exposed to a sudden gust of wind. With a fraction of her old confidence returning to her voice, she continued, 'But one thing is sure, Dewan-ji. I am not going to accept this annexation decree as easily as they may imagine I have. I still intend getting someone to examine the legality of their decision. There may still be the chance this could be overturned in an appeal, do you not think?'

Dewan Rao Bande nodded, taking heart in his queen's determination. 'Yes, what have we to lose, Rani-sahiba? Let us fight this but as astutely as they do.' He considered his next words carefully before adding, 'Rani-sahiba, forgive me for suggesting that you do not spurn Major Ellis's requests to meet you any more. His friendship with Jhansi has been genuine, I believe, and he remains the last link we have with the British. We have no reason to believe he supports his government in their heinous policies, Rani-sahiba. Perhaps it is his friendship that will save us from further trouble.'

Lakshmibai contemplated Dewan Rao Bande's words carefully. She had thought of Robert Ellis every day in the time she had avoided him. Remembering his concern and his kindness over the years that he had been Jhansi's political agent, unable to accept that he had been dissembling and unfaithful, despite all her angry warnings to herself.

She now felt a curious surge of hope and relief at hearing her wise old prime minister's opinion. Even he believed that Robert Ellis was essentially a good man who loved Jhansi in his own way. Perhaps dewan-ji was right that Ellis would at some point feel able to face his own government's policies against Jhansi with courage. There may still be some miracle, just out of reach, that may yet transform the bleak landscape of Jhansi's future.

She raised her chin and nodded. 'Dewan-ji, you know how deeply I care for Jhansi. Major Ellis disappointed me with his failure to save us from annexation but perhaps I have not given him enough time. Yes, we need him to remain our friend. We also need his knowledge of British law and can only hope that, one day, he will share our hatred of it.'

She pulled herself up in her chair, straightening her shoulders before adding in a firm, clear voice, 'I have an apology to make, Dewan-sahib. My behaviour to Major Ellis has been remiss. Please invite him to our court tomorrow. I am sure he will understand that it was my pain over the annexation that caused me to behave so discourteously to him.'

๛ 25 ๛

Ellis returned to Lakshmibai's court, vowing that he would never do anything to cast him so unhappily in her disfavour again. He became a regular visitor to her palace, even moving some of his things temporarily to Motibagh, one of Ranimahal's new guest annexes, to facilitate his work in the library. Despite the dangers, they continued to ride out into the forests together whenever they could, careful to avoid the cantonment area. Ellis wondered sometimes at his own rashness, accepting finally that it sprang from sheer inability to return ever again to those unbearable weeks when Lakshmibai had distanced herself from him. Of course, he knew he had fallen hopelessly in love and knew, even as he did, how dangerous such a liaison would be, both for her and for him. But he was like a dying man who had been given a palmful of water with due warning that it may be poisoned—what had he to lose by drinking it?

In those days they had taken to working late, examining Jhansi's archived documents in the hope of finding something that could overturn Dalhousie's annexation order. That night—one that Ellis would never forget—was filled with the kind of summer torpor that made the world seem purged of all life, save for the clamour of nocturnal insects outside. As dark deepened over Motibagh's garden, the rasping of cicadas faded, replaced by the cloying scents of night flowers. Ellis looked up from the papers that had been spread out on the satinwood davenport. In the dim light of the brass lantern at his elbow, Lakshmibai's eyes were dark and intense, scanning his face to read his thoughts as she spoke.

'Please tell me it is not hopeless. Is it worth showing it to a British lawyer? Nanasahib tells me about a man called John Lang who recently won a case against the Company in Agra...' Ellis could hear the desperation in her voice that indicated how bleak she really knew their case was.

'Not hopeless, Rani-sahiba,' he said as kindly as he could, 'but it would be disingenuous for me to suggest that it's going to be anything but very, very difficult.'

'Why should it be so? Does the 1829 treaty not state quite clearly that all Ramchandra Rao's heirs have the right to rule in perpetuity?' She carefully pulled out a rolled-up parchment from under the others. 'Here it is, with the Governor-General's seal clearly visible.'

'Rani-sahiba, 1829 was a long time ago. Twenty-five years. More water has since flowed under the bridge than should have been allowed and those events cannot be undone now. Going strictly by the law, your case should be easily won. But we cannot forget that it will be heard by the Company directors in the first instance and will probably get dismissed even at that stage.'

'How can they dismiss it if it is a rightful suit?' she demanded.

'Because they have already done so with numerous other similar cases. We both know about the Peshwa's suit and you also know of the case of Maharaja Raghu-ji of Nagpur. Then there is Satara...Sambalpur...this will not be the first legitimate appeal to be summarily dismissed.'

'Are you saying there's no point in even trying to lodge an appeal?' Her voice sounded so forlorn, Ellis did not have the heart to give her his honest opinion.

'What I am saying, Rani-sahiba, is that the only way to embark on an appeal is with the expectation that it may fail. And you will have to give me time...'

'Time,' she laughed hollowly. 'Time, Robert, is a quality that in this land we either have in overabundance or not at all.'

'I understand, Rani-sahiba, but we need time to try and appeal to their good sense first.'

'Whose good sense?'

'Lord Dalhousie's,' Ellis replied, seeing her face instantly cloud over, her shoulders slump.

'He seems to be such a heartless man, Robert,' she said despondently, 'he does not even do me the courtesy of replying to my letters.'

'Let me draft a letter to him this time, Rani-sahiba. We would have to be certain they do not see my hand in it, of course.'

Lakshmibai looked into Robert Ellis's gentle grey eyes, searching for the firm intentions she was desperate to see. Although there were other men whose loyalty she could rely on implicitly—Moropant, Dewan Rao Bande, Nana—Robert was the only man who could actually help her, being himself British. Only he could guide her through this, only he had the power she needed. She was sure he could not be pretending his concern and had long stopped questioning her conviction in it.

'Yes, I trust you to do what is best for Jhansi, Robert,' she said, not unlocking her gaze with his, wanting him now to clearly see her faith in him. 'Please help me to write again to Dalhousie. Even if we do not win our case, Jhansi will honour your help forever.'

She felt a rush of tenderness as Robert Ellis bent his head over the papers to study them again. The soft diffusion of light from the candelabra on the bureau was turning his hair the colour of Bundelkhand's crisp golden sands in the summer months and the temptation to reach out and touch it with her fingertips was immense.

After a few moments, he picked up the paper on which he had been writing and blew softly on it to dry the ink, before reading the paragraph he had just written out loud to her.

> I would make known unto your Lordship that Jhansi is a powerless Native state, for long dependent on the protection of the British Government. My late husband devoted his attention to the art of Peace, avoiding even the semblance of a warlike state; and so if Jhansi is to be absorbed during your Lordship's administration, the five thousand rusty swords worn by the people that call themselves its Army and its fifty pieces of harmless ordnance (harmless except against a power of equal insignificance) will be delivered over to your Lordship's Agent without any demonstration save that of sorrow. That valuable services should be requited by the confiscation of a puny Kingdom or Raj; which has been ever faithful to the paramount power...

'I wonder whether such persistence will impress or irk the great Lord Dalhousie,' Lakshmibai laughed softly.

'If you ask me, Rani-sahiba, irritation might prove a useful thing. Wear his resistance down slowly, that may be the only way. A daily letter until most honourable Governor-General Lord Dalhousie screams, *Please do not bring me any more letters from that dreadful queen! Give her what she wants. If it is Jhansi she wants, she can have it. It is just not worth having to read all these letters she writes to me!*'

Although Ellis smiled as he said this, he knew how keenly Lakshmibai hoped for some kind of miraculous reversal of events. He had tried to be as honest as possible about how fruitless he thought the venture was, sometimes even feeling weakened by her desperation.

'It is very late, Rani-sahiba,' he said as the distant chimes of a clock told him it was midnight. 'I hadn't realized how long we had been sitting here. I think you ought to retire and we can complete this tomorrow.'

She nodded but did not rise straightaway. 'Tomorrow I have a new problem to deal with,' she said abruptly, suddenly pensive. 'I did not tell you earlier because I thought it best not to disturb you when you were working on the Persian translations in the library. I had a letter a few days ago. The governor of the North West Provinces has discovered that Jhansi owes the British government a debt of thirty-six thousand rupees for helping to control an old uprising over land rights. Such a long time ago—in the time of Ramchandra Rao's reign—1832, I think it may have been.'

Ellis was incredulous, 'Which governor...Colvin? No one has told me of this development. The *1832* uprising? But surely they cannot expect you to pay back such a large sum of money in your present strained circumstances! Particularly as that old debt had nothing at all to do with you.'

'Since when, Robert, have I been able to expect understanding or compassion or even logic from your government?' She laughed wryly and Ellis cringed inwardly at the truth of her words.

'You have refused to pay?' he asked.

'Oh yes, I have. I put it to Colvin quite simply that, as it is not a personal debt but one borne by Jhansi state, it is their responsibility as the present guardians of Jhansi's treasury, to pay it.'

'And?'

'And, just this morning, I received a letter from Sir Robert Hamilton confirming that the debt can under no circumstances be paid using the money sealed in the treasury.'

'Have they told you how you should pay it?'

'From my monthly pension, according to Hamilton. What I am not sure is whether he, as commissioner for Central India, gets to decide or whether he too merely takes his orders from Dalhousie. I suppose we have nothing to lose by bringing up the subject in this letter to Calcutta.'

Ellis nodded, feeling suddenly nervous at the impropriety of hearing this news from Lakshmibai rather than his own government. Were the papers regarding this lying on his desk at the cantonment? When had he last been back there to check them? He could barely remember now, with days and nights all blurring into one. He wondered if questions were being asked about his whereabouts these past few days—everyone was, after all, accustomed to his long periods of absence when he toured the countryside for revenue collection.

Ellis dragged his confused thoughts back to Lakshmibai. She was still seated in the pool of soft light cast by the single candelabra, awaiting his reply, and Ellis pulled himself together. 'Forgive my asking you this, Rani-sahiba, but I am not entirely sure of the sums at stake here. If they did take it out of your pension, would there be anything left for you to live on? I am thinking of all the people you support as well...not just your family but the many retainers who rely on your employment too. Dewan Rao Bande, your ministers...'

She nodded her head but seemed suddenly unable to speak. Her eyes looked liquid in the mellow lamplight but Ellis knew it was merely an illusion as he knew her to be a woman who did not allow tears to fall easily. It was possible, however, that she had reached the brink of her endurance. When she spoke again, her voice was brimming with sorrow.

'My father should have been grateful for the unambiguity of Peshwa-sahib's hostility with the British, Robert. At least they never faced the—what can I call it—the *duplicity* that lurks behind so-called friendly treaties.' Her lips twisted with sudden bitterness as she forced herself to stop speaking.

Ellis could not help agreeing silently. Loyal as he essentially remained, his government's treatment of her seemed almost ruthless. He simply could not understand why they insisted on delivering one undeserving blow after another to this queen who, as far as he could see, had striven in the face of great odds to continue her husband's tradition of civility to the British. Widowhood at her young age was misfortune enough but Dalhousie was using that misfortune to deprive her, not just of her kingdom and her child's right to inherit but her very dignity. Had Calcutta grown drunk with its own power? Did overweening authority inure its possessor from common courtesies and ordinary compassions? It was no different to the arrogance Ellis had seen among some landowners back home towards those very tenants and farmers on whose labours they depended for their own comforts.

Lakshmibai had risen from her chair as though unable to bear a prolongation of their conversation. Ellis knew there was no point in stopping her; he had no words of comfort to offer. She pulled her sari around her shoulders and briefly inclined her head to bid him goodnight. He put the forgotten papers down to rise from his own chair and watched her walk out of the room.

Later, unable to sleep for the hot stillness of the April night, Ellis stepped out onto the balcony of his room at Motibagh. He unfastened the top few buttons on his shirt, feeling a brief coolness run over his chest, and looked up at the sky. The drooping immensity of these stars always brought back a dim memory of low-slung summer skies cloaking the fields of Shropshire. The view from this western balcony was truly splendid on nights such as this when the stars seemed to reflect themselves in the abundance of white flowers filling the walled garden below. He inhaled a lungful of perfumed air but a small movement below caught his attention. His eyes, slowly accommodating the shadows of the night, discerned a figure seated on a bench beneath the balcony. It was Lakshmibai. How odd that she had not returned to her chambers after bidding him goodnight. Her back was turned to him and the low-lying branches of the harsinghaar tree nearly obscured her from view. Only the edges of her white sari, its border embroidered with tiny silver sequins now catching the moonlight, was visible in the dark. He did not call out to her for there was clearly some terrible despondency that kept her from returning to her chambers tonight.

Ellis turned to slip back into his room before she became aware of his presence. That would be the kindest thing to do to someone who was as full of anguish as she clearly was tonight. Re-entering his room, he found himself wishing for the first time ever that the British had never come to India at all. If, in a moment as sad as this, he had possessed some power to stanch the tide that had brought them all here—trader and soldier and administrator—he would have willingly used it and never stopped to regret it. He pulled the door to the balcony shut. Perhaps it was best not to lead Lakshmibai into believing the impossible. Perhaps, indeed, she was better off without his presence in her life at all.

He paced the length of his room, agonizing for a few minutes over the woman seated outside, reflecting on how much she had already grown to depend on him. That was clear from the generosity she seemed so willing to shower on him, her attentions and ministrations, the careful way in which she listened to him, her laughter at the things he said. Could it be that her choosing to sit in a spot visible from his chamber was a silent plea for his company, one that she could hardly make openly without embarrassing herself. And what of his own desire for her?

Ellis took a deep breath, standing in the middle of the chamber. He watched moonshadows play like black lace on the door that led out of the room and it was another few minutes before he could bring himself to open it and make his way down the darkened passageway to her.

Even as she had seated herself on that bench, Lakshmibai knew of some new defiance within her. New desires, stretching and unfurling like monsoon vines engulfing bare walls of despair. Even if she stopped to recognize her own rashness, the fear of returning to those swirling choking sorrows of her child's death, her husband's illness, the loss of Jhansi, her worries about money and her son's tenuous future, would only close the door on good sense again. Who had dictated that she was undeserving of simple joys and how could she possibly care that such joys never came unaccompanied by their attendant qualities of imprudence and danger?

And so it was that, as Robert Ellis's tall figure appeared silently from the trees in the walled garden that night, she felt her entire inner being fall with the sensation of a stone plummeting into the dark night. Only later would she attempt to analyse her feelings for all she could recognize at that moment was a strange and immeasurable relief at his presence. How extraordinary that she could sit before him, every last inhibition thrown to the winds, as he beheld her countenance, awash finally with tears. No man had ever seen her so distraught and even Sundar had only ever seen her in that state when her baby had died. But, when Ellis sat down beside her on the stone bench, she looked up at him and allowed her tears to flow unchecked and unwiped as a child would have done, her hands lying limply in her lap. She felt strong arms wind around her shoulders and placed her forehead on his chest, her misery rolling out of her as though it might have been gathering and waiting through the months for this moment.

They sat on that bench for what must have been a very long time, even after her tears had subsided, savouring a pleasure they may never be allowed again. With no words to break the silence, she finally removed his hand from her shoulder, taking it in her own. She examined his lean fingers and neatly clipped nails, suddenly surprised at their proximity. His skin was glowing like marble in the dark of the night and she ran her forefinger along the vein that travelled blue-green up the back of his hand before it disappeared into the fine downy hair that covered his wrist. Then, turning over his hand, she explored the lines on his palm that had brought him so fortuitously to Jhansi and to her. Even in the dark she could see a small ink stain on his writing hand and it was to that that her forefinger next gravitated. Rubbing at it gently, she slowly raised her eyes to look at his face before daring to run a finger over its features, memorizing it for a time when it may not be before her any more. And, at last, she searched for his gaze, but his grey eyes were dark and unfathomable in the fading starlight of the night.

~ 26 ~

Krishna Rao, pacing around the dimly lit corridors of his mansion at Parola, had waited long for this opportunity. How he had longed, all these years, for the chance to regain his lost Jhansi. Squinting with suddenly blurred eyes at the darkened western horizon beyond which the land of his ancestors lay, he felt a momentary pang for the fact that it would be all too late for him. He was too old now for kingship and sensible enough to know that a prize too late was a prize not worth having at all. However, there was his son, Sadashiv. Still young and nearly as ambitious as Krishna Rao himself had been at his age. They had to make their move before it got too late even for him. Having waited so patiently, poised for action all these months, the time was now ripe to spring.

Their earlier forays out to the Rajput kings of neighbouring Orchha and Datia had been successful. Both the dewan of Datia and the son-in-law of the queen of Orchha had been interested in the chance to unsettle Lakshmibai. While Krishna Rao had been uncertain about the depth of Datia's dislike for his neighbouring state, he knew for certain how much the present queen of Orchha had always hated Gangadhar for the help he had given Raja Sujan Singh, her contender for the throne many years ago. He rubbed his hands, sucking in his breath, remembering the careful negotiations, all the mutual promises made...yes, there would be something in it for all of them.

With the foolish besotted Major Ellis being out of favour in Calcutta, Lakshmibai no longer had the ear of those who mattered. To Lord Dalhousie, the rani of Jhansi was now no more than an irritating fly that buzzed occasionally too near his ear for comfort.

Even her people, Krishna Rao reckoned, were clearly disenchanted with her. He had heard of the dwindling numbers in her public durbars that she still vainly tried to hold once a week. And ill-educated people's opinions were so easy to manipulate anyway. All his supporters had to do was send a few whispers out into Jhansi's streets and bazaars about the Englishman that the rani favoured so openly. Why did she afford that Major Ellis such easy access into her private palaces when even legitimate heirs to the throne, like Sadashiv and Krishna Rao, had been prohibited from entering the gates of Jhansi? Krishna Rao would have paid good money to find out what Lakshmibai was up to, now that she no longer had matters of state to attend to, and he suddenly felt most resentful on behalf of the people of Jhansi who were surely entitled to know their rani's every business, especially if it involved these despicable casteless foreigners.

As he spotted Sadashiv riding through the gates of the mansion, Krishna Rao hurried down the stairs, fond smiles wreathing his face. 'So what is the latest news from Dilip Singh, beta?' he enquired eagerly.

Sadashiv nodded but waited until the syces had led his horse away and they had walked up to the veranda. He pulled a chair up to sit close to his father who was musing on the thought that, even though they now lived in Parola, far outside the confines of Jhansi, they still felt the need to whisper when they plotted against Rani Lakshmibai. She had friends and loyalists everywhere and he certainly did not want her getting wind of these latest plans.

'Dilip Singh says he will be ready to move in a few months' time…' Sadashiv said in a low voice, barely audible over the cacophony of the night crickets.

Krishna Rao was aghast. '*Months*? Why the delay…'

'He says he needs some time to gather more ammunition together, he has no grape shot, no musket cartridges—'

'Surely the Orchha armouries are well stocked!'

'Apparently not. The years of peace have made everyone soft. Even army soldiers have been reduced to becoming palace guards.'

Krishna Rao clicked his tongue in frustration. 'That is what we are banking on here…her army reduced…Moropant away, visiting relatives, not that the old fool is of any consequence anyway…'

'Dewan Nathey Khan was worried about the training of the Jhansi army though. He was saying he had heard that Rani Lakshmibai personally trained them every morning, riding out with them for military exercises.'

'You should have told him that she does that only because she has nothing else to do...it is not proper training...what does she know of military training and manoeuvres, she is just a woman...' Krishna Rao's face was distorted with scorn.

Sadashiv got up and impatiently paced the veranda now speckled with tree-shadows that made his features look alternately ghostly and grim. 'I wish we could move right away. How I hate this waiting,' he hissed angrily.

Krishna Rao knew that he had to hold his own zeal back in order to keep his impetuous son in check. Sadashiv was too young to know the virtue of patience, unlike him, who had waited all his life. The plum that had been just out of reach was now ripened and glistening, nearly ready to be plucked. But he knew that moving even a day too early could result in a bitter acrid mouthful rather than the sweetness he had for so long desired.

He threw his head back on the chair, taking a deep breath and holding it for as long as he could manage. Patience, patience, he whispered to himself like a mantra...have patience and Jhansi will soon be ours again.

Filled with a new serenity, despite her continuing strained circumstances, Lakshmibai thought little of the treacheries that were surrounding her. Since that night in Motibagh's walled garden, she had grown ever more tender and trusting of Robert Ellis, reposing in him confidences he was sure she told no others. They were not lovers, although what lay between them, so still and so deep, could only have been love. Yet, like their two countries whose deepest roots lay entwined as one, they were to remain separate in the eyes of the world, parted by their own unspoken fears.

As the days passed, however, it was Ellis who first succumbed to that foreboding. In retrospect, he understood that it was because his double life was gradually wearing him down. When he returned to the cantonment, he was a stranger among his own people and suspected, when he discerned their censure, that they knew where he went when he left the camp for days at a time. When he was with Lakshmibai, he felt gripped with restlessness borne from knowing he ought not to take delight in such unthinking disloyalty to his government. At night, on hearing the ominous ululations of jackals and hyenas beyond the town walls, he thought perhaps it was the dread of uncertainty stalking the countryside that was infecting him so. Like a moth dancing in evermore frightened and diminishing circles around a flame, Ellis was waiting for the pain that must follow joy whenever one has loved against all the rules.

But all that summer he was in Lakshmibai's thrall, with no power to prevent it from tearing to shreds everything he had so far believed in. She was so beautiful and her presence so nourishing that it blinded him to the knowledge of his own treachery. The moment they were parted, however, his demons would rise unbidden again. He tried not to allow doubt to cloud the realization that he would never love anyone so deeply ever again but, in the early autumn, when he received an unexpected order from Calcutta to visit the kingdom of Awadh, it was an odd sort of release he felt. And he announced his departure to Lakshmibai with relief that he failed to mask.

Rather illogically and for long, Ellis blamed Belinda Royle for throwing him into such a foul temper that day. He had bumped into the Royles outside the church on that Sunday morning and sensed immediately that Belinda was in high dudgeon at his presence in the vicinity. Not that he was planning to worship at the church—indeed he had not stepped through its doors in his many years at the cantonment—but Lakshmibai had asked him to deliver a parcel to Sister Agnes and the churchyard on a Sunday morning seemed the best place to find her. Holding the packaged books, he was waiting under the mulberry tree when Belinda Royle accosted him, her shame-faced husband trailing a few steps behind. Later Ellis knew he should have exchanged some small pleasantry and departed their company without further ado but he had lacked the presence of mind and, just a few minutes into a forced conversation, Belinda was unable to contain herself any more. She had stepped forward, the flowers on her bonnet quivering as she spoke with poorly concealed venom.

'May I be so bold as to enquire, Major Ellis, whether you are aware of how widespread the disgraceful knowledge of your *friendship* with the house of Jhansi has become?'

At first taken aback, Ellis replied guardedly but politely, 'I have always been friendly with the royal family of Jhansi, and take pride in it, Mrs Royle. I am, after all, the political agent of the state.'

But Belinda seemed incensed by the coolness of his response. 'I refer, Major Ellis, to your *illicit* liaison that achieves *nothing* but the *betrayal* of those you belong to. I would thank you for not pretending you have failed to understand my meaning.'

'As a matter of fact, I am *not* very practiced at the art of dissembling, Mrs Royle,' Ellis responded coldly. 'I am afraid you will simply have to explain yourself.'

Ellis hoped Belinda Royle would retreat at this point rather than sully herself by voicing the torrid misconceptions crowding her mind but he was astonished to see that she had no intention at all of doing so, despite her husband's feeble attempts to pluck at her sleeve and pull her away. As she shook the hapless Royle off, she stepped closer to Ellis, her face by now quite pink with rage. 'I refer, Major Ellis,' she said, her entire frame trembling, 'I refer to that…that *licentious adulteress* who lives up in that palace of ill-repute. And of your…your *visits*, Major Ellis, your most most shameful, most deplorable visits to her…*boudoir!*'

Had Ellis not been central to this exchange, it may have been one to cause him much merriment later. Perhaps he would even have mimicked Belinda Royle's comical inflexions to someone like Martin or Malcolm over a few tumblers of whisky. But the untruth of her cruel words about Lakshmibai pained him terribly. Heads were turning and staring all around them in the churchyard and even the padre was making his way hurriedly towards them down the steps of the church. But Ellis, rendered speechless by his own rage, merely turned on his heel and strode out of the gates. Collecting his horse, and having nowhere to escape to, he rode straight out to the fort again.

Belinda's cruel words were still resounding in his ears as he walked into the Jhansi courtroom. Lakshmibai was seated among a crowd of men and, suddenly, Ellis could not help a piercing recognition that the wretched Royle woman had not been entirely inaccurate. Lakshmibai was really nothing like any other women he knew. Since becoming a widow, she had ruled her court more ably than her husband or any of his male predecessors had done. She sat now, surrounded by her adoring courtiers, too busy with them to notice Ellis as he stood for a few moments on the fringes of the crowd, his mind still whirling. He watched her conduct her business with the horrible knowledge that she did not really need his support or his friendship—both of which he had so unthinkingly offered at the risk of his own place in the Company. And was that Royle woman right to say that he was betraying his own people by supporting Jhansi's queen in her troubles? Ellis was still mulling darkly over what the ghastly woman had said when Lakshmibai spotted him. Her warm smile made the crowd before him part deferentially but he walked past the courtiers without his usual joy at being so warmly received by her.

He knew he must sound discourteous as he greeted her with his terse announcement. 'I have orders to visit Oudh next month,' he said abruptly, deriving an unconscionable pleasure from the look of dismay that passed almost invisibly across Lakshmibai's face. As she awaited an explanation, he added carelessly, not looking her in the eye, 'Government House has finally decided to take seriously all those rumours that have been emanating from Oudh. And various complaints about the redoubtable Begum Hazratmahal too.'

Lakshmibai, maintaining her composure, replied calmly, 'The begum is a determined woman, more determined than I at saving her kingdom. More determined even than her husband, Nawab Wajid Ali Shah. Nana tells me that the nawab is too fond of his pleasures to see dangers that lie just beyond but the begum sounds more canny. Are your orders to investigate her intentions towards the British?'

Ellis was feeling less belligerent now. 'Colonel Sleeman has been touring the state and has presented a report to Government House that depicts Oudh as being sadly neglected by the nawab. My task is to check how far discontent may have spread among his people.'

'Perhaps Lord Dalhousie is merely seeking reason to annexe the kingdom of Awadh, now that he has Jhansi.' Lakshmibai's face was still tranquil but Ellis could hear controlled anger in her voice.

He hesitated a moment before saying, 'There's no denying that the nawab does not care to leave the comforts of Lucknow and see to the rest of his state. But Oudh is wealthy and perhaps his people do not suffer greatly for his lack of governance.'

She nodded silently as she played with her sandalwood paper-cutter and looked up at Ellis with a sadness he had not seen on her face for a while. She did not say anything and so, still maintaining a carefully blithe tone in his voice, Ellis added lightly, 'Well, I will soon find out, I expect. I look forward too to the famed splendours of Lucknow, never having had occasion to visit the city before.'

He knew his words would wound Lakshmibai and, as she looked away, he saw the sandalwood paper-cutter she held between her fingers bend and snap. She seemed not to notice as she put the broken pieces down on the table before her, her voice remaining calm as she said, 'I have never visited Lucknow either but you can describe it to me in detail when you return, Robert.' After a few seconds, she added in a bolder tone of voice, 'Perhaps you will even find out from Begum Hazratmahal how Awadh and Jhansi can assist each other against Government House policies.'

Ellis threw a sharp look at her face but saw, with relief, that she spoke in jest. He was in no mood for light-heartedness but smiled at the rather far-fetched idea. She started to laugh and soon he found himself joining in, not realizing, even as he heard her voice catch in her throat, that she was despairing in both their capacities to hurt each other for no particular reason.

Less than a week later, he boarded the carriage that would take him to Lucknow, watched by Lakshmibai from the upper windows of her palace. She swallowed the constriction in her throat as she saw his head of golden hair disappear into the buggy, quite unable to fathom why he was leaving Jhansi with anger in his heart for her. She had not asked when he would return, although it seemed as though he was in no hurry to do so. It was true that, so far, he had offered her nothing more than calm and gentle humanity; something to cling to in the midst of all the troubles she was having with his government. But she also knew there would be those who would consider her a fool for not seeing that it had sprung merely from pity.

Trying to shake off her misery, she stood at her balcony, watching Robert leave with the knowledge that he had no reason at all to stay. He was British and she knew that it would take a lot more than the guilt he must feel over her tribulations to keep him close to her. Perhaps one day he would want to stay despite everything and, until that happened, she was too proud to ask. As the horse driver clicked his teeth and tugged on the reins, the carriage trundled out of the cobbled palace yard, Robert's small cabin trunk strapped to the back of it. Lakshmibai stood alone, her hands gripping the marble parapet tightly, reminding herself desolately to be grateful she had her son, her father, her people. What sort of affliction was it to remain unappreciative of such an abundance of love?

৵ 27 ৎ

It was in the manner of a prisoner receiving an unexpected reprieve that Ellis embarked on his journey. He felt relief to be escaping the subterfuge of his double life in Jhansi and excited as he headed for beautiful Lucknow. As the road unfurled behind his carriage, there was little regret at leaving both Jhansi and Lakshmibai behind, the burden of his love for both having grown into an imposition of late.

Scheherazade's Baghdad, he mused, as he caught his first glimpse of the famed city of Lucknow; the city that had been built by the nawabs of Awadh to rival the Mughal splendours of Delhi. The main arched entrance had been built to resemble the great gate at Constantinople and Ellis could see, beyond it, rolling green turf cut by an elaborate system of canals that functioned like a town wall. As his carriage made its way past the splendid dome of the Hussainabad Imambara, Ellis thought that the ornate architecture seemed almost to be admiring itself in the oblong of clear water that lay before it. A few minutes later, he passed the even more glorious Bara Imambara, surrounded by tree-filled gardens and vaulting exuberantly skywards. Remembering a description he had read of Lucknow somewhere, 'a city more vast than Paris and more brilliant', he gazed up at the truly amazing skyline. Comparisons with Paris seemed erroneous for this was more akin to something out of a children's fairy tale. Giant old trees and luxuriant hedges could not hide the arching azure domes, pearly minarets and tall bell-towers that spiralled into the clouds behind them. Down the road came the salubrious residential areas, a parade of mansions with glimpses of cupolas here and colonnades there, pillared fronts of residences that revealed wealth and opulence, if not always good taste.

The roads were wide and well paved and thronging with all manner of horse carriage and rickshaw and the bazaar was teeming with wealthy traders and jewel-draped Muslim aristocrats. As the horse strained to cross a steep iron bridge, Ellis saw the sinuous brown Gomti flow sluggishly beneath. The busy main road stretching before him, Hazratganj, was named after the queen he was due to meet. From here, he knew from the directions he had been given, it was about four miles to Musabagh, the palace north of the city that Hazratmahal had recently moved to with, he had heard it whispered, a lover called Mammo Khan. Ellis now could not wait to see the begum's court of whose grandeur much had been made and wondered if she would be in purdah, unlike the occasion on which she had met Harriet Mead. He had once read a description of the begum that compared her to the Amazonian Penthesilea alongside descriptions of her female guards, whose wont it apparently was to be outlandishly kitted out in military jackets and white duck trousers and armed with a cornucopia of muskets and bayonets, cross belts and cartridge boxes.

Shoulders stiff from leaning forward so much, Ellis sat back in his seat, reflecting on the journey he had made through the affluent Awadh countryside before getting to Lucknow. It had been a most illuminating experience to meet the ordinary people of this state—tea-stall owners and farmers and soldiers. Usually, there was nothing he enjoyed more than communing with ordinary folk but here, in Awadh, he had found himself facing an inexplicably deep distrust. How, he wondered, had Sleeman collected his evidence in the face of such suspicion, especially as his report had reportedly been based on statements gathered from the people and direct observation rather than hearsay. Ellis thought Sleeman's opinion odd for there seemed no overt sign of the people being neglected by their dissolute ruler.

They had all heard the stories of immoderation and self-indulgence emanating from the court but Ellis had been both admiring of and amused by their magnanimous willingness to overlook their nawab's excesses. Perhaps that was because their own lives were by and large prosperous and comfortable. That they did not want the British to take over Awadh's administration was a common thread in all their remarks.

On Ellis's first night in Awadh, he had shared the dining room of his haveli with a group of landlords who had gathered to noisily bemoan British plans to overhaul the old zamindari system. Ellis had uneasily seen their eyes darting towards him as they loudly poured scorn on the new policies that transferred taxation rights that had been theirs for generations to the British. And overheard with more than a little alarm of how incensed Awadh's biggest and most powerful zamindars had grown. He hoped he was not to become the butt of their anger.

Escaping them early next morning, Ellis had thought it strange that neither the wealthy landlord nor the impoverished farmer seemed enthused by the new scheme, despite the idea that the latter at least may have had something to gain from it. From what he could see, even poorer peasants preferred the protection offered to them by the old paternalistic system to being at the mercy of British collectors and sub-collectors who, they believed, understood nothing about their land or lives.

Ellis was similarly perturbed after a chance meeting with a couple of sepoys who seemed oddly unconcerned that they were airing grievances in the presence of an English official. It was as if caution was no longer necessary as, over a few glasses of toddy at a ramshackle grog-shop on the outskirts of the city, they griped about the threat to their future livelihoods if Awadh were annexed as the Punjab had been.

'Once Awadh becomes a British province, like Punjab and Bengal, then I lose my job, my right to appeal, my right to refuse to serve abroad. Five years ago, my foreign service bhatta was taken away, even though it was my efforts that had helped expand British provinces,' the younger of the two asserted, angrily thumping the wooden table as he repeated the words '*my* efforts', glaring at Ellis as he did.

The other sepoy took up from where his comrade left off. 'And I know the next thing our superiors will do is convert us by force to Christianity. Already they are talking of changing the whole system— previously this job was reserved for higher castes only but now, if this new enlistment order comes, there will be no difference between the old sipahi and these new recruits from among Aheers, Jats, Kaits, even Mussalmans, everybody can join in...'

The older sepoy, lacking the passionate anger of his friend, sounded depressed and Ellis, seated at the adjoining table, had joined in their conversation at this point, hoping to explain that forced conversion to Christianity would never happen. He wondered why he bothered as his view was gloomily dismissed by the old sepoy. It was certainly true that, missionaries apart, many Army officers too now came to this country with hopes of converting what they saw as a dark continent to enlightened Christianity. These people were entitled to their fears. Everyone knew that Awadh's annexation by the British was only a matter of time and Ellis could understand how much these people resented the uncertainties. Dalhousie's uncharacteristic indecisiveness was costing everyone dear. So far, Ellis had met no one who thought annexation would do them any good and he was sure that the begum would not be in disagreement.

Ellis's rambling thoughts came to an end as he saw his carriage pull into the massive portico of Begum Hazratmahal's palace. A group of surly guards received him and he found himself being escorted down the miles of honeycombed corridors that had been described by Harriet Mead. At first, all he could think of was of how much more opulent this court was compared with Jhansi's. The walls were either covered with tapestries of gold and silver brocade or hung with yard upon yard of soft damask. Persian and even Axminster carpets lined marble floors. Scattered all around were European-style statues and busts in creamy marble alongside priceless ornaments of gold, silver, ebony and ivory. Enormous crystal chandeliers, crowded with flower-shaped glass candleholders in glowing red and purple, hung from an elaborately gilded ceiling. Ellis could also see thermantidotes, the new style of window fans, in some of the surrounding walls and smelt the fragrance of khus emanating from them.

Hazratmahal was, as Ellis had guessed, in purdah but he got a whiff of the powerful rose attar that had made him feel so ill at the Mead residence. He sensed a strong presence behind the silken curtains. The begum's voice, as she greeted him, was full of the rich gravelly sound belonging either to fat women or those given to years of paan chewing. Ellis also heard the low bubble of a hookah pipe.

'You are a friend of Rani Lakshmibai?' the begum asked suspiciously, the rustling sound of paper indicating to Ellis that she was reading the letter he had handed over to one of her guards. He suspected that she was also using a system of mirrors to observe him.

'Yes, Begum-sahiba. My visit is official, as you know, but I am a trusted friend and emissary too of the Jhansi court,' he said warily.

'What are you doing to help Jhansi with her annexation, then?' she asked sharply.

'The annexation?' Ellis queried in surprise, receiving a grunt in response. 'Well, there's not a lot I can do, Begum-sahiba, such decisions are made in Calcutta as you know. Rani Lakshmibai is considering an appeal and I am advising her on that.'

'Is she likely to win?'

'Her chances are not very good, unfortunately, but she is determined to try.'

Ellis heard the begum sigh dramatically before she said, 'So powerful, so powerful, it is not right.'

Unsure of exactly what she was referring to, he waited for her to say something else, which she soon did. 'Please tell Rani Lakshmibai that I appreciate the sentiments expressed in her kind letter. Poor thing, the annexation of Jhansi must have devastated her.'

'As I said, Begum-sahiba, she is still hoping to find some legal loophole by which she can have it overturned.'

'Loophole, pah!' the begum barked. 'These people in Calcutta are too powerful to let the small matter of legality trouble them. I think states like Awadh and Jhansi would do each other and themselves a great favour by putting up a united front and fighting the Company with force.'

'The East India Company has very powerful armies, Begum-sahiba. Even a principality as big as Awadh will pale into insignificance next to their might. It is best to be cautious before expressing such hasty views,' Ellis responded stiffly.

'Ah but have you considered that the Company's army is made up of our men? Three-fourths of the men in your Company's armies are from Awadh,' she retorted.

'Begum-sahiba, forgive me, but loyalty is not such an unpredictable thing. Men generally consider it fitting to stay faithful to those who pay them and feed them...'

'Aha, my dear Major, but I have learnt cruel lessons about loyalty from the British themselves. Awadh had always remained loyal to the British, as you may know. Not that we could not understand why we were needed, sitting as we do between your Punjab and your Bengal, the great Grand Trunk road cutting right through our state. But still we humoured you, even helping to finance your wars. Do you know that the entire expense for the two-year Gurkha war came out of Awadh's treasuries? Mister Outram and Mister Dalhousie would do well to remember that when they repay our past loyalties with such mockery now. Do you think we do not understand why you now want to possess Awadh in its entirety? Because, Major Ellis, you think we are the last obstacle in your being able to put down the railway lines from Bengal. As simple as that. Do you not think that you take far too much for granted: the goodwill of our royal families and also the loyalty of your own sipahis. You mark my words, Major Ellis, in the end, the sipahis, men of high caste and rank, will align themselves with Awadh against the British.'

Ellis was taken aback by the ferocity in the begum's voice and felt obliged to make his stance clear. 'I am fairly certain, Begum-sahiba,' he said, struggling to stay calm, 'that the Company sepoys know what is good for them. It is best, perhaps, to follow the example set by the rani of Jhansi in avoiding any talk of using force.'

'If you describe yourself as a friend of Jhansi, Major Ellis, perhaps it is your job to advise Rani Lakshmibai to build up her army, as we are doing. Please inform her that one cannot afford to get lackadaisical about security in times like this. You may be interested to let your superiors know that Awadh does not act alone. We are in regular contact with Azimullah at Nana Peshwa's court and also Jung Bahadur, the king of Nepal. Soon we will be making contact with our King Emperor Bahadur Shah Zafar at Delhi too. Government House, far from dismissing us, should be cowering in fear.'

Ellis was not sure at all if this was the truth but felt angered by the barely masked threat. Managing to keep his voice neutral, he asked, 'May I enquire, Begum-sahiba, if Nawab Wajid Ali Shah feels as strongly about this as you do?' He knew he was treading on delicate territory by making such a bold reference to the husband who had, common knowledge indicated, already thrown this vile woman out of his palace.

'The nawab?' she snapped tetchily. 'The nawab is planning to go to Calcutta with some advisors to try and reach a settlement with the British if this infernal annexation comes through. And, if they do not succeed there, they will be going to London, Major Ellis, to discuss it with your Padishah Victoria.' The begum sounded irritable, impatient with the very notion of diplomatic activity.

'The legal route maybe more circumspect, more sensible perhaps?' Ellis ventured carefully, giving her another chance to retract her militant position.

'I have no time for such time-wasting talks, Major Ellis. Where did that ever help either the Nanasahib or even Rani Lakshmibai, you tell me. Haven't they both tried the legal route? I have Bidris Quadr, my son, to think of. He will be the next nawab of Awadh, even if I must die trying to defend Lucknow for him. You believe me, Major Ellis, the British would do well to keep their hands off Awadh. I want you to go back to your Government House in Calcutta and tell them that. Begum Hazratmahal of Awadh has pronounced it so.'

Ellis returned to Jhansi two weeks later and was completely unprepared for Lakshmibai's reaction to his description of Begum Hazratmahal. She was admiring of the begum where he had expected scorn and he felt—even on his first day back—that something about Lakshmibai had changed subtly in the days he had been away. She seemed more remote and less inclined to accept his views without disagreement. Their relationship had undergone an inexplicable shift and he guessed it was at least partially due to the unkindness with which he had announced his departure for Awadh.

Seated near a mirror in her chambers that evening, she was playing with a jewelled hairpin and looked at his reflection as she brought up the subject again, speaking softly, almost to herself, 'I must admit that there will be a part of me that will rejoice for Awadh if they do indeed succeed in defeating the British by force. Perhaps they have learnt from observing Jhansi that there is nothing to be gained by accepting annexation quietly as we did.'

Ellis watched as her chignon slowly unwound, sending a rope of dark hair tumbling down her back. He thought her reaction in some ways unsurprising for how indeed could she have forgotten her resentment at the annexation? But Ellis was also disappointed that his friendship and guidance in all these months had not softened her attitude to the British at all. He felt he was being tested and tried to weigh his words carefully.

'I certainly do know what you mean, Rani-sahiba. You have suffered enough under Dalhousie's policies and it would only be natural to be feeling that way. But war with the Company? Nothing can be more inadvisable for Oudh,' he said firmly.

'Well, what else would you expect them to do, Robert? Given that all other approaches yield nothing but disappointment and humiliation?' She had turned away from the mirror to face him directly.

'Well, there are places where men of honour take their fights. Law courts and hearings and appeals. Battlefields are hardly the place to decide such important things.'

'But how can one hope for justice when the different sides are beset by such inequalities, tell me that, Robert!' She had turned around completely and was now meeting Ellis's gaze squarely, her eyes flashing with smouldering anger.

Ellis paused for a moment before replying coldly, 'What can ever be gained by sending out armies and ordering the killing of people?'

She clicked her tongue and tossed her head impatiently. 'Robert, that is like telling a man who is facing a large cannon that he must shoot at its metal using his puny bow and arrow because the rules of engagement do not allow him to aim for the heart of the man standing behind the cannon. Do you know that even Lord Krishna's advice to Bhima had been to aim for Duryodhana's thigh—when the rules of the Great War were to never aim below the navel? No, of course, you would not know that. It is clear to me that even our gods knew what had to be done in times of unequal wars. But it seems that the British will only learn it the hard way.'

Ellis was taken aback at this sudden militancy in her voice. He had never heard her speak in such a strident tone before and it felt so incongruous emanating from the feminine figure sitting before him, her skin glowing golden in the candlelight, dark curls flowing gracefully to her waist. He watched her get up and walk across the room to open her cupboard doors. She was silent now, her jaw set and her eyes no longer making contact with his. He could sense that some of her anger was aimed at him, the silence between them pregnant with further tacit disagreement.

Ellis got up abruptly, knowing that he had been dismissed. He felt angry and hurt at Lakshmibai's sudden imperiousness, even though, god knows, she was entitled to her resentment. She did not turn around to look at him even when the chair he had got up from fell over with a crash. Bending over to retrieve it, Ellis thought it almost offensive that she had so quickly forgotten that he had always supported her in her fight, even laying his own career on the line. Perhaps her outpourings to him had never really revealed the true depth of her fury against the British and Ellis was suddenly unsure of what lengths she would go to fight her appeal against the annexation, especially if Awadh took the path of force and invited Jhansi to join them. He both wanted and did not want to know all those mysterious thoughts that she had kept hidden from him all this time. He straightened the chair and looked at her one last time, hoping that the expression on her face would have melted and softened into the one he was more familiar with. But her back was still firmly turned as she busied herself with aimlessly arranging some papers in her armoire.

The rigidity of her shoulders and back told him that she clearly wanted him gone. Ellis turned on his heel and left her chambers, striding down the garden path and calling angrily for his horse. He felt not just perturbed at her sudden change of mood but also furious with his own inability to comprehend it.

He rode as hard as he could, returning to the cantonment and trying to divest himself of his anger on that long, empty road. Still sweating from the exertion an hour later, he paced around the veranda of his bungalow, feeling frustration swirl within him. He was sure that Lakshmibai was herself confounded by Begum Hazratmahal's stance. There would obviously be a part of her that would rejoice if Awadh did succeed in slapping Dalhousie's face by going to war with him. That was something he could genuinely understand, given all that she had gone through. But, surely, surely she could see how hopeless such an endeavour would be. Apart from the most terrible bloodshed and destruction, nothing good would ever be achieved. The consequences would be so very much worse than mere annexation.

Looking up at the inky sky, he saw a dense cloud sitting in the middle of it, pressing down on Jhansi like a fist. It was making the air grow close and oppressive and Ellis felt a sudden weight in his chest that made it difficult for him to breathe. Deep in his stomach, the knowledge was growing that Lakshmibai may go much further than he would have ever thought possible in opposing Government House. If she was approached by states like Awadh with a plan for military action, he was beginning to develop a sound idea of the path she would take. And where would he stand in such an event? In a precarious halfway position between his loyalty to his government and his friendship with Jhansi. He had already put himself severely at risk. How could he have been foolish enough to imagine that it would remain possible to juggle love and loyalty when such treacherous chasms were forming all around?

◈ 28 ◈

On a scorching hot morning the following week, Lakshmibai made her customary weekly visit to the Mahalakshmi Temple, stopping as usual to pay alms to the rows of beggars seated outside. After the last of the money had been handed out, she turned to Sundar and Dewan Rao Bande to suggest that they walk through the Halwaipur area rather than use the palanquins waiting to take them back to the palace. There had lately been a lot of talk going around of the temple administration being taken into British control and it was wise to allay the concerns of its residents. But, as they reached the main street cutting through residential area, their footsteps came to a sudden halt as they beheld before them a waste-disposal wagon dragging on its yokes the skin of a large animal that could only have been a cow or a bullock. Only small areas of tan skin were visible as the rest of the creature, including its head and horns, were completely covered in huge, lazily moving clumps of black flies and wasps. As the wagon went over a bump in the road, the insects reluctantly lifted themselves from the sticky carcass, hovering a few inches away in an impatient dark cloud, before quickly settling back down onto the reeking bloodied mess again. The stench was like nothing Lakshmibai had ever known before and, covering her nose and mouth with the end of her sari, she stopped dead in her tracks, with a flabbergasted cry.

'Dewan-ji! What is that terrible thing?'

Dewan Rao Bande and the guards were already running past her. The poor untouchable pulling the wagon, terrified at seeing the rani's entourage, had dropped the wagon handles and already fallen grovelling into the dust.

As Sundar held her back, Lakshmibai watched from a few paces away, unable to hear the conversation between the scavenger and her prime minister. But she could see Dewan Rao Bande shake his head in disbelief as he ordered the man to get up and remove the carcass without delay. As he hurried back to her side, she could hear the shock in his voice.

'Rani-sahiba...what can I say...can it get any worse? According to that poor man, his orders came straight from the British camp to dispose of animal waste material using this very route. He knows nothing else but, from what he said, I gather that a new slaughterhouse has been opened behind the Halwaipur market area that will supply both beef and pork to the cantonment.'

'Slaughterhouse—when Dewan-ji? They never told us...and in *this* area? Halwaipur is full of Hindus, high-caste Brahmins. They could have chosen any area but this one!' Lakshmibai was incredulous.

Dewan Rao Bande shrugged his shoulders and Lakshmibai knew what he was thinking. She put a hand on his shoulder to calm him.

'If they want to shame us completely, this is as good a tactic as any, is it not? I could try summoning Major Ellis but we have heard nothing from him for over a week now.'

She spoke calmly but she felt trepidation at the thought that she may have angered Ellis enough to have him completely realign his loyalties to Calcutta. He was clearly distancing himself from her, his belongings at Motibagh lying untouched these past few days. She knew she had spoken bluntly on his return from Lucknow, but surely the time had come for his allegiance to be properly tested. For if Ellis found himself unable to maintain fidelity to Jhansi's most important needs, what explanation could she make for his continuing presence in her court? Even kindly dewan-sahib's face wore an expression that told her she was only wasting her time if she expected any more help from Robert Ellis.

Having heard nothing from Lakshmibai since their altercation, Ellis had tried to busy himself with the work that had accumulated during his trip to Lucknow. When he finally did hear from the palace, it was a message from Dewan Rao Bande summoning him to the rani's presence. He despatched his reply through her messenger, saying he would visit her court in the evening, hoping he was being called because she wished to apologize for her behaviour last week.

However, one glance at her face as he walked through the doors of the Diwan-i-Khas that evening told Ellis all he needed to know. There was nothing at all remorseful about her stance. Seated on her throne, a few feet above where Ellis stood, she was filled with an incandescence that was almost luminescent, physically quivering with it. He gathered instantly that she had heard of both the takeover of the Mahalakshmi Temple as well as the shameful business of the slaughterhouses. Once again, as with the annexation, it was clear to Ellis that she blamed him for both, bristling with rage as she snapped questions at him through pale, clenched lips. How different she looked—this regal and infuriated queen, clad in glittering silks and diamonds—from the lovely young Lakshmibai who had laughed and ridden by his side in the forests.

Would she understand, he wondered, would she even believe him if he tried explaining things to her? He was himself in disgrace, not just in Jhansi cantonment, but in Calcutta too. Dalhousie had written him a letter, rebuking him for his conduct that 'led to doubts as to the finality of the lapse of Jhansi state in the Ranee's mind'. Rumours of a punishment posting to Panna had come his way too. In the past week, it had become obvious that he was being shunned socially by everyone in the cantonment. There were no more invitations to those luncheons and teas he had always hated but, for some reason, he now minded the affront terribly. Ellis had even seen some people getting up and vacating the mess room as soon as he walked in. Worst of all, he was being overlooked in the most obvious manner in the decision-making process for Jhansi; Colvin, the governor of the North West Provinces, had taken over the administration of Jhansi and his orders were now being executed by Major Erskine, who was the divisional commissioner for Sagar. Ellis was, possibly under direct orders from Calcutta, being left out of the loop completely and quite deliberately. He was, in all their eyes, no better than a traitor.

He wondered if she would believe him if he tried telling her all that? He thought not. Not from the blameful way in which she was looking at him and from the angry words she was flinging so carelessly in his direction. Words that he could barely hear, jumbling as they were so horribly in his brain. Somewhere along the way, the trust she had once had in him had turned to sour and unbearable suspicion and her love for him—for how could he believe it had never been there—had turned to indissoluble hate. Up against so much opprobrium from both sides, Ellis felt he no longer knew what he believed in any more. Suddenly he was disempowered and weakened and very, very tired.

After finishing her say, Lakshmibai watched Robert Ellis turn and walk out of her courtroom without a word in response. She was both astonished and perturbed by his silence and wondered if she may have felt more angered by some long rambling explanations that would have achieved nothing. Was it possible to feel rage and pity for him all at once? From the slope of his shoulders as he disappeared through the courtroom doors, his weariness was apparent. Of course she knew that he too was only a pawn in a bigger game but that was now simply not comfort enough. His failures to her were mounting and by now she knew with utmost certainty that she needed him to swear complete devotion and loyalty to Jhansi; in absolute and unqualified measure and with none of the painful indecisions of the half-love he had offered so far.

❧ 29 ❧

Ellis sat alone at the bar in the Officers' Mess, sipping on his scotch and feeling the alcohol percolate into his benumbed body and mind. For the first time in days he could feel the world recede from him, leaving him with a sensation of weightlessness. Who would have thought…who would have thought even a few weeks ago that resigning from service in India would leave him feeling so relieved? But he had received the affirmative from Government House and now it was all over.

He ought to be devastated but instead felt merely empty. He had come to India a callow impressionable youth who had seen nothing else of the world and had fallen in love with this country's majestic beauty almost straightaway. Even in the most remote outposts, it was always possible to find a nobility and grandeur so stirring as to lift the soul. Most of his comrades, some even younger than him, had felt the same way and, for those who had not fallen into the lively party spirit of the Presidencies and hill-stations, there had been the shikaars and falconry and hunts. But he knew now where they had succeeded and he had failed. While other officers had allowed their minds to grow along with the multiplying stature of British power, to pluck easily at the fruits of bountiful power, Ellis had found himself genuinely unable to do so. Unable, with an inability he sometimes wished he did not possess, to free himself of the guilt that an honourable victor must feel in a vanquished land.

Although the idea of resigning had been taking hold ever since the annexation of Jhansi, it was Ellis's last visit to the palace that had finally decided it for him. His efforts to help Lakshmibai fight off the annexation had not only come to nothing, she would not even allow him to tell her of them. Ellis had only recently discovered that Colonel Malcolm had failed to forward the final impassioned letter Ellis had written to Lord Dalhousie in Lakshmibai's defence. On having accosted Malcolm with that accusation, the man had merely smiled as if acknowledging rather pityingly Ellis's fondness for the rani and his need for protection from it. That had confused Ellis even more than Belinda Royle's fury and the ensuing silence from the whole community had made him question his own loyalties. Was it so reprehensible to have struggled to accept the benighted place his people now held in this country? How could it be that he, for whom country and Company meant everything, was branded dishonourable for simply wanting his Company to act with more honour?

When he had offered them his resignation, he had been both shocked and relieved at the speed with which it had been accepted and put through the bureaucracy in Calcutta. It was clear that the government wanted him out of India as fast as possible. Instructions had already been issued for his replacement to be found and so it would be mere days before he was to leave for Calcutta and board his steamer. Already, he had booked his passage by telegraph and begun the tasks that needed to be completed before departing Jhansi.

He swirled his glass gently, telling himself he ought to be happy that the months of agonizing were finally behind him. He was going back home. To England.

England...he hunched his shoulders on the bar counter. It was a country he could barely remember any more. His father had passed on four years ago and Uncle Herbert had long reverted to the remote figure of his childhood in his rare letters. There was no one at all to return to. And what if England too turned her back on him? After all, he had exulted in leaving her once and had never looked back with longing or regret. What if she too—like Jhansi—regarded him as an ungrateful child, unwelcome at her door?

Ellis closed his eyes, finally allowing Lakshmibai's face to drift into his mind. He tried to remember the pretty smiling face he had fallen in love with, rather than the one he had been confronted with more recently, twisted with hate and anger for him. But it was the latter picture—of her incandescent rage, dark eyes flashing—that kept returning. Ellis felt again that vile blend of anger and sorrow rise up in his throat and push against his eyes. He put his glass down and pressed his palms against his pulsing temples, telling himself bleakly that he should be glad to be getting out before falling any lower.

He forced himself to remember Lakshmibai's unenviable fate, worse—yes, far worse—than his. At least he had another land to escape to. Trapped as she was, it was only natural that she should vent some of her frustrations against British policies on him. Feeling calmer, and picking up his whisky tumbler again, he wondered whether she missed his friendship at all. Did she know that he still faithfully rode out every morning to the Barhwa Sagar lakeside, hoping that she would eventually come? Not that he would have known what to say if she did but it was pointless worrying about that because she had never returned. The place was now imbued with the memory of the day he had broken the news of the annexation to her and it was hard to regain the peace he had once derived from it.

This morning, he had stood on the crest of the ruins and looked out at the distant Betwa. Even mighty rivers moved and changed course, so why should it feel so hard for him? Jhansi's countryside beyond the lake stretched brown and undulating towards distant harvested wheat fields as it awaited its next searing summer. He thought of how Lakshmibai had so suddenly become queen of all this by marrying Gangadhar. Queen of not just this stretch of land and water but all the trees and shrubs that dotted it as far as one could see, of its towns and farms and people, their joys and sorrows, a palace, a fort, a distant silver river...could an act of marriage create a love and a duty towards a land and a people that suddenly transcended all else?

Ellis did not think it possible. After all, the British had proven how easy it was to govern without being burdened by sentimental affection for states conquered. It was a job, a mission that they got on with and performed to the best of their abilities. Administering previously ungovernable lands, bringing the benefits of peace and prosperity to as many imperial subjects as possible and keeping the rewards earned thus for themselves. Nothing more and nothing less. Was that not better than their predecessors, the Mughals, who had set about leaving their stamp so indelibly on the face of India, scarring it forever with some of their atrocities? Ellis had a recollection of Lakshmibai having once compared the British with the Mughals, saying something about how those invaders from Persia had respected the land enough to have integrated and become one with it. But, despite his own fondness for India, and the problems he had had with some of his government's policies, Ellis genuinely could not accept that good governance needed to be anything more than maintaining order within a land as fairly and objectively as possible. He would have wished, of course, for more compassion but perhaps his superiors were right in believing that compassion merely translated into weakness in the eyes of the governed.

Ellis allowed the gloom of the mess room to darken around him, enveloping his body with its cold dank air. Many times in the past few days he had contemplated sending Lakshmibai a note that informed her of his departure, asking if she would meet him just once again, if for nothing else than to forgive him and think of him well in the future, but his pride had prevented him. Perhaps what she needed was time to recover from the annexation and she was not to know that his time in Jhansi was running out. He looked into the golden liquor in his glass, trying to overcome his swelling regret, reminding himself that he would not be the first man for whom love could not come to fruition because of the misfortune of time and circumstance. Even fifty years ago, relationships between British men and Indian women had been barely acceptable; increasing British power had put paid to all that. The missionaries had played their part too, especially the ones more recently arrived in India who preached vigorously against Christians converting to accommodate the wishes of Hindu and Muslim wives and mistresses. And with more Englishwomen coming out to live in India with their husbands, or indeed in search of husbands, it was as if walls of stone had sprung up between the two communities.

As a bearer came into the room to light the lanterns, trophies of animals' heads materialized from the murk, staring glassily down at Ellis: antlered sambhar and tigers and even a wild-eyed snarling black bear, relics of successful past shikaars by the scores of Englishmen who had been here before him, intent only on enjoying all that this bountiful land had to offer them without necessarily becoming one with it. Not for the first time, Ellis wished, foolishly, irrationally, that he had come to India in an earlier time. Perhaps over a hundred or two hundred years before, as a trader of spices, or a mere traveller...when he would have been free to roam the land and the seas...and when love and other such tender concerns would not have been forbidden across cultural divides as they were now. It was possible that such an age would come again but Ellis knew without a trace of doubt that it would be much too late for him.

In the end, Ellis could not bring himself to leave Jhansi without seeing Lakshmibai at all. He nursed a faint hope yet that she would feel heartened if he promised to help, once back in London, to talk to people there who may be sympathetic to her plight. There may be some minister or peer in the House of Lords who could be persuaded, perhaps, to take up her case.

He rode out to her fort through a thin veil of rain. The monsoon had come and gone, leaving all of the countryside a gleaming fresh green. This was a shower that had lagged behind, as though trying to revive his spirits.

After his name had been announced, Ellis walked into her court. He clicked his heels on the deep blue carpet and bowed. Rani Lakshmibai inclined her head and, as he looked up, he thought he saw some of the old softness in her eyes, but could not be sure. Perhaps she regretted her angry outburst to him the last time they had met but she could not very well have apologized for it. Not here, in her court, surrounded by her courtiers. She was looking calm today but regal and unapproachable, resplendent in a gold-bordered sari and a small gem-studded aigrette on her head, so unlike the sprightly figure in tunic and jodhpurs that had effortlessly kept abreast with him on their morning rides. It would be the latter picture that he knew would sustain him once he was far away from her.

A huge brass bowl filled with mogra and kamini flowers had been placed by her throne and sticks of incense on lamp holders built into the wall were making the air heavy with smoky fragrance. In that calm atmosphere, Ellis's voice seemed loud to his own ears, echoing inside his head as though the words were not issuing from his own mouth at all.

'Rani-sahiba, I have come to tell you that I have resigned as Jhansi's political agent. I am returning to England next week,' he said.

He saw surprise on her face and took comfort from seeing what he was sure was a flicker of distress in her eyes.

'Resigned?' she asked. 'England next week? So suddenly, Major Ellis?'

'It is not that sudden, I have been contemplating it for days before finally taking the decision.'

'But why? You cannot mean...' she stopped momentarily, her voice dropping to make a statement rather than ask a question. 'You are leaving India for good,' she said slowly.

Ellis remained silent and this time he was sure he saw sorrow shine in her eyes as she added, her voice turning to a whisper, 'You...your years of service to these lands?'

He kept his voice brisk as he could not bear to let her see his pain. 'I'm not sure I can sum it all up easily, Rani-sahiba. There is too much that is beyond my power to control and even to understand. It will be more advantageous for me to seek a post at the Company headquarters in London.'

There was a pause before she asked, her voice suddenly curving into gentleness, 'Will you not miss India...and Jhansi?'

Ellis observed her changed tone with a piercing feeling in his heart—her voice was now the one from all their old conversations and exchanges of confidences. There was both relief and sorrow at hearing it again. She was clearly remembering that happier time too. This would have been the moment to ask forgiveness for all her recent unhappiness, but, despite his churning emotions, Ellis remained to the last incapable of open disloyalty to Company and government and heard himself reply stiffly, 'There may be many things about your land that I will miss, Rani-sahiba. But I have also missed my own country and it feels as though I have stayed away far too many years. It is time now for me to return to my own home and to my people.'

He looked up at Lakshmibai, squarely meeting her gaze. Her eyes were wide and dark against her face, pale lips parted slightly. He thought he saw her lower lip tremble slightly but could not be sure. She sat terribly still in her throne for a few seconds, the air between them heavy with unsaid words. For one moment, he thought she was about to say something but then she seemed to change her mind. Her lips closed and she raised her chin almost indiscernibly, eyes glinting like the diamonds in her aigrette. It was either a gesture of defiance or acceptance, he could not tell which. With a stabbing feeling in his chest, he clicked his heels on the floor, bowed deeply and then turned to stride out of the room.

Sundar could not believe her ears as she heard Major Ellis's words of farewell to the rani in court. After he had left the courtroom, she ran up the stairs to watch him depart Ranimahal, almost as though having to convince herself this was really happening. She felt a clamouring within her as she saw him waiting for his horse and fought the temptation to call out and stop him. It was plain how afflicted by sorrow the Englishman was from the weariness of his smile as he attempted his usual jocularity with the syces. His shoulders were slumped as he mounted his horse and steered it slowly out of the palace gates.

Sundar, who had never known a man's love and had, for reasons she had not been able to explain to herself, never even been particularly curious about such matters, had always rather oddly liked Major Ellis. Not just for his own graciousness but also for the soft contented expression she had seen on her rani's face as they rode back to the palace, having met him on their first morning rides. He was unfailingly courteous to her and the other maids, accepting their hospitality as though always a little surprised and touched by their dutiful gestures. When he had become a more frequent visitor to the palace, it was Sundar who had arranged his stay at Motibagh without once questioning the propriety of it, aware of how desperately her rani needed friendship and comfort in these sad times. Though she had always held her tongue, she had never once doubted the Englishman's affections for her rani, aware of the depths his careful manner could not always mask. What had gone wrong between them, Sundar wondered, to cause such a sudden dismissal from each other's lives and hearts?

She felt a strange yawning pit opening up in her stomach as Major Ellis's horse picked up speed, cantering down the road and out of sight. She had heard him say in court that he was returning to his country. Did that mean he would never return to Jhansi? England lay far across the black waters; it would surely not be easy to return, even for an English officer like him. And who would be sent to replace him?

Suddenly she heard frantic footsteps running up the back stairs. Turning, she caught a glimpse of Rani Lakshmibai flying up from her courtroom and running to her room in haste. The rani had not seen Sundar standing against the pillar as she slammed the door shut behind her and slid its iron bolt shut before bursting into loud sobbing breaths. Sundar thought it was the most frightening sound she had heard in a long time. Despite all of Jhansi's travails, she had not heard her rani weep so since her baby had died. Panic-stricken, she contemplated going in to comfort her queen but the heavy wooden door was locked from within and, as Sundar stepped back, she realized that Rani Lakshmibai would prefer to think that her grief at Major Ellis's departure had passed unnoticed by all.

∾ *30* ∾

Two weeks later, Sundar walked into the kitchens in search of the chief khansama, Mohandeo. She had to ensure that he was preparing the evening meal as per the rani's instructions. The new political agent for Jhansi, a Captain Alexander Skene, was visiting and Rani Lakshmibai had explained how important it was to develop a good relationship with him. She did not mention the departed political agent at all except for saying that, unlike Major Ellis, Captain Skene was a married man. Tonight his wife and two daughters were coming as well and the rani had seemed pleased that Damodar would have playmates in the two girls. All day the child had been practising and chanting their names...Mary Isabella Frances, Beatrice Cecilia Anne...

In the pantry, Mohandeo was having one of his usual fits. 'Nothing is ready yet, Sundarbai,' he cried on seeing her. 'See how hard these tomatoes are. Fifteen minutes they have been bubbling in this stock and still they will not soften.' He poked with his long wooden ladle at a dozen glistening red tomatoes bobbing cheerfully in the bubbling mulligatawny soup he always produced for his English guests. The tart smell of tamarind floated up to Sundar, making her mouth water instantly. A large dekchi of pulao, baking slowly on glowing coals in the corner hearth, was releasing a fragrance of rice and saffron, the aroma of festivals and celebrations. Over in the corner, she could see a large leg of lamb smothered in mint sauce. Despite his fussing, Mohandeo clearly had everything well in hand.

'Oh give the poor tomatoes time, Mohandeo, perhaps it is because they are not ripe enough that they are slower to cook. But that ghee pulao does smell delicious, I must say. That's what I call the smell of happiness.'

Khuda Baksh, counting plates and cutlery at the far end of the kitchen, called out to Sundar and, as she picked her way past the scullions busy peeling and chopping onions and potatoes, she could see that the old man looked worried.

'Don't tell me Mohandeo has infected you with his anxiety, Khuda Baksh,' she called out merrily, 'you're the only calm soul in this kitchen when a banquet is on.'

'Sundarbai, look at the state of these plates and bowls, how can we use them tonight you tell me?'

She peered at the serving bowl he was holding up and could see that its once white enamel was now a dull cream and covered in a fine spidery network of cracks.

'Are these the best ones we have, Khuda Baksh?' she asked, sharing his concern. Like him, she did not want the rani to lose face in front of the new political agent and his wife.

'We have not bought any new crockery since Raja Gangadhar Rao's wedding to our rani-sahiba. Before Prince Damodar's initiation ceremony, I had asked rani-sahiba to order some more from England, but she refused, saying it would be too expensive and insisting we should manage with what we have.'

'Don't forget, Khuda Baksh, she had to pay for all the celebrations of the prince's initiation out of her personal funds since the British would not let her take anything out of the raja's treasury.'

'Oh I have not forgotten, Sundarbai,' said Khuda Baksh, his normally tranquil white bearded features darkening. 'A travesty, that was nothing less than a travesty. It is only because our rani-sahiba is so forbearing that she still maintains good relations with the Angrez people.'

'Well, I think she feels that it is not these people who are to blame. Decisions are made by the powerful ones in Calcutta and in London who neither know her nor care for her. Why should she hold that against those who are in Jhansi and have always respected her?'

'You are right, Sundarbai. I hope this new agent, Captain Skene, is as good a man as Major Ellis. You know, Sundarbai...' Khuda Baksh put down his dishcloth to lean on the table before saying, 'I sometimes think our rani-sahiba now regrets the way she took out her grief over the annexation on poor Major Ellis. After all, everyone knew it was not a decree he was happy with...'

Sundar, though in agreement with the old butler, remained silent and Khuda Baksh resumed his dish wiping, mumbling half to himself now, 'But why reproach her...everyone needs a person at whose feet they can lay all their sorrow and their blame.'

He lifted the rice dish up to the light and squinted at it again. 'Now Major Ellis, *he* would have understood straightaway about the state of our crockery. So kind he was, so kind. Do you know, Sundarbai, he always made the time to stop and talk to me about my Afghanistan?'

Sundar, who had heard the stories of Khuda Baksh's native Afghanistan many times, nodded before hastily making some excuse to hurry away to her own tasks for the day.

Captain Alexander Skene and his wife Margaret looked up at the fort, dark against the night sky, as they approached it in their landau.

'Certainly doesn't compare with Gwalior fort,' he remarked, under his breath.

'I'm not surprised,' Margaret Skene replied, 'I had understood the Scindias to be far more affluent than the royal family of Jhansi...'

'You're right, darling. Although, if you ask me, all these royals have far too much wealth than is good for them. Some of their personal fortunes are enormous. I'm not sure yet how the annexation has affected the queen of Jhansi, nor how much she has in her personal treasury. Major Ellis was reticent to say the least.'

'That was a strange business, wasn't it? All that gossip about the intrigue between them. It couldn't possibly have been true, could it?'

'One never knows what to believe, Margaret—the mofussil can be quite merciless in such matters. But we all know there's never smoke without some fire...'

The normally placid Margaret Skene turned to her two girls who were prodding each other and giggling on the seat opposite and said sharply, 'Now, I want both of you to be absolute angels when we arrive there. You may be taken off to play in the prince's chambers but Ayah will go with you and she will help you with your laces and petticoats if you need to use the privy. Is that clear, girls?'

Six-year-old Mary nodded and four-year-old Beatrice, given to copying everything her sister did, swiftly wiped the smile off her face and sat up, nodding gravely too.

'Well, we're here now, so you may as well start showing us how angelic you can be from this very moment,' their father said more fondly as both girls peered in awe up at the enormous arching gate their carriage was passing under. A little further down a cobbled path, they were stopped while one of the queen's guards, who had been posted at Sainyer Darwaza to personally escort them to the Ranimahal, conferred with the driver of their carriage. After a few minutes of muttered conversation, they felt the wheels move again.

From the window, Margaret could see the colourful streets of a bazaar, glittering with shiny silks and baubles. Unfamiliar odours of cooking and frying on cow-dung fires drifted through the windows, filling the little carriage with an India the Skenes only occasionally caught glimpses of. Margaret had been similarly enthralled by the sight of the silver bazaar she had once passed inside the Red Fort at Delhi. And had longed to be able to stop the carriage to wander around even though her companion, the doughty old Lady Fraser, had thought her quite mad to even consider it! The cantonment on the outskirts of Jhansi, though a lot smaller than the one they had left behind at Delhi, tried as hard as all other British cantonments to retain an English character and was as resolutely self-contained as all the others, with its own little shops, school, church and mess, giving memsahibs like her little chance to wander further afield. Just six miles down the road and a world away from this colourful melee, she thought with regret.

The carriage had taken a turn and they were outside a set of wrought iron gates that were being opened to let them in. The Ranimahal was a compact but dear little palace, Margaret thought, as she disembarked and looked up at beautifully carved doors and a marble archway inlaid with soft shiny mother-of-pearl glowing in different colours. How like a woman's palace it looked, she reflected, small and exquisite and quite unlike the sweeping splendours of the Mughal palaces she had seen in Delhi and Agra. Once again she wished she had more time to linger and admire the patterns of flowers and climbing vines made of semi-precious stones and coloured enamel chips embedded in marble that decorated the arches. She wanted to trail her fingers in the water canal that was running along the edge of the wall and reach her hand out to catch some of the flying drops of water in the courtyard fountains. But a pair of turbaned guards had arrived to escort them down a carpeted corridor that opened into a large airy room. Once they were seated on carved sofas that occupied one end of the chamber, the guards departed and were replaced by a pair of maids who fussed around them bearing trays laden with all manner of sweet sherbets and tiny silver bowls of cashew nuts and almonds that they lined up on a marble-topped chiffonier that stood against one wall.

Just as the children had shyly helped themselves to a second round of crystallized apricots on the insistence of one of the maids, there was a flurry at the door and Rani Lakshmibai came in through the curtained doorway, holding Damodar by the hand and flanked by two young women. As the Skenes rose from their seats, Margaret was amazed at how young and fragile Rani Lakshmibai appeared at first glance. The description of a coquette and termagant that Belinda

Royle had given her did not fit this grave-faced young woman at all and Margaret could not prevent a rush of sympathy as she realized how early in life this poor queen would have lost her husband and had to deal with matters of state. Rising from a deep curtsey, she saw the rani standing right in front of her, right arm extended in the European style of greeting. As she extended her own hand, Lakshmibai took it in both of hers and said softly in an amiable voice, 'Welcome, Mrs Skene. I am so happy to welcome you to Jhansi.'

After the initial greetings had been exchanged, the queen bent down to look appreciatively at the Skene girls who, Margaret was pleased to see, were curtseying in their little velvet dresses, matching bows in their chestnut ringlets bobbing prettily.

'Oh what beautiful children you have, Mrs Skene,' Lakshmibai said before addressing herself directly to the two girls, 'And am I allowed to ask you what your names are?'

'Mary,' said the older one, dropping in another small curtsey. The rani shook her hand gently before turning to the smaller girl.

'Beatrith,' the younger one lisped through a large gap between her front teeth, causing Lakshmibai to smile as she took her hand.

She turned to the prince lurking behind her with a small laugh, 'My son seems to have suddenly lost the excitement that has overwhelmed him all day at the thought of having new friends.' She pushed the small boy gently forwards with both hands on his shoulders. 'This, Mary and Beatrice, is Damodar. He has been eagerly awaiting your arrival all day and has taken out his best toys for you to play with, haven't you, Damodar?'

The prince nodded reluctantly, looking with awe at the two interlopers in their colourful puffy dresses. The rani turned to Margaret Skene, 'Do you think Mary and Beatrice would like to go inside to play in Damodar's nursery? He has a large collection of toys in there, as also a cage full of lovebirds that they might enjoy feeding. We have even recently acquired a pair of nightingales that Damodar is very proud of, aren't you Damodar?' He nodded again dutifully and Lakshmibai smiled at Margaret. 'Kamlesh and Sundar, my handmaids, can be trusted completely to keep an eye on all three children, if you are comfortable with that?'

'Would it be acceptable, Rani-sahiba, if our ayah went in with them too? It was so kind of you to insist we bring the girls along too but I felt that the ayah would be of help if they needed anything. I hope that was not remiss of me,' Margaret said.

The rani nodded. 'Of course not,' she replied, 'I will send word for your ayah to be escorted to the nursery. Are you happy with that, children?'

She looked down and smiled again at the three sets of obedient nods she received before saying, 'Sundar, escort everyone to Damodar's chambers. Look after Mary and Beatrice's ayah as well and arrange refreshments for everyone. When dinner is ready, you may all come to the dining hall and we shall eat together, yes?'

After the children had departed, accompanied by Sundar, the rani sat down and gestured for Captain and Mrs Skene to be seated on the sofa opposite her. As she enquired how the Skenes were settling down in Jhansi, asking them to inform her if there was anything she could do to assist, Margaret felt herself warming instantly to this unexpectedly serene and gracious woman. She had picked up an entirely erroneous impression from that priggish Belinda Royle who had described the dead king as a barmy old fool and the queen as his child concubine who had developed ideas beyond her station in wanting to be ruler of the state, taking up with Major Ellis to manipulate him in her machinations. Belinda had thought the idea quite priceless, shrieking with cruel laughter, but, as far as Margaret could see, the woman sitting before her was gracious and extremely dignified. It seemed, in fact, rather a pity to Margaret that this queen had not been given a fair chance to rule Jhansi. Alex had told her that, with the Lapse having come into effect, all that remained for the poor woman to do was administer a very diminished contingent of guards and a court denuded of all real power. Even Alex had thought it best to come to an understanding whereby power could be shared with Rani Lakshmibai but the orders from Calcutta to take complete charge of Jhansi had been quite firm. Perhaps their concern was that the rani was altogether still too interested in governance, given the way in which she was now asking Alex a series of questions, her eyes fixed keenly on his face as though it were really important for her to know exactly where his own persuasions lay.

As her husband and the queen talked about improvements that could be made to the old Mughal system of irrigation, Margaret found her mind wandering and looked around the room at the many oil paintings on the walls. The biggest one, dominating the room at its far end was of a thin effeminate-looking man wearing a colourful turban and enormous quantities of jewellery and she guessed that this might have been King Gangadhar. She had heard, although once again her source had been Belinda, that the king had suffered from an unnatural fondness for boys and that a couple of his wives before he married this queen had remained childless too. Prince Damodar, she knew, had been adopted which is what had caused Lord Dalhousie to take over Jhansi. That bit at least Margaret could be sure of!

At dinner, and over the chatter of their children, Margaret Skene remembered the cruel amusement and gossip that had been unleashed in the cantonment about this young queen and the recently departed Major Ellis. She had met him only briefly as the handover had taken place and he had seemed a handsome if rather solemn man, considerably younger than her Alex. A romance was, she supposed, not entirely beyond the bounds of possibility, given how young the pair were and how closely they must have had to work on the administration of Jhansi after the king's death. She had heard too that the queen's father, who was her chaperone in Jhansi, had travelled north of the country recently. Perhaps it was his absence that had caused the rani to draw closer to her political agent, if indeed those rumours about their liaison had been true.

Margaret shot another look at Rani Lakshmibai who was seated at the head of the long mahogany table. Her head was bent as she listened carefully to something her son was saying, the candlelight playing softly on her face. But Margaret could see, from the mauve shadows under her eyes and a smile that did not quite reach her eyes, that she was a woman encased in a strange kind of luminous grief.

❧ 31 ❧

Departing for Kanpur four months before Major Ellis's departure, Moropant had at first been reluctant to leave Jhansi but his daughter's friendship with the Englishman was making him increasingly confused and unsure of how long he could continue holding counsel. There was no doubt that Lakshmibai needed Major Ellis's support to cope with the appeal, but Moropant could not help becoming increasingly nervous of it. When Nana had written inviting Lakshmibai to Kanpur, Moropant had thought that a few weeks away from Jhansi would do her immense good. But she had only briefly considered the offer before declining and asking her father to go instead.

A few months in Kanpur would indeed offer welcome respite from the pall of hopelessness that had engulfed the Jhansi court since its annexation but Moropant had spent his journey reflecting and grieving on recent happenings. Lakshmibai had recently been forced to pension off most of her ministers because there was no longer enough money to pay them. Even petitioners who used to throng to the public durbars had stopped coming, despite their abiding respect for their rani. If they had a problem, it was to the British collector or commissioner of their district that they now went as those were the people with the purse strings and the power. Moropant's own job of training troops had come to an abrupt end too after the army had been disbanded. Lakshmibai had even had to cut back on the number of palace guards she employed in order to save costs, which had left Moropant with no one to train and manage at all.

After visiting Nana, Moropant's plan was to visit Peshwa-sahib's younger brother in Varanasi too. He had never been back, not since old Asharfi-bua had passed away three years ago. But, before that, a month at Bithur would do him no end of good. Tantia was still living with Nana, and Moropant tried to cheer himself as he approached Kanpur by remembering the antics of the two young rapscallions his daughter had grown up with.

The city of Kanpur had grown tenfold since he had last passed through it. Then he had been a young man and the place no more than a sleepy village. Travelling down a newly built macadamized road that curved alongside the river, Moropant could see that a steamer had just arrived, turning the ghats into a hive of activity. Boxes and gunny sacks were being unloaded as piles of packages took their place and an English merchant was shouting instructions to coolies staggering under their loads. On the southern bank, a small leather factory seemed to have sprung up out of nowhere. Polished saddles and harnesses were drying in the sun and, further along, Moropant could hear the whirring of a cloth mill, its emission of fine cotton dust turning the surrounding air a cloudy white.

He counted four army camps on the Grand Trunk Road as he continued on his way to Bithur and marvelled at how big the British army had grown recently. Infantrymen were involved in some kind of drill on a parade ground. All the British soldiers were grouped together on one side, smartly attired in the slate grey uniforms that had replaced the old red ones in some regiments, the senior officer distinguishable by the gleaming pointed helmet he wore. The sipahis were conducting their exercises separately on an adjoining field, clad in their regimental jackets, although some wore turbans and dhotis. Even through the hedges that protected them from passers-by on the road, he could see how prosperous the British army camps looked. So unlike the disbanded army quarters back at Jhansi Fort.

When he finally arrived at Nanasahib's residence, he felt a pang for the days of splendour they had all lost. Time was when this house had been just one of the Peshwa's many palaces but the British had taken over all the rest, leaving only this one for Peshwa-sahib's remaining family members to occupy. Even Saturday House in Varanasi had recently become British garrison headquarters, Peshwa-sahib's brother having been moved to a smaller ghat-side house in the city.

As the gates were opened to let his carriage in, Moropant could see how dilapidated the old Bithur residence had become. An enormous bougainvillea creeper, laden with brilliant scarlet flowers, was masking much of the frontage but Moropant thought it just as well for, behind the creeper, he could see gaping cracks that had formed in the once pristine white plaster of the house. The chandelier in the darkened entrance hall was wrapped up with a large piece of muslin, grey and heavy with dust. Squares of lighter plaster on the walls of the veranda revealed where paintings and tapestries had once hung. Sold, in all probability, he imagined, to those ruthless Calcutta auction-house agents who scoured the countryside looking for nobles who had lost their fortunes in these hard times.

It was almost impossible to imagine that, just one generation ago, the Peshwa had been considered chief of all the Maratha clans—the Scindias, the Holkars, the Gaekwads and the Bhonsles—and had ruled over lands stretching from the River Jamuna in the north to the Kaveri in the south. All gone, all gone, Moropant thought sadly as the rotund figure of Nanasahib appeared through the front door to welcome him, his beaming little daughter by his side.

As they embraced, Moropant felt a rush of affection for this man whom he had known since he was a small boy, adopted by Peshwa-sahib in the same year that Moropant had joined their court. Now here Nana was, with his own daughter by his side, a pretty dark-eyed girl who reminded Moropant of Mani just before she had got married. Those had indeed been happy times at Saturday House, with Mani becoming Peshwa-sahib's surrogate daughter while Nana and Tantia had been the sons Moropant himself had never had. Moropant knew sentimental reminiscing only blurred the sharper edges of memory, but it was hard not to compare those halcyon days back at Saturday House with the bleak fortunes they all faced now.

'Beta, how are you, you do not look so well,' he said gruffly as Nana released him from his grasp to bend down with some difficulty to touch his feet in respect.

'Baba, I am very well disposed. Can you not see the proof I carry here?' Nana replied, jocularly patting his protruding belly.

After Moropant had blessed both Nana and his daughter, Mainabai, he allowed himself to be guided indoors, laughing as Nana said, with mock peevishness, 'Well I certainly hope Mani knows how upset I am that she did not come with you.'

'She is busy with Damodar's upbringing, Nana-beta. You know that is the only joy she has left in life.'

'How has she taken the annexation? In her letters, she only ever sounds positive about being able to get it overturned.'

'Well, she is working on that and still has the support of her political agent although I do not know how long his goodwill will last. I don't prevent her from doing what she thinks is best, even though I believe her chances of winning in court against the British are remote. Without hope, I fear she will go insane.'

Nana nodded sombrely, he knew exactly how Mani felt. As Mainabai was despatched to fetch some tea, the men walked into the back garden where Nana's coterie were gathered. The group of men all rose from their seats on seeing Moropant while Tantia stepped forward, bending to touch the old man's feet in greeting. After blessing him and wiping away a few tears that had sprung unbidden to his eyes at the sight of the strapping young fellow, once such a gloomy little boy, Moropant sat down on the chair that was being pulled forward for him. He wished Mani could have been persuaded to come; she too would have derived comfort from the company of these dear old friends.

Nana's garden was blooming in the spring sunshine with all manner of flowers and vegetables. Moropant inhaled the fragrance of ripening muskmelons as they awaited the hot May winds from the desert that would sweeten them. They were his favourite fruit, making the searing summer months worthwhile in his childhood days in Pune. But he did not think Nana and Tantia would be interested in the maudlin reminiscences of an old man. They seemed ready to get down to some sort of business straightaway, now that the preliminary chitchat had been done with. Posters and pamphlets and recent copies of the *Dilli Urdu Akhbaar* and the *Delhi Gazette* were being spread out on the table in front of them. He heard Nana dispatch a servant with a message for Azimullah to come out from the office within to join them.

Moropant picked up a pamphlet on which something about European missionaries had been printed. There was a picture of a burning church in the corner and the accompanying text said that the British were trying to convert all Hindus and Muslims to Christianity. There was something too about wheat and rice mills being deliberately contaminated with the ground bones of cows and pigs. It explained that the pink cast of Gujarat's salt was from cows' blood. He picked up another pamphlet, bearing closely printed Urdu writing, promising a jihad, not just in India but also in Turkey and Afghanistan where 'mullahs had been hard at work to drum up support'. An Afghan army was being prepared, with the help of Russian guns and artillery, to help overthrow the British. The pamphlet started fluttering, both because of the breeze and the sudden shaking of Moropant's hands. He could hear, through the pounding in his head, how excitedly his boys, Nana and Tantia, talked of revolution and change. Someone was telling him that the pamphlets had done their job well. For a few minutes, he could only hear their conversation in fragments because something like terror seemed to be gripping his heart, robbing him of thought and breath: 'four infantry garrisons'…'cartridges greased with animal tallow'…'feeling against the British presence in Kanpur is definitely spreading'…' but the sipahis actually like General Wheeler, unfortunately'…'not his Christian preaching, though'…'his wife being half-Indian elevates him in their eyes, that cannot be helped'…'but Wheeler's popularity makes him far too confident of his own standing'…'we can work on that…his complacence can only be to our advantage'…'the time has come, the time for jihad has come…'

❧ 32 ❧

Try as he might, Ellis could not help returning over and over again to the coldness of his parting from Lakshmibai. The morning after he had paid her his last visit had brought a noisy and tearful farewell from Karamchand who was to be passed on to the new political agent and it was midday by the time Ellis finally departed his home. However, as his carriage pulled out of Jhansi's cantonment, it was not his bungalow he looked back at but Lakshmibai's fort, receding slowly in the distance. The words of a nearly forgotten poem had been swirling through his mind these past few days—'Had we but world enough, and time…'—and he whispered them now as he looked at her fort one last time, vowing he would return in some happier day. Reclaim land and love in a time when such things were one's own to choose.

But, boarding the steamer at Calcutta a month later, it was his last words to Lakshmibai that he recalled again, picking them up as a child would a carelessly broken toy, re-examining them disconsolately as India slid slowly away over the black choppy waters of the Hooghly. He wondered at his own capacity for detachment and callousness. His lack of grace, his thoughtlessness and all his missed opportunities.

Why he had remained so unable to tell her of his sorrow at parting from her and Jhansi was something Ellis would never entirely be able to explain to himself. During the long voyage home, he found many ways to justify it—the different worlds they occupied, the shifting balances of power, her misery over the annexation—but what he could not forgive himself for were those final words he had spoken to her, so devoid of all the feelings and love he had stored within, both for her and for her beloved land. Nothing would have been lost in revealing that to her, he was to say to himself over and over again in the loneliness of his cabin at sea. There would have been no loss of dignity and no deficit of loyalty. It would have softened her memory of him and her feelings for his people. It may even, as he would later accuse himself relentlessly and unforgivingly, have prevented her bitterness, a massacre and a war.

His journey back to England was nothing like the joyous voyage that had taken him away from it. He kept to himself, thoughts of Lakshmibai and Jhansi continuing to haunt him. Even the scents of India seemed to hang around his person, showing an unwillingness to fall away. He could still discern the smoke of Motibagh's lanterns on his clothes and, once, a whiff of the incense sticks of Ranimahal as he riffled the pages of a book. Even the neem leaves that Karamchand had used to keep silverfish from eating at his manuscripts had India's forests and earth in their smell and, while unpacking them, Ellis had lifted a handful to his face as though terrified he would one day forget the fragrances he had once depended on for comfort.

He found digs at Craven Street on his second day in London, just around the corner from the Northumberland Hotel. They were a small set of rooms at the top of an unremarkable, slightly seedy townhouse, quite unlike his capacious bungalow in Jhansi but it was hard to care about things like that any more. Work had been easily available at East India House for a man who could speak Hindustani with such fluency and soon Ellis was in charge of the daily flood of letters, despatches and messages that were arriving on the new telegraph system. He devoured these like a bereft parent would receive news of a forsaken child. But, when the day was finished, he would wander down to the Thames to stand on its banks for hours at a time, sometimes wondering if anyone would even notice if he stepped off the edge and gave himself up to its stinking depths.

Of course he did not want for the attentions of women, being still young and newly returned from the East. They tempted him in taverns and parlours, pressing warm, inviting bodies against him, offering passing pleasures for a couple of shillings. Sometimes, he took what he was given without much thought, trying to find comfort in infidelity to his own devotion. But there was not much to be had and, as Ellis sunk helplessly into the most intense loneliness, he thought endlessly of the sunlit town of Jhansi and of Lakshmibai. Her memory casting a pall over everything, making wretched life itself. He knew quite simply that there would be no peace until he could raise the money for the passage and return to India someday.

With the annexation of Awadh Ellis could sense, even from so far away, some kind of discontent seeping insidiously across his beloved land. Fancifully, he saw it at first as a slowly spreading stain on an old parchment map, creeping along, silent and unstoppable and infecting with foreboding every piece of news that emerged from there.

It was at first only little things, news of a small peasant uprising in one state, soldiers complaining about their bhatta in another. Like everyone else at India House, Ellis too was unwilling to believe that the mighty Government House machinery in India could ever be caught unawares but, mere months after returning to England, he could finally see what others could not. Perhaps it was due to the trip he had made through Awadh in what now seemed like a distant dream. Even then, he had been able to discern the seething anger against British policies that must have lurked below the surface for longer than anyone knew. Government House had always wanted to believe that the people of India welcomed their rule, even if native royals did not. But Ellis knew, from having observed Jhansi's weavers and dhobis eke out meagre livings in their conurbations, that the annexation of states like Jhansi had, in the end, made no improvements to their lot. And when the hardships of daily life had become all-consuming, it was to their queen and not the British that they would turn. From her at least there was compassion to be had. From their British collectors and magistrates they had long come to expect only cold and uncaring rules.

It was, however, an overheard conversation at India House that first revealed how much there really was to fear. Working quietly at his desk one morning, Ellis had caught the name 'Azimullah' mentioned as the two men who sat across from him in the department gossiped across their desks.

'Lady Gordon. Lucy Duff Gordon,' one of the men said, 'eccentric reputation but quite the society hostess, famed for presiding over political and literary soirées that have gathered some pretty dedicated followers over the years. A right old shine *she'd* taken to the Oriental gentleman when he was here. Rumour has it that they all fawned something terrible over him...John Stuart Mill, Macaulay, Charles Dickens...'

'Why, even the *Times* correspondent, that Howard Russell chap, had been most impressed by the gent's charm, had he not? I read something about this Azeemoolah in one of his articles once. Met him on a ship apparently.'

'Quite unlike a native, of course, so you could see why they were all so taken by him. Urbane, intelligent, able to speak the language as well as any of us. Handsome too, apparently. With all that, the olive skin and beard would have gone down a treat with the ladies, I imagine.'

'Odd that Lady G thought nothing of helping him with his case against our Board of Directors.'

'Well, the silly old bag even despatched him to Paris after he'd lost that case. But I'd have liked to see her face when it was revealed that he carried on from there to bloody Sebastopol!'

'Plenty of trouble to be stirred up there, eh?'

'Too right. And where d'you think he went next...to the court of the Turkish general Amir Pasha! Now what business could he have possibly had there, I ask you?'

Ellis felt his shoulders stiffen, remembering his own encounter with Azimullah at Jhansi on the day of Prince Damodar's adoption. Nanasahib had introduced him as his political advisor. What indeed had taken Nanasahib's man to Sebastopol and Turkey? And was it really true that Azimullah had been celebrated in London's finest parlours? Ellis could imagine the elegant, sharp-faced man he had seen once, surrounded by British sycophants, laughing and joking with them, even as he silently and deeply loathed them all.

But who was really to see the fires brewing under a far land as it lay brooding in its usual summer somnolence that year—not even men like Ellis who understood India well. All Ellis sensed was that there were strange forces already at work, blowing and fanning the tiniest embers of unhappiness into a crackling, spitting fire. Discontent with British rule, both ancient and nascent, were to combine and become a conflagration whose angry, rolling fury would remain invisible to those who refused to see it. Until it consumed them in its rage.

৵ 33 ৯

As the monsoons broke that year, Dewan Rao Bande ushered into the assembly hall a group of sipahis who had arrived from Sagar, asking to be granted an audience with Rani Lakshmibai. They had ridden through the driving rain on a Sunday afternoon and, even though it was not the usual day to hear petitions, the prime minister had thought it wise for Rani Lakshmibai to hear their concerns.

Lakshmibai, supervising Damodar's tuitions in his chambers, signalled to the tutor that he was to carry on with his work while she got up to accompany her guard to the Diwan-i-Khas. Stopping only to give quick assurance to Damodar that she would be back before long, she ran the short distance from her palace to the nearby durbar hall as the rain had temporarily abated.

The spokesperson for the sipahis was a burly native officer, Subedar-Major Gobind Gopal, and after a respectful obeisance to the rani, he opened up in an elegant Hindustani that revealed his high birth and caste.

'Maharani Lakshmibai, we are fully aware of your own concerns with the British policies that have affected your heritage and your son's rights to rule Jhansi. But, at this time, and faced with so many problems of our own, we have come to you for we have nowhere else to turn.'

'Subedar-Major sahib, if you tell me what your problems are, I will see if I can find a solution,' the rani replied, her anxiety apparent only in the manner in which she leaned forward on her throne as soon as she had seated herself. 'But first, please sit down and make yourselves comfortable if it is going to take time...' Lakshmibai waited another few minutes while the men took off their footwear before seating themselves on the cotton gaddas spread out before the throne. 'Do your British officers know that you are here?' she asked, unsurprised to see the men shake their heads, without looking at her. She noticed suddenly that none of them were wearing their regimental tunics.

Subedar-Major Gopal waited for the men to settle before saying, 'Our problems are not recent, Rani-sahiba, but some things we have no control over and we have learnt not to complain about them.'

'Such as?' Lakshmibai queried.

'Oh such as having new young subalterns, straight out of their training college in England, come out on the ships and take immediate precedence over officers like me who have ten–twenty years' service over them and are in no way inferior, bar the colour of our skin, Rani-sahiba.'

Lakshmibai nodded. 'That is a problem very similar to mine that you mentioned earlier. They rule us and they create the law that has made it so, how can we hope for any recourse?'

Another sipahi with a long grey beard cleared his throat before speaking up, 'Rani-sahiba, the new recruits and officers are an arrogant lot, quite unlike the old John Company Officers who knew how to value us and communicate with the men through us. They do not bother to learn our languages any more, unlike the old Company men. These new ones are not even above calling us names...they think we will not understand if they laugh and say "nigger" and "black bastard"...begging your pardon, Rani-sahiba...'

Lakshmibai shook her head ruefully, making no reply and Subedar-Major Gopal spoke again, 'But, even though we have borne all that silently, there are now things happening that we cannot brook any more.'

'Are you referring to the new General Services Enlistment Act?' Lakshmibai asked, knowing what a sore point it had been with most of the Bengal Army when the new rule had been brought in that made it incumbent on the men to serve in foreign places such as Burma. The response from the group of men was a chorus of muttering and it was clear that she had struck a raw nerve.

Lakshmibai heard one of the men expostulate angrily, 'Crossing the black waters is something I have taken an oath I will never do. They will have to put me to death first!'

'Have they no thought that many of us are of high birth and stand to lose our caste by crossing the seas?' another sipahi asked.

'If they cared, would their officers be preaching to us from the Bible on parade days?' a sowar countered.

'Not forgetting too that thirty thousand Sikhs from Punjab have just been enlisted. They want to make us Hindus a minority in the Army and rob us of our status before they rob us of our caste,' a younger sipahi added darkly.

The subedar-major gestured for silence before addressing the queen again, 'It is not just matters pertaining to our caste that are of concern but we know that things are happening that are an insult to our religion itself. What they want, Rani-sahiba, is to convert us all, every one of us, to Christianity. We have it on good authority that the new Governor-General, this Canning, has been sent to India with instructions from their Queen Victoria to have the entire Army, indeed the entire country, converted to Christianity.'

'How can that be possible, Subedar-Major sahib? Would that not be an unfeasible task in a land so vast?' Lakshmibai shook her head, unwilling to believe such a sweeping accusation.

'So I thought as well, Rani-sahiba,' the subedar-major replied quietly, 'until I heard, from the very men who work in the mills, that the British have ordered for bones of cows and pigs be ground up along with our millet and wheat so that we will lose our faiths without even knowing it.'

Lakshmibai was incredulous and she could see that Dewan Rao Bande was as shocked as she. Surely it was impossible to believe that the British would do something as low as pollute their soldiers' religion in such an invidious fashion? But, on the other hand, how had it come to be that an entire body of people, thus far loyal to their Company, had grown so suspicious? Lakshmibai wondered if it were possible that agents with evil intentions were at work, creating false rumours and spreading fears, but the soldiers remained implacable in their conviction that a deliberate plan was afoot to rob them of their caste and religion. Too many factors pointed to it and the British had far too much to gain by achieving that end.

She saw the men off half an hour later, promising to have a discreet word with Captain Skene when he next visited, at least on the matter of animal bones being ground in the grain mills. But, as she returned to her palace, it occurred to her that enough had already happened to make even reasonable people like the subedar-major become willing to put their faith in the unbelievable.

The rain had started again, drumming down incessantly on the tiled terraces as Lakshmibai covered her head with her sari to run indoors. She walked slowly towards Damodar's schoolroom, her mind in turmoil over the things the soldiers had told her. Such implacable belief in their officers' malevolent intentions towards them boded ill for the British, even if all the allegations were untrue.

Her son's small figure was rocking back and forth as he chanted a poem at his desk. It was some pompous little verse about honour and duty that would normally have made her smile but today, watching Damodar's mouth form into little o's as he carefully enunciated every syllable, she could only wonder at the troubles this poor child would inherit from her. What terrible disfavour had she done him by plucking him away from the uncomplicated childhood he had enjoyed with his parents, expecting that he would take joy in a kingdom in which there was nothing left but strife?

The first sign of trouble came in the form of a stack of mouldy chapattis, carefully wrapped and delivered at the European barracks at Jhansi cantonment. Captain Skene had not thought them worthy of being brought to Rani Lakshmibai's court, merely communicating his puzzlement in a casual conversation with Dewan Rao Bande when they had first met to discuss the rumours about the animal bones.

'Chappatis? What are they supposed to mean, Dewan-ji?' Rani Lakshmibai asked.

'It is hard to tell…perhaps a coded message…but a very curious fact that some British people in positions of influence have received them too,' he replied.

'And they come with no message, no warnings?'

'Nothing at all. They come sometimes delivered by police chowkidars and sometimes carried by local children who claim to have been paid coins to deliver them by strangers passing through their villages. According to Skene, a parcel just materialized one morning on the steps of his chowkidar's hut and, having taken one look at the mouldy and rancid contents, he merely ordered that they be thrown away. He only found out later that the padre at the battery church and the magistrate at Almora had received similar packages on the same day.'

Ellis read about the mysterious wheat cakes in a few telegraph messages and knew instantly they were a very bad omen. Similar 'gifts' of mulberry branches had mysteriously appeared in the rooms of British officers in Kabul and Kandahar, placed on their pillows and among their personal belongings just before the outbreak of the Anglo-Afghan war, either to frighten or to warn. But his concern, voiced to a senior, was dismissed, such inexplicable occurrences as usual attributed to the hundred superstitions that plagued India.

Genuine cause for alarm came only with the first of a series of events that began in the eastern troop town of Barrackpore before it would spiral through other cantonments across the central plains. Ellis was confident that Jhansi lay too far west to be caught up in those troubles. That was February in the year 1857. London was cold and beset with the worst pea-souper fogs Ellis had ever seen and he thought of how beautiful Jhansi must look in the spring. He had been back just over a year and now had the money he needed to book his passage to India. Already he had delayed it too long.

'Rani-sahiba, there has been a minor revolt among the troops of the 19th Native Infantry in Barrackpore near Calcutta. Last month, it says here,' Dewan Rao Bande said, reading a small report in *The Calcutta Gentleman* that Rani Lakshmibai had recently insisted on subscribing to, despite its prohibitive cost.

Lakshmibai looked up at him briefly. 'Even when they rescinded the bans on corporal punishment, I thought they were playing with fire.'

She returned to her task of writing the name of the Lord Rama on numerous tiny bits of paper. Damodar, sitting by her side, was rolling them into little balls of wheat dough so that they could feed them to the goldfish in the sacred tank adjoining Raja Gangadhar's tomb. She had been enjoying her weekly ritual with her son, only half listening to her prime minister as he read from the papers of celebratory events in Calcutta that was always of little interest to her. She looked up sharply, however, as Dewan Rao Bande, now sitting up in his chair, started to read more loudly, his voice quickening.

'...the soldiers were convinced that the cartridges had been greased with tallow made from cow and pig fat. As the new model of cartridge involves biting off the top by using the teeth, both Hindu and Muslim soldiers feared contamination of their religious beliefs. Following the refusal of troops in Barrackpore to use the new Enfield rifles, General Hearsey has ordered that they be allowed to revert to the older Brown Bess model.'

Rani Lakshmibai put her pen down, looking at her prime minister in astonishment. 'And I had thought no British policy could surprise me any more! Cartridges smeared with cow fat? Dewan-ji, how can it be possible for these people to be so insensitive? I doubt they would deliberately insult their soldiers' religious sentiments, although there will be people willing to believe that possibility too. But surely an error so gross...is it any wonder the troops are so full of suspicion?'

'Beyond belief, Rani-sahiba. First General Napier—the only general willing to fight for equitable treatment towards all army troops—is sacked, resulting in almost all of the native soldiers drawing lower salaries than before. Then comes Dalhousie's Religious Disabilities Act, giving soldiers who convert to Christianity special privileges not available to Hindus and Muslims, however spotless their records. And now this—cartridges greased with the fat of cows and pigs! It is truly beyond belief.'

Lakshmibai returned to her task as Damodar impatiently jogged her forearm. But she was reminded of the conversation a few days later when the *Dilli Urdu Akhbaar* reported an incident similar to the one at Barrackpore, this time taking place at Berhampore. The report was short but she knew that, under new censorship laws, the vernacular press was under severe restrictions on what it could publish. The report stated merely that, unlike General Hearsey who had ably dealt with the Barrackpore rebellion, Lt. Colonel Mitchell, the commanding officer of the Berhampore regiments, had disbanded the regiments, laying off all native troops without pay.

A month later, Barrackpore was mentioned again in the pages of *The Mofussilite*, the paper carrying a report of a sepoy called Mangal Pandey having shot and injured his British adjutant. Lakshmibai thought it curious that no mention had been made at all of the incident in the English *Delhi Gazette* which carried no more than its usual listings of weddings and births and deaths in the British community, alongside reports from the governments at Calcutta and London.

'Was it the same issue of the greased cartridges that caused this Mangal Pandey to be so agitated?' Lakshmibai asked her prime minister who was seated next to her at the large teak table, all the papers they had been able to gather spread out in front of them.

'I would think that was the cause, Rani-sahiba,' Dewan Rao Bande replied, 'although *The Mofussilite* suggests here that this fellow Pandey was under the influence of a narcotic agent. Bhang, maybe...common enough among the sipahis...' Dewan Rao Bande laughed ruefully as a thought occurred to him, 'One must remember, of course, that an English-language paper would prefer to have the man appear to be deranged or suffering from drug-induced delusions rather than acting out of genuine conviction against them!'

'What will they do to the poor man, I wonder,' Lakshmibai mused. 'His punishment will surely not be lenient for having dared to shoot at an English officer...I have heard that the old Mughal punishment of tying rebels alive to the mouths of cannons before blowing them to smithereens is becoming quite common in some British regiments.' She felt a rush of sympathy for the sipahi. With a name like Pandey, he was surely of high caste and must have felt the disgrace of the contaminating cartridges weigh heavily on his mind to take such a risk.

'I have even heard that in the Punjab, it has not been unknown for the British to order that the bodies of rebels be smeared with animal fat before decimation, so that the loss of religion is total and their own power indisputable.' Dewan Rao Bande returned to his paper, shaking his grey head. 'How that hapless Mangal Pandey would have dreaded such a punishment. He must have been unable to bear that thought because it says here that he turned his gun on his own body and shot himself in the stomach.'

'Imagine when death becomes preferable to humiliation,' Lakshmibai said quietly.

'He survived his own musket ball, Rani-sahiba, but apparently they court-martialled him a week later and hanged him, leaving his body on the parade ground to serve as warning to other mutinous troops.'

Too shocked to respond, Lakshmibai got up and started to pace around the room, a feeling of dread building inexplicably in her stomach. After a few minutes, she stopped pacing to sit down again and look at her prime minister with a look of disbelief on her face.

'Can they really not see their foolishness in creating a martyr for the troops to rally around, Dewan-ji?' she asked, genuinely puzzled. 'They claim to be intelligent rulers, but it seems that they have no knowledge at all of simple human nature. It is so clear to me that they have, by hanging that man, duly provided all those disaffected troops with the hero they have been waiting for these past months. If they do not find some solution quickly, or at least try to make amends, they will soon have not just one Mangal Pandey but a hundred in their midst!'

It was Meerut next, a populous garrison town lying sixty miles northeast of Delhi. The terrifying news of its massacre was brought to Jhansi by the driver of a dak-gadi who had fled the town as it burnt, terrified at being caught up in the sudden events. As his horses were being refreshed in Jhansi's town square, he was brought to Rani Lakshmibai's durbar where she quizzed him for an hour. She could see that, apart from exhaustion, he had suffered no wounds and promised him food and shelter once he had told her all she wanted to know.

He stood before her now, quaking, as he recounted his tale, still clad in his torn and filthy clothes. 'Rani-sahiba, the sipahis' commanding officer had insisted on a drill to teach them how to use the new greased cartridges without putting them to their mouths. But the soldiers refused, partly fearing some trick and also, I think, out of loyalty for their comrades everywhere else…'

'Well, what happened next,' Lakshmibai demanded impatiently as the man broke off to wipe his face.

'They court-martialled eighty-five troops that evening, Rani-sahiba, to ten years' hard labour in jail…summoning a special parade so that everybody could hear the verdict…'

'Ten years of hard labour? For one mistake made by otherwise loyal soldiers!' Lakshmibai gesticulated for the man to carry on speaking despite her interjection.

'My relative was one of the sipahis who was let off, Rani-sahiba, and he said that it was a piteous sight to see his comrades being stripped of their uniforms and fettered with iron shackles before being carted away to the new gaol in the barracks. Some of them were angry, of course, but others...the older sipahis who had put in many years of service...they were heartbroken and weeping and pleading with their British officers that their years of service should count for something. Without their salaries, their families would starve.'

'Did the remaining soldiers protest or do anything in support of their colleagues?'

'Not immediately, Rani-sahiba,' the man replied, his thin frame suddenly starting to shake with the memories of the scene he had fled. 'They were all stunned by the event and, at first, did not know what to do. But, later that night, when the sipahis—including my relative—went into Sadar Bazaar to try to forget the day's terrible proceedings, the townspeople taunted them and shamed them.'

'Taunted them for not having defended their fellow men, I suppose,' Rani Lakshmibai said grimly.

'Yes, Rani-sahiba. Merchants were refusing to serve them, saying that they had no business to be free when they had not thought of defending their poor colleagues from being jailed. Even...begging your pardon, Rani-sahiba...even the prostitutes called them names and refused to conduct business with them, accusing them of being lily-livered and cowardly.'

'And so I suppose they returned to the barracks, intent on revenge.'

'It was the next day, Rani-sahiba. Sunday. The Europeans had attended church as usual and were resting away from the summer heat in their bungalows and messes. First a few British troops who had wandered into Sadar Bazaar were set upon by angry crowds. They were stoned and lynched. One man's body was literally torn to bits even as he screamed for mercy, right in front of Kaka's refreshment shop. And then, as though out of nowhere, the angry crowd just grew and grew, filling the streets of the town. Men seemed to be appearing out of the surrounding fields and villages, armed with knives and sickles. I do not even know who they were. They did not look like Meerut men. First the telegraph lines were cut and the telegraph office was burned down, then they marched to the civil lines, killing every white person in sight. Officers, churchmen, women...no one was spared. Some of the servants of the Europeans tried to protect their masters, hiding them from the rampaging mob, but there was not much they could do. By then, the armoury had also been looted and the prisoners in the jail freed, so it was havoc...and so much bloodshed...I saw a young sipahi stab and stab the dead body of a British officer as though crazed with anger before I took the dak-gadi and fled from that carnage...'

'They cannot all be dead, all the British in Meerut!' It seemed an incredible possibility to Lakshmibai, almost sacrilegious. Even when the Thugee movement had been at its most frenzied, the Thugs had almost always avoided killing Europeans as though unable somehow to break that last taboo.

'I am not sure, Rani-sahiba,' the man replied, his voice now shaking audibly, 'but I think no one was spared...'

'Even the civilian population?'

The man nodded as tears flowed down his face. 'All of them, Rani-sahiba, even women and children...no one with a white skin was spared...'

'And where have they gone now, the mutineers...' Lakshmibai's ears were ringing, a strange echoing sound in her head making her feel dizzy.

'As I left Meerut, Rani-sahiba...when I first dared to look over my shoulder, I saw the cantonment burn, smoke was rising into the sky from the thatched roofs and was visible even when I was one mile away, turning the sky behind me black. I think the rebels' business at Meerut was done in that one afternoon. The troops all seemed to be streaming the other way, headed down the Grand Trunk Road that leads to Delhi...I could hear them cry out to each other to head for Delhi...*Dilli...Dilli chalo*...they were shouting like madmen...' As the man broke down, Rani Lakshmibai asked for him to be led away by her guards and given a place to bathe and rest.

The rebellion she had predicted, with a strange combination of both longing and fear, had finally started. Even where she sat, feeling the serene peace surrounding Jhansi like a winter blanket, she could imagine distant places burn. Delhi, the seat of the old Mughal emperor, that Moropant had told her was filled with both Mughal and British splendours, might already be ablaze. She felt a renewed clutch of panic as she thought of her father who had now been in Bithur for over a year. Realizing how similar to Meerut Kanpur was, with its wealthy European merchants and big British garrisons, it was all too possible that Kanpur would fall next. She would have to send an urgent message to Nana's home, asking Moropant to return before trouble spread in their direction. Who knew if the roads were safe...there was also the possibility of British reprisals that would surely be swift and sharp. She got up from her throne and walked indoors, trying to subdue the quivering that had overcome her body.

Dewan Rao Bande was attending his daughter's confinement in Shivpuri, which would make him unavailable for at least another two weeks. Gripped by sudden loneliness, Lakshmibai found her footsteps taking her towards Motibagh. Perhaps if she went to Robert Ellis's old chambers, she would not miss him as badly as she suddenly did. She had tried so hard to keep his memory at bay since his departure but his face was before hers now, as clear as though he were standing in front of her. Meerut was one of the places he had often visited on his travels out of Jhansi. He might have known some of the people who had been killed there. If he had still been in India, what was to say he would not have been among those who were now dead?

Lakshmibai stood under the jasmine trellis, seeing the Motibagh garden where Robert had liked to work on his manuscripts, spring flowers indistinguishable from the butterflies that hovered above them. If he had still been here, sitting in this garden as she had broken the news to him, would his grief have felt alien to her? How would she have comforted him, while keeping her own feelings apart? Perhaps that was how he had felt on the night she had poured out her feelings to him, sitting on this very stone bench. He had been so tender, even though her grief must have felt remote to one in his position. She clenched her fist, feeling her nails hurt the soft skin of her palms. Time and time again, she had asked herself if she had been too quick to judge him, too hasty in assuming his loss of sympathy. Perhaps it was she who had pushed him away with her anger...

Damodar...she needed to look for Damodar. In his childish prattle, she would find reassurance that her life was still worthwhile. Find comfort in Jhansi's continuing peace, she told herself. These distant mutinies had nothing at all to do with her. She stopped as she reached the archway that led to her son's little garden, hearing his high-pitched chatter as he giggled with Kamlesh over some childish delight. Unwilling to disturb them at their play, she stayed in the dark interior of the room, gazing out at the sunlit garden through a narrow window.

The two children were standing beside the aviary that had been built for Damodar's beloved lovebirds. The child never seemed to tire of tending to the tiny helpless creatures, his tenderness seeming so unusual a trait in a boy of his age. And Lakshmibai could now see that the birds too somehow sensed his gentleness, fluttering and floating around his little figure as he stepped into the cage to feed them.

Lakshmibai gradually felt her trembling subside as she watched her solemn young son lay out platters of water and birdseed, helped by Kamlesh. The tiny creatures they were tending were warbling and tumbling around them trustingly, cheeping their delight. It was almost impossible to believe that there was anything but peace and tranquillity in a world that contained all this too.

She took another deep breath. Whatever was happening in other parts of the country, she was determined to see that none of it would touch the peace of Jhansi. The safety of her family and her people mattered more than anything else and she would let nothing jeopardize it. Not even the possibility being gradually unveiled that in distant mutinies may lie the chance for Jhansi's rule to be returned to her, the achingly tempting prospect that its crown may yet grace her son's head.

It was on the day Ellis was due to book his passage that news of Meerut arrived in London. They had already heard of Barrackpore and Berhampore and hoped that those were isolated incidents. But now, this most fearsome massacre in Meerut. It was incredible. The despatch had taken unusually long to reach, the mutineers having taken the careful step of cutting all telegraph lines out of Meerut on the night before they rose against their officers.

The news affected Ellis deeply. Meerut was a place he was very familiar with from his early days in Jhansi and his mind, still dealing with his other losses, was now filled with the faces of all the people he had known there. It would be weeks before he would know which of them had died. Ellis harked back to the theatre that had been set up and the lively drama group that he had been persuaded to briefly join. The names hastened back, unremembered all these months...Merrydale and Maxwell, the rambunctious Hamilton brothers...and the play they had been rehearsing when he had last seen them—*The Irish Tutor*—its racy humour causing them to fall about in helpless merriment during practice. Could it really be that they were all dead? Cruelly slain by people they did not even know? Young Englishmen and women, intent only on enjoying themselves on dull summer evenings in the mofussil...Ellis felt a shudder pass through him at the thought of the mindless massacre of such innocents. They were his friends, of the same race and blood, they were his people. And, had he still been in Meerut, he would have been dead alongside them too.

✌ 34 ✳

Two hundred miles away from Jhansi, on the outskirts of Kanpur, Moropant was making preparations to depart Bithur at dawn and return home. Dramatic, occasionally shocking news from Meerut and Delhi had been trickling into Nana's offices over the past few days. The news that Delhi too was taken had just arrived, spurring Moropant into deciding finally that his presence would be required by his daughter at Jhansi. Mutinying sipahis had captured Meerut before reaching Delhi in the second week of May, according to Nana's sources. Although both the British and the old Mughal emperor, Bahadur Shah Zafar, had at first tried to keep the rebels out of Delhi's magnificent Red Fort, they had apparently pushed past Rajghat Gate and killed the tollgate-keeper before entering the walled city. After a few minutes of bedlam and confusion, the British contingent, still trying to guard the city, was slaughtered to a man and the citizens of Delhi had thrown open the massive gates in triumphant welcome of the other rebels who were by then pouring down the road from Meerut.

Although Moropant's blood turned cold at the reports of people running frenziedly through the streets of Delhi, shooting and spearing every white person in sight, there was a part of him that could not help joining Nanasahib, Tantia and Azimullah in their excited conjecture that the Company's domination may finally be coming to an end. Surely the fact that the British collector was amongst the first to be killed by enraged mobs in Delhi, spelt the end of the white man's rule? But, as the source's gleeful descriptions of the indiscriminate killings continued, Moropant's knees started to shake so badly, he had to sit down. Through ringing ears, he heard Azimullah's friend proclaim proudly that all the compositors in the offices of the *Delhi Gazette*, the bank officials of the Delhi and London Bank, missionaries in a school and even some women and children had been slaughtered. Although a few Europeans had been taken prisoner and clamped into the dungeons beneath Red Fort, the streets of Delhi were, the man boasted, slimy with the blood of slain Englishmen within a matter of hours.

After a fitful night's sleep, heavy with fevered dreams, Moropant now stood next to Nana, watching his luggage being piled on top of the carriage that would return him to Jhansi, accompanied by two armed guards. Nana turned to Moropant and bent down to touch his feet. Straightening, he spoke in a voice husky with suppressed emotion, 'Baba, go now and inform my sister, Rani Lakshmibai, of these fortuitous events. So far, we have not involved her in our fight against the British because she has had her own concerns to deal with. But now the time is ripe for us to unite, both in spirit and in arms. You have my best guards to keep you safe on your journey to Jhansi and we will, God willing, next meet as comrades in arms against the firangi enemy. God be with you on your journey back to Jhansi.'

It was close on midnight and Lakshmibai lay awake, listening to the uneasy silence of the sleeping palace as she awaited news of her father's return. She had worried about his safety ever since hearing about the Meerut mutiny, knowing that nothing would prevent him returning to Jhansi. When at last, late one night, she heard the gates of Ranimahal creaking open to allow a horse trap through, she knew with certainty that it would only be for her father that the gates would be opened at this time. She got up from her bed, relief flooding through her body, as she wrapped a shawl around her shoulders.

Khuda Baksh was opening the main doors as she arrived to see Moropant descending from his carriage, looking weary and travel-worn. Dear Baba, always so dependable and always there for her, she thought as she ran to touch his feet before warmly embracing him.

'Never again will I let you be gone for so long from here, Baba. I should have known that Nana would not let you go once he had hold of you!'

'God bless you, beti. Yes, Nana needed me there with his own father gone. I must have been both a sad reminder of our dear Peshwa-sahib as well as a comfort to him. Tantia was there too...and Nana's agent, Azimullah, who says he has met you here once. They are good boys, all of them. Good boys and burning with so many ideas, it was a most interesting time and a most illuminating one. But I am glad to be back to the peace of my daughter's household.' Moropant rested his arm around Lakshmibai's shoulders, grateful to be helped up the stairs.

Even though Lakshmibai knew her father needed his rest after his long journey, she escorted him to his chambers. After giving Khuda Baksh instructions to fetch some hot water, Moropant flopped back on his bed with a loud groan, smiling blissfully as his daughter pressed his arthritic knees.

'I must say, despite all of Nanasahib's cosseting, I am glad to be back with you, beti. Maybe I am just too old to be away from home for such long periods of time...'

'Was everything safe on your journey, Baba? We were hearing worrying stories here of the countryside around Meerut swarming with mutineers.'

'With God's blessings we came without meeting any brigands.' Moropant stretched his arms over his head. 'And, as far as I know, mutineers from all the surrounding areas have been converging on Delhi ever since Red Fort was taken.'

Lakshmibai's hands stopped kneading. 'Red Fort has been taken?'

'You did not hear of the fall of Delhi? Bahadur Shah Zafar has been crowned emperor again by the rebel forces. I did wonder whether the news would have reached you before I got here...' Moropant shifted uneasily at the shock in Lakshmibai's widened eyes as the light from the hanging bronze lantern fell on her face.

She stared in disbelief at her father whose face was masked by shadows, confused by his blasé tone. The mutiny had moved much further than she could have imagined in so short a space of time...Delhi and Red Fort...Red Fort was supposed to be impregnable.

'But the Mughal emperor is so old, Baba! And, I thought, completely loyal to the British. I had always believed that, unlike me, he was most relieved when the British pensioned him off because he is only interested in poetry and painting. Even pigeon-breeding was preferable to state administration, I had heard! Where did *he* find the courage to suddenly become leader to an army of rebel soldiers?'

Moropant laughed wryly. 'Yes, poor old man—quite probably over eighty now—I too had it in my heart to feel sorry for him when I heard of how he had been pressed into becoming their leader.'

'So the rebels from Meerut persuaded him to take over their cause.' A picture was already starting to form in Lakshmibai's mind.

'Of course, beti. They need a leader behind whom they can rally and he must have seemed the most likely candidate that the people would be willing to follow. But...'

'But the British...aren't they doing anything to quell this?'

Moropant looked up at the ceiling again, rubbing his fingers on his temples, careful to keep his tone neutral, 'Too late for that, beti. They are all dead. Slaughtered to a man. It must have been quite frightening to the old emperor when he realized that the only people who could have saved him from this fate were dead—and that the killing had been carried out in his name.'

'So all the British in Delhi too are gone?' Lakshmibai cried. 'I had heard about Meerut but who could have imagined that *Delhi*...it is so hard to believe, Baba, that power can lie in one pair of hands one minute and just as suddenly be shifted to another. What of the British in other towns?'

Lakshmibai and Moropant were silent for a few minutes, each lost in their own thoughts. Moropant knew he must tell his daughter of Nana and Azimullah's plans but he was feeling too weary from his travels to face many questions and Lakshmibai was speaking again. 'That poor old Mughal emperor,' she said softly, shaking her head, 'what could an old man like him, a poet and a dreamer, hope to contribute to the plans of such a murderous army, Baba!'

'You are right, beti,' Moropant replied quietly, 'Emperor Zafar's order to stop the killing of European women and children in Delhi was completely ignored. To a man like him, it must be the most terrifying thing to be both leader and follower of such a huge and determined rebel army. No doubt other, more able leaders will emerge before long.'

∼ 35 ∼

Lakshmibai looked out from the battlements of her fort at a fiercely brewing sandstorm in the western sky. She knew she ought to go indoors before the desert cloud descended on Jhansi, turning them all into prisoners as the windows turned dark and grains of sand crackled angrily against the glass panes. Instead she watched the brown veil draw closer, gradually masking the distant forests and now the river from her view. Every mote of dust was carrying more rumour and more uncertainty, all of which would rage around her Jhansi before settling into street corners and over roof tiles and front yards, sticking to everything, impossible to sweep away.

She turned from it only when the storm was nearly upon her, filling her nostrils with its muddy smell and her hair and eyes with pieces of grit, as she hurried down the Amod Garden steps, taking a quick decision to run into the now empty Panch Mahal, nearer than her palace in the city. Spotting a small door flapping on its unfastened latch, she ran in and slammed it behind her, leaning her back against the wooden frame while catching her breath. As the wind rose and whipped outside, moaning as though disappointed not to have snared her, she tried to still her heart that was fluttering like a trapped bird inside her chest.

Her breath gradually returned to normal as she looked around the small hallway of this old palace, remembering its past way of life, considering how much it had all changed. Now, as had never been the case when Gangadhar had been alive, the world outside Jhansi had become one to be feared. Sickened by the indiscriminate killings at Meerut and in Delhi, she had many times contemplated issuing orders for Jhansi's walled town to be closed and barricaded. It was a sad thought as never, since the unhappy reign of Raghunath Rao, had those gates ever been shut to Jhansi's many visitors and travellers, both Gangadhar's and her own belief being that outsiders brought new energy and creativity to the town's population. But, in these uncertain times, every stranger brought with him sinister fears from other places that might infect life in Jhansi. There had been no news from Nana and Tantia for days too. The last she had heard was the news that Moropant had brought on his return from Bithur. From so far away, she could only hope that her two brothers had prudently distanced themselves from the reported killings in Delhi and Meerut.

Whenever she thought of the slain Englishmen at Meerut and Delhi, it was Robert Ellis's face she saw. Just this morning, she had stood at the shrine of Mahalakshmi and prayed silently for his safe return to England. There was always the terrible possibility that he may have left Jhansi for Calcutta only to be transferred elsewhere in Hindustan—Meerut or Delhi even. Strangely, that had at first been the hope she had clung to; that he may only have gone to some other principality and would one day return to Jhansi. But, as that hope had faded, she now wished only to know that he had sailed back to England and safety. The misery of losing his friendship would have been much worse, had it been to this uprising and to death. Such heartless killings that were intent on snuffing out all Christians, be they friends or enemies of this land. But would she ever know if Robert Ellis had left Jhansi as her friend or enemy? There had been so much anger between them in their last few conversations, perhaps it had vanquished all the love and trust there had once been. All she knew now was that such forbidden friendships were like night-flowers; blossoms that so generously perfumed the breezes of the night, only to perish at first hint of light.

Lakshmibai wandered through the darkened room, pulling her sari around herself as she felt its cold mustiness, trying not to dwell on how lonely she suddenly felt. For days, she had been plagued too by the unhappy thought that even her beloved father had not been himself lately. On first mentioning her repugnance to Moropant that the killing of Europeans in Meerut may have been related to religion as much to race, she had caught a passing expression on his face that troubled her—revealing, she was sure, his opinion that she had not fully erased Robert Ellis from her thoughts. He must have heard on his return from Bithur of how much she had come to depend on Robert in the months of his absence and would never believe that she worried equally about all the British in Jhansi: the officers down at the cantonment and Sister Agnes and her fellow Christians at the mission, especially the orphan children whom she had seen grow and thrive over the years.

Unheeding of the fine layer of old dust covering everything, Lakshmibai seated herself on one of the swings that still hung from the ceiling of this empty room, considering sorrowfully the rift that had sprung so suddenly between her and her father. Within his first few days back at Jhansi, it was apparent that he had returned from Nana's house with all sorts of strange and foreign notions in his head; suddenly seeming to have lost much of the gracious wisdom with which he had brought her up, turning into quite another person from the infallible Baba he had once been in her girlish eyes. Perhaps everyone reached a time in their lives when a once perfect parent became suddenly fallible but, recently, she had been unable to agree with Moropant on even the simplest matters—such as whom to post at the city gates to examine all new visitors to Jhansi. Lakshmibai had quickly given in on that issue, agreeing without demur that her father, as head of Jhansi's security, ought to place the guards he most trusted on gate duty but the small disagreement had left her feeling unhappier than it should have done.

Lakshmibai listened to the storm rattling impatiently at all the door and window latches, trying within its brief life to wreak as much havoc as it could. Would that be the fate of this mutiny too? Or was it already waiting to gather pace and roll inexorably across the plains in Jhansi's direction next. She knew she had to be clear in her thoughts well before that happened, sure of the stance she would adopt.

It had not been among her flaws to prevaricate on any matter, but here was one that was already causing her mind to fray into tiny pieces—torn between wanting to pledge blind allegiance to anyone who may help unseat the British at Calcutta and needing at any cost (even if that were her own) to maintain the peace of her land. Whatever had happened in Bithur, it had changed her father in some way she could not fathom, filling him with a strange frightening excitement whenever the subject of mutiny came up, all his old sweet patience replaced by a new intolerance and bitterness. Most of all, it alarmed Lakshmibai to engage Moropant in the kind of debate in which he revealed sentiments that served to only confuse her own often uncontainable thoughts.

She chafed too at Dewan Rao Bande's delayed return from Shivpuri, briefly contemplating sending a request that he depart his daughter's home without waiting to see his grandchild. But this thought was quickly dismissed as she realized how selfish that would be.

Lakshmibai stayed in the darkened room as the dust storm continued to rage outside, pushing her feet gently against the cool tile floor to make the creaky old swing move. There was childish comfort in that motion, transporting her to the rocking arms of her old mango tree. These moments of solitude were rare. But, although she wanted to use this chance to mull quietly over the recent events, trying to comprehend her place in them and the course of action to take if the mutineers came to her fort asking for assistance, she could not stay hidden here for long. They would all be searching for her already, concerned about her absence during the squall. Reluctantly, Lakshmibai stopped her swing to rise and let herself out of the old palace as soon as she heard the patter of the first raindrops on the roof tiles signal that the storm had passed.

It was Major Ellis who sent a message to Captain Skene advising him to turn to Rani Lakshmibai for help if matters took a turn for the worse. Ellis had contemplated writing directly to Lakshmibai, but had eventually decided not to—not just because of the way in which they had parted but because he may thereby make worse the scandal of their relationship. That would not be wise at all in such sensitive times.

Jhansi was never far from his mind as the forces of mutiny gathered angrily around her. His own youth had been dedicated to the upliftment of that beloved town and he could imagine it lying quietly, seeming to slumber in the enervating heat but uneasily, with one eye and one ear cocked, and in full anticipation that it was only a matter of time before the contagion would spread its way too. He thought endlessly of Lakshmibai too, of her unenviable fate to be so caught between what she wanted most of all—the control of Jhansi— and the only way in which it now looked likely to happen, through violence and bloodshed. He could imagine how easily she may be swayed by such rebels. People like Begum Hazratmahal who talked so easily of war and killing. Even when he had been with Lakshmibai, he had not been able to prevent her thoughts from straying down such a dangerous path. Ellis feared deeply for what such a decision would do to her and to her land. Despite the dangers to his own life, he knew he had to return to Jhansi.

In those next few days, Ellis tried his utmost to find a place on a vessel to India but passenger travel had been prohibited in this time of upheaval and troop ships had no room for an officer who had been sent home, not that long ago, in disgrace. He went from port to port, even contemplating travelling as a stowaway, but there seemed no recourse. India now had her back firmly turned to him.

At the end of the month, Rani Lakshmibai received a message saying that Captains Skene and Gordon wanted to visit her. She knew they were going to seek her protection in the event of the Jhansi sipahis rebelling against them and, as the two Englishmen were escorted into the palace, she invited them to follow her into one of the private rooms adjoining her court.

Skene wore an anxious look on his thin face as he took off his pith helmet and turned towards Lakshmibai. Looking her straight in the face, he spoke in a low, tense voice, his words tripping over each other, 'It is hard to know exactly what happened at Meerut and Delhi, Rani-sahiba, but, from what we hear, the mutineers had no compunction in killing all Europeans, even women and children. Many people died in those bloodbaths, not just English but also native troops who had dared to stay loyal. I cannot imagine our men turning so fiendish...our officers enjoy the trust of not just the havildars but the sepoys too...' Skene trailed off, searching the rani's face as though she may have some vital piece of information that would help allay his fears.

'I too have heard about the events, Captain Skene,' Lakshmibai replied quietly. She had liked what she had seen of both Skene and his young wife, and was tempted for one moment to remind him of the delegation of sipahis that had come to see her last year. Although she had relayed their doubts and suspicions to Skene almost immediately, he had in the end given them short shrift, informing her that he would deal with them through his native officers. He foresaw no trouble in scotching rumours as ridiculous as animal bones being crushed in flour mills and she had heard nothing since. There seemed little point in reminding him of that now as he started to pace up and down her room, clinging to his helmet as though it would somehow provide protection in a crisis.

Lakshmibai felt sudden sympathy for his unenviable dilemma. It was an almost laughable irony that the British were suddenly in a position of having to approach her for help and she derived no joy from it, surprisingly.

'Forgive me, Captain Skene, and I hope you do not imagine I wish for such an event at all,' she said gently, 'but I have been wondering how it is that our sipahis in Jhansi have not troubled themselves yet with this issue of the greased cartridges? We have heard about other concerns, as you know, but this business with the tallow on cartridges has never been mentioned here as far as I know and it seems curious that they would not have heard of all the events at other places yet?'

Skene shrugged as though equally mystified. 'I can only think that it is because our garrisons are smaller than those at Meerut and Barrackpore. Trouble is generally easier to anticipate and control here. I also have a lot of personal trust in our native officers, Subedar–Major Gopal in particular. In any event, the new Enfield isn't in use here yet. Of course, there have been murmurings but I do believe we have been successful in keeping them at bay so far.'

Captain Gordon interjected, 'We do hear now, though, that mutineers are out in the countryside, riding madly on horseback from town to town, trying to gather more support. The turbulence is spreading and we still couldn't be too sure of which way either the 12th Native or the 14th Irregular sepoys will eventually go.'

'Yes, you need to take all precautions,' the rani replied contemplatively. After a few moments, she said, 'I will send fifty of my own guards to join your forces. You can be assured of their loyalty as they will come with my instructions. As you know, I don't have much ammunition to give you but I will see what I can spare from my armoury.'

'Rani-sahiba, I thank you,' Skene said, bowing deeply. But as he straightened up, he looked at Lakshmibai and held her gaze firmly. 'I do have one more request, Rani-sahiba...'

Lakshmibai looked into his eyes but did not offer encouragement. She had a fairly good idea of what he was about to say.

Still looking unwaveringly at her, Skene said sombrely, 'Should it become necessary, Rani-sahiba, could I prevail further upon your kindness and ask for our women and children to be given sanctuary in your fort? It would be merely precautionary, you understand, depending on how events unfold.'

Lakshmibai took a deep breath. She knew how inadequate the British cantonment was to house their women and children in case of trouble; villas and bungalows with only grass hedges and picket fences to protect them. If it had been Robert Ellis standing before her, making this request, she would not have thought twice before agreeing. There was enormous risk to herself, of course, but she would think of that only if the rebels did come to Jhansi. She saw the look of relief overcome Captain Skene's face as she silently nodded her assent.

After Skene and Gordon had left the palace, Rani Lakshmibai sent word that all the great gates and darwazas that led out of Jhansi town were to be closed forthwith and barricaded with special rams. Before long, the air was filled with the sound of grinding metal and wood as the ancient city gates were closed, rusted chains and locks clanging into place. They would probably be no match for determined sipahis, nor would those people whose homes had been made on the northern outskirts of the city be protected. But those citizens could be re-housed in the town and the fortified walls would offer some defence. She knew she ought not to feel relief in the knowledge that the cantonment and mission, where almost all the Christians were concentrated, lay well beyond the city walls. She certainly wished them no harm and would assist in saving innocent lives, as she had promised Skene. But it would be naive to ignore the fact that, when the mutiny did come to Jhansi, its spark would lie in that small and very exposed enclave and Lakshmibai's first task was to protect her own people from it.

It was a decision she would soon be grateful for. Just three days after the gates were closed, a fearful hammering was heard on the huge brass-studded doors of Sainyer Darwaza. Fists and sticks were being used to pound so hard on the doors that the thumping was audible even where Lakshmibai sat with Damodar on her western balcony. They both looked up, startled by the noise and, although Lakshmibai guessed instantly what might be causing it, she patted Damodar's hand reassuringly, gesturing that he was to stay seated while she enquired what the commotion was about. As she emerged from her chamber, she saw her longest serving guard, Gul Mohammed, running down the corridor. Between rasping breaths, he informed her that a group of mutineers who had ridden out from Meerut were clamouring to be let into the town, astonished and furious to find its gates closed.

'What do they want from us?' Lakshmibai asked, trying to keep her voice calm.

'They are demanding to know where your loyalties in this uprising lie, Rani-sahiba.'

'Are they mad?' she asked, suddenly incensed at their arrogance. 'This uprising has nothing to do with us. Even if it had, are there ever any easy answers to such questions? Tell them it is no business of theirs, Gul Mohammed. I have no loyalty but to my people and to the safety of Jhansi.' She was standing tall, her eyes blazing with anger.

Although Gul Mohammed cowered at his queen's rage, he replied tentatively, 'Rani-sahiba, they are armed and may return with more people. We have to humour them if we are to avoid a siege.'

'I will not succumb, Gul Mohammed. I will not be threatened by such ruffians. What good reason do we have to even commune with these murderous brutes?'

'If we tell them that we support their cause, they may be better persuaded to leave,' Gul Mohammed reasoned.

Lakshmibai weighed up her reluctance. These were insurgents drunk with the success of their sacking and pillage of Meerut. Even though she shared their desire to unseat the British government, such rebels would be concerned only with their own selfish gains. They had already shown themselves capable of vile conduct towards women and children and would probably stop at nothing. What she needed was time to assess their intent and to keep them away from her own people. Gul Mohammed was right in saying that angry words were unlikely to turn them away from the gates but she was still very sure she wanted to distance herself as far from them as possible.

'I agree that we do not profit by raising their ire, Gul Mohammed, but it is to be made clear that they will not be given access to Jhansi under any circumstances,' she replied. 'Go quickly, before they break the gates down. Tell them we support their cause and do not stand in their way but that we are not in a position to do anything to help them.'

Lakshmibai returned to her balcony, setting Damodar's mind at rest by spinning a quick story about some wandering nomads requiring food and water. But, ten minutes later, after she had instructed Sundar to take Damodar indoors for his bath, she hurried downstairs to see Gul Mohammed returning to the palace.

He looked weary and his voice was rueful, 'Rani-sahiba, they are demanding a token of our support: an elephant, five horses, money and whatever our armoury can spare...they will not heed me when I say we have no ammunition and that our treasury is denuded. They are getting quite argumentative and I fear the situation may escalate.'

Rani Lakshmibai turned away from Gul Mohammed, fear and frustration building inside her. Although he was one of the most dependable guards she had, she could not turn to him or anyone else, for advice—Dewan Rao Bande was still in Shivpuri and Moropant...regrettably, Moropant no longer spoke with the calm wisdom she had so depended on in her younger years.

As she hesitated fleetingly, Gul Mohammed continued speaking, his voice now low and urgent, 'Rani-sahiba, these men are not beyond harming our people if they do not get what they want. More worryingly, some of our guards at the gates appear to be taking their side too. I also heard Krishna Rao's name mentioned by one of the rebels from Meerut. It seems they have already met him at Parola and he has pledged his support.'

Lakshmibai had to think fast. The peace of Jhansi was paramount and it was wise to get rid of these rabble-rousing agitators as soon as possible. It was also deeply unsettling to know that Krishna Rao had been communicating with the rebels. She raised her head and spoke steadily, measuring her words, 'Tell them we will meet some of their demands, but not all, Gul Mohammed. They can have one lakh rupees worth of jewellery, a few guns, three horses and one of the older elephants—not Siddhabaksh. They are to regard it as a token of our support but are honour-bound to accept the condition attached that they are never to return here. Never. We have problems of our own and do not have the resources to spare. That is to be made very clear.'

She watched Gul Mohammed leave again with her message, cold bricks of fear building a heavy tower in her stomach. When he returned a few minutes later to tell her that the offer had been accepted, she breathed a low sigh of relief.

'Please seek out my father, Gul Mohammed. Inform him of this new development and request him to supervise the handing over of money and ammunition to the mutineers. Keep a contingent of our guards at hand to prevent trouble.'

After the faithful guard had departed the chamber again, Lakshmibai sat down heavily on a chair. Even though the matter had been resolved more easily than expected today, it was not over yet. The clawing sense of foreboding that had remained locked inside her ever since the mutiny at Meerut had formed a hard little knot in her stomach that grew a little every day.

She thought of her poor father carrying out the transaction with those rebels, putting himself in danger, even while suppressing his own sympathies for their cause. How she had laboured to explain her feelings to him during one recent tortuous argument: of course, she too, like all the rest of them, longed to finally see the back of the British; she wanted, more than anything else, to have control of her kingdom returned to her, who wouldn't? But men who killed women and children were murderers and there was nothing to be gained by aligning oneself with them. Mutineers capable of such callous acts were never to be trusted for they would just as soon thrust their daggers into the robes of their protectors once the British were all gone.

She had been furious when Moropant had shrugged off all her different lines of reasoning that day, finally reducing her to speechless despair. How indeed had those months in Bithur caused such an unbridegable gulf to form between a doting father and daughter? Was it because he too had heard false rumours about her relationship with Robert Ellis? Although Moropant had not yet spoken directly on that subject, his silences revealed much more hurt than a torrent of angry words would have done. There were days when Lakshmibai dreaded the moment he would finally confront her with his suspicions, and others when she longed, almost childishly, for the liberation of a loving parent's reproach.

Rani Lakshmibai waited for two days to pass, considering her position on the mutineers carefully, before summoning Captain Skene to a private audience. She watched the expression on his face turn to consternation as she told him about the rebels from Meerut having made contact with her, feeling sorry to further deepen his anxieties.

'I had no idea they were already in Jhansi district...they are not still here?' he asked, fear and anxiety twisting his already pinched features. A network of blood vessels had risen on either side of his forehead, throbbing red.

'I think we merely happened to be on their path, Captain. They took what they wanted and have moved on,' the rani replied. 'I am quite certain they are not still here in the district. I did not let them through the town gates at all. The transaction, a purely pragmatic one you understand, was done at Sainyer Gate.'

'How do we know that they will not come back?'

'We do not know that for sure, Captain Skene. But, let us not forget that Jhansi is not exactly famed for its plenitude. Looters and plunderers would much rather head for Delhi or Lucknow where the treasuries and armouries are impressively endowed. What can they hope to get from us?'

'I can only pray you are right, Rani-sahiba. And, no doubt, you were wise in appeasing rather than antagonizing them unnecessarily.' Skene paused before continuing swiftly, 'But, Rani-sahiba, may I request you now to take our women and children in for safety's sake? The time is come for you to keep your promise to us for I fear they are very vulnerable where they are in case of attack. I have nowhere else to take them.'

Skene could see a momentary flicker of misgiving on the rani's face at this request. He knew what a terrible predicament hers was as she could be seen as being too supportive of British interests in the eyes of mutineers, even if it was just the women and children that she helped. Indeed, such an act could even lower her in the eyes of her own people. Who knew where their loyalties lay in all this? But he had to keep the pressure on her for he knew instinctively that this queen was one of the few native royals who could be trusted. Margaret believed that as well, often marvelling at how magnanimously the rani of Jhansi had behaved with them all, given the boorish treatment meted out to her by Calcutta. In any event, there was simply nowhere else for them to go.

Sensing her hesitation, Skene continued speaking swiftly, 'It is far too dangerous, Rani-sahiba, for me to even contemplate sending the women out to take refuge in the Residency at Lucknow or anywhere else. There has been no news from anywhere for days as the mutineers have cut all telegraph lines to stop our communication. These scoundrels are probably scouring the countryside looking for victims and the roads to Kanpur or Lucknow are long...' Skene knew his voice sounded pleading but he had only just this morning heard rumours that the countryside had reverted to the wild old feudal style followed before the British had brought order: grandees fortifying their palaces and training their own soldiers in the use of spears and javelins, forming their own little armies.

'A group of hapless European women and children taken hostage would be a most hazardous situation in such times...' he trailed off, unable to read the expression in the rani's dark eyes. Painfully conscious of having to beg help from someone so recently and churlishly rebuffed by Government House, he thanked his fortunes for having done his part in maintaining a good relationship with the rani of Jhansi as, with immense relief, he saw her purse her lips before nodding.

'Bring them to the fort under cover of darkness tonight,' she said, her voice shaking slightly. 'Do not come to Khanderao Darwaza but use the smaller eastern gate. There is less chance of your being seen entering from there by people who may be unsympathetic to you. I will find the right kind of accommodation where they may be able to hide for a few days. But only a few days, mind. Some better arrangement would have to be made and I will consider the best path, as you must too.'

Captain Skene got up from his seat and bowed deeply with one hand over his heart, words failing him in his wish to express gratitude.

He reminded himself to inform Major Erskine, the commissioner at Sagar or, indeed, Major Ellis back in London, of Rani Lakshmibai's assistance in this time of need once all this had been dealt with. At some point their debt to Rani Lakshmibai would have to be acknowledged and richly repaid. He hoped from the bottom of his heart that the British government would see it fit to reward her assistance by returning the rule of her principality to her when this ghastly mutiny was over.

Later that night, Lakshmibai waited for the British party to be brought to her fort while the rest of Jhansi slept. She wanted to personally supervise their arrival and stood with her bodyguards just inside the small eastern Shahar Darwaza, listening to the first of the carriages pull up outside and unload their occupants. She could hear people whispering urgent instructions to each other in English to be as silent as possible, mothers and ayahs shushing their little ones.

As the carriages rolled up, one by one, the size of the group swelled. There were around sixty people, most of them women, including the maids and ayahs and children. Lakshmibai smiled at Mary and Beatrice, Captain Skene's two little girls whom she saw beaming at her in the dark as they entered the gates, hanging onto their mother's skirts. They had come to know the rani from the few occasions on which they had been to the palace to play with Damodar and Lakshmibai guessed that their mother had kept them up and in good humour by telling them they may be able to play with him tonight. Although she tried to smile reassuringly at Mrs Skene too, she saw that the woman was white-faced and frightened, clutching piteously at the shoulders of her two girls. Behind her was the deputy collector's family, the smallest of them a mere babe-in-arms, gurgling and dimpling from the safety of his pretty mother's arms. Lakshmibai also noticed some of the local Eurasians—teachers from the missionary school, the old school caretaker and the Mutlow men who worked near the cantonment area—and mentally commended Captain Skene for having considered their safety as well. The mixing of blood had always made these poor Eurasians belong nowhere. Being Christian and desirous of being seen as akin to the British, they too would make easy targets for rebels with murderous intentions. The Mutlows were carrying boxes, grunting under their weight and Lakshmibai guessed that the group had brought its own victuals, unaware that she too had ordered the purchase of European foodstuffs.

The last of the buggies was from the church and Lakshmibai nodded at the tall, shambling figure of the padre. Sister Agnes waved distractedly at the rani but did not come across to speak to her, preoccupied as she was with getting the children in her charge out of their creaking carriage as silently as possible. After they were all inside Shahar Darwaza, Rani Lakshmibai nodded at Skene who had accompanied the group along with a few of his men. She saw him pick up each of his girls to give them a kiss and watched while he hugged his wife who was wiping silent tears away. The Skenes had always seemed to Lakshmibai to embody the sweetness and love of family life that had eluded her own fortunes and it was hard not to gaze too intently upon their togetherness.

'Do not be anxious, Captain Skene,' Lakshmibai said as he came up to her for a final goodbye, 'they will be safe in my care.'

Once again, he was lost for words, the lump in his throat moving as she saw tears in his red-rimmed eyes. Her decision to provide sanctuary had been made partly with Robert's memory in mind, rather than for reward or praise, and she turned away, embarrassed by the gratitude on Skene's face.

After the British soldiers had left, the group made its way as silently as possible across the cobbled back street, the stones underfoot gleaming in the light of a swollen full moon that had appeared from behind the clouds. A faint smell of wood-smoke and cooking emanated from the houses they passed although there was no one about as their occupants had long retired for the night. The group was accompanied by Gul Mohammed who had taken along a few of the rani's most loyal guards. Their instructions had been to take the Christians to the building inside the fort that adjoined the ammunition stores, always well-guarded by the longest serving sentries. The top two floors had been chosen as the safest for having no windows and the palace maids had endeavoured to make them as comfortable as possible, laying out beds, mattresses, blankets, water jugs and some basic food supplies. The rani had even thought of sending a box full of toys for the children and some books and reed fans for the women to help them through the hot summer nights.

Having seen the last of the group go upstairs to their hideout, Lakshmibai returned to her palace in the city in her palanquin. She had left the capable Sundar in charge of settling the group in, suggesting that mothers with young children sleep on the lower floor, while the more private chambers be given over to the elderly, the few men and the padre.

On reaching the palace, instead of going straight to her bedchamber, Lakshmibai walked hurriedly down the corridor leading to the kitchens, hoping to reach it before Mohandeo and Khuda Baksh retired for the night. She was not sure if Sundar had remembered to instruct the khansamas to serve the English guests bread, eggs and mutton when they broke their fast in the morning and was relieved to see that these things had already been laid out. The cooks and scullions had all turned in, but a box full of eggs had been placed on a kitchen shelf and a skinned goat was visible, hanging from a metal hook in a far corner of the larder.

With a sense of satisfied fatigue, Lakshmibai walked slowly back to her rooms, holding out a lantern as she silently traversed the darkened corridor. She stopped short as she heard a sound in the passageway just outside her private living room and, lifting her lantern up, was startled to see Moropant's figure emerge from the gloom. He was sitting with his head in his hands but stood up when he saw her. It looked as though he had been waiting there for her to return.

'Baba, you surprised me!' Lakshmibai exclaimed as she neared him. 'Is all well? I was checking the welfare of the English party.'

Moropant seemed hesitant and unable to come straight to the point. His figure looked stooped and Lakshmibai said more gently, placing the lantern on the table between them, 'Forgive me, Baba, I concern myself with our guests' welfare before your own only because they are in danger and we, praise our goddess, still sleep safely in our beds.'

'That is exactly why I am here, beti,' Moropant replied quietly, 'to ensure your security. To beg that you do not endanger it in this way.'

'In what way, Baba? I take one careful step at a time, considering all the options ahead of me. You understand that I must heed my principles too.'

'Principles…' Moropant emitted a hollow laugh.

Lakshmibai was cut to the quick, assuming that the sarcasm referred to whatever falsehoods he may have heard of her relationship with Robert Ellis. But she held her tongue, waiting for Moropant to finish his piece.

Her father's face was only partially visible in the shadows but she could hear the unease in his voice, 'My dearest beti…Mani…ever since you became Rani Lakshmibai, I have considered it my duty to forget the right that fatherhood once conferred on me to tell you what to do.'

Lakshmibai felt a moment's relief that the subject that had simmered uneasily and unspoken between them was finally out in the open. She spoke now in a quiet voice, giving him an unwavering look, 'Is there something you wish to take issue with, Baba? Speak as my father, and I will know it is said with love.'

Moropant took a deep breath before replying, his voice trembling slightly, 'Beti, where it comes to your personal happiness, I will stand by you till my dying breath. Nothing matters to me more than your happiness. Remember, I too was widowed young, and I understand fully the trouble caused by a wilful heart that will not heed the cautions of the mind.'

Lakshmibai felt a lump form in her throat but remained silent as she could see that he had not finished speaking yet.

His voice was still low and tremulous as he continued to speak, now taking her hand in his, 'I care for where you place your heart, beti, only if I can see it will harm you. As a loving father, I stood by and watched my dearest one get drawn into a treacherous friendship as I held silently onto my anguish. But now you must see that there are too many among your own people who view these Christians as our enemy...the hospitality you extend to them will not be easily brooked...'

So he had heard talk about her relationship with Robert, Lakshmibai thought, feeling sad that he had not taken it up with her before this already fraught night. It was true that Robert's memory had led her to offer refuge to the British, but she would surely have found it difficult to turn a group of women and children away from the safety of her fort even if she had never befriended him. How could Baba have lost the humanity he had taught her in such abundance?

Lakshmibai replied pleadingly, 'You tell me what else we could have done, Baba. Most of these people are helpless women and children. Just think how vulnerable a target they would be if the rebellion came to Jhansi...'

'And you don't worry that you have compromised your position by harbouring them here?'

'In this matter, I have no position, Baba. You know that. My quarrel with the British government at Calcutta cannot make me an enemy of their most vulnerable people here. Why should it?'

'*Why should it*? Because, beti, your people expect you to be able to demarcate better in your mind. You cannot choose *some* among your enemy to befriend. That is not the way in times of war.'

Moropant sounded close to tears but Lakshmibai snatched her hand out of his grasp. 'Baba, since your return from Bithur, you have only talked the language of war. That is a business best left to people like Nana and Tantia whose grievances run deep. We are not at war and, consequently, we have no enemies. Yes, we have certain differences of opinion with the British over policy but I will not wage war with them—that has never been my intention. And I most certainly do not have a quarrel with those poor women and children cowering in my fort from murderers abroad. They have shared our salt and are now in my care, just as my own people are.'

The flashing anger in his daughter's eyes, her impractical, stubborn idealism made fear rise in Moropant's heart. 'What are you saying, beti!' he groaned, covering his face with his hands. 'Sharing salt, breaking bread—the time for all that with the English is long gone. And had, perhaps, never existed at all. How can I make you see that those mutineers will merely take your life if you use it to shield the British—'

Moropant stopped short, realizing that he struggled to find the right words to convince Lakshmibai only because her views were exactly those he had himself held dear as a young man. Then it was he who had argued with his old friend, Peshwa-sahib. But now Peshwa-sahib had gone and it was he who had grown old and cynical. How grateful he felt for his trip to Bithur where Nana and Tantia had shown him in what a dreamlike state he had lived his life so far. Even Azimullah—for surely a man of such formidable intellect could not be wrong. What a waste all those letters written by Lakshmibai to Dalhousie had been and how foolish to have trusted Robert Ellis's offers of help. Dialogue and negotiation were for people who were equals, not for ruler and ruled. There was only one path left to them and it both angered and grieved him that his beloved daughter was refusing to see it.

'Listen to me, beti,' he pleaded insistently, dropping his voice, 'the sipahis in the cantonment will mutiny tomorrow. You have to understand what I am trying to tell you. You cannot shelter the British here, it will be the undoing of you. Please, my dearest one, if you do nothing else, do this for me, for your old father and for the safety of the people around you, your own son! Let the British take care of their own. It is not your job to look after them. Your responsibility is to the people of Jhansi and to your oldest friends like Nana and Tantia. You must make arrangements for the English to leave now. Tonight. There will be no mercy for us if the enemy are found in our midst.' Moropant's voice had risen with the last few words, cracking with angry desperation.

Lakshmibai stared uncomprehendingly for one moment at her father, his words echoing in the suddenly unmoving air between them. How had he known exactly when the sipahis were going to mutiny? Since when had he been finding out these things and keeping them secret from her? When had her own father, her own kindly beloved Baba, become this frightening, unrecognizable stranger?

Without another word, she turned and ran into her chambers,

slamming the door behind her. He would not follow her in here and she did not want him to. She could not bear to let her father see the rage she felt overflowing towards him. How could he have lost his last ounce of compassion for ordinary men and women who had done them no harm? Among those he so mindlessly called 'enemy', was Robert Ellis who—whatever else his faults—had loved Jhansi and, yes, had loved her too. That love she had willingly sacrificed at Jhansi's altar, losing perhaps the only such chance life would ever offer.

Lakshmibai walked to the window and saw her town sleeping peacefully in the moonlight. As always, it was a sight that calmed her and gave her strength. Her breath slowly returning to normal, she leaned her head on the window frame, feeling an old sadness replace the anger in her chest. Flicking away the start of a tear with her fingertip, she reminded herself of how little cause she had to regret Robert's departure. He had, in fact, made his own decision to leave her. She had not asked him to go. But, had he still been here, and caught on the wrong side, she would certainly not have turned him out to be murdered in cold blood. That she was sure of. No one, not even the father she adored, would be allowed to send Robert's people to their death.

The following morning, Lakshmibai heard renewed pounding on the city gates as she made her way across to the British hideout in the fort. The sound was so deafening, it was as though the intruders would willingly break down the doors if they were not let in forthwith.

'Hold them there, Gul Mohammed,' she cried, standing under the arched gateway to the fort. 'Why have the rebels come back? Did they not promise that they would go away with what we had already given them?'

'This is another group, Rani-sahiba,' Gul Mohammed called as he ran up to her. 'It is as though the countryside cannot stop producing these endless streams of mutinying sipahis. They are coming from everywhere. These people say they are from Rohilkhand. According to them, the troops of both the 12th Bengal Army and the 14th Irregulars at Sagar have already risen up against their British officers. It would appear that trouble has come to Jhansi too.'

Moropant's words from the night before returned to her in a rush but Lakshmibai remained outwardly calm. She spoke carefully, 'Could it be true, Gul Mohammed—we have heard nothing from Skene and Gordon since they brought the women here.'

'If it is true, we will find out soon enough, Rani-sahiba. Shall I send somebody to see what is going on at the cantonment?'

'These rebels from Rohilkhand...they do not know anything about the women and children we have inside the fort, do they?'

'They don't appear to, Rani-sahiba, but that is not a secret we will be able to keep for very long. There are too many people within the city who now know. And too many of them are unhappy with their presence here.'

'Then my people will just have to understand. Can they not see that compassion demands we take care of the helpless? There are *children* among them, Gul Mohammed!'

'Forgive me, Rani-sahiba, but in times of war and discontent, can one really expect compassion from those who themselves suffer?' Gul Mohammed lowered his voice and added more respectfully, 'Rani-sahiba, you have heard your own people tell you about their loss of trade because of British policy. Can we really expect kindness from poor weavers and peasants, whose children starve every night, towards those of their unsympathetic masters?'

'But these are not those masters, merely their women and children and a few old men,' Lakshmibai cried frustratedly before giving her guard a long look and asking quietly, 'Gul Mohammed, you too think that I have made a mistake in giving the British refuge, do you not?'

The loyal old guard hung his head deferentially but his silence spoke volumes to her. She felt the need to sit down as waves of fatigue washed all over her. How many people should she fight in this wretched matter? People whom she loved and trusted. She was sure dewan-sahib would have maintained a respectful silence had he been here but, who knew, perhaps he too would have felt cursed in having a queen who so resolutely and foolishly wished to protect those whom all else saw as the enemy. Angry confused thoughts coursed through her head...if it were indeed true that the welfare of the British lay at variance to those of her own people, then did she really have a choice at all?

After a long pause, Lakshmibai turned to Gul Mohammed and whispered, her eyes dark against her pale face, 'Very well then. It is not for me to go against the wishes of my people and those whose advice I have always sought.' She turned around and Gul Mohammed could barely hear her as she continued in a low voice, 'Send a message to Captain Skene asking him to approach the maharaja of Datia. He may be in a better position to give the British sanctuary in his fort. Once that is arranged, we will ensure that the women are given safe passage out of Jhansi. That is the least we can do as we turn them out. And let us hope God will forgive us for it.'

Feeling wretched to the pit of her stomach, Lakshmibai retraced her steps back to her own palace, knowing she would not be able to bear the anxious expressions on Sister Agnes and Mrs Skene's faces either. Blameless women—now on her enemy's side—for reasons that had nothing to do with any of them at all.

A young lieutenant, riding furiously through the ripening wheat fields, brought the news to Jhansi town. The rani's guards let him in and, bleeding as he was from a heinous slash on his thigh, tended to his wounds before bringing him to the rani in her palace.

'The mutiny has come to Jhansi, Rani-sahiba,' he stuttered, his pupils still dilated by fear and awe of the killings he had witnessed in the darkness of early dawn—sepoys, alongside whom he had trained, turning on him and his fellow-officers like bloodthirsty strangers.

'Skene...? And Gordon?' Rani Lakshmibai asked, fearing the worst.

'They are both still alive,' the lieutenant replied, his chest still heaving. 'They were given refuge by Subedar–Major Gopal who risked his own life to save theirs...Captain Gordon sends word that you may assume charge of your kingdom once again. He asks that you hold it along with the adjoining territories until this insurrection has been dealt with and the British are in control again...'

Rani Lakshmibai could not suppress a mocking laugh, though the gravity of the situation was all too apparent. 'My kingdom?' she asked. 'How ironic that it is only now that your officers deem it to be mine!' She looked at the bewilderment on the young lieutenant's face and decided to spare him her bitterness. He would never understand it.

The young lieutenant had to be disguised before being sent back to the cantonment. On orders from the rani, he was dressed in a cloak and turban, his skin washed in berry juice to darken it, before being sent on his way. The rani's message to Captain Skene was secreted in the folds of his cloak: '*The dangers that lurk among a people embittered by British policies towards Jhansi are too numerous to stay within my control. The Maharaja of Datia has no such history to overcome and he, at least, will not have the ire of his own people to quell. My people are straining at their perception of my disloyalty to our own fight for justice. I urge you not to leave the women here as I cannot guarantee their safety even within my own palace. At best, I can give you my personal guarantee that the mutineers will not be allowed anywhere near the group when they are evacuated from my fort.*'

News of the mutiny reaching Jhansi was brief. Ellis read the telegram that gave him the bare facts: on the 6th of June, sepoys of the 12th Native and 14th Irregular turned on their British officers and colleagues as though they were some distant enemy they had never laid eyes on before. It was reportedly mayhem as the armoury at Star Fort was taken under the leadership of a Havildar–Major called Gurbaksh Singh, a native officer Ellis could barely remember. Many of the officers were killed, although there were garbled reports of Skene having got the women and children across to Rani Lakshmibai's fort. If they were in her care, Ellis knew her humanity would keep them safe.

As for himself, it was as if the great gates of Jhansi were closing shut before his very gaze. He wondered, as the awful events unfolded, whether he would ever see his precious town again.

৵ 36 ৽

Morning dawned over Jhansi, with the usual distant sounds of dhobis slapping wet clothes against the stone steps of the river, the lowing of the cows as they were led into milking sheds, the frantic chattering birdsong of summer mornings. As the temple bells of Mahalakshmi's shrine clanged for the morning prayers, a man rode up the road from the cantonment in a cloud of dust, arriving at the gates of the town with a message for the rani from Captain Skene.

Lakshmibai, sitting alone at her small writing desk that overlooked the distant hills, read the note that was brought to her by a sentry. Captain Skene and Captain Gordon would arrive later in the morning to escort their women and children away. The raja of Datia had promised them carriages and dolies that would travel under armed guard to his neighbouring state. The carriages would be waiting near the stone temples that stood at the edge of Jhokan Bagh inside Jhansi town at about midday.

Lakshmibai considered the plan. Jhokan Bagh was a quiet secluded area, very near the back gates of the fort and not far from the smallest of the gates leading out of the city. It was a safe arrangement and she wondered if it was Skene who had organized it with such precision. The raja of Datia would have needed little persuasion to give the British sanctuary and Skene would no doubt have promised him numerous rewards when they returned to power. The old raja had, in any case, always regarded British favour as something of a competition between Datia and Jhansi, loathing the fact that Gangadhar had kept in such good favour with the British. Lakshmibai thought regretfully of how she was now giving Datia his best opportunity to prove to the British that they were wrong to ever prefer Jhansi over him.

Even though the sun had risen beyond the curve of the slowly glowing hills, sending its first glancing rays towards her windows, Lakshmibai felt a sudden chill and got up in search of a shawl. Not for the first time in these past few days, she remembered Gangadhar, with intense longing for his gentle wisdom and those happier days of his reign. How fortunate both he and Robert had been to escape all this. Why, Lakshmibai wondered, pressing her fingers over her eyes, why had it become her fate to face this trial alone? How had it come to be that she was forced to choose between her people and her humanity? She thought of the legend of her namesake—the goddess Ganga, whose choice had lain between either keeping herself alive or allowing her children to live. Either way, being condemned to a life without them.

She got up and walked across to Damodar's bedchamber. It seemed to her that waking him up every morning was one of the last remaining joys left in her life. As she pushed open his door, she could hear the steady sound of his breathing. He was curled up in his little bed, unaware of all the events taking place so near, but she wondered how long she would be able to keep him protected thus. She had not even told him of the presence of the little Skene girls in the fort, knowing that he was still too young to keep secrets. Perhaps it was for the best as he would certainly have wept to see them depart so suddenly today. Making room for herself on a corner of his small bed, she slipped under the coverlet, taking comfort from the warmth of his body. She curved one arm around his small waist, enjoying the feel of his back settling into the curve of her lap as he stirred in his sleep. Inhaling deeply into his hair, she thought again of poor Margaret Skene and those other women, waking their children this morning with the news that they would have to flee again. Lakshmibai pressed Damodar's back to her stomach as though it may shield her from some terrible punishment, praying to be forgiven such a terrible decision, made under duress from those who supposedly loved her best.

The afternoon sun was starting its slow glittering descent and still there was no sign of either Skene or Gordon. Lakshmibai was beginning to chafe at the unexplained delay, when a sudden barrage of shooting was heard from the vicinity of the town's main gates. Just as she was calling urgently for her horse to be brought for her to find out the cause, Gul Mohammed came running into the court to give her the appalling news. He was in a state of panic and completely out of breath, wheezing as he tried to speak.

'Rani-sahiba, I was on the ramparts as you had ordered—looking out for the British officers—and was the first to spot them riding hard for Sainyer Darwaza up the Sagar road.' Lakshmibai waited, her heart pounding, as he caught his breath. 'But, Rani-sahiba, even as I ran around the perimeter of the ramparts to issue orders to let them in, I saw a group of men materialize from the southern forests, their guns poised and ready to shoot.'

'Who were these men, not ours surely?'

'I could not recognize them in their cloaks and turbans, Rani-sahiba, but, in the noise and the confusion, I saw Captain Gordon fall in a hail of bullets.'

'O Shiva! And Skene?'

'Captain Skene and one other officer survived that round of firing and rode furiously on for the town gates where our men quickly let them in. But...' The guard stopped speaking, his gaze shifting to his queen's feet, his face suffused with doubt and fear.

'But what, Gul Mohammed?' Lakshmibai asked, her own voice rising sharply.

'Rani-sahiba, before the great gates could be closed again, the rebels pursuing Skene had pushed past the guards and entered the town behind him.'

Lakshmibai put her fist to her chest and closed her eyes momentarily as she felt the world spin around her. She could barely hear Gul Mohammed's next words.

'Fortunately, Rani-sahiba, Captain Skene was not caught and has already been spirited away by two of the palace guards to join the women in their hiding place in the fort.'

Lakshmibai looked up at Gul Mohammed as she gripped the ivory handles of her chair. 'Do you realize,' she asked, her own voice shaking now, 'that the mutineers have got what they really wanted? Can you see that, Gul Mohammed? There is not only a trail of dead Englishmen leading from the cantonment all the way up to Jhansi's doors. But the killers are inside our town, mingling amongst our people as we speak.'

Without another word, she got up and walked out of the court in the direction of the building that housed the British women. She had to calm their fears as, no doubt, they would have heard the firing too. However, as she ran up the stairs to their hideout, she saw that

Captain Skene had got there already and the women were now crowding around him. His uniform was covered in bloodstains and his eyes were wild in his dust-covered face, but she could see that he was unhurt as he sat in the arms of his wife and children who were gathered around him, crying with joy at seeing him alive. Their tearful reunion brought a lump to Lakshmibai's throat and she swiftly turned away from their private exchange of love and concern. Unable to face the tears that would no doubt follow from those women whose husbands had not escaped the firing, Lakshmibai used the commotion caused by Skene's arrival to slip out again, unseen.

As she hurried down the stairs, one of her guards approached her. He looked worried, his brows knit with worry as he fell at her feet, wailing, 'Rani-sahiba, rebels from the cantonment have infiltrated the town, there are at least a dozen who have got in and now they are insisting that we open the gates to let their comrades in too...there is nothing we can do to prevent them entering. Even some of our own citizens are gathering at the gates, clamouring to let the mutineers in.'

'Who was responsible for letting them in? Bring him before me! The order was for Skene and his men to be given passage, not for all the murderers from the countryside to be let into Jhansi.' Lakshmibai's voice was like a whiplash and the guard winced. He did not reply, merely hanging his head and shaking it regretfully. She realized it was not his fault but, enraged with her guards for failing to adequately protect the city gates, she added sharply, 'Tell Gul Mohammed to try to personally confer with these outsiders—rebels from Rohilkhand, Meerut, whoever they are. We need to come to some kind of agreement with them before they start spreading trouble on the streets of Jhansi. Before anything else, I need to speak with Gul Mohammed. Tell him I will be waiting at Ranimahal. Quickly!'

The man ran down the path, his fear and anxiety apparent as he tripped but stumbled on, without stopping. Lakshmibai turned and strode briskly towards the Ranimahal—there was no time to summon the palanquin bearers and it was near enough to walk. Entering the side garden gate, she angrily brushed aside a trailing clump of chameli. It suddenly seemed so ridiculous that the palace maalis had continued to tend these flowers and shrubs in the hot summer months, absurdly watering and weeding even as the countryside around them had burned.

She ran up the stairs to the veranda, pacing restlessly on the polished floor while waiting for Gul Mohammed, planning the arguments to use for the rebels. She would ask them directly what their business in Jhansi was. If it was to get hold of the British hostages, she would explain that they were only women and children and not worthy of their anger. If it was to berate her for supporting them, she would explain that they were already on their way to Datia, that Jhansi had long forsaken them.

Even though she felt physically ill, from both the heat and from her fear, she was determined not to request anyone else for help or advice. Certainly not Moropant, still no doubt annoyed with his daughter for harbouring too much compassion for the British even while she cursed herself for having too little.

As soon as she saw Gul Mohammed riding up from the direction of the city gates, she ran down the steps of the palace again. Dismounting, the guard told her that he had just met some of the mutineers himself. They appeared to be under the command of a rebel risaldar called Kala Khan. Gul Mohammed knew nothing more about him, not which battalion he had come from, nor what it was that he had wanted.

Lakshmibai made a swift decision. The task at hand was clearly far too sensitive to be entrusted with anyone else. Her voice was firm, 'Gul Mohammed, inform Risaldar Kala Khan that I would like his attendance. Do not bring them to the palace. I will ride out to Sainyer Darwaza and we shall meet under the peepul tree there.' Turning to one of her other bodyguards, she said crisply, 'Fetch my horse. Soon. There is no time to waste.'

A few minutes later, she had mounted Sarangi and, accompanied by her personal bodyguards, started cantering down the cobbled pathway in the direction that Gul Mohammed had come from a few minutes earlier.

At Sainyer Darwaza, beneath the hanging roots of the ancient peepul tree, a small dishevelled group of rebel soldiers waited, some still wearing their regimental jackets and insignias. A large bearded man, around whom the group were gathered, dismounted and saluted as he saw the queen. Lakshmibai was relieved to see the subtle sign of respect that he had accorded to her. Perhaps negotiating with these men would be easier than anticipated. She returned his courteous salutation of adaab as she pulled in her reins and halted a few feet away from him.

'Risaldar Khan?' she asked.

He nodded and at first Lakshmibai could not be too sure of whether it was respect that she could see in his eyes as he fixed her with an iron gaze.

'You understand, Risaldar Khan that Jhansi has no quarrel with you,' she said slowly. The man nodded and Lakshmibai felt a silence falling over the rest of the group as they all waited for her next words.

'You may have heard of our own troubles with British policies…the annexation of Jhansi?' she asked and Risaldar Khan nodded again.

'Well, it should be no surprise to you then if I say that we have little support for the British as they now face this uprising.' She had the group's full attention now and she spoke clearly, raising her voice slightly, 'I would go so far as to say that I sympathize with your efforts to oust such indifferent masters.'

She paused for a moment to allow her words to permeate, watching the bearded giant take her words in, nodding his head once. He was silent, waiting for her to finish speaking. After a few seconds, she said with calm deliberation, 'But, in the same way, I have never had any quarrel with the local British garrisons, particularly their women and children. A few days ago, they had come to me, worried about events in the countryside. I offered them shelter on the grounds of humanity. But it was never my intention to keep them forever. We are not their supporters and the plan was for them to leave today and be taken into Datia's care. My only responsibility left to them is to ensure that they leave Jhansi safely and, in this, I ask your assistance.'

There was another lengthy pause as Lakshmibai waited for the risaldar's response. She watched his face as he chewed contemplatively on his lip. His green eyes looked compassionate, she thought, for all his great bulk and impressive beard. After a few seconds, she heard him say in a rasping voice, 'If there are any British officers among them, they should be handed over. Our business is with them.'

An image of the Skenes huddled together flashed into Lakshmibai's mind and, even though she could sense Gul Mohammed shifting uneasily in his saddle next to her, she said calmly, 'There are just two British officers left, Risaldar Khan. The women need those two men to keep them safe on their journey to Datia. Rebels far less reasonable than your men will not spare such a helpless group on the high road, you know that as I do. Let them reach Datia safely and I will request the English officers to give themselves up after that. I give you my word and I am sure they will give me theirs.'

Risaldar Khan gave her a long look that seemed to encompass a sudden deference. Perhaps it was because she had spoken up so boldly but he merely bowed his head briefly before saying quietly, 'The British are free to leave Jhansi, Rani-sahiba. We have no quarrel with women and children. I will speak to Datia once they are there to see what his intentions are and will then take the English officers as captives. I give you my assurance that my soldiers will not harm them on their way there.'

Deeply relieved, Lakshmibai inclined her head at the risaldar to indicate her gratitude and watched while he bowed deeply to her. He too must be a husband and a father, she thought, not needing to be reminded of that most basic code of honour, even among warring men.

'Jhansi will always remain grateful to you, Risaldar Khan,' she said. 'I will ask my soldiers to prepare some food and a place for you to rest tonight. Tomorrow, once the British have left, it is my prayer that your men too will agree to leave Jhansi in peace. We do not have the wealth and riches of Gwalior and our other neighbours to be able to give you anything more than our prayers that you succeed in your mission.'

With that, she bowed once more before turning her horse around to ride slowly back to her palace, conscious of many pairs of eyes watching her depart.

An hour later, Lakshmibai took up position on the ramparts above Shahar Darwaza of the fort to oversee the evacuation of the British. She stood on a platform above the old, disused baradari to get a better view as the group emerged from the building that had been housing them. Some of the women—she suddenly recognized Belinda Royle—were carrying Bibles, their pockets and bags bulging with the jewellery they were probably too frightened to wear or display overtly. They were accompanied by a handful of the palace guards who were helping to carry their belongings. Lakshmibai guessed these were prized possessions from the homes they had left as she saw photographs and paintings and pieces of silver. She had given instructions for the operation to be conducted as quickly as possible and for the younger children to be carried in the arms of the adults. From where she stood, she could see the cluster, including the Skene children, hurrying down towards the Shahar Darwaza in the east and was relieved to note that her instructions were being scrupulously carried out. As the padre's habit and women's dresses billowed in the summer evening breeze, one of the Carshore children waved a pudgy hand over his mother's shoulder at the guards watching from the ramparts. Jhokan Bagh beyond the eastern gate, where Datia's carriages waited, would be a mere five-minute walk away if they continued to go so swiftly.

Captain Skene was leading the party, holding a white handkerchief aloft and dispossessed of all weaponry, as promised to Risaldar Khan. Bringing up the rear was the younger Mutlow man, Sister Agnes and Captain Dunlop, the only other English officer who had survived the morning's skirmish outside the city gates.

Lakshmibai breathed a sigh of relief as she saw Dunlop leave the small arched gateway, herding a couple of children from the orphanage ahead of him. The rebels had got what they wanted, there were no more Christians left inside Jhansi Fort.

But, as Lakshmibai turned away, a deafening volley of gunfire rang out. Unmistakably from the direction of Jhokan Bagh. There were bloodcurdling screams and a flock of crows burst upwards, flapping and cawing frantically, before dispersing into the evening air. Over the ramparts, only the tops of orange grapeshot flashes could be seen, already masked by rapidly spreading smoke. The firing continued, its source masked by the shrines and trees. It was impossible to tell from the noise how many people were involved or who they were. Shocked beyond comprehension, Lakshmibai was barely able to register that rebels hidden in Jhokan Bagh were shooting at the English party. She strained to see what was happening but a billowing black cloud of smoke was curtaining off the events from her view.

Running along the ramparts with the smouldering dusk closing in on her, threatening to choke her, Lakshmibai felt almost as though she had been struck a hard wrenching blow in her stomach as Jhokan Bagh came into view. Straining to see through the grey veils of thinning smoke, the echo of gunfire still ringing in her ears, the first body she spotted was that of Dunlop, then the Mutlow boy, both of them lying sprawled face down, their clothes covered in blood. Further along were other bodies, male and female and some unbearably small…it could not be, Lakshmibai thought frantically…they could never have…why kill small children? Bodies littered the ground and were only slowly becoming recognizable as the smoke cleared. The Carshore children and their pretty blonde mother, the old Mutlow man and his son, Belinda Royle, even dear old Sister Agnes, still surrounded by a small group of children clutching at her habit and her hands…and there, beyond them all, the Skenes, dead, fallen as a loving family ought to fall. The Captain still hopefully holding his white handkerchief, his quiet and serious wife by his side till the end and their children—the little girls that Damodar sometime played with—their tiny bodies were flung on the ground like dolls carelessly discarded after play…

Lakshmibai heard a scream as she looked out at the massacred bodies strewn on the distant ground. The temples were shrouded in silence as though in homage to the dead, crows wheeling soundlessly overhead against the darkening sky. Still she could hear that bestial desperate wailing, realizing with sudden terror that the voice was her own, emerging involuntarily from her gullet as though it had somehow got separated from the rest of her body.

She turned to run downstairs from the ramparts, desperate to see if anyone may have survived, but felt herself being held by her shoulders. Looking back, she saw through her tears that it was Moropant. 'Stay back, beti,' he implored gruffly, putting his arm tightly around her, 'it is too late to help them now.'

Lakshmibai fell gratefully into his arms to weep as though she were a child again but, as he rocked her, she recalled that he had been one of those who had insisted she make those poor women and children leave the safety of Jhansi Fort. He was to blame, then. Her own father...who had taught her the very first lessons she had learnt in honour and kindness. How could such a day have come, she thought, still weeping with her head on Moropant's chest, when even a loving father's advice could turn so treacherous, so dishonourable.

Deep into the night, Lakshmibai stood in her bath chambers, the pallav of her sari getting soaked as she threw another lota of water over her burning face. A distraught Sundar was trying desperately to get her back to her room but Lakshmibai refused to move, holding trembling palms over her fevered brow and eyes. Anything, *anything* to wash away the sight of the Skenes and Sister Agnes at Jhokan Bagh, their bodies lying dead on the cracked summer earth. Still, hot tears rolled unstoppably down her face, sore from the constant washing and the wiping of her punishing hands. Finally, in a daze, she allowed herself to be led back to her bedchamber and undressed, hardly aware of her maids flitting around her with silent concern.

As Sundar draped her in a dry set of clothes and proceeded to gently untangle her hair, Lakshmibai looked blankly at herself in the mirror. A new and frightening thought was piercing her consciousness. Would it not fall upon her now to write letters to Calcutta and to London, telling them about the massacre and explaining how it had taken place within her fort? Normally, in the event of mishaps involving the British, it was someone from their camp who would perform such tasks. Someone like Robert Ellis. But, with the Jhokan Bagh massacre, every last Englishman in Jhansi had perished and the task of informing the British government was hers. She was not even sure whom to contact in the first instance and could only think of Hamilton, the commissioner for Central India. But what if he too was caught up in disturbances further north? Closing her eyes and drawing in a shaky, exhausted breath, Lakshmibai told herself that a letter would have to be written nonetheless. She could only hope that Hamilton would believe her version of events...perhaps he had already heard from Captain Skene of how sincerely she had tried to help them in these past few days. Surely he would understand if she explained her predicament of being caught between angry mutineers, her panicking people and the increasingly desperate requests for help that she had received from Skene and Gordon. More than anything else, she needed to focus her mind on the pragmatic and the necessary. Tasks that would help to keep her mind away from reliving every ghastly minute of this terrible day.

She looked at her maid's face in the mirror. 'Sundar, have the bodies of the English been taken away to be cared for?' Sundar nodded silently and Lakshmibai continued, 'And arrangements made for a Christian burial?'

The maid continued massaging her head, now bending over Lakshmibai to whisper, 'Shhh...' softly into her ear. All this had already been repeated many times over in the past couple of hours but Lakshmibai could not seem to stop traversing the same tortured territory.

'Please summon the court writer to write a letter,' she said, abruptly pushing Sundar's hands away.

Sundar finally spoke, pleading, 'Rani-sahiba, letters can wait, can't they? So much shock suffered...you must rest now. I beg you, let it wait for tomorrow...'

'No, no, it cannot wait. It must be done tonight.'

As Sundar reluctantly put the bottle of hair oil down, Lakshmibai jumped up to pace up and down, wringing her hands, rehearsing the words she would need to put in the letter to Hamilton. Anything, anything to keep her mind from darting back to that fearsome sight. Why did her stupid thoughts persist in returning to that scene, she wondered, like a helpless animal circling and sniffing uncomprehendingly around the carcass of a mate long dead.

She looked around her room—it was all the same as before but she knew everything was transient now. The mellow ochre light of the oil lamp flickering in its niche, those paintings gleaming on the wall, the stars speckling her window—even the tiniest, most ordinary joys of life were now lining up to mock her, taunting her with the possibility that she would soon lose even these. The entire British community in Jhansi had been put to death in her fort, with no one to stand surety of her innocence. What hope did she have of claiming faith from those who already hated her? Even Robert Ellis had left her with revulsion filling his heart. How low would his opinion of her be now?

When Ellis heard of the massacre in Jhansi's fort, he felt the world around him simply stop. For a few moments he had not been able to hear the busy sounds of workaday London—the rustle of papers and scratching of quill pens from the desks around him, the jingling of buggies and horses, the cries of newspaper sellers on the road outside. All the comforting sounds of life sank into some shocked part of his mind that momentarily deafened him to everything else but the blame that he knew would fall on Lakshmibai. Wracked instantly with guilt, he told himself that the massacre would never have happened had he still been at Jhansi. It would surely only have been a matter of time before which he could have earned Lakshmibai's trust again and revived their friendship. Why had he not thought of giving it more time, more heed, more strength of conviction? Why had he so unthinkingly slipped out of her life at a time when she, and Jhansi, most needed him?

On his way back to his rooms that evening, he saw a small chapel around the corner from the thronging Strand. Its glowing stained-glass windows seemed to beckon him away from the pressing crowds. He stepped within and saw the lit candles melting at the altar, gently illuminating the face of a Madonna gazing serenely down at him. Without even thinking, he found himself sinking to his knees. Half-forgotten words that had long since come to mean nothing were flooding unstoppably from his mouth. He had not been a man of prayer for so long, he felt foolish and reprehensible to even be in such a place. But he prayed. He prayed, as he had never done before, that Lakshmibai would somehow be spared the wrath and the vengeance of his people.

๛ 37 ๛

Kanpur was the next place to ignite that same week. Nana was at his front door, watching the gold of an early June dawn spill over the eastern skies of Bithur, when he saw Azimullah's carriage pull up on the road outside. As though unwilling to wait for the guards to open the gates, the man had disembarked his carriage and was now running down the drive. He was shouting and waving his arms but Nana could not discern Azimullah's words until he had neared him, gasping with one hand on his chest.

'The time has come, Nanasahib, all that we have waited these years for! The Kanpur troops have risen!'

He was interrupted as Tantia came rushing out from the mansion, having heard Azimullah's cries. The pair waited for Azimullah to catch his breath before he told them the news. 'Some of our sowars of the 2nd Cavalry in Kanpur were the first to desert the garrison. There is talk of storming the British treasury and armoury but now they are amassing on the Grand Trunk Road just outside Kanpur and will soon march here to Bithur. We must have our plans ready. We must be in charge of the situation before they get here as it is to us they will look for leadership.'

'Are they planning to join the Meerut mutineers on the road to Delhi?' Nana asked, his calm visage showing no sign of the tumult he could feel in his chest.

'I think that may be the plan at the moment. But we can alter the direction of the winds in our favour. Why should we blindly follow an old defunct Mughal emperor in Delhi who has never had a realm, one who has absolutely no appetite to rule? Here is your chance to finally reclaim your stolen title, Nanasahib.'

Nana nodded, putting his arm on his friend's shoulders. 'You are right, Azimullah. Justice is throwing the Peshwas' birthright back into our hands. Would it not be mere foolishness to turn such a glorious chance away? When the men arrive at the gates, I will personally lead the contingent to the British camp.'

Later in the day, Nanasahib saw Azimullah standing almost statue-like on the upper balcony of the house despite the fierce June sun. The man could well afford to take some rest now, having brought the rebellion thus far, but still he looked ready to spring like a wounded tiger. It was as if his body had grown into a permanent state of tautness in all these months of wary, cautious watching and waiting.

Nanasahib turned his brown bay horse around. His guards were gathering excitedly at the gates, making ready to ride out to where Tantia and the troops awaited them near the cantonment. It was hard to believe that in a few minutes he, Nana Peshwa-sahib, would be leading the entire rebel army of the Kanpur garrisons towards General Wheeler's encampment. The thought made him shiver suddenly in the midday heat. It was either exhilaration or apprehension, he could not tell which. But first he had to bid farewell to the womenfolk of the household. They had been waiting for over an hour on the far side of the garden, a small colourful group, holding brass trays full of the religious paraphernalia required to see men off to battle.

As he rode in their direction, his eyes lingered for a moment on little Mainabai, his favourite child, looking so pretty today, a twist of jasmines holding a shiny braid of hair at her neck. All his struggles would be worth it if he could give her the princess's life she deserved and that was her right. He leaned down so that she could mark his forehead with a dab of kumkum, words failing him as she wiped away a quick tear with the back of her free hand. He held her crumpling chin for a few minutes before patting her cheek silently and straightening up again.

The gulmohar trees rustled softly as he turned his horse around, remembering his final adieu before leaving the gates. Azimullah still stood on the balcony, imagining he was unseen, and Nana touched his hand briefly to the jewel in the middle of his turban in salute. There was no telling if Azimullah could actually see him as the sunlight would have been shining straight into his eyes but it was he who deserved congratulation more than anyone else for this turn in all their fortunes.

Nana felt filled with renewed gratitude for the years of quiet service Azimullah had put in, not just here in Kanpur, but in all the stations scattered all across the central plains. Even when the case had been lost in both the Calcutta and London appeals, this dedicated supporter had never once given up hope, only adjusted his methods. For months he had been busy recruiting spies, operating an elaborate undercover system that had infiltrated the East India Company garrisons all across the land. He had also stayed in touch with his friends in Turkey and Russia but, in the past few weeks, his energies had focussed on the Kanpur garrisons and this day brought the fruits of that endeavour.

Nana took his place at the head of the contingent. The elation among his men was palpable. Of course, there had been a few moments of doubt in the past weeks. Major-General Wheeler, the man they marched to meet today, had not been the easiest adversary to be pitted against. An experienced Company man, able to speak Hindi and Urdu as fluently as any of his sipahis and married to a woman who was herself half-Indian, Wheeler had been good to his men from all accounts and, consequently, had more of their support than was customary amongst regiments in these times. He had, in fact, been so sure of his own position that, just last week, he had sent assistance to the Lucknow Residency, forty miles away, from where increasingly frantic messages had been coming from Sir Henry Lawrence to help shore up his arms and supplies. Fortunately, Azimullah had been able to keep his ear close to the ground and had carefully unearthed people with enough resentment towards the British to be recruited to their mission. They had been invaluable in slowly whittling away at the confidence that Wheeler had built up in Kanpur over the years.

This was no time for doubt, though. Their march had started among the clamour of drums and Nana tried to look suitably roused as some of the men at the head of the group took up loud martial chants. Tantia would be waiting with the rebel sepoys at a forest on the edge of Kanpur city and so far they were keeping excellent time. It was Tantia's excitement that had been the most difficult to contain these past few days, Nana recalled, as though everything the fellow lived for had finally come to fruition! He had almost had to be physically held back, unable to contain his fury the day they had heard that General Wheeler was planning to move all the European civilians living in Kanpur to his barracks. That had been in early May and even Azimullah seemed taken by surprise by that piece of news.

'Perhaps Wheeler is being advised by Lawrence in Lucknow,' Azimullah had conjectured, clearly unhappy at not having foreseen the move. 'Apparently Wheeler has stocked up on medicine and food supplies and is now persuading the Europeans at the civil lines that they will be safer leaving their businesses and homes to move to the barracks. I am sure his intentions are to use them as a shield in case of attack.'

Unusually, it was Nana who soothed Azimullah on this occasion. 'He is not likely to have heard of our plans, Azimullah, we have been so careful. No, this is just Wheeler bumbling through a difficult situation again. We will think of something, don't worry.'

Tantia was, as usual, more optimistic than both of them. 'Those barracks are inadequate, even for soldiers, leave alone women and children. Just two solid buildings, surrounded by a collection of outhouses and sitting on an open plain. They will not stand a chance in a siege.'

Nana had been secretly relieved to see that, by the end of May, many Europeans had already left Kanpur in panic, hiring boats and carriages to take them and sometimes their entire household effects down river to Allahabad. Others had just seemed to vanish, going into hiding somewhere in the bowels of the grimy city. But he had heard, with a faint twinge of admiration, that Wheeler had completed his task of evacuating the remaining European residents to the barracks by the end of the month, recognizing the irony of perhaps having helped him along to a certain extent. The posters and pamphlets had clearly done their job well, causing all manner of rumour and intrigue to fly around the streets and bazaars of Kanpur, swelling the dread and uncertainty that would have helped convince the more reluctant to move to the army camp.

It was one of Azimullah's agents in the 2nd Cavalry who had

brought news of more than a thousand people arriving at the barracks one May morning, at least a third of whom were women and children. Many had brought their servants with them, the agent had said, Hindustani maids and ayahs, frightened and confused by their place in the seething confusion, clinging to their small charges, as though keen to emphasize their role in the British camp. Male servants and orderlies had been taken too, to keep their masters in the comfort they were so used to.

Marching towards that camp now Nana felt assailed by a moment's guilt. Along with blameless women and children, those Indian lives too would be lost if Wheeler refused to cooperate and war became necessary. There was not much comfort to be had in Azimullah's grim reminder late last night. 'Those Indians,' he had said firmly, 'those Indians who serve the British are no less dispensable than the British themselves.'

Nana had remained silent, thinking it an inopportune moment to argue. Now he took a deep breath as his men broke out into loud cheers when they rounded a corner and their allies came into view; a huge gathering of rebel sipahis, some still wearing their British uniforms, Tantia at their head. Beyond them in the distance, shrouded in the Kanpur dust and rising up beyond the racetrack on a small hillock, was Wheeler's encampment.

Nana and his men hid in the outlying forest till nightfall, plotting their strategy and meeting their co-conspirators in the 2nd Cavalry. At midnight, as planned, sowars broke into the Kanpur treasury and jail before making for the garrison magazine. Once armed, they stole towards General Wheeler's entrenchment in the darkness, meeting Nanasahib's troops before silently surrounding the British camp on all sides. After last-minute negotiations, they had been joined by the sipahis of the 1st and 56th Regiments too. Only the 53rd still stood by Wheeler, although there was no knowing for how long that would be.

As Nanasahib gave the order for the firing to commence, the British camp—at first in a state of shock—soon gained ground, the whizzing of grape shot and musket fire returning defiantly back to the rebel forces. Wheeler had, fortunately, a few nine-pounder guns at his disposal but he was very vulnerable on hillock, with the enemy forces moving far more easily on the surrounding plains.

Even on the first day, it was clear that Wheeler had one grave problem that would be his undoing. The only water supply available to his camp lay in a single well just off the embankment, pitifully exposed to enemy fire. Seeing this, the enemy placed their guns directly aimed at the well and, in just one morning, three British soldiers and four lascars had been killed while trying to fetch water. It was the height of summer, and with all those women and children needing sustenance in the camp, General Wheeler's Achilles' heel had been easily located.

Still Wheeler held on, hoping for relief from Allahabad or Sind, without any idea of what was going on in all those places. It was only found out much later that Azimullah's well-trained agents were intercepting most of the outgoing messages from Kanpur. Only the messages carried by Gangaprasad, Wheeler's loyal old servant, continued to reach Lucknow, with increasingly frantic calls for help. But they were to remain unanswered too for, by this time, Lucknow had its own mutiny and siege to contend with.

After three weeks of siege, Nana could see that Wheeler's camp had suffered grievous casualties, piles of bodies festering on the southern side of the entrenchment growing into a small hillock. With no proper medical help to treat either the injuries or the spread of cholera and dysentery, conditions in the camp were, from all reports, a veritable hell on earth. But before Nana could send Wheeler an offer to negotiate, news arrived from one of his spies that Wheeler's own son had been decapitated and killed by a stray shot. The young spy from the 53rd trembled with religious fervour as he told Nanasahib that, like Drona in the great Mahabharata, old General Wheeler had been instantly robbed of his last ounce of spirit on realizing that his own son had died in the battle of his making.

Nana knew that surrender was imminent. As rejoicing broke out in the camp, he convened council with Tantia and some of the senior NCOs in his tent. 'Offer the British safe passage to Allahabad,' he said, 'Wheeler will take that under these circumstances.'

Tantia was incredulous, 'Safe passage, Nana? We have our chance to get rid of them once and for all and you want to offer them escape…'

Nanasahib cut in sharply, 'Our motive was never to kill them all off, Tantia, why do you forget that. All we want is for Wheeler and his people to leave Kanpur for good so that we can reclaim the Peshwa's kingdom for ourselves once again. That is all.'

While a storm of muttering broke out among the assembled group, a senior havildar-major, who had been silent through the altercation, raised his head. Standing up and bowing respectfully in Nanasahib's direction, he said, 'Nana Peshwa-sahib is right. As the new ruler, he should not appear tyrannical with the unnecessary shedding of blood. The Peshwas have always been renowned for their honour and may that tradition long continue.'

Nanasahib, grateful for the support, returned the man's obeisance before saying, 'All we want is that the British should leave the treasury untouched and leave Kanpur to us. Apart from that, we have no quarrel with them. They will not refuse our offer as everyone knows that the monsoons will be upon us all in a few days' time. Conditions in that camp must be unbearable already. We should let them go if we have any humanity at all within us.'

General Wheeler gave guarded consent to be evacuated, his conditions being that the survivors be provided with transport to carry the sick and the injured down to the ghats and for boats to be provided that would take the entire party downriver to Allahabad all at once.

Nanasahib agreed to all the conditions and, at the appointed hour on a churning hot summer day, a ragtag bunch of bedraggled survivors limped silently out of Wheeler's camp. They were dressed in torn clothes, some were barefoot and, without exception, they were all living skeletons. One or two of the older women had remembered to carry tattered parasols, as much to shield themselves from the fierceness of the sun's rays as the defiant stares of the rebel sipahis gathered at the gates. Nanasahib issued instructions to Tantia to accompany the group down to the waterside, electing to stay behind with the rest of the troops in order to assess their own casualties and plan the next part of the campaign.

Tantia rounded up the British party, passing on Nanasahib's orders for the weak and the injured to be loaded onto buggies and palanquins while the rest of the party would walk. As the weary procession wended its way across the plain and entered the town, the streets of Kanpur soon grew thickly lined with curious and occasionally jeering people who had turned up to witness the unlikely spectacle of sahibs and memsahibs, until so recently the town's uncrowned kings and queens, now robbed so suddenly of their status. On the way, a soft sobbing broke out among some of the Englishwomen as they passed their old houses, empty shells of the lives they once had, lying burnt and looted. But Tantia's sipahis herded them along, hurrying to get them to Satichaura Ghat on the Ganga before it grew dark.

As the group turned a corner, they saw the ghat, a tree-fringed landing at the mouth of a small ravine. Glimpses of smiles appeared on some of the English faces as a row of barges, tethered and floating serenely on the river, came into view. A couple of the children broke away from their mothers' grasps to run down to the river's edge and splash in the water, the terrors of the past few weeks suddenly forgotten.

The party was greeted at the riverbank by Azimullah who had received Nanasahib's orders to organize boats and have them equipped with sacks of grain and other essentials. As the sipahis began loading the boats with the possessions of the British, General Wheeler shouted orders to his officers to get the women and children onto the boats first, followed by the civilian men and then the soldiers. There was chaos, as women's skirts and shoes got stuck in the squelching mud and children had to be lifted clear onto the decks of the barges but, in a matter of minutes, the British were on their vessels.

General Wheeler, the last man left on shore, began wading towards his boat when a horrible realization dawned on him. He had seen that none of the vessels had their boatmen any more. They had been there a mere minute ago but quite suddenly they had vanished into the dusk. Wheeler whipped his head around but it must have been becoming terrifyingly clear to him now. The rebel sipahis had disappeared too, melting into the edges of the trees lining the darkening ravine.

He looked up, desperately searching Tantia's and Azimullah's faces as they watched from their horses, the expression on his face at first comprehending and then flabbergasted. Containers bearing burning coals were being rushed down to the shore by hundreds of sipahis. They were heaping them onto the reed roofs of the barges. One of the boats had already caught light and the screams of people jostling and trying to throw themselves off were filling the air. A few managed to jump into the water to save themselves, swimming to an unchained boat. There was musket fire too—flashes from behind the trees—and sipahis wielding large swords were charging down towards the people struggling in the water. One of the sipahis plunged a sword deep into General Wheeler's chest and he fell into the muddy water that closed over him instantly. As the firing continued around Wheeler's half-submerged corpse, the river water turned from brown to foaming red. Hundreds of bloodied bodies littered the river, some floating ghoulishly to the surface, their faces turned upwards as though in supplication to the evening sky.

Nanasahib, riding up to the scene half an hour later, could not believe his eyes. Even from a distance he could see that things had not gone to plan. Smoke was rising over the ghats and a terrible smell of burning flesh was heavy in the air. He pulled fiercely on the reins of his horse as he reached the riverbank. Where were all the Europeans?

Where was Wheeler? All those bodies floating in red water...only a group of European women and children were visible, a bedraggled and terrified huddle standing in knee-high water. One of the women started to scream obscenities as soon as she saw him and, as Nanasahib saw a sipahi leap towards her brandishing his sword to silence her, he shouted as loudly as he could. It took a while for his voice to permeate the melee.

'Stop! No more killing,' he roared. 'Where is Tantia? Where is Azimullah? What is all this? You had your orders!'

Emerging from the deepening dusk, Tantia looked sulkily in Nanasahib's direction, not meeting his eye and at first not saying anything. But, when Nanasahib bellowed at him again, demanding an answer, he muttered sullenly, 'The sipahis...their anger could not be contained...'

Nanasahib wheeled around, looking for Azimullah. Surely Azimullah would be astute enough to know how costly such an incident would prove. He could only just discern the calm visage of his trusted emissary in the gathering darkness and, as always, felt reassured by it.

'What is done, is done, Nanasahib,' Azimullah soothed. 'Now we have to work quickly to cover this up. And move on.'

Nanasahib, still confused, turned to the waiting sepoys, 'Take the women and the children away from this place...round them up quickly. How could you have gone so mad? You had been given clear instructions...'

Spotting General Wheeler's wife and young daughter amongst the women being rounded up, Nanasahib rode across to where they stood. Mrs Wheeler's hair was tangled and wild, her blank eyes showing her shock.

'This should not have happened,' he tried to say but the words dried up in his throat. She would never believe him anyway. As he looked at her wounded figure with shame apparent on his face, she drew her mouth together and spat in his direction, her spittle falling into the water before him. Pretending that he had not seen the insult, he turned his horse around, shouting at the sipahis again in frustration, cursing them roundly.

'They are our enemies, not our friends,' a sipahi shouted back from the darkness.

'Do we save our lives or theirs?' someone else called out angrily.

'They started shooting first,' a third voice said.

'Enough said. Just take these women somewhere safe,' Nanasahib spoke gruffly. There was no point trying to reason with men so full of rage.

'Bibighar, take them to the Bibighar, that is not far,' Tantia shouted to the sipahis.

As the women were duly rounded up and instructed to walk, Nanasahib said, 'Please, let us at least give them palkis and dolies to ride in, Tantia, Azimullah, some of them are wounded.'

Azimullah nodded at Tantia who jumped off his horse to call for the palanquins that had brought the wounded from their camp and ordered the women to board them. Although they did not mask the hatred on their faces, they waited silently for the doli-bearers to lower the carts before climbing in without demur. As they started to depart the riverbanks, Nanasahib found it odd that there was no wailing or keening from these women for the men they had just lost and whose mutilated bodies they were now leaving behind in the frothing red river. Was it fear or shock or some inexplicable hardness of spirit that enabled them to put such a brave face on things? Would he ever understand these strange pale-faced women, so delicate of feature and yet so unmoved and proudly tight-lipped?

They arrived at the Bibighar, an elegant old haveli built by a long-dead Englishman for his Mughal mistress, and filed silently into its gates. A leafy tree stood in the centre of the front yard, throwing moonlit shadows over the house. The rooms that lined the central courtyard were large and spacious but the women showed no emotion, except for some muted sobbing, as they were shepherded in and the front and back doors of the house were padlocked. The bars on the window, put in for safety by a solicitous English lover, would prevent them from escaping.

Nanasahib informed them that food and water would be sent, as also a doctor to treat their wounds. He promised too that women from his household, his own wife and daughters, would arrive soon to ensure their further comfort. But the Englishwomen looked at him silently with abhorrence filling their faces. Nothing he said would ever convince them that he was only locking them up for their own safety. He had been unwittingly made an accomplice in today's murders, ensuring that there would be no turning back.

☙ 38 ❧

Nanasahib emerged onto the veranda of his palace in Bithur to drop a few coins into the hand of his waiting scout. The man had to be paid, even though it was terrible news he had brought—a general called

Henry Havelock had set out from Allahabad just a few days ago. He was leading an army of one thousand British soldiers and two thousand of the best Sikh warriors and they were headed straight for Kanpur. Nana knew well that, after the massacre of the British at Satichaura Ghat, mercy was not to be expected but every stray bit of news of the spreading uprising had lent hope, however foolish, that he may actually be spared a reprisal.

He gazed at the empty, waiting horizon, feeling a frisson of fear. Perhaps he ought to summon Azimullah, but the man was a strategist rather than a warrior and had always said he would not be able to help much in times of actual warfare. Tantia, however, already excited at the possibility of combat, was pacing up and down the far end of the corridor, loudly drawing up all sorts of plans with the other men. Nana walked towards them with leaden steps. Although it both irritated and wearied him that Tantia remained so zealous, so blindly optimistic, he could not deny that there was a part of him that was grateful for the dilution of his own dark dread. It was time, perhaps, to contact Lakshmibai for help.

Three days later, on a searing July morning and amidst the pounding of drums and guns, Nanasahib's army met General Havelock's on a crescent-shaped field just outside Kanpur. As the battle quickly degenerated into hand-to-hand fighting, swords and shields clashing like a thousand cymbals, it was soon clear to all that Havelock's forces had swiftly gained the upper hand. With increasing desperation, Nana sensed that his forces were melting into the countryside but, in the terrible mayhem enveloping him, he did not see a small group of his men break away and head off into the nearby forest.

As Nanasahib fled the battlefield, taking his forces towards the safety of the fortress at Kalpi, seven horsemen rode in haste back to Kanpur. They did not need to be told that the most severe retribution already awaited them because of Satichaura and, in the short time they had, they were intent on wiping out as many of the English as possible.

They arrived at the gates of Bibighar, confident that the female members of Nanasahib's family who had been put in charge of the captured Englishwomen would be unable to stand in their way. It was time to deliver the most painful blow that the British could possibly receive.

On hearing bloodthirsty cries at the Bibighar gates, Nanasahib's wife and daughter ran out of the haveli. They knew instantly, from the men's murderous cries, why they had come and tried desperately to keep them out, pleading for mercy, threatening to throw themselves out of an upper window if even one of the English prisoners was put to death. But the killers were unstoppable, pushing past the weeping women before entering the compound.

The hostages cowered inside the haveli, aware that something terrible was about to unleash itself on them. As the doors burst open, they clung to each other, hiding their children inside their petticoats. Momentarily, they saw hope as the two sepoys sent inside to perform the deed balked visibly at the sight of their tears and their terror, laying their guns down at the door before stepping back, shaking their heads. But, in less than fifteen minutes, butchers from the town were summoned and persuaded to take on the task for the right price.

It took four butchers, armed with carving knives accustomed to the tougher flesh of animals, just a matter of hours to complete. Mainabai and her mother fell before their blades, begging for their lives to be taken first, but the screams of the British women and children being chased around the compound gradually spluttered and subsided as, one by one, they were caught and slaughtered. When the final screams were silenced, the only wailing left was that of Nanasahib's women while the murderers leapt on their horses and rode away.

Ellis heard the appalling news alongside the others in his office days later. He had never before seen such anger unleashed at India House. Even normally peaceable men cried for blood and revenge, some sat at their desks and wept. The details had been received from Brigadier-General Neill's camp. After the battle with Nanasahib, General Havelock had moved quickly onto Lucknow to assist the besieged Residency there, leaving Neill to evacuate the Bibighar women along with a small group of soldiers. They had ridden in haste, hoping desperately to find the hostages still alive. But, even as the troops approached from a distance, the resounding silence at the Bibighar and its wide-open swinging gates told them that it was too late for a rescue. They neared it, expecting the worst, but nothing could have prepared them for the sight that awaited them. It was through an uncomprehending blur that General Neill reported seeing the first bits of torn petticoat lace, broken stays and crushed bonnets, remnants of dresses, scattered fragments of makeshift toys and clumps of hair, sticky with blood, clotted to the earth...

As horrified realization coalesced, Neill saw that what he had at first mistaken for pieces of white wood were chopped and scattered disembodied limbs, some lying in pools of crimson blood. And blood was everywhere, spattered and smeared on the walls with a few piteous red handprints visible among the splodges...the floors were thick and slimy with it...the ground outside soaked muddy-red...even the tree growing in the central courtyard looked, he said, as though it was growing out of a pool of blood, sucking it up from the earth before dripping it down again from sodden branches and leaves.

Neill saw one of his soldiers walk slowly up to the tree and touch its blackened bark in disbelief before leaning over and retching at its foot. Even from where he stood, he could see that someone, a child, had been picked up and dashed against the trunk. Bits of bloodied brain matter and hair, shards of bone, even a single staring eyeball remained glued to its coarse, sticky bark, testament to the horrors that those poor women and children had undergone before they had died the most pitiless of deaths.

The well at the back of the house was overflowing with more body parts. Marks were visible on the dusty ground where bodies had been dragged and it was impossible to tell if those poor women had been alive or dead as they were pushed into the well. The water in the well was not visible at all for the mutilated bodies that had been piled into it...blood and guts filled it to overflowing...some bodies were missing arms, some heads. Through it all, strands of hair were fluttering on the thorny shrubs nearby, as though they may yet contain a breath of life.

It fell on General Neill to avenge the Bibighar massacre in a manner that Kanpur would never forget. For three days and three nights, the city was sacked and its surrounding cornfields beaten to exorcize every last rebel in hiding. As fugitives scuttled out from the fields, like hundreds of fleeing partridges, Neill's orders were for every fiendish native to be killed—man, woman, child, guilty or innocent, it did not matter. Mercy was not deserving where no mercy had been shown. Even tender Mainabai, Nanasahib's fourteen-year-old daughter who had pleaded desperately for the life of the Englishwomen and children at Bibighar, was found later, dead alongside her mother and aunts, bayoneted in her stomach, her hands and feet hacked off.

Nanasahib, riding hard with his men through the Bundelkhand forests in the direction of Kalpi, knew nothing of either the merciless retribution or the travesty that had generated it. But, by the time he was to meet the British forces again in the ravines around Kalpi, another whole year later, it would be with the terrible, aching knowledge that the pitiless deaths of all their womenfolk were still waiting to be avenged by both sides.

Before that, however, British vengeance at Kanpur had to be completed fiercely and swiftly and there were only a few, like Ellis, who quailed to see evil only beget more evil. When a few rebel sepoys and sowars had been caught, Neill commanded that they be brought alive to Bibighar. He did not care to ask if they were the perpetrators of the horrors that had taken place a week before. Somebody had to pay an immediate price and it was with grim pleasure that he ordered the captured men to kneel on the blood-encrusted floors and lick it clean. They licked until the blackened crust had turned to blood again and were ordered to keep licking until the floor was cleansed of blood. If they raised their heads to protest or plead, a whiplash or rifle butt was waiting to return them to their incomplete task. And when the floors were finally cleaned thus, those men were put to death.

For the remaining men who were rounded up in the next few days, there were other punishments waiting. Seeing that it had been the business of greased cartridges that had sparked the mutiny, Neill and his men struck upon a worthy retribution. Hindus were to be sewn alive into the carcasses of cows and Muslims into the skins of pigs to rob them completely of their religions before their bodies were stuffed into the mouths of cannons and blown to bits. There was to be no trace left of their bodies, so that they could be completely denied the funeral rites and cremation ceremonies demanded by their beliefs, for was it not those accursed religious convictions that had caused all this trouble in the first place?

As a general warning, on all the main roads in and out of Kanpur and, in particular, the Grand Trunk Road from Varanasi and Allahabad, mile upon mile of gallows and gibbets were erected, from which hung the bodies of sipahis who had dared to rise up against their masters and there they dangled for days, gradually decomposing under the summer sun, pigs from nearby villages feasting on limbs that swung too close to the ground.

By the time news reached Lakshmibai of the massacres and reprisals at Kanpur, the details were garbled and unclear. All she could tell from a few scribbled hand-delivered notes was that Nana and Tantia were both alive but on the run from the British, and probably headed for a sanctuary at Kalpi.

Her own fate remained unclear. The mass deaths of the British as Jhansi had mutinied had brought control of the land back into her hands but Lakshmibai knew it would not be for long. She needed to find out what Nana's and Tantia's hopes for the future were but, as far as she knew, there was no point in dreaming foolish dreams. She had no doubt that the British would be back to avenge their dead in Jhansi.

Lakshmibai's conjecture was accurate enough. From Dewan Rao Bande's nephew, who worked as a clerk at Government House in Calcutta, there were already reports of scattered British forces being swiftly marshalled. The new Governor-General who had taken over from Dalhousie was throwing every effort into controlling the situation, possessing a skill for organization that Lakshmibai was certain could not be shared by the octogenarian Mughal emperor supposedly leading the other side. Her source informed her that, in order to regain control of all the distant affected areas, telegraphed messages had been sent from Calcutta to the governors of Bombay and Madras to hasten the arrival of the troops due to return from Persia and Rangoon. Sir John Lawrence had been instructed to take complete charge of the Punjab. Determined that Calcutta should appear calm, Governor-General Canning had ordered for Queen Victoria's birthday ball to go ahead as planned, although many invitees had apparently stayed at home, in fear of the native soldiers who would be guarding the event.

By now Lakshmibai knew that uprisings had taken place in almost all the central provinces but she guessed that Canning's most important priority would be to regain control of Delhi and remove the Mughal leadership before it became an effective rallying point for all disgruntled sipahis. It was common knowledge that the old figurehead emperor possessed few martial abilities, but there might be some among his own sons and grandsons who could successfully take over the operations and the British could scarcely afford any more complacency.

News and rumour trickled in over the next few weeks of British units from distant places marching on Delhi. Lakshmibai heard that they were leaving trails of destruction in their wake, exacting punishments on villagers who may have helped the rebels. Entire villages were being burnt and anyone suspected of collaborating with the rebels had their heads shaven, their bodies smeared with pork fat and pork juices spat into their mouths before they were hung. As the British forces marched out of some villages, they were leaving behind trees that had bodies hanging from every branch, as though laden with ghastly rotting fruit.

In her more despondent moments, Lakshmibai could imagine hearing the distant keening of women rising on the late summer winds sweeping into Jhansi. She read in the English papers that Governor-General Canning was pleading for a stop to the brutal reprisals, calling for clemency, but the press merely lambasted him for his misplaced mercy.

The Mughal capital of Delhi was the first place that the British would attempt to regain from the mutineers. Although armies led by the sons and grandsons of the Mughal emperor had put up renewed resistance, the British force finally arrived on the outskirts of Delhi and, in London, Ellis waited for news of the recapture of Red Fort.

He had once seen the pretty British suburbs and cantonment of Sabzimandi and could imagine the garrisons marching past them, seeing all those bungalows that had once housed prosperous European merchants and officers lying destroyed; once private and treasured possessions littering gardens and lawns—broken crockery, discarded clothes and toys, torn bed linen, all the stuff of peaceful domesticity lying exposed and begging to be avenged.

A British camp was purportedly forming on the forested slopes of Delhi Ridge overlooking the Red Fort but it was being whispered disconsolately around India House that, despite being joined by the Corps of Guides, the Gurkhas and Hodson's Horse, they were not having much effect. Not only did early reports indicate that the grand old fort was remaining impregnable, news was that the mutinying forces it had become home to were growing and swelling by the day. From places as far flung as Malwa, Nasirabad, Jullunder and Bareilly, rebel armies were arriving, like triumphant ships pulling into port.

By August, the merciless heat of the summer sun and outbreaks of cholera had combined to take so many British casualties that the slopes of the Ridge had become thick with makeshift graves. Ellis was told that the forces now had no choice but to await the arrival of John Nicholson and his men from Lahore. Nicholson's name was one Ellis was familiar with. Among all the tales that had emerged of the reprisals, Nicholson's were the most horrendous, talked of with pride in the clubs and army establishments of London. The forty mutinous sepoys that Nicholson had caught in his regiment had apparently been lined up in front of a bank of cannons on the vast parade grounds as his Peshawar garrison looked on. One by one, each was led before a cannon in which powder had already been placed without the shot. Hands were tied to the carriage wheels so that the stomach directly covered the muzzle. And, while their colleagues watched, the order to fire was given. After all forty men had been thus dealt with, all that remained on the cannons were some pairs of hands, still tied to the wheels, while blackened heads and other body parts lay scattered all across the stinking parade grounds. Such retribution would surely put paid to all future insurgency, Ellis heard people say, as the sickness grew in his heart.

Through late summer, reports of the assault on Red Fort kept coming and the monsoons brought with it news that, after consistent cannon-fire from the British camp, the walls of the fort had finally started to crumble. Once Kashmiri Gate was breached, it was not long before triumphant British forces easily entered the walled city. Despite meeting stubborn resistance, they had fought their way down to Jama Masjid and the silver bazaar of Chandni Chowk where the Delhi Bank was triumphantly recaptured. It was rumoured that Nicholson had taken a fatal shot in the battle but, by the end of September, Delhi was once again in British hands. No one knew how much was truth and how much conjecture but reports reached London that Delhi's mutineers had been furiously dealt with, until the streets of that elegant old city ran with rivers of rebel blood.

Ellis heard that the Mughal emperor was still alive even though his sons and grandsons had been put to death. He read a triumphant report in the *Times* of how Hodson had tricked them out of hiding and could not help wondering how the frail old Mughal emperor would have felt at seeing the mutiny he clearly wanted no part in finally coming to an end. The papers said that he had been placed under house arrest in his own fort, although no one knew yet what fate would finally be chosen for such a feeble old poet and pigeon-fancier, briefly and unbefittingly commander of a rebel army that had dared rise up against the British.

Amongst such triumphant news, it was the people trapped inside the Residency at Lucknow that captured the attention of all at India House most vividly. They had been under siege for four months when Delhi had been retaken and Ellis wondered if the Meads were safe amongst them. Sir Henry Lawrence, chief commissioner of Awadh, had wisely taken early charge as soon as the events at Meerut earlier in the summer had become known and had cannily made it his first priority to shore up the sixty acres of buildings and gardens that made up the Lucknow Residency, creating a safe haven into which he had ordered all the local Europeans to move. Faced with no other choice,

Sir Henry had recalled all the sepoys who had been disbanded at the first sign of trouble, even recruiting one hundred and seventy native pensioners who had responded to his desperate call for help.

Thus the longest siege of the Mutiny would begin and Ellis could imagine poor terrified Harriet Mead, sleeping alongside other women on reed mats laid out on the floor of the ruined ballroom, listening night after night to the booming of the guns in the city, tinkling and rattling the chandeliers above their head whenever the Residency took a direct hit. He thought of how desperately women like her would regard such an awful event, quite probably completely unable to understand why their happy lives had been transformed so suddenly. It must have been horrible indeed for poor Harriet to comprehend how her husband's loyal sepoys had turned into murderous rebels. Ellis had heard that the fighting in those days had been so fierce that the first Englishmen to be killed had not even been buried properly, their bodies, along with those of their horses, being thrown down the side of an escarpment to be left to feasting vultures and hyenas.

On the sad day in July that Sir Henry was mortally wounded by a Howitzer shell, Begum Hazratmahal had allegedly conducted the coronation of her twelve-year-old son Birjis Qadr to mass exultation in the city of Lucknow. Nawab Wajid Ali Shah, in Calcutta to appeal against Awadh's annexation, had been arrested by the British and imprisoned in Fort William. But no one had bargained for the fight that would be put up by his wife who had stayed behind to rouse the mutinying forces. Ellis, of course, remembered the grim promise she had issued in his presence once, one he had been so quick to dismiss.

Even when Henry Havelock and James Outram arrived at the Residency in September, the siege merely wore on and it took General Campbell's army another two months to finally end it. As the first troops of the 93rd Highlanders entered the gates of the Residency, they later reported being both amused and horrified to be set upon by a group of deliriously happy but filthy and bedraggled waifs. They had never seen Englishwomen in such a state, dressed in tatters, unwashed skeletal arms and shoulders showing unheedingly through gaping holes in their clothes. The luckier ones were wearing dresses made out of the Residency's curtains and tablecloths and Ellis imagined a weeping Harriet Mead among them, her turquoise bracelet, a gift from Begum Hazratmahal of Awadh, still gracing one emaciated wrist.

He met Harriet weeks later, spotting her in the foyer of East India House. She was with her mother and wore the weeds of a new widow, a pale shadow of the girl she had been. Even though Ellis had not

enquired the nature of their business at India House, she made
reference to her widow's pension, dropping her eyes to the ground
when she realized that Ellis had not heard of James Mead's passing.

'Killed at the Residency in the very first week of the siege,' her
mother explained gently, 'at the hands of his own sepoys.'

Ellis was shocked. 'I haven't the words to express my regret...' he
stumbled and halted, seeing Harriet's blue eyes swim with sudden
tears.

He felt dreadfully sorry now for so many things; for having left
the Mead residence on the last occasion he had seen them in such
abrupt fashion, for having not cared enough to find out how they—
his own people—had fared in the weeks leading up to the mutiny, for
all their luckless lives.

But there was not the opportunity to express any of that for
Harriet and her mother were already excusing themselves and taking
his leave. From across the crowded lobby, Ellis watched the two ladies
depart the building before they were swallowed up by the crowds on
Leadenhall Street. He thought, with both anger and sorrow, of how
India continued so relentlessly to infect them all with her pain.

❧ 39 ❧

Jhansi's peace in the weeks following the revolt was uneasy and
fragile, memories of the massacre and news of distant British reprisals
laying bare the hopelessness of being spared.

It was on one such morning, when tranquillity seemed to tremble
uncertainly in the still air, that Sundar and Kashi sat on a durrie in the
rani's chambers, a small pile of jewellery spread out on the white
muslin cloth that stretched between them. As their fingers gently
worked through the tangled mess of gold chains heavy with precious
stones, they kept their voices low.

'What do you think made rani-sahiba fling this jewellery box on
the floor, Sundar? Such a fit of temper. Even in worse times, she has
not been known for anger.'

Sundar pretended not to hear as she wiped a bracelet with a piece
of velvet before placing it carefully in a tiny silk drawstring pouch.
She too had been astonished and then distraught when she had
walked into the rani's room in the morning and seen the queen's
dwindling stock of jewellery so carelessly discarded on the carpet. But
Rani Lakshmibai had merely looked up from her table, as though

nothing were amiss, and given Sundar uncharacteristically curt instructions to sort the jewellery out, adding almost as an afterthought that it was to be kept somewhere safe for Damodar's future wife.

Sundar did not wish to speculate but, as Kashi held up an exquisite multilayered tanmani, trying to untangle its looped pearl strands from jewelled bars dotted with white sapphires and pigeon's-blood rubies, she started to weep silently. She could remember the rani having worn it at her wedding—how young, how hopeful they had all been then. Now, years after the king's death, she was embracing widowhood as though she believed she had been punished for not having done so sooner.

'What can I say, Kashi,' Sundar replied finally, gathering her emotions together, 'ever since the massacre at Jhokan Bagh, our rani-sahiba's behaviour just makes me despair.' She put down a silk pouch to wipe her eyes and blew her nose on her dupatta before continuing, 'I simply cannot persuade rani-sahiba that there is no need to rise before dawn and bathe herself in the Amod Garden tanks—it will be punishingly cold before long. But will she listen?'

'Why don't you just refuse, Sundar? Insist she goes with you to the bathing house where the water can be warmed.'

'Oh the last time I tried, I saw her face tighten so angrily. Even in the half-darkness, it was clear to see. Never has she ever looked at me with such rage, Kashi. She did not say anything but merely gestured for me to continue. I felt so terrible pouring from the copper ewer as she stood there, trembling under the onslaught. She has never liked to bathe in cold water after the summer months have passed.'

'It is as though she wishes to punish herself. All those hours now spent in prayer and meditation. She was never one to waste time on prayers before.'

'And kneeling on those cold steps of the water tank. It is only when she turns to the eastern skies to feel the first rays touch her face that I see a glimpse of pleasure. That dear face, once so ready to break into smiles...'

'Remember how we all used to bathe in the water tank together? The walls echoing with laughter as we played our games...it was not so long ago.'

'But, do you know, Kashi, I now cannot even remember when rani-sahiba last allowed me to weave a flower chain for her hair or decorate her hands and feet with henna. Do you think it possible for one to return to a state of complete happiness once one has suffered pain?'

Kashi sighed as she arranged an enamelled choker in its box. She knew Sundar did not really expect an answer and so took up the conversation again after a few minutes. 'Now, it is as if it pains our rani-sahiba to even sit with us women. Straight to the exercise yard to join the guards in military and equestrian practice after the morning prayers. Three or four hours of exercise every day, is it any wonder she is losing weight?'

'Oh barely will she stop to eat or rest, Kashi. And even that only if I remind her. So frugal are her meals now, we might as well close down the royal kitchens. Military practice, meetings with her ministers and the prince's education—that is all she is concerned about.'

'Perhaps it is only because the administration of Jhansi has once more become her concern in the absence of the British, Sundar,' Kashi offered comfortingly.

'You may be right, Kashi. But I think our rani is now behaving like a widow because she hopes that, by doing so, she can wipe out everything that has happened since the raja's death. That is why, if you ask me, she has also taken to wearing white garments, divesting herself of this jewellery. But what can that achieve, you tell me?'

'Maybe, it is merely rani-sahiba's way of expressing gratitude for Jhansi's future having been delivered back into her hands. Maybe she thinks it is an act of God and believes that her penance and prayers can prevent her losing it again.'

Sundar shook her head sadly. 'No,' she said, stacking the wooden boxes to one side, 'if you ask me, I think our poor rani-sahiba has never been able to get over that terrible sight of the slain English at Jhokan Bagh. It is to rid herself of that awful spectacle that she is exhausting herself thus.'

As they got up from the durrie to start putting the jewellery boxes away, Sundar looked out of a window at Jhansi's surrounding land slumbering peacefully. She would not say it out loud, but she believed that her rani missed Robert Ellis more than perhaps even she knew. And was haunted by the most undeserving guilt for having loved and trusted, in times when love and trust were unreliable things. Sundar would not express such a thought before even Kashi but she had noticed how at times the rani's father too observed his daughter with a sorrowful expression on his face. He too must know that it was the evening hours that were likely to bring back memories of the man in whose company the rani had sometimes sat on the balcony of the courthouse, watching the distant hills glowing like a row of amethysts before they would melt into the dusk. In the early days, Moropant had watched his daughter leave for the rides on which she had met Major Ellis with barely masked apprehension and

Sundar knew that he had wished then for something, anything, to take the foreign interloper far away from the naive love of his daughter. But now that the Englishman had gone and everyone could see unhappy shadows form on their beloved rani's face, under her eyes and in the hollows of her cheeks, Sundar wondered if even Moropant may have prayed for a kinder outcome.

It could not have passed unnoticed that Lakshmibai had never let Robert Ellis's name pass her lips after his departure and, although there were many who had always wanted his presence to be expunged from her life, Sundar wondered if they now felt any of the pleasure they had expected to gain from it.

Sundar also suspected that Lakshmibai's decision to move back to Panch Mahal inside the fort came from the same stubborn desire to erase happier times from her mind—and had only half-believed the rani's explanation that it was safer for her retinue to return to the confines of the fort in these times of rebellion and war. But, without demur, Sundar and Kashi and the rest of the predominantly female staff of the queen had packed their belongings before the winter and moved out of beautiful Ranimahal whose bejewelled walls had echoed so briefly with laughter and love. Moving back to the darker corridors and cloisters of Panch Mahal had been like moving back in time for Sundar, memories of Raja Gangadhar's illness and the dead baby returning to haunt her night after night.

It was in that grieving half-light that Jhansi waited for its own future to be resolved, sometimes with an almost uncaring resignation that the British would be back to avenge their dead. News from Delhi and from Lucknow had trickled in and everyone now knew that the British Army was slowly sweeping back to power, exacting grim reprisal wherever their people had suffered. How could Jhansi hope to escape such systematic vengeance?

Perhaps it was that bleak but certain knowledge that robbed Lakshmibai too of sleep. While the rest of the palace would sink into slumber, as the palace clocks chimed the midnight hour and all the reassuring sounds of daily life slowly faded away, Sundar would see the rani's figure still seated in a lonely pool of light at her writing desk. She sometimes spent hours there, scribbling letters under the fading glow of a flickering lamp, refilling it with oil herself if the hour was too late to summon one of her maids. Although Sundar knew that the act of letter writing would only underline the absence of Robert Ellis, she did not ask the rani to desist, knowing that some comfort may be found in labouring with the words she needed to explain things to other people and to herself.

Sometimes Sundar looked at the names and titles on the envelopes when she was given them in the morning to be delivered...Major Erskine, Commissioner for the Sagar and Narmada Territories...Sir Robert Hamilton, the Governor-General's Agent for Central India. Sundar, of course, had no acquaintance with any of these people but guessed that the letters contained pleas on behalf of Jhansi, and feared to imagine that all their futures now lay in the hands of these English strangers.

Lakshmibai's first task, if Jhansi was to be spared a reprisal, was to explain how the massacre at Jhansi had come to be. She needed to seek the ear of Major Erskine, even while desperately hoping that Captain Skene had conveyed her genuine desire to help him before he had been killed. In her first few letters she had attempted to explain her helplessness to Erskine—her lack of an army to take on the rebels who had arrived at her gates, the growing dissatisfaction of her own people—but had received no response. Then, in the middle of July, a reply had come. Erskine had responded with sympathy, miraculously entrusting her with the care of Jhansi district! His instructions to her were to collect revenue, raise a police force and do everything in her power to prevent the spread of anarchy in her realm. Lakshmibai's eyes sped joyously over Erskine's writing, closing in relief at the final words that promised Jhansi 'liberal' treatment when the British returned.

Lakshmibai exulted in the credence Erskine seemed willing to confer on her version of events, not knowing that among the people who had written to British authorities in her defence was Robert Ellis.

However, her joy in receiving Major Erskine's reply was short-lived as she became gradually aware that the British were in fact surreptitiously investigating her part in the massacre. Hope filled her again, a few days later, when Dewan Rao Bande informed her that two captured rebels at Kanpur—one of whom had been the warden of Jhansi jail—had confessed to the British under interrogation that they had decamped to the rebel side during the Jhansi uprising only on realizing that Rani Lakshmibai would never join the mutineers.

However, as the weeks passed, Dewan Rao Bande's source indicated that more and more fingers were now pointing accusingly at Rani Lakshmibai's part in the Jhansi massacre. Government House in Calcutta had already grown uncomfortable with Erskine's early assessment of her innocence and, as the tone of Major Erskine's letters started to slowly shift, Lakshmibai was too perceptive to miss it.

Ellis had written letter after letter to all the people who mattered, in London and in Calcutta. He could not, of course, write directly to Lakshmibai without attracting further suspicion on her head, especially given the undeserved dishonour of their relationship. Perhaps it was the notoriety earned by his friendship with her, but he received no reply from the government and soon understood that no one really wanted those views that did not help to make the pieces fit.

Soon he would find out that others had written too, and with malign intent. Colonel Malcolm who, though no longer in Bundelkhand, had always wanted to believe in Lakshmibai's infidelity to the British; Mr Thornton, the deputy collector of Samthar; John Sturt, the deputy commissioner of the Salt Division at Almora—their disbelief of the rani's version of events based largely on hearsay and anecdotal evidence but far more credible and useful than Ellis's view, under the circumstances.

Sir Robert Hamilton had also received direct evidence of Rani Lakshmibai's culpability from a survivor of the Jhokan Bagh massacre— a Mrs Mutlow who, being Eurasian, had been mistaken for an Indian and had escaped the shooting with her ayah. It was clear to Ellis that, as the rest of the Mutlow family had died at Jhokan Bagh, their relative not only wanted retribution but, more importantly, a promise of protection from the British, given the poor Eurasian's halfway status between two unwelcoming societies; but Ellis wondered whether Hamilton would deduce such a simple fact.

Lakshmibai's future looked grim but, even if he had been able to get on a ship and sail the seas to her, Ellis knew there was by now nothing more he could do to help her.

❧ *40* ❧

Sitting in her court, Lakshmibai could see an almost identical mix of hope and pleading on the faces of all three men standing before her as she looked up from the letter. They were now her chief advisors, these three elderly men—her prime minister, Dewan Rao Bande; her head of security, the dependable Gul Mohammed; and, her father, Moropant. Although the three of them more often than not disagreed with each other, today it felt as though she was up against the combined influence of all three.

She returned the letter to Dewan Rao Bande who put it away carefully in the cloth file he held in his hands. It was from the raja of Banpur, a Bundela Rajput who had used the mutiny to take control of nearby Sagar district. He had written to suggest that Rani Lakshmibai join forces with him in order to jointly wrest more territory for themselves before the British came back.

'I think he is probably quite right when he says more territory will mean better control and a better state of preparedness to face the British when they return, Rani-sahiba,' Rao Bande said carefully.

Lakshmibai looked beyond them to the pale northern hills that she could see from the Panch Mahal windows. The acquisition of land, so dear a proposition to most rulers and the British, had never interested her. For her, the peace and prosperity of the people of Jhansi was the principal thing, a lesson she had learnt so many years ago from Gangadhar.

'I think we all know that it is only a matter of time before the British do return,' she said pensively, 'perhaps there is already an army coming our way, convinced as they seem to be of our guilt in the killings. By aggressively taking up more surrounding territory before that, we will only ruin an already precarious position with them.'

Gul Mohammed cleared his throat. 'Rani-sahiba, from what we hear, our position with them can be made no worse. We are already condemned by them.'

'Condemned, when they return, to either hand over Jhansi entirely to them or face them boldly on the battlefield,' Moropant added quietly.

'Rani-sahiba, there is also the danger that others like the raja of Banpur will emerge. Not with friendly offers like his but with their sights set on Jhansi instead,' Rao Bande said, now wearing a very troubled expression on his face.

Lakshmibai knew he was referring to rumblings from the nearby kingdoms of Orchha and Datia that had been getting louder of late.

'And we know well how quickly men like Krishna Rao and Sadashiv would rush to assist our neighbours to move against us,' Moropant added. 'Months of exile from Jhansi having given them ample time to sharpen their knives.'

Lakshmibai nodded. 'Their animosity is to be expected. I have never expected anything but trouble from Krishna Rao. How he must rejoice at hearing of our tribulations.'

'I would not be too surprised, Rani-sahiba, if it is he who persuaded Orchha and Datia that, while we are in British disfavour, we make a much easier target for their combined forces than ever before,' Rao Bande said.

'Perhaps the British too would be easily persuaded to help them against us, seeing that they believe we have killed their people—' Moropant said before Lakshmibai cut him short.

'The British have not confirmed that yet and let us not rush to assume our own undeserved guilt in their eyes,' she said firmly. 'I wish to give it another chance. Perhaps if I wrote to Major Erskine, requesting assistance in the event of an attack from Orchha and Datia, he will realize that we still welcome British involvement in Jhansi. I am not against that and would merely wish that they do not deprive Damodar of his rightful inheritance this time.'

The letter was written but Major Erskine's reply, arriving before the end of October, made it sufficiently clear that Jhansi was not a priority for the British at all. What chilled Lakshmibai's bones were the words with which Erskine had ended his letter: '... *when the British return to Jhansi, they will first examine the conduct of everyone involved in the mutiny and massacre before dealing with them accordingly.*' It was an ominous warning and one that they did not even bother to couch in dissembling words any more.

Lakshmibai gave it one last chance, this time writing to Sir Robert Hamilton, the Governor-General's own agent for the central provinces, telling him that the chiefs of Orchha and Datia as well as rebel thakurs and landlords were taking advantage of her disturbed state to attack her and cause unrest in the areas that she was trying to keep peaceful until the British could return.

But Hamilton did not even bother to reply to that letter. Governor-General Canning's orders to conduct a full-scale investigation against the rebel queen Lakshmibai had lain on his desk for days and he owed her no more correspondence. By now, her contact with the meddling raja of Banpur had been reported to Calcutta too. And her troubles with Orchha and Datia presented as hostility by a traitorous rebel towards those states that had attempted remaining loyal to the British during the mutiny. Even though loyalty was a quality that could not be easily separated from expediency, already lists were being drawn up in the Governor-General's office to mark out those deserving of support and those for whom vengeance would be at its most merciless. Lakshmibai, who everyone was more and more convinced had viciously massacred a helpless group of women and children under false promises of refuge in Jhansi Fort, was a marked woman in British eyes.

She sat alone in the darkened sanctum of her temple, leaning on the carved stone pillar in a corner. There was no one she could share such momentous decisions with and no one, she realized with sorrowful incredulity, with whom she particularly wanted to. Perhaps such self-reliance was something to be grateful for but then how could she explain this fear rising up from the far reaches of her fingers and toes and washing over her entire body, transmuting into an aching blend of remorse and dread.

Earlier in the morning, before the palace had awakened, she had slipped out unseen and walked under the jasmine trellises, down the path flanked by flaming oleanders, to stand before Motibagh. The annexe that Robert had so briefly occupied as he worked on his manuscripts had remained closed since he had left...she could not recall if it had been she who had given the orders for it to be so. Cobwebs brushed her face and arms as she walked slowly up its stairs and the main door creaked loud objection to being opened after so long, the sound echoing sadly through vacant corridors.

Who had covered up the sofas and bureaus with dust sheets, turning them into small ghostly relics of another time? Who had painstakingly removed every little belonging of the last occupant...his writing materials, his clothes that had hung in the wardrobes...his very presence?

For a moment, Lakshmibai had sat on the edge of his chair imagining the many people who would have been relieved to see Robert go—her father, perhaps even dewan-ji, too respectful, too kindly to ever tell her she would eventually suffer from her refusal to accept divides that were already there.

It was they who were right, she thought, feeling shame wash over her at not having heard what, in many different ways, they must all have tried to tell her. Why had she not seen them before—those barriers that had sprung up years ago—before Robert had left her, before the annexation, before she had become Jhansi's young queen, maybe even long before those white traders had first sailed across the black waters on their ships and pulled in on ancient eastern shores...

Only she had not seen, or had not wanted to.

Getting up hastily from the chair, Lakshmibai ran out of the room, as though in a futile bid to escape mistakes already made, down the corridor, into the shrouded living room, out onto the veranda, not able to shut away the sound of her own fleeing footsteps resounding like guilty drum-beats against her ears. Never again, never again, never again, they seemed to be saying, never again will you ever offer love where it is simply not due.

๛ 41 ๛

There remained only one path to take and Lakshmibai was determined to take it with whatever dignity she had left. She had tried everything in her power to salvage the situation with the British, even resisting advice from the people closest to her, but now her intentions towards them needed to be signalled unambiguously. As a first step, she called for Gangadhar's family standard to be brought out of the fort's storeroom. After the palace maids had cleaned and repaired it, an auspicious date was assigned for it to be raised and Jhansi's citizens were duly informed.

Against a glorious saffron dawn and the chanting of temple priests, the citizens of Jhansi gathered in small, excited huddles. They watched while the royal standard was hooked onto the flagstaff by the palace sentries, their cherished queen standing nearby. The metal pole on the fort's tallest turret had remained empty from the first day of the uprising when the rani had thought it safest to bring the British flag down. But now, as the distant hills lit up like a row of flaming torches, Jhansi watched Raja Gangadhar's old ruby-red pennant rise slowly upwards before beginning to billow proudly in the breeze. Its symbols of the kettledrum and ceremonial royal fan, glittering in gold thread, were visible from the farthest reaches of the town and Lakshmibai could hear her citizens cheer and ululate joyfully at this final symbol of their freedom.

That afternoon, with help from a delighted Moropant, Rani Lakshmibai embarked on an energetic conscription process. The few hundred palace guards with whom she had managed since the annexation would not suffice for the preparations that were at hand. Advertisements were put up in the town and leaflets distributed in the surrounding towns and countryside. The rani needed soldiers to help her in her defence against her Rajput neighbours' unfriendly advances and possibly future British hostility as well.

It was the latter prospect that made volunteer soldiers turn up in droves from across the countryside, some of them rebels who had escaped British reprisals. On recruitment days, the queues grew longer and longer outside the camp set up by Moropant in the field bordering the town. And, from the interviews they conducted, Lakshmibai saw how many of her people had come to hate the rule of the firangi. Even women were volunteering to serve, stating the courage of their queen as good enough reason for them to be recruited as soldiers too. Lakshmibai saw no reason to turn them away and was especially touched when a peasant woman, who was exactly the same height and complexion as her and even had a son of about the same age as Damodar, came before them to declare that it would give her immense pride to be allowed to stand in for her rani during battle. She said her name was Jhalkaribai and Lakshmibai saw some of her own confident demeanour mirrored in the woman who stood tall and straight, declaring her determination to confound the enemy out of their wits, even at risk to her own life.

In a matter of weeks, Jhansi's reborn army had swelled to include ten thousand Bundela and vilayati warriors in addition to two thousand trained sipahis who had left the British army during the recent rebellion. Gul Mohammed was made army commander and, alongside him, Rani Lakshmibai took personal charge of training her new soldiers, joining them in their exercises and drills, men and women working side by side. While teaching them how to aim and shoot from horseback, Lakshmibai insisted that all her maids, including Sundar and Kashi, join them too. 'These are skills everyone must know in times of trouble,' was her angry exhortation whenever one of her maids tried crying off using household duties as an excuse.

While the men and women of Jhansi rallied to the support of their queen, the town became a hive of activity. The streets filled daily with the arrival of carts bearing sack-loads of saltpetre that had been ordered from Gwalior for the manufacture of gunpowder. The fort's old cannons, buried under the soil of peaceful years, were unearthed, cleaned and polished. The two largest, Karak Bijli Thope and Bhawani Shankar Thope, were wheeled out of their storage chambers and given pride of place on the fort's largest bastions. Volunteer gunners, among whom was the king's old Afghani retainer Khuda Baksh, were given special training in the rapid loading of powder and cannonballs.

The disused mint was commissioned again and local coins brought back into currency; the town's granaries stocked up with dals and wheat and rice. Flour and ghee and sugar were distributed to the poor, with instructions to hoard as much of it as possible in case of a siege.

Jhansi was like a busy thriving beehive as masons toiled to strengthen the fortified walls with granite blocks and mortar and people buttressed their own dwellings with bricks and mud-filled sacks. Lakshmibai ordered that people occupying houses along the edge of the city be evacuated to safer buildings, their mansions given over to soldiers who could patrol the boundaries day and night. Newer, smaller cannons and guns, assembled in the city's old foundries were mounted on all the batteries that had been erected on the taller buildings of the city so as to command every possible approach while providing enfilade for each other.

Guards were trained in espionage skills and sent out into the countryside while trusted messengers rode back and forth between Kalpi and Jhansi bearing coded letters from Nanasahib and Tantia Tope, informing them of Rani Lakshmibai's plans and keeping her abreast of their own. A secret passageway was dug beneath the Shiv Temple inside Jhansi Fort that would provide a direct route to the Kanpur Road in case, despite such formidable preparation, the British did indeed succeed in infiltrating Jhansi.

By the time Orchha and Datia had made their incursions into Jhansi's surrounding territory in the winter, Lakshmibai's forces were so ready for battle that the enemy was seen off in a matter of hours. It was only a skirmish but Rajput troops were sent scurrying back to the safety of their own borders, having met Jhansi's fiercely determined defences.

With a new-found confidence in her ability to defend Jhansi against attack, Lakshmibai thought of a new strategy. It was one that in private moments of contemplation pained her grievously but, as night fell on the rout of Orchha's and Datia's forces, Lakshmibai commanded that the countryside surrounding Jhansi be burnt to the ground. This was the only way to ensure that her guards on the fort's ramparts would have a clear view of the British army when it finally arrived.

That night, Lakshmibai stood on the roof of her fort and watched the greedy orange flames rage through her beloved countryside with immense sorrow welling up in her chest. She had loved every leaf on every tree that she passed on her rambles in happier times. It was their abundant shade that had protected her, not just from the summer sun, but also from the gaze of those who would have objected to her early meetings with Robert Ellis. To see those silent old trees now burn in her defence was almost like seeing her men and women fall in battle and, as a queen who loved every inch of Jhansi, she very nearly could not bear the loss.

It was this blackened landscape and an eerily empty cantonment that General Hugh Rose saw as he rode into Jhansi district with his troops on a late March evening. Ellis read the missive Rose had written to the

Board of Directors and his sense of loss was great too. The forests and trees surrounding Jhansi had been his escape and his sanctuary, providing him with some of his most blissful moments in India. General Rose's descriptions of the devastated cantonment that had been his home for so many years shattered him. The cantonment that he had helped develop, always so immaculately kept, now apparently lay in ruins. Rose had written that the mess-house roof was burnt to rafters, the new church building of St. Jude's a mere shell, its broken pews and pulpit scattered in the churchyard. Star Fort had been ransacked and emptied of the vast ammunition stores it had housed and once beautifully maintained houses were laid open and bare, looted of all possessions. Ellis remembered his bungalow, hoping desperately that Karamchand, his faithful old orderly, would have escaped it alive. Hugh Rose's despatch ended expressing anger that in the distance Jhansi's Fort was visible on its hillock, the rani's crimson standard arrogantly flying from its main turret in place of the British flag.

It was still impossible for Ellis to believe that Lakshmibai could have been responsible for what had happened to the British at Jhansi, despite all the reports he saw blaming her. He knew her too well to see her hand in such unthinking cruelty and destruction but could not very well state that to anyone without seeming even more traitorous than before. He feared for her, feeling weak and helpless in his inability to protect her, as General Rose's army approached her fort. And completely powerless about the sorrow he knew would overwhelm him if his people succeeded in killing her.

The numbness he had felt all these months now finally gave way to grief. A grief so sudden and fierce, it was as physical as a blow. After reading General Rose's despatch, Ellis had left his office on Leadenhall Street and wandered aimlessly for hours, confused by the city's capacity to keep going regardless of his pain.

Sleep had finally silenced the streets when he returned to his rooms much later that night. King's College was almost invisible behind curtains of fog and a huddled figure called from behind its gates, for alms or with an illicit offer. He kept his head down and walked on in the direction of Craven Street, barely noticing by then how mercilessly the icy river winds sliced across his body. The cobbles beneath his boots were black and wet, echoing a hollow sound in the quiet of the street as he approached his doorway. Sapped of energy, he walked slowly up the stairs to his meagre accommodation and dropped half-dead onto his cold bed.

Sleep would not come that night and Ellis lay for hours reflecting on how he had come to love Lakshmibai and then lose her. That in itself was not so unusual, but now the two of them were at war; how had they come to face such retribution?

The despatch had said that she had burnt the forests surrounding Jhansi's fort. Ellis closed his eyes, despairing at the thought. Those forests had belonged to both of them, green havens given to them like gifts. And she had torched them. Was her fury against him perhaps? Had she grown to hate him so much that she had turned their earth— the land they both loved—to a charred wasteland lying in wait of an invading army. He opened his eyes again but saw the shadows on his ceiling, cast by the gas lamp outside, turn to blackened branches raised skywards in supplication as they burnt.

They had ridden to those lakeside forests every morning, slowing their horses only as they ducked under the darkened safety of their thick leaf canopy. He could still feel the searing heat, his voice clogging up in his throat as he longed to draw her into his arms, his desire remaining futile while she talked of something else. She had spoken, in those far days, of her childhood and of similar rides with those she had loved as a child.

Those names, those childish names now chilled Ellis's blood. How did once laughing children ever grow into murderers? Little Mani and her friends, Nana and Tantia. Now murderers, mutineers of the worst sort.

❧ *42* ❧

Rani Lakshmibai stood under the arches of her public hall, an eerie silence pervading this once busy space. Jhansi's citizens, aware by now that the British were approaching, had emptied the streets, seeming to want to stay in their houses, close to their families and loved ones.

Only four people from the rani's diminished council of ministers had attended her meeting this morning but, as they discussed methods of payment to the soldiers and workers in Jhansi, they were interrupted by a sentry. The man handed an envelope to the rani, informing her that it had been delivered to Khanderao Darwaza just a few minutes before by a rider from the British camp, carrying a flag of truce. It was a letter from Sir Robert Hamilton.

Lakshmibai read it swiftly, aware that her ministers were waiting for her to explain its contents. She looked up at the concerned expressions on their faces, informing them incredulously, 'Sir Robert Hamilton wishes to invite us—he specifies my name and yours, Dewan-ji, and yours too, Baba. It is supposedly a secret rendezvous. They are willing to negotiate a settlement.'

She handed the note to Moropant who scanned it slowly, his disbelief evident as he pursed his mouth and shook his head. 'It is a trick. That's the only way they know they can capture us,' he said, as he finished reading the letter and passed it to the prime minister.

'Possibly,' Lakshmibai replied slowly, 'but it may also be that, having seen our formidable defences, they have become apprehensive about taking us on in battle.'

Dewan Rao Bande looked up from the letter on hearing that. 'Rani-sahiba, I looked out at their forces arriving on the plains this morning and they are not inconsiderable either. They have at least three thousand sipahis, if not more, who have stayed loyal. And who knows how many more are already being sent as reinforcement...with such a large army, they are not likely to be in fear of us...no, this is something else.'

'Treachery, I am sure of it!' Moropant exclaimed, pained that no one else could see what was so clear to him.

'Maybe that but maybe also a willing settlement. Who knows? Is it not at least worth finding out what they want? Of course, we will ensure our safety, refuse to go to their camp and ask them to present themselves here instead.' Lakshmibai turned to Gul Mohammed, 'What do you think? Is it not a tempting thought to spare all the lives that will be lost in war?'

The newly appointed army commander looked steadily at the queen he had grown to respect deeply in the past few months. 'I am a soldier, Rani-sahiba. To put the enemy before me is reason enough to fight. But, like you, I have no wish to shed the blood of our brave warriors without very good reason. Perhaps it is worth asking the British what their terms are.'

Moropant could not believe his ears. '*Terms*? Have they ever offered us fair terms? Even in times of peace? Here we have just recovered our land, as though in an act of divine providence, and you want to give it *back* to them now on a silver platter?'

Lakshmibai interjected, 'We are not giving it back, Baba, merely trying to find out how much sovereignty they are willing to offer us in order to avoid a battle that even they, surely, must wish to prevent.'

Lalu Bakshi, the rani's paymaster, intervened with a new line of reasoning. 'Rani-sahiba, it may sound odd but, although we worry about shedding our soldiers' blood, I think that sentiment may not be shared by the soldiers themselves. I have heard them say that they will demand their arrears of pay if we do not fight the British. I sense a lot of restlessness on their part to move on and fight so they can finally reap the rewards of being soldiers.'

'That is true,' Lakshmibai conceded, 'if we are to offer our people any future prosperity at all, that can only be achieved by vanquishing the British completely and taking their possessions. I can see that our soldiers have many good reasons to want to fight the British and two very important ones—pride and control of their own prosperity. Their months of preparations should not have been in vain. I had sworn to myself that I would lead my people into war only if I absolutely had to. That time has come. We will fight.'

She saw the looks of satisfaction on the faces of the men who sat in front of her as she turned to the waiting sentry and said resolutely, 'Take a message back to Sir Robert Hamilton that we are not willing to negotiate.' She turned next to her prime minister, 'Dewan-ji, please draft a reply. It is to state that the British cannot despise us one minute and attempt to negotiate the next. Jhansi was blameless when it gave refuge to their people. They have responded to our kindness with blame and suspicion and now cannot expect us to open our doors to them again. And, if it is Jhansi that they want, tell them they will have to take on its rani first.'

At first light of day, Gul Mohammed looked out over the ramparts of the fort at the amassed ranks of the British troops below. Their preparations for attacking Jhansi were impressive indeed. The army commander could see that the enemy had surrounded the town on the southern and eastern perimeters of the town wall. Artillery sites, gleaming with the metal barrels of guns and cannons, were now being constructed all around, elephants and camels churning up dust as they pulled the heavier weaponry. Further away, tents were being pitched. It looked as though they would be willing to stay for as long as it took Jhansi to fall.

Gul Mohammed did not need the benefit of the intelligence he had received to see that only about a fourth of the British contingent were white soldiers and officers. The rest were Hindustani and he wondered at the unquestioning, unthinking allegiance of these sipahis to the foreigner in the midst of this rebellion. What made them fight their own brethren and countrymen? Money? Security? Was that all it took to purchase loyalty? Perhaps it was some misguided notion of what was good for Hindustan. But Gul Mohammed felt his stomach burn with a slow anger as he saw sipahis from the Gwalior contingent that had stayed loyal to the British accepting commands from a red-coated officer who was pointing this way and that. One could not blame the British alone—the fault lay with all of them for allowing the pale-faced foreigner to create these divisions that so easily pitted brother against brother.

Gul Mohammed steeled his heart as he looked again at the British army, spreading like an angry red wound on the breast of Jhansi, and vowed that anyone who attacked his homeland—Christian, Sikh, Hindu or Mussalman—would be considered a despicable foe, worthy only of death.

Lakshmibai took up position beside Gul Mohammed on the tall southern tower to assess for herself the British forces gathered on the southern flank of the city. She had been warned—they were indeed a formidable presence. As she scanned the endless rows of tents in a camp teeming with soldiers and horses and saw the glint of their guns and cannons, she felt a rush of incredulity again at the thought that this army had marched miles across the country to assemble at her door. How indeed had things come to such a pass? She turned to her commander with a more pragmatic concern.

'Is it not strange, Gul Mohammed, that they have not taken advantage of the more vulnerable northern and north-eastern fringes, where the newer parts of our city lie?'

Together they looked below the southern tower that had the protection of its deep moat. To the west, where the walls of the fort fell away in a steep chasm to the ground below, the British had set up a huge artillery site, all its gun barrels trained on the fort.

'It may be possible, Rani-sahiba, that they will attempt distracting us on this front while mounting a surprise strike in the north. But we have that part of the city well covered too,' Gul Mohammed replied confidently.

'It is probably only my head they are after—in which case they would be far less interested in the town than in this fort where they know they are likely to find me.'

Gul Mohammed looked at his queen's face, unable to fathom from her serene profile if she was really as unafraid as she sounded and she turned to look at him reassuringly. 'I would rather they fought us here, Gul Mohammed, than attack my people in the town,' she said.

Using a telescope, she watched the enemy camp start to stir as the skies above them turned soft pink. Tiny figures of soldiers swam into her view, emerging from their tents, donning their belts and holsters and scabbards, polishing their guns, standing in huddles, no doubt discussing their battle plans. Campfires were sending grey spires of smoke into the now crisp clear air as the morning chapattis were roasted.

As the sun rose higher over the hills, Jhansi waited, poised, aware that Rani Lakshmibai had ordered them not to shoot first. But, as Lakshmibai continued to watch, her eyes taking in everything, she noticed that levels of activity had suddenly quickened on the plains with the soldiers falling into ranks. There was a distant shouted order. And then the unmistakable crack of musketry as soldiers on the British side started firing, choosing a raised bastion on the town's southern wall to aim at. The battle for Jhansi had started.

Lakshmibai took a deep breath before nodding at Gul Mohammed and the five guns that had been mounted on the attacked bastion returned fire with a resounding boom. She wanted to be sure the British would see that there had been not even the hint of hesitation in her response. For every shot of theirs, she would return five.

Now, on Gul Mohammed's orders, all batteries opened fire, the air filling with the deafening boom of guns and cannons. In return, the walls of the fort were fiercely cannonaded but Lakshmibai nodded in satisfaction at Gul Mohammed as their defences returned shot for shot. It would be patent to the British that Jhansi was short of neither artillery nor ammunition. She hoped too that the English general could see, even from where he stood, how keenly focussed her troops were on that imperative task that even the sharpest of generals sometimes forgot, which was the prompt repair of damaged defences and guns. She watched her men and women scurrying back and forth, bearing trays of slaked lime and mud and mortar on their heads as breaches in the wall of the fort were swiftly patched up with palisades almost as soon as they had been damaged.

All morning neither side seemed to gain an advantage but Lakshmibai was sure that the afternoon heat of these plains would soon become unbearable for the enemy troops. This fortuitously early start to the summer would give her troops the advantage they needed. The enemy may even have to retire to their tents, in the absence of forests, if the sun grew too hot, which would be the time to escalate the strikes on them. But she watched, her heart sinking, as afternoon came and the English general instructed his men to wrap their heads with wet towels and pugrees to cope with the sun while they fought on.

By evening, there was still no sign of either side giving up. The skies above Jhansi continued to rain fire and, every ten minutes, a shell would land on another of Jhansi's buildings or stores. With each roof and thatch that exploded, sending angry flames spiralling upwards, Lakshmibai could hear the enemy on the plains cheer wildly. She gave renewed reminders to her troops that it was early in the battle yet, but could feel her own spirits sink at the damage being inflicted on her beloved town. Aware of the importance of keeping morale from flagging, she asked for Sarangi to be brought to her and rode swiftly out into Jhansi's besieged streets to check on the fate of her citizens.

Dusk was falling but, on this terrible night, the twinkling lamps that usually punctuated the courtyards and gateways of houses at sundown had not been lit. Instead, the entire city was blanketed by a choking, smoke-swirled darkness, pierced only by the light from embers of burnt-out buildings. There was no chanting of evening prayers in childish high-pitched voices from gardens and verandas, just the wailing of women who had already, so early into the battle, lost loved ones.

Lakshmibai moved from house to house, tirelessly comforting the families of the dead, trying to find words of encouragement for those who had survived. She visited the makeshift hospital that had been set up in the public halls to ensure that her vaids and doctors were coping with the hundreds of wounded being brought to their door. But there was not much she could do for her suffering smoke-shrouded city. She had to return to her fort and to the fighting, a new kind of trepidation growing inside her. If this was the price in just one day for prideful courage, she did not want any part in it.

Inside Jhansi Fort, people were darting about, fetching more ammunition supplies from the stores, putting out fires with the help of bullocks that had been commissioned to draw water from the Amod Garden well and preparing fresh material to repair the damage done to the fort's southern walls. Soldiers, wounded as they had held their posts on the ramparts, were being tended to under the arches of the outhouses where the palace vaid tirelessly worked. Lakshmibai could see that an air of excitement still covered her camp. She could hear in her soldiers' voices little of the desperation that her own mind felt gripped with as they shouted words of encouragement across the quadrangles to each other. It was not for her, as their queen and leader, to reveal her worries that their enthusiasm may be short-lived. Tonight she would send a rider out to take up Nana's offer of support.

After four days of consistent shelling, the parapets of four southern bastions in the town wall were torn down and the guns atop them suddenly lay cold. Lakshmibai, who had left the ramparts just a few minutes before to ride around the city and supervise relief work, looked up at the silent cannons, trying frantically to recall which of her gunners had manned that post. She hoped distractedly that old Khuda Baksh, trained to be a palace butler and not a gunner, had not perished in the morning's defence for she had not seen him all day. Already too many of her warriors had died in the fighting and the smoke of battle had been replaced by that of cremations in the northern end of the city where the priests at the Lachhmitaal ghats had not stopped burning pyres for Jhansi's brave these past few days.

On hearing another loud booming sound, Lakshmibai looked up to see that a breach had become visible on a part of the wall that was nearest to the fort but, as British soldiers on the other side cheered loudly, she issued quick orders to stockade the gap. More than a dozen of her men and women could be seen swiftly running for the southern wall, while others covered the breach with gunfire.

Where, thought Lakshmibai desperately, where were the reinforcements promised by Nana?

On the fourth day, General Rose was interrupted by one of his subedar-majors delivering an important piece of news. Nanasahib's army, led by Tantia Tope, had been spotted marching towards Jhansi. It ought to have been fortuitous, as this was exactly the trap that both Rose and Robert Hamilton had wanted Nanasahib's forces to walk into, the plan having been to capture them as they rushed to the rani's aid. But the subedar-major reported that Tantia had already crossed the Betwa and was accompanied by over twenty thousand men. Twenty thousand, among whom would be the vicious warriors responsible for the Kanpur massacres. Rose was now up against an enemy that had not just multiplied but was of the most formidable and ruthless variety.

Just before nightfall, Tantia's men arrived on a hillock to the west of the British forces, accompanied by elephants and camels towing enormous cannons. Some of the rebel sipahis were still wearing their old uniforms and waved their rifles defiantly at the sight of the British camp, the bold glint of their bayonets visible to General Rose's watching troops. Within an hour of their arrival, Tantia's army had built a massive bonfire to signal their presence to their friends inside Jhansi town. As the flames shot into the night sky, a great cry of relief was heard emerging from Jhansi Fort. From where they stood on the plains, the British could hear the raucous cheering of the fort's defenders and the people inside the town, alongside the celebratory booming of their guns.

Inside Panch Mahal, Moropant smiled for the first time in days.

'We are safe now, beti! I knew Tantia would not fail to come. Jhansi will be defended.'

But Lakshmibai could not immediately share her father's sense of relief. 'Baba, please summon the war council, we will have to rethink our strategy with this new development.'

As it would take ten minutes for them to gather, she ran down the stairs of Panch Mahal to reach the small courtyard where a small temple had been built for her to offer worship in these times of war. The Shivalingam had been washed for the evening ablutions, the lamp ready with its oil and wick. Today she wanted to light the holy lamp herself as thanksgiving. Folding her hands and feeling relief flood her body, she thanked Lord Shiva who was always there for the righteous and the brave. She prayed too for Tantia's protection. 'Please give him strength, please give him courage, please keep my brother safe,' she whispered, eyes tightly closed.

She opened them swiftly as she heard a small rustling sound in the oil-smudged depth of the temple. As her eyes adjusted themselves to the darkness, she saw a small figure cowering behind the Shivalingam. Who had dared to step into the sanctum, she wondered, her hand going instantly to the poniard she always carried by her side. But, as she heard a small sniffle, she saw it was her son and took a quick step forward to catch him as he stumbled out towards her.

'Damodar, my child, what are you doing in here, what is it?' she cried, clasping his head as he buried it in her waist.

He replied in a tearful torrent, 'I'm scared...I do not like the guns, Ma. I ran away from Kamlesh who was saying we are going to kill all the British. Why are we killing them, Ma? And why do they want to kill us?'

She held his arms and knelt down to face him. What was the easy answer to that? Cupping his tear-stained face in her palms, she said gently, 'My darling, sometimes we have to kill just to keep ourselves safe—can you understand that?'

'Will we really kill them all—even Mary and Beatrice and Major Ellis?'

Lakshmibai gathered her son up in her arms, her heart bleeding with both pity and relief at his innocence. Kashi and Kamlesh had kept their promise of protecting Damodar from everything, even though she knew that it would fall on her to explain things to him someday. She had no words but continued to kneel on the floor of the temple, feeling her son's body grow slowly calm against her own. Perhaps she ought to think of sending him to his parents' house while her own attention was taken up with the siege. Perhaps he was safer in the confines of the fort, if his parents could be moved into Panch Mahal to care for him and bring him comfort. But now she had to tear herself away from him to return to her ministers who would be waiting for her. With the arrival of Tantia's forces, new hope was dawning on Jhansi. She got up and silently took Damodar's hand before leading him back to his chambers.

In the end, the battle of Betwa between General Rose's army and Tantia's forces was briefer than anyone thought it would be. Hugh Rose's men, a fearsome blend of infantry and cavalrymen, armed with artillery, howitzers and field guns, took the offensive and Tantia's first line floundered early on. It was soon clear that their second line was too far behind to provide an effective rearguard. As Tantia's forces retreated in confusion into the forests, they set fire to the trees in order to prevent the enemy from following but the British army, now intent on victory, pushed on ahead, their horses leaping over the smoking undergrowth in their enthusiasm.

After just a few hours of fierce hand-to-hand combat, the burnt forests on the banks of the Betwa were thick with the bodies of the dead, both sides losing vast numbers of men; the British in hundreds, Tantia's forces over a thousand. Forest clearings, sometimes the refuge of lovers, now lay strewn with dead bodies. Earth patterned once with dappled sunlight was now stained with blood and a tumbling silver river turned foaming red.

An escaping rider brought the news to Lakshmibai in her fort; Tantia's remaining men were in hasty retreat. Though maintaining a brave face before her war council, Lakshmibai felt desperation flood her again. Jhansi's chances were receding so rapidly. Without Tantia's help, and given the beleaguered state of the town's defences, she could already see defeat hovering over her beloved city like an evil impatient spirit.

Jhansi waited in shocked silence for more news of their allies but it looked, from the lack of communication, as though Tantia's remaining numbers may have returned to Kalpi to nurse their wounds and regroup. Lakshmibai had no way of knowing how terrible their casualties had been, nor even whether they were in a position to offer her help any more. But she knew it fell upon her to rouse her own depressed and saddened forces to face the next wave of attacks that were sure to take place in a day or two.

General Rose had already given the order; the breach that had been made in the south wall of the town looked big enough to justify their first assault on Jhansi town. It was to take place early in the morning and the plan was for one column to storm the breach while the other would use the distraction to scale the walls of the town further away on the east.

British sappers laid ladders against the southern town walls that were still dark and untouched by dawn-light. But sleepless eyes on Jhansi's ramparts had been looking out for them. In a matter of seconds a ferocious bombardment broke over their heads. Metal trays carrying burning coals were tipped over the edge of the walls, accompanied by round shot and grape and musket fire. It was as though hellfire was falling from angry skies and many fell screaming back to the waiting earth. But still the advance continued, brave men scrambling over ladders and through the breach. Before long, dozens of British soldiers were inside the walls of Jhansi town.

Inside Panch Mahal, Rani Lakshmibai was awakened with the news that her people were directly under attack on the streets of Jhansi. She sprang out of bed and, brushing away Sundar's offer of sustenance, ran to get herself ready for battle. Sundar, who for the past few days had been getting her rani's uniform and armour ready to be worn first thing in the morning, had laid everything out the previous night and they now waited, gleaming in the dim morning light.

Silently, Sundar helped Lakshmibai into her tunic and breastplate but, by the time she came to tying on the armour plates on her arms, her face was frozen with fear. Lakshmibai remained silent in the face of Sundar's unbearable anguish, merely using her scarf to silently wipe a stray tear off the girl's trembling chin. Even if there had been more time, she lacked the words to comfort her devoted companion. Once she was ready, Lakshmibai turned from her, walking rapidly to the central chamber where Moropant and Dewan Rao Bande were already waiting.

'It is time to use our Afghan battalion,' Lakshmibai said without any other preliminary talk. 'I will lead them myself,' she added, indicating by the tone of her voice that there was no time to waste and that she would brook no argument.

'Beti, let Gul Mohammed…'

Lakshmibai turned sharply to face her father. She understood his fear but she would not indulge him now. Looking at him steadily, she replied calmly but with as much compassion as she could muster, 'Baba, I must do my duty. You have trained me yourself and you know that I am as capable as any of my soldiers, including Gul Mohammed. Please let me join them now. I would rather die in defence of my people than have them give up their lives in order to protect me.'

Sundar watched Moropant's shoulders sag as he stepped back to allow his headstrong young daughter to stride out of the room.

Ellis heard about the vicious counter-attack led by Rani Lakshmibai and her thousand Afghan volunteers. General Rose, taken by surprise, had admitted watching in vain as his men fled for cover behind buildings and temples. Against the backdrop of a burning building, he had caught a sudden glimpse of the figure of a petite young soldier, eerily beautiful, silhouetted against glowing fires as her chestnut horse reared up against the flames. The jewelled scabbard of the talwar she was brandishing looked like molten gold, the expression on her face full of fearless hauteur. This was, he said, the infamous queen of Jhansi and, when Ellis read his description of her beauty and courage, he thought his anguish would finally consume him.

That afternoon Robert Ellis wrote his resignation letter before walking under the grand Doric columns of India House for the very last time. He did not look back once, feeling only merciful release. For too long had he laboured under the yoke of beliefs no longer shared with his Honourable Company. Now he was no longer too young to know any better.

Leadenhall market was still busy with traders and punters but to Ellis, suddenly, the bustle and noise was less unbearable. He took his usual route through the narrow cobbled alleyway leading to the Jamaica Coffee House, past the pubs and chophouses, heaving on this Friday night with well-attired bankers, brokers and merchants from the city. He reached the Royal Exchange but found crowds gathered even in the normally quiet square that lay behind it. A new statue was being erected and Ellis stopped for a few moments, watching. No home or hearth awaiting him and now no business to attend to either. As the stone figure of a man was unveiled, he heard the small gathering cheer. The soft sunshine of an early summer day was casting a glow over their happy faces and a breeze blew through his hair, as though offering comfort. He sat on a bench and thought he would stay there for a while before deciding where to go next.

℘ 43 ℘

At dawn, Lakshmibai stood at her window, facing the unbearable. Jhansi had tried everything to keep the enemy out but they had proven too determined and too powerful. Her father stood quietly by her side as she gazed out at her city, exhausted and wearied by the nine-day siege. Yesterday, they had somehow mustered up enough strength to beat off the British onslaught, fearlessly driving the invaders off their streets and back to their camp. But even she had to concede that Jhansi did not possess endless reserves of resilience.

'It is really me that the British are after, Baba,' she said quietly, 'once they have Rani Lakshmibai, they will leave Jhansi alone.'

'You cannot possibly be thinking of giving yourself up to them!' Moropant chided sharply, even though he recognized the painful truth of her words.

'If it meant that they would then leave Jhansi untouched...' Lakshmibai trailed off, not daring to look her astounded father in the eye. Without turning to meet his gaze, she continued swiftly, 'I need not give myself up to them, Baba. All I would have to do is make another foray out into the streets, as I did yesterday, only this time allowing them to shoot me down.'

Moropant closed his eyes and took a deep breath. It was a few moments before he spoke again, his voice emerging loudly hoarse in the stillness of the room. 'And what if they took you alive? You know as well as I do that there must be a rich reward on your head!'

She paused before replying, 'Perhaps it would be better then to embrace death in the manner of Rajput princesses who so bravely give themselves up to the holy fires of jauhar when their honour is at stake. In this case, it would be the rape of Jhansi I could hope to avert with my death.'

As Lakshmibai turned away from the windows, her father grasped her arm, speaking urgently, 'If they find you dead, their fury will be magnified and Jhansi is even less likely to be spared.' She could hear the desperation clogging his throat. He continued talking quickly, falling over his words, as though desperately trying to catch her thoughts before her mind was irretrievably made up. 'Instead, if you flee, they will try to chase you and leave our people here unharmed. Take Damodar with you. Gul Mohammed can cover your escape. I will stay to control things here in your absence.'

Lakshmibai looked at her father. His face seemed to have acquired hundreds of new lines in the past few days.

'*Go*,' he urged again, 'I will stay with the defence. Take Damodar, we will follow.'

He was right. It was her life the British wanted. They would surely come in pursuit of her and so the farther away she could get from Jhansi the better it would be for her people. It was best to leave now, before they started ransacking the town, she was the only possible decoy her people had.

She nodded, thinking aloud as she rapidly issued her orders. 'We will leave without delay, taking the secret passageway to the Kanpur road. I will take Damodar, Sundar and Kashi with me, and a few soldiers. The rest can stay and guard the fort and palace. Gul Mohammed and the other soldiers can join us at Kalpi by the time the British come chasing after us. Inform Jhalkaribai that the time has come for her to keep her promise. Tonight she will disguise herself as me and leave with another entourage. She will have to make sure she is spotted by the British while escaping, so that they follow her, imagining she is the queen. Jhalkari is a fast rider, they will not be able to catch her. By then my party would have already gained enough of a lead to reach Nana's camp and Jhalkari can join us there. While we make preparations to depart, send a messenger, our fastest rider, to Nana and Tantia telling them to expect us at Kalpi by nightfall.'

She stopped to look at her father's face. He suddenly looked so old, her poor dear baba, so anxious on her behalf. She reached out an arm to place it tenderly on his shoulder. 'Baba, you too must come with me, you are wounded and cannot stay behind,' she said softly, making her voice more firm as she saw him shake his head. 'No, do not look at me like that; you are in no state to fight such a rapidly encroaching enemy. Besides…I need you with me, Baba. How could you even imagine I would leave without you?'

In her chamber, Lakshmibai found that Sundar had already given young Kamlesh instructions and the young maid was darting about, pulling clothes out of the wardrobes.

'Sundar is getting Prince Damodar ready, Rani-sahiba, and I am to look after you,' the girl said breathlessly, her eyes dark with dilated pupils.

Lakshmibai tried to smile reassuringly at the poor child but she caught a glimpse of her own face in the mirrored panels of the wardrobe and saw how white it looked. How could she inspire courage in her people when she herself looked so drawn?

Sitting on the edge of her bed so that the little maid could reach the top buttons on her tunic, she asked softly, 'Have you had a chance to say goodbye to Damodar, child?'

Kamlesh, furiously concentrating on pulling out the pearl buttons, nodded, her small lips pursed.

'Do not fret, Kamlesh, for your separation from the prince is only temporary. Once the enemy has been drawn away from Jhansi and defeated in battle, we will return. And then life for you and Damodar will be just as it was before this fighting started. Perhaps even better.'

The poor girl was still unable to respond and so, as she waited for her armour plates to be hooked into place, Lakshmibai continued to speak, keeping her voice as comforting as possible. 'I am leaving you with great responsibilities, my child, as both Sundar and Kashi have to come with me. You are now in charge of the royal household. Ask Mohandeo to distribute the grain and rice stored in the royal granaries among the poor. Lead the other maids to the hidden bunkers under the prison. And the prince's lovebirds. Take care of them, tell them he will be back. And when we are back, we will buy another hundred birds to fill our gardens with their song. Perhaps we will celebrate our return by not having tuitions for one full week. You would like that, wouldn't you?'

Finally getting a small smile in response, Lakshmibai placed a hand on the girl's head. 'More than anything else, Kamlesh, be brave. We all need courage to face the days that lie ahead.'

Getting up from her bed, Lakshmibai wondered from where she herself would draw the courage she needed for the ensuing journey. A journey that would be putting miles between her and Jhansi with every galloping step they took.

She caught her reflection as she turned—a brave young soldier in male attire and armour. What a burden to be acclaimed for qualities of courage that had not even been tested. She almost smiled at the irony of it. How had it ever come to be that she was so hailed for valour and yet so fearful; so loved and yet so alone...

She cast a quick look around her bedchamber bathed in early morning light, its brocades and tapestries glittering more brightly than ever before, murals and mirrors all freezing in a strange hard and golden brilliance. Even the Lucknow glass globes and mirrors that lined the room seemed filled with that same blazing light, as though conspiring to ensure that the image burnt itself forever in her memory before she would leave it.

In less than an hour, the small entourage was ready to leave. Offering one last prayer at the temple, Rani Lakshmibai gave instructions for Damodar to be brought out. He had been moved to the innermost chambers of the palace when the siege had started and, despite her plan to move his parents into the fort, there had not been the time to make the necessary arrangements. She watched the small figure emerge from a doorway, his hand in Sundar's, and tried to quell the rush of maternal concern she felt at the terror that covered his innocent face. He was not even nine yet...how different his childhood was to the sunlit one she herself had enjoyed. And how sad that she, with all her wealth and position, had not been able to give her son the simple joys that her father had so abundantly showered her when she was small.

As Damodar was lifted up by Gul Mohammed and tied to his mother's waist with instructions to hold on as hard as he could, Lakshmibai only briefly patted the small arms that wound tightly around her waist, fearing that any show of concern on her part would only deepen his own.

Damodar turned back to look instead at the window of his mother's room from where Kamlesh had promised to wave him goodbye. The light and shade of the morning was playing tricks with his eyes, making it impossible for him to see if his friend was standing there at all. Sundar had promised him that Kamlesh would follow them later to Kalpi as the group this morning had to be as small as possible so as not to be detected by the British. He had been scared and unable to sleep these past few nights, despite Kashi agreeing to sleep in his room. He was sure the shelling from the British camp had worsened over the past few days as the enemy had seemed to crawl closer on the far side of the city. Even at night, as the firing sputtered away, the silences were uneasy and even the sudden cry of a dog could make him jump awake in a sweat. The poor horses too seemed not to be able to rest, waking him as they stirred early in the morning, snorting, demanding their feed. From that point on, even as the summer dawn broke like an egg over the distant hills, shimmering yellow and white in the heat haze, the inside of the fort had churned with ceaseless and frightening activity this past week. This morning he had been awoken even earlier than usual by the neighing and stamping of the horses gathering outside, their smell of sweat and fear rising up with the dusty air and floating into his room. But, it always reassured him to look at his mother's calm face and he gripped her waist now as tightly as he could, pressing his forehead against her back.

She gave the signal and the small group of horse riders set off as quietly as possible, out of the palace yard and towards the fort's secret passageway hidden under its northern ramparts. As creepers were moved aside and a small locked door opened, they entered a dark, cold tunnel. There was a musty smell and a few bats flapped away in fright. Damodar shivered, imagining he was entering the very bowels of the earth as the long corridor snaked before them. But, after fifteen endless minutes, they emerged into the cool sunshine of a wood on the other side and an empty road became visible through the trees. As they cantered out of the quiet copse, Damodar noticed how still the countryside around them was; they must already be miles away from the fighting at Jhansi. He looked back over his shoulder to see if he could see the town or the British camp. Only the fort was visible over the trees, glittering silver as it sat atop its hill. His mother's royal standard was fluttering gently in the morning breeze as the riders spurred their horses and started galloping down the Kanpur road.

Only too late was it deduced that someone disguised as Lakshmibai had provided a decoy for the royal party to escape and the information was kept under wraps for fear of exposing General Rose's folly. As that second entourage created a deliberate distraction, they were spotted by the night guards at Bhanderi Gate. The troops had earlier in the day deliberately removed a picket from the cordon surrounding the town to tempt the queen into leaving her fort and were pleased to see the ease with which she had taken the bait. As the group rode swiftly past, Lieutenant Bowker fired at them but was dismayed to find that, in his desire to capture the queen alive, he had missed. A battalion of the 14th Light Dragoons was sent in pursuit but it had not reckoned for the horsemanship skills of the predominantly female entourage and soon lost them in the darkness of the night.

A couple of hours later, still following the trail that had been carefully set, another soldier of the Light Dragoons spotted the person he too was sure was the queen, unmistakable on her chestnut horse and with a child tied to her back. Guessing that they had stopped to get some rest, he galloped up to them, hoping to capture them alive but was knocked off his horse by their firing of a matchlock ball. As he staggered back to his feet, he saw them escape into the forests on their horses. They had left behind the food they had stopped to eat, along with an embroidered royal parasol and some baggage, all of which was taken back to the camp and confirmed as belonging to the queen as it bore her insignia. The soldier was mortified to have to report to General Rose that, although he had captured some of the queen's clothes and baggage, their royal owner had decamped.

In his fury at having lost Rani Lakshmibai, General Rose ordered that Bhanderi Gate from which she had escaped be locked and nailed shut forever. The remaining town gates were, however, to be thrown open for the British forces to enter, and an enraged command was issued for the sacking of Jhansi to commence.

It was as if they were entering a ghost city. By now the town had too many dead and too many injured to hold its head up any more. Despite all the preparations, nine days of relentless fighting had robbed it of its spirit and last feeble bursts of resistance had spluttered like a dying fire before finally growing cold. It was fear and certainty of death that was spreading through the streets now, like an inescapable contagion infecting every silent house.

Gates forced open, British troops started going from house to house, pulling out their occupants, shooting and bayoneting them in the streets. As bodies started piling up on the roadside, some men were taken to Jhokan Bagh to be put to death there to remind everyone of those other slain innocents being avenged. Death had to spawn a worse death; those were simply the rules.

For the next four days, Jhansi was pillaged. The first wave of attacks was in Halwaipur district that soon became a giant cremation ghat with fires burning everywhere. While dead bodies clogged the streets, dogs and survivors wandered from pile to pile in search of their loved ones. A few people had managed to take refuge in hidden underground bunkers where the airless stench of fear and perspiration was preferable to the carnage outside. Huddled in their subterranean haven, their feet immersed in their own bodily wastes, these few citizens of Jhansi could hear the terrifying cries of women trying to protect their husbands as they were dragged out of their hiding places in storage granaries and rafters of buildings and barns. As the men were shot indiscriminately, their women went down with them. The city's temples, into which people had crowded hoping for sanctuary or miracles, were ransacked. Temple idols, bells and jewellery were taken and the halls of worship were left piled high with bodies, the floors slippery with blood. The peaceful waters of Lachhmitaal turned pink as bodies littered its edges. Gangadhar Rao's necropolis on the edge of the lake had become an open stinking and putrid graveyard, already attracting greedily preying vultures and jackals. In the weaver's conurbation, the soldiers went berserk as here there were no treasures, only human life to rob. Men and women were shot down alike and, when people were found hiding inside hayricks on the edges of the city, orders were given for a match to be put to every single hayrick that still stood. As dense smoke filled the air, the looting began.

The first round was the prerogative of the British officers and all they wanted was jewellery, silver and money. If they found none, they killed, sometimes gunning down entire families. The bank in the marketplace was plundered, officers stuffing their pockets with silver and gold, discarding worthless Jhansi currency on the ground.

As soldiers ransacked the public library for its leather and silk bindings, hundreds of books and manuscripts on philosophy and art, epic stories of the Ramayana and Mahabharata, copies of the Bhagwad Gita and Upanishads, learned volumes on arts and sciences carefully translated into Marathi and Sanskrit and scores of volumes of lyrical Persian poetry, some translated into English and proclaiming tenderness and love, were thrown into the flames and burnt.

Beautiful Ranimahal and its adjoining Motibagh, every inch of which had been planned and perfected by a hopeful young queen, was invaded next; carpeted floors of public assembly halls covered in the red mud of blood-crusted boots, the famed hall of mirrors smashed to smithereens, white buds in its garden of pearls spattered with blood. After the building was divested of all its treasures, it was set alight, its old timber roof sending flames leaping skywards as it blazed with unearthly light, presiding like an angry goddess over a punished city.

Finally, the soldiers stood before Khanderao Darwaza, the main gates of the fort. Finding it unmanned, they streamed up the rise, looking for the rani's quarters. After a short battle with fifty of the palace guards, the doors to Panch Mahal were flung wide open. It was clear immediately that the rani and her coterie had already left, their scattered belongings revealing the haste with which they had departed. The few occupants who had stayed back were found hiding in kitchens and stables and were put swiftly to death, among them a small maid cowering in a cage full of lovebirds. The chief gunners, Khuda Baksh among them, firing to the last, were set upon and hacked to pieces, their limbs thrown into the Amod Garden well and women's bathing tank. In the main kitchen, a fierce fight was put up by the queen's chief khansama, Mohandeo, who had waited for the British forces, a cleaver in either hand. Despite the pleadings of the kitchen hands, he had refused to flee, these kitchens being the only place he had ever had to call his own. In just a few minutes, he was overpowered by six men, his arms and legs chopped off, his decapitated head placed triumphantly atop one of his own cooking pots, a chapatti shoved into his mouth.

The soldiers now crowded joyously into the empty halls and courtyards of Panch Mahal, intent on destroying everything that could not be taken away. Plate glass decorations on the doors, Lucknow mirrors on the walls, giant chandeliers, old carved archways, marble fountains and tessellated flooring were all pulverized and turned to dust. Semi-precious stones embedded in the walls were gouged out with bayonets and knives before being stuffed into pockets. Even the shrubs and creepers in the queen's walled gardens were not spared, swords furiously flying to cut and chop whatever came in their way. The prince's large birdcage in a corner of the eastern garden was thrown open but tiny fluttering creatures, with no knowledge of escape, stayed on the safety of its seeded floor, hopping over the body of a dead child.

Anything that could be taken away was picked up and carried off...silver wine goblets once reserved for honoured English visitors, jewellery boxes, one holding an old layered pearl tanmani, a wooden throne, a velvet swing, the royal cradle, carved furniture, gold leaf boxes and ivory artefacts, marble columns, window frames, paintings, books, manuscripts, silk rugs, wall-hangings, cushions, drapes, clothes...nothing of any value was left.

When that was done, the Indian sipahis were sent in to finish off the rest. After the innards of the palace and the wealthy merchants' houses had been cleaned out, even the poor were not spared...copper cauldrons, brass utensils, stoves, charpoys, water pots, door hinges and bolts were all carried off. Next they took all the clothes and textiles that could be piled onto bullock carts...bales of silk and muslin and half-finished carpets from the weavers' houses. Finally they took the food, arriving with large sacks and containers to empty the granaries and houses of all the rice and lentils and grain that had been carefully stocked up to last Jhansi through the siege.

The Light Dragoons and Bombay Regiment, the first to enter the palace, had not found Rani Lakshmibai and her entourage, nor any of her closest retainers, except the body of a grey-bearded old man lying on a couch inside the old courtroom. His turban had been taken off and laid carefully by his side and it looked as though he may have poisoned himself before they had broken in. They had no idea who he was but guessed that it may have been the queen's prime minister.

Rani Lakshmibai had fled, they said scornfully, but it was the general's order to ensure that there would be nothing left for her to return to. Not her beautiful Ranimahal, not its fountains and courtyards, not Motibagh which gave refuge on a secret night, its garden of pearls filled with the white of night-flowers and moonlight. All of Jhansi, once alive and thriving, its bazaars ringing with the sounds of prosperity, its streets thronging with people going about their daily business. All of that life and grace and beauty was reduced in those four days to nothing.

❧ 44 ❧

Lakshmibai's group stopped in confusion on the outskirts of Datia—it had just been noticed that the rani's father and her paymaster were both missing. Taking refuge in the cool dark of the forest interior, the group waited anxiously, listening for the sound of approaching horses.

'When did you last see them?' Lakshmibai asked her men, aware that some of them would be chafing against this delay. It could cost them their lives but she could not ride on without waiting for her father and Lalu Bakshi to catch up.

'About twenty miles outside Jhansi, Rani-sahiba,' one of the guards replied. 'It was a safe place to stop. I heard Moropant-bhai say he had to dress his wound and Lalu Bakshi offered to assist him.'

'Did anyone actually see them dismount? Why did no one tell me? We should have stayed together,' Lakshmibai said angrily. The unfamiliar sound of tears in her voice silenced her men.

After a few minutes, one of the soldiers spoke up. 'Somehow they just became separated from the group, Rani-sahiba...'

'I only just noticed their absence, when I informed you, Rani-sahiba...'

Lakshmibai surveyed the surrounding countryside, now suddenly terrifyingly empty of people.

'Shall we wait awhile, Rani-sahiba? We should be safe under the cover of these forests. Maybe they are only a little behind us.'

'But the British army could already be in pursuit of us...'

Lakshmibai gestured for silence, listening desperately for the sound of her father's horse, but all she could hear were the cries of birds and monkeys among the trees. 'We cannot wait here merely hoping they will catch up,' she said finally, 'it is better for someone to turn around and go in search of them.' She looked at one of her faster riders and watched him promptly turn his horse around without even awaiting instruction.

'Godspeed,' she whispered under her breath, the sound of receding hooves like a small drumbeat of hope. Stopping to dress her father's wound could have delayed them by up to an hour. Perhaps they would soon be catching up.

Less than an hour later, the guard who had gone in search of them returned and Lakshmibai's heart stopped to see he was alone as he emerged through the trees. The expression on his face was grim. Panting, he delivered his news, 'Rani-sahiba, villagers tell me they were captured. By a zamindar loyal to the British. They saw them being taken away. No one knows where. Probably back to the English camp.'

Each word jolted her chest. A rescue would be impossible with the small number of troops she had with her. It would merely jeopardize their safety. And there was no telling how close behind them the British army might be. They would certainly now be hoping she would return to her father's rescue, thereby walking straight into their trap. Lakshmibai looked at the faces around her; she had to be decisive, even in the face of such unbearable torment.

'We cannot turn back,' she said, her voice low but firm. 'If Gul Mohammed and his soldiers arrive in time, we may yet be able to send a party out to rescue my father and Lalu Bakshi. For now, we have no choice but to ride on to Kalpi where we are awaited.'

She turned her horse around, spurring it to lead her men through the darkening forest. Cold dread was building in her heart as they rode into the dusk. Things were not going to plan. Her Baba in British hands! What would they do to him to get information on her? She worried about Jhalkaribai's safety too and was desperate to know of what may have transpired in Jhansi after she had left. Was Jhalkari leading the British out of Jhansi, as planned? Lakshmibai wished she could stop the voices screaming in her head to turn back, to rescue her father and return to her beloved Jhansi.

Damodar, clinging to her waist, thought he felt his mother's body racked with silent sobs but no one else noticed her heaving terror and grief as they galloped on towards Kalpi.

Four hours on, Lakshmibai and her small entourage finally stopped their exhausted horses on the crest of a small cliff. Below them, rising up from the moon-bleached countryside, was the dark looming shape of the citadel of Kalpi. And, in its shadow lay the tents of Nanasahib's camp, glowing with the light of lanterns and campfires, like a scattering of gleaming jewels.

As the group from Jhansi emitted joyous whoops to behold the welcome sight, Nanasahib, Tantia and all their troops emerged from their tents in a welter of excitement. Brave Lakshmibai, clad in gleaming white, was riding down the hillside towards them followed by her small contingent of soldiers in a cloud of dark dust. A great cheer broke out in the camp. Who else but this beautiful young queen could be their talisman of luck in their final bid to defeat the British?

The welcoming troops surrounded Lakshmibai with cries of joy and she was warmly embraced by both Nana and Tantia as soon as she dismounted. While Damodar was taken away by Sundar and Kashi to be bathed and given sustenance, Lakshmibai joined Nana and his senior commanders in his tent. Once all the important news had been exchanged, Nana, seeing her exhaustion and the unnatural glittering brightness of her eyes, suggested she get herself washed and rested before joining them for their evening meal. But Lakshmibai shook her head. She had no appetite for food and was not even sure she would have the capacity for rest. She knew she would not have to explain to Nana how the absence of her father lay cold and heavy inside her chest, like a slowly sinking stone.

In the two weeks following Lakshmibai's arrival at Kalpi, the primary task was to prepare troops for battle. Nanasahib, watching Lakshmibai's prowess with cavalry manoeuvres, smiled broadly as she rode up to him after a series of exercises one morning.

'My sister, let me say again how ably you have taken charge of training my men,' he said as she neared.

'They are good soldiers, Nana, very eager to learn,' she replied.

'Unfortunately more endowed with enthusiasm than discipline,' he laughed. As he saw Lakshmibai's face remain unsmiling, he added gently, 'Your baba will come, Mani, I have no doubt of that. Why, did Jhalkari and Gul Mohammed not turn up unexpectedly a day after your arrival? Just when we were beginning to think we had lost them too? And, if Baba doesn't escape, we will send our forces to rescue him when we take on the British, yes?'

Lakshmibai remained silent, biting her lip to stop from crying. They both knew that if Moropant's and Lalu Bakshi's identities were discovered, it would be they who would hang for the massacre at Jhokan Bagh. It frightened Lakshmibai too that the British were taking so long to follow her to Kalpi. She had been so certain that they would set off in immediate pursuit of Jhalkaribai, imagining she was the queen, and almost could not bear to imagine what might be keeping them back. Jhalkari too had been certain that her ruse had gone exactly as planned.

'And what of Jhansi, Nana?' she said finally. 'There has been no news at all since Jhalkari came. Nor of the soldiers who had been deputized to stay back to mount Jhansi's defence. Two whole weeks?'

'Do not be so anxious, Mani,' Nana said comfortingly, 'they will surely not waste time in ransacking Jhansi. It is not a town that has the riches of Delhi and Lucknow.'

Lakshmibai turned away, not wanting to show her anguish at that thought. Her poor townsfolk had nothing to offer the British and perhaps Nana was right that in the penury of her weavers and traders would lie their salvation. She thought of her fort and her beloved palace for only a moment before deciding that she cared not a whit if they were pillaged and looted. The important thing was that the people who had stayed behind should remain unharmed—little Kamlesh and gentle Khuda Baksh, even poor loyal Dewan Rao Bande who had felt he was too old for escape and urged them to go without him.

A week later, Nanasahib's camp awoke to find an army of four thousand foot soldiers, led by the nawab of Banda and recently defeated by the British, limping their way across the plains of Bundelkhand in their direction. They were hungry and footsore and desperately short of ammunition but the arrival of these new allies brought a renewed optimism to the camp.

Yet still they waited for General Hugh Rose and his army who should have come out in search of them days ago. As they languished under the punishing summer sky, Lakshmibai suggested that they use the time by opening up the disused underground foundry at Kalpi fortress. They would need more ammunition for their guns and shot for their cannons. The coming battles were not going to be easy.

For another two weeks, they awaited news of the approaching enemy, keeping their soldiers exercised and ready. And, finally, as April slipped into scorching May, they received the welcome message that the British army had been seen on the Jhansi–Kanpur road a week before, making steady progress towards Kalpi. Tantia, eager to embark on the campaign, urged Nanasahib to allow him to lead their forces on an offensive and, although Lakshmibai felt such a course of action was inadvisable, she held her silence as Nanasahib gave order for the army to march. He himself would stay back with the camp-followers, ready to arrive with reinforcements when necessary. At dawn, Tantia and Lakshmibai were to lead the first front out to stop the British advance at the town of Kunch, twenty miles south-west of Kalpi.

As the morning sky turned yellow with heat, Lakshmibai took her place next to Tantia at the head of their army. From this vantage point, she could see multiple ranks of enemy forces stretching endlessly across the searing Kunch plains. Sensing Tantia's restlessness, she wondered at her own lack of fear. There had even been laughter back at the camp this morning as she had bid Damodar goodbye, promising him she would be back by nightfall, amused as he solemnly saluted her and refused to bestow the requested kiss.

'It is strange that I feel relief, Tantia, to have arrived finally at this point,' she said, patting her restless horse's sweating neck.

'Well, it is not my first head-to-head conflict,' Tantia replied, turning to her. His face was tense and unsmiling. 'My previous experiences bring me courage.'

Lakshmibai laughed softly. 'I do not know if it is courage on my part, Tantia, or merely the liberation of finally facing my task. The possibility of direct combat has hovered over me for months in which each day has felt as long as a year.'

Tantia did not respond and Lakshmibai shot a quick look at his profile. Preparations for battle in recent days had been marred by arguments as Tantia had become resentful of the trust invested in her leadership abilities by Nanasahib. Though quick to understand Tantia's wounded pride, Lakshmibai worried that he would once again make the error that had cost him the battle of Betwa, becoming overconfident in his frontline's abilities to manage without their flanks being adequately protected. Contrary to her advice this morning, Tantia had once again put his faith in the natural fortifications afforded by Kunch's woods and gardens. Lakshmibai knew, from what she had seen of the wily English general and his determined assault on her great stone fort at Jhansi, that the woods of Kunch would offer little protection. Even now she could see that, despite having marched through the night, the enemy troops were eager and ready for battle, their front a long gleaming colourful line, restless with the impatient bucking and swaying of their horses.

Lakshmibai felt a sudden quiver of apprehension on behalf of poor Sundar who had drawn in her horse close behind her. Loyal, gentle Sundar, whose hands were meant for ministering and caring rather than the hilt of a sword. She cast a quick glance at the woman who had dedicated her life to her comfort, feeling suddenly angry at her stubborn refusal to stay behind in the camp. Seeing the delicate beauty of Sundar's mien, her tiny diamond nose-pin sparkling as it caught the sun, resembling a fragile dewdrop about to vanish in the morning light, she felt unbearably saddened. How she would grieve if wounds were to mar that lovely tranquil face, the face she had looked to for all manner of help ever since coming to Jhansi. Sensing the rani's eyes on her, Sundar turned her head and for a split second the two women looked at each other as though seeing for the very first time how much they had really meant to each other in the strange journey they had made together.

But there was no time for words of love or farewell, if indeed the time had come for that. Tantia had already given the war cry.

Lakshmibai spurred Sarangi forward, feeling the gathering speed of her hooves echo the beat of her own heart. As she heard her army thundering behind her, she raised her voice in a rousing cry of 'Har Har Mahadev', her sword raised high above her head. She was right at the frontline as the two sides came together on the Kunch plains in a massive clashing of swords and shields.

The shouts of men and high-pitched whinnying of horses were deafening. The stench of powder smoke and burning flesh choked Lakshmibai's throat and nostrils. But, remembering her childhood lessons, she quickly transferred her reins to her mouth, feeling its sour taste as she clenched the leather between her teeth. Now that both her hands were free, she pulled out her second sword, squeezing her eyes to see through the swirling smoke. The figure of an enemy soldier loomed before her, large, red-coated, raising the muzzle of his gun to point it at her. Without a further thought, she whirred the sword in her right hand through the air as she rode towards him, feeling it stop as it met the flesh of his shoulder. Despite her own churning gut, she pointed her second blade right at the man's belly, driving it in as hard as she could. The reins dropping from her mouth, her cry was piercing: 'My baba, where is my baba!' She knew her enemy would have no answer as she saw the flashing whites of the soldier's eyes, the foam gathering at the corners of his mouth as he fell.

One by one, she toppled enemy soldiers, numbing herself with the thought of how easily they would torture her poor father, reminding herself furiously of the old anguish of her beloved Peshwa-sahib, thinking of how they had bombarded the walls of her poor Jhansi. And faced with such wordless fury, men collapsed before her like easily hewn trees.

But the British were equally determined and, after three hours of battle, Lakshmibai could feel her body grow heavy and soaked in perspiration, the muscles in her arms aching with agonizing fatigue. Even as she wondered if she ought to give the command to retreat, she saw to her horror that some of Tantia's men had already turned around to flee in the direction of Charkhari. Frustrated with Tantia's lack of communication, and recognizing that it would be foolhardy to carry on fighting without the support of his troops, she swiftly gave the order to her own soldiers to withdraw and return to Kalpi, shouting out reminders to retreat in the manner that had been practised many times over in the past few days.

Looking over her shoulder, she was relieved to see that the British forces were not giving chase and guessed that they too were suffering from the fierceness of the midday summer sun. She watched her men organize themselves into an orderly retreat, the last line stopping at regular intervals to turn around, calmly take aim and shoot any stray pursuers as they fled. Once the last of her soldiers had left the battlefield, she galloped after them, returning with them to camp.

Back at the safety of Kalpi fortress, there were recriminations over Tantia's second lost battle. Barely waiting for the privacy of closed doors, Nana let his fury descend. 'How can you be so obtuse, Tantia?' he yelled. 'How can you forget that communication on the battlefield is the key to efficient warfare?'

Lakshmibai could see a familiar sullen look overcome Tantia's features. The expression on his face was that of the child whom Nana had always picked on and she had always comforted. There was no point rebuking him for Lakshmibai knew better than anyone else that Tantia responded stubbornly to anything but words of love and encouragement.

She placed a cautionary hand on Nana's arm to stop his tirade. 'My brothers, time is at a premium. Let us not argue. We need to prepare for the next assault before they are upon us.'

As they turned their attention back to the maps spread out before them, she knew it would fall upon her again to gather Tantia back into Nana's circle.

'I still think Tantia should be commanding the next attack, Nana. The only new tactic we should employ this time is to have a second front, which I must be allowed to lead. That will take the British by surprise.'

She saw with relief that Tantia's face had brightened slightly as the heads of the officers gathered around the table nodded in agreement.

Now named 'Warrior Queen' by the British, Lakshmibai made a second surprise pre-emptive attack at Gulauli where General Rose and his troops had gathered after the first battle. But they were soon forced to retreat as their troops were met with the fierce artillery defences of Rose's camp. As her army floundered, General Rose advanced swiftly, using horse artillery, cavalry and field guns. The British were confident that Tantia's men would turn around and flee to Kalpi, as before, unable to face the ferocity of the counter-attack, but Lakshmibai came to the fore, charging with her horse to lead a combined cavalry and infantry attack on the right of the British lines. Seemingly inspired by their rani's fearless charge, her troops fought with renewed desperation and for a while it looked as though the

British were losing ground. As Lakshmibai's forces came within feet of Rose's field batteries, skirmishes and hand-to-hand sword fights broke out. Horses and men fell all over the battlefield, the sounds of human screams, neighing of horses, clashing of swords and firing of bullets combining to make the most fearsome clamour.

Through air thick with smoke, General Rose gave the order for the bayoneting to begin. Lakshmibai, watching with horror as some of her best soldiers fell, accepted that she could not afford to carry on. She had to take a quick decision to retreat before further casualties were suffered but did not even know where Tantia was in the melee. Gul Mohammed was nearby and she called out to him.

'My Sarangi has taken a gunshot wound and is bleeding hard, I must take her back. Call for a retreat, Gul Mohammed.'

She could barely hear his shouted reply through the noise, 'I will see you at Kalpi, Rani-sahiba.'

Lakshmibai looked down at her mare's right flank that was now bleeding profusely as she slid off her panting body. Spotting a riderless horse wandering forlornly along the fringes of the heaving battlefield, she pulled Sarangi behind her before springing on to it. Briefly she looked back to see that her trusted Gul Mohammed was organizing the retreat before pulling her horse away from the devastation, one hand holding poor, struggling Sarangi's reins. Ash was falling like drifting grey rain, covering the dead and wounded until they formed ghostly mounds, unmistakable from the boulders that had lain peacefully on this field before it had become a battleground.

On returning to the camp beside the craggy hilltop fortress of Kalpi, and handing Sarangi over to be tended by the grooms, Rani Lakshmibai stormed into Nanasahib's tent. She found him sitting with a handful of his men.

'What is wrong with Tantia,' Lakshmibai opened up, unable to hold her patience this time, 'again he has done this, leaving the battlefield without communicating anything to me.'

'Ah, on this occasion it is probably my fault,' Nana replied. 'I sent word that I needed him to go on to Gopalpur to persuade the nawab there to join his forces with ours.'

Though momentarily aggrieved by the haphazardness of Nana's commands, Lakshmibai decided that recriminations within their own command structure would only damage the morale of their soldiers.

She found herself agreeing half-heartedly with Nana, 'I suppose our depleted numbers makes it incumbent on us to look for new allies. We need to regroup with other armies and take the British on with renewed vigour.'

'I think we should march westwards now, to Gwalior,' Nana said. 'The Gwalior forces can be persuaded to join us by the time Tantia comes from Gopalpur.'

'But Nana, Scindia of Gwalior has remained steadfast in his support of the British,' Lakshmibai exclaimed in surprise. 'Why would he join us now? Has he not much more to gain by staying away from the uncertainties of rebellion?'

'I am going to win Scindia's loyalty by reminding him of our old Maratha ties, Mani,' Nana replied confidently. On seeing Lakshmibai's doubtful expression, he added, 'Even if Scindia shows reluctance, Azimullah had made enough secret visits to Gwalior, much before the rebellion had even started, to secure the loyalty of the men. We have the word of Scindia's soldiers that they would be ready to join the uprising even if their maharaja refuses to support us. Tomorrow we will march to Gwalior.'

Sitting on a bale of hay in a damp stable block, Lakshmibai wished she could shut out the laboured breathing of her poor Sarangi. What was war but the loss of loved ones? And in the name of those abstruse things that Nana and Tantia seemed so keen on—pride and territory and titles. Was any of that worth the fact that her father was still missing...and now the loss of poor Sarangi too, her beloved mare who had brought her nothing but joy all these years and then carried her into the terrifying heat of battle before exhaustedly laying down her own life. For something she would not even understand. The wound the poor horse had taken had festered and swollen with pus in the heat and she was now in no state to make the onward journey to Gwalior.

Lakshmibai held a sobbing Damodar in her arms as he stroked the horse's barely moving chest, knowing that the doctor had administered a drug that would soon put Sarangi to sleep forever. As the heaving of Sarangi's chest gradually stilled under the flat of Damodar's palm, Lakshmibai rose from her haunches, still holding her son in her arms. He was now too heavy for her but she carried him out of the stable, feeling his hot tears soak into the collar of her angarkha as he made little whimpering sounds against her ear. Perhaps the child needed to cry his heart out, not just for Sarangi but the whole sorry state of his life. So far he had held on, showing remarkable restraint for a child so young, calling himself her 'brave little soldier' in the few moments they snatched together whenever she was back in her tent.

But time was of the essence today as Nanasahib's men were

already waiting for her to begin the long march west. Damodar's comfort would have to wait for later, whenever and wherever they stopped for the night. It would be easier to console him when they lay under a vast star-filled sky that would stretch around them so limitlessly that their labours and tribulations would suddenly seem small.

As she mounted her new horse, her son taking his place behind her again, Lakshmibai resolved that, in some unhurried peaceful time and in a future that would one day surely belong to them, she would try to be a good mother again to Damodar. And, like a good mother should, she would then teach him all those important lessons about life, as her own father had so carefully done for her in a sunlit faraway river town, now entire worlds removed.

Lakshmibai could feel Damodar's small figure slumped against her back, strapped as he was to her waist to prevent him tumbling off their horse if he fell asleep on the journey. When he awoke, he would want food and water, she thought with panic, feeling far worse for the fact that he had tried so hard to remain uncomplaining so far.

The sky above them was an unforgiving sheet of brass, glittering yellow and hot, as she and Nanasahib led the remaining five thousand men and women of their army westwards. Already their journey had taken three long days and they were forced to go even slower as they crossed the Gwalior hills, the sun beating mercilessly down on their heads.

These were the very hills that she had been able to see from the upper floors of Panch Mahal and Lakshmibai remembered their purple hue on clear airless days. How distant those peaceful days now seemed when she had looked at these huge folds on the horizon to assess such simple things as the seasons, the impending monsoons, the time of day.

Looking ahead, she could see the River Sind in the distance, dried to a mere a trickle in places due to the blazing summer heat. As they chose a shallow stretch to ford it, allowing their horses the luxury of drinking from the cool water and wading through its depths, she realized that they were now in the territory of Maharaja Jiyajirao Scindia of Gwalior. Despite Nana's assurances, she felt very uncertain of Scindia's machinations but they rode on, picking up speed as the beautiful carved walls of Gwalior Fort rose before them in the far distance.

One of the riders called out excitedly that Maharaja Scindia had sent out emissaries to greet them. Squinting into the heat, Lakshmibai saw tiny specks on the horizon but, as the horsemen neared, she could hear them shouting that the rebels were to stop further progress forthwith. They met in a cloud of dust and, within minutes, found that Scindia's instructions were unambiguous: the rebels were to leave at once or face immediate attack by the Gwalior army. Shock and anger were written all over Nana's face but the emissaries were instructed to return with a message that Nanasahib's troops were only looking for reinforcements of clothing and supplies. They would not stay long, Nana averred, although Lakshmibai knew he was dissembling. She wondered, as they rode on towards Gwalior, whether Scindia, cowering in his fort, would be as wily as Nana and have already called for assistance from the British.

Eight miles from Gwalior, Nanasahib's army was attacked by Scindia's forces who had remained British allies. Taken by surprise with the unexpected aggression, the advancing troops were about to turn back, but Lakshmibai rode forward, rallying her men behind her. Leading the way with two hundred cavalry, she faced the Gwalior troops, her horse rearing up while she shouted encouragement. As her cries of 'Deen!' and 'Har Har Mahadev' were picked up by her soldiers, their voices ringing in unison across the battlefield, a sudden shift in mood became apparent and, to Scindia's astonishment, the cries could soon be heard ricocheting back from his own army as well. Within minutes the two sides had thrown their swords and rifles down to rush across the field and hug and embrace each other, brothers bonded by a common enemy. It was as though the Gwalior troops had waited long for an inspiring figure of resistance and finally found one in the fearless figure of the rani of Jhansi, her small son strapped behind her back.

Maharaja Scindia, on witnessing the astounding spectacle of his entire army deserting him to join the rebels, fled for the British camp at Agra where he and his family were given refuge. He reported that he had seen the rebels riding in the direction of his abandoned fort and palace.

Nanasahib and Lakshmibai entered Gwalior city in triumph and its citizens turned out in full strength to cheer them, waving date palm leaves and mango branches to signify their admiration of such brave and fearless warriors.

After Gwalior had been occupied, Nanasahib's first decision was to organize a grand durbar in the magnificent Phoolbagh Palace. Lakshmibai knew it was not supposed to be a celebration as Nanasahib too had suffered his share of agonies since being informed of the massacres at Kanpur. She had seen his bitter tears and had not been able to tell if it was for the sacking of his city or the horrible suffering of the women at the Bibighar or the loss of his beloved Mainabai that he cried. The durbar, he assured her, was merely to serve as a symbolic coronation of his renewed status as Peshwa and head of the Marathas. It was an important title, he said, one that would rouse their troops to fight the hardest battle that still lay before them. They both knew that the British would never let them have the strategically placed Gwalior. Attack on their new position was imminent.

So it was with dismay that Lakshmibai saw preparations for battle stopped so that everyone's energies could be redirected to Nana's coronation. A huge canopy was erected inside the fort and festooned with all the Maratha flags and standards. Hundreds of men and women were toiling to decorate the palace with marigold garlands and auspicious leaves of mango and banana trees. Palm flowers were being plunged into barrels of grain to signify prosperity and oil lamps and incense sticks were already making the air heavy with smoke and fragrance. In one of the grand halls, freshly tonsured priests, wearing dhotis and tulsi-seed necklaces, recited verses from the Vedas to invoke the blessings of the gods and their chants now resounded within the walls of the fort.

Lakshmibai knew she ought to be pleased to behold the joy of her old friend but could not help feeling deeply uneasy instead. Much as she too wanted to enjoy their victory, she knew that hard work lay ahead. The troops could do without the distraction of a celebration. A celebration that was far too premature when Rose's army were mere miles away, no doubt planning their next move. She worried, though, that voicing her displeasure at this time would only make it appear as though she wanted some of the glory for herself. This was Nana's moment, the one he had waited for all his life and, when he appeared in the hall, dressed in his ancestral robes and jewellery to ascend Scindia's throne, Lakshmibai told herself firmly to be happy for him. She watched the glow of satisfaction come over his tired face as the screaming of conch shells and shehnais proclaimed him the new Peshwa and remembered suddenly the scribbled entry in his childhood diary that had promised himself this moment even as a ten-year-old boy.

Turning away from the brightly lit hall, with a sudden stab of unshed tears behind her eyes, she hurried towards her chambers before anyone could witness her distress. Suddenly all she wanted was to spend the night quietly with Damodar, Sundar and Kashi. They had all turned in for the night and she crept into her room, anxious not to wake them. She lay down on her bed, unable to take comfort from the soft breathing of her sleeping son. The booming of the gun salute from the ramparts of Gwalior Fort, celebrating the rebirth of the Maratha confederacy, filled the room like an eerie death knell. Try as she might to focus on victory and battle, she could not seem to erase from her mind the as yet unknown fates of both her father and Jhansi, too scared to openly acknowledge that she had probably lost them both forever.

She looked at Damodar as he slept fitfully in the curve of her arm, flinching in his sleep at the booming cannon shots. He had asked her just this afternoon whether she would go with him to the dried riverbed of the Morar river to search for its famously sweet watermelons and she had promised, knowing that such small pleasures would never be theirs again. Why, she wondered, pressing Damodar's head to her chest and trying to cover his ears with her palms, had she ever brought the child into her life at all? What sort of curse was it that, instead of being able to shower him with a mother's blessings, her love had been like a terrible pestilence that had blighted his young life forever? And, having loved him and taken him into her life, here she was now faced with the task of writing him out of it again. For wasn't that the most compassionate thing to do in these circumstances? To let him return to his parents, to ease him out of her life again, to have him forget somehow that he had ever loved her at all?

The following day, Lakshmibai was desperate to get a few moments alone with Nanasahib but whenever she looked at him, he was surrounded by his brand new set of sycophants, eager for the attentions of their new Peshwa. She observed, with sadness and with trepidation, Nanasahib's beaming smiles, his unwary satisfaction, wondering at his ability to allow present happiness to so completely cloud both the past and the future. Finally she managed to drag him away from the attentions of his followers, pleading for a few minutes of private conversation.

'What is it, my little Mani?' he said flippantly, 'I hope you are not going to give me one of your delightful lectures! These are such glorious times for our Maratha clans, I will not allow you spoil it with your worries.'

'Nana, my brother, I speak with love, please listen to me…'

'Very well then, let us sit here for a few minutes,' he said, stopping in a shady courtyard and patting the space next to him on a marble bench.

'Nana, please let us not forget that it isn't over yet. We still have work to do. Have you forgotten, Nana, that the British forces will be regrouping somewhere and are possibly already on their way to us?'

Nana's face had gone serious. He knew sensible little Mani was right. She was always right, unlike that great blundering fool Tantia, still trying to form some sort of alliance with the nawab of Banda. There had been no news from him for a while and Nana knew it was probably best to lay his faith in the young woman who sat beside him. Who would have thought that the little girl who had trailed after him and Tantia when they were children would grow into such a brave commander?

'What do you think we should do, Mani?' he asked, uncharacteristically full of sudden humility.

'Capturing Scindia's treasury and being delivered his army so miraculously are almost like God-given blessings, Nana. First we have to pay Scindia's troops some form of indemnity to ensure their loyalty and, of course, we must pay our own troops handsomely for all that they have undergone these past weeks. That will stoke their enthusiasm for more warfare. Then we have to shore up the defences of this town, organize the garrisons under capable commanders, maintain the discipline of the forces, post troops along all the roads that lead into Gwalior...'

Nanasahib got up from the bench. 'You are right, Mani. We have plenty to do. I would like you to take personal charge of organizing our troops. Before that, though, I have something I want you to take. I have carried it around inside my robes for the past two days because I had really wanted to give it to you on the night of the coronation but you were nowhere to be seen then.'

Lakshmibai shook her head disbelievingly as Nana took a beautiful old pearl chain from around his neck and held it up in front of her. She could not even remember when she had last worn such heavy jewellery...not since Gangadhar...not since...but stubborn, loving Nana was already pulling it over her head. There would be no arguing with him. She lifted up the heavy ruby pendant and looked into its blood-filled depths feeling immeasurably moved. There were still those who loved her. It was true what her father had told her—years ago, when she had been small and, more recently, when she had thought she could befriend the British. It was people like Nana and Tantia who would be with her when all else was lost and times turned bad. How right her poor baba had been and how unthinkingly she had rebuffed his warnings against putting her trust in a man like Robert Ellis. Ellis, who had left her at her moment of gravest need, never once trying to save her from the murderous intentions of his country's invading army.

As Nana's attention was taken up with some other distraction,

Lakshmibai returned quickly to her chambers and, in the privacy of her room, looked in the mirror at the heavy pearl chain on her neck. In the half-darkness, she could almost fool herself into believing she was back to being a queen again and not a military commander! Tomorrow, however, she would ask Sundar to put it back in Gwalior's treasury. The weight hanging on her neck would only hamper her in the battles to come. Nana had asked her if she would lead the next attack against the British in place of Tantia, and she had willingly agreed.

At midnight, Lakshmibai stood next to her son's bed, feeling anguish wash over her at the sight of his sleeping face. These recurrent departures for battle were so fraught only because they involved bidding him goodbye each time. She ought to feel thankful he was asleep this time.

In repose, Damodar's features had lost that air of anxiety he had worn ever since the siege of Jhansi had begun. She had tried to answer some of his early probing questions, struggling herself to believe in exhortations about the protection of their land. Was it not true that the only real protection of a land lay in preserving its peace? But that kind of simple notion seemed to have no place in this time of war. A war she had never asked for. Why, even the people whose peace she most wanted to preserve had urged her to fight for their honour. And so she had kept her ideas to herself, her disquiet eventually silencing even her young son.

She knelt by Damodar's bedside, wondering whether she had been wrong to shirk the explanations she owed him. Had he really been too young to understand? And, if he was, then how had he so quietly accepted his new life, so far from the home and the playmates he must surely miss. It had been just a few days after leaving Jhansi that Damodar had stopped quizzing her altogether. Sometime after reaching the camp at Kalpi, those relentless questions to which she had no answers had suddenly stopped and the child had finally lapsed into bewildered acceptance of everything that was put his way. Even attempting recently to put a brave face on it. That had somehow been so much worse than his earlier insistent inquiries.

Lakshmibai reached out her hand and smoothed Damodar's pillow near his face, sorely tempted to wake him up and make one last attempt at explaining everything before she left. Would it be worse for him to wake up in the morning and find that she had left for battle without even bidding him goodbye? Or to be roused now, and perhaps not be able to sleep again, imagining with terror his mother riding out with her invading army in the shadows of the night?

She gently moved a curl that lay across one temple, withdrawing her fingers as he stirred and mumbled in his sleep. The troubled little crease that appeared on his forehead at this interruption was suddenly heartbreaking and she pressed her fist tight against her mouth, feeling an immense wave of sorrow well up within her. She had to get up and leave before she woke up this peacefully sleeping child. Leaping up, she stumbled out of the room, almost unable to see where she was going for the unbidden tears now flooding out of her eyes. On her way out, she could do no more than touch a stricken Kashi wordlessly on her shoulder, leaving the maid hitting her head repeatedly on the doorjamb, as though that pain could somehow prepare her for the anguish that lay ahead.

❧ 45 ❧

Rani Lakshmibai was in complete charge of Nanasahib's forces as they gathered on the scrubby plains of Kotah-ki-Sarai to face General Rose's army in that final battle. She was tireless on her horse, riding up and down the ranks of her soldiers, issuing instructions, orders, encouragement. The sun was high in the sky and she hoped that, by delaying the battle, the heat would fatigue the British before they had even started. She had also carefully chosen for her position a part of the field where a series of entrenchments already existed along the base of the hills. Hills south of Gwalior that had been visible from Jhansi's fort on cloudless days.

Rose's army approached and took up its station on the far side of the battlefield. As the British column began a slow advance, the first shot was heard from one of Lakshmibai's field posts and an officer's horse collapsed from under him with a terrified whinny. The man sprang to his feet, an expletive emerging from his lips at the accuracy and temerity of the shot, before he snapped an angry order for his infantry to charge. They rushed forward, baying for blood as Lakshmibai's troops responded with a barrage of fire. Even while many British troops were seen to fall, exposed as they were on the plain, their swift approach brought them near enough to Lakshmibai's artillery to engage them in hand-to-hand sword combat. After a few hours of fierce fighting, her forces were pushed back onto the hills behind them. From here, regrouping, they made another attack, this time on the British rearguard. Now the British retreated hastily, allowing Lakshmibai's army time to creep back from the exposed slopes and take up their field positions again.

It was during the second British advance that it happened, this advance comprising a combined infantry and artillery force of the 8th Hussars. Lakshmibai's men, fighting to the point of exhaustion, had been pushed back into the hills. Now they were given no time to take stock for, waiting for them among the hidden folds of the land, was the 95th Foot Brigade. Lakshmibai's forces were chased further up the slopes but fought wildly, repulsing the British troops who retreated briefly into a series of nullahs behind the hills. But there was no mercy and, yet again, the Hussars used the lull in battle to push forward. It was when they made their swift reappearance so soon after the first two advances, that Lakshmibai was suddenly taken unawares. As her soldiers scattered, she was caught without her escorts. She looked around for just one split second before riding forward, disappearing into a black veil of smoke.

It was a young Hussar who got her. At first, confused by the smoke, the soldier had felt his flank scraped excruciatingly by the tip of an enemy sword. He swung around, the stinging pain in his leg making him instinctively raise his own sabre, seeing through the grit and dust that a uniformed rebel was turning back to ride towards him again. He heard a carbine shot and the advancing soldier jerked forward in the saddle, as though hit from behind. As their two horses passed each other, their hooves thundering like drums in his frightened ears, he reached out with one hand clinging onto the reins. He felt his arm jerk back as the blade of his sword met flesh and, swiftly, as he had been taught, he drove it as deep as he could before twisting the hilt to cause utmost damage to the organs within. Despite the resistance of the flesh and muscle caught on his sword, he made, once again, a piercing motion, almost able to feel the life that lay under the blade of his sword slip away. As he turned his horse around again, eager to know the effect he may have caused, he saw, through the ash-filled air, that his victim had slumped and was now sliding off a frightened, rearing horse. To ensure the rebel's death, he rode up again but saw, as armour plates dislodged and dropped away, that the soldier was a woman. His horrified gaze took in the sight of her body lying bleeding and draped across her horse, eyes already glazing in a pale and beautiful face. As he spurred his horse to move on to the next enemy soldier, it was with shocked and muddled comprehension that he realized he had just killed a young woman. Only later was he informed that his victim had been the feared warrior queen of Jhansi.

She had felt the crunching blow of the musket ball slam into her shoulder before white-hot pain radiating from her stomach flashed everything else into oblivion. Still, as her brave horse carried her forward, she kept her talwar pointing before her, hoping she could take one more of the enemy before she fell. Instead, he had got her— a soldier so young she was suddenly grateful she had not killed him. He was little more than a boy himself, confused and traumatized by what should have been his moment of triumph. Only a few years older than her Damodar.

Damodar would have woken up by now. She thought with sudden panic, the world spinning around her, that she ought to have instructed Kashi last night to take him back to Jhansi, to his own parents. They would surely understand that she had only borrowed their son's love for a while and would be glad to claim him back. But what of her own unkept promises; to search for sweet watermelons on a dry riverbed, to explain away his fears some peaceful night under a roof dusted with stars. As her father had once done for her...

How strange that she could hear her baba call her now...his dear voice echoing among the trees, calling out through hot green evenings for bath and tuition and other things worthy of escape.

But voices faded as the putrid smell of death filled her nostrils. She slipped off her saddle and felt herself falling towards the blackened burning earth. Slowly, as a dove's feather from a high turret, she was falling and stopping, floating and retreating, drifting, drifting towards the beckoning earth. Her blood was dripping over the flanks of her horse and onto the earth below. She could see drops scatter to the ground looking, for all she knew, like rubies glittering in the dust. As though that were their place; blood and earth, earth and blood, the two belonging together as much as a pair of lovers destined to bring each other anguish.

She tried to flutter her eyes open, still hanging upside down from her saddle, and could see, through the tears and perspiration swimming in her eyes, floating ashes of war fill the sky above. Was this what snow was like then...each flake catching the sun, like the silver tinsel of her wedding day, scattered by a Jhansi that had loved her unconditionally from that very first moment. If I am content to die, it would be to have saved you, my Jhansi: the peaceful streets of Halwaipur, the fish in your temple lake, most of all, the shining happiness on each and every face in your thronging bazaars.

What a terrible fate for a queen to know that the salvation of her people could come only from her abandonment of them. Like poor tormented Ganga-devi who sacrificed her life so her children could live.

Now she was being hauled up and carried on horseback, every galloping stride sending shafts of pain coursing through her body.

Sometimes she lapsed into blissful sleep but would just as quickly snap awake, the throbbing of her wounds reminding her she was still alive and on some interminable journey.

They were putting her down on a bed of leaves; high over her head was a canopy of green silk spangled with sun. Someone had flung gold-dust into the evening air as though for a queen's welcome.

She knew these forests—he had waited for her in them. His tall figure on a chestnut roan, both man and horse impatient as she wended her way through the trees in their direction. His gaze coming to rest on her face with what she had thought was tender concern at her safe arrival. He had loved her once and now he wanted her dead.

Dark veils were falling again as the light faded and the trees grew close and forbidding and she could smell the burning flesh of men and horses once more, the stench filling her nostrils, her eyes hurting with the grit of ash and gunpowder, her breath forcing itself out in short painful bursts.

Someone was unhooking the protective plates on her arms and slipping off her shoes. Her headscarf, sour with perspiration, was being placed over her brow, the thinness of its silk failing to shield her eyes from the sun glancing just above the trees. A cloth turban was slipped gently under her neck. The smallest movement caused pain to nudge into every pore but the words she needed to tell her soldiers this were stuck, clogged and throbbing in her parched throat.

A hand caressed her hair. Was it him? How she had loved him. She arched her neck with the ache of old wounds, worse than these she bore now. She had wanted to love him with all the desperation of a young heart and at first thought that was love. She had wanted to return his goodness tenfold when he was kind to her and had tried not to mind when he had not—was that not a kind of love? She could feel a hand wipe her escaping tears and wanted to tell whoever it was that she cried not out of despair. Would they believe her if she said that she had not meant to forget him, nor disrespect his memory? It was just that, when love came at last, she had not felt able to turn it away...

Her eyes would not open but faces and voices were shuttling before her, unravelling frantically like spools on a weaver's loom, beckoning and echoing through the trees by a sweet old pet-name, tempting her by the future she may yet have, begging her to live...

When Gul Mohammed saw the rani fall at Kotah-ki-Sarai, he rode over the smoking earth, unheeding of whizzing bullets and screams of death, to scoop her off her horse. Along with a few of his soldiers, he had then ridden furiously, clinging to her body with his arms, holding the reins in his teeth. He was intent on getting his queen as far from the British as possible, fearing they would defile her body in some terrible revenge. He had heard there was a reward of one lakh rupees on her head and knew they would be pleased to get her alive or dead. Sundar had already stabbed herself in a frenzy, as she had often threatened to do if she ever saw their rani fall. Her body too had been picked up by one of the sipahis on horseback and the small group of horsemen rode furiously together towards a forest at the edge of the hills, the thudding of hooves urgent on the silent earth.

Dismounting only after they were hidden in the darkest depths of a jamun grove, Gul Mohammed sent his fastest rider to get help from Gwalior, while the bodies of the two women, friends unto death, were gently laid side by side on leaf-beds on the forest floor. Someone had unfurled a turban to cover Sundar's body from the gaze of the living and already its muslin was stiff with blackened blood.

In this gladed green haven, sounds of the battle they had just left could not be heard at all. Here there was only evening birdsong and the laboured breathing of the rani, surrounded by her soldiers as they awaited defeat.

Fragments of the men's conversation flitted across the forest clearing like frightened moths:

'Nanasahib will surely send a doctor as soon as he receives our message.'

'Not a moment will be wasted when he knows our rani's life is at risk...'

'...like a sister to him, she is...'

'But the British must already be on their way to Gwalior Fort to capture Nanasahib.'

'Will our brothers know of their own impending deaths, hai Allah!'

'Maybe Nanasahib will not receive our message at all. Maybe he has already fled to save his own life.'

'Then, Allah, who will rescue us? Who will even know that we are all bleeding to death in this godforsaken place, so far from home?'

Gul Mohammed looked down as the rani moved slightly. She was conscious and using one arm to pull at the ornament on her neck. Wiping her tears and begging her in frantic whispers to stay still, Gul Mohammed lifted the chain from between her limp, bloodstained fingers. He stared blankly at the large pearls, marbled maroon by her blood. Perhaps she thought he could sell them to gain a reprieve for the soldiers, as though sea creatures may have wept for years to buy them mercy.

She was still losing blood, the earth beneath her soaking it up, possessed by an insatiable greed for it. It would take a miracle to save her now. Gul Mohammed looked distraughtly up at the jamun tree. It had been bristling thick and black with returning birds, their clamour drowning soldiers' groans and the scuffing and fidgeting of thirsty horses. But now even last heedless crows were being silenced by the deepening evening. Shadows unfurled and ran rapidly across the forest floor, long fingers warning mutely that it would be dark before long. He turned his head, still listening for the help that was awaited from Gwalior, with the bleak knowledge that it was too soon, much too soon. At least another hour must pass before he could hope to hear the thudding of hooves...how could he stretch her laboured breathing to last till then?

The battle was lost too. Confusion would reign among the forces on the plains of Kotah-ki-Sarai with neither the rani nor him present to issue orders. He was sure it would only take a few hours for the British to gain the upper hand. From then it would be a matter of time before they moved into Gwalior city to reconquer it and he felt suddenly that it would be merciful for his rani to die without the knowledge of their defeat.

Looking down at her face, anguish piercing his heart, he saw that her eyes were suddenly wide open, depthless dark pools in a pale face. She was struggling to speak.

He put his head down and heard her voice crack and whisper, barely able to discern her words.

'He awaits me...' she said, but he could not know of whom she spoke.

Epilogue

It seemed to Ellis that battles were crazed games that neither side could possibly win. He, who had never actually fought in one, could only imagine Lakshmibai caught in the midst of those warring armies as later, like a man depraved, he set about gathering as many details as he could find of her last stand.

It was a strangely beautiful place—the battlefield of Kotah-ki-Sarai—or so it comforted him to think; an arena darkened with curtains of silver smoke, cinders drifting through the sky like soft black snowfall, the earth beneath scattered with beads of blood and coins of sunshine.

That was how Ellis saw it and, for months afterwards, he could not close his eyes without seeing Lakshmibai's lonely figure on horseback in that terrifying theatre. It was utter helplessness he felt as, time and time again, his mind would replay the scene of her likely death like a single bar of sad music stuck on the tip of a gramophone needle. For years they had been separated by the silk veils of her purdah and, now, there was nothing at all he could do to stop her as she turned her horse around to begin her slow final ride, vanishing behind falling smoke curtains forever.

Ellis thought many times in those days of stepping into the river near his lodgings to allow it to claim his body and poor tortured soul. But something always stopped him; the memory, perhaps, of a distant land that still beckoned. He could not accept that its doors would remain closed to him, despite his failed efforts at trying to book a passage to India in the week of his resignation from the Company. Those frantic trips to docks across the country had been abandoned, however, when the terrible events of 1857 had overtaken him. And, imagining that his feeble and belated efforts to return to Jhansi were being mocked, he had finally given up.

When he first saw newspapers emblazoned with jubilant accounts of General Hugh Rose's successful campaign in Bundelkhand, he had felt physically sick: gloating editorials making much of the dastardly deeds performed by the rebel leaders, most of all the rani of Jhansi. And then that horrible day when every single paper carried news of her death. The words had leapt off the page like small knives embedding themselves in his heart, even while the world around him celebrated the death of the Rebel Queen and the end of Mutiny.

Mere days later, the *Times* had published a copy of the letter General Rose had written to the commander-in-chief of Queen Victoria's Army after Gwalior had been taken. The dark weight of a rain-soaked evening closed in on Ellis as he read Rose's account of having personally witnessed Rani Lakshmibai's cremation ceremony and seen her turn to ashes. The thought of Lakshmibai's warmth and beauty reduced to dust was truly unbearable to Ellis, there being no comfort in the thought that she, at least, had been returned to her beloved land. How could there be when that land had no room for him any more. He thought that General Rose's description would haunt him forever and it certainly did, for many years crippling his ability to partake of life's most mundane pleasures—music and conversation, even the simple joy of human relationships. Not for a moment in those sorrowing days did he imagine that the report could have been untrue.

It was only in 1864 that Ellis could finally bring himself to return to India, motivated by a growing desire to find those people and places that had once made him so happy—his old orderly, Karamchand, Barhwa Sagar lake, Jhansi. By now he had learnt of grief's capacity to grow over the years into something calmer and deeper that edges silently into the soul forever. A weight wrapped around the heart that one can learn to live with. After all, there were others too who had suffered grievous losses in the uprisings of 1857. In the summer, Ellis heard about Harriet Mead's remarriage to a cloth merchant called Thomas Pinkerton, discovering that she had returned to India three years ago in order to raise a tombstone to James Mead within the grounds of the Residency in Lucknow.

That winter, Ellis too booked his passage, making again the same journey he had made as a young man—over the seas to Calcutta, overland to Banda and then, across the dusty swathes of central India, to Jhansi.

Many things were different, not least the trains that could now carry him through parts of his journey. The people were different too; Indians and Europeans more divided perhaps than before India had become Britain's. It was while boarding the train that would carry him from Calcutta to Allahabad that he first noticed the careful segregation; British officers and gentlemen in the first-class carriages, all the Indians, rich and poor, crowding into the others.

He remarked on it wryly to the man sharing his compartment, a young lieutenant who did not look a day over twenty. 'Hadn't realized they'd keep us so separate,' he said, gazing out of the train window at the red ropes that divided the platform into two discrete areas. This time, as a mere traveller with no Company or government business to attend to, Ellis felt he could speak freely, with little to fear. But he noticed uncertainty overcoming the pleasant features of the young officer sitting on the berth before him. He had no wish to embarrass or confuse the young man who reminded him rather poignantly of himself at that age: blonde, strapping and oddly uncomfortable in the restrictive uniform.

'Hasn't it always been that way, sir?' the lieutenant replied politely.

Ellis thought for a moment before nodding. 'You're quite right, my dear fellow, it probably has.'

'You're not newly arrived here are you, sir?'

'Well, yes, in a manner of speaking,' Ellis replied briefly, 'although I have been here before.'

The young man now looked interested, 'Really, sir? When?'

'Oh a long time ago, it now seems. Nine years. I returned to England in 1855.'

'Before the Great Mutiny then?'

'Yes, before the Great Mutiny.'

'That's rather a pity, sir,' the lieutenant said, adding cheerily at the blank expression on Ellis's face, 'Imagine missing out on that!'

Ellis pulled back the wooden shutters of the window to let in some breeze. The platform was still crowded with people leaping on and off the train as a whistle rent the air. The compartment lurched alarmingly as they began pulling out of the station in a great cloud of steam. Ellis's companion was fortunately silenced by the noisy spectacle, his blonde head almost hanging out of the window in excitement as the platform with its hawkers and shops started moving past. But, after all that had been left behind and the train gained speed, settling down to a comfortable swaying motion, the lieutenant pulled the window shutters closed and turned to face Ellis again. He smiled and offered his hand, 'Sorry, sir, I should've said before. I'm Lieutenant Corby. HM's Thirteenth Light Infantry.'

'Ellis, Robert Ellis.' He had stopped using his rank years before, seeing it as lost along with so much else. There was no point burdening this jovial young man with any of that. 'Thirteenth Light Infantry,' he asked, 'isn't that at Dinapur?'

Lieutenant Corby looked surprised that he knew. 'Used to be, sir. But we were sent recently to Allahabad to occupy the new cantonment there. South of Cannington—you might have heard of it? The civil area, newly built on a grid system by the riverside. We even have a railway line linking North Cantonment with New Cantonment. It's all very smart.'

'Yes, I had heard that the government had undertaken to build hundreds of new barracks.'

'And vastly increase the proportion of British soldiers to Indian,' Lieutenant Corby said, adding, 'Good thing too. They never did catch the main villains of the Mutiny, you know. I guess the government was rightly nervous there could be another uprising somewhere which is why they packed off the old Mughal emperor to Rangoon in such haste.'

They were silent for a few minutes before Corby spoke again. 'Rajputana,' he said, 'that's where I'd put my money. After all that was where they finally caught that guerrilla leader, Tantia Tope, still trying in vain to keep embers of mutiny alive. He was hung to death, of course, but the chap he worked for, the old Peshwa's son—well, *he's* still at large. There's every chance he'll resurface at some point. Those slippery Marathas are not to be trusted—been to war with us thrice already, not counting the Mutiny.'

Ellis had heard the stories of Nanasahib's escape from Gwalior. There had been numerous false sightings these past few years, news and photographs of lookalikes regularly making the papers, but it seemed that Nanasahib had actually managed to get away and the most likely hiding place was reckoned to be Nepal. Apparently, the king of Nepal had given Begum Hazratmahal sanctuary too, although there were incredible rumours that she now lived the life of a pauper. Young Corby was still talking and Ellis hoped he would not mention Lakshmibai's name. He had not heard it uttered out loud for years now.

'...there's a great example of just how canny they are. That Peshwa's political advisor was a Muslim called Azimullah. His story of escape is the stuff of novels. Apparently he got out of India by travelling incognito with an Englishwoman who had fallen in love with him. The last we heard was that he had got to Constantinople and become emissary to the sheriff of Mecca. Imagine that, sir!'

Ellis smiled briefly and looked at the swathes of brown land outside the window—huts and villages and, in the distance, a small mud-fort. All the Indian nobles who had remained loyal during the uprising had been given land and properties belonging previously to rebel kings and queens, along with titles such as 'Choicest Son of the British Government'. Jhansi itself had been handed over to Maharaja Scindia of Gwalior, along with three lakh rupees, as a reward for his loyalty to the British.

'Luckily they got the rebel queen,' Lieutenant Corby piped up again. 'She was the one who was truly dangerous. Fearless, they said. And merciless too. Put seventy of our women and children to death in her fort before riding out in battle against General Rose. Imagine the arrogance.'

As Corby shook his head ruefully, Ellis kept his gaze on the far horizon. His eyes hurt terribly from the heat and the bits of dust and grit that were flying through the window. But, inside, all was numb. Poor Corby, he was not to know.

'It was the Hussars who got her, sir. They'd kept her father captive in case she managed to escape, in order to lure her back. But, once she was killed, there was no point keeping him and so they hung him too the next day. Took him back to Jhansi, in fact, to the very same gardens where the massacres had taken place and put him to death right there, along with a whole host of others who had been complicit in the murder of our people.'

Ellis dragged his gaze back to the young face before him, so open and honest and quite animated by his storytelling skills. He tried to look impassive as he asked softly, 'There was a son, wasn't there?'

'Oh yes, the rebel queen's adopted child. That's rather a sad story actually, seeing how she just abandoned him for battle. Apparently he lived the life of a fugitive for many months, hiding in the forests of Bundelkhand along with a few faithful retainers. When they finally emerged, hoping to return to Jhansi, they were told that the child's real parents had been killed and so they eventually went somewhere else. Indore, I think it might have been. But he was officially pardoned by Queen Victoria, of course, seeing that he really had nothing to do with his adoptive mother's dastardly deeds. Our queen's been really awfully generous to the native royals since the Mutiny. Proclamations and treaties being signed every day promising that their territories will from now on be protected. And their right to adopt, of course.'

'Too late,' Ellis whispered under his breath, looking out of the window again. Too late for Jhansi. Too late for Lakshmibai.

Corby looked startled but regained his equanimity quickly. 'You're probably right, sir. It was a bloody time. Took over a year to put down. It's acknowledged now in some circles that Lord Dalhousie was misguided in pursuing his Doctrine of Lapse to such an extent. But now he's dead too and, with India passing to the crown and a state of peace having been declared, all should be well hence. Good times lie ahead. I'm certainly glad to be here.'

Ellis smiled at the young man's confidence. It was not such a long time ago that he had been filled with similar hope. He took a deep breath, feeling relief at having passed his first test in India, quite unable to believe that he had managed to sit with a stranger and hear him talk about Lakshmibai like that. Perhaps his poor broken heart had indeed healed sometime during the passage of the years.

Onwards to Jhansi, Ellis spoke to everyone he came across, as though making up for his years of enforced exile and silence. He knew he must seem eccentric and perhaps even a little sad to the people he accosted, especially the Indians who had clearly grown unused to having English sahibs commune with them so informally. But he was no longer in uniform, had no civil duties to take care of and cared little if people thought him quite mad.

However, on his very first day back in Jhansi, he discovered that Corby's was the British view and not one shared by the people of Jhansi at all. Only the British seemed convinced that Rani Lakshmibai had taken a mortal wound in battle. All the Indian people whom Ellis spoke to, on the other hand, pointed out that General Rose and his army had been fighting the battle at Kotah-ki-Sarai when the rani's bleeding body had been taken into the forests, never to be seen by the British again. A funeral ceremony had certainly taken place at the Rock of Gwalior, under the shade of a tamarind tree—there was no disagreement on that. The ceremony had been attended by a small handful of the rani's soldiers but these men later put it about that it had not been Rani Lakshmibai's funeral at all.

It was the khitmudgar at the dak bungalow where Ellis stayed who was the first to declare quite vehemently that Rani Lakshmibai was still alive, claiming that the cremation had been that of the queen's handmaiden—Sundar. Ellis knew better than to argue with such certainty, mulling silently as he finished his dinner on the easy manner with which hope gave over to myth.

In the next few days, the more people he spoke to, the more evident it became: it was those who loved her best who could not bear to think of her as dead, their disbelief apparently setting off rumour and legend even as the smoke had risen from the burning sandalwood of Lakshmibai's funeral pyre, even as her ashes had been gathered up and immersed in river water.

But Ellis put the story again to a teashop owner in the old part of the city two days later and that old man too swore on knowing someone who had been acquainted with one of the rani's soldiers.

'Sahib, that soldier, Liaquat Ali, was among the group that helped our rani-sahiba escape the forests on the night Gwalior fell,' the teashop owner said firmly as he placed a tumbler of frothy sweet tea before Ellis. 'Our rani-sahiba lives, we all know that. Of course, she must wear a burkha and live the anonymous life of a Muslim woman, mind, for you never know if the British generals might still want their revenge. But she is in a city not that far from here. And, sometimes, she returns, sahib. She returns to her beloved Jhansi, cloaked and veiled, as she did once with the raja. To see how we fare, to share still in the joys and sorrows of her people.'

From under the eaves of the old teashop, Ellis looked up at Jhansi's empty fort on its hillock. It had always had a certain brooding presence but, today, overlooking the busy sunlit city, it looked more secretive than ever before. He had heard only that morning that the British were planning to move a garrison into its compound and use Panch Mahal as its office. Their continuing anger towards Rani Lakshmibai had been clear enough earlier in the day, when he had stood in the shadow of the great wooden gates of Bhanderi Darwaza— kept permanently shut and barred on General Rose's orders ever since Lakshmibai had escaped the Jhansi siege through it. On his wanderings, he had seen too that Ranimahal was mostly destroyed and Motibagh completely burnt down, shops and offices having sprung up on its site. Only remnants of the garden were visible through the trees, its walls now blackened and decaying, splashing fountains stilled, great branches heavy with white flowers growing uncontrolled and wild.

It was clear to Ellis that Jhansi itself, in the wont of cities, had overcome much of its trauma in the six years since its destruction. The burned-out cantonment had been rebuilt and become an important and elegant British enclave. A new railhead was being developed to the west of the city, bringing prosperity back to the traders and merchants. And people, as people do when they too are intent on regenerating their lives, seemed to have forgotten the terrors of the bloody massacres that had beset both sides in the Great Mutiny. Despite all of that, how curious that they could not bring themselves to forget their beautiful young queen. It was touching to say the least, this unshakeable belief among Lakshmibai's people that she still lived. Clearly borne from the love they still held for her, but Ellis had no wish to demean such precious, closely held beliefs with more deliberation.

As the sun started its slow descent behind Jhansi's fort that evening, Ellis was still sitting in the teashop, his tea grown cold and congealed in the glass before him. He continued to silently watch the crowds filling the streets of the bazaar as the fasting hours ended; people purchasing food, customers in search of bargains, tradesmen and hawkers busily at work. Innumerable horse carriages were cantering in through the town gates too, travelling in from nearby Shivpuri or Deogarh on this festival day. Hordes of women and children clad in colourful, tinsel-edged clothes were disembarking noisily from big landaus and smaller tongas. One small carriage, a veiled woman its lone passenger, stopped just a few yards from where Ellis sat.

He watched the woman disembark from the tonga, only a flash of ankle visible under her burkha as she lifted it to tread in the dust. Holding a small purse close to her, she too joined the crowds streaming past the havelis, unaware of being watched. She appeared to inhale in pleasure on entering the bustling sweet market, where sevaiyan whirls were being soaked in sugar syrup and blocks of sohan halwa lay stacked high in greasy glass boxes. But she bought no Eid sweetmeats, stopping instead at a hawker's stall to buy a pair of conch earrings and a few glass bangles. He watched her slip them onto her wrist as she made her way up the road towards Bara Bazaar, its shops and kiosks beckoning brightly with colourful bales of Kharua cotton and glittering Chanderi silks. Ellis's heart began to pound at the manner in which she carried herself. He observed her graceful gait, a certain familiar tilt of the head.

He got up hastily and stepped out of the teashop, keeping his eyes on her, wondering where she would go next. Following her at a distance, he saw her pass the gates of what remained of Motibagh. Her footsteps slowed down for just one fraction of a second as she glanced into its overgrown garden before quickly moving on. Was she remembering, like him, a night of forgetfulness? Or was she thinking perhaps of how that palace had rung once with the laughter of her maids, the durbar halls echoing with the hopes of her people?

He was still some way behind her and halted as he saw that she had stopped again. She was now standing just outside the jeweller's shop and seemed to be looking in his direction, although he could not see her face for the veil covering it. He considered going up to her to speak to her. To say that he had seen her pause to look into Motibagh. To tell her how often he too remembered their beautiful garden of pearls. Even if she had forgotten it, perhaps he could find some comfort from knowing that she yearned no more for those lost times, growing contented with a poorer, more serene life. Maybe there had been solace in being able to retreat again to a world in purdah. To a life where there was finally peace. He wanted, quite desperately, to ask her about all of that. More than anything else—if given just one question—he would have asked her whether she ever remembered a man called Robert Ellis. And had forgiven him for loving her and letting her down in equal measure.

But Ellis did none of that. Instead, as the woman turned to walk away from him, he stepped back into the celebrating crowd and watched her enter the noisy chaos of the bazaar. In just a few moments, she had disappeared from his view.

Bibliography

BOOKS

Allen, Charles, *Soldier Sahibs: The Men Who Made the North-west Frontier*, London: Abacus, 2001

Dalrymple, William (selected and introduced by), *Begums, Thugs and Englishmen: The Journals of Fanny Parkes*, New Delhi: Penguin Books, 2002

————, *The Last Mughal*, New Delhi: Viking/Penguin Books, 2006

David, Saul, *The Indian Mutiny*, London: Penguin Books, 2003 (New edition)

Devi, Mahasweta, *The Queen of Jhansi*, translated by Sagaree and Mandira Sengupta, Calcutta: Seagull Books, 2000 (Originally published in Bengali as *Jhansir Rani*, 1956)

Farrell, J.G., *The Siege of Krishnapur*, USA: Harcourt, 1973

Ferguson, Niall, *Empire: How Britain Made the Modern World*, London: Penguin Books, 2004 (New edition)

Fraser, Antonia, *Warrior Queens*, London: Weidenfeld & Nicolson, 1988

Fraser, George Macdonald, *Flashman in the Great Game*, London: HarperCollins Publishers, 1999 (New edition)

Gupta, Pratul Chandra, *Nana Sahib and the Rising at Cawnpore*, Oxford: Clarendon Press, 1963

Hibbert, Christopher, *London: The Biography of a City*, London: Penguin, 1983 (Revised edition)

Hibbert, Christopher, *The Great Mutiny India 1857*, London: Allen Lane–Penguin, 1978

Hodson, Major V.C.P., *Officers of the Bengal Army 1758–1834*, United Kingdom: Naval and Military Press Ltd, 2001 (New edition)

Holmes, Richard, *Sahibs: The British Soldier in India, 1750–1914*, UK: HarperCollins, 2006

James, Lawrence, *Raj: The Making and Unmaking of British India*, New York: St Martin's Press, 1999

Judd, Denis, *The Lion and the Tiger: The Rise and Fall of the British Raj 1600–1947*, New York: Oxford University Press, 2005

Kaye, John, and G.B. Malleson, *History of the Indian Mutiny of 1857-58*, 6 volumes, London, New York: Longmans, Green, 1896–99

Keay, John, *India: A History*, New York: HarperCollins Publishers, 2000

Lang, John, *Wanderings in India: And Other Sketches of Life in Hindostan*, London: Routledge, Warne and Routledge, 1859

Paul, E. Jaiwant, *Rani of Jhansi, Lakshmi Bai*, New Delhi: Roli Books, 1997

Raikes, Charles, *Notes on the Revolt in the North-Western Provinces of India*, London: Longman, 1858

Rousselet, Louis, *India and its Native Princes: Travels in Central India and in the Presidencies of Bombay and Bengal*, London: Chapman and Hall, 1875, Reprint, New Delhi: Asian Educational Services, 2005

Roy, Tapti, *Raj of the Rani*, New Delhi: Penguin Books, 2006

———, *The Politics of a Popular Uprising: Bundelkhand in 1857*, New Delhi, New York: Oxford University Press, 1995

Russell, William Howard, *My Indian Mutiny Diary*, London: Cassell, 1957

Sen, Surendra Nath, *Eighteen Fifty Seven*, New Delhi: Publications Division, 1957

Seton, Rosemary, *The Indian 'Mutiny' 1857-58: A Guide to Material in the India Office Library and Records*, London: British Library, 1986

Taylor, P.J.O., *What Really Happened During the Mutiny: A Day By Day Account of the Major Events of 1857–1859 in India*, New Delhi: Oxford University Press, 1997

Ward, Andrew, *Our Bones are Scattered: The Cawnpore Massacres and the Indian Mutiny of 1857*, London: John Murray Publishers, 1996

Wild, Antony, *The East India Company: Trade and Conquest from 1600*, London: The Lyons Press, 2001

Wilson, A.N., *The Victorians*, London: Arrow Books, 2003 (New edition)

WEBSITE

www.copsey-family.org/~allenc/lakshmibai/index.html

Acknowledgements

Immense gratitude is owed to a small band of people on whose time and support I unashamedly leant in my search for that abstruse, sometimes all too elusive thing: readability.

Judith Murdoch and Rebecca Winfield who so patiently and enthusiastically waded through endless early drafts, Diya Kar Hazra who made valuable suggestions, and Shantanu Ray Chaudhuri who perfected the final one with calm meticulous clarity and a head for figures and dates that I really could have done with during history exams in school. Big thanks too to all the other Penguins who unfailingly bring such vibrant energies to the business of commissioning, editing, proofing, production, art, publicity and sales, all vital processes in the birth of a book.

Thanks too to Maria Misra, who, despite her own writing and teaching commitments, kindly helped pick out many historical sore-thumbs from the first draft of the book; Khushwant Singh, for keeping me smiling from afar with canny observations on 'filling in the holes left behind by history'; Shomit Mitter, whom a far better writer than me once described as 'the best reader a writer can hope to have' (I know now why); Anshu Jain, who so generously brings his incisive boardroom style to even the humblest of projects; Tony Hunt, neighbour, back-up printer, cheer-upper and friend; David Austin, for his valuable diplomat's double-vision on British–Indian history; Helen Yuet Ling Pang, for making the space I needed in my day-job to help keep creative fires burning; and Renu and Pavan Varma, for good times, good advice and keeping my sometimes all too fervent imagination firmly reined in.

To Peter Brown too a special thank you for opening the doors to that most excellent archive at the *Times* offices in Wapping as also to staff at both the National Archives in New Delhi and the British Library's Oriental and India Section in London, eternally patient and long-suffering with my inability to crack computerized archive codes.

Of course, there are many historians and writers, some long gone, to whom I owe a different sort of debt—one of borrowed scholarship and hours of pleasure offered by their own books and, now, websites. While their works, listed in my bibliography, enabled numerous imaginary journeys around nineteenth-century India and Britain from a small South London study, my actual travels to Jhansi were enriched and illuminated by my very dearest Daya Misra and Omana Nair...to both of you, as ever, my love and appreciation for sacrificing your own comforts to ensure mine.

Finally, a big thank you to my husband and daughter, who have not just kept from swatting away my annoying writing bug but have even helped create a nice warm nest for it. To the former—ever a generous advocate for female courage—is dedicated this book. And the latter its eagerly awaited 'book-lunch'.